JOEL P [ROSENBERG]

"His penetrating knowledge of all things Mideastern—coupled with his intuitive knack for high-stakes intrigue—demand attention."

PORTER GOSS
Former director of the Central Intelligence Agency

"If there were a *Forbes* 400 list of great current novelists, Joel Rosenberg would be among the top ten. . . . One of the most entertaining and intriguing authors of international political thrillers in the country. . . . His novels are un-put-downable."

STEVE FORBES
Editor in chief, *Forbes* magazine

"One of my favorite things: An incredible thriller—it's called *The Third Target* by Joel C. Rosenberg. . . . He's amazing. . . . He writes the greatest thrillers set in the Middle East, with so much knowledge of that part of the world. . . . Fabulous! I've read every book he's ever written!"

KATHIE LEE GIFFORD
NBC's *Today Show*

"Fascinating and compelling . . . way too close to reality for a novel."

MIKE HUCKABEE
Former Arkansas governor

"[Joel Rosenberg] understands the grave dangers posed by Iran and Syria, and he's been a bold and courageous voice for true peace and security in the Middle East."

DANNY AYALON
Israeli deputy foreign minister

"Joel has a particularly clear understanding of what is going on in today's Iran and Syria and the grave threat these two countries pose to the rest of the world."

REZA KAHLILI
Former CIA operative in Iran and bestselling author of *A Time to Betray: The Astonishing Double Life of a CIA Agent inside the Revolutionary Guards of Iran*

"Joel Rosenberg is unsurpassed as the writer of fiction thrillers! Sometimes I have to remind myself to breathe as I read one of his novels because I find myself holding my breath in suspense as I turn the pages."

ANNE GRAHAM LOTZ
Author and speaker

"Joel paints an eerie, terrifying, page-turning picture of a worst-case scenario coming to pass. You have to read [*Damascus Countdown*], and then pray it never happens."

RICK SANTORUM
Former U.S. Senator

JOEL C. ROSENBERG

A J.B. COLLINS NOVEL

WITHOUT WARNING

TYNDALE HOUSE PUBLISHERS, INC., CAROL STREAM, ILLINOIS

Visit Tyndale online at www.tyndale.com.

Visit Joel C. Rosenberg's website at www.joelrosenberg.com.

TYNDALE and Tyndale's quill logo are registered trademarks of Tyndale House Publishers, Inc.

Without Warning

Designed by Dean H. Renninger

Without Warning is a work of fiction. Where real people, events, establishments, organizations, or locales appear, they are used fictitiously. All other elements of the novel are drawn from the author's imagination.

For information about special discounts for bulk purchases, please contact Tyndale House Publishers at csresponse@tyndale.com, or call 1-800-323-9400.

ISBN 978-1-4964-0620-0 (SC)
ISBN 978-1-4964-2329-0 (mass paper)

Printed in the United States of America

23 22 21 20 19 18 17
 7   6   5   4   3   2   1

To our youngest son, Noah—you have such an inquisitive and creative mind and, oh, what a storyteller you are! Your mom and I cannot wait to see the great things the Lord will do in and through you, young man, as you follow him with all your heart.

"'For I know the plans I have for you,' says the Lord. 'They are plans for good and not for disaster, to give you a future and a hope.'"

JEREMIAH 29:11

CAST OF
CHARACTERS

★ ★ ★

JOURNALISTS

James Bradley "J. B." Collins—national security correspondent for the *New York Times*

Allen MacDonald—D.C. bureau chief for the *New York Times*

Bill Sanders—Cairo bureau chief for the *New York Times*

AMERICANS

Harrison Taylor—president of the United States

Martin Holbrooke—vice president of the United States

Margaret Taylor—First Lady of the United States

Carl Hughes—acting director of the Central Intelligence Agency

Robert Khachigian—former director of the Central Intelligence Agency

Paul Pritchard—former Damascus station chief for the Central Intelligence Agency

Lawrence Beck—director of the Federal Bureau of Investigation

Arthur Harris—special agent with the Federal Bureau of Investigation

Matthew Collins—J. B.'s older brother

Lincoln Sullivan—attorney
Steve Sullivan—attorney, grandson of Lincoln

JORDANIANS
King Abdullah II—the monarch of the Hashemite
    Kingdom of Jordan

ISRAELIS
Yuval Eitan—Israeli prime minister
Ari Shalit—acting director of the Mossad
Yael Katzir—Mossad agent

EGYPTIANS
Wahid Mahfouz—president of Egypt
Amr El-Badawy—general, commander of Egypt's
    special forces
Walid Hussam—former chief of Egyptian intelligence

TERRORISTS
Abu Khalif—leader of the Islamic State in Iraq and
    al-Sham (ISIS)
Tariq Baqouba—commander of ISIS forces in Syria

OTHERS
Prince Mohammed bin Zayed—head of intelligence
    for the United Arab Emirates
Dr. Abdul Aziz Al-Siddiq—onetime professor and
    mentor of Abu Khalif

PREFACE

* * *

From *The First Hostage*

The camera zoomed in on the president.

And then, on cue, Taylor spoke directly to the camera.

"My name is Harrison Beresford Taylor," he said slowly, methodically, wincing several times as if in pain. As he spoke, Arabic subtitles scrolled across the bottom of the screen. "I am the forty-fifth president of the United States. I was captured by the Islamic State in Amman on December 5. I am being held by the Islamic State in a location that has not been disclosed to me, but I can say . . . I can say honestly . . . I can say honestly that I am being treated well and have been given the opportunity to give *ba'yah*—that is to say, to pledge allegiance . . . to the Islamic State. I ask my fellow Americans, including all my colleagues in Washington, to listen . . . to listen carefully . . . that is, to listen carefully and respectfully to the emir, and to follow the instructions . . . he is about to set forth for my safe and expeditious return."

When Taylor was finished, the camera panned back to Abu Khalif, emir of the Islamic State.

"Allah has given this infidel into our hands," Khalif said in Arabic. "O Muslims everywhere, glad tidings to you! Raise your heads high, for today—by Allah's grace—you have a sign of his favor upon you. You also have a state and caliphate, which will return your dignity, might, rights, and leadership. All praise and thanks are due to Allah. Therefore, rush, O Muslims, to your state. Yes, it is your state. Rush, because Syria is not for the Syrians, and Iraq is not for the Iraqis, and Jordan is not for the Jordanians. The earth belongs to Allah.

"I make a special call to you, O soldiers of the Islamic State—do not be awestruck by the great numbers of your enemy, for Allah is with you. I do not fear the numbers of your opponents, nor do I fear your neediness and poverty, for Allah has promised your Prophet—peace be upon him—that you will not be wiped out by famine, and your enemy will not conquer you or continue to violate and control your land. I promised you that in the name of Allah we would capture the American president, and I have kept my word. The king of Jordan will soon be in our hands. So will all the infidel leaders in this region. So will all the dogs in Rome. The ancient prophecies tell us the End of Days is upon us and with it the judgment of all who will not bow the knee and submit to Allah and his commanders on the earth."

Khalif now turned to his right and faced a new camera angle. Behind him was a shadowy stone wall. When he resumed speaking, it was in English.

"Now I speak directly to Vice President Holbrooke. Fearful and trembling, weak and unsteady, you and the infidels you lead have lost your way. Now you have three choices—convert to Islam, pay the *jizyah*, or die. You must choose your fate and choose it quickly. If you and your country choose to convert, you must give a speech to the world doing so under the precise language and conditions of Sharia law, and you will be blessed by Allah and have peace with the caliphate. If you choose to pay the *jizyah*, you must pay $1,000 U.S. for every man, woman, and child living in the United States of America. If you do not, or if you act with aggression in any matter against me or against the caliphate, the next video you see will be your beloved president beheaded or burned alive. From the time of this broadcast, you have forty-eight hours, and not a minute more."

PART ONE

1

★ ★ ★

I had never been in the Oval Office before.

But I'd always imagined my first time going differently.

The tension wasn't immediately apparent as I stepped into the most coveted executive suite on the planet. But it would come. It had to. I would force it. And when it did, my fate would be sealed.

At first, the president and I were both on our best behavior. As far as he was concerned, our past battles were water under the bridge. Yes, in Amman he had been blindsided by an enemy he neither truly understood nor saw coming. But in his eyes, the successful rescue effort had been enough to shift the balance of power, and he had adapted quickly. Tonight, as he addressed the nation and the world in a live televised speech to a joint session of Congress, he was at the top of his game. Soaring in the polls. Confounding his critics. Seemingly destined to leave the American people the legacy of peace, prosperity, and security they so desperately longed for.

The president beckoned for me to be seated, then took a seat himself behind the *Resolute* desk, built from the timbers of a British naval vessel abandoned in a storm in 1854. As he did, he opened a black leather binder embossed with the presidential seal. He picked up a Montblanc fountain pen and excused himself for a moment to make a few final edits to his speech before we loaded into the motorcade to head up to Capitol Hill together.

With every passing moment, my anxiety grew. In less than an hour, Harrison Beresford Taylor, the nation's forty-fifth president, would deliver his annual report to the legislature. He would assert unequivocally, as he had on every other such occasion, that "the state of the union is strong."

Yet nothing could be further from the truth.

I could take it no longer. It was time to say what I had come to say.

"Mr. President, I very much appreciate you inviting me here. I know you have a great deal on your plate right now. But I have to ask you, not as a reporter, just as me. Do you have a plan to kill Abu Khalif or not?"

It was a simple, direct question. But it immediately became apparent that Taylor was going to avoid giving me a simple, direct response.

"I think you're going to be very pleased with my speech tonight, Collins," he said, leaning back in his black leather chair.

"Why?" I asked.

"Trust me," he said with a smile.

"That's not exactly in my nature, sir."

"Well, do your best."

"Mr. President, are you going to lay out for the American people a plan to take down the ISIS emir?"

"Look, Collins, in case you haven't noticed, in the last two months we've ripped ISIL to shreds. We're targeting all of their leaders, including the emir. We've stepped up our drone strikes. We've taken out twenty-three high-value targets in the last six weeks alone. Is it going as fast as I'd like? No, and I'm pushing the Joint Chiefs. But you need to have patience. We're making great progress, and we're going to get this thing done. You'll see."

"Mr. President, with all due respect, how can you say we're making progress?" I shot back. "Abu Khalif is on a genocidal rampage. As we speak, he's slaughtering Muslims, Christians, Yazidis, and anyone who gets in his way: beheading them, crucifying them, enslaving them—men, women, and children. We're getting reports of unspeakable acts of cruelty, worse every day. He's murdered your friends and mine. This is the guy who held you captive. If we hadn't gotten there when we did, he would have taken a knife and personally sawed off your head—or put you in a cage and burned you alive—and uploaded the video to YouTube for the entire world to see."

"And now we have them on the run," Taylor countered. "We're blowing up their oil fields. We're seizing their assets. We're blocking their ability to move money around the world. We're shutting down their social media accounts and cutting off their communications."

"It's not enough, Mr. President," I insisted. "Not unless you're going after the emir directly. You're hitting his men and his money, but, sir, you can't kill the snake unless you cut off its head. So I must ask you again: have you signed a presidential directive to take Abu Khalif out, or not?"

2

★ ★ ★

The president leaned forward and glared at me.

"I was *there*, Collins. I was *in* that cell. I was *with* those children. Every night their faces haunt me. Every morning I hear their shrieks echoing down these hallways. Don't stand there and make it sound like I'm doing nothing. You know full well that's not true. I'm not sitting on my hands. I put American boots back on the ground in Iraq. I sent America back to war in Iraq—against the will of my party and much of my cabinet. My base went ballistic, but I did it. Because it was the right thing to do. And we're winning. We're taking out ISIL's forces. We're cutting off their supply lines. We're taking back land. We've got them on the run. What more do you want?"

"Simple. I want Abu Khalif's head."

"It's *not* that simple, Collins."

"Mr. President, do you really understand who this man is, what he wants, how far he's willing to go?"

"*Me?* Do *I* understand?" Taylor bellowed,

suddenly rising to his feet. "You're honestly asking if *I* understand who we're up against?"

"Sir, this is not Saddam Hussein. It's not bin Laden. It's not Zawahiri or Zarqawi. Abu Khalif is not like any enemy we've ever faced before. This is a man who thinks he was chosen by Allah to bring about the end of the world, a man willing to use genocide to hasten the coming of his messiah and establish a global caliphate."

Taylor was seething. But I didn't stop.

"And he's coming here, Mr. President. *Here.* To America. To our streets. He's said so. He's promised to kill you and as many Americans as he possibly can, and he will—unless you take him down."

Taylor shook his head in disgust and walked over to the windows. As he looked out at the snow falling on the Rose Garden, I stood as well.

"You're a real piece of work, Collins, you know that? You need to take a deep breath and calm down and show a little trust in the armed forces of the United States and their commander in chief. We're winning. We have the enemy on the run, and we're not going to let up."

"Mr. President, I watched Abu Khalif behead two men. I saw him test sarin gas on prisoners who died a grisly, gruesome, horrifying death. I've looked in his eyes. I know who he is. And he told me exactly what he was going to do."

Taylor didn't say anything. He just glanced at his watch and then again stared out the window into the icy darkness that had descended on the capital.

"Look, Mr. President, I know you've gone

against your party, your cabinet, even your own campaign promises by putting U.S. forces back into Iraq. I'm not saying you're sitting on your hands. You want to win. I see it. But, sir, don't underestimate this man. Abu Khalif has kept every threat he's made so far. How many times has he bragged how his experienced, trained, battle-hardened jihadists are coming here carrying American passports, fighters who will easily slip across our border and blend into society until they're ready to strike? He's coming here, Mr. President, and unless you stop him, it's going to be a bloodbath."

At this, Taylor turned to face me. "You think I don't know that, Collins? Are you really that arrogant?"

"Then tell me you've signed a presidential directive to hunt down the emir of the Islamic State, wherever he is, whatever it takes. Give me that, and I'll back off."

"I'm not going to get into operational matters, Collins—not with you. Not with any reporter from the *New York Times*."

"So I'll take that as a no."

"Don't play games with me, Collins. Don't twist my words. I didn't say no. I said I'm not going to discuss it—not with you."

"Off the record," I said.

"Nice try. This entire conversation is off the record."

"But—"

"How many ways can I put it to you, Collins? I get it. Abu Khalif is a thug, a cold-blooded killer.

He's the face of ISIL, I grant you. But you're making too much of him. He's just one man. We'll find him. We'll take him out. But don't kid yourself. That won't be the end of it. There's going to be another thug after him, and another after that, and another after that. And we'll find them and neutralize them as well. But I'm not going to paralyze my administration in the hunt for just one guy. We're going to go after the entire ISIL leadership and their infrastructure and their money—systematically, step-by-step, until we're done, until it's over. But you've got to understand something, Collins. ISIL is a threat, but it's not an existential threat to America. They can't destroy us. They can't annihilate us. I don't care about all their talk of building a global caliphate. It's never going to happen. You want to talk about a potential existential threat? Then let's discuss climate change, not ISIL."

What in the world is he talking about? I asked myself. I hadn't called ISIS an existential threat. And how on earth did this compare to climate change? "Mr. President, Abu Khalif is not *just one guy*. He's different—brilliant, savvy, charismatic, irreplaceable."

"Nobody's irreplaceable."

"This guy is. He's not some back-alley street tough like Zarqawi. This is one of the smartest foes we've ever been up against. He's got a doctorate in Islamic theology and another one in Islamic eschatology. He's fluent in seven languages. He's a genius with social media. He's casting a spell over the entire Islamic world. He's a magnet, attracting jihadists from 140 different countries. He's mobilizing and training and deploying foreign fighters on a scale unlike anything we've ever seen. This is no longer just a terrorist movement. Abu Khalif has built himself a full-scale jihadist army—a hundred thousand men consumed by the notion that Allah has raised them up to conquer the world. His forces may be in retreat in Iraq, Mr. President, but they're spreading like a cancer across the Middle East and North Africa, they're penetrating into Central Asia and Europe and Latin America—and they're coming here next."

3

A Secret Service agent entered the Oval Office.

"Mr. President, it's time. The motorcade is ready."

Taylor, the hard-charging former governor of North Carolina and onetime founder and CEO of an enormously successful tech company in the Research Triangle near Raleigh, was not a man accustomed to being challenged to his face. He kept his eyes locked on mine for a few more moments.

"Mr. Collins, I invited you here to thank you for all you did to save my life. I asked you to be my honored guest tonight at the State of the Union. Tomorrow you will receive the Presidential Medal of Freedom in the ceremony we have planned, and this is how you thank me, by telling me I'm not doing enough to keep Americans safe? We're on the verge of a great and historic victory against the Islamic State, and you're standing here in the Oval Office asking me for vengeance."

"No, sir—I'm not asking for vengeance. I'm asking for justice."

The president shook his head. "I'm an antiwar

Democrat, Collins, yet I went to Congress and demanded they pass a formal declaration of war against ISIL. I'm the man who pulled the last of our forces out of Afghanistan, yet I just sent thousands of American ground forces back into Iraq. Why? To crush ISIL once and for all. And that's precisely what we're doing. Did we find Abu Khalif in Alqosh? No. Did we find him in Mosul? No. But are we going to keep hunting him? Absolutely. And for you to suggest I'm not serious about getting this guy is not just crazy. It's downright offensive."

"Are you going to attack Raqqa?" I asked, speaking of the ISIS capital in Syria.

"We're focused on Iraq right now, and you know it."

"Are you going to take Homs? Aleppo? Dabiq?"

At this, the president's entire demeanor shifted. Instead of fuming at me, he laughed out loud. "Collins, have you completely lost your mind? I'm trying to put *out* the forest fire in Syria, not pour gasoline on it. I'm working night and day with the Russians and the Iranians and the Turks and the U.N. to try to nail down a cease-fire that will hold, something that'll actually stop all the killing, not increase it."

"But, sir, don't you see? Agreeing to a cease-fire before destroying Khalif would be a disaster. You'd be giving him a safe haven. You'd be effectively handing him enormous swaths of territory he alone would control, territory he could use as a base camp to launch attacks against the U.S. and our allies."

"So what would you have me do, exactly?" Taylor asked as he took his suit jacket from a hanger in the corner. "You want us to get sucked into a bloody ground war in Syria? Because that's exactly what Abu Khalif wants. He's practically begging me to put a quarter million American troops smack-dab in the middle of Syria's civil war. He *wants* me to attack Dabiq. He *wants* me to get caught in a quagmire. And why? To bring about the end of the world, right? You said it yourself. He's consumed with establishing his global caliphate. He's transfixed on slaughtering the 'forces of Rome' and ushering in the End of Days. And now you really want me to play into his sick, twisted game? I took you as smarter than that."

This was going nowhere. But I took a deep breath, and one last shot. "Mr. President, I'm asking you a simple, straightforward question. And you still haven't given me a simple, straightforward answer. So let me ask you one more time: Do you have a plan to hunt down and kill Abu Khalif, wherever he is, whatever it takes, or do you not?"

The president didn't say anything. Instead, he buttoned his suit coat, walked back to his desk, and picked up the loose pages of his speech. He scanned several of them closely, as if looking for a particular section. Then he scribbled a few notes in the margin.

"Sir?" I asked after several moments of silence.

Taylor ignored me for a while longer, making more changes before putting all the pages into the binder.

"Yes, we have a plan," he said finally, quietly,

closing the binder and looking back at me. His voice was once again calm, collected, and presidential.

He pushed a button on his phone, then turned back to me and kept talking. "Abu Khalif came after me personally. Why? Because we'd actually hammered out a comprehensive peace treaty between the Israelis and the Palestinians. My predecessors tried to get it done, and they failed. I was *this* close. And then Khalif and his thugs came along and blew it all to kingdom come. I won't forget that, Collins. Not ever. And as long as I am the commander in chief, I won't rest until we take these guys down—all of them. On that, you have my word."

He looked sincere. He sounded sincere. But I wasn't convinced. Harrison Taylor was a consummate politician, and the simple fact was I didn't trust him. It had been two months since the forces of the Islamic State had blown up his peace summit in Amman. Two months since ISIS forces had launched a chemical weapons attack in the Jordanian capital and captured the leader of the free world. Two weeks later, Congress had declared war and a coalition of U.S. and allied forces had "reinvaded" Iraq—albeit this time at the invitation of Baghdad—and made a big show of it on worldwide television. But ISIS was still slaughtering thousands of innocents. Its leader was still a free man. And it was now increasingly clear to me that this president had neither a plan to bring him to justice nor the will to see one through.

For years, the Taylor administration's approach to the Middle East and North Africa had been a disaster. Foreign policy was driven by press releases and photo ops. Taylor had been repeatedly warned about the magnitude of the threat posed by the Islamic State, yet he'd been caught off guard by the ISIS onslaught in Amman. Now much of the region was on fire. The cost in human lives had been catastrophic. Yet there had been no political cost whatsoever. To the contrary, Taylor was more popular than he'd ever been.

The president loved to say that ISIL was on the run and that the caliphate had been cut in half. But he hadn't asked Congress to authorize the use of force in Syria. He refused to conduct bombing raids there or send Special Forces to find Abu Khalif or any of the rest of the ISIS psychopaths. And yet, for now, at least, the public was giving Taylor and his administration tremendous credit for freeing Iraq and returning millions of refugees to their homes. The homecoming Iraqis cheering the American and allied forces and even bowing down before the cameras and kissing the land that had been returned to them made for great television, I admit, and I'm not saying it wasn't a victory. It was. But it was a Band-Aid on a severed artery.

The region was bleeding to death, and ISIS was causing the bleeding. This wasn't the Cold War. The jihadists couldn't simply be driven out of Iraq and back into Syria and "contained" there. They were bloodthirsty lunatics, driven by an apocalyptic, murderous brand of Islam unlike anything the world had ever seen before. Abu Khalif and his men chilled me to my core. They were a lethal virus that had to be eradicated before they spread to every part of the planet, leaving a trail of death and heartbreak in their wake.

I had braved a mounting winter storm to come here to the Oval Office to see the president of the United States in person for the first time since we'd been airlifted together out of Erbil at the beginning of December. I had come at the president's personal request. I had hoped to find a man sobered by reality, a leader who had truly learned and absorbed hard lessons from all that had transpired. Instead I saw a risk-averse politician basking in the glory of an adoring nation, disturbingly unaware of the catastrophe I sensed was coming next.

4

★ ★ ★

"Why, James, what a pleasure to see you again," the First Lady said in her typically warm and gracious manner as she entered the Oval Office and eased the mounting tension.

"Thank you, Mrs. Taylor," I replied as she gave me a quick hug and a kiss on the cheek, leaving behind a smudge of pale-pink lipstick in the process. "It's an honor to see you as well."

"Please, James, it's Meg," she said as she drew a white cotton handkerchief from her purse and dabbed it on my cheek until the lipstick was gone. "How many times must I ask you to call me Meg?"

"Sorry, ma'am," I said. "Guess I'm just not used to being on a first-name basis with a First Lady."

"Hush—you're practically family now, James," she said in her distinctive Southern lilt. "Harrison and I can never repay all you've done for us, and we want you to feel welcome and at home in this house. Now, how's your mother? Did her surgery go well?"

Whatever her husband lacked in Tar Heel charm, Margaret Reed Taylor made up for in spades. Now fifty-eight, the eldest daughter of a former North Carolina senator—and the grand-daughter of a onetime president of UNC Chapel Hill—was as politically savvy as she was lovely. She'd earned her MBA from Wharton and her law degree from Harvard, and my colleagues on the White House beat swore she was the administration's chief strategist, though she was far too clever to let anyone get a clear look at her maneuverings. Tonight, she wore a modest but elegant robin's-egg-blue suit and a gorgeous string of pearls, and clearly she knew how to extricate her husband of thirty-two years from a delicate moment like a seasoned professional.

"It did, ma'am," I said, impressed that she was aware of my mom's hip surgery less than two weeks earlier. "Thanks for asking."

"Is she up and about yet?"

"Not quite yet, but it could be worse."

"I hear she's one tough cookie."

"She'd be glad to hear you say it, ma'am. She sure wishes she could be here tonight, and not so much to be with me as to meet you."

"Well, bless her heart. Tell her I'd love to give her a call in a few days, and I'd certainly love to have you both come for a meal when she's up to it."

"That's very kind, ma'am. She'll be tickled pink."

"Good. Now have your brother and his family come to Washington for all the festivities? Will they be in the chamber tonight?"

"Matt came, and I'll meet him over there. He was having dinner with Senator Barrows," I said.

"And his wife?"

I shook my head. "Annie felt she needed to stay with Mom and the kids. But she also would have loved to meet you."

"You bring her with your mother and we'll all do lunch. They'll be watching you on television tonight, I'm sure?"

"Absolutely—and tomorrow, too," I said. "It's the biggest thing that's ever happened in Bar Harbor. I can tell you that much."

"We hear you've become quite a hero up there." She smiled, then turned to brush a few pieces of lint off her husband's freshly pressed navy-blue suit and adjust the Windsor knot in his red power tie.

Just then, another Secret Service agent stepped into the room. He said nothing. But he didn't have to.

"It's time, sweetheart," the First Lady said. "We mustn't keep all your fans waiting." At that, she turned to me and smiled. "The American people just *luuuv* my husband, James," she said with a wink. "Don't forget that now, you hear?"

She held my gaze until I nodded. She didn't say another word, but she'd made her point. *My husband is beloved and thus more powerful than ever. You're just a reporter. Don't ever forget that, James—ever.*

It was true that the president's approval ratings were soaring. But on the issue of Abu Khalif, the American people were with me. It was a small comfort at the moment, but it was true. Earlier in the day, Allen MacDonald, my boss at the *Times* who had recently been promoted to D.C. bureau chief, had e-mailed me an advance look at the latest numbers from a *New York Times*/CBS News poll fresh out of the field. The survey found that 86 percent of the American people wanted the president to "use all means necessary" to bring the leader of the world's most dangerous terrorist movement to justice, and 62 percent said they would be "satisfied" if the ISIS emir was captured, convicted, and sent to Guantánamo. But fully nine in ten Americans said they wanted Abu Khalif hunted down and killed in retribution for what he had tried to do to our country.

I was sure Taylor was aware of the numbers. Yet they'd apparently had no impact at all. Did the president really think the American people were going to believe him when he looked them in the eye tonight and told them he was doing all he could, even if he was clearly dead set against sending U.S. and allied forces into Syria under any circumstances? Did Taylor really think Abu Khalif was going to abandon his very public—and oft-repeated—pledge to assassinate him and raise the black flag of the Islamic State over the White House?

For nearly two months, I had lain in a hospital bed, endured multiple operations, struggled through rehab, and tried to recover physically and emotionally from all that I had witnessed in Alqosh. Almost seven hundred ISIS jihadists had been killed, but two Delta squads had also been wiped out in one of the deadliest battles in the history of Delta Force. And I had been right in the middle of it.

The one thing that kept me going every day—despite wrenching pain and utter exhaustion—was the certainty of hearing one day soon that Abu Khalif had been captured or killed.

Now, it seemed, that hope was all but gone.

As the president and First Lady stepped out of the Oval Office and headed through the West Wing to the foyer on the north side of the White House, I pulled out my gold pocket watch, a gift from my grandfather, and glanced at it as I followed close behind. It was 8:27 on a dark and snowy night in February. I was going to my first joint session of Congress. I was about to be a guest of the president during his State of the Union address, one in which I was going to be prominently mentioned. I completely disagreed with the president about his policies toward the Islamic State. I was increasingly fearful that Abu Khalif was preparing to strike again, perhaps even here inside the United States. But for now, I had a genuine sense of excitement about what lay ahead.

This was going to be an evening to remember.

5

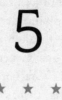

This was my first time in a presidential motorcade.

It was a sight to behold. Amid the gusting winds and blowing snow and unusually bitter temperatures—hovering at a mere eight degrees, at last check—seven D.C. Metro police motorcycles gunned their engines at the head of the pack, preparing to exit the northeast gate of the White House complex for the two-mile journey to the Capitol. Next in line was the lead car, a police cruiser with its red-and-blue lights flashing, and its two officers—wearing thick winter coats and sipping what I assumed was strong black coffee from a thermos—ready to clear the way for the rest of the team.

Behind these were two identical black stretch Cadillacs, covered in white powder and a bit of ice. The first, in this case, served as the presidential limousine. The second served as the decoy car to confuse any would-be attackers as to which vehicle actually carried the chief executive.

Given my little contretemps with the president in the Oval Office, I suspected I was no longer going to be invited to join the First Couple, and I quickly learned my instincts were right on the money. As I came through the North Portico, I watched as three-star General Marco Ramirez, the commander of Delta Force, wearing his full dress uniform under a thick wool overcoat, got into the president's limousine with the commander in chief and First Lady.

As an agent closed the door behind them, I have to admit I found myself a bit jealous. It wasn't that I wanted more time with the president. He wasn't going to say anything more to me tonight on or off the record, and that was okay. I'd said what I'd come to say. Still, I would have loved an inside look at the car they called "the Beast." The specially built Cadillac clocked in at about a million and a half dollars. Each door had eight inches of armor plating capable of surviving a direct assault by a rocket-propelled grenade or an antitank missile. The windows were capable of taking direct fire from automatic machine guns without shattering. The chassis was fitted underneath with a massive steel plate designed to withstand the blast of a roadside bomb. The vehicle was even hermetically sealed to protect against biochemical attacks.

Or so I'd been told. I wasn't going to get to see it for myself tonight. But that was fine. I was at ease with my conscience, and for the moment that was all that mattered to me.

Behind the two limousines were five black Chevy Suburbans, all awash in red-and-blue flashing lights, all being constantly brushed off by agents trying to keep their windows as clear from the elements as they possibly could. I knew from my research that the first Suburban was known as "Halfback" and was filled with a heavily armed counterassault team. The next carried classified electronic countermeasure equipment. The rest I wasn't entirely sure about, though I knew they carried more agents, a medical team, and a hazmat countermeasures team. These were followed by a vehicle known as "Roadrunner," which carried the White House communications team, and an ambulance.

I donned my black leather overcoat and matching leather gloves and pulled a black wool cap over my bald and freezing head. Not three steps out the door of the White House, I could see my breath, and my glasses were fogging up. A deputy press secretary directed me into one of several black Lincoln Town Cars that would carry White House staff. Behind these were a number of white vans for the White House press corps, more Secret Service Chevy Suburbans, three or four additional police cars, and more motorcycles.

Fortunately, the driver of my Town Car already had the heat running. It felt good to get inside, shut the door behind me, and take shelter from the storm. I'd expected that. What I hadn't expected was to see anyone I knew waiting for me.

"Good evening, Collins," said the man in the backseat. "Good to see you again, and good to see you getting out for a change. How are you feeling?"

"Agent Harris, what a pleasant surprise," I said,

genuinely happy to see him once I'd cleaned the lenses of my glasses and put them back on. "To what do I owe this pleasure?"

Arthur Harris was a thirty-year veteran with the FBI and part of a rapidly growing unit of special agents hunting ISIS operatives in the U.S. and abroad. We'd first met in Istanbul when he was investigating the car bombing that had taken the life of one of my colleagues at the *Times*. Later, he'd been involved in the mole hunt that had led to the stunning arrest of CIA director Jack Vaughn, his mistress, and a top intelligence analyst at the NSA back in December. It was Harris who had come to find me at the Marka air base in Amman, and it was Harris who had cleared me for release from Jordanian custody when I had been briefly suspected of being complicit in the attack on the royal palace. As such, Harris and I had spent quite a bit of time together in recent months. We were among the few Americans who had survived all that had happened in Jordan and Iraq, and I was honestly glad to see him again.

Harris smiled. "Between us, I believe the president would like you arrested and beaten. That's off the record, of course."

I laughed as the motorcade rolled, but I wasn't entirely sure he was kidding.

6

★ ★ ★

Almost immediately Harris's mobile phone rang.

As he took the call, we exited the White House grounds through the northeast gate, turned right on Pennsylvania Avenue, then immediately took another right onto Fifteenth Street just past the Treasury Department. Moments later, we turned left, rejoining Pennsylvania Avenue, and from there it was a straight shot to the Capitol building.

Looking out the window at all the snowplows working feverishly to keep the president's route clear, I resisted the impulse to check the latest headlines on Twitter. I already knew the news was grim. Turkish military forces were bombing Kurdish rebels in northern Syria. A series of suicide bombings had just ripped through Istanbul, Ankara, and Antalya, mostly targeting government offices and hotels frequented by foreigners. A petrochemical plant in Alexandria, Egypt, had just come under attack by as-of-yet unknown militants. Rather than be reminded of all that was going wrong in the world, however, I simply wanted to enjoy this moment.

Against all odds, I was actually heading to the U.S. Capitol building to be the president's guest at the State of the Union address. I was under no illusions. I didn't deserve to be there. In fact, given all that had happened in the past several months, I should probably be dead, not still working as a journalist and winning awards. For the first month and a half of my recovery, I'd been certain I'd never go back to my life as a foreign correspondent, and even if I did, I had no desire to cover wars and terrorism. I'd seen too many friends get killed and wounded. I'd seen too much horror.

The bitter truth was I'd given my entire career to being part of an elite tribe of war correspondents, and it had cost me nearly everything. Now in my early forties, I was divorced. I had no kids. I barely saw my mom or my brother and his family. I was a recovering alcoholic. My neighbors didn't know me. The doorman at my apartment building across the Potomac barely even recognized me. Wasn't it time for a change?

But a change to what? I had no idea what I'd do if not write for the Gray Lady. Teach journalism to a bunch of lazy, spoiled twentysomethings who had no idea how the world worked? Cash in with some Wall Street gig—VP of public affairs for some multinational bank or investment firm? I'd rather drink poison. In theory, a change sounded great. But what exactly would I do next? What *could* I do that I would actually enjoy?

Unbidden, my thoughts abruptly turned to Yael Katzir, the beautiful Israeli agent I had met in

Istanbul and with whom I had survived the grueling events in Jordan and northern Iraq. I'd barely
seen her since we'd been evacuated together on Air
Force One after the attack in Alqosh. Yet I had to
admit she was never far from my mind.

As a senior chemical weapons expert for the
Mossad, Yael had been at the top of her game.
She'd been right about ISIS capturing chemical
weapons in Syria. She'd been right to warn then–
Prime Minister Daniel Lavi that ISIS was planning
a coup d'état in Amman. He hadn't listened, and
now he was dead. What's more, she'd been spot-on
in her analysis that President Taylor was being held
by ISIS forces not in Mosul or Homs or Dabiq
as many U.S. intelligence analysts had believed at
first, but in the little Iraqi town of Alqosh, on the
plains of Nineveh. She'd nearly paid with her life.
But she'd been right, and now she was a rock star
at the highest levels of the Israeli government. The
last text she'd sent me, almost three weeks before,
was that the new prime minister, Yuval Eitan, had
asked her to serve as his deputy national security
advisor. It was a big job, a heady promotion. She
wasn't sure she wanted to take it. But it was evidence of the enormous respect and influence she
held in Jerusalem.

She had sent me a note asking me what she
should do. I'd written back immediately and told
her to take it and to make sure she got a big raise to
go with it. I couldn't have been more proud of her,
I told her. She deserved every accolade and more.

Selfishly, however, it was hard not to think of
her promotion as my loss. I knew there was likely

no future for us. She had a job, and she wasn't going to leave it for me. And honestly, what was I going to do? Move to Israel? Learn Hebrew? Convert to Judaism? The fact was, I'd only known her for a few months. We had only just begun to be friends. Still, I missed her. But with her new responsibilities, I had no idea when I would even see her again.

Harris finally finished his phone call and turned back to me. He didn't look well.

"What was that all about?" I asked.

"Want a scoop?"

"You kidding?" I asked.

"No," he said, dead serious.

"Sure. What've you got?"

"State police in Alabama just took down an ISIS sleeper cell near Birmingham."

"Seriously?" I asked, pulling a notebook and pen from my pocket.

"Four males, all Iraqi nationals, and a woman from Syria."

"What were they doing in Birmingham?"

"Weird, right?"

"Very," I concurred.

"That's not the half of it," Harris said. "When the troopers got a search warrant for their apartment, what do you think they found?"

I shrugged.

"Almost five hundred mortar shells—not active ones, mind you, just dummies, the kind the military uses for target practice."

"What would they need those for?" I asked. "And where would they get them in the first place?"

"Well, that's the thing," Harris said. "We have no idea."

"Does the president know?" I asked.

"No, not yet—I don't think so," he replied. "We're just getting this ourselves."

"Well, somebody better tell him before he starts speaking."

The motorcade soon pulled up to the parking plaza on the north side of the Capitol and came to a halt. Photographers and news camera operators recorded the president and First Lady and General Ramirez being greeted by the Speaker of the House and led inside. I glanced at my grandfather's pocket watch. It was almost 9 p.m. The networks would go live in six minutes.

7

★ ★ ★

THE U.S. CAPITOL BUILDING

"Mr. Speaker, the president of the United States!"

The sergeant at arms of the United States House of Representatives shouted the words at the top of his lungs. When he finished, the room erupted. Everyone in the House Chamber jumped to their feet and launched into deafening and sustained applause. Members of both parties from the House and the Senate were whooping and hollering and cheering the leader of the free world, and they did not stop. Indeed, by my reckoning, Taylor received the longest recorded standing ovation in the history of any State of the Union address.

No wonder the man wasn't listening to me. Why should he? The president's approval ratings were now in the mideighties. It was a stunning, neck-wrenching turn of events, given that two months earlier—just before the ISIS attack on the peace summit in Jordan—his approval ratings had been drifting down into the midthirties, imperiling the administration's entire agenda and threatening to bury dozens of House and Senate

Democrats in a political avalanche in the next elections. But since then, the world had dramatically changed. No longer was Taylor politically dead and buried. He had been resurrected, and tonight he was taking a victory lap.

I watched it all unfold from the section of the second-floor gallery reserved for the First Lady and the guests of the First Family. General Ramirez stood directly beside Mrs. Taylor, two rows ahead of me. To their right were the fifteen Iraqi children we had rescued from Abu Khalif's underground prison in Alqosh, all cheering the president, along with several of the social workers who were caring for them after their traumatic ordeal and helping them get adjusted to their new lives in America. In the row behind the First Lady stood members of her Secret Service protective detail, and beside them stood the wounded but surviving members of the Delta squad who had rescued the president in Alqosh.

Standing beside me was my brother, Matt, also cheering enthusiastically. I was glad he could be here. He'd been with me every step of the way since this ordeal had begun. He had come down from Maine every week, sometimes for two or three days at a time, to spend time with me at Walter Reed. He'd sat with me for hours and let me talk about what I'd been through, what I'd seen and heard in Alqosh and Mosul and Abu Ghraib. Together we'd theorized about where Abu Khalif could be holed up. I thought Khalif was probably in Raqqa. Matt was convinced he was now somewhere in Libya. We'd argued about where Khalif might strike next and how the Taylor administration might respond. He'd read me every newspaper and magazine article he could get his hands on about the allied offensive in northern Iraq. He always prayed with me when he arrived and before he left, and whenever I let him, he read the Bible to me too, working his way through the Gospel according to John. I listened politely. Sometimes I asked questions. Matt always had answers—good ones, interesting ones, compelling ones—but he hadn't pushed me, and for that I was grateful.

Matt clapped and hollered for the president like just about everyone else in the room, and I understood why. He was a patriot, and he was being swept up in the moment. We'd all thought this president was dead in Jordan, and then in Syria or Iraq, and then—almost miraculously— he'd been rescued, and these dear, precious children had been liberated from the clutches of those ISIS monsters. What's more, millions of Muslims and Christians and Yazidis in northern Iraq had been liberated from a dark, oppressive force. It was a great story, one for the ages. From most of the country's vantage point, it all looked like one giant success story. Why shouldn't they celebrate? They didn't see what was coming.

But I did.

Abu Khalif had promised he would come to the U.S. Brazenly, proudly, smugly, he'd told me he had American and Canadian jihadists fighting for him in Syria and Iraq. He'd bragged to me that such men would be able to enter the United States undetected. And now they were here. In Alabama, anyway. Sure, some in Birmingham had been caught. But there were others. Many. I was sure of it. When and how and where they would strike, I had no idea. But I had my guesses. It wasn't going to be a workplace shooting like in San Bernardino. It wasn't going to be the attempted assassination of a lone police officer sitting in his patrol car on the streets of Philadelphia. I doubted it was going to be an attack on a satirical newspaper office like *Charlie Hebdo* in Paris or even an international airport like in Brussels or Istanbul. No, this was going to be bigger. Much bigger. And I suspected Abu Khalif had set his next action into motion even before the attack on the peace summit in Amman.

That's why he'd gone on the record with me. That's why he had laid out his entire wicked strategy when I interviewed him in the Abu Ghraib prison outside of Baghdad. That's why in Mosul he had demonstrated for me that he was fully capable of carrying out his threats. The attacks in Jordan were just a trailer. The coming attacks in America were the main attraction.

So I clapped politely. I knew I was on live worldwide television. I needed to be respectful. I would give Taylor his due. But I could not bring myself to do more. I was deeply grateful we'd found the president alive and gotten him out safe. At the same time, I was more convinced than ever that he didn't truly understand the nature and threat of the evil that was coming. Unless the FBI and the CIA were at the top of their game, the president was about to be blindsided again. We all were.

I discreetly glanced over to Matt's right. Agent

Harris stood politely but did not clap. Perhaps he couldn't, I thought. Perhaps that was part of the bureau's code of conduct, like that of the Secret Service. The agents protecting the First Lady weren't clapping either. They weren't showing emotion of any kind. I wasn't sure why, exactly. I didn't spend much time in such circles. But I must say, I was a bit envious.

Grinning broadly, the president shook hands and posed for selfies with congressmen and senators of both parties as he worked his way down the center aisle, clearly enjoying every moment. Had he been briefed on the takedown of an ISIS cell on American soil? If so, I wondered whether it would affect anything he was about to say.

Eventually Taylor reached the well of the House—the open area in front of the rostrum—where he greeted the assembled Supreme Court justices, all of them seated, and embraced each of the members of his cabinet, all of them standing. From there, he shook hands with each of the Joint Chiefs before finally making the turn and climbing the rostrum, where he was reintroduced by the Speaker of the House and greeted by even more tumultuous applause.

8

Finally the chamber settled down and people again took their seats.

The president looked at the teleprompter screen to his left and at the other on his right. Then he glanced down at the printed pages of his remarks in the three-ring binder on the podium—the one I'd seen him making notes on in the Oval Office less than an hour earlier—and his broad smile faded somewhat. I tried to imagine what he was thinking. I wanted to believe that the argument I'd made to him—and what he'd hopefully just heard from his national security advisor—was weighing heavily on his mind. But I couldn't read him. Not from where I was sitting.

When he looked up, he surveyed the audience, all four hundred thirty-five members of the House, all one hundred members of the Senate, ambassadors from nearly every nation, members of his administration, official guests, and of course, the members of the Fourth Estate. For almost a full minute, he said nothing. But then he cleared his throat as he took out a handkerchief and dabbed his eyes.

"Mr. Speaker, Mr. Vice President, members of Congress, distinguished guests, and my fellow Americans," he finally said, his voice shaky at first but gradually gaining strength. "Over the course of this past year, the American people and our government and our military have been tested as at few other times in our history. The forces of freedom have come under a vicious assault by the forces of violent extremism. Our enemies have tried to murder our leaders. They have sought to terrorize and blackmail our people and force us into submission to their perverted vision of global domination. They have done so at the point of a gun, at the tip of a sword."

The room was deathly quiet. Taylor reached for a glass of water. He took a sip. He cleared his throat once more. And then he turned back to the teleprompters.

"When I was seized by the forces of ISIL, it wasn't just I who was taken hostage. We all were. America was held hostage. But America did not surrender. You did not surrender. You did not give in. No, you came together. You united as one people. You fought back against the terrorists. You fought back against the forces of darkness, and you won—America won—and if we stay united, America will keep on winning!"

This brought the house down. What ensued was a two-minute-and-twelve-second standing ovation.

I timed it.

"You did *not* surrender," the president continued when the audience had just barely settled back in their seats. "You stood tall and true, and the forces of freedom prevailed. The American armed forces prevailed. The American people prevailed, and the state of our union has *never* been stronger."

Back to their feet they jumped. They whooped and hollered. Some stamped their feet. It was a good old-fashioned political revival meeting, and it struck me that Taylor should probably just say thank you and good-night. No good could come of trying to go on any further. Then again, the man was a politician, and what politician had ever quit while he was ahead?

"In my capacity as commander in chief, I asked Congress—the people's representatives—to formally declare war on ISIL, and you agreed," the president said when everyone was seated. "With your full support and approval, I sent fifty thousand of America's finest soldiers, sailors, airmen, and Marines back into Iraq."

I couldn't help but be impressed. Taylor was skillfully tying Congress's fate in the Middle East to his own. They loved him now. They were with him now. But if things went bad, the president was making sure they couldn't throw him under the bus. They had made these decisions together, he told the country, Republicans and Democrats. The election breezes were already blowing.

"Together we sent five hundred tanks and more than two hundred aircraft to the region. Together with our Sunni Arab allies—the Iraqis, the Jordanians, the Egyptians, the Saudis, the Gulf Emiratis, and the Kurds—we built a powerful military, diplomatic, and economic coalition. And tonight I can report that together we have achieved impressive results. We have liberated the city and people of Mosul."

Applause erupted again.

"We have liberated Alqosh."

More applause.

"We have liberated the province of Nineveh—indeed, the entire nation of Iraq is now free from the black flags of ISIL."

Still more applause—and then came the coup de grâce.

"We have accomplished what our critics said was impossible," the president declared. "We have cut the caliphate in half, and now ISIL's days are numbered."

Another standing ovation.

"He's crushing it," Matt shouted to me as we both rose to our feet.

I said nothing, just made a perfunctory smile for the cameras. Apparently the president hadn't been told, or he didn't care. Either way, I knew at that moment he wasn't going to mention the capture of an ISIS cell on American soil. He had a narrative: Victory. Success. Glory. And what had unfolded in Alabama didn't fit it. It raised too many questions. *If America was truly winning against the forces of Abu Khalif in the Middle East, what was ISIS doing here, in the South, so deep inside the homeland? Were there more of them? How many? Where were they? What were they planning? And what were they doing stockpiling empty mortar shells?*

As I scanned the audience, another line

of questions came to mind. Where was King Abdullah II? Why wasn't the Jordanian monarch— our most faithful Sunni Arab ally—here as an honored guest of the president? Where were Palestinian president Salim Mansour and Egyptian president Wahid Mahfouz and the Saudi king and the Gulf emirs? If I was here, why weren't they? Why weren't we honoring our Arab allies who had done so much of the heavy lifting in the fight against the forces of darkness? And where was Yuval Eitan, Israel's new prime minister? Was the president going to acknowledge his late friend and ally Daniel Lavi? No country had stood with the U.S. more faithfully during the current crisis than Israel. So why weren't the Israelis being honored? Why was the president taking all the credit for himself?

Just then, however, Taylor asked everyone to be seated while he honored every American who had fallen in Amman and Alqosh. He read the list slowly and respectfully, giving not just the names but several sentences of description about each. And he paused after each one, offering the audience and the nation time to absorb the details and remember their sacrifice. Still, why hadn't he invited our allies? Wouldn't that have been a powerful demonstration of solidarity in a time of great darkness and turmoil?

When he had finished reading every name, the president called for a moment of silence. Most people bowed their heads. I'm sure Matt prayed for the families and friends of the slain. I just stared blankly as the horrific images from Amman and Alqosh came flooding back.

After a few quiet moments, the president turned and looked up to the gallery. He asked General Ramirez and his Delta commandos to stand. He recounted what they had done in Alqosh. He thanked them for their loyal, sacrificial service. Then he asked the nation to join him in honoring "these unsung but unmatched American heroes." The tall, burly, freshly shaven men—all dressed in new suits with crisp white shirts and neckties—looked uncomfortable as they received such a sustained standing ovation that I actually forgot to check my watch and see how long it lasted. These were rough men. They were used to operating in the shadows, in faraway places. They had no experience in the spotlight. They had no desire to walk the corridors of power. Yet they were being celebrated tonight, and as the applause went on and on, each of them seemed deeply moved. And I have to admit that even as a cynical war correspondent, I found my eyes welling up with tears. These guys had saved my life, and I would be forever grateful.

The president turned next to the Iraqi children. He briefly explained who they were, though he omitted the details of the cruelest things that had been done to them. But he made it clear enough how much they had suffered. He did not ask them to stand, but everyone in the room stood for them. We all cheered them, me included, as if hoping that the applause might somehow wash away the more nightmarish moments from their memories.

As much as I didn't want to, I had to concede

Taylor was a master at this. Yes, there were still threats out there. Yes, ISIS was still a clear and present danger. But the president wasn't entirely wrong. America had won some real successes on the battlefield. We were doing some things right. These were all bona fide heroes, and they deserved the president's attention and respect and the respect of the nation. I could hardly fault Taylor for the address he was delivering. It was beautifully crafted and touchingly delivered. I hoped he would still lay out the enormous challenges ahead of us. But the American people had been through a terrible ordeal. There was a time and a place to come together and celebrate what was going right. This was that time. This was that place. Even I was moved by it all.

When we all sat down again and the room had settled, the president surprised me by asking me to stand. I wasn't sure exactly why I was caught off guard. I should have known it was coming. It's why he had invited me. It's not that I thought he'd cut me out of the speech given the dustup we'd just had in the Oval Office. But my thoughts were elsewhere. I'd been caught up in the moment, in the tributes to the others, in my emotions, and I had temporarily forgotten that I, too, was going to be singled out.

The president began to explain the role I had played in the hunt to find him and in saving his life and the lives of these children. His words were simple and direct but exceedingly generous and kind, especially given the history between us.

But as he spoke, something happened that I

did not expect. I heard a boom. We all heard it. It shook the House chamber. Then we heard another and a third.

At first it sounded like thunder. But as the shaking intensified, I knew exactly what was happening. I shot a look to Harris, and it was clear he knew too.

The Capitol was under attack.

9

It took Harris only a fraction of a second to react.

"Get them out—all of them—now!" he ordered the head of the First Lady's detail.

For a moment, the agent hesitated. Technically, this wasn't Harris's call to make. The agent looked at me, then down at the president. I was still on my feet, not sure what to do. When the booms had begun, the president had briefly paused, mid-sentence, distracted by the sounds and the vibrations. But then—perhaps assuming he was merely hearing thunder—he had once again found his place on the teleprompter and continued delivering his speech.

Now, however, hearing the commotion in the gallery, he stopped again and looked back up at me and those around me. He could see Harris—whom he knew personally—talking to the agent in charge of his wife's safety. From that distance, he couldn't have heard what Harris was saying. But he didn't have to hear the words. He could see the look in Harris's eyes. This wasn't thunder. Washington was under fire.

It all seemed to be happening in slow motion. I saw the First Lady's lead agent talking into his wrist-mounted radio. Then he was on his feet. I turned and saw two enormous Secret Service agents bound up the stairs of the rostrum. They grabbed the president and pulled him away from the podium. I stared as they literally lifted him off his feet by several inches, carried him down the stairs, and whisked him out a side door. The First Lady's detail started moving as well. They pulled her out of her seat and raced her past us, up the stairs and out of the gallery. As I watched them go, I just stood there, frozen in place, paralyzed with fear and shock and disbelief. Then I saw more Secret Service agents race to Vice President Holbrooke and pull him out of the chamber, even as the Capitol police detail assigned to protect the Speaker of the House moved to evacuate him as well.

I was still standing there, not moving, not running, not reacting at all. And it wasn't only me. In those few seconds, no one in the chamber except the Secret Service and the Capitol police was reacting. Not yet. We were all too stunned by what we were seeing and hearing around us.

Suddenly I could hear Harris shouting my name.

"Collins—Collins—do you hear me? We need to go, now!"

I heard the words but couldn't think, couldn't move. Harris's voice seemed distant and hollow. But then I saw my brother jump up. He grabbed me by my suit jacket and pulled me into the aisle. At the same time, I saw General Ramirez and his men jump to their feet. And then everything snapped back. It was as if I had suddenly reconnected to time and space—to reality.

"Move, J. B.—go!" Matt shouted.

But I couldn't leave—not yet—and it wasn't because I was in shock. *"The children!"* I shouted back. *"We need to get them out!"*

Harris hesitated. He was trying to get me to the door and back to the motorcade. But Matt and the Delta guys were already moving toward the kids, and I was right behind them. I could see the fear in the children's eyes, but they responded quickly and obediently as Matt and I motioned to them to get up and follow us out of the gallery.

Just then, an immense explosion rocked the chamber. Chunks of plaster and Sheetrock came raining down on the House and Senate members below.

We burst into the hallway, where we met a team of Capitol police officers rushing toward us. They assured us they would take the children and their chaperones to a secure location. A moment later, they were moving the Iraqi kids and their handlers down the hallway and soon they had all disappeared around a corner.

Another explosion rocked the building. The hallway lights flickered. More plaster fell from the ceiling. People were screaming and scrambling to get out of the building. Harris ordered us to follow him, and Matt and I raced for a nearby stairwell. When we reached the ground floor, we slammed through the doors and followed Harris down another long hallway.

Now we were hearing one explosion after another in rapid succession. The entire building was shaking. The Capitol was taking direct hit after direct hit, and I suddenly had flashbacks to the ISIS onslaught against the Al-Hummar Palace in Amman.

How many attackers were coming? How soon would they be here? Were the mortar rounds raining down on us filled with chemical weapons, as they had been in Amman? If so, was there sarin gas pouring through the halls of the Capitol? We'd never be able to see it or smell it. Had we already inhaled it? If so, how much longer did we have?

As we rounded a corner, we were halted by Capitol police and Secret Service agents brandishing automatic weapons. Some of them were donning full chem-bio suits, blocking our path back to the motorcade. A chill ran down my spine. We had no protection from poison gas, and I had no idea how we were going to find any. Harris flashed his FBI badge and credentials. He was cleared to pass, but Matt and I weren't.

"They're with me," Harris shouted.

"I don't care," a lieutenant shouted back. "I can't let them through."

"They're guests of the president," Harris insisted. "We're supposed to be in the motorcade."

"I have my orders," came the reply. "No civilians in or out of this checkpoint."

Harris was enraged. I could see it in his eyes. But he was a government man, first and foremost. Moreover, he wasn't an idiot. He wasn't about to storm through a checkpoint in a crisis. Instead, he turned and motioned for Matt and me to follow. We backtracked down the hallway, took a left at the next corridor, then a right and another left, running at full speed. Still recovering from my injuries, I wasn't entirely able to keep up with either him or Matt, but I wasn't too far behind. I'd been faithful in doing my rehab exercises, and fortunately it was paying off.

A moment later we reached another exit. Two heavily armed Capitol police officers—also in chem-bio suits—were guarding the door. They checked Harris's credentials, then urged him to stay inside.

"*No, we have a car!*" Harris shouted over the deafening, nonstop explosions. "*We're supposed to be in the motorcade!*"

"*The motorcade's gone, sir!*" one of the officers yelled.

"*Gone?*"

"*Most of it. They had to get POTUS out.*"

"*Fine—but I need to get back to the bureau immediately. I'm part of the ISIS unit. And I suspect that's who's hitting us.*"

"*Maybe, but it's not safe out there, sir,*" the officer shouted back.

"*We'll take our chances,*" Harris insisted. "*Now move aside—that's an order.*"

I wasn't sure Harris was making the right move. Yes, the Capitol was under a withering assault. But weren't we safer here than dashing out into a massive winter storm with mortars raining down death and sarin gas possibly blanketing the Capitol grounds?

Before I could say anything, though, both officers stepped aside and Harris bolted out the door. Matt dashed out after him. For a moment, I couldn't move, once again paralyzed with fear. I'd seen this film—twice—and I hadn't liked it either time. But as I watched Harris and my brother reach the sedan we'd arrived in, I didn't want to be left behind. If I was going to die, it was going to be with them. So into the storm I went, bolting across the plaza.

10

* * *

Our driver hit the gas.

We peeled out, fishtailing on the ice. Harris was in the front passenger seat, on his phone and already briefing someone back at the bureau on the nightmare unfolding around us. Matt was sitting to my right, staring out the window as round after round of mortars smashed into the roof and the walls of the north wing of the Capitol, where the Senate offices were located. I had my phone out. I was speed-dialing my bureau chief, Allen MacDonald, over and over again but kept being directed to voice mail.

Unable to complete a call, I opened Twitter instead and started writing dispatches, 140 characters at a time. I quickly described the scene I'd witnessed inside the Capitol moments before and what was unfolding outside as well, putting specific focus on the fact that the attack was being waged by mortar fire, something I couldn't remember ever happening inside the continental United States. Then I tweeted out my "breaking news" exclusive: authorities had arrested members of an alleged ISIS sleeper cell in Alabama that was stockpiling hundreds of mortar shells. I didn't say where I'd gotten the information. Nor did I add other details. I hadn't, after all, had the opportunity to find a second source. But I trusted Harris; he hadn't steered me wrong yet. Given that the site of the State of the Union address was now under mortar attack for the first time in U.S. history, it seemed imperative to me to get the word out there that the U.S. government knew for a fact that ISIS operatives had apparently been in possession of—and thus had presumably been experimenting with—mortar rounds on American soil.

Those were all the facts I had at the moment. But I hoped that by my getting them out there, other enterprising reporters would pick up the trail and hunt down more.

Suddenly the driver stomped on the brakes and turned hard. We found ourselves twisting, turning, sliding twenty or thirty yards across the ice- and snow-covered pavement, barely coming to a halt in front of a Capitol police cruiser. Our driver put his window down and demanded to be let through. But he was told this exit on the north side—leading to Constitution Avenue and from there to Pennsylvania Avenue—had been sealed off until the president's motorcade made it safely back to the White House. Harris flashed his badge and explained we urgently needed to get back to FBI headquarters, but the officer told us there was nothing he could do. The orders had come from the top. The only way out, he told us, was on the opposite side of the Capitol grounds.

Infuriated, Harris ordered the driver to back-track. He did, slamming the sedan into reverse, spinning the car around, and racing for the south-east gate, swerving to avoid the craters caused by errant mortar rounds.

As we spilled onto Independence Avenue and headed west, lights flashing and siren blar-ing, I looked back at the Capitol. The scene was surreal, like something out of Hollywood. The entire north wing—the Senate side—was ablaze. Through the blowing, swirling snow, I could see additional mortar rounds arcing in from multiple directions. Several smashed into the great dome, which was soon engulfed in flames as well. Police cars, fire trucks, ambulances, and hazmat teams were racing to the scene from all directions, even as we raced away at ever-increasing speed.

Our driver took a hard right turn on Third Street and headed for the intersection with Pennsylvania Avenue just a few blocks ahead. Matt and I were riveted on the Capitol out the window to our right. But when we heard Harris gasp and drop his phone, we both turned to see what in the world he was reacting to.

Then I gasped as well. The president's motorcade—what was left of it, anyway—was straight ahead, trying to advance westward on Pennsylvania, back to the White House. But it was under attack from RPG and automatic-weapons fire. At least four of the police cruisers that had been in the lead had smashed into one another. Now they were a raging inferno piled up in a way that blocked the path forward for the rest of the team, including the Beast and the decoy car. Both limousine drivers were trying to back up, but they had at least a dozen Chevy Suburbans behind them, also trying to back up and creating a logjam.

Out of the corner of my eye, I saw a brilliant flash of light. It originated from a high window of a large office building to the right of the Labor Department. Next I saw the contrail, and then one of the Suburbans behind the Beast erupted in a massive explosion. The SUV was lifted into the air and then flipped over, landing on its roof. A fraction of a second later, there was another flash of light, another contrail, and another Suburban was blown sky-high.

Our driver slammed on the brakes and we went skidding for a good thirty or forty yards. Fortunately, with all the roads blocked off and cleared of traffic, there was no danger of smashing into anyone else. But we still were watching the president's motorcade come under assault, and we were horrified at the sight.

With a clear view of everything that was unfolding, I used my phone to take multiple pictures of both the motorcade and the Capitol and immediately tweeted them out. Just then I saw members of the Secret Service's tactical unit open fire on the office building. Two agents fired RPGs into the window from which the incoming fire was emanating. At the same time, another agent popped out of the roof of one of the remaining Suburbans. He was armed with a .50-caliber machine gun. He pivoted toward the office building and let her rip, though not before a final rocket-propelled grenade was launched at the Beast. Switching my iPhone to video mode, I was filming as an RPG hit the side of the lead limo and burst into a ball of fire, even as both that limousine and the one behind it maneuvered to get out of the kill box, onto a sidewalk, and around the burning wreckage of the lead cars in front of them.

Our driver started shouting into his wrist-mounted radio. He was explaining what he was seeing, and while I couldn't hear what he was being told in return, it soon became obvious. *We* were now supposed to act as the lead car, a blocking force to get the president back to the White House. Our driver gunned the engine, and we raced for the intersection, fishtailing when we got there but narrowly making the left onto Pennsylvania Avenue. We couldn't see anything but the snow-storm ahead of us. Luckily the boulevard was clear of traffic. D.C. Metro police cruisers blocked most of the access streets on either side of us, and several massive white-and-orange D.C. snowplows and salt-spreader trucks blocked the remaining ones. I figured we ought to be home free once the presidential limos worked their way around the burning vehicles currently blocking their path.

"Here they come," Matt said as the first limo found an opening and began to catch up with us.

Harris and I craned our necks to get a look. For a moment, I saw only one of the limousines, but soon the second emerged through the flames and billowing smoke as well.

"Floor it!" Harris shouted, and the driver did just that.

Soon we were racing west on Pennsylvania, past the Canadian embassy, past the Newseum on our right and the National Gallery of Art on our left. But when we got to the Navy Memorial, all hell broke loose. I heard automatic gunfire erupting to our right. It seemed to be coming from one of the adjacent office buildings. But before I could pinpoint the exact location, one of the D.C. snowplows blocking a side street suddenly surged forward and pulled directly into our path. Our driver mashed the brakes and swerved left, but I knew instantly there was no way we were going to clear it, and I was right.

11

We slammed into the driver's side of the enormous truck.

There was a deafening crunch of metal on metal, and the windows in our car blew out. We all lurched forward. I saw the air bags deploy in the front seats, but in the back, neither Matt nor I wore seat belts. In the intensity of our exit from the Capitol, neither of us had even thought of it, and now we were being thrown around like rag dolls. The limousine behind us tried to swerve out of our way but couldn't turn fast enough. It clipped the rear of our Lincoln Town Car, sending us spinning out into the middle of the street, where we were then broadsided by the second limousine seconds later.

When we stopped moving, everything grew quiet. We were all choking on the smoke emanating from the explosive charge of the air bags, badly rattled by the crash. But we were still alive, and as best I could tell, I hadn't broken any bones.

"Everyone okay?" I asked, kicking open my door.

We were hit by a frigid blast, but at least we could breathe.

"I'm good," Matt said. "But my door—it's stuck."

I glanced over at him. Matt wasn't good. He'd cracked his head. Blood was pouring down his face. I offered to help him, but he waved me off. He insisted he must look worse than he felt. He pulled out a handkerchief and applied pressure to the gash across his forehead.

"Get out on my side," I said, gritting my teeth against the bitter wind and snow.

As my brother scrambled across the broken glass covering the backseat and exited through my side, I checked on Harris. He said he was fine and focused on our driver.

"He's not moving," Harris said.

"Does he have a pulse?" I asked.

Harris checked, then shook his head. "No, he's gone."

Just then I heard gunfire erupt again. It wasn't close, but it wasn't far enough away for comfort either. I scanned the sidewalks and the buildings around us but couldn't find the source. Harris drew his service weapon, a Glock 9mm handgun. That wasn't going to provide much protection if our attackers stormed into the street with automatic weapons, but it was better than nothing.

Suddenly a pistol fired. This *was* close, directly to my left. I turned quickly and stared in horror as the driver of the snowplow—clad in a black parka and black ski mask—climbed out of his cab and fired twice more, aiming at Harris. The FBI agent wheeled around and fired once but then went down.

The snowplow driver had also been hit by Harris's return fire. He landed with a crash on the crumpled hood of the sedan. He was groaning in pain, but he was alive and began pulling himself to his feet. To my right, I saw Matt hit the deck. I knew I should have done the same. The gunfire to our right was getting louder by the second, and the snowplow driver with the pistol was no more than ten feet away. But with Harris down and in mortal danger, I instinctively climbed back into the car. I reached for our driver's service weapon and yanked it from its holster under his jacket. The assailant was on his feet again and stumbling toward Harris. I didn't know if Harris was dead or alive, but there was no time to hesitate. I fumbled for the safety, flicked it off, aimed through the shattered windshield, and fired four times. At least one and maybe two of the rounds hit their mark. The man snapped back violently, then went crashing to the snow-covered pavement.

I immediately got out of the car and raced around the rear, the pistol in front of me, ready to fire again. But before I could, I saw Harris—on his back, on the freezing pavement—firing three more rounds into the hooded man.

"Clear on this side!" he shouted.

"Clear on this side too!" I shouted back.

Harris scrambled to his feet. He grabbed the gun from the man. There was no doubt he was dead. A crimson pool was now growing around him.

Harris tossed the terrorist's gun to me. Harris

himself was covered in snow and ice, but he was moving with ease. He didn't look injured. It took me a moment, but then I realized he hadn't been shot; he'd merely slipped on the ice while whirling around. The fall had probably saved his life. He urgently signaled for me to double back and move around the front side of the snowplow while he went around the other side, just in case the driver had a wingman. I quickly did as I was told. I motioned for Matt to stay down and gave him the extra pistol, just in case someone got by me.

Then, as I peered around the front of the truck and the giant orange plow, Harris's instincts proved right. There was a wingman. Standing no more than two yards from me was an enormous figure—at least six-foot-five—also wearing a black parka and a black hood and holding a submachine gun.

He opened fire. I was able to duck just in time, but I could hear the rounds pinging off the cab and engine block. I could also hear the man running toward me, his heavy boots crunching in the snow. I crouched down and aimed around the corner, my hands trembling in fear as much as from the cold.

But just as the man approached, I heard Harris shout into the night. *"FBI—freeze!"*

The man didn't comply. A split second later I heard three shots ring out and a body crashing to the ground.

Again Harris yelled, *"Clear!"*

My heart racing, adrenaline coursing through my system, I forced myself to stand. Then I cautiously stepped out around the front of the plow to find Harris standing over the corpse. He kicked the machine gun in my direction and pulled the hood off the dead man. He looked Libyan to me, or perhaps Algerian. Either way, with the dark eyes and the oversize beard, it was obvious he was either from North Africa or the Middle East, and I had no doubt he was ISIS, working for Abu Khalif.

Two black Suburbans quickly arrived on the scene. In the distance, I could hear sirens coming from every direction. At first, I assumed the FBI had sent a team to help us. But the Suburbans didn't come to a stop. They weren't from the bureau. They were from the Secret Service. They'd come to rescue the president and get him and the First Lady back to the White House safe and sound.

But no sooner had they arrived than automatic gunfire erupted again. This time the source was clear: an upper floor in a nearby office building. Again I could hear rounds pinging off the snow-plow and the Suburbans. Harris and I ran for cover, but just then I heard the sizzle of another RPG streaking through the air. The force of the explosion sent Harris and me flying. I landed flat on my back and hard, in the middle of Pennsylvania Avenue.

The wind had been knocked out of me. Burning pain shot through my back and legs. Wincing, I forced myself onto my right side. I looked back at the Capitol, now completely engulfed in flames. I could see Harris several yards away, closer to the plow, dazed and trying to get to his feet.

Then suddenly I found myself blinded by

headlights. One of the limousines was headed right for me, but I was in too much pain to move. With bullets whizzing by us, I felt someone grab me and pull me aside just as the first of the two limos whooshed by. When I looked up, I found Matt standing over me. But over his shoulder I saw another flash of light, another contrail, and another RPG streaking through the air.

"Matt, get down!" I yelled.

The second Suburban exploded on contact. It flipped through the air, landing not more than twenty feet from us and directly in the path of the second limo as it was roaring by. This time it was I who grabbed Matt and pulled him toward me as the second limo rushed past, missing Matt's left foot by inches. The driver of the second limo then hit the brakes, fishtailing past us. Right behind them were the Secret Service tactical units. They were returning fire, engaging the terrorists in the building beside us. But the president and his team were boxed in. With the storm, there were no choppers in the air. There would be no air support. Sharpshooters were trying to suppress the RPG fire, but they weren't having much luck.

How was this possible? I wondered. We were just blocks from the White House. But that didn't really matter just now. All I knew for sure was that we had to get off this street, and fast.

12

★ ★ ★

These were not amateurs.

Someone had been planning this attack, likely for months.

I forced myself to get up, despite the pain. I could now see that Harris was, in fact, wounded. His trousers were shredded, and he was holding his leg. Matt rushed to his side and assessed his wounds. Then he took off his scarf and wrapped it around Harris's left leg as a tourniquet. They were both hunched down behind the smoking wreckage of the sedan as the bullets kept flying in all directions.

Clearly the sedan we had been riding in was undrivable. It had been totaled. It was also leaking gasoline, putting us in additional peril. Just as clear was that none of the other vehicles on this street were going to stop for us. They had one mission only—to protect the president of the United States—not to get us to safety.

I turned to the snowplow. The lights were on. The windshield wipers were still running. So was the engine. I scrambled across the icy pavement, opened the door of the cab, and then returned to Harris's side.

"Matt, let's get him in the truck," I shouted across the firefight. *"We ought to be able to punch our way through in that."*

Matt looked back at the snowplow. He said nothing. I could see the skepticism in his eyes. But he nodded. This was our only shot, and he knew it. He also knew there was no time to overthink it. We had to move fast. Harris was losing blood, and if another RPG was fired at this sedan, we'd all be finished.

Careful to stay low, out of the line of fire, we dragged Harris through the snow, then lifted him up and laid him along the bench-style front seat. Matt climbed over him, shielding Harris's body while at the same time taking care to keep his own head away from the passenger-side window. Once they were in, I climbed into the driver's seat, put my seat belt on, revved the engine, and threw the Western Star 4800 into reverse. We jolted forward rather violently. I'd never driven anything so big and lacked any finesse whatsoever. It was all Matt could do to keep Harris from sliding off the seat. When I hit the brakes, we were thrown back. Grinding the gears something fierce, I finally jammed the stick into first gear, and now we were lurching forward—slowly, but we were moving.

That said, my driving was the least of our worries. The bullets were coming hard and fast, as if we were heading into a rainstorm of gunfire. The longer we stayed on this street, the sooner we'd be dead. So I hit the gas, using the massive engine and the plow blade to push the fiery wreckage of the Suburbans out of our way. That, in turn, cleared a path for both limousines, and as I braked, the first limo shot forward immediately. To my surprise, however, the second limo pulled alongside us. I waited for it to catch up to its decoy. Instead, as I looked down through the blowing snow, I saw the agent in the front passenger seat frantically waving me to move forward. Baffled but in no position to ask questions, I depressed the accelerator and again we lurched ahead, heading west down Pennsylvania Avenue. Rather than drop in behind me, however, the Beast hugged my left flank, and then it became clear. This limo held the president, and the Secret Service driver was using us as a shield.

We were taking withering fire on our right side, but we pressed on. Suddenly the passenger window exploded. Glass flew everywhere and I tromped harder on the accelerator. Despite the snow and ice, I had no problems with traction in this massive truck. Likewise, the Beast had no problems keeping up. We soon passed Freedom Plaza on our right and the Ronald Reagan International Trade Building on our left.

Fifteenth Street was coming up fast. I had a decision to make. Should I be taking a hard right by the Willard Intercontinental hotel and the Treasury Department, heading eventually for the northwest gate of the White House? Or should I continue straight through the southeast checkpoint? The former was the classic route, the usual route, but for that very reason I suspected it was also the most perilous. It would snake us through a canyon of hotels and office buildings, any one of which might have more terrorists waiting for the president. I had no way to contact the Secret Service team in the presidential limo. But I did have Harris. I gave him both options, and he ordered me to go directly to the southeast checkpoint and then slam on the brakes, letting the Beast blow through the lowered gates, and then using the snowplow's bulk to seal off the checkpoint from anyone else who might try to crash through.

That was fine with me. The only problem was that I had now built up a head of steam and badly miscalculated how long it would take to stop.

"Hold on!" I shouted as I slammed on the brakes.

We all braced for impact, and the last thing I remembered seeing was Secret Service agents diving out of the gatehouse before we hit it directly, smashing it to smithereens.

PART
TWO

13

* * *

I awoke groggy and disoriented.

"Welcome back," said a kindly looking older gentleman.

I said nothing, and he didn't press me. I just stared at him and tried to figure out where I was. The man was probably in his mid- to late sixties. He was clearly a physician, wearing a white lab coat and a stethoscope around his neck. He was standing over me, holding a clipboard and checking my pulse.

"How are you feeling?" he asked.

Again I said nothing.

"Can you tell me your name?"

I tried to form words, but nothing came out. He handed me a cup of room-temperature water. I took a small sip, and he asked me again.

"Collins," I whispered.

"Is that your first name or last?"

"Last."

"And your first?"

"J. . . ."

"J. what?"

"J. B."

"What's that short for?"

I stared at him blankly.

"What's your full name, son?"

"James," I said finally. "James Bradley."

"Do you remember your birthday?"

"Yes."

There was a brief pause while the doctor waited for the answer, but I said nothing. A moment later, with great patience, he asked me again to tell him the exact date of my birth.

"Oh, uh . . . May—May 3."

"Good," he said, apparently checking my answers against whatever was written on his clipboard. "Where?"

"Where what?"

"Where were you born?"

"Maine," I said. "Bar Harbor." I was finally starting to feel more like myself, my head clearer and the answers to his questions coming more easily now.

"What's your mother's name?"

"Maggie."

"And your father?"

"Next question," I said tersely.

He raised his eyebrows. "I need it for the files."

"No, you don't," I said, then noticed his name badge. "I'm not a minor, Dr. Weisberg. My father hasn't been in the picture for over thirty years."

"Okay," he said, shifting gears. "Do you know what day this is?"

That took me a moment. "Tuesday—er, no, Wednesday, probably."

"Good," said the doctor. "What's your brother's name?"

"Matt—Matthew—where is he? Is he okay?"

"A few stitches, a slight concussion, but yes, he'll be fine," he said.

"Can I see him?" I asked.

"Of course," Weisberg said, nodding. "He's in the room next door. You can see him in a few hours. Now, the other man you came in with? Do you remember his name?"

"Harris?" I asked.

"You tell me."

"Yeah, Harris," I said. "Arthur Harris. Works for the FBI—and how is he?"

"He'll be fine."

"He was shot," I said.

"True, but he was lucky—only grazed," Weisberg said. "It was a bit messy, but we patched him up. He'll be good as new in no time." He shone a penlight in my eyes and checked to see if my pupils were properly dilating.

"So where exactly am I?" I asked.

"GW," he said, apparently knowing that I lived in the area and would understand that he meant George Washington University Hospital on Twenty-Third Street, just minutes from the White House. "It's been a tough night. Considering the rest of the folks I've seen tonight, I'd have to say you guys are pretty lucky."

It was all coming back to me.

"The president?" I asked. "Are he and the First Lady safe?"

The doctor said nothing.

"I'm not asking for anything confidential," I insisted. "I don't need to know where they are. I just want to know if they're okay."

"They are," he said. "Now, just a few more questions. Do you have any allergies?"

"No."

"Do you have a heart condition?"

"No."

"Diabetes?"

"No."

"Are you currently on any medications?"

I shook my head.

"Do you use any illegal narcotics?"

"No."

"What about alcohol?"

"What about it?"

"Do you drink?"

"I used to."

He waited.

I didn't want to say any more, but I knew he could already see where this was going. "A lot."

He said nothing.

"I'm a recovering alcoholic," I conceded.

Again he waited patiently. So finally I told him. There was no reason not to. "Two years, five months, and twenty-eight days."

"Good for you—one day at a time," he said. "Now look: you need to get some rest. There's a team of agents from the bureau outside your room, and your brother's room and Agent Harris's room, to make sure you're all safe. I'll check back on you in a few hours, when the sun comes up. In the meantime, if you need anything, press this button and the nurses will take care of you."

"Got it," I said. "And, Doc . . . I'm going to be okay, right? I didn't lose a limb or a lung or something?"

"Nothing so dramatic," Weisberg said, writing a few final notes on my chart. "You got banged up pretty good out there. You have a mild concussion—certainly understandable. Still, given the injuries you sustained in December in Iraq— bullet wound to the right shoulder, significant burns due to a hand grenade, significant loss of blood, dehydration, and the like—I'd like to keep you for the next twenty-four to forty-eight hours for observation, just to be safe."

There was no way that was going to happen. Too much was at stake. I had a story to chase and I couldn't do it from a bed at George Washington University Hospital. But I knew better than to get into an argument I was sure to lose with my attending physician. So I just nodded. "Can you at least bring me my phone and turn on the TV?"

"No, Mr. Collins," he replied. "Right now you really need to rest."

"I realize that, Doctor, but I'm a reporter. I need to know what's happening out there."

"The worst of it is over," he said. "But there's nothing you can do about it right now in any case. You don't work for the *Times* tonight. Tonight you're a patient. My patient. So get some sleep, and I'll see you in a few hours."

I glanced at the wall clock. It was 4:23 a.m. The sun would be coming up in about two and a half hours over a capital and a nation traumatized by the deadliest terror attack on American soil since September 11, 2001. But the question that kept haunting me was: What was coming next?

14

I was awakened by two investigators from the FBI just after 6 a.m.

They had come to get a complete statement from me as to what I had seen and heard as the terrorist attacks unfolded the previous evening at the Capitol building and along Pennsylvania Avenue. The "taciturn twins"—they were about the same age, nearly the same height, similar build, similar off-the-rack suits (ugly ones, at that), with equally dour demeanors—interviewed me for about thirty minutes. They took detailed notes. They covered every conceivable angle but refused to answer any of my questions in return.

"You sent out a Twitter message last night about an ISIS sleeper cell in Alabama," one said.

"*Alleged* ISIS sleeper cell," I clarified.

"Fine, alleged ISIS sleeper cell," he replied. "You reported that authorities found hundreds of mortar shells in the perps' apartment."

"And?" I asked, unclear where he was going.

"How did you know any of that?" the

investigator asked. "The news wasn't public yet. No press release had been issued. You don't live in Alabama."

"That's my job, gentlemen," I said. "That's what I do—report things other reporters haven't yet."

"But where did you get the information?"

"Nice try," I said. "You're not really asking about my sources, are you?"

"Mr. Collins, we need you to cooperate."

"I am cooperating," I noted.

"We need you to cooperate *fully*. We're asking how you knew when so few people did at that point."

"Lots of people knew," I countered. "The state police knew. The local authorities knew. The bureau knew. So did the White House, the CIA, Homeland Security, and the Joint Terrorism Task Force." I was spitballing, trying to throw them off the trail. But I had no idea if it was working.

"So, Mr. Collins, does it ever seem odd to you?" the lead agent now asked, trying a different tack.

"What?" I asked.

"That you keep winding up in the middle of terrorist attacks?"

"No," I said calmly.

"Why not?" the agent asked, incredulous.

"I'm a national security correspondent for the *New York Times*," I responded. "I cover war and terrorism. I don't expect to live a simple, easy life. If I did, I'd be writing for *Travel + Leisure* or *Better Homes and Gardens*."

"And it doesn't worry you?" his partner pressed.

"Of course it worries me," I shot back. "It

worries me that ISIS operatives are able to slip across our borders and make it to Washington and fire mortar shells at our Capitol, and nobody stops them. It worries me that you guys can't protect the seat of our government from an attack everyone knew was coming. It worries me that the president of the United States doesn't seem to have the will to crush ISIS once and for all even though they took the man captive, put him in a steel cage, threatened to douse him with kerosene and set him ablaze. It worries me that they tried to convert the entire country to their insane vision of Islam. It worries me that Abu Khalif is on a genocidal killing spree and the U.S. government doesn't seem to have a plan to hunt him down and put a bullet between his eyes. Should I go on? You got all that? Or am I going too fast for you guys?"

"We're guessing you're done talking?" said the lead agent.

"Oh yeah, I'm done," I snapped.

"Here's my card," he said. "Please let us know if you think of anything else."

I took the card and put it down on the bed without looking at it.

When they were gone, a nurse brought me a Styrofoam cup of black coffee. It wasn't the worst I'd ever had, but it was close. I drank it anyway. It was going to be a long day, and I needed all the fuel I could get.

Then came a knock on my door and my brother popped his head in. "You decent?" Matt asked.

He looked pretty banged up—scrapes and bruises all over his face and nine stitches on his forehead—but when I asked, he said he felt fine. I waved him over and gave him a hug, grateful we were both still alive.

When he asked about me, I was tempted to lie and say I was fine too. I didn't want to look weak. Least of all in front of my big brother. Instead, I told him the truth, what I hadn't even told Dr. Weisberg. I felt horrible. My neck was in wrenching pain from whiplash. One of the disks in my lower back was pinched and it was killing me. The muscles in both my legs were severely cramped. My backside was bruised. I wasn't trying to complain, I insisted. I was just answering his question.

Matt stared at me for a moment. I think my candor caught him off guard. Then he said, "Well, the good news is you don't really look like you've been through a major terrorist attack."

At first I thought he was being sarcastic. But that wasn't Matt's style. It was mine. I hadn't actually looked in a mirror yet. Now I did. I pulled myself out of bed, walked into the bathroom, and stared at my reflection. Behind my designer prescription glasses, my eyes were bloodshot. My salt-and-pepper goatee needed a trim. My bald head needed a fresh shave. But Matt was right. I had only the mildest of scrapes and contusions on my face. What injuries I'd sustained were real enough, to be sure, but my bruises and contusions weren't immediately visible. In a day without much to be grateful for, I would take it.

Harris came in just then. He was hobbling around on crutches, but as Dr. Weisberg had predicted, he was going to survive. The look on his face, however, told me immediately there was trouble.

"Turn on the television," he said without any pleasantries.

"Why?" I asked.

"The president is about to address the nation."

15

* * *

"This is CNN Breaking News."

I moved over to the bed and sat down and urged Harris to take the chair to the right of the bed, as it was the only one in the room. He hesitated, but when I insisted, he finally accepted. It was clear he was in more discomfort than he was letting on. Matt came over and stood in the corner to my left.

Soon we were transfixed as CNN showed a split screen. On one side was a live shot of the still-smoking U.S. Capitol; on the other was a view of the East Room of the White House and an empty podium bearing the presidential seal. On the lower portion of the screen, scrolling headlines noted various world leaders sending condolences to the American people. Moments later, Harrison Taylor—looking somber yet resolute—stepped to the podium and began to speak. It was surreal to think that I had been with him just a few hours earlier. How fast the world had changed.

"My fellow Americans," the president began,

staring directly into the camera and looking like he hadn't gotten any sleep at all. "Last night, enemies of the United States unleashed a cruel and cowardly attack. The attack occurred without warning. The terrorists targeted the heart of our capital, intending to decapitate our national leadership. But I am pleased to report that they were completely unsuccessful."

I was shocked. *"Without warning"?* How could he say such a thing? How much more warning did he need? A blind man could have seen ISIS coming. Abu Khalif couldn't have been clearer. I'd published his words verbatim, for all the world to read. Surely the DNI and the directors of the CIA and DIA and FBI and Homeland Security and their tens of thousands of employees had read them. I knew the president had read them. Last night I'd practically taken a yellow highlighter and pushed them in his face in the Oval Office. Okay, so Khalif hadn't given us the exact place and time of the attack, but was Taylor really so naive as to think he would?

"Fortunately, I am safe and unharmed," the president continued. "As you can see, I am here in the White House, at my post, doing the work of the nation. The vice president is also safe and unharmed, as is the Speaker of the House. Neither are in Washington at the moment. Both are currently in secure, undisclosed locations, but I can assure you that they, too, are hard at work. Indeed, during the night, I conducted a secure video conference with both of them, as well as the National Security Council and the Joint Chiefs of

Staff, assessing the damage and mapping out our response.

"Moments ago, I finished another video conference, this one with the secretary-general of the United Nations and the leaders of Canada, Great Britain, France, and Germany, as well as the supreme commander of NATO. Each of them have pledged their full support to me as I manage this crisis, and to the people of the United States as we recover from these attacks and plan our response.

"In less than an hour, I will be meeting with my full cabinet and will be conducting additional calls with the leaders of our allies around the world, all to make sure they have a clear and detailed understanding of what has been unfolding here and so that I can answer their questions and enlist their assistance.

"In a moment, I will brief you on the damage that was inflicted last night and what is being done to bring those responsible to justice. But first I want to assure you that every step is being taken to prevent other attacks from happening on American soil.

"First, I have directed the secretary of Homeland Security to shut down all civilian aviation to and from the United States and within the U.S. and our territories for at least forty-eight hours. This should give federal, state, and local authorities time to make sure no terror threats are being plotted in our skies and to plug any potential holes in our air-defense systems.

"Second, I have ordered that our borders with

Mexico and Canada be closed for the next forty-eight hours. All seaports will be closed to incoming vessels—cruise lines, commercial container ships, private yachts, and so forth—during the same period. This will give the Coast Guard time to make sure we are on top of any possible new threats.

"Third, I have directed the secretary of the Treasury to suspend trading on the New York Stock Exchange and NASDAQ for the remainder of the week. It is my hope and expectation that the markets will reopen on Monday morning. But for now I'm asking the Treasury Department and the SEC to take all measures necessary to safeguard our financial systems against the possibility of terrorists exploiting these attacks or trying to exacerbate their effect to bring harm to the American economy.

"Now I want to be crystal clear—there is no credible evidence that other attacks are coming by land, air, or sea. I am working very closely with the director of National Intelligence, our entire intelligence community, and our allies to review every conceivable threat and every possible lead that will guide us to those responsible. I assure you, we will bring them to justice. I have great confidence in the men and women of our law enforcement community and our military. They are working around the clock to keep us all safe. However, out of an abundance of caution, I am using my authority under the Constitution as your commander in chief to take the measures I deem appropriate to defend every

American—and all the visitors under our care—against all threats, foreign and domestic.

"That said, let me take a few moments to share with you some details of what happened last night. At approximately 9:36 p.m., as I delivered the State of the Union address, terrorists unleashed a bombing campaign against the Capitol building using mortar shells fired from artillery pieces positioned in various places around Washington, D.C. Some of the explosive devices were filled with chemical weapons, specifically sarin gas. The damage to the Capitol was extensive, and I regret to inform you that there was significant loss of life. According to the latest information I have been provided with by the secretary of Homeland Security, a total of 136 people died in last night's attacks. Another ninety-seven were wounded, some of them critically. Among the dead are forty-nine members of the House, nineteen members of the Senate, seventeen members of the press corps, twelve foreign ambassadors, thirty-three guests, three police officers, two D.C. firemen, and one member of my Secret Service detail."

The number hit me like a punch in the gut. *A hundred and thirty-six dead? Ninety-seven more injured? How in the world could this have happened in the most secure facility on the face of the planet, in the heart of the American seat of government?*

"Authorities are still notifying the next of kin for a number of these folks," the president noted. "At the appropriate time, we will post every name on the White House website. When the moment is right, we will hold a memorial service to honor these brave men and women, all of whom deserve our deepest respect. For now, would you join me in a moment of silence to remember these fallen heroes?"

The president bowed his head and closed his eyes. Matt and Agent Harris followed suit. I just stared at the television. *A hundred and thirty-six dead in Washington, D.C., at the hands of Abu Khalif.* My blood was boiling. I had no doubt every American felt the same.

But for me, this was personal.

16

★ ★ ★

I should have turned off the television right then.

For when the president began speaking again, what he said absolutely infuriated me.

"My fellow Americans, rest assured that as I speak, the FBI, the Department of Homeland Security, and other federal law enforcement agencies are engaged in a monumental investigation that spans multiple locations, including multiple states and even nations. While it is too early to say who is responsible for these attacks, you have my word that I will keep you updated on critical developments in the hours and days ahead."

Too early? What in the world was he talking about? There was no question in my mind this was the work of ISIS. I didn't have solid, incontrovertible proof yet—the kind I could publish, the kind someone could use to prosecute—but I'd bet everything I had this was the work of Abu Khalif. It had his fingerprints all over it. Surely the president had been briefed on the capture of the ISIS cell in Birmingham by now. Surely he knew far more than I did. Why was he hedging? Why not just tell the American people the truth?

"I urge every American to show restraint at this difficult hour," the president continued. "We must not make the mistake of jumping to conclusions that this was the work of a single organization. And even if it so proves to be, let us not make the mistake of concluding that there was a religious motive to these attacks, much less that this was the work of a single religion."

Again I recoiled in disgust. Restraint? Was he kidding? Why weren't we already carpet bombing Raqqa, the ISIS capital in Syria? And no religious motive? What did the president think the *I* in ISIL stood for anyway?

I bit my tongue, not wanting to explode in front of Harris. The FBI agent had become a valuable source. I didn't dare risk offending or alienating him. But the president's equivocation in the face of direct attacks on the American people, our leaders, and our honor made me physically ill.

What's more, I felt nauseated by his genuflections at the altar of political correctness.

No one in his right mind was accusing the *entire* Muslim world of trying to kill us. Not the Republicans. Nor the Democrats. So why was the president determined to set up such a straw man?

When the president insisted the vast majority of the Islamic world didn't want to kill us, that was true, and good—wonderful, even. But survey after survey showed that while some 90 percent of Muslims around the world did *not* subscribe to the philosophy of violent jihad, somewhere between 7 and 10 percent of Muslims did. I was very glad that nine out of ten Muslims had little or no inclination to violence. But in a world of 1.6 billion Muslims, 10 percent represented some 160 million people. That was equal to half the population of the United States! A nation with a population that large would be the ninth most populous country in the world. This was a big deal. This was a real and serious threat, for it was precisely this pool of 160 million sympathizers and supporters of violence from which ISIS was recruiting.

Yes, Americans wished it could all be over. Taylor certainly did. So did I. We were all exhausted by the conflicts in the Middle East. But the problem wasn't going away. It was actually getting worse. The last twelve hours proved it. To stick our heads in the sand and pretend we weren't engaged in a global war of guns and bombs and ideas was as foolish as it was dangerous.

Not once during his State of the Union address—nor during his address to the nation this morning—had Taylor mentioned the Islamic State by name. Rather, last night, as always, he had used the abbreviation ISIL. The acronym was accurate enough. It stood for the "Islamic State of Iraq and the Levant." But by only using the term ISIL and avoiding the full name, the president was purposefully avoiding using the words *Islam* and *Islamic* and *Muslim*. He was specifically avoiding any mention of the caliphate or any discussion of the theological and eschatological precepts driving Abu Khalif.

In one speech several months earlier, he had actually explained why he refused to say the full name of Khalif's emerging empire. "The Islamic State is neither Islamic nor a state," he had argued.

Such nonsense made my blood boil.

How could the president defeat an enemy he refused to define?

17

Then came the bombshell.

"The U.S. and our coalition allies have achieved remarkable victories in the Middle East in the last few months, and we must not allow what has just happened to drive us off target," the president continued. "As I said last night, we have liberated Mosul. In fact, we have liberated all of northern Iraq and made that entire country safe again. Our work there is nearly finished, and we can be proud of our success. We should be pleased with our progress, and we should stay the course. We must not change our strategy or weaken our resolve. We must not allow our enemies to force us to live in fear. Nor are we going to let them lure us into a quagmire that could bog us down for a generation. Our mission is nearly complete. We will bring to justice those who perpetrated this dastardly attack. But when our work is done, I won't delay for one moment bringing our troops home once again. I will not let terrorists dictate our national security policy. We will not become embroiled in the Middle East forever. We will do our job, and we will move on. To this end, you have my solemn pledge."

I couldn't believe what I was hearing, and as I glanced at Matt, it was clear he couldn't either. Harris was inscrutable, but my brother was livid.

The president's constitutional mandate was to protect us from all enemies, foreign and domestic. It was, therefore, the president's solemn responsibility to help the American people understand exactly what we were up against. For Taylor to pretend that ISIS wasn't involved in these new attacks—or that the fighters working for ISIS, or ISIL, or whatever he wanted to call it, weren't Muslims and weren't driven by their interpretation of Islamic theology—was just asinine.

As anyone who had studied their books and speeches and websites and videos could see, the leaders of the Islamic State professed over and over again to anyone who would listen that they didn't simply want to expel the infidels from the Mideast and North Africa. They wanted to either convert or exterminate the infidels, usher in the coming of their messiah known as the Mahdi, and establish the Islamic kingdom or caliphate that would rule over the entire globe. They weren't simply trying to conquer the "filthy Zionists" and the "ugly apostates" and "diabolical Crusaders." They wanted to force every person on the planet to bow down and submit to their version of Islam or be slaughtered. They were diabolically obsessed with bringing to fulfillment the Islamic prophecies supposedly uttered by Muhammad fourteen centuries ago, and they believed they could accelerate the

End of Days by engaging in all-out genocide. And not only were they trying to hasten the end of the world through their own violent actions, they were absolutely convinced that Allah required this of them and that they would burn in hell if they did not destroy their enemies.

This was what Abu Khalif and his inner circle believed. This was what drove them. This was what they preached, what they talked about, prayed about, wrote about. This was what they studied, what they thought about, what they rallied their forces around and indoctrinated into their children and their newest recruits. This was what energized and enthused and enraged them. And this was what made Abu Khalif so much more dangerous than Osama bin Laden or any of his colleagues or predecessors. Khalif was not simply a terrorist. He was the head of an apocalyptic, messianic, genocidal death cult, and in his head was a ticking clock counting down to doomsday.

With a plethora of Islamic texts in hand—real or otherwise—Khalif was explaining to his followers and the whole of the Muslim world his view of Allah, his view of mankind, his approach to the End Times, and why it was urgent for all Muslims to get off the sidelines and come join the caliphate.

And it was working. Abu Khalif was winning Muslim recruits in droves.

He had publicly pledged to decapitate the American government. Twice now, he had come dangerously close to achieving his objective. Yet twice in twenty-four hours, the president had refused to mention his name or the name of his movement.

Who was the commander in chief trying to convince by such obvious denial? I wondered. Did he really believe that what had just happened was evidence of our "success" in the war against the caliphate rather than a damning indictment of our failures? The president was living in fantasyland, and it was getting Americans killed.

None of this would be happening, of course, if he had thrown the entire weight of the American intelligence community and military into hunting down and destroying the emir of ISIS. Yet rather than vowing to ramp up our attacks and destroy every last vestige of Abu Khalif and his genocidal forces, the president was repeatedly signaling his intent to end our involvement in Iraq and bring U.S. troops home from the region as rapidly as possible.

That was tantamount to surrender, and I was about to explode.

18

I went straight to the nurses' station, dressed only in a hospital gown and slippers.

I demanded my suit and my phone. The head nurse said that wasn't possible. I could get my things back when I was released, and only my attending physician could authorize that, and he wouldn't be available for another ninety minutes.

"This is still America, isn't it?" I asked her. "This is still the land of the free and the home of the brave?" Through gritted teeth I made it clear she had two minutes to turn over my personal effects. She dug in her heels.

I was about to go ballistic when Agent Harris stepped up behind me and calmly intervened.

"Ma'am, my two colleagues and I are leaving here in five minutes," he said in that firm, authoritative, no-nonsense tone they must teach new recruits down at the FBI training center in Quantico. "Now, we would be grateful if you would provide us our personal effects immediately."

It worked. Within moments, Matt, Harris, and

I had everything we needed. Less than five minutes later we were in a cab heading straight to the J. Edgar Hoover Building.

Harris kept his cards close to the vest. He wouldn't tell us what he had in mind, but he didn't disabuse me of the notion he was taking us to look at some of the evidence the bureau had compiled so far on who might be responsible for these attacks so I could write a story for the *Times*. For the moment, though, he merely assured us that at the bureau we could get a change of clothes and a shower before we went any further.

The District of Columbia looked like a ghost town. In normal times, the five inches of snow alone would have led to the shutdown of all government buildings, schools, shops, and private businesses. But these were clearly not normal times.

The fires at the Capitol building had finally been put out, but all of Capitol Hill was now a hazmat disaster area. Specialists in chem-bio gear were swarming over the grounds and through the rubble of the Senate Chamber.

The cab driver had a local news station playing. We learned that every unsecured building in a twenty-block radius of the Capitol had been evacuated due to the threat of chemical weapons contamination. Meanwhile, the entire corridor between the White House and the Capitol had become a crime scene. It had been cordoned off from the public as the FBI, Secret Service, D.C. Metro police, and other law enforcement agencies gathered evidence. At the same time, a massive manhunt was under way for any and all suspects who had participated in the highly coordinated attacks.

Harris sat in the front and made several calls. Matt and I sat in back, with Harris's crutches across our laps. Matt immediately called Annie. He assured her—and our mom, who was on the extension—that we were alive and safe and had just been released from the hospital. He apologized that we hadn't been able to call earlier and explained what we'd been through.

Meanwhile, I speed-dialed Allen. After assuring him I was okay, I dictated an eyewitness account of what it had been like to be inside the House Chamber and on Pennsylvania Avenue during the attacks. It was all I could do not to let my personal outrage at the president come through, and for the most part I was successful. Allen was relieved to know I was all right, and he was grateful to get my first dispatch. He told me it would be posted on the *Times* homepage within the hour. I told him I was en route to FBI headquarters and would keep him posted on what I learned.

Moments later, we arrived at the Hoover Building. The main entrance was closed and heavily guarded, so the cabbie pulled up to the E Street entrance. I got out first and helped Harris with his crutches, then turned to Matt and suggested he head to my apartment in Arlington and get some rest.

"No, J. B. I want to stay with you," Matt insisted.

I shook my head. "I need to focus. And you need to rest. Go to my place. I'll link up with you as soon as I can."

"You sure?" he said.

"Absolutely," I said, then had an idea. "In fact, you should find a way to get up to Bar Harbor. You need to be with Annie and the kids. Don't worry about the cost. I'll cover it."

"You're serious?" he asked.

"Hey," I said. "It's the least I can do."

I hoped this might ease my conscience a little. My pursuit of the ISIS story had put my family in danger. I was single, making decent money, and had very few expenses. Matt, on the other hand, was a seminary professor. He wasn't exactly swimming in cash, and he had a wife and two young kids to support. I was sure he'd blown a good part of his meager savings to buy last-minute airline tickets to evacuate himself and his family out of Amman. Paying for him to get to Bar Harbor really was the least I could do.

"Let's go, Collins," Harris said, glancing at his watch. "We need to move."

I nodded and paid the cabbie the current fare plus enough to get my brother back across the Potomac to Arlington. I gave Matt my apartment key and my Visa card. He thanked me and made me promise I'd call home and tell Mom I was okay. Then the cab pulled away.

"Come on," Harris said. "There's something you need to see."

19

* * *

We cleared security and boarded an elevator.

Harris positioned himself so I couldn't see what button he had pushed.

"Why are you doing this?" I asked.

"Doing what?"

"Taking risks. Feeding me information."

Harris said nothing. The elevator headed up.

"The two agents who took my statement," I said.

"What about them?"

"They wanted to know who'd leaked me the info about the mortar shells."

"What'd you tell them?"

"I think you know exactly what I told them," I said. "In fact, I think you *told* them to ask who fed me the information and to keep pressing me to see if I'd crack."

"And why would I do that?" he asked as we passed the second floor and kept heading up.

"To see if I could be trusted."

Harris said nothing as we cleared the third floor.

"Can you be?" he asked finally.

"You tell me," I said.

The elevator dinged. The doors opened. We had reached the fifth floor.

"Guess the answer is yes," I said, then stepped off.

I nodded to several uniformed agents holding automatic weapons, but they neither stopped nor searched me. Then I followed Harris to a suite of offices on the Pennsylvania Avenue side of the building. A secretary waved us forward. The security men posted nearby nodded but didn't say a word. The name on the door was *Lawrence S. Beck, Director*.

Beck was a legend in D.C. He had been a special agent for the bureau for almost twenty years before being appointed to serve as the U.S. attorney for the southern district of New York. Later he served for three years as U.S. assistant attorney general. During his career, Beck had successfully prosecuted some of the most notorious serial killers, embezzlers, mobsters, and terrorists in the country's history. At fifty-six, he was tough as nails, straight as an arrow, and as bald as I was after a fresh shave.

We'd actually met once in Baghdad at an embassy function in the Green Zone just after the liberation of Iraq in the summer of 2003. He was helping advise the Iraqis in how to set up their justice department. Tall and lanky, brimming with energy, he hadn't been real chatty. Instead, he'd chain-smoked through the evening, and given that he didn't really affect my beat directly, I'd not paid any more attention to him. Now I was standing in his office.

"Mr. Collins, have a seat," the director said.

I did as I was told. Harris sat beside me. Beck didn't sit at all. Rather, he paced and chewed—constantly—what I guessed was nicotine gum. I saw no ashtrays in the room. There was no smell of smoke. No stains on his fingers. Just the telltale signs of a man who wished I were offering him a light.

"Impressive work on tracking the ISIS story, Mr. Collins—the chemical weapons in Syria and all," he began. "Three separate intelligence agencies were pursuing that story. But you're the one who confirmed it."

"Lot of good it did," I said, in no mood to take credit given all the carnage that had ensued.

"Not your fault," he said, striding over to the enormous plate-glass windows overlooking Pennsylvania Avenue and the crime scene five stories below. "Those were political decisions, and—off the record—foolish ones. Nothing you could've done about that. You got the facts. You got them right. You put them out there for the world to see. There was nothing more you could do."

He was right. But so what? Where was he going with this? I was tempted to ask but held my tongue. Beck had summoned me. He had something to say to—or ask—me. He'd get to it in due time. There was no point seeming overeager.

"Did you catch the president's speech this morning?" he asked.

I glanced at Harris, then back at Beck.

"Of course," I said.

"Any initial reaction?"

It seemed a strange question for the director of the FBI to ask any reporter, especially a *New York Times* correspondent. His was an apolitical position. So was mine. At least, it was supposed to be. What *should* my reaction be? And why would he care?

I shrugged. Beck stopped pacing. He just stood behind his desk and waited for me to answer. But I said nothing.

"You had no reaction at all?" he asked.

"I'm not sure what you're asking, sir," I said cautiously.

"It didn't seem odd to you the president didn't accuse ISIS, didn't mention Abu Khalif, didn't suggest this was the emir's payback for Alqosh?" Beck pressed.

For a moment I stayed silent.

Beck didn't move. Didn't resume pacing. Didn't say a word.

"Okay," I said finally, seeing nothing to lose. "Off the record, yes—it did seem odd."

He waited for me to go further.

It wasn't just odd, of course. It was insane—an epic dereliction of duty. But why did Beck care what I thought? Again, I wasn't a columnist. I wasn't a pundit. I was a news reporter. My personal views were supposed to be irrelevant.

"Look, Director," I said at last, "if you've got something to tell me, I'm all ears. But I'm afraid I can't comment on the president's speech. Yes, I found it odd. But beyond that, I'm trying my best to stay objective."

Beck nodded. "Fair enough," he said. Then he

opened a file on his desk and began sliding one
eight-by-ten glossy color photo after another over
to me. And one after another, I gathered them
off the desk, reviewed them, and passed them to
Harris to look at. The photos showed an abandoned facility, a relic of D.C.'s history.

"You're looking at what used to be the
Alexander Crummell School," Beck said. "It's a
twenty-thousand-square-foot building set on two
and a half acres on Galludet Street."

"Just off of New York?" I asked.

Beck nodded.

"The Ivy City district," I said.

"That's right. You know it?"

"Sure." I had recognized the neighborhood
immediately. "I had an apartment near there years
ago when I first started with the *Times*."

"Then you might know the school was built in
1911 and shuttered in 1977," he continued.

I didn't. Nor did I care. I was waiting for the
punch line.

Beck slid more photos across the desk. The
first three weren't interesting in the slightest. They
showed several angles of an unmarked tractor
trailer bearing Alabama license plates, sitting in the
snowy parking lot of the abandoned school. The
fourth photo, however, sent a jolt of adrenaline
through my system.

20

* * *

"You found the weapon," I said, stunned.

I stared at the photo, trying to take it all in. When I didn't immediately hand it to him, Harris leaned over and gasped.

"One of them," Beck confirmed. "What you're looking at, gentlemen, is a World War II–era U.S. Army M114-model howitzer. It's capable of firing 155-millimeter shells—each weighing about ninety-five pounds—up to a maximum range of about nine miles."

"How far is the school from the Capitol?" I asked.

"Just over two miles," the director noted. "And there's more." He handed us more photos. "Now you're looking at Our Lady of Perpetual Help Parochial School—or what's left of it. It was a Catholic elementary school for, I don't know, half a century or more. Three stories. Playground. Parking lot. Used to take in hundreds of kids, mostly African American, but it's been abandoned since 2007."

"Where is it?" I asked.

"1409 V Street Southeast."

"Anacostia," I said.

"Right," Beck agreed. "Just a block from the Frederick Douglass National Historic Site. Used to be a jewel. But the diocese ran out of money and shut her down."

"How far is it from the Capitol?" I asked.

"Two and a quarter miles," Beck said.

"Straight shot, no obstructions?" Harris asked.

"'Fraid so," Beck said, nodding, then showed us a photo taken from the roof of the school. The smoking wreckage of the Capitol Dome was clearly visible, and every muscle in my aching body tightened.

Next Beck showed us photos of another abandoned, unmarked 18-wheeler, also bearing Alabama tags, and another M114 howitzer.

"Unbelievable," I said, shaking my head. "Please tell me you've got suspects in custody."

"Not yet," Beck said, but then he corrected himself. "Not exactly."

"What do you mean?" I asked.

Rather than telling me, Beck simply passed more photos across the desk. These next shots had been taken at a construction compound just off of Douglass Road in Anacostia, not far from the Suitland Parkway. Another 18-wheeler. Another set of Alabama plates. But unlike before, these photos revealed stacks of intact, unfired 155-millimeter mortar shells—nineteen, by my count. Then came a photo of an African American security guard, graying, probably in his late fifties. He'd been murdered, double-tapped to the chest.

"Where's the howitzer?" I asked.

Beck handed me more eight-by-ten glossies. One showed the twisted, scorched remains of a World War II–era howitzer. Others showed bits and pieces of the howitzer spread all over the compound.

"What happened?" I asked, my thoughts racing.

"Apparently one of the mortar rounds exploded inside the barrel of the howitzer before it could be fired. Or perhaps it blew up as it was being fired. Our technical teams are still on site, doing their analyses."

"And whoever was manning this thing fled when the howitzer blew up too?"

Beck shook his head. "Worse."

The final seven photos were each more gruesome than the last. They revealed dead men in their mid- to late twenties. Each had dark skin and a beard. And they all had clearly been killed by exposure to sarin gas. I had seen it before—in Amman, in Mosul, and in Alqosh. I knew the signs. Their eyes were glassy and dilated. Their hands and fingers were twisted. Some were curled up in a fetal position. There was unmistakable evidence that each of them had lost control of their bodily functions in their final moments. They had urinated and defecated all over themselves. Several were covered in their own vomit. They had died just the way they had intended their victims to die, the way they had intended the president to die, the way they had intended my brother and me to die.

I couldn't look any longer. Shuddering, I stood, walked over to the windows, and looked out at the fresh snow falling on a city reeling from the latest wave of evil. The death toll—at 136—wasn't as high as the 9/11 attack on the Pentagon, which had claimed 184 lives. But the al Qaeda attacks had taken place almost two decades earlier. A generation of young people had been born and raised since those attacks. They'd only heard about them through textbooks, documentaries, and annual memorial services. These attacks by ISIS were as fresh as they were horrific, and since they had come on the heels of the disaster in Amman, every American knew two things: First, it could have been much worse. And second, it wasn't the end; much more was surely coming.

Abu Khalif had launched an unprecedented chemical weapons attack inside the heart of the American democracy. This was the first time weapons of mass destruction had ever been used against the American people inside the American homeland, and it had taken place in prime time, during a nationally televised State of the Union address, when an estimated 70 million Americans had been watching.

"Have you ID'd the seven yet?" I asked, fixated on the smoke still rising from the House Chamber but forcing myself to do my job.

"We have," Beck said. "Five are recent Syrian refugees. Each entered the U.S. in the past year as part of the president's program to welcome and absorb fifty thousand refugees fleeing ISIS. The sixth was an Iraqi national. He was captured by U.S. forces as a member of AQI and sent to Abu Ghraib. He got out the night Abu Khalif escaped."

"The night I was there, interviewing Khalif?" I clarified.

I saw Beck's reflection in the window as he nodded.

"And the seventh man?" I asked, turning to see Beck handing his entire file over to Harris.

This time Harris answered, reviewing the notes. "Jordanian. Twenty-six. Graduate of MIT. Studied chemical engineering. Son of a Jordanian member of Parliament."

"You're kidding me," I said.

"Wish I were."

"What else?" I asked, my thoughts reeling.

"They're all ISIS," the director said. "Every single one of them. None of them were carrying passports or other forms of ID. But we've recovered their phones. We've got their fingerprints. We're still crossing the t's and dotting the i's, but the evidence is overwhelming. They're all in our databases. They've all sworn allegiance to the caliphate and to Abu Khalif personally. Several of them posted videos of themselves doing so on YouTube. And if these seven are ISIS, we can be pretty sure the teams who ran the other two locations were ISIS as well."

"So the president was lying," I said. It wasn't a question. It was a statement of fact.

"I wouldn't say that," Beck countered.

"Of course you wouldn't," I argued. "You're a career lawyer, and you're the director of the FBI, personally chosen and appointed by the president. But facts are facts."

"Let's stick to what we know for now, Mr. Collins," Beck replied.

"Didn't the president just tell us it's 'too early to say who is responsible for these attacks'?"

Neither Beck nor Harris responded.

"Didn't he say, 'We must not make the mistake of jumping to conclusions that this was the work of a single organization'?" I pressed.

"Mr. Collins, the president is operating in the midst of a fast-moving crisis," Beck replied. "He didn't say it wasn't ISIS. He merely said it was too soon to point a finger. And he's right. Our investigation is still ongoing."

"Sir, with all due respect, Abu Khalif just tried to take out the entire American government," I said. "Then he and his men tried to slaughter me and Agent Harris in front of your own building, blocks from the White House. The president should be ordering the annihilation of ISIS strongholds in Syria. He should be unleashing the entire might of the American military toward finding and killing the head of ISIS. You know it. The entire country knows it. Don't start making excuses for him. Not now. Not after all we've been through."

"He's not making excuses," Harris responded. "He's telling you to keep your head in the game and stay focused on the mission at hand."

"Yeah? And what's the mission?" I asked, my face red, the back of my neck burning. I knew I was about to lose it.

Harris held up the file. "Putting everything he just told you on the front page."

21

★ ★ ★

"J. B., wake up."

I groaned, rolled over, pulled the blankets up over my head, and flipped my pillow to the cool side. But then I heard it again.

"Come on, wake up, J. B.—listen to me—it's important."

Was that Matt's voice? How could it be? It was way too early. I had to be dreaming. But then I heard it again.

"J. B., seriously—you need to get up."

That was definitely the voice of my big brother. I forced my groggy eyes open.

The room was dark and quiet but for the howling winter winds rattling my windows and the low hum of a space heater a few feet away. I glanced at the clock on the nightstand next to me. *You've got to be kidding me,* I thought. It was 4:36 in the morning. I'd been back in my apartment for less than three hours. There was no way I was getting up now.

"Go back to sleep," I mumbled, then shut my eyes again.

Suddenly all the lights came on and Matt kicked the side of the bed. I sat up, shielded my eyes with my arm, and tried to imagine why in the world Matt would want to provoke me into punching him in the face.

"Are you crazy?" I snapped. *"Turn it off."*

"Here," Matt said, tossing a fresh copy of the *Times* on my lap. "Check out the front-page headline, top of the fold."

Annoyed, I tried to rub the sleep out of my eyes and concentrate on the paper in my hands. **Evidence Strongly Suggests ISIS Responsible for Chemical Attack in D.C., Says FBI Director**, read the headline.

"It's all over cable news and it's blowing up Twitter right now," Matt said.

My exclusive interview with FBI Director Beck was the lead story, along with insider details of the bureau's ongoing investigation. Below the fold was my two-thousand-word firsthand account of the terror attacks. Allen had been ecstatic. These stories were going to drive the national news cycle. But they were no cause for getting up at zero-dark-thirty.

"Drink up," Matt said before I could snap at him again. He handed me a piping hot Starbucks mug.

"Not bad," I said, taking my first sip and savoring the perfect aroma. "Now what in the world is going on?"

"Didn't you get my note?" he asked.

"What note?"

"The one I left on your bathroom mirror last night."

"Why—what'd it say?"

"How could you not have seen it?"

"I don't know," I said. "I just didn't."

"What time did you get in?"

"I don't know—one fifteen, maybe one thirty."

"And?"

"And what?"

"Didn't you brush your teeth?"

"What are you, Mom?" I asked, my annoyance growing.

"I left you a note."

"Fine—but I missed it. What does it matter?"

He just looked at me like I should know what he was talking about. "What's today?" he finally asked.

I shrugged. "Thursday."

"Yeah, but what day?"

"Who cares?"

"I do."

"Just let me go back to sleep."

"What day is it, J. B.?"

"I don't know—the sixteenth."

"No, it's the seventeenth—it's right there on the front page."

"Okay, fine, it's the seventeenth. So what?"

"So it's February 17," Matt said.

I just stared at him.

"Three days after Valentine's Day?" he said. "Ring any bells?"

I sighed and took another sip of the coffee. It

had been a long time since I'd thought or cared about Valentine's Day, and Matt knew it. I was divorced. I wasn't seeing anyone. The only woman I really cared about had nearly died in my arms on the other side of the world, and now I barely ever heard from her. Then it hit me. Matt and Annie had gotten married three days after Valentine's Day, three months before she graduated from college.

"Got it," I said finally. "Your anniversary's today. So are you flying home today?"

"I can't," he said. "The airports are all shut down, remember? Trains, too. But . . ." Rather than finish the sentence, he dangled the keys to my new Audi in front of me.

"You're not serious," I said.

"I am," he replied.

"You want to drive all the way to Maine?"

He nodded.

"Today?"

Another nod. "I plotted it all out on MapQuest. It'll take us eleven hours and forty-five minutes door to door, without stops."

"Us?"

"With fuel stops and bathroom breaks, I'm guessing we can be there in thirteen hours. If we get on the road by five, we can be there by six tonight. We'll surprise them. It'll be fun."

"And then what?" I asked, in no mood for a thirteen-hour road trip.

Matt smiled. "I take Annie out for a nice romantic dinner, and you . . ."

"What?"

"You and Mom can babysit," he said, like it was the greatest idea in the world.

"You've really lost your mind."

"It'll be great. You and Mom can catch up. She'll love it. The kids'll be so excited to see you. You can hang out for a few days, then drive back on Sunday."

This was a terrible idea. I hated it. All of it. I had a job. I had a story to pursue. I couldn't afford to be diverted. Not now. I'd been off my beat far too long already.

But I stopped myself. I really did owe Matt. What's more, I owed Annie and Katie and Josh. I owed my mom, as well. I was on the front page today with two big stories. The least I could do now was take Matt up to see his bride and his kids and spend a few days together as a family, something we hadn't done since . . . I couldn't remember when.

"Okay," I said at last.

Matt stared at me. "Really? You're serious? You're not just messing with me?"

"Nope—I'm serious," I said. "I'm in."

"Wow," he said, visibly dumbfounded.

"Just give me a few minutes to pack," I said.

"Already done," Matt replied.

"What do you mean?" I asked.

He nodded to my garment bag on the floor.

"You packed for me?" Now I was the one who was dumbfounded.

"Last night, while you were working," he said. "It's all in the note."

"The one on the bathroom mirror?"

Matt shrugged.

"Guess you thought of everything," I said.

"Not quite," he replied.

"What do you mean?" I asked.

"I never thought you'd really say yes."

22

★ ★ ★

Matt gathered our bags and took them down to the car.

I threw on jeans and a flannel shirt, brushed my teeth, read the note on the bathroom mirror, and shrugged. I was going on a road trip. The timing couldn't have been worse. But I knew I had to do it.

Matt offered to take the first shift driving, but I said no. With a good, strong cup of coffee and a double shot of adrenaline, I was wide-awake now. In my head I was already working on my next story, and I needed time to think, not talk. So Matt adjusted the passenger seat in the Audi until it was all the way back and drifted off to sleep. I'm sure he was thinking about celebrating his wedding anniversary with Annie. I had other things on my mind.

My lead article for the *Times* that morning would, I knew, make a big splash, and for good reason. It told the public for the first time about the three howitzers and the three locations in D.C. where they'd been positioned to fire mortars at the

Capitol. It also broke the news about the murdered night watchman at the construction company in Anacostia, the identity of the seven dead Arab men, and the solid, conclusive evidence that each of them was a member of the Islamic State.

With Director Beck's permission, Agent Harris and I had visited the crumbling Alexander Crummell School, the boarded-up Catholic school, and the construction company. Allen MacDonald had sent along a *Times* photographer to take crime scene pictures. Then Harris and I had visited the city morgue. I'd seen the bodies of the seven ISIS terrorists for myself. I'd interviewed the D.C. medical examiner about the cause of death. I'd been allowed to look at her notes. The science was clear. All seven had died of complications triggered by sarin gas poisoning, and initial tests strongly indicated that the chemical fingerprint of the gas found in the remaining mortar shells matched the gas used during the attack in Amman.

It was good info, but I knew Allen would want more soon.

I figured once Matt got a few hours of rest, he could drive and I could write. By midafternoon, I could probably have a new draft that I could send, a draft that could significantly advance the story. But I was going to need Agent Harris's help.

Dawn rose and the sky brightened. Before long we had passed the city of Wilmington and were crossing the Delaware Memorial Bridge. I checked my rearview mirror again. I'd been doing so constantly since we'd pulled out of my parking garage.

Nothing seemed out of the ordinary. But I couldn't shake the feeling that something wasn't right. I told myself the jitters in my hands and stomach were just frayed nerves from all that had happened to me in recent months.

But I had to admit that for the first time in my life I was scared. Abu Khalif had promised to kill me. And I believed him. He had just demonstrated to the entire nation that his reach extended deep inside the United States. Who could say he couldn't reach me?

I checked the mirror again. Still nothing suspicious, so as I got off I-295 and onto the New Jersey Turnpike, I put on a mobile phone headset and dialed Harris's number. It was early, but I was in no mood to wait.

"Collins, is that you?" Harris asked.

I could hear the fatigue in his voice. But I could also hear phones ringing and people talking in the background. He wasn't at home. He was already at work at the bureau. Maybe he'd never gone home.

"I need your help," I said.

"For what?"

"I need more info on some of the things we came across last night."

"Sorry—I can't," he replied. "You've gotten all you're going to get out of us."

"Harris, come on; your boss gave me this story on a silver platter," I said calmly. "He wants this stuff out there. I just need a little more."

"Can't do it, Collins," Harris said, speaking almost in a whisper. "You got your story, and it's breaking big inside the administration. You had details the president and NSC didn't even have yet. And they're furious. The AG has already called the director and read him the riot act. There's no more. That's all you're going to get."

"Wait," I said. "At least tell me how the ISIS guys got the howitzers."

"I can't."

"Just give me a clue, a lead—something—and I can do the rest."

There was a long pause.

"Harris, you still there?" I asked.

"Write this down, Collins."

"What?"

"Three words—you ready?" he asked.

"Ready," I said, and Harris spoke the three words slowly, enunciating clearly.

"Lowell, Coon, Marion."

Then I heard a click, and the line went dead.

23

★ ★ ★

I speed-dialed Allen immediately.

He didn't pick up the direct line in his office, so I tried his mobile phone. He picked up on the second ring but said he wasn't in the newsroom yet. The snowstorm was still wreaking havoc on D.C. area traffic, and he was sitting in gridlock on the Beltway, still trying to get downtown. "Why, what've you got?" he asked.

"Do you have a pad and pen handy?"

"Of course."

"And are you stopped right now?"

"Yes, unfortunately."

"Good. Take this down—three words," I said. "Lowell. Coon. And Marion."

"Got it," he said. "What does it mean?"

"I have no idea," I conceded.

"Then why are you telling me?" Allen asked.

"I got them from a source—a good one—who says they're clues to finding out how ISIS got their hands on howitzers. Can you get someone to run a search and see if anything pops?"

"Sure," he said. "I'll text Mary Jane and get her

working on it right away. What else have you got? We're already getting great feedback on your pieces from this morning."

For the next ten minutes, while Matt slept, I laid out for Allen the contours of my next story—the feverish federal manhunt for the remaining ISIS terrorists, the ones who hadn't accidentally blown up their howitzer and killed themselves with sarin gas. It was all material I'd gotten from Beck but hadn't fit in this morning's article.

I explained to Allen that according to the bureau, all three 18-wheelers that had been abandoned at the three crime scenes had been rented. Each was from a different rental company, but the rigs had all come from Alabama. The FBI was working with local and state investigators to determine exactly who had rented them and when.

Then I shifted to the howitzers themselves. "Apparently the terrorists needed tractor trailers to transport the howitzers because each one weighs about six tons," I said. "Beck told me all three were World War II–era, built in the early 1940s. All three saw action in Europe—two in France and one in Italy."

"How do they know?" Allen asked.

"They've got serial numbers on them," I said. "Somebody in the basement of the Pentagon was actually able to look up their records and figure out where they'd been used."

"So how does one go about acquiring a howitzer?" Allen asked.

"I wouldn't think there's much of a black market," I said.

"How about an Army surplus store?"

"For a seven-decade-old weapon that weighs six tons?"

"Right—so then how would a terrorist get his hands on one, much less three?"

We discussed all kinds of scenarios—private collections, auctions, Hollywood studios, museums. None of them struck us as particularly plausible, but Allen promised to get some people on it.

Then he abruptly changed the subject. "Listen, J. B., I need you to go back to Amman."

"What?"

"Someone needs to interview this Jordanian member of Parliament," he explained. "Who is he? Why was his son found dead in Anacostia with a group of ISIS jihadists? Did the father know his son was involved in terrorism? Have the Jordanians arrested the father? Who else is he linked with? You know the drill. And you know the king. You need to get on this angle right away."

"Allen, I—"

"I've got you on the next plane to Amman. It's all booked. Lufthansa flight 9051 out of Dulles. It leaves at 5:20 tomorrow afternoon, assuming the Homeland Security secretary lifts the travel ban. You'll route through Frankfurt and arrive in Amman by dinnertime Saturday. Mary Jane will e-mail you the details in a moment. And don't worry; I talked to the brass in New York. They know what you've been through and they're very grateful. They let me bump you up to first class.

122   ★   WITHOUT WARNING

No need to say thank you. Just pack a bag and make sure you're at Dulles tomorrow by three."

"Allen, I can't do it," I said.

"This isn't a request, J. B. This is a huge story, and no one on my staff has better sources in the Middle East—and certainly not in Amman—than you."

"I get it, Allen, but . . ."

"But what?"

I took a deep breath.

"I'm not in D.C."

As I said it, I glanced down at the dashboard, saw the fuel gauge, and realized I was running low. I started looking for a service station where I could top off the tank and get some coffee and maybe a breakfast sandwich.

"What do you mean you're not in D.C.?" Allen asked. "Where are you?"

"My brother and I are driving up to Maine to see our family."

"Without telling me?"

"It was, you know, spur of the moment."

"What time did you leave?"

"Five this morning."

"So where are you now?"

"Not far from Philly, heading north on the New Jersey Turnpike."

"And when were you planning to tell me?"

"I'm telling you now."

"When will you be back?"

"Sunday, I guess. Maybe Monday."

Allen sighed. "Okay, listen," he said. "I'll make a deal with you. You need to go see your family. I get that. Really, I do. Take a day or two with them. Then fly out of Boston on Saturday evening. I'll have Mary Jane reissue the tickets. But you're going to Amman, J. B. I need you there."

I took a deep breath.

"What?" he asked, clearly sensing my resistance and somewhat uncharacteristically trying hard not to express his frustration.

"What if I take a leave of absence?" I said.

"You just had a leave of absence."

"Then how much vacation time do I have saved up?"

"No, J. B. You need to do this, and you're going to do it. I'm saying this for your sake, believe me. If you give up on reporting now, you're going to regret it for the rest of your life. I know you. And I'm telling you, my friend—you need to get back on the horse."

"How much vacation do I have coming to me, Allen?" I pressed.

"Forget it, J. B."

"It's got to be at least twenty weeks," I said. "I never take time off."

Another sigh. "Twenty-six."

"Then I'm taking a vacation, effective immediately."

"J. B., please, you need to stay on this story," he insisted. "Hunt down these killers. Run them to ground. Force the administration's hand. Make them bring Abu Khalif to justice. And *then* take the rest of the year off if you'd like. Write a book. Go to the Caribbean. Sleep on a beach. Marry that Israeli girl you're so fond of. But not now, J. B.— not right now."

24

★ ★ ★

"What was that all about?"

My heated conversation had just woken Matt up. I glanced over at him as I finally found a service station and pulled off the main highway. "Nothing. You want some breakfast?"

"Sure, that sounds good," Matt replied as I pulled up to the gas tanks and asked the attendant to top us off with premium unleaded. I still couldn't believe New Jersey prohibited self-service gas fill-ups, but given the brutal weather, I certainly wasn't going to complain today.

"So what exactly can't you do, and why?" Matt asked.

"Forget about it," I said. "It's nothing."

"J. B., give me a break. It's obviously not *nothing*. You just talked about taking a leave of absence from the only job you've ever loved. Now what's going on?"

"I said forget it!" I snapped. "Now do you want some breakfast or not?"

It came out far more harshly than I'd intended. But rather than apologize, I just glared at Matt.

He'd seen this before, and far too often, I'm afraid. So he sighed, shook his head, and let it go. "Whatever," he said, getting out of the Audi. "Text me what you want. I'll be back in a few."

As I watched him head inside, I felt guilty and confused. I'd barely spoken to Matt for the better part of a decade. Now things were finally beginning to thaw between us. Why had I just lashed out at him? Why was I reverting to my old patterns? I wasn't sure. I didn't like it. But I didn't know how to change it, either. I knew I should apologize to him. At the same time, I didn't want to waste any time psychoanalyzing myself. I had work to do.

I picked up my phone and checked my e-mails. There were five new ones.

None were from Yael.

The first was from an old friend, Youssef Kuttab, senior advisor to Palestinian Authority president Salim Mansour. He was checking to make sure I was safe after the terror attacks in D.C. But he was also updating me on Mansour's recovery. In December, the Palestinian leader had been shot twice in the back by ISIS forces right in front of me during the attack on the royal palace in Amman.

At the time, the official story put out to press said President Mansour had been lightly wounded, but I knew the truth was far more serious. One bullet had missed the man's spine by less than a centimeter. The other had ripped through the left shoulder and caused a tremendous loss of blood. Only the fast actions of the impressive IDF medics on the chopper out of Jordan, multiple blood transfusions, and later three highly complicated operations in Ramallah at the hands of skilled Palestinian surgeons had saved Mansour's life. Trying to downplay the seriousness of the president's injuries, every few days the P.A. press team released a new photo of Mansour resting in a hospital bed, smiling, laughing, chatting with his wife and kids, talking by phone with one world leader or another, reading briefing papers, and so forth. But not one of the photos had actually been taken during the days following the attempted assassination, I knew. They'd all been taken nine months earlier when Mansour had undergone a rather simple hernia operation. Yet the P.A. media team now put them out there—to great effect, I might add—and no one was the wiser.

During those dark days when Mansour's life hung in the balance—and could have literally gone either way—I had kept in close contact with Youssef Kuttab, who himself had only narrowly escaped being severely wounded or killed in the Amman attacks. I gave him my solemn word that nothing he told me would be published. I just wanted to know how the man was doing, as I had such tremendous respect for Mansour. The Palestinian president was one of the most humble, strong, and wise leaders I'd ever met. He was a true man of peace, and I genuinely and deeply feared the prospect of his death.

The president is doing much, much better, still off the record, Kuttab's e-mail began after inquiring about my safety. *The last few weeks have seen a nearly miraculous recovery. He's not just walking now; he's actually exercising. His appetite is returning. His color looks good. He still struggles with severe pain and, between us, even more severe depression. He smiles for the cameras, for the videos, for the media. But the man you saw in Amman—the man you remarked on who seemed so relaxed, even full of joy—that man, I'm afraid, is gone. Will he return? I don't know. We have seen other miracles, so I guess anything is possible. Inshallah.*

With every sentence, I found myself wincing. My heart grieved for Mansour. He had sacrificed so much to serve his people and try to hammer out a comprehensive peace accord with the Israelis, only to see the process literally explode in his face just before the final deal was signed. Now there was nearly zero interest in reviving the peace process among the Palestinian and Israeli populations, or among their leaders. Everyone knew ISIS was responsible for the terror attacks in Amman. But conspiracy theories had metastasized. Suspicion ran deep on both sides of the Green Line. Bloggers and activists on both sides blamed the other side for sabotaging the peace process, and emotions were running high.

At the end of Kuttab's note was an invitation to come and visit him and the president at my earliest convenience. I appreciated the gesture, and I liked the idea of sitting with these dear friends and sipping mint tea and seeing firsthand how they were doing. Perhaps if I headed over to Amman, I should go to Ramallah, too, and do an exclusive interview with Mansour—something to make Allen happy. Or at least get him off my back.

But then I glanced in my rearview mirror and suddenly my blood ran cold.

25

★ ★ ★

A black Mercedes pulled into the service station, covered in snow.

It eased into the line behind me, about six cars back. I was pretty sure I'd passed it several times before, but each time it had caught up with me. About twenty minutes earlier, I thought I'd seen it exit the turnpike. Now it was back.

The snow had turned to sleet. Visibility was getting worse. The Mercedes's windshield wipers were going full blast, and its front windshield was fogged up. I strained to see faces, but there were too many cars between us to get a good look. Then, in my side mirror, I saw the back passenger door of the Mercedes fling open, and despite the cold I broke out in a panicked sweat.

But out of the car came two figures I did not expect. They weren't Syrian or Iraqi men. They were two blonde little girls with pigtails and a puppy. They were wearing matching pink snowsuits, boots, mittens, and scarves, and they bounded out of the car without a care in the world. They didn't seem bothered by the cold and the sleet. Nor were they paying attention to the traffic around them.

In my rearview mirror, I stared in horror as the girls started racing across the parking lot toward the front door of the restaurant, oblivious to a Ford F-150 pickup bearing down on them. Their mother was now out of the car. She was screaming as the driver of the pickup laid on his horn and hit his brakes. Every driver in every car watched helplessly as the truck—which had been coming off the highway far too fast—fishtailed and skidded across the ice toward the girls, who stopped in their tracks, paralyzed in terror. I expected to see the truck smash into the girls and at the last moment turned away. I expected to hear the impact, but it never came. I expected to hear more screaming, but everything grew quiet.

Finally I forced myself to look again. To my amazement, the truck had come to a full stop just inches from the girls. The mother bolted to her daughters and grabbed them. The father was right behind her. Eventually I started breathing again. My heart started beating again.

But then I was startled by someone tapping on my window. I turned quickly only to find it was the service attendant, a young Hispanic kid no more than nineteen or twenty, motioning me to roll down my window. "Sixty-three bucks," he said.

Had I been in a different frame of mind, I might have asked this kid why the state of New Jersey didn't trust ordinary citizens to pump their own gas without blowing the place up, why the governor and the legislature were stuck in the twentieth century. Instead, I pulled out my wallet and handed him my Visa card. When it came back with a receipt, I pulled over to the rest area's entrance. Matt hadn't come out yet, so I returned to my e-mails.

I sent a quick note to Kuttab, assuring him that I was okay and telling him I would be honored to come see him and his boss soon. But for the moment, that's all I said. I knew I could work that into a trip to Jordan. But I genuinely had no desire to go to Amman. What I really wanted to do was go see Yael in Tel Aviv or Jerusalem. If I did that, a stop in Ramallah might still make sense. For now, however, a visit with the Palestinian president would have to wait.

The second e-mail was from Allen MacDonald's executive assistant. As promised, Mary Jane had sent me the details of the flights she'd booked for me from Bar Harbor to Boston, and then from Boston to Amman, via Istanbul, on Turkish Airlines. I didn't respond. I didn't know what to say. So I just moved on.

The third e-mail in the queue was from someone claiming to be a top aide to General Amr El-Badawy, commander of Egyptian special forces. I had met the general on a remote Jordanian air base in the final hours before the joint assaults on Dabiq and Alqosh. We hadn't spoken much then. I hadn't heard from him since. But now his aide was writing to tell me El-Badawy wanted to speak to me. The subject was too sensitive to discuss by e-mail, the message writer indicated, asking if I could please call the general—through him—at the private number he provided. I glanced at my watch. I couldn't call now, of course. Matt would be back at any moment. But I was curious, so I sent a note back that I would call at my soonest opportunity.

The fourth e-mail was a somewhat-cryptic message from a partner in the law firm claiming to represent the estate of Robert Khachigian. The firm apparently had "important business" to discuss with me concerning the final will and testament of the former senator and CIA director, who had been assassinated the previous November in D.C. This, too, was apparently a sensitive matter and required an in-person meeting in the firm's office in Portland, Maine. The partner indicated it was not something he could discuss by phone. I couldn't imagine what that was all about, nor did I care to guess.

Normally I'd be nowhere near Portland, but as fate would have it, I was about to be. Maine's largest city was a mere 175 miles south of my hometown of Bar Harbor, roughly a three-hour drive, depending on traffic. I decided I would find the time to make the trip. Khachigian, after all, had been a dear friend of our family and a personal mentor of mine. He had been shot and killed right in front of me while helping me track down one of the most important stories of my career: the capture of chemical weapons by ISIS forces in Syria. Whatever this lawyer had to say about my old friend, I would hear him out. I owed Khachigian and his memory and his family nothing less.

The newest e-mail was from Allen. He apologized for getting testy with me. He assured me that he understood what I was going through, and was ready to request a two-month sabbatical of sorts for me—not counted against my vacation time—so long as I would first go to Jordan and then take the next few weeks to follow this story about the manhunt for the ISIS jihadists that had just hit Washington. After that, he said, he would fully support me taking a "much-needed" break. I read it twice but didn't reply. My answer hadn't changed, and frankly I was peeved at him for pushing. I wasn't going to Amman, and that was final.

Again I glanced at my watch. Matt still wasn't back. I was about to put the phone down and turn the radio on. But suddenly—and somewhat oddly—I found myself thinking of our home in Maine. It occurred to me that I was actually looking forward to the visit. I craved a hot, home-cooked meal, prepared in that old kitchen, served on that old wooden table, in that old drafty house—the house I grew up in—with my mom and Matt. I couldn't wait to play with my niece and nephew, to laugh and giggle with them, maybe play hide-and-seek. Most of all, I wanted not to talk about ISIS or the manhunt or my work or anything related to Washington or the Middle East. Instead, I wanted to sleep in my childhood bed, and awake to a blanket of new-fallen snow and the smell of fresh coffee and bacon and sausages frying in the kitchen. I couldn't remember the last time I'd had anything like that, and the fact was I missed simple times and a quieter life.

I made a snap decision and sent a quick e-mail to my mom. I briefly described the anniversary surprise Matt was plotting, gave her our location and estimated time of arrival, and said I was looking forward to seeing her. Then I swore her to secrecy and hit Send.

Matt finally got back in the car with to-go cups of steaming black coffee for both of us and a couple of breakfast sandwiches. It dawned on me that I hadn't texted him like he'd asked, hadn't told him what I wanted. But rather than apologize, I said nothing. I just nodded my thanks, drank in the infusion of caffeine, and pulled back onto the turnpike.

26

★ ★ ★

We had no music playing.

The interior of the Audi was silent, save the *whoosh-whoosh* of the windshield wipers and the hum of the road beneath the treads. Matt, still annoyed or at least disappointed in me, had eaten in silence and then quickly drifted back to sleep.

I was thinking about nothing in particular, just doing my best to stay alert, when I glanced at a passing road sign. I thought we might be getting close to Newark, but the sign didn't say anything about Newark. It didn't mention Trenton or Shore Points or Manhattan either. It wasn't a mileage indicator. It simply noted that VFW Post 8003 in the town of Lawnside had adopted this stretch of the turnpike to keep it free of litter.

Lawnside. *Lawnside.* Something about the sign caught my attention. But why? Did I know anyone from there? I didn't think so. Had I ever been to Lawnside? Not that I could recall. So why had I noticed that sign? Why had it caught my attention? Why did I care? Was there any reason at all, or was I just growing exhausted? Maybe it was time to switch with Matt and let him drive. After all, we still had nine hours to go.

Suddenly I realized it wasn't the name of the town but the organization on the sign that had tickled my subconscious. I grabbed my phone, hit Redial, and got Allen on the third ring. He was finally in the office.

"What about a VFW post?" I asked.

"What?"

"Or an American Legion post?"

"I'm not following you, J. B. What are you talking about?"

"We have them all over Maine," I said. "Some of these places have old Revolutionary War cannons out front. Others have World War II tanks and other vehicles. Maybe some have howitzers. Maybe that's where ISIS got them from."

"Hmm, okay, that's interesting," Allen said quickly, catching up with my otherwise-random train of thought. "My father-in-law landed on Omaha Beach on D-day, and he was very active in the VFW in Topeka."

"Did his post have a howitzer?"

"No, an old half-track," he said. "But you're right; maybe some do."

"Agent Harris mentioned three names—Lowell, Coon, Marion. What if they're towns with VFW posts and missing howitzers?"

"I knew a town called Lowell when I was growing up in Wisconsin," Allen said. "It was about seventy miles northwest of Milwaukee, along the Beaver Dam River. My grandpa used to fish not far from there. But it's small. I mean, really tiny. I bet there's not a thousand people in the whole town."

"Did they have a VFW post?" I asked.

"I don't know—maybe," he said. "A lot of those small towns do."

"Can you look it up?"

"Right now?"

"Absolutely. This is important."

"Fine," he said. "Hold on."

The sky was brightening, but I couldn't see the sun. A layer of thick winter clouds obscured the sky. The digital display on my dashboard said the temperature outside was a mere nine degrees above zero. The forecast called for more snow, but it wasn't coming down at the moment. The turnpike was pretty clear, considering, but the snowplows and salt trucks were out. More was coming, and they were ready. Was I? It occurred to me then that I didn't have snow tires on my car. Why would I? Washington rarely had this much snow, and when it did, it usually melted away within a few days. Now I was headed to Maine in a sports car I'd bought well below the Mason-Dixon Line.

A moment later, Allen was back on the line. "Get this," he said. "Lowell's population is a whopping 340."

"That's it?"

"Yeah—just eighty-nine families and a post office."

"And a VFW post?"

"Yes—Post 9392."

"And are they missing anything?"

"As a matter of fact they are," Allen said. "I just

pulled up an AP story from January 2. That's, what, six weeks ago? Turns out your instincts were right on the money. According to the story, an M114 U.S. Army howitzer used in World War II was stolen from outside VFW Post 9392 sometime after midnight on New Year's Eve. A police officer is cited saying the evidence suggests this may have been some kind of high school prank. They found empty beer cans and cigarette butts at the scene, rocks thrown through windows, spray paint on the walls, that sort of thing."

"Pretty smart," I said, "making it look like some kids out to goof around on New Year's."

"Right. I bet the theft wasn't even reported to the Feds. Why would it have been? No one could have imagined a World War II–era howitzer was going to be used in a terrorist attack."

Other pieces quickly started falling into place. Searching the *Times'* database of news stories from all manner of publications all over the country, Allen pulled up several promising articles. One was about a howitzer stolen on January 9 from a VFW post in Coon Valley, Wisconsin, population 765. Another concerned a howitzer gone missing from a VFW post in Marion, Massachusetts, population 4,907. The articles were brief, little more than curiosities mentioned in the police blotter of obscure newspapers. In each case, the thefts were described by authorities as apparently the work of local youths. The details of the crimes were nearly identical—beer cans, cigarette butts, spray paint, and other forms of vandalism, all suggesting a high school prank of some kind. There was no indication that the police in any of the jurisdictions were aware of the other stolen howitzers. And there certainly was no mention of any notion that a larger plot was being set into motion.

Allen promised to work with his counterpart on the national desk to send *Times* reporters and photographers immediately to each location. For the moment, we were operating on a hunch. It was a good one, a plausible one—indeed, one Harris himself had set me onto—but before we went to press, we needed more hard information. We couldn't rely on old stories in local papers. We needed our own people to talk to the VFW folks in each town and interview the local cops. We also needed to confirm that the FBI had been talking to the local authorities and try to pick up any other useful tidbits that would help our readers better understand the ISIS plot.

After I hung up, I drove for another hour.

Then Matt's phone rang—the ringtone of a dad, some song from *Toy Story*. He woke up instantly and groggily fumbled to take the call. It was Annie. He motioned for me to be quiet, not wanting me to spoil the surprise of our visit. But no sooner had he said hello than I saw the anxiety in his eyes. He said only a few words before ending the call and reaching for the car radio.

"What is it?" I asked. "What's going on?"

"Annie says there's been a terrorist attack in New York."

27

★ ★ ★

Matt quickly found a news station out of Manhattan.

The attack had occurred in the subway system. But it wasn't a stabbing, a shooting, or a bomb. We tuned in just in time to hear a reporter broadcasting from outside of Penn Station say that this was another chemical weapons attack. Terrorists had somehow pumped sarin gas into the subway tunnels through the ventilation system.

"One transit official has confirmed to me that there have been simultaneous and closely coordinated attacks at nine different subway stations in Manhattan, Brooklyn, and the Bronx," the reporter said. "We have no casualty figures yet, but hundreds of ambulances are being called in and hazmat teams are being deployed."

As the minutes ticked by, the situation devolved from bad to worse. The news anchor said the Associated Press was now reporting that Washington D.C.'s Metro system had been hit as well. Soon there were reports of chemical weapons attacks in Philly, Boston, Chicago, Minneapolis, Dallas, and Atlanta.

The first detailed reports came from Atlanta. There, the city's transit systems hadn't been targeted. Instead, several large luxury hotels had been hit, including three Hiltons, a Marriott, and a Ritz-Carlton. The news station played a sound bite from the Atlanta fire chief, who said the terrorists had apparently employed some kind of aerosolized dispersion system to pump the gas through the hotels' ventilation systems. In so doing, they had effectively reached every room in the building and had killed nearly every guest and employee. Hundreds were reportedly dead in Atlanta alone, and several hundred more were wounded and battling for their lives.

Then came an update from Boston. The correspondent—reporting live from an emergency command center that had been set up at city hall—said that terrorists had found a way to pump sarin gas into the city's underground train system known to locals as "the T."

"I'm standing here with Police Chief Ed McDougal," the reporter said after setting the scene. "Chief, this is a fast-moving, fast-changing story. What can you tell us so far?"

"Thirty years on the force and I've never seen anything like it," the chief responded. "This is without question the worst terrorist attack in the history of the city. As of five minutes ago, we had over six thousand casualties. We're calling in ambulances from all over the state to come help us right now."

"Did you say *six thousand* dead?"

"No, no, I said *casualties*—six thousand *casualties*," the chief clarified. "I don't have an exact breakdown right now between dead and wounded."

"Can you give us your best guess, based on the information you're seeing?"

The chief refused to speculate, so the reporter asked, "And do you know at this point who is behind this attack?"

Again the chief refused to comment.

"But you suspect it's connected to the attacks in Washington, is that correct?" the reporter asked.

"That seems like a reasonable guess, but at the moment that's all it is—a guess. Give us some time. I've got my best officers and detectives on this. We're getting lots of help from federal and state authorities. We're going to figure this out and bring the people who did this to justice. You can take that to the bank."

"How many first responders have fallen to the gas?"

"I don't have any figures on that, but quite a few."

"And we're talking about sarin gas, like the kind that was used to hit the Capitol building on Tuesday night?"

"That seems to be the case, but again it's too soon to be definitive," the chief explained.

"You think it's ISIS?" the reporter pressed.

"I'm not going to speculate," the chief replied. "Like I said, we have no suspects at the moment. We're just trying to respond to the crisis. But the mayor and I are planning a press conference later in the day once we have more hard information."

On the radio, we could suddenly hear more sirens rapidly approaching. "Look, I've got to go—sorry," the chief said, and he was gone.

The reporter summarized what she'd heard for listeners just tuning in, then threw it back to the anchor in the main studio in Manhattan.

I reached over and turned the radio off.

"What are you doing?" Matt asked, incredulous. He'd never seen me turn off a breaking news story, probably because I never had.

"I don't know," I said. "I just—I can't listen anymore."

I realized I was gripping the steering wheel so hard my knuckles were white. I saw Matt glance at my hands and then look away. He didn't say anything, didn't press. We were both traumatized. We'd both seen things no one ever should. Now more people were dying, all over America. It just never seemed to end.

The phone rang. The caller ID said it was Allen. I knew what he wanted. This wasn't about going back to Jordan. This time he was calling to draft me into covering this fast-breaking story. He knew I was approaching Manhattan. He needed all hands on deck. But the last thing I wanted to do was head into the scene of another terrorist attack. My hands were shaking. My heart was racing. I just couldn't do it. I let the call go to voice mail and kept driving.

Matt and I continued in silence for more than an hour. We didn't talk to each other about the attacks or anything else. I think I was in shock. Too many thoughts were racing through my head, and I wasn't ready to share them. But eventually I couldn't help myself. I turned the radio on again.

The updates came fast and furious. In Chicago, several elementary and high schools had been hit. In Minneapolis, the Mall of America had been targeted. In Dallas and Philly, several luxury hotels were attacked. There were no hard numbers on casualties, but the numbers of dead and wounded were mounting rapidly.

For a long time, Matt and I said nothing. We just listened in complete shock. I kept thinking about the 1995 attack on the Tokyo subway. That had been sarin gas as well. Only twelve people had died, but more than 5,500 others were injured. That attack, though carefully planned, had not been nearly as effective as the terrorists had hoped.

Somehow I knew Abu Khalif had studied the planning and strategy of those attacks in Japan. Clearly, he'd found a way to make his attacks far more deadly. So what was coming next?

28

"I'm going to call Annie," Matt said, giving up on the element of surprise.

We were nearly through Connecticut, heading for Massachusetts. Matt tried several times, but no one answered. Finally he left a message, then called the house, and after that Mom's phone. Getting no one, he sent them a few texts, gave them an update on our progress, and noted that according to our GPS we should be in Bar Harbor by around seven and that he couldn't wait to give her and the kids a big hug.

Just then, my phone rang. Again the caller ID said it was Allen. Again I let it go to voice mail. But a few moments later, Matt's phone rang.

"It's your boss," he said. "Should I take it?"

The newest D.C. bureau chief was nothing if not persistent.

"No," I said and kept my eyes on the road.

"You going to tell me why?" he asked.

"Allen wants me to cover the attacks in Manhattan and then catch a flight to Jordan."

"To do what?"

"Interview the MP whose son was involved in the attacks in Washington."

"And?"

"And that's why he keeps calling. He says he's got no one else to interview this guy, and he's insisting I do it."

"And you don't want to?"

"You're kidding, right?"

"No, I'm not," Matt said. "That is your job, isn't it? And he is your boss, right?"

"Matt, you really want me to stop driving to Maine and cover sarin gas attacks in Manhattan? And then you really think I should go back to Jordan? You can't be serious."

"What if I am?"

"Are you?"

"J. B., when have you ever listened to my advice?"

"Well, I'm listening now."

"You're serious?"

Actually, I was. Perhaps it was my clumsy way of apologizing for being so distant for so many years or so rude earlier in the day. But Matt wasn't buying it, and I could hardly blame him.

"Listen—I'm in a jam," I said. "Allen's right; this is my story. But given all I've been through, I don't want anything to do with it."

"I understand that," Matt said. "It is Manhattan, after all—the *Times* certainly has more than enough reporters to throw at the story. But why not go to Jordan? That I don't get."

"Matt, tell me you're kidding."

"Why?"

"Because honestly, I can't imagine anything worse than going back to Amman right now."

"Don't the king and his forces have everything back under control at this point?"

"Yeah, pretty much."

"So it's probably not so dangerous anymore."

"Not like it was, no."

"Couldn't you see the king again while you're there and, you know, after interviewing the MP, do a story on how His Majesty and the royal family are doing two months after the crisis, what he sees for the future, how he views the fight with ISIS at this point?"

"Maybe."

"Don't you want to see him again?"

"Of course I do."

"I thought you were impressed with him."

"I am. I was before I met him, but even more so now."

"So what's the problem?"

"What do you mean?"

"I mean those all seem like pretty good reasons *to* go to Amman, even if you don't cover the attacks in Manhattan," Matt said.

I didn't respond. I just kept driving. After another few miles, Matt tried again.

"Answer me this, J. B. Is your job on the line if you keep defying Allen's orders?"

I shrugged. "Maybe."

"Didn't you tell me you and Omar and Abdel snuck into Syria when Allen ordered you not to?"

Reluctantly I nodded.

"And Abdel died on that trip, in Homs, and Omar died later in Istanbul?"

I said nothing, but it was all true.

"And you nearly got killed too."

"Your point is?" I asked, feeling more and more defensive.

"I just don't want you to lose your job; that's all," Matt said.

"Since when?" I shot back.

He looked surprised and a bit hurt. "Why would you say that?"

"Face it, Matt—you and Annie and Mom never approved of me being a war correspondent. You all think I've put my career ahead of everything else—my family, my marriage, my spiritual life, you name it. So maybe it'd be better if Allen canned me and it was over and done with, right?"

"J. B., you're a great reporter, but you're a real piece of work, you know that?" Matt said. "I've always read your stuff, and I've always been proud of what you do. And as long as you keep pursuing the truth, I'll always be proud of you. If you decide to give this thing up, that's your call. But don't get fired for blowing off your boss. Don't get canned for acting like a jerk."

I grew quiet and kept driving without looking at him.

"What's the matter?" Matt asked after a while.

I didn't respond.

"You don't like my advice?" he asked.

"No, as a matter of fact, I don't," I said.

"Okay, fine—I can take it—but why not?"

"I don't want to talk about it," I snapped.

JOEL C. ROSENBERG ★ 149

"Of course you do," Matt said. "You just asked me for my advice for the first time in . . . well, forever. You may not like it, but you asked for it, and I'm telling you—you should do what your boss wants and go to Jordan. After that, should you step down from your job and do something else with your life? Maybe. *Maybe.* But for heaven's sake, don't get fired. Do what Allen wants you to do. Then go see Yael and take some time to figure out what you really want, what she wants, what the future might hold. *Then* make a decision about your job. But not right now. Not like this. Not when all hell is breaking loose and all your instincts are telling you Abu Khalif is the one responsible. Right now you need to stay focused, or you're really going to mess things up."

We drove in silence for several miles. Then Matt tried again. "J. B., come on; I've known you for too long. This isn't about some quick trip to Amman. Something else is wrong. Talk to me—what is it?"

29

Matt was right—something else was eating me.

I was just too embarrassed to admit it.

But who else was I going to talk about it with? This was my brother. I'd barely talked to him, or even seen him, since we were in college. I wasn't used to confiding in him. But I had no one else, and we still had a good six hours to go before we got to Bar Harbor.

"It's Yael," I said at last.

"What do you mean?" Matt asked.

I tightened my grip on the steering wheel, took a deep breath, and checked my mirrors again. "She hasn't written back."

"At all?"

"Well, hardly at all."

"I don't understand. I thought you two were getting close."

"So did I."

"Wasn't she the one who insisted you be allowed to go into Iraq with the Delta team even though one of the generals was against it?"

"Forget it," I said. "Let's talk about something else." I reached for the radio and turned it back on.

But Matt turned it off. "J. B., you obviously want to talk about this. So go ahead. We're off the record. I'm not going to tell anyone else—not even Annie or Mom. You have my word."

We drove in silence for several miles. Then I finally began talking again.

"She sent me an e-mail during Hanukkah."

"Okay."

"She thanked me for reaching out to her so many times," I said. "And she apologized for not writing back sooner."

"Well, that's good, right?"

"I guess."

"What else did she say?"

"She said she hoped I had a good Christmas."

"Okay, that's nice."

"Two sentences, really, you think that's nice?" I said. "I'd written her probably four or five pages' worth by that point."

"J. B., she was lucky to be alive. She'd already been in the hospital for a month. And she'd had three or four surgeries by then, maybe more. Isn't that what you told me?"

"I know, but—"

"But what? Cut her a break. Was that the last time you heard from her?"

"No, she sent me a text message a few weeks ago."

"All right, now we're getting somewhere. What was that one about?"

"She'd just been offered a new job."

"Doing what?"

"Working for Prime Minister Eitan as his deputy national security advisor."

"And she wanted you to be the first to know?"

"No, she wasn't sure if she should take it."

"Really? She was asking you for advice?"

"I guess."

"Why would she do that unless she valued your opinion?"

"I don't know."

"Certainly she has other people to ask, right?"

"I would hope so."

"But she asked you."

"Well, yeah."

"And what did you say?"

"What could I say? I told her to take it."

"That's it?"

"I told her I was proud of her, she deserved it, what a cool job, that kind of thing."

"Okay, so what's wrong with that?"

"Nothing."

"But there's something you're not telling me."

"Like what?" I asked.

"I don't know," Matt said calmly. "You tell me."

"I *am* telling you."

Matt shifted in his seat and tried another tack. "Did you really want her to take the job?"

"Why wouldn't I?" I asked. "She deserved to be promoted. She's amazing at what she does."

"I'm sure she is, but that's not what I asked."

I drove in silence for a while longer. "Look, I wasn't *against* her taking the job," I finally said.

"I mean, who am I to be against her getting a big promotion?"

"Okay, I get it, but you would have *preferred* she not take the job, right?"

"I couldn't tell her that."

"Why not?"

"It wasn't my place."

"She was asking you."

"Yeah, but this was a huge honor. It was a really big deal for her. I didn't want to stand in her way. What kind of jerk do you think I am?"

"J. B.?" Matt said, clearly trying to choose his words carefully.

"Yeah."

"Let me ask you something."

"Okay," I said, bracing myself.

"Did it ever occur to you—I mean, seriously, did you ever consider the possibility that Yael wanted you to tell her *not* to take the job?"

"No, of course not," I said instantly. "That's ridiculous."

Matt was quiet.

"You don't understand," I protested. "She was perfect for this job. I mean, she'd have been crazy not to take it."

"Then why did she ask you?"

"I don't know," I said. "Just being polite, I guess."

I glanced over and saw Matt raising his eyebrows quizzically. He obviously wasn't buying my analysis.

"What are you saying, exactly?" I asked, seeing

where he was heading but needing to hear it spelled out all the same.

"You said Yael was hardly in touch at all after her surgery, right?"

"Right."

"And when she did reply to your messages, it was just short responses?"

"Exactly."

"And then suddenly—out of the blue—she asks you this huge question, a really personal question about her future."

"So?"

"So you really still think she was just being polite?"

30

I grew quiet.

We were making decent time. The snow was coming down harder now, but the plows and salt trucks were out, and in the immediate aftermath of the attack in New York, traffic was light.

"You think she was testing me?" I asked finally.

"I don't know about *testing*," he said.

"But you think she wanted to see if I'd say no?"

"Maybe."

"You think she wanted to see if I'd tell her she *shouldn't* take the job?"

Matt didn't say a word. But when I glanced at him, he shrugged. "It's possible, isn't it?" he asked quietly.

Was it? I wondered. *Had she really wanted me to give her a reason to retire from the Mossad and . . . and what? What did she want? What did I want?*

"After you told her to take the job, did you hear back from her?" Matt asked.

"No."

"She never told you whether she took the job?"

I shook my head.

"Do you think she did?"

"I don't know—I mean, I assume so," I sputtered, suddenly realizing how ridiculous I must sound. I was an award-winning journalist for the world's most influential newspaper. Wasn't it my job to figure out the facts, not make assumptions or jump to conclusions?

"But you don't know for sure?" Matt asked.

"No," I said, embarrassed. "I guess I don't."

"So for all you know, she could have passed on the offer."

"Why would she?"

"You're saying the bottom line is you believe Yael Katzir is currently serving as the prime minister's deputy national security advisor?"

I hesitated. I really didn't know. When I didn't respond, Matt shifted gears.

"J. B.?" he asked.

"What?"

"Do you love this woman?"

I was startled by his directness. But he was right. That was the question.

"I don't know. Maybe."

"You're not sure?"

"I've touched that stove before; you know that," I said.

"And you're not exactly eager to get burned again."

"Of course not."

"Just because of Laura?" he asked.

Yes, Matt, "just" because my cruel, heartless ex-wife ripped out my heart and drove over it with the SUV I'd just bought her. I didn't say that, of course.

I didn't need to. He could see my whole body stiffen.

"Okay, fine—you're not sure if you love her," he said. "That makes sense. You hardly know her. But you want to *get* to know her, to see if there's really something there. Right?"

"Yeah, I guess—yeah."

"So?"

"So what?"

"So isn't that a good reason for getting on a plane, going over to see the king—and while you're over there, seeing Yael—and letting the *New York Times* pay for the trip?"

★ ★ ★

Matt took the next shift.

The snow had stopped falling, and the road crews had been able to keep the streets clear, but our prospects of getting to Bar Harbor more or less on schedule were dimming. We still had almost five hours to go.

I climbed into the backseat, stretched out as best I could, put in my earbuds, and zoned out to Paul Simon's *Graceland* album. Scrolling through my e-mails, I found several from Allen and a blizzard of messages from other *Times* reporters comparing notes about the terror attacks. But for the first time I could ever remember, I had no interest in reading them. I didn't want to scan the headlines or track the story. I didn't want to reach out to any of my sources by e-mail, text, or phone. It wasn't that I didn't care. I did. Deeply. But I was spent. I simply didn't have the emotional, physical, or intellectual energy to engage in any of it. It was as if all my circuit breakers were going off. There was nothing I could do about any of it, and so I set down my phone and faded off to sleep. And kept sleeping for hours.

I don't remember the sound of the road or even the music in my ears. I don't remember Matt stopping again for gas or my phone ringing, which, according to the log, it did several times, as Allen continued trying in vain to get ahold of me. What I do remember was Matt suddenly shaking me and a sudden blast of winter air.

"J. B., wake up."

"Why? What's going on?" I said, trying to get my bearings and wondering why it was so dark.

"I need you to drive," he said. "I'm starting to weave all over the road."

The brutal cold of Maine quickly snapped me back to reality. "Where are we?" I asked as I forced myself out of the Audi, stretched my legs, and let Matt climb into the back.

"Just outside of Bangor," he said.

It had been a long time since I'd been home, I realized, and longer still since I'd driven all the way from D.C. The few times I had been up here in recent years I'd flown to Bangor and rented a car. Feeling decently rested, I agreed to take the next shift, then climbed into the driver's seat, shut the door, turned on the seat warmer, and tried to get comfortable. The LED display on the dashboard indicated the temperature outside was in the single digits. Inside it was only seventy.

I turned up the heater a few notches to get it to seventy-five.

I pulled back onto I-395, heading southeast now, having skirted Penobscot Bay. I kept my speed around fifty, well under the state limit. It was snowing hard again. The roads were slick. The last thing I wanted to do was wipe out so close to home. We had less than ninety minutes to go.

I glanced in my rearview mirror. Traffic was light. No one seemed to be following us. But for some reason I couldn't shake the feeling that someone might be. I didn't say anything to Matt. I didn't want to worry him. His anniversary had already been ruined by a day of terror attacks ten times worse than 9/11. There was no point adding my paranoia to the mix.

The clock on the dashboard said 7:27 p.m. Matt had fallen fast asleep. With the rough weather, we were well behind schedule. Pulling out my phone, I noticed the battery was running low, so I connected it to the car charger. I didn't need the GPS. I knew my way from here. But I did want to give my mom a call and let her know we were coming. I tried twice but got voice mail both times. I tried Annie's cell phone too but got her voice mail as well. I left brief messages on our whereabouts and let them know that at the rate we were going, we would likely pull in sometime after eight thirty. Then I kept driving through the darkness and the blowing snow.

31

* * *

My phone rang.

I hoped it was my mom or Annie. But it was Allen MacDonald again. I ignored him. Then he called again, and a third time and a fourth, in rapid succession. He was determined to reach me. I was determined not to let him.

Then Matt's phone began ringing, and Matt woke up in a fog. "Good grief, doesn't your bureau chief ever give up?" he said from the backseat.

"I wish," I said.

"Maybe you should take it this time."

"Not a chance," I said. "I'm still mulling what you said. But I'll get back to him tomorrow, I promise."

Then Matt, too, got a second call from the *Times'* Washington bureau, and a third.

"Maybe something's going on," Matt said. "Seems pretty important."

"No, it's not important," I said. "Just annoying. Turn off your ringer and go back to sleep. We'll be there soon."

"You sure?"

"Absolutely," I said. "I'll wake you as soon as we're close."

"All right, thanks." Matt yawned again, then hunched over, pulled his coat up over his face, and went back to sleep.

Before long we passed the Hancock County Airport and then drove through the sleepy town of Trenton, population less than fifteen hundred. This was the last stop on the mainland. It swelled in the summer but was practically a ghost town this time of year. There was no reason to pull over. We had plenty of fuel, and we were anxious to get back to our family. So I continued driving, over Trenton Bridge and onto Mount Desert Island, hugging the shoreline and snaking along Highway 3 around the north side of Acadia National Park. We passed through Salisbury Cove and Hulls Cove until the highway turned into Eden Street, which led us directly into the town where Matt and I had both been born and raised.

I tried to recall the last time I'd been there and concluded it had to have been at least three years, though it might have been four. I'd never thought of myself as particularly nostalgic, but just seeing the sleepy coastal town with its ubiquitous churches, their steeples covered in a fresh blanket of snow, brought back a rush of warm memories. Hunting and fishing with my grandfather. Making blueberry pies with my grandmother. Cross-country skiing with Matt and hiking Cadillac Mountain with our friends. Christmas caroling in bone-chilling temperatures with the church youth group. My mom making us hot cocoa with marshmallows afterward. Sitting in front of a roaring fire in the parsonage while Pastor Mike regaled us with all kinds of crazy stories from his childhood. And his wife, Sarah, serving us bowls of her homemade chili. I hadn't thought about such things in years.

Now, as I turned right on Main Street, I could see the streetlamps glowing yellow in the frosty-blue air and the white lights illuminating a giant wire outline of a moose set atop one of the shops. Most establishments were shut down for the evening. At this hour, no one was shopping for gifts or getting their hair done or buying supplies from the hardware shop or taking letters to the post office. But all of the town's restaurants were open and doing a brisk business, perhaps packed with couples celebrating a belated Valentine's Day. Despite the attacks, people here were still trying to live normal lives. They were a resilient, rugged people. I envied them. And though I was loath to admit it even to myself, I missed them.

In the distance, a siren broke the Norman Rockwell–esque tranquility. Soon a fire truck raced up behind me. I slowed and pulled to the side of the street to let it pass. Moments later two more fire engines were tearing down Main Street as well. As I began to drive again, I was cut off by two police cars and an ambulance coming down the street, each with lights blazing and sirens blaring. Matt woke up and asked what in the world was going on. I had no idea, but clearly it was a big deal and would undoubtedly be the lead story in the next morning's edition of the *Mount Desert Islander*.

We passed the hospital on our left and on our right the snow-covered Little League fields where we'd played ball for so many springs and summers. Soon we reached the south side of town and took a left on Old Farm Road. It had been freshly plowed, which was good. Then we saw flashing blue lights ahead and a police squad car blocking our path. I rolled down the window to ask what the problem was and immediately smelled the smoke.

"Sorry, gentlemen, 'fraid I can't let you through," one of two uniformed officers said as he sipped a thermos of coffee.

I didn't recognize him, nor he me.

"House fire?" I asked.

"'Fraid so. And a nasty one—three alarms."

Matt and I peered through the snowy forest around us but couldn't see any fire trucks, much less the house in question.

"Whose house?" I asked.

"Dunno," he said. "I'm kinda new here. Moved here from Portland. Just two months on the job."

"So you got roadblock duty?"

"'Fraid so."

"What number, then?" I asked.

"Uh, I don't exactly . . . Eighty-five, maybe?"

My heart stopped. "Which street?"

"Sols Cliff," he said.

"That's *our* house," Matt shouted from the backseat, the fear in his voice palpable.

"*Yours?*" the young officer asked, skeptical.

"We grew up there," I said, my heart racing

but trying to keep my voice calm. "Our mom's still there. Please, we need to get through."

"Let's see some ID," he said.

I had no time for this guy. I knew exactly what was happening. I knew why my calls to Mom and Annie hadn't connected. I knew why Allen had been calling me repeatedly for the past hour. I threw the Audi in reverse, then shifted gears again and hit the gas. We shot around the back of the squad car and raced up the road, taking a sharp left onto Sols Cliff Road. Suddenly I had to slam on the brakes. The road was full of emergency vehicles, and I could see our family's home—and the woods around it—going up in flames.

32

★ ★ ★

Matt bolted out of the car and ran toward the house.

Shutting down the engine, I threw open my door and raced after him. Matt was nearly tackled by a uniformed police officer trying to keep him from reaching the inferno. By the time I caught up to him, two more officers had blocked our path.

"My family!" Matt screamed. *"They're in there—my wife, my kids, my mom."*

"Who are you, sir?" one of the officers asked.

"Matt—Matt Collins," he stammered, his face ashen, his body shaking. "Please, I have to get to them."

"Do you have ID?" the officer said.

Matt stiffened. His eyes went wide. I'd never seen him like this. I actually thought for a moment he was about to throw a punch. So I stepped forward, put myself between Matt and the three of Bar Harbor's finest. I showed them my driver's license and my press pass. Then I explained again who we were and why we were here.

"Okay, boys, I've got this," said a voice from behind us.

I turned around, expecting to see the young officer whose roadblock we'd blown through. Instead, I found an older gentleman, probably in his sixties. He wasn't dressed in a police uniform but had on a black North Face snow jacket, a black ski cap, a red plaid flannel shirt, faded jeans, and old boots. He flashed his badge and identified himself as the chief of police. I didn't recognize him. But then again, I'd never had any run-ins with the local cops—not since leaving for college, anyway.

"You're J. B. Collins?" he asked.

"Yes, sir."

"And you're Matthew Collins?"

"Where's our family, Chief?" Matt shouted, blowing off the question and causing each of the officers around him to tense.

The chief waved them off and took a step forward. "I'm afraid I have very bad news for you two boys," he said over the roaring of the searing flames as ash and embers swirled around us like snowflakes.

"No," Matt said, shaking his head and backing away.

I grabbed my brother's arm to hold him steady. All the bravado in his voice had evaporated. His knees were beginning to buckle. I was afraid mine might too.

"Two are gone," the chief said. "Two are severely wounded."

My grip on Matt tightened, as did his on me.

He was shaking his head but could no longer speak.

"What do you mean, gone, Chief?" I asked, my voice trembling. I resolved to stay strong for my brother's sake, knowing full well what was coming next.

"There's no easy way to put this, gentlemen— your mother is dead," the chief said without emotion, looking first at me, then at Matt. "And, Mr. Collins, I'm afraid your son is dead as well."

"No—no, I just—" Matt stammered, nearly inaudible, shaking his head, tears streaming down his face. "That can't—that's not—"

An explosion on the north side of the house suddenly sent all of us, including the first responders, scrambling for cover. I pulled Matt to safety behind one of the pumpers. A moment later, I heard one of the firemen say the heating-oil tank had just blown.

I stared in horror as the flames consumed what was left of the historic home. Our great-great-grandfather had built it in 1883 in a Greek Revival style. The half-acre waterfront plot alone was now worth a thousand times what he'd paid for it. The house had been enormous, with thirteen rooms, including six bedrooms, four and a half baths, and a grand living room with huge bay windows looking out over the Atlantic. Not a month went by without someone inquiring if it was for sale. But Mom would never sell. She had always said she was going to die in this house, and now she had.

"Annie? Katie?" Matt demanded. "They're still alive—the chief said so."

So he had. I grabbed Matt's jacket and we found the chief again and demanded to know what had happened to my sister-in-law and niece.

"They're alive," the chief confirmed. "But they're in critical condition."

"Where are they now?" I asked.

"We airlifted them to Maine Medical Center not ten minutes ago," he said.

"In Portland?"

"Yes."

"Come on, Matt, let's go," I said, turning back toward my car.

"Follow me, gentlemen," the chief insisted. "I'll give you an escort."

PART THREE

33

The next seventy-two hours were a blur.

Matt and I split most of our time between the ICU at Barbara Bush Children's Hospital, part of the Maine Medical Center, and the adult ICU in the hospital's other wing. The doctors urged us to remain hopeful, but both Annie's and Katie's situations could hardly have been more dire. Both were unconscious, badly burned, and suffering from severe smoke inhalation, and though I didn't dare say it to Matt, I had little hope for their recovery based on what we'd been told so far.

On Friday evening, Agent Harris came to see us at the hospital. Unbeknownst to us, he and a team of investigators from the bureau had arrived in Bar Harbor early Friday morning. They'd spent the day collecting evidence and interviewing witnesses.

"I'm going to tell you something few others know at this point," Harris told us as we stood outside the ICU, surrounded by uniformed local police and armed federal agents who had been personally tasked by President Taylor with providing round-the-clock security for our family. "You can't print this, J. B., any of it. I'm letting you know this as a member of the family, as a courtesy, *not* because you're a reporter."

"I understand," I said, and Matt nodded as well.

"Look, this is hard to say, but I think you need to know," Harris said. "The deceased victims were double-tapped with a 9mm pistol."

"Double-tapped?" Matt asked.

"Shot twice in rapid succession," I explained, then turned back to Harris. "You're saying this was a professional hit."

Harris nodded. "The ME determined from his autopsy that your mom and Joshua died instantly from the gunshot wounds. Their bodies were severely burned in the fire, but they didn't feel a thing. There was no smoke in their lungs, indicating that they were killed before the fire was started."

The image of Matt's face at that moment—as pale and queasy as when we'd first arrived on the scene of the fire—would be forever seared into my memory. I put my arm around him and helped him sit down in the waiting area. He looked terrible. He was unshaven. He'd barely eaten. His eyes were bloodshot and moist, but thus far he was containing his emotions. Barely. Under the circumstances, he'd been remarkably strong, but I wasn't sure how much more he could take.

"And Annie? Katie?" he asked. "Were they shot too?"

"I'm afraid so," the agent explained. "Your wife was shot twice. Your daughter only once. Whoever did this apparently thought they were both dead.

But when the firefighters found them, they weren't in the kitchen like the others. They were huddled in the basement, in a closet, bleeding and unconscious but away from the worst of the smoke."

Neither Matt nor I said anything, so Harris continued. "As best we can ascertain, when the shooters left, your wife must have checked the others, realized Katie was still breathing, and dragged her downstairs to where she hoped they'd be safe until help came. We found a cordless phone in her hand. Turns out she managed to call 911 before she passed out."

"She called 911? What did she say?" Matt asked.

"She told the dispatcher there were four terrorists in the house and that they'd been there for quite some time. She said they were all wearing black hoods, all speaking in Arabic, though the leader spoke some broken English. They were ransacking the place. And the leader kept demanding to know where you were, J. B. He kept shouting that you were supposed to have gotten there by seven. He thought you were hiding and that the family was lying to protect you or had warned you away somehow."

Now I had to sit down. I felt light-headed and shaky. The bitter truth was now crystal clear—my mother and Josh had been murdered because of me. Annie and Katie were fighting for their lives because of me.

Harris then told us that the arson investigators believed the fire had been set around seven thirty. Matt and I knew full well what that message was and who had sent it.

"Seven thirty, you're sure?" I asked.

"Give or take ten minutes," Harris said.

I was coming to the painful realization that if we'd gotten home when Matt and I had originally planned, we might have been able to break up the attack—or been killed with the others. The storm had slowed us down, and in doing so it might also have saved our lives. But that was little comfort.

"What else can you tell us, Agent Harris?" I asked. "Please tell me you have some suspects."

"Not yet, but we've got some leads," he replied.

"Like what?"

"The clerk at the Shell station on Main Street said two men in their thirties came in yesterday around dinnertime. They looked Middle Eastern. One used the restroom. The other bought bottles of water. He paid with cash. But we ran the video from the closed-circuit cameras and came up with a car and a license plate. We've got an APB out and my team is looking at footage from every camera in Bar Harbor. We'll find it—I promise you that."

Six hours later, they did, on some side street in Augusta. Little good it did, however. There were no security cameras in the area, so the FBI had no idea what these two were driving now, who they were, or where they were headed. As far as I was concerned, the trail had gone cold.

On Sunday morning, I sat with Annie and Katie, who were now in the same ICU. I insisted Matt take a break, go get a hot shower, and get some sleep or at least lie down for a while and rest. He'd been understandably reluctant to leave his wife and daughter, of course. But there had been no movement, no progress, no news, and the two of them didn't even know he was there. I promised to call him if either or both of them woke or if there were any developments at all. Finally he agreed.

By Sunday evening, Matt was back at the hospital and it was my turn to take a break. I sat on my bed in a Motel 6 on the outskirts of Portland, surrounded by containers of half-eaten Chinese food and empty bottles of Coke Zero and craving a real drink more intensely than any time in days. But there was no minibar, and with killers out there somewhere hunting for me—and a messy nor'easter bearing down on us—I wasn't about to head out to find a liquor store. I took a shower instead.

Just after nine, a text message came in from Allen. It said the president was about to give his third press conference in as many days, and the press pool was picking up rumors there might be an important update on the hunt for the terrorists. I thought of the two FBI agents parked in the room next door, assigned to watch my back, and the dozen federal agents and handful of local cops at the hospital, watching over Matt and his surviving family.

I didn't think ISIS was likely to come after me again—not now, not with a media feeding frenzy surrounding us.

But Harris refused to take any chances. And I was grateful.

34

★ ★ ★

As I waited for the president to speak, I was going stir-crazy.

For much of the last twelve hours, I'd been responding to a blizzard of e-mails concerning the memorial service, and once again my circuit breakers were blowing. For one thing, my mom's church was in the midst of extensive renovations due to a burst water pipe several weeks earlier, and the sanctuary was in no condition to host an event that was drawing national media attention. That necessitated finding another church facility, and I eventually chose St. Saviour's Episcopal Church, located close to the center of town. The building was beautiful and historic, and its sanctuary held 280 people, making it one of the largest on the island.

That, it turned out, had been the easy part. Now I was dealing with a torrent of questions from the director of the funeral home, the church secretary, the florist, the driver of the hearse, and dozens of my mom's friends and hundreds of other well-wishers.

Hour by hour, the condolences kept pouring in by e-mail and text message, not just from the local area but from all over the country. I couldn't keep up. I wasn't cut out to be a social secretary. But I knew I had to keep it all off of Matt's shoulders. He was proving himself stronger than I'd feared, but he didn't have the bandwidth for any of this right now.

I finally sent a text to Allen, apologizing for not being in touch sooner. He wrote back immediately, offering his own condolences and saying he'd already had Mary Jane cancel my flight to Amman. He told me I didn't need to come back to work anytime soon. He knew I couldn't write about what I was going through or be a source for other *Times* reporters covering it, even though this was big, front-page news. He was just happy to know I was still alive.

As I hit Send on a response to yet another e-mail, President Taylor entered the White House pressroom to a thousand camera flashes. I set my phone down, picked up the remote, and turned up the sound on the TV perched atop the dresser.

"Tonight I want to update you on the tragedy of the past few days," the president began. "As you know, terrorists have unleashed attacks in nine American cities and towns, beginning with our nation's capital and most recently in the small seacoast town of Bar Harbor, Maine. These cowardly attacks came without warning and without remorse. These are despicable, cold-blooded acts. They were unprovoked and unconscionable, and they will not be tolerated."

There it was again. *Without warning.* Was this really what the intelligence community was telling him? No attacks in American history had been more clearly telegraphed. Abu Khalif had done everything but fax a map and a timeline to the White House Situation Room. The president and his national security staff simply didn't want to believe it. They still had no idea what they were really up against, and we were all paying the price.

"As of this hour, some 4,647 American citizens and residents, and 62 foreign nationals—not counting the perpetrators—have been killed in terror attacks on the American homeland over the course of the past week," the president continued.

It was a chilling statistic. It represented 1,651 more deaths than the 2,996 people killed during the 9/11 attacks in 2001. I could only imagine Abu Khalif's twisted pleasure upon hearing the news that he had, in one day, killed half again as many Americans as his onetime mentor, Osama bin Laden.

The president then added that the sarin gas had wounded an additional 6,114 people, many of whom were in critical condition. He asked the nation to send "thoughts of peace and healing" to the families of the deceased and to those "suffering from the cowardly actions of these violent extremists."

Even with the nation under attack, he refused to utter the phrase *Radical Islam*, much less *apocalyptic Islam*.

Disgusted, I reached for the remote to mute the TV and get back to work. But then the president said that he had ordered U.S. bombers and fighter jets to attack ISIS positions inside Syria. That caught my attention. A map flashed up on the large monitor mounted over his left shoulder. The graphics indicated the position of the most recent air strikes, just inside the Syrian border with Iraq. The president claimed that in the last twenty-four hours, American forces had killed 612 fighters loyal to Abu Khalif, all of whom were hiding out in these border regions. Most of them, he said, had previously fought in Iraq but had been pushed back into Syria due to U.S. operations to liberate Mosul and other northern Iraqi towns and villages.

Did this represent a fundamental shift in U.S. strategy against ISIS, or a weekend diversion? I wondered. Now that Abu Khalif had struck inside the American homeland, was Taylor finally heeding my advice to take the gloves off and go after ISIS and its leader inside Syria, regardless of how much the Russians and Iranians and the U.N. secretary general protested?

For the moment, I could only hope. The president didn't say. Not exactly. Instead, he offered another tantalizing nugget. He explained that he was expanding authority for the CIA to use drone strikes against high-value ISIS targets inside Syria as well as in Yemen, Libya, Afghanistan, and the Bekaa Valley in northeastern Lebanon. Then a face flashed up on the screen. I recognized it instantly: Tariq Baqouba.

"I can report to the American people that these expanded drone strikes are already having a devastating effect on the enemy," the president said. "Just hours ago, U.S. forces identified, targeted, and killed Tariq Baqouba—ISIL's number-three-ranked leader—in a drone strike near the Syrian-Iraqi border. In recent months, Baqouba was ISIL's operations chief, responsible for terrorist activity throughout the Middle East and North Africa. While we do not believe he was the mastermind of last week's attacks inside the United States, we have solid intelligence indicating he played a key role in executing those attacks. Last fall, Tariq Baqouba led ISIL forces in a raid against a Syrian military base near Aleppo. It was this incident that allowed the group to capture precursors for chemical weapons—specifically for sarin gas—and thousands of artillery shells to deliver them. Tonight, a savage killer was brought to justice, and you have my word: there is more to come."

At this point, Taylor took a few questions.

No, the FBI still had not made arrests of anyone in connection to the attacks in Washington or in any of the six cities where chemical weapons had been unleashed against the American people.

No, the FBI had made no arrests in the attack on the Collins family in Maine.

Yes, the bureau had offered a $5 million reward for information leading to the arrests and convictions of suspects in all of these cases.

Yes, there had been a huge spike in calls to the FBI tip line.

No, he couldn't comment any further on ongoing investigations.

Then it was over.

That was it? I thought. *That's all the detail you're going to give us?*

I shouted something profane and threw an ashtray at the wall. I didn't need vague answers to meaningless questions. I needed real results, and I needed them now.

35

★ ★ ★

Suddenly there was rapid knocking at the door.

The two agents assigned to protect me had come to check on me. They'd heard my yell and the crash of the ashtray and wanted to know if I was all right. I cracked the door open, apologized, and told them I was fine. They looked skeptical but eventually went back to their room.

When I heard them open and shut their door, I walked over to the windows. I pulled back the curtains, ever so slightly. It was snowing hard. The cars in the parking lot were covered with another several inches of fresh powder. What I wouldn't give to be free for a few days and head to Killington with some friends on a ski getaway.

My mobile phone rang. The number was Allen's.

I was about to ignore it but thought better of it. Maybe my brother was right. It wasn't exactly a wise career move to chronically blow off the boss. If I was going to leave the *Times*, then I should do so on my own terms, with a plan of what I was going to do next. To get myself fired for no good reason was just plain stupid.

"Hey, Allen," I said, my voice hoarse and laced with fatigue.

"Hey. I didn't actually expect to reach you. How are you?"

"I honestly don't know how to answer that," I admitted.

"I'm so sorry. I can't imagine what you're going through."

"No, look, I'm the one who's sorry—about Jordan, about not answering your calls, about being, well, you know."

"Forget it, J. B. You don't have to apologize. I understand. Believe me."

"Thanks," I said. "And thanks for your text, too, by the way. I appreciate it. So what's up?"

"Well, I just landed in Bangor, just rented a car. I should be in Bar Harbor in about ninety minutes."

"You're serious? You're going to Bar Harbor?"

"Of course," he said.

"Well, thanks, but—and please don't take this the wrong way—but why?"

"I spoke to your mom's pastor this afternoon," he explained. "He and his staff have gotten calls from every network and every national paper, the AP, Reuters, you name it. They're all coming up to cover the service. CNN wants to broadcast it live. It's becoming a major media event. Plus, with the VP flying up, the Secret Service is getting involved. The pastor's being deluged. He asked me for some advice. I said I'd be happy to come up and help, and he jumped at the offer."

"The vice president is coming?" I said, my stomach tightening.

"You didn't know?" he asked.

"No, but then again, why would Holbrooke tell me? I'm just running the thing."

"Well, according to my source at the White House, he's coming. Anyway, the pastor said he needed someone to manage the media at the memorial service—said it's going to be a madhouse. He didn't know anyone else who could do it, so I decided I would."

"That's very kind of you, I guess," I said.

"It is, actually, but that's not even the reason I called."

"What is?"

"I have news."

"What kind of news?"

"A front-page exclusive."

"By whom?"

"Bill Sanders."

"On what?"

"The hunt for Abu Khalif."

"What are you talking about?" I said. "Why is Sanders writing about Khalif?" Bill Sanders was the Cairo bureau chief for the *Times*. ISIS and Khalif were not his usual beat.

"Because you aren't," Allen said. "And because after you, he's the best Mideast correspondent we have. I asked him to work his sources and find out what's being done to track down the emir of ISIS and bring him to justice."

"And?"

"You'll see when you read the article. Make sure to pick up a copy of the *Times* bright and early tomorrow. Look, I gotta go. I'll call you in the morning."

With that, Allen MacDonald was gone. But there was no time to process all that he'd just said. For no sooner had Allen hung up than the phone rang again.

"Hello?" I said, not recognizing the number. I wondered if it might be the VP's office.

"Is this J. B. Collins?" asked the man on the other end of the line.

"Who's asking?" I said.

It was not a voice I recognized.

"My name is Steve Sullivan."

"Okay." The name was familiar, but I couldn't immediately place it.

"I'm the lawyer in Portland who's representing the Khachigian estate. I've written you a number of e-mails but haven't gotten any replies."

Now I remembered the name and the e-mails. I'd fully intended to write back, but I guess I never actually had. Sullivan's first e-mail had been rather cryptic. He'd indicated that he'd had important business to discuss with me concerning Khachigian's will. He'd said it was a sensitive matter that necessitated meeting in person. The rest of his e-mails were all variations on that theme. Since I had no idea what Khachigian's will could possibly have to do with me, it hadn't seemed that urgent given everything else going on.

I apologized and started to explain what had happened with my family.

"Yes, I know, and I'm very sorry for your loss, Mr. Collins," he said. "Truly, I am."

"That's very kind, Mr. Sullivan," I replied. "So you'll understand why I'm not in a position to meet at the moment."

"Actually, Mr. Collins, I must inform you that this is an urgent matter that cannot wait any longer," Sullivan countered.

Generally I applauded tenacity. But this was going too far. "Well, it will have to, Mr. Sullivan. I'm afraid I'm far too busy for this right now. But please, have a good night."

Before I could hang up, however, Sullivan quickly explained that he was in possession of a sealed envelope that I needed to see. "It's marked in Khachigian's own handwriting," he said. "The note reads, 'If I am killed in mysterious circumstances, please get this to James Bradley Collins immediately.'"

36

* * *

My return to Bar Harbor would have to wait.

I arrived at the offices of Sullivan & Sullivan, attorneys at law, at precisely 8 a.m., briefcase in hand. The firm didn't typically open until nine, but I didn't care. I'd told this guy if he really wanted to meet with me, that's when I'd be available. Not a moment later.

I'd been driven by two agents from the bureau, and the agent behind the wheel of our unmarked bureau sedan kept the engine running while his partner went inside to check things out. Five minutes later, he exited the three-story brick building and gave us an "all clear" signal. The driver parked and escorted me inside.

The decor was humble but tasteful. This wasn't a high-powered firm with a lot of Washington and Wall Street connections. Indeed, I suspected Robert Khachigian had been the Sullivans' highest profile client by far. The walls needed a fresh coat of paint. The chairs in the foyer were ready to be reupholstered. The magazines were out of date.

The computer on the receptionist's desk looked like it had to be a good ten years old. The aroma of pipe smoke, carpet cleaner, and instant coffee wafted through the air.

Steve Sullivan greeted me with a firm hand-shake. He was younger than me, no more than thirty-five, I thought, despite the receding hair-line that no doubt came from too many hours and too much stress. He wore a gray three-piece suit that looked like a throwback to a different generation, despite the brand-new and rather stylish dress shoes that squeaked when he walked. He asked if I wanted some coffee or a glass of water, both of which I declined, and then he ush-ered me down a hallway and into a moderately sized corner office overlooking Portland's main thoroughfare.

An elderly man, surely in his eighties, stood when I entered.

"Mr. Collins, please meet my grandfather and the founding partner of this firm, Link Sullivan," the younger man said.

"Link, did you say?" I asked as I reached out to shake the grandfather's hand.

"Lincoln, actually, but my friends call me Link," he said.

He was gray and balding and frail but had a warm smile and trustworthy eyes. As he offered me a seat, it occurred to me to wonder whether there was another Sullivan. Where was Lincoln's son, Steve's father? I glanced around and saw no pic-tures of the three men—separate or together—in any of the many frames on the large executive desk or on the walls. I was tempted to ask but decided the best thing was to get through whatever they wanted to talk about as quickly as possible and be on my way. There was too much else on my plate; getting to know the history of the Sullivan family wasn't exactly on the list.

The grandson sat in a weathered wooden chair across from his grandfather. I followed his lead and sat in a similar chair a few feet to his right. The FBI agents stepped back into the hallway and shut the door. The three of us were now alone.

"We understand you're pressed for time," the elder Sullivan began after verifying my identity by checking my driver's license. "We would not have insisted you come here unless it was of the utmost urgency."

"The sealed envelope," I said.

"Yes, the envelope. And one other matter," he said.

"What's that?" I said. "Your grandson didn't mention anything beyond the envelope."

"Mr. Collins, are you aware that my client left nearly his entire estate to you and your brother, Matthew?"

For a moment I just stared at him. "I beg your pardon?" I finally said.

"It's true."

"I don't understand. What about his family?" I asked.

Sullivan leaned back in his creaky leather executive chair. "As you know, Robert's wife, Mary, passed away three years ago from ovarian cancer. They had no children. Their parents are deceased.

Robert's sister, Ellen, died a decade ago. And Ellen's children . . ." He looked at me expectantly.

I said nothing.

"I believe you knew Ellen's son, Chris."

"Yes," I said guardedly. "He was an Army Ranger. He was killed in Afghanistan in 2006."

"Exactly," the elder Sullivan said. "And you and Ellen's daughter were . . ."

He paused. I tensed. He was referring to Laura.

". . . married, I understand," the grandfather continued.

"And divorced," I hastened to add. I stood, walked over to the window, and stared out at the snow and the traffic and people hustling and bustling, to and fro.

"As the executor of Mr. Khachigian's estate, I can tell you that has no bearing on his final will and testament."

"But shouldn't she inherit everything?" I asked, turning now to face the two Sullivans. "I mean, Laura is his only living heir, right?"

"A man is entitled to leave his estate to anyone he so chooses," said the elder Sullivan. "In this case, my client chose to leave his estate to you and your brother."

"His *entire* estate?" I asked, incredulous.

"Well, no. Not quite. Laura will receive one quarter of the assets, once the house is sold and everything else is liquidated." Lincoln Sullivan pulled a copy of the will out of a folder and handed it over to me. "You and your brother will receive equal shares of the rest. We will need to have the house reappraised, of course. But it's quite valuable, as is his portfolio of stocks and bonds. All told, we believe you and Matthew will each receive about $15 million, give or take, before taxes."

I took the thick document in my hand. I tried to read it over but my thoughts were reeling and my vision was blurring. "And Laura?" I finally asked. "What will she receive?"

"About $10 million, give or take."

I didn't know what to say. "I had no idea."

"That the Khachigians were that wealthy, or that you and your brother were in the will?"

"Either—both," I said, rereading the first paragraph of the document before me for the third time and still not absorbing it. My eyes were filled with tears but I was fighting them back, embarrassed to show such emotion in front of two complete strangers. The grandson reached for a box of tissues on the desk and handed it to me. That embarrassed me even more, but I nodded my thanks, took a tissue, and wiped my eyes. "So this is what was in the envelope you mentioned? The will?" I asked, fighting to compose myself.

"No, the will was always in my possession, in my safe," said the grandfather. "That wasn't what was in the envelope. That's something entirely different."

"Meaning what?" I asked.

"I can't say," Sullivan said.

"Why not?"

"Because whatever he put in the envelope, he chose not to show me," Sullivan explained. "Frankly, I have no idea what's in there."

"But that's what you used to get me here."

"It was very important to my client."

"So may I see it?"

"You may," he said, reaching for his cane and rising—shakily—to his feet. "I'll be right back."

37

Lincoln Sullivan hobbled over to a door I hadn't previously noticed.

With Steve at his side, helping him keep his balance, he opened it to an adjacent conference room and disappeared from view.

Alone for the first time, I suddenly noticed that the office was dimly lit and quite chilly, as though someone had forgotten to turn the heat on, or perhaps the heater was broken. The whole situation seemed a little odd, and I wondered why in the world I had come. My mother had been murdered. So had my nephew. My brother was in a hospital across town, pleading with his God to save his critically wounded wife and daughter. I'd barely had time to accept what had just happened, much less grieve. Yet here I was in some dilapidated old law firm I'd never heard of, being told that Matt and I had just inherited thirty million dollars from a man to whom we had no blood relation. I hadn't come for money. I didn't even want it. I just wanted my family back, and now I regretted coming here at all.

I considered bolting but thought better of it.

I'd come here for something far more valuable to me than money. There was something Khachigian wanted me to know, some bit of information he wanted me alone to see. Not Matt. Not even his attorneys, though he clearly trusted them a great deal. Could it be clues to the identity of whoever had leaked him the information about ISIS capturing chemical weapons in Syria? Or even clues to who might have ultimately killed him? Whatever it was, Khachigian had obviously left something deeply important to him, in my name, with the executor of his estate, and he'd done so shortly before his death. For that reason alone, I forced myself to stay and see this thing through.

As I waited for the Sullivans to return with the mysterious envelope, I checked my phone. There were dozens of new text messages and e-mails, but only two were critical. Allen's caught my eye first. He noted that Vice President Holbrooke had just confirmed that he was, in fact, going to attend the memorial service. Air Force Two would be wheels down at 7 a.m. the following morning, and the VP would arrive at the church by motorcade. Allen also said that he had found a place to set up a full-blown media filing center and was now trying to track down card tables, mult boxes, and a lot of extension cords. Lastly, he asked if I'd seen the front page of the *Times* yet. I had not. In fact, with everything else going on, I'd forgotten to look, so for now I moved on.

The other significant e-mail was from Agent Harris. He reported that his colleagues had lifted partial prints from the car abandoned on that side street in Augusta. They belonged to an Iraqi national who had served as a translator for U.S. forces in Fallujah in 2003 and 2004. Later, he'd been arrested as a mole. It turned out he'd been secretly working for Abu Musab al-Zarqawi, the leader of al Qaeda in Iraq, the forerunner of ISIS. He'd been tried and convicted and sent to the Abu Ghraib prison facility near Baghdad in 2005. But he'd escaped along with Abu Khalif the previous November. While Harris conceded the FBI couldn't yet prove in court that this guy was a member of ISIS or that he had been personally sent by Abu Khalif to kill my family, he said the evidence was moving steadily in that direction, and he wanted me to be in the loop.

I opened the attachment Harris had sent. There was a thumbnail picture of the guy from the FBI's most wanted list. In the photo, he was no older than thirty with dark, soulless eyes, closely cropped black hair, a dark complexion, and a thick scar across his neck. I burned the image into my memory. This guy had slaughtered my family. I had no doubt who had sent him or that he was coming for me next. He had a mission. It wasn't yet accomplished. And this wasn't the kind of guy who just gave up and went home.

When Lincoln Sullivan reentered the office, he was holding a small sealed envelope—the envelope I'd come for. He set it on the desk and slid it across to me without a word. Then he excused himself and departed again through the same door.

I sat there by myself for a long moment,

listening to the ticking of my grandfather's pocket watch, staring at Khachigian's handwritten scrawl on the outside of the envelope, and wondering what I would find inside.

38

* * *

Two minutes later, I blew out of the Sullivan firm and headed straight for the car.

"Gorham Savings Bank," I said to the two agents hustling to catch up. "172 Commercial Street—*let's move.*"

On my lap sat the envelope from Khachigian. I held its entire contents in one hand. There wasn't much—just a brass key and a business card for the manager of the Gorham Bank branch on Commercial Street. That was it.

We pulled up precisely at nine o'clock, just as a security guard was unlocking the front door. I grabbed my briefcase and dashed out of the car and into the bank, only to find that the branch manager whose name was on the business card was out sick. Nevertheless, a young assistant manager offered to help me. She led me to a vault filled with safe-deposit boxes, and soon I had Khachigian's box in my hands. The assistant ushered me to a small room containing only an oak table and a swivel chair, then left me there so I could open the box and examine its contents in privacy.

I nervously fumbled with the key but finally opened the steel box and found myself astonished. Inside were stacks of crisp, new one-hundred-dollar bills, wrapped in rubber bands. In all, I counted nine thousand dollars, all in U.S. currency. Underneath the cash was a brand-new satellite phone. There were also three different passports—one Canadian, one Australian, and the third from South Africa. The passports had different pictures of me and different fake names for me. Beside these were three leather wallets. In each I found a half-dozen credit cards with the same names as the ones on the passports, along with driver's licenses, business cards, and various other materials corresponding to the fake names and appropriate countries of origin. There was also close to a thousand dollars in local currency in each of the billfolds.

Underneath all this were two more sealed white business envelopes. I opened the first one to find a handwritten letter, personally signed by Khachigian. I glanced back at the door to the windowless office to make sure it was fully closed, then sat down in the chair, facing the doorway in case someone suddenly entered, and began to read the letter.

Dearest James,

If you have this in your hands, then I am dead and you have met the Sullivans. Please know that you can trust them implicitly, as I have.

*Link was my father's banker and worked with
your grandfather years ago as well. I doubt
he told you that. He is far too discreet. Link's
grandson, Steven, is as trustworthy as any young
man you'll meet. Before returning to Portland,
he used to work for the Treasury Department—
specifically the Secret Service—for nearly a
decade, handling dozens of bank fraud and
other cases and putting countless crooks and
international terrorists behind bars.*

*If I know you, you're probably wondering
about Steve's father, Link's son. We'll get to
that in a moment. You're also likely reeling
from what the Sullivans just told you about
my estate.*

*There is a reason for all this. Whoever has
killed me did so to silence me, to keep me from
telling the world urgently important facts about
ISIS and its plans. So the torch now passes to
you. Below I have listed three people whom
you need to contact immediately. Go visit them
in person. Show them this letter. I trust them.
They're good people. Now you must win their
trust. Learn what they know, and tell the
world as quickly as possible.*

*Do not wait. Do not hesitate. I believe far
greater attacks are coming against the American
homeland. Perhaps your reporting can save
many lives, including your own.*

*By now it has become painfully clear to
me that Harrison Taylor has no idea what he's
doing. He won't listen to wise counsel. He doesn't
understand the nature and threat of the evil he*

faces. And I fear he—and the nation—will soon be blindsided as a result.

Over the many years of my career, I have known many presidents, good and bad. But I have never feared for the future of America as I do right now. We are not merely in a rough season, James. We are hurtling toward implosion. The president is selling out our allies and appeasing our enemies. He is gutting our military and dispiriting the brave men and women throughout the intelligence community and the military. Too many are giving up and moving on. And the more that leave high-level government service, the more danger America is in. People with such tremendous experience cannot easily be replaced.

Meanwhile, our enemies smell blood in the water. They see weakness, and they are probing, probing, probing, looking for vulnerabilities to exploit and waiting for the right time to strike. I fear they are planning something catastrophic.

Go stop them, James—before it's too late.

And one other thing. Whoever killed me is coming after you, James. Make no mistake. They're coming after Matt and his family and your mom as well. Your family is not safe in Bar Harbor. Not anymore. Persuade them to leave. Get off the grid—out of sight, out of mind. It's that serious. They need to hide. You need to help them. This is why I've left you and Matt the lion's share of my estate. Matt must use the money to get his family to safety. But you must use your share to defeat ISIS. To that end, I have left you with cash, new identities, and access to your own jet.

I know you want to go get these guys. Especially now. Good for you. That's what I've always loved about you. You're not afraid to go on offense, to seize the initiative. I can't promise you won't meet my same fate. I just hope you'll do a lot of damage to the caliphate before all is said and done.

Last thought: I'm not a preacher. I'm not a pastor. But as your friend, I need to urge you, James—please read your Bible, humble your heart, and give your life to Christ. I let too many years go by before I got serious about the things that matter most. I don't have many regrets about my life, but this is one. If it weren't for Matt patiently answering my questions and guiding me through the Scriptures and urging me to make a decision for or against Christ once and for all, I don't know where I'd be. I'm not a humble man by nature, James. It was excruciating for me to admit I needed a Savior. But I did. I do. And so do you. Go find him before it's too late.

I leave you with the verse that changed my life, the words of Jesus, from the Gospel of John. "Greater love has no one than this, that one lay down his life for his friends."

Godspeed, son—I hope to see you on the other side.

Your biggest fan,
Robert

For a moment, I just sat there, staring at the pages. There was so much to take in.

For starters, so much of it was too late. The catastrophic attacks had already come. So had the hit on my family. Why hadn't the Sullivans brought me all this sooner? Why hadn't they come down to Walter Reed right after I'd gotten back from Iraq? On the other hand, why hadn't I responded sooner to their calls and e-mails? The weight of my failures was almost overwhelming. I set the letter down in the box, leaned back in the chair, and closed my eyes. Everywhere I went, people were getting killed, and I knew I bore a great degree of responsibility.

That said, I feared Khachigian had me all wrong. Clearly Khachigian wanted me—expected me—to personally go after Abu Khalif and these ISIS devils. Given all that he'd done for me—in the past and certainly now—how could I refuse? Yet I wasn't sure I had the energy or desire to go back on offense. What's more, how could I leave Matt, Annie, and Katie now, after all that had happened? They were all the family I had left.

Then there was the mention of his faith. Of all the conversations we'd had over the years, I couldn't recall any about his religious beliefs. I knew Matt had had a profound influence on him, but Khachigian himself had never discussed his faith with me. He was a secretive man by nature. It's what had made him an effective keeper of the nation's secrets. But that only made his urgent appeal that I follow his spiritual journey and wrestle through the claims of Christ for myself all the more surprising. He was urging me to study the Gospels and make a decision, once and for all, for or against, before it was too late. Was I going to listen to him . . . or ignore him?

I sat silently for several minutes, then suddenly opened my eyes and picked up the letter again. I reread it, more slowly this time, word for word, sentence by sentence. Then, on instinct, I flipped the page over, and there on the back I found three names: Paul Pritchard, Walid Hussam, and Mohammed bin Zayed. Beside each name was a mobile phone number. None of the names rang a bell. I didn't recall Khachigian having ever mentioned them before. But these were his sources for the chemical weapons story. Of this I had no doubt.

Which left me with two questions: Who were they, and would they talk to me?

39

* * *

We raced the 175 miles back to Bar Harbor.

The bureau was transferring me from the Motel 6 in Portland to someplace in my hometown, where I could make the final preparations for the funeral. As I sat in the backseat of the bureau's sedan and watched the snow-covered trees and hills and barns of rural Maine blur by, my thoughts raced as fast as the car. I felt conflicted about heading back to Bar Harbor. My brother needed me with him at the hospital in Portland. But someone had to finish planning the service. He couldn't. I owed him. The memorial service was set to begin in less than twenty-four hours.

On a good day, the drive took less than three hours. But with so much snow falling overnight, I knew we'd be lucky to get there in four.

With my briefcase resting on my lap, I pulled out my grandfather's watch. It was 9:47. I made a quick call to Matt to check on him. He said he was just about to go into the ICU and would have to call me back. He would be making the trip to Bar

Harbor in a couple of hours with another team of FBI agents.

Next I called Allen but got voice mail. I didn't leave a message. Then I called Harris, hoping for an update.

"How are you holding up, Collins?" he asked, answering on the first ring.

"Surviving," I said.

"How did the meetings with the Sullivans go?"

"Fine."

"Anything interesting?"

"Just some loose ends they were trying to clear up."

"So what was in the safe-deposit box?" Harris asked.

"Personal stuff."

"Nothing relevant to my investigation?" Harris pressed.

"No," I said. "Just some private things, family things."

"Don't lie to me, Collins. You know it's a crime to lie to a federal agent, right?"

"So I've heard."

I hadn't crossed that line, not exactly, but I had come pretty close. The letter *was* personal. It contained Khachigian's thoughts, emotions, and desires for me and Matt and our family. It included his personal assessment of the president and the administration. It didn't contain evidence relevant to a murder investigation—not precisely, anyway. I certainly wasn't going to tell Harris that I now had new passports, driver's licenses, and credit cards. Khachigian had given me those for the very real possibility that I would need to slip away unnoticed, undetected by the ever-watchful eye of the American government. Telling Harris would obviously and completely undermine that intended escape hatch.

As for the three names, at the moment I had no idea who they were. Clearly they were old friends of, and trusted sources for, Khachigian. But beyond that I knew nothing about them, and as far as I was concerned, I was under no obligation to disclose them to the FBI. I wasn't under investigation. I hadn't been served a subpoena. I didn't have to tell Harris anything I didn't want to, and for the moment, I didn't want to tell him this.

Harris had no new information for me, so I ended the call and thought more about the three names. I was dying to know who they were. At the moment I had no time to do a background search on them, much less contact them, but I needed to connect with them soon. I needed to know what they knew and follow whatever clues they could give me. Yet I hesitated even to do a basic Google search for these names on my own mobile phone. Partly I was concerned that Harris might be monitoring my calls and online activity—mostly to protect me, of course, but perhaps also to keep an eye on me. Was that paranoia? Maybe. But for the moment, I decided extra caution was prudent.

I was even more concerned that ISIS might somehow be monitoring Matt's and my phones. How else had the terrorists known we were supposed to be at my mother's home by seven o'clock that Thursday night? If they'd been physically trailing us, I was pretty sure I would have spotted them somewhere during our fifteen-plus-hour drive from Arlington. The more I thought about it, the more likely it seemed that they must have intercepted the e-mail I'd sent to my mom from the service station on the Jersey Turnpike, giving her a heads-up that we were coming home and estimating our time of arrival. Matt had also sent a text to Annie telling her we'd be there by seven. They must have intercepted that one too.

On the other hand, what about the voice messages I'd left later, updating both Mom and Annie on our progress and telling them that due to snow and traffic we likely wouldn't reach Bar Harbor until closer to eight thirty? If the terrorists were truly tracking our calls and text messages, wouldn't they have intercepted those messages as well? Then again, I'd made those calls at 7:27 p.m. Based on what Harris had told me, maybe it had already been too late. Maybe by then Abu Khalif's men had already struck.

Just then, I remembered there was still another envelope from Khachigian I had not yet opened. Fortunately, the agents in the front seat were engrossed in a conversation of their own. I wasn't paying much attention, but from the fragments I'd caught so far, they were discussing the arrival of the vice president and how they were being instructed to interface with the Secret Service. That seemed as good an opportunity as any to investigate further without the FBI looking over my shoulder, so I opened my briefcase and pulled out the other sealed envelope. Opening it carefully, so as not to attract their attention, I was stunned to find paper-work detailing my new fractional ownership of a private Learjet.

I quickly scanned the documents in my hands and learned that Khachigian had prepaid for 100,000 flight miles, including fuel costs, pilot time, landing fees, taxes, and other assorted fees. Included in the envelope was a membership card. It did not have my name on it. It didn't have anyone's name on it. It just had a membership number and a PIN code. Reading through the instructions, I learned that all I needed to do was call the 800 number on the back of the card—or the international toll-free number from anywhere outside the U.S.—and punch in my number and PIN. At that point, I would be immediately con-nected to a flight coordinator who would simply ask where I wanted to depart from, at what time, what my destination was, and how many passen-gers would be accompanying me. The entire pro-cess was anonymous. They didn't care who I was. They just needed the number, the PIN, and six hours of advance notice before departure.

That could come in handy, I thought as I fin-ished reading. Then I put the card in my wallet, the paperwork back in the envelope, and the enve-lope back in my briefcase.

40

An hour later, we were tearing up I-295, heading north.

I used my iPhone to check the financial markets. They were up and running again as of that morning, after having been shut down for several days by the Feds. But already they were tanking. The Dow was down more than six hundred points. The NASDAQ was down more than 5 percent. It shouldn't have been surprising, given how bad the Nikkei, Hang Seng, and other international markets had been in recent days. But seeing everything so deep in the red—and knowing the satisfaction that must be giving Abu Khalif—sent a chill down my spine.

I knew I should be responding to the avalanche of e-mails and phone calls that were pouring in regarding the service, but all I wanted to do just then was play hooky. I'd had no time to think, no time to grieve. I wasn't sleeping well and had no one to talk to. Matt was in even more pain. Allen had his hands full with all the media inquiries.

And I certainly wasn't going to pour out my emotions to these agents from the FBI.

Thinking of Allen reminded me of the article he wanted me to read. I pulled up the *Times* app on my phone and looked for the front-page piece by my colleague Bill Sanders. The headline immediately caught my attention: **Egypt Emerges as Unexpected Ally in Hunt for Abu Khalif**. It was datelined Cairo.

As I scanned the story, it became immediately apparent that congressional leaders on both sides of the aisle were furious that the Taylor administration was doing so little to bring the ISIS leader to justice. Yes, the president had ordered new bombing runs and drone strikes. But according to Sanders's reporting, this was not a fundamental change of U.S. strategy. Rather, unnamed congressional leaders—and the unnamed head of a foreign intelligence service—said these attacks were "short-term fixes" aimed at "satiating America's bloodlust for revenge." The air strikes might last for a few weeks, said an anonymous member of the Senate Armed Services Committee, but they would be curtailed again once all the anger at ISIS had calmed down a bit.

"President Taylor has no appetite for a serious and prolonged war against the Islamic State inside Syria," said the unnamed senator. "It doesn't fit his strategy of containing the caliphate rather than crushing it."

Now, Sanders wrote, attention was shifting to Arab intelligence services for help in taking out ISIS leaders and operatives, and Egypt was emerging as chief among equals.

There were several more quotes by Republican senators speaking on background, chastising the White House and State Department for "not being serious" about winning the "great war of our time" and for "seeking sensational headlines, not serious solutions."

This struck me as shoddy journalism. Why was Sanders giving cover to GOP lawmakers, letting them take unnamed potshots at the president? If the Republicans had something of import to say, Sanders should have required them to say it on the record.

Far more interesting was a scathing—and very much on-the-record—statement by the ranking minority member of the U.S. Senate Select Committee on Intelligence, excoriating the administration for not taking specific and decisive action against Abu Khalif in the aftermath of the widespread ISIS attacks inside the U.S.

"Run this [expletive deleted] to ground and blow him to kingdom come," said Jane Oliphant, the senior senator from Rhode Island and former chairwoman of the Democratic National Committee. "What the [expletive deleted] is the White House waiting for? Are we really going to outsource this to the Israelis, the Jordanians, and the Egyptians? All three are great friends and capable allies. But we're the [expletive deleted] United States of America, for crying out loud. It's time for the president to show these [expletive deleted] what Uncle Sam is truly capable of."

Sanders dutifully quoted the president's national security advisor insisting that "every possible measure is being taken" to track down the emir of ISIS and counseling patience for "those in the peanut gallery who perhaps have read a few too many spy thrillers and think hunting terrorists is easy and quick."

However, Sanders also cited an unnamed CIA official who admitted that the fear of ISIS moles in senior positions in government agencies was "nearly paralyzing" the U.S. intelligence community. "No one knows who to trust," he said. "So no one is sharing information and things are getting missed."

"Enter the Egyptians," Sanders wrote. "Working quietly but in remarkably close cooperation with the Israeli Mossad and the Jordanian General Intelligence Directorate, senior officials in Cairo have made the hunt for Abu Khalif a top priority. In the past thirty days, Egyptian police and security forces have arrested twenty-three ISIS operatives. In the process they have scooped up an enormous amount of intelligence about ISIS methods, and more raids and arrests are expected in coming days."

As I kept reading, I forgave Sanders for letting a few Republican senators snipe at their political adversary on background. The rest of his reporting was as riveting as it was detailed. He described intense interrogation sessions of ISIS terrorists by Egyptian agents, the seizure of cell phones and laptops, the cracking of passcodes and encryption software, and even a list of confirmed locations where Abu Khalif had been sighted over the past two months. On that list were the Iraqi cities of Mosul and Dohuk and the Syrian cities of Raqqa, Aleppo, Deir ez-Zor, and al-Mayadin. Given that I myself had theorized that Khalif might be in Raqqa, the ISIS capital in Syria, the story rang true. But Sanders had pieces of the puzzle I did not.

He cited a senior Egyptian intelligence official saying he had actually been privy to grainy photos of Abu Khalif getting into the back of an ambulance in Raqqa, reportedly headed for Deir ez-Zor. However, the official noted, none of the witnesses indicated that Khalif was injured.

"The ISIS leader appears to be using Red Crescent ambulances as his personal taxicabs to obscure his movements," said the Cairo-based official, speaking on the condition of anonymity.

The article didn't quote any sources saying the Egyptians, Jordanians, or Israelis were close to actually finding the ISIS leader. But in the infuriating absence of American leadership, the three countries had apparently banded together on a mission each regarded as vital to its own national security.

Clearly the hunt for Abu Khalif was on. But according to Sanders, the White House wasn't exactly taking the lead.

41

We arrived at the Harborside Hotel, and I checked in.

The agents secured my room, then left me to myself and occupied the rooms on either side of mine, though not before cleaning out the minibar, at my request.

"Two years, six months, and three days," I told them as they removed all the alcohol from my room. "One step at a time. One day at a time."

I said it. I meant it. But there was no question I intensely wanted to drink and drink heavily. The pain of the last few days was sinking in more and more, and I desperately wanted an escape. The brutal truth was that I was an alcoholic. It had nearly destroyed me in the past. It was a constant temptation, and though I was determined to manage it, I genuinely feared I was going to crack.

My phone buzzed. It was a text message from my friend Carl Hughes, the longtime deputy director of intelligence at the CIA. In December, after the arrest of then-Director Jack Vaughn on charges of espionage, the president had named Carl the agency's acting director. I immediately dialed the number he gave, eager to hear his voice.

I'd known Carl, now fifty-two, for nearly twenty-five years. We'd first met at American University, where I was an undergrad majoring in political science and he was a grad student studying international affairs. We'd become friends and kept in reasonably close touch over the years as he'd gone off to work at Langley while I'd gone to Columbia for an MA in journalism before taking a job with the *New York Daily News* covering local crime stories prior to landing a position as a foreign correspondent for the Associated Press. We'd both done well for ourselves. Eventually I'd moved over to the *Times* and emerged as the paper's chief national security correspondent. Carl had proven himself one of the most impressive analysts who had ever risen through the ranks of America's intelligence community. Now he had finally been named to the top spot.

His secretary answered. I gave my name and said I was returning Carl's message and wanted to thank him for his condolences. She immediately transferred me to his executive assistant, a man with a military background who, among other responsibilities, was tasked with making sure not just anyone got through to the acting director. Again I explained who I was and why I was calling. I stressed that I was calling as an old friend, not as a journalist. Finally Hughes came on the line.

"J. B., I'm so sorry not to have called sooner," he began. "I just . . ."

His voice trailed off, and as it did, the weight of all that had happened hit me again, and hard.

"Don't worry about it, Carl," I said. "You've got a very full plate."

Nevertheless, he apologized profusely for not being able to come up for the funeral. I told him that was fine, but he insisted on explaining. He'd initially arranged to join the vice president on Air Force Two the following morning and surprise me, but the president had suddenly decided to send him to Moscow on agency business. He was leaving in a few hours.

He asked me how I was doing. He asked how Matt was holding up and what the doctors were saying about Annie and Katie. I told him what I knew, which still wasn't much, then took a deep breath and shifted gears.

"Carl," I began. "I have to ask—"

But he immediately cut me off. "Don't, J. B."

"What?" I said, taken aback. "You don't even know what I was going to say."

"Of course I do—we've known each other too long. You want to ask whether the president is serious about hunting down Abu Khalif. But you can't."

"Why not?"

"Just don't go there."

"Because you can't tell me anything?"

"No, of course I can't," he said. I expected him to say he needed to take another call and let me go. But to my surprise, he continued, perhaps taking pity on me. "Look, I can't say it on the record, of course, and you can never repeat this, but your instincts were spot-on. All the warnings were there. Every light on the dashboard was blinking red. We didn't know certain pieces, but we knew enough. We knew something was coming. We knew it for weeks. We knew ISIS had people here. It was inevitable with all the refugees the president's been welcoming into the country with open arms. We didn't know which ones, of course. There were too many to vet—more than fifty thousand—it was an impossible situation. But I personally briefed the president and the NSC on five separate occasions. I urged him to shut down the airports and seaports. I pleaded with him to delay the State of the Union. He wouldn't hear of it. Any of it. And then the NSA intercepted two calls and a text message. I personally called Larry Beck at the FBI. That's how they found the cell in Birmingham. We were hot on their trail, J. B. Another twenty-four hours, and we would have had them—some of them, anyway."

I was floored—not just that the head of the CIA was telling me so much, even as a friend, but much more by the damning nature of what he was saying. If the president had known all this before any of it had gone down, then he had stood there in the Oval Office and lied to my face. He had stood there in the House Chamber and lied to a joint session of Congress and the country. The state of the union was not strong. ISIS was not on the run. Abu Khalif had not been contained. Rather, he and his minions were coming to kill Americans, and the commander in chief wasn't doing all he could to stop them.

I'd gotten my answer. No, the president wasn't serious about hunting down Abu Khalif. Someone else was going to have to do it. Maybe the Egyptians were up to the task. Or the Israelis. Or perhaps the Jordanians.

But Harrison Taylor could not be trusted to do the job. That much was clear.

42

* * *

I worked straight through the afternoon.

No lunch. No breaks. I was burning pure rage and fighting a lust for hard liquor. My only hope was to stay busy.

By sundown, I'd finalized the service order, edited and signed off on the program and made sure it got to the printer on time, and talked to the florist multiple times, answering myriad questions while trying not to go insane. All the while, I did my best to make sure everything was coordinated with the pastor, the local police chief, the head of the advance team for the Secret Service, and the vice president's chief of staff. And there were still twenty-six e-mails remaining that had to do with the service, not to mention another thirty-nine from colleagues in D.C. and sources around the world offering their condolences or giving me leads I ought to be following up on.

Rubbing my eyes, I plugged my phone into a wall charger and stood for a moment to stretch. Then I stepped into the bathroom. I splashed warm water on my face and dried myself off with a towel and tried to decide what to do next. Order some room service? Turn my phone off and watch a movie on pay-per-view? Go down to the gym and work out? None of the options sounded attractive. I had no appetite. No interest in the latest garbage from Hollywood. No desire to be babysat by my FBI handlers while I spent an hour on the treadmill. What I ought to be doing—what I wanted to be doing, I decided—was tracking down everything I could find on Paul Pritchard, Walid Hussam, and Mohammed bin Zayed and finding a way to contact them. The clock was ticking. The information was valuable, Khachigian had made clear, but it might also be perishable. *Use it or lose it.* I had to move quickly.

I still didn't want to use my own phone for anything sensitive, in case anyone—the FBI or ISIS—might be watching. Instead, I grabbed the satellite phone Khachigian had left me in the safe-deposit box. Powering it up, I quickly got a signal, pulled up Google, and ran a search on the three names mentioned in the spymaster's letter to me.

The first was Paul Pritchard. I didn't immediately find a LinkedIn bio for him, but I did find a 2012 profile on him in the *Washington Post* that would have to suffice for now. Pritchard, it said, was a former intelligence officer in the U.S. Army who had served in both Iraq and Kuwait in the first Gulf War before joining the CIA. From there, he'd been recruited into the Clandestine Service, working his way up to the rank of station chief in Damascus. But this was odd. The *Post* article said that Pritchard was ultimately fired from the agency by Khachigian for reasons that weren't immediately clear. Then, in 2013, the *Wall Street Journal* reported that he had been killed in a car bomb in Khartoum. Was that possible? Was he really dead? Then why was he on Khachigian's list?

I found several mentions of Walid Hussam, who, according to Al Arabiya, was a former chief of Egyptian intelligence back during the days when Hosni Mubarak was president. Once again I was confused. At first glance, it seemed like Hussam had been out of the spy game for a long time. He'd written a book on the Arab Spring that hadn't sold many copies, though I found a few unflattering reviews. He'd briefly taught at the American University in Cairo. Then he'd dropped off the radar screen. I couldn't find a single news story about him, or even mentioning him, from the past half decade. Why, then, would Khachigian send me to him?

The third name on Khachigian's "must-see" list was Mohammed bin Zayed. The name was vaguely familiar to me. I knew he was a member of the royal family in the United Arab Emirates, but I couldn't remember anything else about him. The Google search, however, struck pay dirt. I found a wealth of stories about him, all indicating he had served for almost two decades as the UAE's ambassador to Iraq before being severely injured in a bomb blast in Baghdad almost three and a half years earlier. That, apparently, had retired him, which was likely why I hadn't ever done any business with him. More recently, however, he had been named the UAE's chief of intelligence.

So, I thought, at least one of the people on Khachigian's list was still active in the intelligence business. The others seemed to be out of the game or, in Paul Pritchard's case, maybe even no longer alive. Was it possible the old spy chief's information was out of date?

Just then I heard footsteps in the hallway and a soft voice outside my door. *"You sure that's the room?"*

I quickly powered down Khachigian's satphone and put it back in the briefcase and tucked the case under the bed. Then I turned and faced the door, my heart pounding fast and hard. I waited for a movement and noticed flickering shadows under the door to the hallway. Someone was pacing. I couldn't tell exactly if it was one or two, but whoever they were, they were deciding what to do next.

Rising to my feet, I moved quickly across the carpet and pressed myself against the wall to the left of the door, straining to hear more of their conversation. I expected them to burst into my room at any moment, and I had no idea what I would do when they did. Everything got quiet. The pacing stopped. So did the talking. Whatever was happening, it was happening now.

I decided not to wait. Grabbing the handle with my left hand, I gave it a hard turn and flung the door open, determined to face the threat head-on.

I was prepared for the worst. Instead, standing in front of me—startled and alone—was Agent Art Harris, holding a cell phone against his ear.

"Never mind," he said to whoever was on the other end. "It's the right room. I'll call you back."

I started breathing again.

"Hey," Harris said calmly. "Expecting someone else?"

"Wasn't expecting you, that's for sure," I said.

He stood there for a moment, waiting for me to say something.

"Would you like to come in?" I asked finally.

Expressionless, Harris entered, and I shut the door behind him.

"Please tell me it's not that easy for someone to approach my room," I said.

"No, don't worry," Harris replied. "There are agents stationed in the lobby, at every exit in the hotel, and at both ends of your hallway. And video cameras feeding into a makeshift operations center on the first floor. Believe me, we've got you covered. I just forgot your exact room number, that's all."

"So why are you here?" I asked.

"We have a problem," he said.

"What's that?"

"We've arrested a suspect."

"That's a good thing, isn't it?" I said.

"Yes and no."

"Meaning what?"

"Meaning, yes, we've captured an ISIS operative. Wonderful. The problem is that from the information we've pulled off this guy's phone, we now believe there are at least two more ISIS sleeper cells operating in New England."

"And you're worried they're going to hit the memorial service tomorrow?"

"No. Between the Secret Service, the bureau, and the local authorities, we're confident the service will go safely and without a hitch."

"Then what?"

"We're worried about what could happen after the VP goes back to D.C. and the circus leaves town," Harris said. "We believe these two cells may have orders to kill you and the rest of your family."

It was as if Harris had just sucker punched me. "You're saying they're coming to finish us off?"

Harris didn't say anything just yet, but I could see it in his eyes.

"I see," I said, forcing myself to take deep breaths. "So what exactly do you recommend?"

"You're not going to like it."

"I already don't like it."

"I wish there was another way, but honestly, I don't see one."

"What is it?"

"We need to move you into WITSEC," Harris said.

"Into *what*?"

"The federal Witness Security Program."

43

"You've got to be kidding me," I snapped.

I had barely eaten. I had barely slept. I was completely overwhelmed by everything I had to do to get ready for the next day. And now this?

"That's your plan?" I asked. "You and a bunch of geniuses in Washington want the four of us to put on fake mustaches and move to Utah or New Mexico or Alaska or wherever, and change our names and raise ostriches and be completely cut off from our friends, our relatives, and everything connected to our previous lives? Are you nuts?"

"Well, I'm not sure about the ostriches and fake mustaches, but if you'll just take a moment and listen—"

"No," I said, suddenly feeling claustrophobic. "That's not something I have time to listen to."

"J. B., you need to sit down and listen to me very carefully," Harris said calmly but with authority. "You and your family are being systematically hunted down by ISIS. Why? Because you know Abu Khalif. Because you've seen him. Because you've talked to him. Because you've watched him—personally watched him—kill people. And because he personally told you his plans to attack Americans inside the homeland. No other American citizen that we know of has met him. No other American could actually identify him in a lineup, could identify his voice. That's why he wants you dead. He needed you at the beginning to get his message out. And now that he's done with you—now that you're no longer of value to him—he's going to kill you. You're a threat to him. When we capture Abu Khalif—and we will; make no mistake about it—he's going to stand trial. He's going to give an account for all the blood he has spilled, all the lives he has destroyed. And then you're going to testify against him. If my colleagues and I do our job right, he will pay for his crimes against humanity. He will be executed by lethal injection. But that's going to take time, and at this moment, you and your family are in grave danger. And that's why I'm saying—"

"Forget it," I said, cutting him off. "You're wasting your time."

But Harris would not be dissuaded. "That's why I'm saying we need you as a federal witness. If you agree to this—"

"I said forget it. I'm a reporter, not an informant for the FBI."

Harris wouldn't let himself get derailed. He just kept on talking. "If you agree to testify, the federal government is empowered to protect you and your family. We can't force you. But if you agree, we can relocate you. We can give you all new identities. We can make sure Abu Khalif and his men never find you or your family. But only if you sign this." He pulled a document out of his breast pocket and handed it to me.

"What's this?" I asked.

"It's a memorandum of understanding," he said. "It explains exactly what will happen, how it'll all work, and what your responsibilities will be."

"Keep it," I said. "I don't want it."

"What about Matt?"

"He doesn't want it either."

"And Annie and Katie—what about them?" he countered. "You're saying they don't want federal protection after all they've been through? You're saying they don't want a chance to heal from their wounds and go on with their lives free from fear that one day Abu Khalif and his men will come and finish what they've started? Are you really going to blow this off and put their lives—all of your lives—in jeopardy again?"

I didn't want to hear any of it.

"Come on, Collins. You owe it to them—and to yourself—to at least read this over, talk to Matt, think it through, and then decide. But you're going to need to move quickly. We don't have much time."

My mind was reeling. I couldn't believe what I was being told. On the face of it, it all sounded ridiculous, like something out of the movies. But as much as I didn't want to admit it, Harris had a point.

"So how would it work—big picture?" I asked.

"First, you and Matt would need to read and

sign this agreement. Second, we'd put you all on an air ambulance—preferably tomorrow afternoon, after the memorial service. I've been instructed to personally take you to the location we've chosen for you."

"Which is where?"

"You'll know when we get there."

"Don't we get to choose?"

"It's better if you don't."

"Why?"

"Less chance you'll pick someplace you've already talked about with family and friends, someplace people might know—or guess—where to look."

"Fine," I said, even less happy with that scenario. "What then?"

"You'd have a medical team taking care of Annie and Katie twenty-four hours a day, seven days a week, until they recover. You'd have private tutoring for Katie when she starts to recover, until she's well enough to go to a local school. You and Matt would each receive a stipend of about $60,000 a year for the first few years, until you find jobs and get on your feet. And of course, you'd all have new identities. You'd be completely off the grid—no linkage with your past life whatsoever."

"No contact with family?"

"No."

"Friends?"

Harris shook his head.

"Colleagues from work?"

"I'm afraid not," Harris said. "If you agree to this, it means you agree to all the stipulations—first and foremost that you can have absolutely no contact with anyone from your past. I realize that's hard to contemplate, but believe me, it's for your own safety."

"And if we do this, you think it'll work?" I asked. "You can really keep us all safe?"

"We can," Harris insisted. "Since we started the program in 1971, we've protected nearly twenty thousand people."

"And how many have you lost?"

"Of the people who followed the rules?" he asked.

"Yeah," I said.

"None."

44

Matt arrived at the hotel just after ten.

I'd already spoken to him briefly by phone to give him a summary of what Harris was proposing. Neither of us was permitted to use our own cell phones. So Harris had insisted I use his phone and that Matt use the phone of one of the FBI agents guarding him.

The bureau's technical division was still trying to determine how the terrorists had known we had been planning to be home by seven o'clock that fateful night. Until they could rule out the notion that ISIS had somehow tapped either or both of our numbers, Harris said we needed to be extra careful.

Matt greeted me in the lobby of the Harborside with a bear hug and wouldn't let go.

"You look horrible," I whispered, trying to break the ice.

"Thanks," he whispered back, finally releasing me.

"You eat anything today?" I asked.

He looked at me for a moment, then shook his head.

"I didn't think so," I said, motioning him to follow me down the hallway to the hotel's main restaurant. Since the bureau—in cooperation with the U.S. Secret Service—had commandeered the entire hotel, there were no other diners. I asked Harris if he could get someone to whip up a couple of omelets, some sausage and bacon, and a fresh pot of coffee. He radioed for one of his guys to make it happen. Then he and his colleagues took a few tables by the door.

Matt and I sat at a table in the back. As Matt removed his coat, scarf, and gloves, I asked about Annie and Katie. There was still nothing to report. Nothing good. But nothing bad either. I asked if Matt had been getting any sleep. Not much, he said. He'd tried, he insisted. But sleep simply would not come. He'd experienced too much horror, and now the FBI was telling us we had to give up our very identities and all contact with family and friends.

"So what do you think?" I began, bracing myself because I already knew the answer.

"What do I think? *What do I think?* I think Harris is insane," Matt replied. "Who does he think we are? Cowards? He thinks we're just going to give up our lives? Absolutely not. No way."

"That's what I told him," I said calmly.

"What we need is for the president to go after Abu Khalif and take him out—period," Matt continued. "Khalif should be on the run, not us."

"You're right," I agreed.

"Then why are we even having this conversation?"

"Because the president isn't going to do it," I said. "The country might be buying this latest bombing attack—and the new drone strikes—but it won't last. He's not serious. You know it. I know it. Abu Khalif knows it. And though he won't say it, Harris knows it too. That's why he wants to get us out of harm's way now, while there's still time."

"But it's crazy, J. B.—completely nuts."

"I know."

"I'm not going to do it—*I'm not*," Matt insisted. "Are you?"

Just then one of the agents brought over a pot of coffee, two mugs, some fresh cream, and some sugar. I kept quiet.

The moment the agent had gone back to the kitchen, Matt pressed me for an answer. "Is that what you want to do, J. B.? Hide for the rest of your life? Is that how we were raised?"

"It's not just about us, though," I said in a hushed tone, leaning toward him. "It's about Mom and Josh. More important, it's about Annie and Katie. If we stay out in the open, they're going to hunt us down and kill us. That's it. That's the deal."

"Can't these guys protect us?"

"Yes, if we go into the program."

"And if we don't?"

"Then pretty soon we're on our own."

Matt said nothing. He poured us each a cup of coffee, put a packet of sugar in his, and started stirring with a fork, as the agent had forgotten to bring us any spoons. But he didn't take a sip, and neither did I.

"Look—if it was just me, I'd probably take my chances," I said quietly. "And maybe if it were just the two of us, we'd do the same. But if we could wind the clock back and give Mom and Annie and the kids the chance to slip away and live safely in Montana or Arizona or wherever, just the six of us, don't you think they'd have taken that in a millisecond?"

Matt remained quiet, and in the silence I suddenly realized I was talking myself into a decision I couldn't have imagined making just a few hours before.

"Matt, this is my fault. I know that, and I'm sick about it. But I can't undo what's happened. This is it. This is our reality now. And you and I can't simply think about what we want. We need to do what's best for Annie and Katie, and as much as we're resisting it, I think we both know what that is."

45

The agent brought us the omelets and the side dishes.

We nodded our thanks and waited again for him to leave us.

"There's something else I have to tell you," I said.

My older brother just looked at me. He was already on information overload. What I was about to tell him wasn't going to help.

After making sure there was no one approaching us, I told him about my visit to Sullivan & Sullivan, about the will and the $30 million—give or take—we had just inherited. I didn't tell him about the fake passports or my new fractional ownership of a Learjet. Those weren't details he needed to know right now, or maybe ever. The first part was enough.

"Even as we speak, the Sullivans are setting up two untraceable bank accounts in the Cayman Islands, one for you and one for me," I said. "At the same time, they're liquidating all of Khachigian's assets. The house will take time to be sold, obviously. But the rest will be in our accounts in the next twenty-four hours."

He looked pale, close to being in shock. "What about Laura?" he asked.

I nodded. "I asked that too. She'll get a big share as well."

"And taxes?"

"I've already instructed the Sullivans to set aside whatever they think we'll need to pay into a separate account and to pay our tax bills as soon as possible."

"And their share as executors?"

"All taken care of."

"J. B.—I can't believe this," Matt said. "I don't even know what to say."

I shrugged. "I know. I had the same reaction. I've just had an extra day to process it."

"And you told all this to Harris?"

"Of course not."

"Why not?"

"He doesn't need to know. It's none of his business."

"But if we end up going into the Witness Protection Program—which still sounds ridiculous to me, by the way—isn't he going to find out eventually?"

"I don't know. Maybe. We can worry about that later. For now, all we have to worry about is keeping you and Katie and Annie safe. And that means we have to come up with an answer for Harris."

"But you're not—"

"Keep your voice down, Matt."

Harris and his colleagues turned toward us. I smiled and nodded.

"Fine," Matt said, more quietly this time. "But you're not *seriously* considering this, are you?"

"Yes, I am, actually. But that's not the point, Matt. It's not about what I do. It's about keeping you all safe. If I don't go into the program, none of you can. I'm the witness. I'm the one they need to protect."

I could see in my brother's eyes he couldn't tell whether to laugh in my face or get up and punch Harris in his.

"You wouldn't be able to write for the *Times* anymore."

"No."

"You couldn't write your memoirs."

"No."

"Couldn't write op-eds."

"Not if I want to have a long and happy life," I said softly, knowing how hard it was for him to hear it. "Eat your omelet."

"It's cold."

"Whose fault is that?"

Matt stared at the eggs, then at me. Finally he sprinkled on some salt and pepper and wolfed down the entire meal in just a few minutes. I took a few bites of my own meal but couldn't summon any appetite.

"So how does this play out?" Matt asked when he had finished and had washed it all down with another cup of coffee.

"What do you mean?"

"I mean they have to get rid of us, right? So how do they do that?"

I took that as a good sign. Despite his resistance, he was asking questions, which meant he was finally considering the idea, which meant he might actually get to yes.

"Once we're safe in wherever they're going to resettle us, the news will come out that we've all been killed in a car bombing just outside of Portland."

"Kinda grim."

"Yeah."

"When would that happen?"

"Next few days."

"And then?"

"There'll be another memorial service, I guess. I imagine there will be a lot of press. Big story, right? Another terrorist attack and all? And then that's it."

"Everyone we know will think we're dead."

"Yeah."

"And that's all right with you?" he asked again.

I pushed my plate away angrily. "No, it's not all right with me. But, Matt, how many ways can I say it? The guy the FBI caught? He had your private mobile phone number. He had mine. He had floor plans of Mom's house. He had dozens of photos of your family, notes on their daily routines, friends, acquaintances, church attendance, favorite restaurants, you name it. And he had a trunk full of automatic weapons and plastic explosives. The guy was a professional. And there are three more just like him in his cell—three more the FBI haven't caught yet. Harris says the guy was also in contact with two other cells in the region. He isn't just being dramatic. This is real."

"Can't they catch these guys and be done with it?"

"Maybe, maybe not," I said. "Harris says they've got more than three hundred agents hunting them down. So yeah, he's confident they'll catch them. He's just not confident that will be the end of it."

"'Cause he's never going away," Matt said, half under his breath, looking out the windows again at the twinkling lights across the water.

There was no hint of a question, just a statement of a bitter reality. And he was right. I couldn't tell him what Carl Hughes had told me. But it wasn't even necessary.

"No," I said quietly. "Abu Khalif is never going away."

46

★ ★ ★

BAR HARBOR, MAINE

It was the dead of night, and I lay in my bed, tossing and turning.

Unable to sleep, I just stared up at the ceiling fan as the moonlight streaming in through the windows cast long, dark shadows across the stucco surface. The fan itself was off, of course. After all, the temperature outside was well below zero and sinking. A new storm was approaching. I could hear the howling winter winds gusting across the North Atlantic, rattling the windows.

My hands mindlessly toyed with my grandfather's pocket watch, which now read 3:18, but my thoughts were a thousand miles away—well over five thousand miles away, actually, in Israel. Against my better judgment, I'd sent Yael a text. Told her I missed her. Asked what she was up to. Told her I wished she would write and hoped she was well. In Jerusalem, it was now after 10 a.m. on a workday. She was, no doubt, immersed in meetings, perhaps with the prime minister, perhaps with the full security cabinet. I didn't really expect to hear from her. But if I was about to "die" in an FBI-staged car bombing, I guess I just wanted to say good-bye. Inside, I raged against the notion that I would never be able to see her again, never be allowed to talk to her again. Not that we'd interacted much in the last few months anyway. But *never*? If not for the need to make sure Matt and his family were finally and truly safe, the thought would be inconceivable.

The latest news from the hospital was not encouraging. Annie's vital signs were stable. But earlier that night, Matt had received a call from the ICU that Katie's breathing had suddenly stopped. They'd caught it instantly, thank God. They'd gotten her breathing again within seconds, and she was now on a respirator. At this point there was nothing we could do but pray. And try to sleep.

If only I were following my own advice.

I got up and got a glass of water. However frigid it was outside, I was soaked with sweat. Was I coming down with something? Did I have a fever, or was I just consumed with anxiety? I had no idea. But one look at my bloodshot eyes in the bathroom mirror was enough to make me wonder if I needed to check into the hospital for a few days myself.

Matt was clearly going through the five stages of grief. At the moment, he seemed to be shifting from denial to anger. I, on the other hand, was calm and functioning better than Matt. But that was simply because I was still fully immersed in a state of denial—and not just because of the murders of my family members, but because of the murders of so many people I loved.

All around me, the death toll kept mounting, and I just kept moving. Somewhere deep in the recesses of my mind, a faint and distant voice was telling me I had to stop. I couldn't keep up this pace. I couldn't keep living off adrenaline. I had to face the reality that my world was crashing down all around me, or I was going to crash too. Everything I'd known, everything I'd trusted, everything I'd ever taken for granted, was rapidly coming to an end. My career. My connections with everyone I'd ever worked with or befriended. Even my name, my very identity. I knew it, but I certainly hadn't accepted it. How could I?

Clicking off the bathroom light, I walked back through the bedroom to the windows overlooking the water and pulled aside the drapes. I stared out into the oncoming storm. Thick, heavy clouds rolled in off the sea, obscuring the full moon and shrouding my room with darkness.

I still had no idea what I was going to tell Harris in the morning. Matt and I had spent more time arguing about it before going to bed. He'd kept trying to convince me how ridiculous the FBI agent's plan was. And everything he'd said had made perfect sense.

There was only one argument I could make in response: We were all going to die unless we accepted Harris's offer. It was a compelling argument because it was true. But that didn't make it any easier to accept.

I flipped on the television and roamed through

a hundred and fifty channels, but there was nothing I wanted to watch. I scrolled through my iTunes account, but there was nothing I wanted to listen to. I checked my messages again, but Yael hadn't responded. Why would she? She had a life of meaning and purpose. I was about to give mine up.

★   ★   ★

I suddenly woke up to someone pounding at my door.

Groggy and disoriented, I forced myself out of bed and stumbled to see who in the world was making such a racket so early. It was Matt, and the look on his face told me I was in serious trouble.

"J. B., what are you doing?"

"Sleeping," I said. "Why aren't you?"

"We're waiting for you."

"For what?" I asked.

"It's 9:15."

"And?"

"You were supposed to meet us in the lobby ten minutes ago—it's time to go."

47

Fifteen minutes later, Matt and I were in the lobby.

I told Harris we'd have an answer for him after the memorial service. Then I told him Matt and I were going to drive ourselves to the church, not be driven by him and the agents he'd assigned to us. He didn't like it. But I refused to budge. I told him he could follow behind us, but my brother and I needed to be alone before the service, and that was final. We weren't under arrest. We weren't employees of the federal government. We hadn't yet agreed to enter the Witness Protection Program. The FBI had no legal basis to prevent us from doing what we thought was best, and at the moment, this was it.

We immediately exited the hotel, not waiting for Harris's response. I headed straight for the driver's side of the black Lincoln Navigator assigned to us. Matt headed straight for the passenger's side.

"Out," I told the agent behind the wheel.

He just stared at me with a blank expression.

"Please," I added.

A moment later, he pressed on the wire running to his ear. He radioed back, asking if he'd heard right. Apparently he had. Mystified at such an unprecedented turn of events, he got out. I got in, and Matt climbed in beside me. The agent moved to get in the back, but I hit the gas and shot out onto the street without him. I turned left on West Street, then took a right on Main, as the agents scrambled into their vehicles to catch up.

"Good work," Matt said as he quickly fastened his seat belt and held on to the handle over the door. "Now you've got the FBI mad at us. Brilliant."

It was snowing again. Another inch and a half of fresh powder had fallen overnight. The forecast was calling for another few inches throughout the day, and the temperature was a mere twelve degrees. I notched up the heater and flipped the headlights on. "We need to talk," I said.

"About your driving or your manners?" he asked.

"About Harris's offer," I said.

"I thought last night you said we had no choice, that we'd die if we didn't accept."

"I did say that. But I was up most of the night thinking about it from every angle, you know, to see if there was any other way."

"Is there?"

"I haven't come up with anything yet."

"Then we have to say yes, right?"

"Maybe not," I said.

"But what about Annie? What about Katie?" he asked. "You kept saying we had to put them first."

"We do—absolutely," I said as we approached

the first of several police checkpoints in a town that today looked like an armed camp.

"And?"

"And I don't know," I admitted as I slowed to a halt. "As far as I can tell, we have until the service is over to come up with an alternative, or we're going to have to say yes. And I don't want to say yes. I really don't."

We both handed over our photo IDs to the heavily armed officer, then showed him the pins we were wearing, one from the FBI, the other from the Secret Service, indicating that we had all-access clearance for the event at the church and the reception to follow back at the Harborside. The officer checked them carefully, then nodded and told us to pop our rear cargo door.

"I got the first good night's sleep I've had in days last night," Matt said as we idled. "You know why? Because I stopped fighting this thing and decided to believe you."

"That we'd be safer by saying yes?"

"Yeah."

"That this is the best chance—and maybe the only one—to protect Annie and Katie?"

"Exactly."

The officer radioed ahead our names and the license plate number. Meanwhile, a K-9 unit sniffed for explosives as another officer used a mirror attached to a long metal pole to check the underside of the car for explosives. Finally we were waved through, just as Harris and his men pulled up behind us in two more Navigators.

I took a right onto Mount Desert Street and

passed the church parking lot that Allen was using as a media staging center. It was lined with rows of satellite trucks and cars bearing the logos of dozens of media outlets. Then we turned into the parking lot beside St. Saviour's Episcopal Church. There were local police and Secret Service agents everywhere. But beyond their vehicles with all their flashing red-and-blue lights, the lot was mostly empty, and there were no reporters or cameras in view. This clearly was not the parking area for the general public. Not today.

An officer wearing a bright-orange safety vest pointed us to our spot. I parked and turned off the car but didn't get out.

"Matt, do you remember what I told you in Amman?" I asked.

"You mean that Abu Khalif had threatened to kill you and all of us if you didn't report exactly what he wanted you to report?" Matt asked.

"Right."

"Of course I remember. How could I forget?"

"Well, before we go in there, I just need to say this face-to-face."

"What?"

"I'm sorry."

"For what?"

"I never should have written those stories. It wasn't just my life at stake. It was all of yours. I had no right to put you all in harm's way."

"No, don't say that, J. B.—you had to do those stories. I know that."

"No, I didn't."

"Yeah, you did—the world had to know."

"But I got Mom killed. I got Josh killed. And for what?"

"This isn't your fault, J. B.," Matt shot back with a vehemence I didn't expect. "You did your job, and I'm proud of you. This isn't your fault. It's Abu Khalif's and his alone."

"But I—"

"Stop it. Seriously—just stop. You've done a lot of stupid things in your life, a lot of stuff I would never have done. But telling the world who ISIS really is—who Abu Khalif really is—wasn't one of them. Yeah, it cost us—more than we ever imagined. But it also saved a lot of lives. And the truth is, I know where Josh and Mom are. They're in heaven, right now, with Christ. They're safe. They're free. And someday Katie and Annie and I are going to be there with them. No more pain. No more sorrow. No more tears. God will wipe them all away. The only thing that really scares me—terrifies me, actually—is the thought that you won't be there with us."

48

★ ★ ★

As we got out of the Navigator, Harris and his men pulled into the lot.

A moment later, we could hear the sirens and the motorcycles, and soon the motorcade roared up, stopping just a few yards away from us. Secret Service agents in long winter coats and black Ray-Bans fanned out to set up their perimeter. I watched as the head of the detail surveyed the scene and received a status check from each of his agents. Then he opened the door of the armor-plated and snow-covered black Chevy Suburban. Immediately Vice President Martin Holbrooke stepped out and came directly over to Matt and me.

"Mr. Vice President, thank you for coming," I said, taking off my gloves and shaking his hand.

"Gentlemen, it's an honor to be here," Holbrooke replied. "I'm so sorry for your loss. On behalf of the president and me, I hope you'll accept our sincerest condolences."

"Thank you, sir, that's very kind," I said. "I don't believe you've ever met my brother, Matt."

"No, can't say I have had the pleasure—good to meet you, son," the VP said, turning to shake Matt's hand. "I can't pretend to understand the pain you're both going through. But I want you to know how much the president and I—and the nation—respect you both and how committed we are to bringing those responsible to justice."

I stiffened—not visibly, I hoped. I wasn't looking for a fight. Not here. Not now. I just wanted to make it through the day and help Matt do the same. But to hear the second most powerful man in the world lie to my face—on the grounds of a church, no less—was almost more than I could bear. Neither Holbrooke nor the president was serious about tracking down and terminating the emir of the Islamic State.

Why not just admit it? I thought. *Why not just walk into the press center down the street, gather a bunch of reporters around, look into the cameras, and say to the American people, "Look, the president and I feel really bad about all the terrorism that Abu Khalif and ISIS have unleashed over the past days, months, and years. We didn't see the attack on the peace summit in Amman coming. We didn't pay attention to the warnings about the coming attacks on the Capitol or the rest of the country, much less on this little fishing village on the coast of Maine. Sure, we feel bad for the Collins family—and for all who have suffered at the hands of Radical Islam. And sure, we're comfortable lying and telling you we're winning, that we'll never rest until we make Abu Khalif pay. But the truth is we've got better things to do than be obsessed with Abu Khalif. Dealing with the Middle East isn't why we*

ran for office, and frankly we're getting tired of think-
ing and talking about it constantly. There are much
bigger priorities to deal with here at home than wast-
ing so much time and money on events half a world
away. So we're cutting our Sunni Arab allies loose.
We've offered the Jordanians barely any financial
assistance to rebuild their capital. We're not providing
the Egyptians enough helicopters or drones or night-
vision goggles or other state-of-the-art equipment to
hunt down ISIS leaders. Neither of us attended the
funeral of the Israeli prime minister. We're slashing
the American defense budget. We're demoralizing our
armed forces and intelligence community. We're forc-
ing a whole lot of good, experienced, irreplaceable
men and women out of the military at a time we
need them most. And we really couldn't care less. This
is what we're doing. And there's nothing you can do
to stop us."

As far as I was concerned, *that* was the truth—
and it made my blood boil.

But I held my tongue.

It wasn't as much of a struggle for Matt. It's
not that he didn't have strong views, but he was
a genuinely nice person. He didn't hold a grudge.
He simply didn't see the value in it. And for all his
disagreements on policy, he really was grateful the
vice president of the United States had traveled
from Washington to attend a memorial service
for his family members. So as we stood there in
the parking lot, the snow swirling about our faces,
he thanked Holbrooke with a sincerity that both
impressed and eluded me.

At the encouragement of the Secret Service,

we began walking up the freshly shoveled sidewalk and across a courtyard, Matt and Holbrooke taking the lead, me a few steps behind.

As we entered a side door, we were greeted by Pastor Jeremiah Brooks, my mom's pastor, and the rector who officiated here at St. Saviour's, a kindly silver-haired woman. She handed each of us a program, and then the bells started ringing. It was precisely ten o'clock. Everyone but us was in their seats. The service was set to begin.

49

* * *

Pastor Brooks led Matt and me out into the sanctuary, to the pew in the first row.

The vice president and his security detail followed right behind us.

The first people we saw were Annie's parents and two younger sisters, all of whom had arrived in town just a short time earlier after visiting the hospital in Portland. They were sitting in the second row, dressed in black, right behind our assigned seats, and they were a picture of grief. The youngest, still in her teens, was sobbing. Matt handed her a handkerchief I suspected he'd planned to use himself. Annie's mother was barely keeping it together. Her mascara was already smeared and the service hadn't even started. Annie's father, a one-time Anglican priest and now an Indiana farmer with a tanned, leathery face and thick, calloused hands, was doing his best to be the stoic comforter for his family, but he looked like he'd been run over by a truck. He gave Matt an awkward hug. This was not a man comfortable with any displays of affection, least of all in public.

When we were all seated, the rector stepped to the front. She welcomed everyone and then introduced Pastor Brooks.

Brooks, a lanky man in his sixties, looked somber as he stepped to the pulpit, opened his Bible, and organized his notes. "Thank you all for coming," he began, taking his reading glasses off to look out over the crowd of nearly three hundred people. "We are gathered this morning to honor, remember, and celebrate the lives of Margaret Claire Collins and Joshua James Collins."

The two caskets—one long, one short, each adorned with flowers—stood on metal supports at the front of the sanctuary. That put them about two yards away from us, and I found myself staring at the caskets as the pastor continued his opening remarks. Brooks explained that he had been my mother's pastor for more than thirty years. He thanked Matt and me for asking him to officiate, and thanked the St. Saviour's rector and staff for their hospitality. Finally he thanked the vice president for "honoring us with your presence." Then he began his message.

I had no intention of listening. If I was going to come up with an alternative to the plan proposed by Agent Harris, now was the time to do it. Still, I was sitting in the front row, directly beside the vice president. I couldn't exactly flip the program over and begin sketching out my plan. I had to at least look interested, and for me that posed a distinct challenge. Because I wasn't.

To make matters worse, Brooks kept looking at Matt and me. Not the whole time, of course.

He was addressing the entire congregation, but his gaze kept returning to us again and again, and it made me uncomfortable. After today, I couldn't imagine I'd ever see this man again. I didn't need him preaching to me. And yet he did.

"In the New Testament, the apostle Paul teaches us that 'to be absent from the body' is 'to be present with the Lord,'" Brooks explained. "If you knew Maggie and Josh at all, you know that both of them had placed their simple trust in the shed blood of Jesus Christ on Calvary and that they are with him now and forever."

His accent suggested southern New Hampshire roots, possibly even Boston, not Maine. It was vaguely reminiscent of how my grandfather used to talk.

"Both Maggie and Josh knew they were deeply loved by God. They truly believed the Word of God as recorded in the Bible: 'I have loved you with an everlasting love; therefore I have drawn you with lovingkindness.' They truly believed what the Lord said through the prophet Jeremiah: 'I know the plans I have for you, plans for good and not for evil, plans to give you a future and a hope.' What's more, they both believed that Jesus was, in fact, the Messiah, the Savior, who fulfilled the messianic prophecies, who died on the cross, and who rose from the dead on the third day. I had the privilege of kneeling down and praying with Maggie the day she received Christ as her Savior and Lord by faith, the day she was forgiven of her sins and born again by the Holy Spirit. And almost three decades later, I had the great joy and honor of praying with

Josh as he, too, decided to give his life to Christ. I know what they prayed, and I know how their lives changed as a result. That is why I can say with absolute certainty that they both knew the blessed hope of the gospel message."

Again Brooks looked at Matt and me. I looked away.

"Now, there are many things I loved and admired about Maggie Collins. But perhaps at the top of the list was that she was a faithful member of our choir. She was there every Sunday morning, rain or shine, and she sang with all her heart. She sang not for me or the congregation but to her Savior. You could hear it in her beautiful voice. You could see it in her lovely, sparkling eyes. She didn't just believe she was going to heaven when she died—she *knew* it. She believed Christ's promise, 'I am the resurrection and the life; he who believes in Me will live even if he dies.' She believed his words to the repentant thief on the cross that 'today you will be with Me in Paradise.' Without a shadow of any doubt at all, she absolutely *knew* that when she breathed her last breath here on earth, she would take her first breath in heaven in the very presence of her God and Redeemer forever and ever—and frankly, she couldn't wait."

Memories of my mom singing in the choir came flooding back. And she didn't just sing in church. I suddenly found myself remembering her singing or humming old hymns of the faith all the time—while she was cooking, while she was cleaning, while she was driving to the supermarket. The woman simply wouldn't stop. It used to drive me crazy. But what I wouldn't give now to hear her hum "It Is Well with My Soul" one more time.

"And little Josh—oh, what a heart for Jesus," the pastor continued. "He would come up to Bar Harbor in the summers to visit his grandmother, and he would participate in our vacation Bible school, and he was such a joy. Two summers ago Josh memorized sixty-two Bible verses in six weeks. *Sixty-two!* His favorite was not exactly one you'd expect for a young boy. It was John 15:13— the words of our Savior: 'Greater love has no one than this, that one lay down his life for his friends.' Now, I have to say, I've been pastoring a long, long time, and I've met a whole lot of kids, but I never met anyone quite like Josh."

The more the pastor spoke, the deeper my remorse became. I thought about how little I really knew Matt's kids and how much I had missed in their lives. I'd never known Josh had memorized so much Scripture. Nor that he'd had a favorite verse. Nor what it was. And then it struck me that this was the very verse Khachigian had quoted in his letter to me.

"Last Thursday night, what looked like a tragedy to us was not a tragedy for Maggie and Josh," the pastor continued. "The spirits of these beloved family members and friends were taken from us. But they are not lost. Oh no. Maggie and Josh are gone, but they are not dead. They are more alive today than they have ever been. These two saints are alive and well in the throne room of heaven. Right at this moment, Maggie and Josh are worshiping at the feet of the King of kings and the Lord of lords, our great God and Redeemer, Jesus Christ. Their race is finished. Their mission here on this earth is complete. They are home, safe and sound, awaiting us to join them, if we, too, are in Christ. But, my friends, your only hope of seeing them again is to give your soul to the God they entrusted their souls to, and to do it before you breathe your last here on earth."

As I stared at those coffins, the finality of it all hit me hard. For the past several days, I'd been living on adrenaline, duty, and denial. But sitting there in that church, looking at those wooden boxes, the brutal, unfair, cruel reality finally came crashing down on me. Mom and Josh were gone. Forever. They were never coming back. And all the family events I'd missed, skipped, ignored—they were gone too, never to be recaptured.

"My friends, one day, whether we want to or not, whether we're ready or not, you and I will stand before the judgment seat of Christ," the pastor continued, his voice unexpectedly calm, his manner surprisingly gentle, not like the hellfire-and-brimstone preachers of my cynical imagination. "We're all going to pay the piper. If you're still an unforgiven sinner when you die, the Bible says you'll be the one who pays for your own sins. That is, you'll go to hell, forever, with no way of escape. But the Bible also says that if we repent and receive Christ, then he pays for our sins—in fact, he already did, when he died on the cross in Jerusalem two thousand years ago.

"So today you have a choice to make: say yes to

Christ, receive him as your Savior—as Maggie and Josh did—and God promises in his Word to forgive you. He'll adopt you as his child. And when you stand before him one day, you'll stand there as one forgiven, not one condemned, and he will welcome you into his open arms—just as he so eagerly and lovingly welcomed Maggie and Josh on Thursday night. Or say no, and roll the dice. It's your choice. But I beseech you as a man of the cloth: don't gamble with your eternal future."

I shifted uncomfortably in the pew. As much as I wanted to resent the pastor and all he was saying, I couldn't. He was speaking to me, and he was connecting. I was trying not to listen, but I simply couldn't help it.

When the pastor finished, we sang a hymn, and then it was my turn to speak. I had a pit in my stomach as I stared out at the congregation through tear-filled eyes, feeling racked with guilt so overwhelming I could barely breathe. In pursuit of my dream of being an award-winning foreign correspondent like my grandfather, I had essentially abandoned my family. I hadn't been there when they'd needed me. I hadn't been there for the big moments in their lives. And now, because of me, two of them were dead, and two others were lying in an intensive care unit, fighting for their lives.

The truth is, I don't remember what I said for the next few minutes. I hope I thanked the pastor for his beautiful words. I hope I said some nice things about Mom and about Josh. I honestly cannot recall a single word that came out of my mouth. It couldn't have been too bad. I do remember people coming up to me after the service, in the receiving line, thanking me for honoring my family so beautifully.

But I'll never forget what the vice president said after me because it so infuriated me. Holbrooke dutifully expressed his and the president's condolences to Matt and me and to our family and assembled friends. Somebody had fed him a few details about my mom and Josh—even some tidbits about Annie and Katie—that he sprinkled throughout his prepared remarks as though he'd known them personally, as though he'd been an old friend. That didn't bother me. Nor did it bother me—too much, anyway—that he was using the administration's boilerplate language about "the scourge of violent extremism," and about the "cowardly attacks of those who claim to speak in the name of Islam but have no idea what this great religion of peace is truly all about." What did bother me—what absolutely enraged me—was something he said almost in passing toward the close of his remarks.

"As we lay to rest these two heroes—not victims, but true American heroes—let there be no doubt: We are winning the war against ISIL. We have liberated Mosul. We have liberated northern Iraq. We are killing their leaders. We have them on the run. What we have seen this past week is tragic, but rest assured, these are among the last violent spasms of a cruel but vanquished movement."

The last violent spasms? A cruel but vanquished movement?

What planet was he living on? Nearly twice as many Americans had just died at the hands of the Islamic State as had on 9/11. Nearly as many Americans had perished in one week at the hands of Abu Khalif as in ten years of fighting in Afghanistan and Iraq. ISIS was hardly "vanquished." It might have lost its grip on northern Iraq, but it was solidifying its grip elsewhere. It was expanding its caliphate into Yemen, Somalia, and Libya. It was recruiting tens of thousands of new foreign fighters and raising millions of dollars for its jihad against the West. Yet this administration couldn't or wouldn't see it. They simply refused to throw their full might into crushing this evil force once and for all.

At that moment, something in me snapped. I was suddenly consumed by a toxic and rapidly intensifying feeling of humiliation, compounded by guilt and fused with rage. By the time the service was over, I was seething. Something had to be done. Abu Khalif was engaged in nothing less than genocide. He had to be stopped. Who was going to do it? The president? The vice president? Not a chance. They were abject failures, and nothing about that was going to change. The world couldn't wait for a new administration and a new plan. Neither could I. Neither could what was left of my family. That much was clear, and that certain knowledge left me with no other choice and not a shred of doubt.

I knew what I had to do, and I now had a plan.

PART
FOUR

50

TEL AVIV, ISRAEL

A brutal winter thunderstorm was bearing down on Israel's largest coastal city.

I sat in the Royal Executive Lounge on the fourteenth floor of the Carlton Hotel, a few blocks north of the U.S. Embassy, nursing a Perrier as I watched the driving Mediterranean rains pelt the windows. Outside, palm trees bent in the forty-mile-per-hour winds. Streaks of jagged lightning illuminated the dark sky, and crashes of thunder rocked the building.

My pocket watch said it was five o'clock. I'd come to the same place, sat in the same leather chair, looked out the same window for the fourth day in a row. My contact had yet to show up. Maybe this was a complete waste of time. But I didn't see any other way. So I sat, and I waited, and I tried to be patient. Not exactly my strong suit.

What bothered me most was that I'd nearly blown up my newly mended relationship with my brother to get here. Matt was furious with me. And I certainly understood why he felt betrayed.

Initially he'd liked my plan, but that's only because I hadn't told him all of it.

The part I told him about when we were alone in the rector's office after the memorial service had been straightforward enough. We would accept Harris's proposal to put us into the Witness Security Program, but with one caveat: the FBI couldn't kill us off.

We would agree to disappear from our daily lives for several months, perhaps even a year or more, until Abu Khalif was arrested and my testimony was needed or until Khalif was dead and my family and I were no longer in danger. I'd take an indefinite leave of absence from the *Times*. Matt would take an indefinite leave of absence from Gordon-Conwell Theological Seminary. With the bureau's help, we would slip away unnoticed, undetected, and undetectable. Harris would provide us with new identities, complete with driver's licenses and passports and credit cards and mobile phones. We'd have fake names. We'd live by the aliases Harris provided. We would live, in other words, like anyone else in the Witness Security Program, with one difference. We would not be "dead." There would be no car bomb. There would be no funeral. The world wouldn't think we were dead. They would just think we'd gone away to recover from the attacks and get the physical and psychological and spiritual help we so obviously needed. When we were better, we would come back.

My plan provided my brother full anonymity and protection and first-rate medical care for his wife and daughter. But it also provided Matt the ability to reenter his life at some point. It was almost elegant in its simplicity. It was the best of both worlds, and Matt loved it.

Harris? Not so much.

For the bureau, it was the worst of both worlds. We would be costing the American taxpayers just as much as if we were entering the formal program and playing by all the rules, except that we wouldn't be entering the formal program and we wouldn't be playing by the rules. We'd get all the benefits, but the bureau would still face many of the risks. Abu Khalif would know we were still alive. He'd do his best to track us down and take us out. If we made a single mistake—and we probably would, Harris insisted, given that we weren't intelligence professionals—then I might not even be alive long enough to testify.

So my plan called for a compromise. We would split the costs of our "disappearance" fifty-fifty with the bureau. Yes, the U.S. government would be going to considerable expense. But Matt and I now had sufficient financial resources to defray some of these costs. I didn't think we should have to pay for all of it. After all, I would eventually be providing an enormously valuable service to the government by way of my testimony. But we would agree to cover half the costs to defray the added exposure for the FBI.

Harris had blown a gasket when we presented him with our counteroffer. He told us in a dozen different ways that he could never sign off on such a foolish and pathetic plan. But Matt and I held our ground. We made it clear we appreciated the bureau's concern for our well-being, and we were willing to hide for a time, but we weren't going to hide forever.

It was near midnight on that Tuesday by the time Harris finally met us back at the Harborside. He told us the request had gone all the way up the chain of command. Neither the director of the FBI nor the attorney general liked the idea, Harris said, but in the end they had agreed to it, provided Matt and I sign waivers indemnifying the U.S. government from any criminal or civil liabilities in what they called "the not unlikely possibility" that one or all of us were murdered by ISIS.

We had, of course, signed the waivers. In triplicate. On video. With a half-dozen federal agents there to sign affidavits as witnesses.

The next thing we knew, we were being rushed by helicopter to the Portland International Jetport in the dead of night. There, we boarded an unmarked Gulfstream IV business jet that had been retrofitted to serve as an air ambulance. Annie and Katie were already on board. They were lying on stretchers, hooked up to IVs, respirators, heart monitors, and who knows what else, attended to by a doctor and a nurse, both of whom worked for the FBI.

As we gained altitude, Matt had sighed, then leaned over and thanked me. We were safe from ISIS, and we were together as a family. Given the alternatives, that wasn't bad, he said. Then he leaned his seat back, pulled a blanket over himself, closed his eyes, and drifted off to sleep, a calm and peaceful man.

I knew it wouldn't last. I'd have to tell him the rest of my plan. But not just then. He needed his sleep, as I'd needed mine.

51

* * *

"Sir, can I get you anything from the bar?"

The twentysomething waitress who had just interrupted my daydream had kind eyes and a pleasant, gentle manner. She meant no harm. She was just doing her job. But she had no idea what she was asking.

Yes, I want a Scotch on the rocks with a twist.

Yes, bring me the whole bottle.

Yes, please deliver a case to my room.

There were only a handful of people in the lounge, and none of them knew me. I'd been here four days, and my contact hadn't even called me back. Or sent an e-mail. Or a text. Yael hadn't responded to any of my messages either. She knew I was here. She knew I wanted to see her. She was just blowing me off. *So why not have a drink?* I asked myself. I deserved one.

"Maybe just a cappuccino," I said, forcing myself to smile.

Another boom of thunder, and the hotel trembled once more.

I checked my pocket watch again. It was closing in on six. I'd been here almost nine hours. For the fourth day in a row.

How much longer was I going to wait? What was I even doing here? Khachigian had, after all, drawn me a road map. He'd given me names, sources he trusted. Yet instead of tracking down the contacts he had given me, I was wasting time in this hotel lounge.

I got up to stretch and walked around the lounge for a bit. There was nothing to see. There was no one I wanted to talk to. A happy couple on a date, drinking champagne, laughing it up. A handful of executives discussing a telecom deal. Two gray-haired ladies, clearly tourists. One was reading Agatha Christie's *Murder on the Orient Express*; the other was leafing through a copy of the *National Enquirer*.

Really? I thought. *You've come all the way to the Holy Land and you're wasting your time with tabloid trash?* Then again, what was she supposed to be doing? She hardly wanted to be outside just then. Nobody did. The storm bearing down on Israel's coastline was unbelievable.

I sat down and opened the Bible app on my phone. With nothing else to do the past four days, I'd finished reading the Gospel of John, not because I had really wanted to but because I'd promised Matt I would. In fact, when I'd finished John, I'd read through the other three Gospels, too, and then much of the rest of the New Testament. It was actually kind of interesting to read it here in Israel, where so much of it had taken place. I'd found myself particularly intrigued by Luke's account. Luke was a Gentile. A physician. An educated man and a good writer. He hadn't been an eyewitness like the apostles, apparently, but he'd set out to write an "orderly account" of the life of Christ. Like a journalist. A foreign correspondent. And a good one. His report provided a compelling narrative. Rich in details. Direct quotes. Colorful anecdotes. I'd never read anything quite like it.

The waitress came back with my coffee. I paid her, then tried to stare out at the storm. But the sun had set. Darkness had fallen. All I could see was my reflection in the window, and I winced in regret. I took a sip of my coffee, closed my eyes, and suddenly the clock turned back and I could feel the Gulfstream touching down.

I remembered Matt being startled awake. I remembered him trying to reestablish exactly where he was. I remembered his sudden sense of anticipation as he rubbed his eyes and checked his wristwatch, then leaned over to me and whispered, "Ten bucks we're in Wichita."

"Kansas?" I'd said, rubbing my eyes as well. I hadn't slept at all.

"Yeah."

"Why Kansas?"

"I don't know. We were flying for about four hours, give or take. If we were heading west, I'm thinking that puts us around Wichita."

"Why not Oklahoma City?"

Matt had shrugged. "You'd rather live there?"

"Hardly. But I'm sure we're not in Kansas."

"How do you know?"

"It's not nearly cold enough."

In my mind's eye I pictured Agent Harris opening the door near the cockpit. The cabin had been flooded with brilliant sunshine and a warm, sultry breeze. We hadn't flown west. We'd flown south.

"Your new home, gentlemen," Harris had said, standing beside the open door. "Welcome to St. Thomas."

As we exited the plane and headed toward a white Ford Explorer that was waiting for us, Harris explained, "Your wife and daughter will be taken to a specialized medical clinic on the other side of the island. You can visit them this afternoon, but first I need to show you the house, get you settled in, and explain a few things. Then I've got a noon flight back to D.C."

"Why did you bring us *here*?" I asked, more coldly than I'd meant, as we wound our way up narrow roads, covered in dense foliage, driving on the left side of the street as if we were in Great Britain.

"Ever been here before?" Harris asked. "Either of you?"

I didn't bother to answer.

"That's why you brought us here?" Matt asked. "Because we've never been?"

"Think about it," Harris replied. "You don't know anyone here. No one knows you. Not a lot of people read the *New York Times* down here. You can't imagine yourself visiting, much less living here. It's not you. I get it. I can see it in your faces, your body language. You're mountain people. Lake people. You like to ice fish and hunt. You don't hate deep snow and bitter winters. In fact, you love both. You'd be skiing at Killington right now if I'd let you. Which is why this is perfect. No one would think to look for you here. Wichita? Maybe. Oklahoma City? Perhaps. But the Caribbean? Never."

We'd come to a fork in the road. To the right was a sign to Magens Bay, but we took the road heading left, snaking up the mountain, heading north toward a place called Tropaco Point.

"You're actually still on American soil, gentlemen," Harris continued. "These are the U.S. Virgin Islands. You don't need a passport to fly from here to the mainland or back. You can operate in U.S. currency. And there are plenty of pasty-white tourists and businessmen—just like you two—who visit here, live here, retire here. So you're not exactly going to stand out."

I had to admit, Harris was right. Neither Matt nor I had ever had any interest in coming down here. But as we pulled into the driveway of a three-story house painted in a pale yellow with blue shutters, I could see Matt was warming to it.

And why not? The temperature was a perfect eighty-one degrees. The view from each of our three balconies was absolutely spectacular. The clouds were white and puffy. The bay, directly below us, was the most gorgeous shade of azure I'd ever seen, rimmed by white sandy beaches and dotted by sailboats gliding along in the lovely tropical breezes.

We'd never even imagined living in a place so gorgeous.

Inside, things got even better.

The tour started in the basement, where Harris showed us the secure room—or "panic room"—which by Middle Eastern standards was a full-blown bomb shelter. Hidden behind a sliding bookshelf, the room had a cement floor and two-foot-thick reinforced concrete walls. The ceiling was also concrete-lined with steel plates to prevent attackers from drilling into it from the first floor. The door was made of thick steel and Kevlar, and the entire structure was blast resistant and hermetically sealed to prevent smoke, tear gas, or other toxins from entering.

The room had sets of bunk beds that could sleep six, a separate toilet and shower facility, a small kitchenette, and a supply of water and canned and freeze-dried food that could last for up to thirty days. There was also a communications console that would allow us to monitor video cameras positioned all over the house and connect with local authorities, including the St. Thomas FBI field office, just in case. Harris walked us through the system of high-tech batteries that could provide all the power we needed if somehow we were cut off from the local grid.

The rest of the massive six-bedroom house—complete with a fully equipped medical suite—was no less impressive. The place was furnished and had all the linens, towels, dishes, silverware, and other necessities we might need. There was a large entertainment center in the basement and TVs in every bedroom, all hooked up to a satellite dish on the roof. And in the back, there was a two-car garage, where we found a bronze Toyota RAV4 and a forest-green Jeep Grand Cherokee.

The bureau, it seemed, had thought of everything.

"Have you ever seen anything so beautiful?" Matt asked later that evening after Harris left and we were finally seated together, looking out over Magens Bay.

"Can't say I have," I said, glad Matt was happy.

And then I told him the next stage of my plan.

52

★ ★ ★

TEL AVIV, ISRAEL

I paid my bill at the front desk and headed out the front door of the Carlton.

It was windy and wet and gray, but sometime in the night the rains had stopped. The bellman whistled for a cab and it pulled up momentarily. It was just before seven in the morning. There had been no time for breakfast or even a good cup of coffee, but I wasn't staying in this country a minute longer. I'd wasted almost four and a half days, and I was done.

"The airport," I said, and we were off.

I still felt bad about the way I'd left things with Matt. When I told him I wasn't staying on St. Thomas, he'd been furious. "Are you crazy?" he'd said. "You just got here."

"I know, but I never planned to stay. I wanted you and Annie and Katie to be safe, to enter the FBI program, albeit with modifications, and now here you are. You've got this great house—better than either of us could have imagined. You've got first-rate medical care for your family. You've got new passports, new IDs, everything you need. So you'll be fine. But I can't stay."

"You can't go," Matt had replied. "I know I did everything I could to persuade you to do what Allen asked and go write those stories about the MP's son and the king and his family and all. But everything's changed. We negotiated with Harris. We made a deal. It was approved by the attorney general of the United States. You can't just renege on it now."

"Look, Matt," I'd said, "what you and I agreed to was that the only way this *ever* ends—the *only* way we ever get our lives back—is if Abu Khalif is taken out once and for all. Now you and I both know the president's not going to do that. But the Egyptians might. The Jordanians might. The Israelis might. Maybe a few others. Khachigian gave me information that might help take Khalif down. I need to go make sure this thing gets done right. Then we can all go home."

"Help? You?" Matt had asked. "J. B., have you completely lost your mind? What, you suddenly think your initials stand for James Bond? Jason Bourne? Jack Bauer? What are we talking about here? You're not an assassin. You're not trained for any of that. You're going to get yourself killed. And then you're going to get us all killed."

But in the end, I had left anyway. I had no other choice. I'd come to Israel first, hoping to link up with folks at the Mossad who might be able to make use of the information I had. But that hadn't happened. I was on my own.

It was going to take a while for my taxi driver

to work his way through the morning rush-hour commute to Ben Gurion International Airport, but at least the plane would wait. I was no longer flying commercial, after all. There was a Learjet waiting for me on the tarmac, fueled up and ready to go, a jet I partially owned. By lunchtime I'd be in Istanbul. By dinner I'd be in Dubai, having hopefully secured a meeting with Mohammed bin Zayed, the UAE's intelligence chief.

I had no intention of reaching out to bin Zayed directly until I arrived. He had no idea who I was, and I didn't want to give him much time to find out. But if everything went according to plan, I'd be sipping coffee with him soon and discussing the hunt for Abu Khalif.

I pulled out my iPhone—a new one I'd picked up en route to Tel Aviv—and checked the headlines. This was a phone even Agent Harris didn't know about and thus one he couldn't trace.

My eye was drawn immediately to the lead story in the *Washington Post*, our fiercest competitor, though never our equal. It was an exclusive, lengthy, and stupefying interview with President Taylor, conducted in the Oval Office. In it, the leader of the free world had just gone on the record as saying some of the most incendiary comments of his presidency.

"Yes, this is a difficult moment," Taylor had told the editorial board of the *Post*. "We have been hit by extremists who fundamentally reject modernity, who reject our values and our way of life. And I grieve for the families who have suffered losses. But we must maintain a sense of perspective. We are waging a war against these extremists, and we are winning. We are taking back the lands they've ravaged. We are killing their leaders. We are cutting off their money supply. And they are reeling. So they are lashing out, and these recent attacks, as terrible as they are, are simply death spasms of a movement whose day is over. Let me be clear: my job, and that of the American military and our allies, will not be over until these extremists are shut down once and for all. But they are trying to lure us into a much-larger conflict. They want us to come back to a full-scale war in the Middle East. And that's not going to happen. America's days of fighting endless wars in the Middle East—for the oil companies, for Israel, for democracy, for freeloader despots, or for whatever other reasons the neocons and the warmongers and the foreign policy establishment in this town are itching for—those days are over. They are over. And we are never going back."

This was a new low. In a single paragraph, the president had once again demonstrated his absolute unwillingness to properly defend the American people and our national security interests in the world's most dangerous and volatile region. That was nothing new. But now he had unleashed what amounted to an unprecedented anti-Semitic slur, and from the Oval Office no less, by accusing our Jewish allies in Israel and the "neoconservatives" in Washington—referring primarily to conservative Jewish foreign policy experts, many of whom were Republicans but some of whom were Democrats—of dragging America into war time and time again.

Not Osama bin Laden and al Qaeda and the 9/11 hijackers.

Not the Mullah Omar and the Taliban.

Not Saddam Hussein, the Butcher of Baghdad.

Not Abu Musab al-Zarqawi and the forces of al Qaeda in Iraq.

Not Abu Khalif and the forces of the Islamic State.

No, in the president's worldview, apparently it was the Jews—in Israel and the United States—along with the oil companies and also our "free-loading" Sunni Arab allies (presumably Jordan, Egypt, the Saudis, and the Gulf emirates)—who were responsible for every war the U.S. had ever fought in the region.

The implications of the president's remarks were far-reaching, but for the moment I couldn't go there. I was still trying to understand the mind-set of an American leader—a Democrat backed by more than 70 percent of the American Jewish community—turning so harshly against people who had so wholeheartedly supported him.

There was no time to think about any of it much further, however, for suddenly the taxi lurched onto some Tel Aviv side street and then down a series of ramps into the bowels of a dark parking garage, and before I knew it, we had screeched to a halt.

My door was opened by one of several large, swarthy men, all wearing black leather jackets and jeans. "Excuse me, Mr. McClaire," he said. "Would you please follow us?"

For a moment I thought they had the wrong guy.

"Mr. McClaire, please—your contact is a busy man, and he has a schedule to keep."

Finally I recognized the alias. I had used it, along with one of the fake passports Khachigian had left me, when I'd flown to Israel several days earlier.

I stepped out of the taxi, hoping these men were connected to my source and that they weren't going to double-tap me and stuff my body in the trunk of one of the dozens of cars and minivans parked all around me. Either way, there was no point resisting. I wasn't armed. I wasn't trained in self-defense. No one even knew I was here. Why not just get on with it?

I followed my escorts through the garage, through a filthy exit door, into a putrid stairwell, and up several flights of concrete steps. The more steps we climbed, however, the less concerned I was about getting shot in the back of the head execution-style and the more certain I was that my fishing expedition had been successful after all.

We soon exited on the ground floor. The air was chilly but fresh—almost sweet—as my handlers walked me across the street. Yesterday's storm had subsided. We were in the heart of the ancient town of Jaffa, just south of Tel Aviv, and once we entered a park overlooking empty beaches and crashing surf, they told me to sit down on a wooden bench. One of them lit a cigarette. The other pretended to tie his shoes.

"Mr. McClaire," said a kindly, older voice just

over my right shoulder. "What an unexpected pleasure. Welcome to Israel."

I turned and found Ari Shalit, the head of Israeli Mossad, coming around the far side of the bench, bundled up in a long navy-blue winter coat, a plaid Scottish cap, a scarf, and leather gloves.

"Ari," I said, standing to greet him and shake his hand, as surprised as I was relieved. "It's so good to see you. Thanks for making some time."

"Of course—you didn't really think I'd let you fly off to the Gulf without saying hello, did you?"

I held my tongue. That was exactly what I'd thought, but I was glad to be wrong.

"So," he said, "how's life in the Caribbean?"

I was so stunned I didn't know how to respond. My mouth opened, but no words would form.

"Don't look so surprised," he said. "It's my job to know such things, is it not?"

It took me a moment to recover. "Is it really that easy?" I finally asked.

"If you know what to look for, yes."

"Does Abu Khalif know what to look for?"

"No, not yet," said Shalit. "Besides, he has his hands full right now. For the time being, your brother and his family are safe."

I stared out at the whitecaps on the roiling Mediterranean, unsure whether to be relieved or worried.

"There is one thing I don't understand, and I must ask you," Shalit said. "Why did Agent Harris let you come? I mean, your being here is quite a risk for someone in the Witness Protection Program."

"He didn't let me," I said.

"I don't understand."

"I didn't tell him."

For once, it was Ari Shalit who didn't know what to say.

"Although," I continued, "if you know I'm here, the CIA probably knows. And if the CIA knows, the FBI must know. And if they know, Harris knows. Am I right?"

"I doubt it."

"Why?"

"Because you did everything right," Shalit said. "Flew to New York—not commercial but by private plane. Then changed planes. Flew to London. Bought a new iPhone. Changed planes again. Flew to Madrid. Changed again. Came here. All different tail numbers. Different names, different passports, different credit cards. You were careful. I've been impressed. It was like you'd been a spy all your life. I doubt the guys at Langley saw any red flags."

"But you figured it out."

"Yes, but we were expecting you to come," Shalit said, staring out at the sea. "They were expecting you to stay."

53

★ ★ ★

"You were expecting me to come here?" I asked, once again surprised.

"Of course."

"Why?"

"We were right to do so, weren't we?"

"Yeah, but if you knew I was coming, why did you just let me sit alone at the Carlton for four days, doing nothing, without even responding, without even telling me you'd gotten my message?"

Shalit shook his head. "You weren't alone."

"What's that supposed to mean?" I asked.

"Everyone in that executive lounge was Mossad," he explained. "We were watching you. Testing you. Waiting to see if you'd start drinking again. To see if anyone was following you. See how you'd react to disappointment. And to see if you had a plan after us."

"And what did you learn?" I asked.

"You booked a flight to Dubai. So you did have a plan. And you hadn't been drinking. And you had been quite patient, after all. And no one was following you. So here you are."

"Then you know why I came?" I asked.

"I think so," Shalit replied. "But I want to hear it from you."

"Fair enough," I said, then paused for a bit, watching the waves crash against the rocky Jaffa shoreline. "I want in."

"In?" he asked. "What exactly does that mean?"

"You're hunting for Abu Khalif," I said in a hushed tone, even though at this early hour, and season and temperature, no one but the bodyguards was around. "He murdered your prime minister. You want to make him pay. But you're getting almost no help from Washington. Or the Europeans. And ISIS is still on the move. They're still slaughtering innocent people, still on offense, still planning bigger and more deadly attacks. You know they're coming here, to Tel Aviv, to Jerusalem, to Haifa and Tiberias. You know they don't just want to kill Americans. They also want to murder Jews—Israelis in particular—and as many as they can. So you need help, and you need it fast. That's why I've come."

At this, Shalit turned and looked directly at me. "You came to *help* us?" he said, appearing genuinely perplexed.

"Yes."

"To help us find and kill Abu Khalif?"

"Exactly."

"This is why you've risked your life, and your brother's and your sister-in-law's and your niece's lives, to crisscross around the world, to come all the way over here, to meet with me, to tell me you want to join the Mossad and help us assassinate Abu Khalif?"

"Why else?"

Shalit sat there for a long while, searching my eyes, trying to read me. It was rare to see him caught off guard. The fifty-seven-year-old spook had built his career on knowing everything about everyone, on knowing all secrets, large and small. This was what had made him one of the most interesting operatives I'd ever met in the Middle East. The fact that we'd been friends for almost two decades had made him an invaluable source. But right now I wasn't looking for a story. I was looking for a job.

"I am not easily surprised, *Mr. McClaire*," he said, emphasizing my new alias. "But I must confess, today I am. I thought you were here for something else—something else entirely."

"Like what?" I asked.

He smiled. "Honestly? I thought you were here for Yael."

"Yael Katzir?" I asked.

"Who else?"

"Well, who says I'm not?" I asked.

"You haven't brought her up."

"What are you, her father?"

He laughed. "No, no, of course not."

"Then with all due respect, why would you care?"

"I'm her boss," he said.

"I thought she was working for the prime minister."

"You thought wrong," he said simply. "She turned that job down. You didn't know?"

"No," I said. "Can't say I did. Why didn't she take it?"

"Why didn't she tell you herself?" he replied.

"I have no idea," I said.

He shrugged. "Then it's not my place to say. For that, you'll have to talk to her directly. But for this other topic, I can honestly say I did not see this coming."

"Clearly."

He turned back to the sea. "You're not a spy," he said after a long silence.

"True."

"You haven't got the training."

"Obviously."

"And you already have a job."

"*Had,*" I corrected him.

"You quit?"

"Not exactly."

"Fired?"

"Let's just say I'm on an extended leave of absence."

"Paid?"

"No."

"Then how can you afford not to work?"

"Again, Ari, with all due respect . . ."

"You think that's none of my business?"

I shrugged.

"Think again. If you want to work for me, Mr. McClaire, *everything* is my business."

There was no guarantee he was going to let me in if I told him, but I was guaranteed to be shut out if I refused to say anything. So I explained as concisely as I could what Robert Khachigian had done for my brother and me.

"J. B.," he sighed, finally abandoning the pretense of my alias. "If this were anyone else, I wouldn't even be giving you the time of day. You have no training. You have no security clearances. You're not Israeli. You're not Jewish. The list of reasons I should be putting you back on your private jet to the Caribbean is a mile long."

"But . . . ?"

"You tell me."

"What do you mean?"

"Make the case," he said. "Sell it to me."

"It's simple," I said. "I'm the only Westerner on the planet who has ever met Abu Khalif. I'm the only Westerner to have ever spoken with him at length. I know what he looks like. I know what he sounds like. I've met his closest advisors and spoken to them. I've read everything ever written about him. I know how he thinks. I know what he wants. I speak Arabic. And he thinks I'm in hiding. That's my competitive advantage. I'm in his blind spot—he doesn't see me coming."

"Maybe not," Shalit said. "But I've got a pretty sharp team. They've studied him too. They're trained. They're experienced. They've been doing this a long time. How are you going to find him if they can't?"

"They can, and they will, but they need my help—and so do you," I said. "Before Bob Khachigian died, he wrote me a letter. He made it clear that his final wish was for me to track down Abu Khalif. And he gave me several leads."

"What kind of leads?"

"Names," I said. "Three of them, to be exact."

"What names?"

"Not so fast," I said. "First you agree to put me on your team."

"But why come to us? Why not go to the CIA?"

"I can't."

"Why not?"

"Because the acting director's hands are tied."

"By whom?"

"By a man blaming your country for all the wars in the region."

"No comment," Shalit said.

I nodded.

"To be fair, your president says he wants to take down all the ISIS leaders. He's authorizing drone strikes, bombings. And ISIS leaders are dying— two more just yesterday."

"The president wants headlines," I snapped. "I want Abu Khalif's head."

Shalit said nothing.

"We've known each other for a long time, Ari. You trust me, and I trust you. That's why I'm here."

Again Shalit looked out at the Mediterranean. "Do you really understand the risks you're taking, my friend?"

"I'm willing to die for my country," I said as though I meant it, though I wasn't entirely sure I did. The truth was, death flat-out terrified me. I had no idea what the afterlife really held or how to determine my eternal fate. Maybe my mom and

Josh were right. Maybe Pastor Brooks was. Maybe not. But that was all a different subject for a different time.

"Perhaps you are willing to die for your country, J. B., but are you willing to die for mine?" Shalit asked.

"Honestly? No. But this isn't about me dying for anyone's country; it's about making Abu Khalif die for all he's done."

"So you're here for vengeance?"

"No," I said. "Not really."

"Justice, then."

"In part," I said.

"What else?" Shalit asked. "Why do this? Why take such risks?"

"I want my life back, Ari," I said. "But even more, I want Matt and Annie and Katie to have their lives back. I want them to live free and safe and without a care in this world. I owe them that. Actually, I owe them much more. But I have nothing else to give them than this. Now what do you say? Are you going to let me help you guys hunt down Abu Khalif or not?"

54

The Mossad chief abruptly stood.

"It's time," he said, adjusting his scarf and collar to protect himself from the wind.

"Time for what?" I asked, standing as well.

"Let's go for a little ride," he said, pointing to a black sedan that had just pulled up, followed by two black Chevy Suburbans.

"Where?"

"You'll find out soon enough."

"What about my luggage, my briefcase, my laptop?" I asked, picturing them in the trunk of the taxicab in the nearby parking garage.

"Don't worry," he said. "All your belongings are safe. But I will need your new mobile phone."

When I asked why, he explained he was going to take the battery out of it so no one could track our movements.

"We're going someplace no one can know about," he added. "Now come. We don't want to be late."

Our driver worked his way out of Tel Aviv's morning gridlock and got us on Highway 2, heading north along the coast toward Haifa. Just before we reached Herzliya—the elite seaside community filled with enormous overpriced homes owned by high-tech Israeli CEOs and former government ministers now serving on their boards—he took a right on Highway 5, then turned north on Highway 6.

Eventually we arrived at the Ramat David Air Base in the Jezreel Valley. This was the country's main air base in the north and home to some of Israel's most advanced fighter jets, including the new F-35i stealth fighters.

I pulled out my pocket watch. It was a little before ten. Our driver turned off the main road, pulled to the first guard station, and came to a halt. Young soldiers holding machine guns watched us carefully as we all handed over our photo IDs—even the acting director of the Mossad.

A few minutes later, we were cleared to proceed. The gates opened, and our driver eased us forward.

We took a quick right and wound around the inner perimeter of the base. In the distance I could see rows of F-15s and F-16s being cleaned and refueled, and I could hear several taking off and landing. Then we reached the far side of the base and stopped in front of a nondescript, unmarked concrete building with a few cars parked out front and a sentry standing post.

Two of Shalit's bodyguards got out, surveyed the area, nodded to each other that the coast was clear, and then opened Ari's door and mine. The base was remarkable in how unremarkable it looked. All the buildings were badly in need of fresh paint and basic repairs. The pavement on the roads and tarmacs was cracked, and weeds were growing everywhere. The barracks for the rank-and-file soldiers looked like they hadn't been spruced up since the Independence War, and even the accommodations for the pilots and other officers were largely unimproved. The reason was obvious enough. The Israelis had no money to spend on improving their bases. They were funneling every shekel into the planes themselves, their weapons, their avionics, and the training of the men and women who flew and serviced them. Little else mattered, so little else got funded.

Inside the nondescript building we were greeted by a major who led us through a series of electronically locked doors, down a long hallway, and onto an elevator.

"Okay, Mr. McClaire," Shalit said as the doors closed and we descended, "you asked for it. You got it. You're in."

"Thank you, Ari," I said, suddenly feeling the weight of such an honor and enormous responsibility.

"Don't thank me now," he said. "You have no idea what you just signed up for, my friend."

The elevator door opened, and Shalit led me into a rather spacious but windowless office. "Have a seat," he said. "The major here will help you fill out some paperwork. I'll be back to get you when you're done."

Shalit wasn't kidding about the paperwork. The waivers and nondisclosure forms and all kinds of other legalese took me almost an hour to read through carefully. The short version was that I was not an employee of the State of Israel. I was not an employee of the Mossad. I was not an independent contractor for Israel or the Mossad or any other government or private institution in Israel. I was not being paid or compensated in any way by the State of Israel, the Mossad, or any Israeli entity. I was not receiving from Israel any medical insurance or any life insurance or any of two dozen other listed benefits. What's more, I agreed to completely indemnify the State of Israel, its citizens, and its agents from all future claims of liability related to my volunteer services. I would not disclose the names, ranks, or other personal or professional details of any Israeli citizen or resident I met during the course of my volunteer work. I would treat all paperwork and electronic documents as the property of the State of Israel, handle it all as highly confidential and sensitive, and not share, give, pass, transfer, transmit, or in any other way communicate their existence or their substance, even in a redacted or summary fashion, to any unauthorized foreign national, including my own lawyers, family members, or friends, without express written permission—which I would never receive. *Ever.* And on and on it went.

Counterintuitively, perhaps, the more I read, the calmer I became. Shalit knew what I was asking. He knew my weaknesses and liabilities. He knew the risks I was taking as well as the risks he and his government were taking. Yet he was bringing me in anyway. It wasn't out of charity.

Shalit had to sincerely believe I brought something critical to the table and possessed something he urgently needed. It wasn't just the three names. It was my unique set of experiences and insights. I really did know Abu Khalif in a way no other Westerner did.

When I finished reading the final page, I went back and signed each document one by one. When I was done, the major led me along a darkened basement corridor to a lounge, where we met Shalit.

"All set?" he asked.

I nodded.

"You're sure?" he pressed.

"I'm sure."

"Good."

Shalit led me through a labyrinth of corridors and past a series of workstations where analysts quietly labored on computers displaying satellite images of various remote towns and villages. Then we arrived at a large conference room. A guard holding an Uzi stood outside the door. At Shalit's command, he stepped aside. Shalit then entered a password into a keypad and opened the door.

The moment we entered, everyone stood to attention.

Even Yael Katzir.

55

* * *

RAMAT DAVID AIR BASE, ISRAEL

"At ease," Shalit said, taking a seat at the head of the large oak table.

The group of five—four men and Yael—just stared at me. One guy's mouth literally dropped open. Yael's hand shot to her mouth, perhaps to prevent a similar reaction. I scanned each face and forced myself to look at her last. I saw shock in her eyes along with a flash of anger. The shock I could understand. She knew I was here in Israel because I'd told her in numerous e-mails and text messages over the last few days, though clearly Shalit hadn't told her he was bringing me to Ramat David. But the hostility? Where was that coming from?

"I said, at ease," Shalit repeated.

The team members took their seats. Most of them were dressed casually—jeans, sweaters, and a few plaid wool shirts over white cotton T-shirts—suggesting that none of them were military. Not currently, anyway, though they certainly all had been and probably still held fairly senior ranks in the reserves. They were older than most of the others I'd seen on the base, ranging in age from late forties to early sixties, making Yael—still in her early thirties—the youngest person in the room.

I tried to pick out the team leader. A guy on the far side of the table struck me as the most likely suspect. He was the oldest of the group, aside from Shalit. He was also the only one wearing a crisp, white oxford shirt and had a pair of reading glasses dangling from a chain around his neck. His small, intense eyes stayed locked on me even as the others shifted their attention to the head of the table.

Shalit motioned for me to take an empty chair to his left. The table was cluttered with open notebook computers, thick three-ring binders, and half-filled ashtrays. The walls were covered with maps, satellite imagery, and eight-by-ten black-and-white photos of various ISIS commanders, all high-value targets. A much-larger photo of Abu Khalif—a screen capture from the video of him speaking to the American people from Alqosh—was hanging front and center.

I noticed, too, photos of Jamal Ramzy and Tariq Baqouba, each with a big red X drawn over their faces. Ramzy had been the commander of ISIS rebel forces in Syria until Yael and I had gunned him down in the king's palace in Amman. Baqouba, his replacement, had been taken out by an American drone strike just days earlier.

As I sat down, I looked back at Yael. Her eyes were riveted on me. I couldn't read what she was thinking. Her expression was inscrutable. But one thing was clear: until sixty seconds ago, the last thing she had expected was for me to walk through that door.

"I'd like you all to meet Mr. Mike McClaire," the Mossad chief began.

The room was deathly quiet. *Was this a joke?* they were wondering. They didn't say it, but I could see it in their eyes.

"Officially, Mr. McClaire is an ISIS specialist on loan to us from NATO—from the Canadian government, to be precise," Shalit said. "That's our cover story. Of course, like everything else that happens in this room, on this floor, in this building, and on this base, Mr. McClaire's presence here is classified. You won't discuss his presence or reveal his identity to anyone outside this room. Not to your best friend on this base. Not to the janitor in the mess hall. Not to the minister of defense. Not to the prime minister himself. And certainly to no one on the outside. Any violation will be prosecuted to the fullest extent of the law. Are we clear?"

Everyone nodded.

"To anyone who asks about him, he's just 'the new guy.' If anyone has questions—they shouldn't; they know better, but if they do—you tell them to come to me. Understood?"

More nods.

"Good. Now, we all know who this really is," Shalit continued. "And you are all well aware that aside from the president of the United States, there is no one Abu Khalif wants to kill more than Mr. Collins here. His life and the lives of his family are in grave danger. Thus, I need you to treat him as one of the team and protect him like family. Am I clear?"

Reluctantly I scanned the room and made eye contact with each one as they all nodded again. Even Yael.

Still, Shalit could read the room better than I could, and he addressed their understandable cynicism head-on. "Okay, now why have I brought a civilian—an American, a goy, and a journalist, no less—to our illustrious little base camp here on Ramat David? One reason and one reason only: James Bradley Collins is the only person in this room who has ever actually met Abu Khalif. He's the only one of us who has ever spoken to him, ever looked into his eyes. He's also the only one of us who has had family members murdered by Khalif's men. He found him before. He's going to do it again with our help. And together we're going to take him out once and for all. Any questions?"

There were none. Or rather, there were a thousand, but no one was stupid enough to ask them.

"Fine," Shalit said. "Now let's get to work. Miss Katzir, would you introduce your team to Mr. Collins?"

Her team?

Shalit hadn't mentioned that.

56

* * *

"Of course, sir," Yael replied.

She took off her reading glasses and set them on the notebook in front of her. Then she went around the table and gave me the first name and brief background of each of her colleagues. I assumed the names were false and didn't even try to remember them. The backgrounds, though, were fascinating.

First, on my immediate left, wearing the oxford shirt, was a dark-skinned and somewhat brooding Sephardic Jew of Yemeni origin with closely cropped graying hair and two fingers missing from his right hand. He'd lost them when wrestling a hand grenade away from a Black September member in Beirut, Yael said, and he was lucky to be alive. Now in his early sixties, I guessed, the man was a thirty-two-year veteran of the Shin Bet, Israel's domestic intelligence service, roughly equivalent to the American FBI. He was, Yael noted, the most experienced tracker of high-value targets in the Shin Bet and had been highly decorated.

Sitting beside him was a Russian immigrant

who, to me at least, bore a striking resemblance to Leon Trotsky, one of the leaders of the Russian Revolution and the founder of the Red Army. Thin and wiry—almost gaunt—he had a salt-and-pepper mustache and matching goatee even uglier than mine. But unlike me, he had a wild, unkempt shock of graying hair and wore round, black-rimmed spectacles. Yael explained that years before, the man's father had been the KGB's station chief in Baghdad, Cairo, and later in Damascus before being posted in Vienna, where he walked into the Israeli embassy one fall Friday and defected. Remarkably, nobody in the Kremlin had ever so much as suspected that the family was Jewish. Today, she concluded, this "son of the KGB" was now the Mossad's most senior analyst of Islamic terror movements.

Across the table sat a short, stocky redhead in his mid- to late fifties who Yael said was a major general in the Israeli military and one of the top analysts from Unit 8200, Israel's signal intelligence–gathering operation, roughly equivalent to the NSA. His father had been a top Mossad agent serving in Arab lands, and his mother was an English teacher who, despite her husband's job, was a peacenik through and through. Little did she know what her only son had grown up to do. Even today, his mother thought he was an executive with HOT, the Israeli cable TV company. Instead, he'd become one of the best Arabic speakers on her team, Yael said, not to mention the best chef she'd ever met in Israel. "His ginger couscous is to die for," she concluded.

I'd just learned I had made another mistake. Not only had I wrongly ID'd the guy in the oxford as the team leader, it now turned out that we actually did have an active military man—a senior officer, no less—in our midst, despite the fact that at the moment he wasn't wearing a uniform. Zero for two, I thought. How exactly was I supposed to add value to this team?

Next to the redhead sat a rather tall, well-built man in his late forties, perhaps early fifties, with thinning, sandy-blond hair and a face that struck me as Swedish or Danish or perhaps Norwegian. Yael explained he was a highly decorated—but now officially retired—former commander of the Sayeret Matkal, the IDF's most elite commando unit. No Israeli had personally captured or killed more high-value targets than he had, Yael said, and his ability to drive the intel-gathering process in order to produce hard, clear, actionable, accurate information that led to the actual takedown of HVTs was unparalleled in the Israeli military. And by the way, she added, he's from Holland.

Well, I thought, I'd been close. Still, it had been a foul ball, at best. At this point my batting average was .000. At least no one else in the room knew it.

So here they were—the team Yael had assembled to hunt down Abu Khalif—Israel's best and brightest. Fingers, Trotsky, Gingy, and Dutch.

All but Dutch were native Arabic speakers. They'd learned the language growing up, not in the army or university. They all had significant time operating in the Arab world as spies or commandos. And they had real-world military experience, including decades of experience searching for high-value targets.

As Yael added some details and explained their mandate, I had my first chance in two full months to look at her. She was breathtaking in a chocolate-brown sweater, black bomber jacket, faded blue jeans, and brown leather boots, and it was all I could do to stay focused and listen carefully and retain all the details she was saying. Even with the scars on her face and neck, visible despite the fact she was growing out her hair to cover them up, she was beautiful. Even with her left arm in a cast. Even though she had clearly lost weight. Even with the obvious lack of consistent sleep, the sadness in her eyes, and the dark rings underneath them. I found her stunning. I couldn't help it. I was falling for this girl, no matter how little she reciprocated.

"Thank you," Shalit said when Yael was finished. "Now, as all of you except Mr. Collins know, I've just gotten back from London, Paris, Berlin, and Rome. I met with each of their intel chiefs. I reviewed all they have on ISIS. And the bottom line is I'm coming back empty-handed. Their files are virtually blank. None of them have any real assets in Syria to speak of. None of them have penetrated any ISIS cells. They have no idea where Abu Khalif is, and frankly they don't seem to care all that much."

"Then what are they doing all day?" Fingers asked.

"Hoping against hope they can identify and thwart the next terror attack in their own countries," Shalit replied. "They're purely in defensive mode and have little interest in going on offense. The head of MI6 told me ISIS has weaponized the Syrian refugees coming into the U.K. He and his team are tracking twenty-two different ISIS cells right now. The Brits are identifying a new one every few days. He said he and his team are drowning in refugees. His people can't possibly vet them fast enough. They're trying to watch to see who links up with these terror cells. They're trying to keep them from buying weapons. But they're completely overwhelmed. Yet the prime minister keeps letting more and more refugees into the country despite all the polls that show the public's concern rising. And in every other capital, I heard essentially the same story."

"So once again, we're on our own," said Dutch.

It wasn't a question. It was a cynical, almost bitter statement of fact, and Shalit made no attempt to tell him he was wrong.

57

★ ★ ★

"Okay, now tell our guest where we are at the moment," Shalit ordered.

"Honestly?" Yael replied. "Nowhere."

"Why?" I asked.

"Where do I start?" Yael replied, her body tense and her eyes cold. "Lots of reasons, but at the top of my list at the moment would be the Americans."

"Meaning President Taylor isn't taking the hunt for Abu Khalif seriously, isn't willing to sign an executive order to take him out, and isn't willing to authorize an invasion of Syria to find him?" I asked, sure we agreed on that much, at least.

But Yael threw a curveball. "No, meaning the White House is obsessed with drone strikes," she replied. "They keep finding ISIS leaders and killing them, one after another after another."

Now I was confused. "Isn't that a good thing?"

"No, Mr. Collins, it's not a good thing—not if the objective is finding the head of ISIS," she said. "Last week my team tracked down Tariq Baqouba, the number-three guy, head of all military ops for the caliphate. We hunted him down. We knew exactly where he was. Then, as good allies, we dutifully briefed the Americans, told them his precise location, and asked for their assistance in capturing him. Next thing we know, Baqouba is killed in a drone strike and President Taylor is boasting about it on TV. There's just one problem. You don't kill a man like Tariq Baqouba. You snag him and shake him until he tells you everything. Killing him gives you a headline for a day. Capturing him gives you a gold mine of intelligence that can keep you going for weeks, sometimes months. And this wasn't the only instance. Yet no matter how hard we protest, the president won't listen to us. He's become Mr. Drone Strike, and I'm telling you, that's never going to get us to Abu Khalif."

"Whoa, whoa, Katzir, let's pull this thing back," Shalit said. "We're not here to bash the chief executive of our most important ally. Let's focus on what we know and don't know. A month ago, you all thought Khalif was in Mosul. Walk Mr. Collins through what you've learned since then."

"Fine," she said, glaring at me, clearly unhappy with the request but even more unhappy, it seemed, with my very presence. "Well, we know for certain that Khalif was in Mosul last November, because you interviewed him there, right? And we know for certain that he spent at least some time in Alqosh because after President Taylor was captured in Jordan, the video ISIS released showed both the president and Khalif together there. Unfortunately,

Khalif somehow slipped away in the hours before coalition forces took Alqosh and rescued the president. So the first question is, where did Khalif go after Alqosh?"

"Do you believe he went back to Mosul?" I asked.

"We do," Yael confirmed. "Mosul was the perfect place to hide. It used to be a city of about two and a half million people, one of Iraq's largest. When ISIS took over in the summer of '14, a good deal of the population fled. Still, there were hundreds of thousands of Iraqis living in Mosul last December. Khalif had allies there. He had a network of safe houses there. He had money, weapons, communications equipment, everything he needed to hunker down and ride out the storm."

"But Khalif obviously heard the rumblings that U.S. forces were coming to retake Mosul," I said.

"Correct," Yael agreed. "For some bizarre reason that eludes everyone around this table, including yours truly, the White House and Pentagon were telegraphing the impending military operation for the better part of a year. President Taylor—big surprise—had been dithering, refusing to sign off on the operation for this reason or that. But the ISIS attack on the summit in Amman and the president's capture were the last straw. The moment Taylor was safely back in the White House, he finally authorized the formation of a Sunni Arab alliance—Kurds, Egyptians, Saudis, and the emirates, plus whatever King Abdullah could spare from Jordan—to come help the U.S.

liberate Mosul and all of northern Iraq. The Arab leaders all said yes. They all sent men and matériel. But when the coalition stormed through Mosul, Khalif was nowhere to be found. He'd slipped the noose again."

"To where?" I asked.

"Well, that's the billion-dollar question, isn't it?"

Yael looked at Trotsky.

The Russian immediately took the baton. "We all would have said Raqqa," he began, referring to the Syrian city east of Aleppo with roughly a quarter of a million people, making it the sixth-largest city in a country that was imploding by the hour.

"But . . . ?"

"But we've found no trace of him. No sightings. No signals. Just rumors."

"Still, it makes sense that he'd be there."

"Maybe yes, maybe no," Trotsky said. "On the plus side, Raqqa has certainly been the capital of the caliphate for the past several years. We're picking up lots of SIGINT out of there. The Americans keep finding and killing top ISIS commanders there in one drone strike after another. It's practically become the drone strike capital of the world, there are so many high-value targets coming in and out. On the minus side, why would Khalif hunker down in a place so carefully watched? It's not his style. And for all his talk of martyrdom, we don't see him volunteering to lay down his own life for his team or his cause."

"Then why do all the other HVTs keep going there?" I asked.

"Good question," Trotsky said.

"And one we don't have the answer to," Yael added.

"Why not?"

"Because we've got no assets on the ground," said Gingy, the guy from Israel's Unit 8200. "We've got no spies, no moles, no human assets inside Raqqa to explain what's going on. We're trying to monitor calls and e-mails and movements of thousands of jihadists all across Syria, Lebanon, Iraq, Gaza, Iran, you name it. But our systems are overwhelmed. We don't have the manpower to sift through everything we have."

"What about the NSA?" I asked. "Aren't they vacuuming up everything? Can't they help?"

Yael took that one. "I'm sure they are, but they're not exactly sharing what they have with us. And frankly, over the last two months, retaking Mosul and northern Iraq has been the top priority in Fort Meade and Langley and certainly at the White House."

"Not finding Abu Khalif," I said.

"No," Yael said.

"Could that mean Khalif might actually be in Raqqa, but you just haven't isolated him yet?"

"No, he's not there."

"How can you be so sure?"

"It doesn't fit his profile."

"What do you mean?"

"The man just launched a devastating series of attacks on Washington and seven other American cities and towns," she noted. "The American administration's position notwithstanding, these were *not* the last gasps of a dying movement. This was a brilliantly designed and almost flaw-lessly executed series of terrorist operations with precision timing and deadly effect. You can't put a plan like that together in a city that is being watched 24-7 by the Americans, the Russians, the Iranians, us, and the bulk of the Sunni Arab world, not to mention one that's being bombed every few days. Everyone knows Raqqa is the ISIS capital, which means Khalif isn't there. He may not be far away, but he's not in Raqqa."

"Then where?" I asked again.

"We have no idea."

My first reaction was raw anger. This was the best this elite Mossad team could come up with? *He's not in Mosul. He's not in Raqqa. Beyond that, we're clueless.* Every armchair analyst in the world writing a blog in his underwear could come up with that. With a two-month head start, spy satel-lites, drones, thousands of spies and analysts on their payroll, and billions of dollars a year in U.S. military aid, how in the world could one of the premier intelligence forces in the world not be closer to catching the man who had killed their prime minister?

I wanted to scream at someone—all of them.

I'd left my brother and his family for this?

I knew I had to calm down, take a deep breath. Of course they didn't know. Not yet. That's why I'd come. That's why I wanted to help.

But these weren't kids. These were highly trained, highly experienced combat intelligence veterans. They'd hunted down a whole lot of bad guys in their day. They'd also been the team that had turned the eyes of the Mossad—and thus the Americans and the Jordanians—to Alqosh in the first place. These were good people—sharp, clever, outside-the-box thinkers. So why weren't they further down the road?

The answer—once I'd cooled down enough to accept it—was entirely obvious.

Their prime minister and nearly his entire protective detail had been killed in Amman two months before, and the entire Israeli security establishment was suffering vertigo. Two weeks after the attack, the head of the Mossad had died of pancreatic cancer, further destabilizing the Israeli intelligence culture. Then came the joint U.S.–Sunni military push into Mosul and across northern Iraq. On top of all this, the new leader of this new unit was a woman who'd nearly been killed in Alqosh. How long was it since she'd been released from the hospital? How long since she'd turned down the new prime minister's offer and been approved to take this post? Having come on board, hadn't she needed to be brought up to speed on everything she'd missed while in the hospital and in rehab—mountains of field reports, cable traffic, satellite imagery, telephone intercepts, e-mail intercepts, and text message intercepts, not to mention countless meetings, verbal briefings by each of her new team members, and intense pressure from on high to deliver results?

All of it took time.

And then, of course, the White House—as risk

averse as any I'd ever seen—was taking out every valuable source with a Hellfire missile before the Israelis could snag 'em and bag 'em.

No wonder the team was running behind.

I needed to calm down and cut them some slack—starting with Yael.

58

* * *

There was a knock on the conference room door.

Shalit glanced at a security monitor, then pushed a button, electronically unlocking the door. A colonel burst in with breaking news—Abu Khalif had just released a new video, and it was about to be shown on Al Jazeera.

Yael quickly turned on a bank of monitors behind her. On the largest flat-screen, mounted on the center of the wall, she put a live feed from the Arab news network based in Doha, Qatar. On four smaller screens, hanging by steel mounts from the ceiling, she brought up Israel's Channel 2, Al Arabiya, CNN, and Sky News. Then she grabbed her chair and moved it to my end of the conference room, setting it down to Shalit's right. This gave her a clear view of each of the screens. It also put her about five feet away from me.

Yael turned up the sound on the center screen, and every eye in the room turned to Al Jazeera—except for mine, which I admit lingered perhaps a moment too long on this woman who had all but captured my heart yet was still treating me like a stranger.

The new video was not yet running. Instead, the network was showing a still photo of Abu Khalif wearing his signature kaffiyeh and flowing white robes while their commentators were discussing what he might say.

Shalit was riveted on the screen, undoubtedly listening for any tidbits of hard news the anchors might have. But Yael glanced at me quickly, awkwardly, and then looked away. I was dying to talk to her alone, to really know what she was thinking, to know why she was being so hostile. What had I done wrong?

But then I heard the voice of the man who had murdered my family.

"My name is Abu Khalif," he began, looking straight into the camera. "I greet you in the name of Allah, the most beneficent, the most merciful, the only ruling judge on the Day of Recompense, the day of coming judgment. Truly all praise belongs to Allah. We praise him, and we eagerly await the day that he sends Imam al-Mahdi, the promised one, the rightly guided one, who will expand the caliphate over the entire globe and send the infidels into the hellfires forever."

The emir now went off on an interminably long and nearly incomprehensible rant about some ancient battle that occurred in the seventh century. I tried to focus, but my mind soon wandered back to the day I'd met Abu Khalif in Abu Ghraib, Iraq's most notorious prison. I'd been hunting for an exclusive, and to my regret, I'd gotten it. Even now,

I could still see myself stepping into that barren interrogation room. I could see the face of the man in handcuffs, wearing the orange prison jumpsuit. He had struck me as part religious fanatic, part terrorist mastermind—a serial killing lunatic and by far the most dangerous and disturbing man I'd ever met.

Back then, Khalif had sported a wild, unkempt black-and-gray beard. Now the beard was neatly trimmed. But those eyes had not changed. They were full of murder. They still haunted me, and I could literally feel the hair on the back of my neck stand erect.

I forced myself to look away from his eyes, and only then did it strike me that this video wasn't a wide shot like in Alqosh. This was a tight close-up on Khalif's face. There was a bookshelf behind him, but it was empty. Apparently he had learned from his past mistakes. The last video had shown Khalif standing in the courtyard of a crumbling mausoleum, and Matt had immediately recognized the location. Then he'd quickly contacted me to let me know Khalif was in the town of Alqosh, on the plains of Nineveh, in the heart of northern Iraq, standing in the ruins of the tomb of Nahum, the ancient Hebrew prophet who had foretold the coming judgment of the wicked Assyrian capital. This time, there was nothing for foreign intelligence analysts to focus on, no clues as to what kind of building he was using or what city or even country he was in.

Suddenly the emir's message shifted gears, and I tuned back in.

"Let all of humanity know the words of the holy Qur'an, that 'he who deceives shall be faced with his deceit on the Day of Resurrection, when every human being shall be repaid in full for whatever he has done, and none shall be wronged.' When Imam al-Mahdi comes, when the final judgment comes, every infidel will see the error of his ways. Every infidel will experience the flames of justice. But even now, the infidels have begun to pay for their crimes—in Amman and throughout the kingdom of Jordan; in Washington, D.C.; in Philadelphia and Boston and Chicago and Minneapolis and Dallas and Atlanta; and even in the remotest village in Maine. As of this recording, more than 6,300 criminal American souls have perished at the hands of the jihadists of the caliphate in just the last few weeks. We can praise Allah for his faithfulness."

The number jumped out at me. The president had told the nation that the number of deaths was 4,647. Taylor had also said another six thousand Americans had been wounded in the ISIS attacks. Maybe more had succumbed to their injuries. Then again, I wasn't exactly about to depend on facts and figures provided by Abu Khalif.

"I tell you today, let all who abide in the caliphate know—let the entire world know—this is only the beginning," the emir continued. "Soon—very soon—the faithful warriors of jihad, along with all Muslims everywhere, will celebrate the festival of *Isra* and *Mi'raj*. This will be a celebration like no other. Together we will celebrate not just the journeys of the Prophet, peace be upon him.

No—together we will celebrate the fall of the apostates, the slaughter of the infidels, the fulfillment of the prophecies, and the coming of the end of the age. O Muslims everywhere, glad tidings to you! Raise your heads high, for soon—very soon—you will see what the faithful have longed to see for so many ages. Keep your eyes fixed on *Isra* and *Mi'raj*. Remember what the Prophet, peace be upon him, saw on that blessed journey. Remember the night visions. Remember what was revealed in the heavens. It is coming, O Muslims. It is coming, and it cannot be stopped."

What was coming? I wondered. *What was ISIS planning next?*

"All praise and thanks are due to Allah," Khalif concluded. "Therefore, rush, O Muslims, rush to do your duty; rush to join our jihad. Time is short. The end is nigh. What will you say on the Day of Judgment? What will the scales of justice reveal? As our brother from Jordan—Abu Musab al-Zarqawi—first told you: the spark of the consuming fire was lit in Iraq. It spread to Syria. Now it has spread to Jordan. And it has spread to America, but more is coming—so much more. This spark has become a raging, uncontrollable fire. And this fire will intensify until it burns all the crusader armies in Dabiq. Let there be no doubt, O Muslims—Rome is falling. The Caliphate is arising. The hope of all the ages is truly coming to pass."

59

★ ★ ★

"Thoughts?" Shalit demanded when the video had ended.

Yael muted the TV, and for a moment there was quiet as everyone processed what they had just seen and heard.

"Clearly another attack is coming," Trotsky said. "Khalif says a celebration is coming because more infidels are going to be killed."

"I'm afraid he's right," Yael said, getting up and walking over to a large whiteboard hanging on the wall in between the maps and photos of ISIS leaders. "Khalif boasted that 6,300 Americans have already died at the hands of the jihadists, but he said, 'This is only the beginning.'"

"Plus he said, 'More is coming—so much more,'" Gingy noted.

"Right," Fingers said. "And he said the attacks are becoming a 'raging, uncontrollable fire.'"

"So we're agreed that he's not just bragging about the attacks in the U.S. but signaling more attacks to come?" Shalit asked the team.

Everyone nodded.

Shalit turned to Yael. "Now it's a question of location. Is ISIS going after the Americans again or heading to Europe—or coming here?"

Yael said she was going to reserve judgment until she'd had the chance to review the transcript and go over precisely what was said, word for word. But her instinct was that Khalif meant both—more attacks in the States as well as more around the world, specifically in the West.

"Why do you say that?" Shalit pressed, not indicating she was necessarily wrong but trying to better understand her thinking.

"Khalif wasn't clear, and he wasn't clear for a reason," Yael replied. "He's not trying to give away his game plan. He's trying to dominate the global news cycle. He wants to be larger than life, larger than bin Laden. He wants to be seen as the most important and most powerful Muslim in the world. He sees himself as the leader of the caliphate—not just the Islamic State but the global Islamic empire. He truly believes he is going to take over the entire world. He's trying to inspire more Muslims to join the caliphate, become jihadists, and bring their expertise and their resources to the team. Where he hits next is important, but I don't believe that was his central point."

"You think this was a recruitment video?" Shalit asked.

"Not primarily," she clarified. "Though I'm sure it will function as one. Given all the success ISIS has had in recent days, I expect he's going to have ten thousand new recruits by the end of the week. But I don't think that was his main objective."

"Go on."

"I think Khalif put this video out not to tell his followers *where* he was going to strike next," she said. "He put it out to tell them *when*."

"Soon," I said.

"Very soon," Dutch clarified.

"Yes, yes, but it was more than that," Yael prompted. "He was clear. He was precise. Did anyone catch it?"

The room was silent, and then Trotsky spoke up. "He mentioned the festival to celebrate *Isra* and *Mi'raj*."

"Exactly," Yael said. "But why? What's important about this festival?"

She was circling the room now, trying to get the group energized, thinking, participating. Her entire demeanor had shifted. Her body language was no longer cold, no longer reserved. She was engaged, even passionate. Her eyes had lit up. It was clear she respected the men in this room enormously and loved leading this team.

"The festival marks Muhammad's journey to the Al-Aksa Mosque and his supposed visit to heaven," Trotsky said.

"Right," she said. "This is a big deal in the Muslim world—the Night Vision and the Ascension. Where does it come from?"

"The Qur'an and some of the hadiths," Fingers said.

"Good, good—which sura?" she pressed.

Gingy took that one. "Seventeen. But why does it matter?"

"Because we're hunting a man who has a doctorate in Islamic jurisprudence," she insisted. "He memorized the Qur'an before he was nine. This is a man who eats, thinks, and breathes the Qur'an and the hadiths. I'm not saying he's interpreting it correctly. But he knows his stuff. Everything he says comes from his religious beliefs, and we're not going to find him unless we can understand him. We need to outfox him, people. We need to get ahead of him, anticipate where he's going next."

I glanced over at Shalit. He was sitting back in his chair and I detected a slight smile on his face. He, too, was enjoying Yael's energy, her passion, her commitment to this mission. If Shalit had ever had any doubts about his choice to head up this team, I suspected they were long gone.

Still, I wasn't clear where she was going with this. But before I could ask her, she turned to me.

"Now, Mr. Collins, since you supposedly have so much to offer us," she said, her demeanor rapidly cooling, "perhaps you would like to enlighten us on the story of the Night Vision and the Ascension and why Abu Khalif might be referencing it?"

Her voice held an edge once again. She was standing at the other end of the room, under the video monitors. I looked into her eyes. They were hard and unforgiving. She loved this team, but she wasn't welcoming me onto it. She wasn't accepting Shalit's decision to bring me in without consulting her, without giving her the courtesy of a heads-up before springing me on her. Indeed, she was challenging my very qualifications for being in this room at all.

I looked at her, then at the others in the room. They were waiting for me to answer. I could feel the tension mounting, and I was under no illusion that Shalit was going to step in and bail me out.

This was my test, and I had about ten seconds to pass it.

60

* * *

I didn't claim to have a PhD in Islamic theology, and Yael knew it.

I certainly didn't know much about the brand of Islamic eschatology driving the leaders of ISIS, though I'd been scrambling to learn everything I could over the last few months. I'd studied the Qur'an and the hadiths as an undergraduate majoring in political science. And I'd studied them more closely on my assignments in Iraq and Afghanistan. I'd discussed them at length with various Arab government officials, scholars, and even terrorists I had interviewed in the field over the past decade.

But this wasn't about my education or my job or my qualifications or lack thereof. Something else had angered Yael, and I still had no idea what. For the moment, I needed to stay calm and pass her test.

"Well, Miss Katzir, let's see," I began. "As a young man in his thirties, Muhammad used to climb up into the caves of Mount Hira, not far from Mecca, to pray and to meditate. As I recall, he began having dreams and visions in the year AD 610, which would have made him about forty years old. At first he couldn't decide if it was Allah or Satan speaking to him. I think it turned out to be his first wife, Khadijah, who convinced her husband he was hearing the voice of Allah. She ended up becoming his initial convert. She encouraged him to keep going to the cave and listening to the voice. And soon Muhammad came to believe that Allah was commanding him to proclaim a new message to the pagans on the Arabian peninsula."

I paused for a moment to gather my thoughts, then looked back at Yael. "It was about ten years later—around the year 620—that he experienced what became known as the Night Vision and the Ascension. Muslims believe the angel Gabriel appeared to Muhammad in Arabia and gave him a mystical winged horse, or maybe a donkey, named Buraq. If I remember, one hadith says that Buraq bucked when Muhammad tried to mount him, but Gabriel put his hand on the winged creature and rebuked him. Anyway, this creature ostensibly flew through the night sky and took Muhammad to 'the farthest mosque,' otherwise known as 'the mosque in the corner.' Today it's called Al-Aksa Mosque."

"In Jerusalem?" Yael challenged, showing no evidence she was impressed by my answer thus far.

"Well, nobody actually knows for sure where 'the mosque in the corner' was located," I replied.

"What are you talking about?" Yael snapped, suddenly pacing again. "Every Muslim on the planet claims Jerusalem is their third-holiest city, right after Mecca and Medina."

"They do," I agreed. "But the Qur'an never actually mentions Jerusalem. Not by name. Not even once. And of course, there was no mosque on the Temple Mount in AD 620. When the mosque was later built there, it was named Al-Aksa to comport with sura seventeen. So how could Muhammad have flown to a mosque that didn't exist? But that's a different discussion."

"Go on," she said, circling the table. "What about the Ascension?"

"Well, again, according to the Qur'an and the hadiths, once he arrived at the mosque in the corner, Muhammad prayed and earnestly sought the counsel of Allah," I explained, straining to remember everything I'd ever read or been taught on the subject. I tried hard not to ad lib or embellish, knowing I couldn't afford even one false step. "As I recall, it was at this time that Allah supposedly reassured Muhammad that he was on the right path, that he was doing the right thing, that despite all the opposition he was encountering, he was in fact submitting to the divine will. Then Muhammad was told to climb up a ladder—the *Mi'raj*—right up into the seven levels of heaven, where he met and spoke with the prophets of old—prophets like Abraham and Moses and even Jesus. These revered holy men, according to the ancient Islamic texts, assured Muhammad that he was one of them, that he was a true prophet just like they were, and that he was truly hearing the voice of God."

Every eye turned back to Yael. It was as if we

were playing singles at Wimbledon. *Serve. Smash. Return. Smash.* But I wasn't done yet.

"What I find particularly interesting is that this all came during—or perhaps right after—what Muslims call the Year of Sorrow. That was the fateful year that Muhammad's beloved uncle died. Then his first wife, Khadijah, died as well. This was the wife he truly loved, the wife he'd apparently been faithful to. In fact, he didn't marry another woman until Khadijah passed away. So these dreams and visions were occurring during a time when Muhammad was grieving—and facing many other challenges as well. Most Jews and Christians, unsurprisingly, were rejecting his insistence that he was their rightful religious leader and that Islam was the divine successor to Judaism and Christianity. Some people were saying he was a heretic, that he was listening to the voice of Satan, not God. So this was a time of great distress and confusion. Muhammad was in deep mourning. He was desperately seeking a sign from Allah, and in the Night Vision and the Ascension, he suddenly believed that he had received what he had asked for."

Yael just glared at me, and that's when Shalit stepped in. "Perhaps it's fair to say Mr. Collins knows the story of the Night Vision and the Ascension after all," said the Mossad chief.

"Maybe so, but I'm still waiting for him to answer my questions," Yael shot back.

"Which were what exactly?" Shalit asked. "Remind me."

"She's asking why," I said before she could

respond. "Why would Khalif reference the festival marking these events? What exactly is he trying to say? Is he hatching a plot connected somehow to the Al-Aksa Mosque or the Dome of the Rock? Is he going to attack Jerusalem?"

Yael stood motionless.

"And?" Shalit prompted. "Do you have an answer, Mr. Collins?"

"My answer is Yael's answer," I said, wanting her to know I'd been listening.

"Meaning what?" Shalit asked.

"Meaning I can't say whether Khalif is planning to strike Jerusalem and the Temple Mount," I said. "But Yael said it herself. The reason Khalif released this video isn't to tell Muslims *where* he's going to strike next. It's to tell Muslims *when* he's going to strike, during the festival marking the Night Vision and the Ascension."

"Precisely," she said. "And when is that?"

Everyone looked at me. I struggled to recall the date. I so wanted to pass this test. But in the end I simply could not remember. "I'm sorry," I said. "I don't know."

"Do you?" Shalit asked, turning back to Yael.

"Of course," she said.

"Then when?" he asked.

"This year the festival occurs on April 3."

My stomach suddenly tightened.

That was only thirty-three days away.

61

Yael's analysis sparked a firestorm.

For much of the next hour, the group dissected every sentence—every word—of Khalif's statement. For now the group was split. Fingers and Dutch agreed with Yael that Khalif was marking April 3 as the date of the next attacks. Trotsky and Gingy weren't convinced. Shalit didn't take a side. Nobody asked me for any further analysis.

In the end Shalit told the group he wanted them to test their theories against every other piece of intel they had on Khalif and ISIS. He said he was supposed to brief Prime Minister Eitan in person at four o'clock that afternoon. Thus he needed the best they had no later than three, when he would be boarding a chopper to the Kirya—the IDF's headquarters—in Tel Aviv.

Soon everyone had been dismissed, leaving the conference room and racing back to their workstations. It was closing in on noon. They had less than three hours, and the stakes were high.

"So what do you think?" Shalit asked me as he pushed away from the table.

I hadn't left the conference room. I had no workstation, no place to go.

"I think you've put together an impressive team," I said.

He nodded. "With an impressive leader, no?"

"Very," I said.

"Not so happy with you."

"Apparently not."

"Don't forget she's got a very personal stake in the success of this mission," Shalit added. "That's why she's good. That's why I have no doubt she'll succeed."

"That's why you recruited her away from the prime minister's office."

"That's why she said yes."

"And that's why you let me join your team—because I've got a personal stake in this too?" I asked.

"Of course," Shalit replied. "You've just met the best of the best, J. B. These guys are in a class of their own. But you two are the key. You and Yael will work harder and longer, drive deeper, look more thoroughly, and think about this mission every moment of every day, because it's not a job for you. You're not here because you're experts. Neither of you. You're here—both of you—because you want Abu Khalif found and taken out even more than I do."

He leaned forward. "Now tell me: does it concern you that the team is divided?"

"You mean that they almost came to blows over the significance of April 3?"

"Exactly."

"Welcome to Israel," I said. "Five Israelis. Six opinions. Right?"

"For better or for worse," Shalit said, nearly smiling, though not quite.

"For better," I said. I was actually glad to see how divided the team was. It required each side to dig hard, fast, and deep into all the intelligence they had at their disposal to see if there was anything that would bolster their case. That was good. Skepticism in the face of even the most impressive intelligence analysis was not only justified but essential.

Groupthink, by contrast, was dangerous, especially when it came to national security. Too often it led to blind spots, caused people to be unaware of their own misguided assumptions and biases. Too many in Washington had been blindsided by the catastrophic attacks by the Islamic State. Some of the best and the brightest intelligence, security, and political officials in the world had tragically missed the signs of what was coming.

Shalit motioned for me to come and sit beside him. When I did, he said very quietly, "James, it's time. Tell me what you have."

I nodded. He was right; it was time. I walked him through the three names Khachigian had left me, the research I'd done on them, and all the information on each that I'd been able to track down.

Shalit listened carefully but looked disappointed. When I was finished, he sighed. "I'd expected more."

"More names?"

"More quality. More depth. These men are fine. I know two of them—Pritchard and Hussam. They were competent operatives in their day. But Pritchard was fired and now he's dead, and Hussam was jailed, and these are the names you bring me?"

"I'm not giving you these names," I clarified. "Bob Khachigian is. I don't know any of the three. I have no idea what they can tell me. But if Bob says these guys can help me, I believe him."

Shalit sighed again. "I certainly agree with your assessment of Bob. He was a great spy. He was a great analyst and one of the finest men to lead the CIA, certainly the finest I ever knew. I'm skeptical about these names, but clearly he must have known something I don't."

"So?" I asked.

"So let's get moving," he replied. "We trusted him in life. Why not trust him in death? I'm putting you and Yael on a plane to Cairo this afternoon. You're going to start with Walid Hussam and find out where this trail leads."

62

* * *

Walid Hussam was not the first name on Khachigian's list.

But Shalit had insisted on sending us to see Hussam first. Initially I'd pushed back, arguing Yael and I should go first to Dubai and meet Mohammed bin Zayed, the UAE's intelligence chief and the only name on the list who was still an active intelligence agent. That had been my original plan, and I thought we should stick to it.

But Shalit had overruled me. "Cairo first, then Dubai," he'd said, explaining that he had better contacts in the Egyptian capital.

Upon hearing this new development, Yael was not happy, to say the least. I could clearly hear her even through the closed conference room door as she told Shalit she had better things to do than go off on a wild-goose chase, spending what could be upwards of four or five days crisscrossing the Arab world with me. But in the end Shalit outranked and overruled her, just as he had me. She might not like it—she didn't, in fact—but Yael was stuck with me now.

Just after 3 p.m., with the initial written assessment of Khalif's videotaped address complete, Yael and I said good-bye to the team, headed upstairs to the flight deck, and approached the Sikorsky S-76 executive helicopter piloted by two Israeli air force colonels who would fly us to the airport where my private jet was waiting. I stepped forward and offered to help Yael, who looked a little uncomfortable with the cast on her left arm, into the chopper. She ignored me and did just fine on her own, taking the leather seat immediately behind the pilots. *So much for chivalry,* I thought as I scrambled into the back and slid across the leather bench to the left window seat. Two security guys climbed in next and sat beside me. Then one of the ground crew shut the door behind us and tapped the fuselage twice. The moment we were all buckled in, we lifted off and headed south.

As the chopper banked to the right—southwest—I snuck a glance at Yael. She looked exhausted, and while the wounds to her face and neck were healing nicely, short of extensive plastic surgery, they were going to leave some serious scars. It didn't matter. She was still the most beautiful woman I'd ever met, even though she hadn't said a word to me since storming out of her meeting with Shalit.

I gazed out the window at the Jezreel Valley below and thought of Matt. I tried to picture what he was doing just then. It was only eight in the morning on St. Thomas. He was probably having breakfast and reading his Bible out on the veranda overlooking Magens Bay. He was probably praying for me, and even though I still didn't believe what he believed, I was grateful.

I grabbed my briefcase from the floor and retrieved the briefing paper I'd prepared at Shalit's request, summarizing my research on Walid Hussam. If I was going to meet this guy, Ari had told me, I might as well know as much as possible about him.

Hussam had been born in 1954 in the Egyptian port city of Alexandria. He was only thirteen in 1967, too young to fight in the war against Israel. But in 1973, when Egypt launched a surprise attack against "the criminal Zionists" on Yom Kippur, the holiest day of the Jewish year, Hussam was on the front lines as a nineteen-year-old deputy commander. When his superior officer was mortally wounded in a ferocious firefight with IDF forces near the Gaza Strip, Hussam had to take over. His bravery in combat caught the attention of those up the chain of command.

In time, Hussam became the aide-de-camp for Omar Suleiman, the notorious head of the Egyptian General Intelligence Service. After Suleiman fired two of his deputies and another was later mysteriously murdered on a visit to Tripoli, the spy chief named Hussam his new deputy in late 2009. But soon the Arab Spring erupted in Tunisia and rapidly spread to the streets of Egypt. Egyptian president Hosni Mubarak promoted Suleiman to vice president on January 29, 2011. That same day, Mubarak promoted Hussam to become head of EGIS.

But by then all hell was breaking loose. Millions of Egyptians had taken to the streets, burning cars, burning police stations, calling for Mubarak to step down, calling for the entire Egyptian government to be arrested and tried on charges of treason. To Hussam's astonishment, even the White House was openly calling for Mubarak to step down. Once that happened, it didn't require being an intelligence professional to read the handwriting on the wall. Mubarak was going down.

On June 30, 2012, the once unthinkable occurred. The Muslim Brotherhood was swept into power, and that very day, Hussam found himself arrested, thrown into prison with thousands of other Mubarak loyalists, tortured, and left to rot and die without a trial.

What no one had foreseen that day, not even Hussam, was how rapidly the Egyptian people would then turn against the Brotherhood and their leaders. Less than a year later, a stunning 20 million Egyptians—roughly a quarter of the population—signed a petition calling for the Brotherhood to relinquish power. Many turned out on the streets, demanding the same. They didn't want Sharia law imposed on them. With Egypt teetering on the brink of full-blown civil war, the army finally stepped in, launching a coup in late June of 2013. It was bloody but successful. Within weeks, the military was in full control of the capital and the country. Most of the Brotherhood leadership was dead or in prison, and suddenly Hussam and thousands of his colleagues found themselves released from prison.

Now sixty-four, Hussam was out of the intelligence game. He hadn't reentered government but had started teaching at various universities. He wrote a book on the Arab Spring, though it sold poorly. He joined a few corporate boards, probably making a few bucks, and spent far more time with his children and grandchildren than he ever had.

How he was going to help us find Abu Khalif, I had no clue. But like Shalit, I was operating on the basis of my confidence in Robert Khachigian. He hadn't steered me wrong yet. Except perhaps with Laura.

Just then our chopper touched down. When the door opened, it was immediately apparent we were not at Ben Gurion International Airport but rather at an airfield in Herzliya, the upscale community up the coast from Tel Aviv. I saw my Learjet being fueled up and readied for departure. How it had gotten here, I had no idea. Who had authorized the flight, I had no idea. Why I hadn't been told a thing about it, I also had no idea. But frankly, at the moment, I didn't care. I was in the world of the Israeli Mossad. They operated differently than the *New York Times*. I knew I'd better get used to it, and fast.

63

★ ★ ★

Yael and I hurriedly boarded, took our seats, buckled up, and roared down the runway.

The whole process from start to finish took less than fifteen minutes, and it was a good thing we'd moved so quickly. It was 4:37. It was already getting dark. A storm was rolling in, and winter rains were pelting the plane.

As we reached cruising altitude, I was tempted to lean my chair back and get some rest, which I desperately needed. So did Yael. Instead, Yael opened her laptop and buried herself in her work.

I stared out the window, trying desperately to think of something to say. "Yael, do you remember General El-Badawy?" I asked.

I knew full well she remembered the commander of Egyptian special forces, whom we had first met in the war room with King Abdullah as he and his fellow Sunni military commanders made their final plans to assault Dabiq and Alqosh.

Yael kept typing furiously, albeit only with her right hand.

"Well, the other day I got an e-mail from someone saying he was an Egyptian colonel who worked for El-Badawy. Said the general wanted to speak with me. The subject was too sensitive to discuss by e-mail."

Again, nothing.

"I was thinking we should probably call him when we get to Cairo," I continued. "Maybe you're right. Maybe Hussam is a dead end. But El-Badawy is a key player. What do you think?"

Zero.

I didn't know whether to laugh or scream, but this silent treatment was getting ridiculous. I glanced around the cabin. The cockpit door was closed and surely locked. The pilots couldn't see or hear us. There were no other passengers on the flight, and unlike on the helicopter, we could actually hear ourselves think. We could have a conversation if we wanted to, and I wanted to. This was the first time I'd been alone with Yael Katzir since the underground bunker with the king and his generals in northeastern Jordan, before we headed out to Alqosh, and there were things that had to be said.

"Yael," I began, "we need to talk."

"Not now," she replied, hunting and pecking on the keyboard with her right hand since her left was still healing.

"It's not even an hour-long flight."

"I said, not now."

"Look, you're not happy with me being here, with Shalit putting me on this team. That much is clear. But you owe me the courtesy of telling me why."

At this, she looked up. "The courtesy?" There was astonishment in her voice. "The courtesy? Seriously? Where do you get off, *Mr. McClaire?*"

"What are you talking about?" I said. "I thought we were friends."

"I thought so too."

"Then what happened?"

She just shook her head. "You've got a lot of nerve, Collins, you know that?"

"I've obviously done something to offend you. But I have no idea what. So just tell me."

"No, J. B., this isn't the time or the place. People's lives are at stake. So just give me some space and let me do my job."

No matter what I said, it was clear I wasn't going to break into the ice palace. I regretted it, but there was nothing I could do about it. Except perhaps one thing—keep talking. If she didn't want to tell me what was bothering her, fine. But I hadn't come halfway around the world to get shut down. We both had a job to do. She didn't like it, but that was tough. At this point, I didn't care. Shalit had brought me onto this team. He'd forced her to work with me, over her numerous—and vociferous—objections. So we'd better get started. I pulled out my grandfather's pocket watch. We'd be on the ground in twenty-two minutes.

"Did your team find any intercepts referencing *Isra* and *Mi'raj*?" I asked.

"No," she said, still typing.

"Did they find anything in Israeli databases indicating any terrorist detainees have referenced *Isra* and *Mi'raj* in recent months?"

She mumbled something.

"What's that?" I asked. "I'm sorry; I didn't catch that."

"*No*, they didn't," she replied.

"What about the U.S. or Interpol databases?"

"Nothing."

"What about historic connections between *Isra* and *Mi'raj* dates and acts of war or terrorism?" I pressed.

"What about them?"

"Did your team find any?"

"Not yet."

"But they've picked up chatter about coming strikes in the U.S.," I said.

That stopped Yael cold. She quit typing and looked at me.

"What do you mean?"

"The papal visit," I said. "The pope is coming to the States soon for Palm Sunday in Chicago, Easter in Los Angeles, then back to New York to address the U.N. Your guys are picking up chatter from ISIS operatives. You think Abu Khalif is plotting to take out the pope?"

Yael looked astonished. "Who told you that?"

"I'm on your team," I said. "I think you were supposed to."

"How did you find out?"

"I didn't," I said. "It was a guess. A pretty good one, as it turns out. Remind me to play poker with you someday."

She cocked her head to one side, then nodded and leaned back in her seat. "Touché," she said at last. "You saw the Reuters story out of Vatican

City that the pope had just accepted an invitation to return to the States. You saw the dates. You saw all the flurry of activity, and you guessed."

"Khalif doesn't even have to hit the pope—not directly," I said. "There are 69 million Catholics in the U.S. They're 22 percent of the population. Bomb a few dozen churches around the country—all soft targets with little or no security—and you'll create enough panic."

She looked at me long and hard, then closed her laptop. "Unfortunately, you're dead-on. Ari already briefed the PM, and the PM is going to call the president. Given everything that's unfolded in recent weeks in the States, I suspect the Vatican will call the trip off. But there's more."

"Like what?"

"We're picking up all kinds of chatter that ISIS is plotting major attacks against theme parks across the U.S.—Disney World, Disneyland, SeaWorld, Universal Studios, Kings Dominion, Six Flags, you name it."

"Spring break," I said.

"Exactly. Schools let students off for a week at a time, right?"

I nodded.

"But different schools in different states take different weeks?"

"Right."

"So all together it's about a five- to six-week period—and it's coming up fast," she said. "And while you're thinking about that, think about this: Three hundred million guests visit American theme parks, water parks, and amusement parks each year. These businesses are responsible for over $220 billion in overall economic impact and something like six hundred thousand jobs. If Khalif successfully targets that industry, he's going to do real and lasting damage to the American economy."

"When does the spring break season begin?" I asked. It had been at least two decades since I'd gone down to Miami or Daytona or Panama Beach.

"This year it starts on Saturday, March 12," she said.

That was only eleven days away.

PART
FIVE

64

* * *

"I thought we were going to Cairo," I said.

"We are," Yael replied.

"Then why are we flying southeast? Cairo is southwest."

"Because we're making a stop on the way."

Yael explained that the Sinai Peninsula had become infested with jihadists of all stripes. ISIS was there. As was al Qaeda, Islamic Jihad, members of Hamas, and factions of the Muslim Brotherhood, among others. And some of them, she said, had shoulder-mounted surface-to-air missiles.

"But I thought the Egyptians were rooting out the jihadists," I said.

"They are. And President Mahfouz is making progress. The Mossad even provides targeting assistance and other aid sometimes. Still, it's not safe for a business jet coming out of Israel to fly across the peninsula. There's too high a risk we'd be shot down, and I for one don't want to wander in the desert for forty years."

"Okay, so why aren't we arcing out over the Mediterranean?" I asked.

"We're heading to Aqaba first," she said, referring to Jordan's resort city at the northern tip of the Red Sea.

"Why?"

"We'll land. We'll refile our flight plan. We'll change our transponder number and even our tail number. *Then* we'll head to Egypt."

"I don't understand. Israel has a peace treaty with Egypt."

"True. And we have a close working relationship with Cairo on the security side. But it's not normal for business flights to emanate out of Tel Aviv and head straight to Cairo. Not at this time of year. Not in this weather. We don't want to draw attention."

"So, what? We're going to play an Arab couple flying to Cairo for a few days?"

"Canadian, actually," she said. "You're Michael McClaire. I'm your wife, Janet. We're from Edmonton—on holiday."

"No wonder you're not happy," I laughed.

"This wasn't my idea, believe me," she snapped.

"Oh, I believe you. This has Ari's name written all over it."

"Shut up, and just let me do my job."

"Fine," I said. "When do we land in Cairo?"

"We're not landing in Cairo."

"Isn't that where Hussam is?"

"Yes, but we're flying to Asyut."

"Why?"

"Again, security precautions. We should land around seven."

"And then?"

"We'll drive to Cairo."

"You and I are renting a car together?"

"Of course not," she said. "We'll have a driver."

"Well, won't this be interesting."

★ ★ ★

We landed a few minutes ahead of schedule.

By my watch, it was now 6:48 p.m. As we disembarked, we were met by two Mossad agents. Our driver and bodyguard was a tall and lean young man who never smiled and introduced himself as Mohammed, though I was certain that wasn't his real name. He struck me to be about Yael's age—early thirties. The Mossad's station chief in Cairo was a somewhat-older and somewhat–less fit guy who looked to be in his early forties, about my age. He introduced himself by the name Abdel.

I would never have suspected these men were Jewish or Israeli or worked for the Mossad. Both looked like the native-born Egyptians they were, and both spoke fluent, flawless, native Egyptian Arabic. Whoever had recruited them had done a remarkable job, and I had no doubt we were in good hands.

"What time do you think we should get to Cairo?" Yael asked as our large black Mercedes crossed a bridge over the Nile and flew along the Asyut Desert Highway.

"Just before eleven," the station chief said.

"So when do you think Michael here should reach out to Hussam and ask for a meeting?"

"I'd do it now," Abdel replied, turning to me. "Say you're having dinner with a source in Alexandria but you need to see him immediately, at Khachigian's insistence. Say you could meet him anywhere in Cairo at, I don't know, eleven thirty tonight. Say it's very important and very time sensitive."

"Why lie about being in Alexandria?" I asked. "The man is a former spymaster. Won't he be able to find out where we're coming from?"

"You'd better hope not. Because if he gets so much as a whiff that you're with the Mossad, you'll have big problems."

"I thought you all were close."

"Not that close, my friend," Abdel replied. "Not right now."

"But your prime minister went to Amman to sign a comprehensive peace deal with the Palestinians, with President Mahfouz's full approval," I protested. "When Amman was attacked, Mahfouz sent the head of Egyptian special forces to Jordan to be part of the coalition to rescue President Taylor. I was there. We both were. We met him. We spoke with him. Everyone was working so closely together."

I looked at Yael to back up my assessment, but she wouldn't—or couldn't. "That was then," she said. "Now everything's changed. After the slaughter in Dabiq, there was a tremendous backlash against Mahfouz and the government. People were angry that Egyptian forces had died fighting in Syria, of all places. Then Mahfouz made a mistake. When Yuval Eitan was sworn in as the new Israeli prime minister, Mahfouz immediately called to congratulate him, and it leaked."

"And what?" I asked. "I don't see the problem."

"It was too quick," Yael said. "Emotions were too raw. The street was red-hot, and Mahfouz looked like he was being too friendly with 'the Zionists.' It was like lighting a match and tossing it into a sun-scorched forest. The country erupted. Demonstrations in front of the Israeli embassy. People burning tires, cars, Israeli flags. It got ugly fast. I think it rattled Mahfouz and his team. They recalled their ambassador and made us pull ours out too. Mahfouz stopped taking the prime minister's calls. The defense ministers stopped talking. The spy chiefs stopped talking. It's been like that for almost two months."

"So despite the fact the Egyptians are scooping up dozens of ISIS fighters, you don't know what they know?" I asked.

"Just what we read in the *New York Times*, I'm afraid," Yael replied.

So here we are, I thought.

I looked back at Abdel. He nodded and glanced at my phone.

I made the call.

65

Unfortunately I got Walid Hussam's voice mail.

I left a message, then sent a text and an e-mail as well.

By the time we approached the outskirts of Cairo, I still hadn't heard back.

Yael told me to call Hussam again. Again I got voice mail. I was getting worried. Yael told the station chief to call his men who were trailing Hussam and find out what was going on.

Two minutes later we got the report. The former spy chief and his family had been at a party but were just now leaving the restaurant and getting into cabs. "They should be home soon," Abdel reported. "What do you want to do?"

"We proceed as planned," Yael said. "Take us to the hotel. There's not going to be a meeting tonight. We just have to hope we can arrange something tomorrow morning."

A few minutes later, we pulled up to the entrance of the Mena House, the oldest and most beautiful privately owned resort in all of Cairo. Sitting in the shadow of the Great Pyramid of Giza, it looked more like the grand palace of one of Egypt's ancient pharaohs than a modern luxury hotel.

Yael pulled a wedding ring out of her pocketbook and put it on her left hand. Then, to my surprise, she gave one to me. It fit perfectly. Shalit had thought of everything.

"I do," I deadpanned.

She didn't find me funny in the slightest.

Playing my part as doting husband, nevertheless, I opened my door and got out of the Mercedes. The rain had stopped, but the pavement was wet and the air was cold and the brisk winds made it feel colder still. I stepped around the back of the car, opened the door for my bride, and offered her my hand. This time she took it, smiling at me for the first time all day, and even kissed me gently on the cheek.

I knew she was only acting, but I liked the role, and I liked the scene.

We walked into the lobby with Yael leaning on my arm. We passed through the airport-like metal detector, and Yael put her pocketbook through the X-ray machine—standard operating procedure at hotels in the Middle East these days.

I went to the reception desk and checked us in as a couple and made sure to pay with one of the credit cards under the name McClaire. Abdel, playing the role of the dutiful valet, brought in our bags and helped us up to our room. He unlocked the door and motioned for us to wait. Then he drew a silencer-fitted pistol I had no idea how he got past security and entered the room without us. We watched as he checked the closets, the bathroom, under the bed, behind the curtains, and outside on the veranda. When he was certain no one was waiting for us, he wheeled in our luggage and handed Yael the pistol.

"Sweet dreams," he said without expression. "I'll be in the room across the hall. Mohammed will be in the room to your right. Let us know if you need anything."

Then he walked out the door and shut it behind him, and Yael and I were alone.

We looked around and found ourselves standing in an enormous suite overlooking the palm trees and the heated pool and the dazzling four-thousand-year-old pyramids rising high and proud and surreal into the night sky. I glanced at Yael, then at the king-size bed with its soft Egyptian cotton sheets and small chocolates wrapped in gold foil sitting atop the pillows.

"I'll take the floor," I said.

Some things were not in the script.

★ ★ ★

Suddenly I heard my phone buzz.

I'd fallen almost instantly into an uneasy sleep. Now, bleary-eyed and disoriented, I fumbled around in the darkness for my glasses and my phone. It was 11:53, and there was a text message from Hussam. He said he'd been at a family gathering and had just seen my e-mail. He apologized for not getting back to me sooner. Khachigian had been an old and dear friend, he said. He'd be happy to meet me. Was I available now?

I texted back saying of course and asking where to meet him.

A few moments later, Hussam sent back his address. I recognized it immediately. It was a high-rise building right on the Nile, close to the American embassy, close to the Hilton where I'd stayed a few months earlier to write the story that had started it all, the one revealing that the Islamic State possessed chemical weapons.

I found Yael asleep on the bed, still in her jeans and brown sweater. I woke her up, explained the situation, and then called the guys on their mobile phones. Ten minutes later, we were rolling.

★ ★ ★

"So, Mr. Collins, what brings you to Cairo on such urgent business?"

The introductions and small talk were over. So were the condolences for the deaths in my family and so many other Americans in recent weeks. So were the condolences I gave him on the loss of fifty-three Egyptian commandos who had participated in the daring—and disastrous—raid in Dabiq. We had covered it all, but it was time to get down to business.

Hussam poured us both cups of freshly brewed mint tea as we sat looking out over the twinkling lights of Egypt's largest city from his thirtieth-floor penthouse suite. It was now past one in the morning. Much of the capital was asleep. But I had clearly piqued Hussam's curiosity.

I was alone, of course, and operating under

my real name. That's how I'd known Khachigian, and that's how I'd initially reached out to Hussam. Yael had stressed again how important it was that I not be connected in any way, shape, or form to the Mossad. My alias, Michael McClaire, was to be used only when I needed to present a passport. Under no other circumstances should I mention that name.

Since Yael and her team needed to be able to hear everything I said and everything that was being said to me, I was wearing a wire that was beaming an encrypted version of our conversation down to a communications van parked a block from the apartment. That signal, in turn, was being transmitted directly and in real time to the Mossad safe house in Cairo, which was sending it back to the bull pen at Ramat David. There it was being digitally recorded and would be carefully analyzed by Gingy, Trotsky, Fingers, and Dutch.

I took a sip of the piping hot tea. It was too sweet for my liking, but it was laced with the caffeine I desperately needed, so I quickly took two more sips. Then I set the glass cup down and leaned forward in my chair. "Mr. Hussam, I came because I need a favor."

"Of course, Mr. Collins. Whatever can I do for you?"

"We had a mutual friend," I said, referring to Robert Khachigian.

"We did."

"And before our friend was murdered, you

tipped him off to the fact that ISIS had chemical weapons in their possession."

"Go on," he said, not confirming my instincts but certainly not denying them.

"That's why he was murdered," I continued. "Because ISIS decided he was a real and immediate threat."

Silence.

"You both instinctively understood what could happen if Abu Khalif were to gain control of weapons of mass murder."

Hussam sat stone-faced.

"And now your worst fears have been realized," I continued.

At this he nodded.

"This is not the end," I said.

"No," he replied. "I'm afraid not."

"He will kill many more unless he is stopped."

"That is why you've come?" he asked.

"Yes, Mr. Hussam," I said. "I need you to help me find him."

66

★ ★ ★

CAIRO, EGYPT

"Why me?" Hussam asked. "I've been out of the game a long time."

I shook my head. "Not that long. And clearly you're still wired in. That's how you knew ISIS had seized that base near Aleppo with the sarin gas precursors. That's how you saw the satellite and drone photos and heard the audio intercepts. That's how you became convinced of the gravity of the situation—because you'd seen the evidence. You gave it to Robert. Robert gave it to me. I put it on the front page of the *New York Times*. Suddenly the whole world knew, while you stayed under the radar the whole time."

Hussam did not respond immediately.

"Mr. Hussam, please understand—I don't blame you for his death. Not in the slightest. You absolutely did the right thing. Robert knew the risks, and he was more than willing to take them. Because he trusted you implicitly and because he loved his country and had devoted his life to keeping her safe."

Hussam rose and walked over to the sliding-glass door to the balcony.

"You just made one mistake," I continued. I saw his head turn ever so slightly. He was listening—carefully. "You calculated that once the story was out there, the president of the United States would take action, that he would order military strikes on ISIS forces in Syria and Iraq, that America would destroy a mortal enemy of the Sunni Arabs once and for all. Except it didn't happen. ISIS crossed the red line, but the American president refused to take action."

"No," Hussam said quietly, still staring out at the Nile. "You're right. I honestly never seriously considered the possibility he wouldn't act. I'm not sure I considered it at all."

I stood and walked over to him. "The world has taken a very dark turn, Mr. Hussam," I said softly. "The America you thought you knew—the friend of Egypt, the ally of peaceful Arabs, the superpower who confronts evil with courage and overwhelming might—I'm afraid that America is gone."

"You're saying it's just us now?" he asked.

I nodded but said nothing.

We stood there in his living room, silently looking out over a city of some eight million souls, a once great and mighty regional power—the world's only superpower for a long stretch in ancient times—now humbled and teeming and increasingly endangered. Then I said, "It was you, wasn't it? You're the one who e-mailed me and asked me to contact General El-Badawy."

He didn't respond.

"So call him," I said.

Hussam thought for a moment. Then, to my surprise, he walked to his kitchen, picked up a phone, and started dialing. "General, it's me. Yes. . . . I did. . . . I think so. When? . . . Fine—bye." He turned to me and sighed. "Okay. You have a driver?"

"He's waiting downstairs."

"Then let's go. It isn't far."

Encouraged, I asked to use the restroom while Hussam put on a sweater and a coat. He pointed me down the hallway. Locking the door behind me, I quickly sent a text to Yael and the team to confirm that we were heading to see General Amr El-Badawy, commander of Egypt's special forces. I thought it was likely El-Badawy had given Hussam the critical intel on ISIS that Khachigian had passed to me. If Cairo's intel on ISIS operations in Syria had been that good several months ago, they might very well be able to help us track down Abu Khalif now.

Then I asked Yael to forgive me for what I was about to do next.

Unbuttoning my shirt, I quickly ripped off the microphone that had been taped to my chest and the transmitter that had been secured to the small of my back. I tossed both into the toilet and flushed. I had no idea what that had just cost the Israeli government, nor did I care. I wasn't going to be caught wearing a Mossad wire when I entered the Defense Ministry—period.

I washed my hands, took a deep breath, stepped out of the bathroom, and turned off the light.

"Ready?" Hussam said, waiting for me in the vestibule.

"I am," I said, and we were off.

By the time we walked out the front door of the high-rise into the brisk night air, Mohammed was alone with the Mercedes, standing at attention and holding the rear door open. There was no sign of Yael or Abdel or the communications van, and for this I breathed a sigh of relief.

Hussam gave Mohammed the address and we began cruising down nearly empty city streets. Ten minutes later, however, we did not pull up to the Defense Ministry. Rather, we stopped at a small café in a suburb called Heliopolis, just blocks from the presidential palace. The café was closed. The lights were off and there was no movement inside. It was, after all, 2:17 in the morning. Yet Hussam insisted that this was the place.

Mohammed stopped the car and let us both out. Then Hussam guided me down a dimly lit alley, past two Dumpsters overflowing with putrid garbage, to a back door, where he knocked twice.

I could only imagine what Yael and the team were thinking. They had no way to see where I was, what I was doing, or whom I was about to meet. Nor did they have any way to listen in to my conversation, as per the explicit plan. But when the door opened, I knew I'd done the right thing. Three large bodyguards greeted us and pulled us inside. I was immediately given a pat-down that was, in a word, thorough. The wire would have been found instantly, and the meeting would have been blown. But in the absence of the wire, I was cleared and led down a hallway, with Hussam, to a small private dining room where the fifty-six-year-old general was waiting.

El-Badawy greeted me warmly and told his men to step outside and interrupt us only to bring in some coffee. When they left and closed the door, he bade Hussam and me to sit down.

"Thank you for coming, Mr. Collins," he began.

"Forgive me for not coming sooner," I replied. "I am so sorry for your loss."

"And I am for yours."

He nodded and tapped his right hand to his chest. "It is not easy to lose those you love."

"No, sir," I said. "It is not. Still, I wish I could have come sooner."

"Not at all," he said. "Obviously when I heard of what had happened to your family, I knew I could not expect you to come."

"So you gave the story to Bill Sanders," I said. "You told him about how closely Egypt is cooperating with Washington in the hunt for Abu Khalif."

"Perhaps," he said.

"You made the right call. Bill is an excellent journalist. The story made a big splash."

"Maybe," El-Badawy said, "but it's not true."

"Pardon?"

"You heard me. The story is fundamentally untrue."

"You're not helping the Americans?" I asked, suddenly puzzled.

"We want to," he said. "We're trying to. But the fact is . . ."

He stopped midsentence as someone knocked on the door. Coffee was brought in. Thick, strong Turkish coffee. With a plate of baklava. And a bowl of crisp red apples, bananas, and fresh pears. This wasn't going to be a quick meeting. We were going to be here for some time. When the agents were finished serving, they stepped back out of the room and again shut the door.

"Mr. Collins, are we off the record?" El-Badawy asked.

"I'm not here for a story."

"Then what are you here for?"

"I want your help."

"With what?"

"Finding the man who killed my family."

"The man who killed my men."

"The very same."

"And when you find him?"

"That's my business."

"Not if I'm helping you."

"Then let me be clear, General," I said. "Abu Khalif is not going to Guantánamo. Not if I can help it. If you help me find him, he's going to die."

67

★ ★ ★

"So you're not here on behalf of the *Times*?" the general asked.

"No," I said.

"Then you're working for Langley?"

"No, this is personal."

"But you and Carl Hughes are old friends, and he now runs the agency, right? By all measures, he's itching to take the gloves off and go after Khalif— whatever it takes, however long it takes, wherever the trail leads. And I'm supposed to believe he didn't send you?"

"He didn't."

"Does he know you're here?"

"I hope not."

"Then who are you working for?"

"I told you: this is personal."

"Don't insult me, Mr. Collins. You want my help? Then answer my questions. Somebody sent you. Somebody's helping you. Who?"

I'd known the question was coming. It was obvious. Inevitable. Still, I wasn't fully prepared to give a plausible if not entirely accurate answer.

Frankly I didn't know what to say. So I froze. I wasn't trained for this. All I knew was I had to keep the Mossad out of it. "I'm not at liberty to say."

It was all I could think of, and even to me it sounded lame.

"Suffice it to say," I quickly added, "that if we find Khalif, I have people who can take him out."

"People?" the general asked, his eyebrows raised.

"Yeah."

"What kind of people?"

I didn't reply.

"Editors from New York?" he pressed. "Reporters in tweed jackets?"

I kept silent.

"Hunters from Maine?"

I sipped the coffee and almost instantly felt the jolt of caffeine.

"The boys from Blackwater?" he probed. "Mossad? The Jordanians? You sure aren't working for the Saudis."

"General—" I began, but he cut me off.

"I know," he said. "You're not at liberty to say."

"No."

"Mr. Collins, do you remember what I said in the bunker, in Jordan, about Khalif's endgame?"

I remembered all right. "You said Khalif wants Mecca. He wants Medina. He wants Cairo. He still wants Amman. And that's just for starters."

"And do you remember what your guy, General Ramirez, said to me?"

"He said something like, 'I don't have time to

get sidetracked.' The president of the United States was being held by ISIS. We only had sixteen or seventeen hours to find him and rescue him before he was executed on YouTube."

"Correct. So it's understandable that Ramirez wasn't interested in the long-term goals of Abu Khalif at that moment. But I am. Khalif is indeed coming after Mecca. He is coming after Medina. But he's also coming after Cairo. He wants to do what the Brotherhood failed to do. He wants to make the world's largest Sunni city—and largest Arab country—part of his caliphate. I can never allow that to happen. But your government doesn't seem to get it. You've had 9/11. You've had the attacks in Amman. You've just had all these attacks inside the American homeland. And still your president thinks ISIS is less of an existential threat than climate change. How can he dare say such a thing?"

"That's why I'm here, General. That's why I need your help."

"And that's why I can't give it. Not if you aren't going to tell me who the information is for."

I was desperate. This meeting was sliding off the tracks. "General, you need to trust me," I said. "You gave me critically important information on ISIS, and I put it on the front page of the paper of record. You asked me—admittedly, indirectly—to do something that advanced your interests, and I did it."

"Because it advanced yours, too."

"And now I'm back. I didn't come on my own. You invited me. And even if you hadn't, Bob Khachigian sent me. Because he trusted me. And

I'm telling you: you can too. Give me what I need, and I'll make sure Abu Khalif pays for his crimes. I promise you that."

"Look, Mr. Collins, with all due respect, I invited you here as a reporter. You're not a spook, not an assassin. Don't get me wrong. I see what Khalif has done to your family. I know you're out for vengeance, and I don't blame you."

"Not vengeance," I said. "Justice."

"Call it what you want, but if you're not here on behalf of the Central Intelligence Agency, then you can't possibly assure me that if I help you track down Khalif, you'll be able to bring him to justice. That's impossible. You'd never get close to him— not you or the mercenaries you've hired."

"I haven't hired any mercenaries."

"Then they've hired you—or the Mossad recruited you, or the GID did," he speculated, referring to Jordan's General Intelligence Directorate.

"Don't be ridiculous, General," I retorted. "You know I'm not Jewish. How could I have been recruited by the Mossad?"

It was a deceptive question, but it was true in a way. After all, I hadn't been recruited by the Mossad. I'd volunteered.

"So you're working for King Abdullah," he concluded.

I shook my head. "I've met King Abdullah. I admire him enormously. I think he's doing a remarkable job under horrific conditions. And I think if the cards had been dealt a little differently, he'd be leading the charge to get Khalif. But his hands are full just now rebuilding his country."

"Which is why he's outsourcing the job to you."

"You're fishing, General, and you're wrong. I don't begrudge you asking. You have to ask. But I can't tell. But that doesn't mean we can't work together to find Khalif and bring him to justice. I'm not just asking for your help. I'm offering to help you. I know this man. I've met him. I've studied him. And I truly think we can help each other."

"I'm sorry, Mr. Collins."

The general took a final sip of coffee, then stood. It was over. I'd blown it. My only hope now was to tell El-Badawy about my connections to Mossad. It was my only shot. It could backfire. But wasn't it worth trying?

"Wait," Hussam suddenly said in Arabic, standing as well. "Listen to me. Collins found Jamal Ramzy. He found Abu Khalif once. He found the president. Maybe he really can find Khalif again."

"He's just a reporter," the general shot back.

"Maybe so, but his instincts are spot-on. You know it. That's why you invited him here."

"Be serious. He didn't use his own instincts—he had help."

The general moved toward the door, but Hussam physically blocked his path. *"And what do you think he's asking for now?"* he asked, directly in the general's face. "Look, Amr, this guy is good, and we need him. What's the worst thing that could happen? We work with him. We hunt for Khalif together. If he finds him, maybe you and your men get to go kill him. Imagine what that would do for the country, for Egypt's standing in the world. Remember, Wahid personally tasked us with getting this done. We can't just blow it off. We need to try. I'm not saying it's going to work. But it's clear the White House isn't going to help us. The Kremlin isn't going to help us. This is it. This is our last play."

They were arguing in heated, rapid-fire Arabic. I wasn't catching all of it, but what I did get was chilling. Both men believed that what had happened in Amman and in Washington was going to happen in Cairo—Abu Khalif and his forces were coming to kill Egyptians, in large numbers, unless someone stopped him.

What's more, it was quickly becoming clear that the directive to find me and bring me into the mix had come straight from the top. Hussam wasn't out of the game after all. And he wasn't simply an old friend and confidant of the commander of the Egyptian special forces. Formally or informally, Hussam was working for Wahid Mahfouz, the president of Egypt.

And I was their last option.

68

The next thing I knew, I was being hustled out the back door of the café.

We spilled out into a deserted alley, under the hazy glow of a streetlamp. Two black SUVs awaited us, doors open, armed guards at the ready. It was raining again—a biting, sleety, gusty mist. I turned up the collar of my coat as Hussam and I hurried into the second vehicle. The general and his men piled into the first. A moment later, we were peeling down empty streets. The windows were tinted. I couldn't see much. I certainly couldn't see the black Mercedes or the communications van anywhere, and as much as that worried me, it had to be driving Yael crazy.

"Text your driver," Hussam said, apparently noticing me looking in both directions and craning my neck to see out the back. "Tell him to stay put."

"Where are we going?"

"I can't say."

"So what should I tell him?" I asked.

"Tell him you'll stay in touch—you just have

a quick detour. When we're done, this driver will drop us both back at the café."

I did as he suggested, increasingly sure where we were headed.

A moment later came the reply.

U safe?

That had to be Yael, not Mohammed.

Yes, I wrote back. **All good.**

Lost contact.

I know. I'm sorry.

Boss very upset.

Yes, I wrote. **Gotta go.**

I put away the phone and noticed Hussam eyeing me, but he didn't say anything more.

Just then we pulled off the main street and passed through a heavily guarded security checkpoint. Soldiers in full combat gear atop armored personnel carriers gripped .50-caliber machine guns while other soldiers in ceremonial garb stood erect and saluted. Seconds later, without any words being spoken, the steel barriers ahead of us were lowering into the pavement and a massive steel gate was electronically opening.

"Welcome to Al-Ittihadiya Palace, Mr. Collins," Hussam said.

I had never been to the presidential residence in Cairo, but I'd heard of it. In the early 1900s, this immense building was the largest and most luxurious hotel in all of Africa. At the peak of its private glory, kings and queens, presidents and prime ministers, movie stars and business tycoons from all over the world stayed here. Today it was the Egyptian White House.

We followed the general's SUV around to the back of the monumental structure. I glimpsed the gorgeous dome, beautifully illuminated by a large flood lamp. As we pulled up to a rear entrance and were led into the foyer, the thought occurred to me that this had never actually been the palace of a Middle Eastern potentate. More likely, it was what some European architect had imagined such a palace should look like.

Inside, I was again carefully searched, and I again found myself grateful I had ditched the wire, no matter how angry Shalit was.

The interior of the palace was even grander and more exquisite than the exterior. An aide met the general, Hussam, and me at the security center and walked us down marble corridors, each wall covered with ancient artwork, swords, and various archaeological artifacts. Then we took a right into another labyrinth of corridors adorned with framed photographs of President Wahid Mahfouz being sworn into office, Mahfouz speaking to the masses, Mahfouz meeting with the king of Saudi Arabia, Mahfouz meeting with the emirs of Dubai and Abu Dhabi, Mahfouz meeting with the presidents of Russia, China, and India, and on and on it went. What I didn't see—though maybe I just missed it—was Mahfouz with President Taylor.

We reached another security checkpoint. When we were cleared, we were ushered into an enormous office, at least two stories high and a hundred feet long. The walls were wood paneled and lined with grand bookshelves, and above us hung not one but two enormous crystal chandeliers. I had barely looked around when a half-dozen bodyguards entered the room. The general and Hussam immediately stiffened, and there—entering from a hidden door behind one of the bookshelves—was President Wahid Mahfouz.

"Mr. Collins, thank you for coming to Egypt," he said, shaking my hand vigorously and with a warmth I had not expected from a man so routinely attacked in the media as a ruthless authoritarian. "It's a pleasure to finally meet you. I've read most of your work, especially over the past year. I am a great admirer."

"Thank you, Mr. President—that is very kind," I said. "I just wish more of it was good news rather than bad."

"So do we all, Mr. Collins," he replied. "So do we all."

69

* * *

I knew Mahfouz had an agenda.

It was obvious from the way Hussam and El-Badawy had been vetting me. They'd been determining whether I merited this meeting. Clearly Hussam thought I did. The general wasn't so sure. So undoubtedly it had been the president's call, and he'd decided yes. It was a risk, to be sure. We were about to discuss very sensitive matters, matters the Egyptians most certainly did not want splashed across the front page of the *New York Times*.

Complicating matters further, the editors of the *Times* had not exactly been kind to Mahfouz and his administration. An editorial the previous summer had charged that "human rights abuses under Egyptian president Wahid Mahfouz have reached new highs" and that "thousands of Egyptians have been arrested and imprisoned without due process, without fair trials, and some have been tortured and killed." Another recent editorial urged the White House to "increase pressure on the Mahfouz government," possibly even suspending the $1.3 billion in aid the U.S. annually gave to Egypt.

I was not on my paper's editorial board, of course. Nor did my views always reflect theirs. I wasn't paid to opine. I was paid to report. In print, I had always kept my opinions to myself and striven to be as fair and neutral as humanly possible. But would Mahfouz know that? Wasn't his view of me likely to be tainted by the opinions of my employer? Personally, I *was* concerned about allegations of human rights abuses in Egypt, of course. But I wanted this man to know I was grateful that he and the Egyptian military had, in fact, seized control of their country back from the Muslim Brotherhood. I was glad he'd worked so hard to restore order in the streets and to get the economy moving again, sluggish though it still was. I was glad he was building closer security ties with the Jordanians, the Israelis, the Saudis, and the emirates. And I was glad he was taking ISIS—and all of the Islamic extremists—as seriously as he was.

A few years earlier, Mahfouz had delivered an address at Al-Azhar University, the Harvard of Sunni Islam, located in the heart of Cairo. The speech was absolutely riveting, unlike anything I'd heard from any other Muslim leader. He'd stood before the intellectual and spiritual hierarchy of the Sunni world and demanded that they make serious, radical, sweeping reforms. He had called for a religious revolution.

"It is inconceivable to me that the world should see Islam as a religion of violent jihad, extremism, murder, mayhem, beheadings, and wanton cruelty," he'd bellowed before the stunned gathering of clerics, scholars, and students. "This is not Islam! Yet the extremists are making the world believe this is who we are. On Judgment Day, you will have to answer for what you did and did not teach. You imams are responsible to teach peace. Show the world that our religion is made for peace, not for war. The burden is on you!"

I couldn't say firsthand whether the human rights abuses the *Times* and many others were writing about were as bad as portrayed or whether they were being exaggerated by media. Was Mahfouz using harsh and heavy-handed tactics to restore calm in a country nearly undone by the Brotherhood? I didn't know, but I wasn't about to bring such matters up. They were important, to be sure. But they were not my immediate concern. Right now I had to stay focused.

But before I could say anything at all, the president cut me off.

"Mr. Collins, I've asked you to come because I want your help," Mahfouz began.

I kept quiet and listened carefully.

"When I was elected by the people of this great country, I thought nothing could endanger Egypt and the Islamic world more than the Muslim Brotherhood and the extremist rhetoric they were preaching and exporting all over the region and the world. But since taking office, I have come to believe that what Abu Khalif is doing and saying is far, far worse."

70

I nodded for the president to continue.

"This notion that mankind can somehow speed up the coming of the Muslim messiah—the Mahdi—and hasten the establishment of Allah's kingdom on earth—this is foolish, dangerous talk," Mahfouz said. "Yet this seed has taken root in many Muslim men, and not a few women, and it is bearing poisonous fruit. This apocalyptic thinking would be toxic enough on its own, of course, but the way Khalif teaches it, the way he and his men practice it, is pure evil. Khalif has convinced himself that committing outright genocide is the surest and most effective way to speed up the coming of the caliphate. This notion should be dismissed by all Muslims as sheer lunacy. Yet it has metamorphosed into a lethal virus. The number of ISIS-related Egyptian deaths in the past few days alone is evidence of that. Khalif's sick ideology is spreading—rapidly—across the region, across the planet, and we must stop it before it's too late."

"I agree," I said.

"And ISIS is not the only threat," he continued.

"The Iranians—at least the Ayatollah and his inner circle—they, too, want to bring about the End of Days. Yes, they want to resurrect the glory of the Persian Empire. But what they really want is to hasten the establishment of the caliphate and the appearance of the Mahdi. They come at it all from a different angle, of course. Their theology and eschatology is not precisely the same as ISIS, though it might look the same to you, to the West. But that is not the point. The point is they are just as dangerous. They have a whole country, a whole nuclear industry, and a missile-building complex. And now—thanks to your country—they have international legitimacy and another $100 billion to make mischief with. I know you've come to talk about ISIS. I know your focus is Khalif. But you must understand how I look at the world. The ayatollahs threaten Egypt and our way of life. They've said as much. They're not hiding it. One of the Supreme Leader's top advisors just said the other day, 'We have captured three Arab capitals. We're working on a fourth. And we have another in our sights.' What do you think those three capitals are, Mr. Collins?"

"Beirut, Damascus, and Baghdad."

"Precisely. And do you know the fourth capital Tehran is trying so hard to capture?"

"Sana'a," I said, referring to the largest city in Yemen, "but I'm guessing you fear Cairo is next."

"Cairo and Amman—they want us both," Mahfouz said. "But ultimately we are not their primary objective. Whom do you think they want most of all?"

"Jerusalem," I said.

The Egyptian leader shook his head. "No. Remember, Israel is only the Little Satan to them. You—Washington, America—you are the Great Satan, and they're coming after you. ISIS and Khalif have already struck. The ayatollahs want to be next."

"So what are you doing to stop them?" I asked. "And how can we work together?"

"Egypt is facing the most serious internal and external threats in our modern history, but there are limits on how much we can do. We have our hands full with the jihadists in the Sinai. We are fighting them, and we are gaining ground. But the situation there is far worse than most people realize. Your president isn't giving us enough arms and ammunition. I have asked repeatedly. He has repeatedly said no. What's more, your own newspaper's editorial writers are urging him to cut off American aid to us."

So he did read the *Times* editorial page.

"But back to Khalif," Mahfouz said. "We aren't just killing ISIS jihadists on the battlefield. We're capturing them. We're inducing them to talk to us, to tell us what they know. Don't ask me how. Just know that we are developing solid, actionable intelligence on Khalif and his forces in real time."

Now we were getting down to it. I could feel my heart pounding. This was really happening. I was exhausted. I was grieving the deaths of my mother and nephew. I was battling clinical depression and craving a drink so badly it was physically painful. But I was also in Cairo. Inside the presidential palace. Shalit and Yael had told me exactly what to ask for if I got to this moment. "Find the couriers," they had said. "Ask about the Baqouba brothers."

Tariq Baqouba, recently killed by an American drone strike, had been the third highest ranking man in the ISIS hierarchy. His brothers, Faisal and Ahmed, were both trusted deputies. Yael suspected one of them—probably Faisal—was a courier, possibly *the* courier for the ISIS leader himself. If we could find Faisal and Ahmed, she had argued, we would find Khalif.

"Do you have anything on either or both of the Baqouba brothers?" I asked. I needed something concrete. Something I can use. A phone number. A location. And I was about to hit pay dirt.

"Of course," Mahfouz said. "I'll give you everything we have, on one condition."

My stomach tightened. "And what's that, Mr. President?"

"You need to tell me whom you're working with, or I'm afraid there's nothing more I can say."

71

I could hardly blame him.

Who was I that he should give me state secrets when I wouldn't even tell him whom I was working for or what exactly I was going to do with the information? This was highly classified intelligence that some Egyptian agent might very well have paid the ultimate price to secure. Still, I needed to know.

"Mr. President, I completely understand your position," I began, trying to build trust while finding a way through this minefield. "But I'd be grateful if you would keep in mind a few things—"

Mahfouz cut me off. He wasn't curt. I can't say he was impolite. But he made it clear this wasn't a negotiation. "We aren't in the souk, Mr. Collins," he said calmly. "Even if we were, you want to buy something, but you have no currency and no credit. You want to make a purchase you can't pay for."

"I realize that, sir, but—"

Mahfouz held up his hand. "Tell me something, Mr. Collins. How did you arrive in my country?"

The question jarred me as it seemed to come out of nowhere. "Why do you ask, Mr. President?"

"I find it curious that we have no record of a James Bradley Collins landing at Cairo International Airport, or any airport in Egypt, in the last two months."

I felt as if the wind had been knocked out of me. Suddenly I wished Yael and Shalit were listening to this and feeding me answers. I wasn't trained for this. I was tempted to blurt out the truth right then and there, to tell Mahfouz that I'd gone to the Mossad, that Ari Shalit wanted to work with him—in the shadows if necessary—to bring down Khalif before it was too late. I was sure it would be well received. But the stakes were too high to violate the confidence of my only allies and patrons at the moment.

"You obviously slipped into my country with false papers," Mahfouz said. "Which, I'm sure I don't have to tell you, is illegal. You have committed a crime. Perhaps I should just lock you up and then wait to see who—if anyone—would come to bail you out. You're walking a dangerous line, Mr. Collins. So let me remind you. This is not a game."

"I understand," I said, my mouth bone-dry.

"Good."

"If you'll give me some time, Mr. President," I said, desperately trying to recover, "I'll confer with my colleagues and see if they will agree to let me share their identity with you."

The president stood, and the rest of us followed suit.

"I will give you till noon," Mahfouz said. "Walid is your contact. Let him know what your friends decide."

★ ★ ★

Dawn was rising as Hussam and I headed back to the café in silence.

Morning rush hour started early in Cairo. It wasn't in full swing yet by any means, but with the rain, which was coming down harder now, and the growing traffic, the drive took us longer than it might normally have. The silence was awkward, and I was glad when we turned onto Baghdad Street, for I knew we were now just a block from our destination.

I pulled out my phone and texted Yael and Mohammed that we would be there momentarily. A large delivery truck partially blocked our path. Annoyed, our driver laid on the horn, but two men were wheeling large crates of something into an open garage. They weren't going to be getting out of our way anytime soon. We eased around the truck and finally reached the café.

As we pulled to a stop, the retired spy chief broke the ice, telling me he wouldn't need a ride back home. The president wanted him to return to the palace. I assumed they were about to have a debriefing. I could only imagine what they were going to say. As one of the bodyguards opened the door for me, I thanked Hussam for his time. "If it were up to me, I would have already told you whom I'm working with. It makes sense. But . . ."

"You have your orders," he said graciously. "We all do. You must be a loyal soldier. There is nothing more important than loyalty, James. Nothing."

"Life was simpler when it was just me and the Gray Lady."

"Maybe so. Just do what you have to do—and let me know by noon."

"No hard feelings?" I asked.

"Of course not," he said. "None at all."

The next moment, I spotted the Mercedes. It was parked a block down from the café. Mohammed stood in a doorway, smoking a cigarette and waiting for me. I started to get out. But Hussam grabbed my shoulder.

"What is it?" I asked, turning back to him. "What's wrong?"

"You asked about the Baqouba brothers," he whispered.

"What about them?"

"They're the key," he said. "Whatever you decide to do with us, that's fine—but I want you to know you're on the right trail. That's all I can say for now. I hope that's enough."

I looked in his eyes. He seemed sincere, like a father giving a son a gift. I sensed I could trust him. "Thank you," I said. "Stay safe."

"Inshallah," he replied. "You, too."

I turned toward the Mercedes and motioned for Mohammed to start the car. He quickly dropped his cigarette, stamped it out with his shoe, jumped in the car, and started the engine. I looked up and down Baghdad Street but didn't see the communications van. I had no idea where Yael was. I hoped she was close. I didn't want to debrief her by phone, but the forty-five-minute drive back to the hotel was too long to wait. There were decisions to be made, and they wouldn't be made by her. I doubted even Shalit had the authority to make this call. I guessed the prime minister himself would have to be informed.

As I approached, Mohammed got out and moved around the hood to open the rear passenger door for me. Thunder rumbled in the distance. It was as cold here as it was back in Israel.

But as I crossed the street, I suddenly saw a flash of light to my left. My first thought was lightning. But it was too low, too isolated. And then came the massive concussion. The SUV I'd just stepped out of—the one Hussam was still in—exploded. It flipped through the air and came back to earth with a deafening crash. The resulting shock wave sent me soaring. I smashed into the side of the Mercedes. Then I heard the distinctive whoosh of a second rocket-propelled grenade and once again felt the earsplitting explosion and the searing, scalding fireball.

I couldn't move, couldn't think, couldn't breathe. I couldn't hear or see. Thick, black, acrid smoke filled the sky, filled my eyes, and the last thing I heard was the *rat-a-tat-tat* of machine-gun fire.

And then everything went black.

72

★ ★ ★

When I came to, I was lying on the wet pavement, covered in glass.

My clothing was soaked and torn. My eyes stung. My ears were ringing. I had no idea how long I'd been out. As I pulled myself to my knees and then to my feet, I saw that all the windows in the Mercedes had been blown out. Then I saw Mohammed sprawled out on the sidewalk, his body ripped to shreds, a pool of crimson surrounding him. I stumbled over to him and checked his pulse. He was gone.

I looked around and stared at the carnage before me. The roaring, flaming wreckage of the SUV. The charred bodies of Hussam, his driver, and the bodyguard. The gaping, jagged holes where the windows of the café had been. They'd all been blown to bits, and the building was on fire. It was then that I realized I couldn't have been unconscious very long. There were no police cars on the scene, no fire trucks or ambulances. But they'd be here any moment.

Looking to my right down Baghdad Street,

I noticed the delivery van was gone, and a chill abruptly ran down my spine. Did Abu Khalif somehow know I was here? Had he sent jihadists to kill me before I found him? How was that possible? How could he have known? Was one of the Israelis a mole? Someone in Mahfouz's office? That didn't seem likely, but there were still only a handful of people who even knew I was here. That meant there were only a handful of possible suspects, and four of them were dead.

I felt my phone vibrating in my pocket. I took the call, but whoever it was, I couldn't hear what they were saying. A moment later a text message came in. It was from Yael.

Get out of there now! she insisted. **Meet at the safe zone—go!**

My head was pounding. My right knee was bleeding. I felt foggy and disoriented. I knew we'd discussed a rendezvous point, a safe zone, just in case something went wrong. But right now it was all a blur. I couldn't remember the name. I couldn't remember the address. But I had no time to think about that. I had to get moving. Yet I couldn't leave Mohammed there. I couldn't leave the body of a fallen Mossad officer on a Cairo side street.

I opened the back door of the Mercedes. Then I picked up the six-foot-one, two-hundred-pound Israeli and wrestled him into the backseat, even as a crowd was beginning to form. As I shut the door, I noticed that his pistol—equipped with a silencer—had fallen out of his holster. It was sitting in the gutter, in a puddle, and just the sight of it—along with the blood on the sidewalk, and the blood that was now all over me and all over the car—triggered a shot of adrenaline through my entire system.

I grabbed the pistol and raced for the driver's side. I could hear again—not perfectly, but it was slowly coming back. Sirens were approaching from multiple directions. Behind the wheel, I gunned the engine and took off, leaving the growing crowd of onlookers and knowing they were all witnesses.

As I barreled down Baghdad Street heading for El-Orouba Street, a major thoroughfare, I knew people had seen me. They'd seen my face. They'd seen the car, shot up with machine-gun fire. They'd seen me put a body in the backseat. And someone had surely taken down the license plate number. Someone always did.

I raced up the ramp, onto the highway and into thickening traffic. I tromped on the accelerator, weaving from lane to lane when I could, but knowing all the while I was running the risk of attracting the attention of the police. I couldn't afford to be stopped. Not the way this car looked. Not with who I had in the backseat. Not with the information I had to get to Yael.

The phone rang. I didn't want to answer it as I raced westward onto Salah Salem Street, heading for the Nile. But it was Yael and she could tell me where I was supposed to be going. So I put the phone on speaker and dropped it into the cup holder by the gearshift, knowing I would need both hands on the wheel from this point forward.

"You've got a tail," she yelled before I could even say hello.

"What are you talking about?"

"You're on Salah Salem, heading west, right?"

"Right."

"Someone's following you—a silver Audi—it's eight, nine cars back and it's coming up fast."

"How do you know?"

"'Cause Abdel and I are six or seven cars behind him."

"Cops?" I asked.

"No," she said.

"Secret police?"

"I doubt it, not with that car."

"Then who is it?"

"I have no idea, but you need to lose them."

"I can't," I said. "You need to get them off me—now."

I glanced in my rearview mirror and then in my side mirror. Yael was right. Whoever was in the Audi, they were coming up way too fast. I shifted into a higher gear, broke left and roared around a dump truck, then cut back to the right. In the process two other cars braked hard to miss hitting me, which temporarily blocked the Audi's view of me as well as its approach. But I doubted it was going to be enough.

Edging to my right, I checked my side mirror again. I could see the Audi. It was only five cars back but boxed in between a Ford Expedition and a large moving van. This was my chance. I pulled onto the shoulder and then hit the gas.

Fifteen seconds later, I reached an off-ramp and took it.

"No, no, don't get off!" Yael screamed over the speakerphone. *"What are you doing?"*

"I had to," I yelled back. *"They're gaining on me."*

"And we're gaining on them!" she countered. *"Now you'll be on smaller streets. More traffic. More lights. Get back on the highway."*

I braked and downshifted as I roared down the ramp and came to a dead stop. Yael was right. The traffic was brutal in both directions. Everything was gridlocked. Fear threatened to overwhelm me.

"I don't know what to do," I said. "I'm stuck."

"Don't worry," Abdel said into the phone. "I don't think they saw you."

"You sure?"

"Either way, they're trapped in the left lane. No wait—"

"What?" I yelled.

He swore loudly.

"What?"

"They just shot at the Ford. The Ford's braking. They're smashing into the Ford, pushing around him. They saw you. They're heading for the off-ramp."

I was still not moving. Traffic was at a standstill. And then I saw the Audi barreling down the ramp, coming straight for me. Inside were two men, both wearing black hoods. And they would be on top of me any second.

I should have panicked, but instead I had an idea. I grabbed for Mohammed's silenced pistol on the seat beside me. I would shoot these two just before they reached me, and that would be the end of it. But the pistol wasn't there. Frantically I searched everywhere, then realized it had slid off the passenger seat and onto the floor. I could see it, but with my seat belt on, I couldn't reach it.

73

* * *

I was out of time.

The Audi smashed into the back of the Mercedes at full speed. This should have driven me into the Volkswagen van that had been idling directly ahead of me, but at that moment traffic started moving again. The VW turned right and got clear just in time. I went straight ahead, but instead of folding up like an accordion from impacts on both sides—crushing me in the process—my Mercedes went ricocheting through the intersection.

I clipped the back of one car and the front of a pickup. But the velocity from being hit so hard from behind still sent me hurtling completely through the intersection and up the on-ramp on the other side. How the driver's side air bags weren't triggered, I had no idea, but I hit the gas and the Mercedes poured back onto Salah Salem Street, leaving the Audi trapped by the new chaos its driver had just created.

I could hear Yael and Abdel cheering over the speakerphone, but they were abruptly drowned out by the sound of automatic gunfire. At the same time, I could hear the Audi smashing its way through the intersection, and when I glanced in my rearview mirror, I saw the Audi surging back onto the thoroughfare behind me and one of the terrorists aiming an AK-47 at me.

For the moment, I was a good ten to twelve cars ahead of them, but they were fighting hard to close the gap. I pushed the accelerator down and zigzagged through the morning rush-hour traffic at forty, fifty, sixty miles per hour. Often I was on one shoulder or the other. But the guys in the Audi weren't just keeping up—they were gaining. I roared past the National Military Museum on my right and an enormous mosque on my left. Still the Audi kept coming, and now Yael and Abdel were nowhere to be seen, stuck in the mess the Audi had left behind.

Traffic was getting worse. My speed was dropping from fifty to forty to thirty miles per hour and then all I could see ahead of me was a sea of red brake lights. When I looked again, the Audi was only six cars back and coming on strong. Fearing I would soon be trapped, I again broke right at an off-ramp and began weaving through various side streets at ever-increasing speeds.

The Audi never missed a beat. My pursuers were tracking my every move as I increasingly feared for my life. These guys clearly knew who I was. They weren't going after Hussam. They'd been coming after me. When they saw me sprawled out on the street by the café, they must have initially thought they'd done their job. They couldn't have known I'd only been knocked unconscious. But someone had told them after I'd gotten up and driven away. Someone in that crowd. And now they were closing in for the kill.

"Where are you? We can't see you," Yael said over the speakerphone.

I had absolutely no idea. Office buildings and restaurants and parks and street signs were blowing by too fast for me to process, much less report them. I was trying not to get sideswiped by the traffic around me, and that was increasingly becoming a fool's errand.

Up ahead the street I was on was ending. Railroad tracks lay dead ahead. But there was no crossing. Not here. Just a cement wall on the other side of the tracks. I hit the brakes and pulled hard to the right, spilling into oncoming traffic and going the wrong way up a one-way street. I laid on the horn and flashed my lights as I wove my way forward.

Cars, trucks, and motorcycles were swerving to get out of my way and then, all of a sudden, the road completely cleared. I figured there must be red lights ahead. In another sixty or ninety seconds they would turn green, and then cars and trucks and motorcycles would be hurtling straight for me once again.

A freight train was now speeding past on my left. I was picking up speed on this clear straightaway—forty, fifty, sixty miles per hour—so I was slightly gaining on the train. But the Audi was gaining on me. They were a mere three car lengths behind me. Then two. And soon they were right on my tail and about to smash into me.

Then I heard something beeping. I glanced down at the dashboard and saw the gas gauge on empty. Just my luck. I'd made it through half of Cairo with ISIS butchers on my tail, and it was all going to come to an end because I ran out of gas. It had to be a leak, I knew. There was no way the Mossad guys had forgotten to top off the diesel before rolling out on this mission. Which meant I'd been leaking fuel since coming under machine-gun fire at the café.

A single spark, and the whole car could erupt.

I heard the train's horn blow twice. It was a sharp, piercing sound—the sound of danger, the sound of warning. And that's when I saw the rail-road crossing ahead. Now I knew why the traffic was stopped. It wasn't for a traffic light. They were stopped for an oncoming train.

Less than a quarter mile ahead of me the road veered slightly left and crossed the tracks at an angle, and I could see the gates were down. I could see the lights flashing, and I knew I had a choice to make. Floor it and try to outrun this thing. Or slam on the brakes and get hit from behind by the Audi, a collision that could easily ignite what leaking fuel was left and blow me to kingdom come. And that's if I was lucky. More likely, if I could even come to a full stop before the crossing and not get boosted onto the tracks by the Audi, the ISIS guys following me would capture me and take me back to Abu Khalif. That would be a fate far worse than death, I knew, so the choice was clear.

As the train horn blew two more times, I pushed the accelerator to the floor. I was doing nearly seventy miles per hour as I pulled ahead of the locomotive—half a car length, then a full car length. Better still, I was pulling away from the Audi. Not much. Not enough. They were still far too close. But rather than right on my bumper they were about a car length back, and then two.

I looked ahead at the crossing. It was coming up fast. Again came the blast of the train's horn— and not just once or twice. This time the engineers laid on the horn and wouldn't stop. I glanced in my side mirror. I could see their faces. Looks of sheer terror. They could see what I was trying to do. They were sure I was suicidal. But there was nothing they could do to stop me, and there was certainly nothing they could do to stop their engine and the hundred fully loaded freight cars they were pulling.

A split second later, the moment of truth arrived.

At the speed I was going, the rubber-coated crossing and the slight rise over the tracks sent the Mercedes airborne. In my periphery I could see and feel and hear and even smell the rush of the oncoming locomotive. But I cleared it. It was close. Far too close. But somehow I cleared and slammed down on the pavement on the other side, metal crunching, sparks flying, and then I hit the brakes and closed my eyes. The car—shuddering, smoking, skidding, weaving—finally slammed into the side of an idling but empty city bus.

The air bags exploded. But the Mercedes didn't. Not yet, anyway.

The interior of the car instantly filled with

smoke. Coughing, choking, gasping for air, I groped about blindly for the firearm and my phone. I somehow found both and kicked open the driver's-side door and crawled out of the wreckage. Gripping the silencer-equipped pistol in hand, I turned back to confront my pursuers.

But then I saw the Audi—or what was left of it. Flaming chunks of German engineering were raining down from the sky. The Audi was gone. The men inside it had been vaporized. What's more, the train hadn't derailed. It had survived, and for the moment, so had I.

74

* * *

A crowd was gathering.

That was a problem. The police were already on their way. I could hear the sirens approaching. There were witnesses. They would be interviewed. The Mossad agent's body would be found in the backseat of the Mercedes. And I might be found too.

I pushed my way through the crowd, limping and in pain, yelling in Arabic for people to get out of my way but careful to keep my head down and avoid eye contact. Without stopping, I made sure the pistol's safety was on and then shoved the gun into my belt and pulled my shirt over it. Then I made my way to a subway station. I hustled down the stairs as quickly as I could, mopping sweat from my brow and trying desperately to suck in fresh air and get hold of my spiking heart rate.

I knew countless people had just seen me go into the subway station and would therefore point the police in my direction, so I hobbled my way to the other end of the station and took an escalator back up to ground level. The moving stairs ended inside an office building, out of the direct sight of anyone who was gathering around the crash. Immediately I bolted out the building's back doors, crossed a busy street clogged with rush-hour traffic, and passed through the lobbies and back doors of three more office buildings and then a shopping plaza. At that point I flagged down a taxi, jumped inside, thrust a handful of cash into the driver's hand, and told him to get me to the campus of Cairo University. Speaking in Arabic, I promised the man a very generous tip if he could get me there quickly, and he readily complied.

Soon we were weaving through traffic and crossing the Abbas Bridge, heading west. I texted Yael, telling her I was alive and where I was headed. Seconds later, she texted back with the address of a supermarket on the north side of the campus. I relayed the information to the driver and asked how long it would take to get there. He said ten to fifteen minutes, depending on traffic, and I shot that information back to Yael.

I'm on my way, she said. **I'll be there in no more than half an hour.** Then she gave me exact instructions about what to do when I arrived. **Pay the driver in cash. Go directly into the supermarket café, but don't order. Don't sit down. Head straight for the men's room. Step into a stall. Lock the door. Turn off the ringer on your phone. Wait there. And whatever you do, don't attract any more attention.**

Everything took longer than promised. The taxi driver's estimate was way off. So was Yael's. But I did as I was told, and eventually Abdel met me in the men's room. I gave him the gun, and he gave me a clean, dry set of clothes and a new pair of leather shoes. I washed my hands and face and changed quickly as he stuffed what I had been wearing into a duffel bag and rushed me through a back door into an alley, where Yael was waiting in the van.

Moments later, with Abdel at the wheel, we were working our way through traffic. Abdel was careful to maintain the speed limit, careful not to attract attention, and before I knew it, we were on the Ring Road heading north.

As we drove, I told Abdel and Yael everything that had happened in excruciating detail. She had me on speakerphone with a secure line directly back to her team at the Ramat David air base and Shalit at Mossad headquarters. They were firing questions at me left and right. *Had I seen the men who had fired the RPG that killed Hussam? How good a look had I gotten at the Audi that had followed me? Did I know what color it was? What specific model? What was the license plate number? Could I remember any other details about the attack?*

Unfortunately the answer to everything was no. I hadn't seen anything. I couldn't remember anything. I had nothing specific, much less actionable, to report. And then I began firing questions back at them. *How in the world could ISIS have tracked me to Cairo? How could they have known I was with Hussam? How could they have known my exact location? Even on the off chance that ISIS had picked up some whiff of intelligence that I was in Cairo, how could they have possibly known I would be at that café at that moment?*

JOEL C. ROSENBERG ★ 399

I was angry, and I was scared. The attack made
no sense whatsoever. I could count on one hand
the number of people who had known precisely
where I'd be that morning and when. No one on
this call had known. Not even I had known.

"Maybe there's a mole inside the Egyptian palace?" one of the analysts mused.

The very notion sent a chill down my spine,
especially as I explained to them everything I had
just discussed with Hussam and the general and
President Mahfouz. Shalit wanted to know what
exactly Hussam and Mahfouz had said about the
Baqouba brothers and whether I believed the
Egyptians had specific intelligence on their whereabouts. He wanted to know if I had admitted, confessed, hinted at, or intimated in any possible way
that I was working with the Mossad. He wanted
to know why I'd destroyed my wire and flushed
it down Hussam's toilet. And on and on it went.

I answered every question numerous times, but
Shalit and the others kept asking in different ways,
from different angles, both trying to force me to
remember every single little detail but also trying
to break my story. It was clear that some of them—
Dutch and Fingers in particular—didn't believe
me. "Why would you discard the wire unless you
were planning to give them information you didn't
want us to know?" Fingers demanded.

At that I went ballistic. "What exactly do you
think would have happened when the general's
men searched me? How would I have explained a
wire? El-Badawy is the head of the Egyptian special
forces, for crying out loud. If he caught me trying

to secretly record our conversation, he would have had me thrown into a cell!"

Yael finally intervened and cut off the call. As we exited the Ring Road onto the highway bound for the Egyptian city of Ismailia, she turned to me and repeated the question Shalit had asked me. "Did you believe Mahfouz when he said he had solid intel on the Baqouba brothers?"

"Absolutely," I said.

"Why?"

"I don't know," I replied. "I can't give you anything definitive. Call it intuition. Call it a gut instinct. All I can say is, I've been doing this for a long time—interviewing subjects, assessing their honesty, assessing their motives and reliability— and I'm telling you, this is legit."

"So you think they know something important."

"I do."

"Because they're scooping up bad guys in the Sinai?"

"Among other places."

"Human intel?"

"You mean as opposed to a telephone intercept or an e-mail?" I asked.

"Or a hard drive or pocket litter or anything else," Yael replied.

"You want to know if they have an actual source with firsthand knowledge of where one or both of the Baqouba brothers are?"

"Right."

"That I can't say," I confessed. "I don't know what they have, and I don't know how they got it.

But it's something. It's big. It's real. But I have no doubt it's perishable."

"Meaning if we don't get it today, it might not be true tomorrow?"

"Exactly."

Yael was quiet for several minutes. Then Abdel piped up as he drove. "You think Mahfouz is serious about helping bag these guys?" he asked.

"Yeah, I do," I said.

"He really wants to take down Abu Khalif?"

"Not directly," I said. "He said his hands are full with the jihadists inside Egypt and in the Sinai. But he's got something he wants to give to somebody. He just feels he has to be careful who that somebody is. He wants to work with the Americans, but they're not playing ball, and he doesn't trust them anymore. Why else would he meet with me? I wasn't asking for a meeting with him or the general. I only wanted to talk to Hussam because Khachigian told me to. Even you guys weren't sure if Hussam was an active player."

"Turns out he was," Yael said.

"I'll say—the man was working directly for President Mahfouz. It was Mahfouz who learned ISIS had chemical weapons. It was Mahfouz who wanted to get that intel to President Taylor. It was Mahfouz who wanted the world to know what Abu Khalif was planning. So he gave the intel to Hussam. Hussam gave it to Khachigian. And Khachigian leaked it to me."

"That was months ago," Yael said. "Doesn't mean they've got the goods now."

"Maybe not," I said. "But look at the article

my colleague Bill Sanders wrote. The Egyptians told him they had photographs of Khalif getting into Red Crescent ambulances going in and out of Raqqa. Did you guys have that?"

"No," Yael conceded.

"Do you believe it?" I asked.

Yael shrugged.

"Well, do you?" I pressed.

"Probably."

"Then Mahfouz and his team are doing their job. They've got the sources. They want to help. They're willing to play ball. But not unless I tell them who I'm working for. Which is why I need to tell them."

"Absolutely not," Yael said. "That's never going to happen."

"We don't have any choice," I countered. "I need to call them back and make sure they don't suspect me for Hussam's death. And I need to tell them I'm working with you guys and why we all need to work together. I can't wait until noon. If ISIS really was responsible for that attack, then they could very well know what I'm fishing for, and that means the Baqouba brothers know or will soon. Whatever hard intel Mahfouz has on them is going to be useless unless we move fast."

75

★ ★ ★

Abdel dropped us off at the Ismailia airport just before 11 a.m. local time.

The business jet lifted off minutes later, bound for Dubai. As soon as we were in the air, I demanded Yael get Ari Shalit back on the phone. At first, she told me this was impossible, but when I threatened to call Carl Hughes at the CIA and get ahold of Shalit through him, she finally relented and put me on a secure phone to Mossad headquarters.

For much of the first hour of our three-hour flight to the commercial capital of the United Arab Emirates, Shalit and I battled over the efficacy of informing the Egyptian government of my connection to the Mossad. I was adamant that every minute going by was wasted time that could blow the only real lead we had to the killer of the Israeli prime minister, not to mention thousands of Americans. Shalit, however, countered just as forcefully that the future of the entire Israeli-Egyptian peace treaty lay in the balance.

"Listen, James," he said, "if Mahfouz thought

for a split second that Mossad was running operations inside Egypt, the entire treaty could come unglued. Yes, it's that sensitive. And don't forget: your involvement has already led—directly or indirectly—to the death of Walid Hussam. Israel has enough crises to worry about without opening up an entire new front with the Egyptians."

I could not dissuade him, and when I raised my voice, Shalit hung up on me. Had I been a politician, I might have turned to Yael and spun the whole thing as a stalemate. But I wasn't a politician. I had no energy or desire to call this anything other than what it was—a complete and utter defeat. I'd made my case, and I'd lost, and now I was done. I'd put my life on the line to try to make a difference, to find leads that could help the Mossad crack this case and find Abu Khalif. And now we had a lead. With a single phone call from Ari Shalit to General El-Badawy, we had the potential to blow this thing wide-open. Yet Shalit refused to listen. He had his reasons, of course, but they weren't nearly good enough for me.

I slumped into a seat in the back of the plane and stared out the window at the vast expanse of the Saudi desert below us. I could see no cities, no towns, no villages—not even bedouin outposts. There were no trees, no rivers, no vegetation, no signs of life in any direction as far as the eye could see. I saw no roads, no cars, no people, no power lines. No evidence of human existence at all. It was like I was staring down at the surface of the moon. Uninhabited. Uninhabitable. Barren. Empty. And unforgiving.

In that moment, I felt more alone and help-less than at any other time in my life. I was doing everything I could to bring Abu Khalif to justice, to safeguard my family, to give us a chance at a life of freedom and security. But I was failing. I'd almost died—again. I'd seen far too many others die before my eyes—again. And for what? What good had any of it done? What, if anything, had I accomplished?

I thought about that as I looked down at the desert from thirty-nine thousand feet. I thought about that as we streaked through the atmosphere at five hundred miles an hour. And nothing at all came to mind. A half hour went by. Then an hour. And then two.

We were approaching the Gulf. We were told that in a few minutes we would need to fasten our seat belts and prepare for our descent. Absent-mindedly I did both, but I just kept staring at the desert floor, and try as I might, I couldn't see any good that had come from this mess. Nor could I see a way forward. I was out of plays. Out of options. Yael had shut down on me and I didn't know why and she wouldn't say. Shalit wasn't listening to me and I did know why, but I wasn't wrong, yet I couldn't budge him. I owed the president of Egypt an answer I wasn't allowed to give. So what was the point of it all? I had no idea.

I was suddenly overwhelmed by the intense desire to get back to Matt and Annie and Katie. I missed them so badly it was physically painful. I'd wasted so much of my life covering other people's lives that I'd blown much of my own. My marriage. My relationship with my mom. My relationship with Matt and his family. I knew I couldn't go back and change the past. But maybe I could start fresh. Maybe, at the very least, I could go home, or to whatever passed for home at the moment, and make amends. Or try, anyway. At that moment, I resolved to book my flight back to St. Thomas the moment we landed in Dubai, and only then did I finally begin to breathe again.

I turned away from the window and found myself glancing at Yael. She was sitting toward the front of the plane, hunched over her laptop. I was dying to know what had gone wrong between us. Whatever spark I'd felt in Istanbul and then in Amman and even on that base in eastern Jordan just before we'd headed into Iraq was long gone. I wanted to fix it. I wanted to make it right. I wanted to go back to the way it was before, when even the mere prospect of a few moments with this fascinating, beautiful, mysterious woman was tantalizing and electric.

This was the moment. I had to know. And I had to know now—before we landed, before I boarded a flight back to the Caribbean, before I walked out of her life forever, never to see her again.

76

* * *

I was about to unbuckle my seat belt and go talk with her when we hit some serious turbulence.

The plane began to shake violently, lurching from side to side. The pilot came on and insisted we remain in our seats with our seat belts fastened and not attempt to move about the cabin. Yael's laptop suddenly slid off the tray in front of her and went crashing to the floor. I could see her trying to decide whether she should grab it or not, but as the jet shook even more intensely, she decided against it. She glanced back to make sure I was all right. I nodded that I was fine, but it wasn't true. Not even close.

I was feeling nauseated. I was beginning to perspire. I reached up and opened the vent above me to get more air, and then I closed my eyes and leaned back and tried to steady my nerves and my stomach. I was not prone to air- or sea- or carsickness, but I remembered that on the few occasions I had experienced motion sickness as a kid, my mother had always told me to focus on something else, something specific, something good. Now, as I closed my eyes, it was my mother's face that came to mind—not hazy and gauzy and distant but as crisp and vivid as if she were really with me. It wasn't a mystical experience. She wasn't speaking to me. I wasn't hearing her from the grave. It was just a memory, and after a split second the image faded, replaced by a feeling of intense regret. I missed my mom. I wanted to see her. I wanted to talk to her. I wanted her to tell me everything was going to be okay.

From the time I'd left for college at the age of eighteen, I'd always been a man in a hurry. Always on the go. Always making excuses why I couldn't come home, couldn't see her, couldn't even call home enough and say hi. And the sadness I felt was excruciating.

And then I began to cry. Sob is more like it. I felt embarrassed and ashamed but I couldn't help it, though I did everything to stay quiet and not draw Yael's notice. Still, I was completely overcome with emotion—with loss, with regret, with fear—and from the inner depths of my soul I wept. It wasn't only for my mother. I think it was for all the people I'd lost in recent months. I hadn't really grieved for any of them. Not properly. But at that moment all that I had kept buried came rushing to the surface.

Wave after wave swept over me, the tears accompanied by images. My father storming out our front door when I was twelve—the last time I ever saw him. Me walking past my mother's room when I was seventeen and seeing her on her knees, praying through tears. My friend and photographer Abdel Hamid stepping on a land mine in Homs. Omar Fayez starting the rental car in Istanbul and it blowing to smithereens. Matt in Amman, driving me to the airport, pleading with me not to go to Iraq.

All these and many others flashed like a strobe light through my mind and heart. There didn't seem to be a rhyme or reason, no theme or common thread that bound them all together.

The last image in the rapid-fire series was my mom's pastor, speaking at her memorial service back in Bar Harbor. In my mind I again heard one of the last things he'd said.

"Maggie and Josh are gone, but they are not dead. They are more alive today than they have ever been. . . . But your only hope of seeing them again is to give your soul to the God they entrusted their souls to, and to do it before you breathe your last."

Those words thundered in my heart. They shook me to my core. And in that moment, I knew they were true. I can't explain how. I just knew that everything I'd heard the pastor say that morning was true. Everything Matt had been trying to explain to me for years was true. All of it. Jesus' life. His death. His burial. His resurrection. The way to heaven. The way of salvation. My sins. My need for a Savior. It all made sense. All at once, everything I'd been reading in the Gospels and the rest of the New Testament began to click into place. For the first time in my life, I could see it. And I wanted it. I wanted *him*. I wanted to be saved. To be adopted into God's family. To know beyond the shadow of a doubt that I would spend eternity with him and with my family.

So through my tears—silently but earnestly—
I begged God to forgive me, to change me, to fix
me, to rescue me and adopt me.

And something happened. I didn't see a vision.
I didn't hear angels singing. I didn't see fireworks
or have some out-of-body experience. But I felt
clean in a way I'd never felt before. I had peace I
couldn't begin to explain.

I was different. One moment I was lost and
dead and grieving and alone. And the next moment
I wasn't. In the blink of an eye. In the space of a
prayer. I was different.

I was free.

77

We touched down at Dubai International Airport at precisely 4 p.m.

It was sunny and breezy and eighty degrees, and as we taxied, I composed myself and tried to process all that had just happened to me. I wanted to call Matt. I wanted to tell him what I'd done. I wanted him to pray for me, and I had so many questions. But first I wanted to talk to Yael. Not about my newfound faith. Not yet. I just didn't want there to be any bad blood between us. Whatever I'd done wrong, I wanted to apologize to her and do what I could to make it right. She clearly didn't have any feelings for me. That hurt more than I cared to acknowledge, especially to her, but I wasn't going to make a thing of it. I just wanted to book my flight back to St. Thomas and say my good-byes on good terms.

Ignoring the still-lit seat belt sign, I moved up to the seat next to hers. She had just recovered her laptop and was putting it into her carry-on bag, but before I could start the conversation, her satellite phone rang. She answered it, then handed it to me, a surprised look on her face.

"Don't tell me that's Ari calling to reconsider," I said.

"Not exactly," she said.

"Calling to fire me, then?" I asked. "No need. I'm done."

She shook her head. "Quiet—it's not Ari."

"Then who?" I asked.

"It's the prime minister," she whispered.

A moment later I found myself on the line with the new Israeli premier, Yuval Eitan.

"Mr. Collins," the prime minister began, "I understand we have a problem."

"I guess we do, sir," I replied. "But I'm sorry you had to be bothered with this."

"Well, I'm not sure how it works in Washington, but around here the head of the Mossad tends to get the PM involved when, you know, the fate of a treaty with a major Sunni Arab neighbor is on the line."

"That would make sense," I said, not knowing what else to say.

"Ari tells me you two really got into it this morning."

"I'm afraid so, sir."

"Gave him quite an earful."

"Yes, sir. I was pressing him to put you on a call with President Mahfouz as quickly as possible."

"About?"

"Look, sir," I said. "I'm only doing this for one reason. I don't want money. I don't want attention. I don't even want vengeance. I want justice. I want to see the man who murdered my family stopped before he can hurt anyone else. I want this monster who's committing genocide stopped once and for all. That's why I dropped everything and came to you guys. I thought I could help. I thought I had something unique to contribute. Ari agreed. And he put me in the field. And I came back to him with a lead. A big lead. A serious one. But it requires your team coming clean with President Mahfouz, and apparently you're the only one who can authorize that. But Ari is dead set against you doing anything of the kind, and that's pretty much where things derailed."

"So now what?"

"That's up to you, sir," I said. "I'm going home."

"Unless I do what?"

"Pardon?"

"You heard me," the prime minister said. "Just say it plainly. What is it you want?"

I paused for a moment, caught off guard by the question. "Didn't Ari tell you?" I finally asked.

"I want to hear it directly from you," Eitan said.

I thought about that. It was a fair request. Surprising, but fair.

"Very well, Mr. Prime Minister," I said. "You need to call Mahfouz directly—and immediately. You need to tell him how and why I'm connected to you. You need to be clear, and you need to be precise. I came to you. You didn't recruit me. I don't work for you. I don't answer to you. But I want the same thing you want, the same thing he wants, and you're calling to offer to work together with him and his people to take down Abu Khalif before he does any more damage. You understand he's got information that could lead to the capture of the Baqouba brothers. And you understand he's offered to provide that information so long as he knows how it's going to be used. Then assure him there are no measures you're not willing to employ to see this job through to the end."

"That's it?" he asked.

"That's it," I said.

"That's a pretty high-risk proposition, Mr. Collins, given Cairo's stiff-arm toward us since the Amman attacks," Eitan said.

"No, sir," I countered. "With all due respect, the high-risk scenario is letting this moment pass. President Mahfouz was clear with me. You are not Egypt's problem. Israel doesn't threaten Egypt's way of life. Abu Khalif does. The ayatollahs do. He believes the next Arab capital that ISIS and Iran are coming after is Cairo. That's what Mahfouz told me. He told the same thing to Washington. He's been trying to reach out to the White House. He's even used the *New York Times* in recent days to send the message right to the top. But the White House isn't listening. President Taylor's convinced he's done all he needs to do. He doesn't want to take any more risks. He certainly isn't going into Syria to find Abu Khalif and take him down. He doesn't think the reward justifies the risks."

"And you think this creates a unique moment for us?" Eitan asked.

"I do, sir," I said. "Do what President Taylor

won't. Make the first move. Reach out to Mahfouz. Show him you respect him. Show him you want to be his partner. Offer to work together on a major operation that will make both your countries safer. And do it right now—before the window closes."

There was silence on the other end of the line.

I was tempted to keep talking, to push him, to try to seal the deal through the force of my reasoning, but something held me back. So I kept quiet. I just waited. And waited. And finally the prime minister spoke.

"All right, Mr. Collins, I'll make the call on one condition," he said.

"What's that, sir?" I asked.

"That you stay in the game and see it through to the end."

78

★ ★ ★

"So what do you think?" I asked Yael when I'd briefed her on the call.

"Why ask me?" she said as we finished taxiing and came to a complete stop.

"I value your opinion."

"You certainly seem to have no trouble *giving* your opinion," she said, getting up the moment the seat belt light was turned off and pulling her suitcase out from under her seat.

I just looked at her. "The job with the PM's office?"

"What about it?" she asked curtly.

"You asked me what to do," I replied. "I told you I thought you should take it. What's wrong with that?"

"Nothing. Get your things. We need to go."

"Yael, come on, what in the world is going on here?"

"This isn't the time, J. B."

"You brought it up."

"My mistake."

At that moment the cockpit door opened.

The pilots introduced themselves, and I was surprised to learn that our plane had been piloted by the station chief and deputy station chief of the Mossad's Dubai office. They had orders to help us get through security and to our hotel and then link up with the head of UAE intelligence. To do that, we needed to change clothes, change IDs, and follow their lead.

Ten minutes later, the four of us exited the plane to blue skies and white wispy clouds. I was now dressed in a five-thousand-dollar Zegna suit, a gold Rolex, beautiful Italian handcrafted leather shoes, and sunglasses I suspected cost more than my first car. The cover they'd given me was that I was an Arab—a Sunni—and a highly successful CEO of a British hotel chain. I was coming to the Gulf to visit friends. The whole thing seemed implausible on the face of it and I nearly laughed in their faces when they first explained it to me. But the station chief—going by the pseudonym Ali—insisted we needed a reason I was flying into the UAE on a Learjet, and this was it. Once we made it through passport control and customs, he said, we could change our image and our cover for the rest of our stay. But for now I was an Arab businessman and Yael was my wife.

To her they gave a black silk *abaya*, the traditional floor-length dress worn by devout women in the Gulf, and a black *niqab*, a veil that covered her head and face completely except for a small slit she could see through. This was the only option, they insisted. Yael's facial scars, and the fact that her arm was in a cast, would raise too many questions unless we went this route. Yael had no problem with it. I did. But it was clear we didn't have a choice. So down the stairs and onto the tarmac we went.

The pilots handled all our paperwork with the local officials. My job was to keep checking my watch, look annoyed, and pay no attention to my wife, who was always several steps behind me.

Ali was right. It worked like a charm.

The moment we were cleared into the country, we were met by a silver Rolls-Royce and a black Toyota Land Cruiser. Out of the SUV jumped several aides who took care of our luggage and our personal effects. The driver of our Rolls opened the back door for me and Yael while the pilots got into the chase car. The whole process took less than fifteen minutes, and soon we were off to the Burj Al Arab Jumeirah, the most beautiful hotel I'd ever seen, much less stayed in, anywhere in the world.

Located on an artificial island in the Persian Gulf, the hotel—the third tallest in the world— was designed to look like the sail of a ship. Our rooms were on the twenty-fifth double-story floor, looking out over the city of Dubai. But we had no time to savor the place or explore the amenities. The moment I'd gotten off the phone with the prime minister, I'd sent an e-mail to the private account of His Royal Highness, Prince Mohammed bin Zayed, the chief of intelligence for the United Arab Emirates and the third name on Khachigian's list. As I'd done with Walid Hussam, I briefly explained my connection to the former CIA director and described the letter he'd left me upon his death.

By the time we checked in to the Burj Al Arab, I'd already received a message back to meet His Highness for a nine o'clock dinner at Al Muntaha, a restaurant located on the twenty-seventh floor of the hotel. That gave us a little over four hours to prepare, and we did our best to use the time wisely.

The first thing I did was send a text to Paul Pritchard's phone number. Pritchard, a former CIA operative, was the top name on Khachigian's list. He was also supposedly dead, as far as anyone knew. But I didn't buy it. Khachigian wasn't sending me to a corpse but to a trusted confidant. The man was alive. The only question was whether he'd respond to my message at all, much less come out of hiding and actually meet with me.

Yael handed me her laptop and instructed me to read a forty-three-page encrypted dossier she'd just received on the Islamic State. It had been developed by her team back at Ramat David, specifically authored by Trotsky, and updated overnight. The first section contained info on attacks perpetrated by ISIS over the past three days:

- Three car bombings in Baghdad— 129 dead, 53 wounded
- An attack on a petrochemical plant in Egypt—more than 600 dead, more than 1,000 wounded, and some 10,000 people evacuated

- A suicide bombing at a Coptic church in Alexandria, Egypt—46 dead, 78 wounded
- A suicide bombing in a Catholic school in Luxor, Egypt—21 dead, 35 wounded
- Two suicide bombings in two Coptic churches in Cairo—64 dead, 212 wounded
- Two truck bombs at two different hospitals in Yemen—113 dead, 301 wounded
- And now, of course, the RPG attack near the presidential palace in Heliopolis—6 dead (including the two men driving the Audi)

What struck me immediately was that the pace of the attacks was accelerating. The second section of the dossier included a chart noting the number of ISIS attacks month by month for the last year. In the previous February, there had "only" been sixty ISIS attacks outside of Syria and Iraq, killing a total of 416 people and wounding 704. Yet as this February had come to a close, the chart noted there had been more than two hundred ISIS attacks—including those in the United States—for a total of more than nine thousand people dead and more than fifteen thousand wounded. Clearly the tempo was increasing, and so was the urgency of stopping these monsters.

The good news came in the third section of the report. This provided a summary of ISIS fighters killed and captured in the month of February, country by country.

- Iraq—3,102 jihadists dead, 26 captured (reflecting the ongoing allied operations to liberate northern Iraq)
- Syria—119 jihadists dead, 0 captured (reflecting limited allied bombing runs along the Syrian border with Iraq, and the lack of allied ground operations in the Syrian theater)
- Yemen—403 jihadists dead, 33 captured (reflecting the Saudi offensive there)
- Egypt—104 jihadists dead, 23 captured (primarily reflecting the Egyptian campaign against ISIS in the Sinai Peninsula, as well as raids against ISIS sleeper cells in several major Egyptian cities)
- Libya—63 jihadists dead, 2 captured
- Jordan—25 jihadists dead, 0 captured

The Jordanian figures appeared shockingly low until I sifted through the data more carefully and saw that in December and January, the Jordanian security forces had killed more than five thousand ISIS fighters and captured well over three hundred. By the beginning of February, the battle to retake Jordan was essentially over. So the low number reflected the stunning and rapid success of the king's campaign to secure his country, not his failure.

The remainder of the report provided summaries of the latest intel gleaned from interviews with ISIS detainees, material pulled off their phones

and computers, and a review of their "pocket litter"—material taken from the jihadists upon their
capture, ranging from airline boarding passes and
used bus tickets to meal and purchase receipts to
handwritten notes to or from their colleagues. The
material was a treasure trove, but the amount of
information—some valuable, some irrelevant—was
overwhelming. Forty-three pages from just the past
three days, and this was only a summary. Back on
the Ramat David air base were hard drives full of
thousands of hours of interrogation tapes, tens
of thousands of transcript pages, audio recordings
of intercepted phone calls, intercepted e-mails,
intercepted text messages, reports by human agents
and sources, satellite photos, drone footage, and on
and on it went. All of it had to be carefully processed and collated and tagged and reviewed and
analyzed and then stored in a way it could be readily
found and searched and cross-referenced with other
material. And more was coming in by the hour.

There was just one glaring problem. As potentially helpful as all of it was, none of it gave us
a single actionable clue to where the Baqouba
brothers or Abu Khalif were hiding.

79

* * *

The view from the twenty-seventh floor was exquisite.

I arrived at the restaurant a few minutes early but did not need to wait. The maître d' immediately led me to a private room in the back. Seated outside were two plainclothes security men. They patted me down and checked my ID, then radioed to more agents inside the room who opened the door and let me in.

The room was all glass from floor to ceiling, except for the wall I'd just entered through, and the twinkling lights of Dubai were dazzling to behold.

Wearing crisp white linen robes and a white headdress bound by a thick black cord, Prince Mohammed bin Zayed quickly rose from the table and greeted me warmly. But he was not the only person in the room. A tall, fit man stood right beside him. I wondered if he was a bodyguard—until he introduced himself.

"Paul Pritchard," he said, extending his hand. To say I was startled would have been an understatement. Not only was Paul Pritchard alive, but he and the prince had come to this meeting together. They were friends. Probably allies. Very likely business partners. This was going to be quite an evening.

As I sat down, I adjusted my glasses. They were not my usual pair. Before I'd headed to dinner, Yael had asked—again—that I wear a wire. I'd refused. But Yael had insisted that the situation was far too sensitive for her team to simply depend on my memory. She said they needed to hear, record, transcribe, and analyze the entire conversation, beginning to end. I pushed back just as hard that the risk of being detected was far too high. Prince bin Zayed was no amateur. This guy was the top spy in the Gulf region. He was going to have bodyguards. They were going to search me. They were, therefore, going to find the wire, and we'd be shut down before we even got started. What was the point?

In the end, however, the local station chief had proposed a compromise. Out of his briefcase he had produced a pair of eyeglasses that looked exactly like mine. Embedded into the frames was a highly sensitive microphone with a small transmitter that could broadcast the audio via an encrypted signal up to a half mile away. The lenses themselves, it turned out, weren't exactly my prescription, he'd conceded, but when I put them on, they were pretty close. I was impressed with his creativity and forethought, and in the end I agreed to wear them, ending the showdown.

Though younger than Paul Pritchard by a good

decade, Prince Mohammed bin Zayed nevertheless dominated the room not simply by virtue of his office but by the sheer force of his personality. He did not strike me as arrogant, but he definitely had a commanding way about him. When he asked you to sit, you sat. When he asked you questions, you answered. When he gave you an answer, you believed him. He just had an air of authority without swagger or showiness that I actually found reassuring.

Like me, the prince was in his early forties. Unlike me, he was a billionaire several times over. He was a member of a royal family that was sitting on an ocean of oil. Even when prices fell, he was still wealthier than I could even imagine, a high-ranking member of the *Forbes* 400 list though he'd never worked a day in the private sector.

That said, I detected nothing in his manner that seemed consumed with material things. Admittedly, we were sitting in the most expensive restaurant at one of the most expensive hotels on the planet, but he didn't strike me as pompous or distant. Rather, he had a firm handshake and sharp, quick eyes that flashed with an intelligence that both impressed and somewhat intimidated me. When a young waiter approached, the prince ordered a Coke Zero with lots of ice, not a fancy bottle of wine, champagne, or liquor. When it was time for dinner, he ordered a simple garden salad. Pritchard, on the other hand, ordered the king crab and ratatouille ravioli accompanied by the 200 gram Wagyu fillet, cooked medium and

served with a glass of the house cabernet sauvi-
gnon. I split the difference, ordering a salad and
a bowl of lobster bisque.

For his part, despite the lavish dinner order,
Pritchard wasn't playing the role of a flashy, jet-
setting businessman. He wasn't wearing Zegna
or Armani or some other designer suit. Instead,
he wore a crisp new light-blue dress shirt under
a navy-blue blazer, cotton Dockers, and loafers
without socks. Graying at the temples and
clean-shaven, he was lean and looked like he
could handle himself with a weapon or in hand-
to-hand combat. I had questions for him. So
many questions. But for now those would have
to wait.

The prince offered his condolences on the
deaths of my mother and nephew. Then he asked
about Khachigian—details about his death, how
we'd known each other, and how I thought ISIS
had discovered his efforts to expose their acquisi-
tion of Syrian chemical weapons. I answered all his
questions as best I could while Pritchard listened.
It was a professional yet relaxed conversation and
I was grateful for their interest.

At the same time, I knew the prince was testing everything I said to see if I was being truthful and candid, and I suddenly felt self-conscious
about having used an alias to enter his country.
Surely as the head of UAE intelligence, he knew,
but if it bothered him, he didn't let on.

Our meals came, but only Pritchard seemed
interested in the food. The prince and I mostly just
kept talking. He barely touched his salad. I barely

touched my soup. In time, I apparently passed his test.

When the waiter finally removed our plates and served us coffee, we moved from the dining table to several leather chairs looking out over the water. When I commented on how lovely the Persian Gulf looked from such a vantage point, and especially at night, His Royal Highness gently reminded me that this was "not the Persian Gulf, but the Arabian Gulf, thank you very much."

I quickly apologized for my faux pas.

When it came time to get down to business, I started things off with a direct question of my own. "So do you guys know?"

"Where Abu Khalif is?" the prince replied.

"What else?"

"No," he said. "Not for certain."

I took a sip of coffee. "But you must have some idea, right? I mean, obviously we can rule out Mosul. The allies have gone through the city street by street, house by house. And we can pretty much rule out Raqqa. It's been scrutinized up and down for the past two months, and it's not that big to begin with."

"He's been there, though, in Raqqa," the prince said. "We've had multiple sightings, just like the Egyptians. But no, we don't think he's there now."

"Then where?" I pressed.

Bin Zayed did not reply. Instead, he turned to Pritchard, who floored me.

"At this point, we think he's with his wives and kids," the former Damascus station chief said. "Find them, find him."

"Whoa, whoa, what in the world are you talking about?" I asked. *"Abu Khalif is married?"*

"I just found out a few days ago myself," the prince said, clearly amused by my reaction.

"I had no idea," I said.

"Join the crowd," Pritchard replied. "Turns out he's got four wives and seven children."

"How do you know?" I asked. "How did you find out?"

"For the past several years, my firm has been working closely with the prince on making sure the UAE is safe from terrorism—from ISIS, Iran, and other chief threats," Pritchard explained. "Last week we picked up the scent of an ISIS cell operating in Abu Dhabi. We shared it with the prince, and as you can imagine, that got the leadership pretty spooked."

I could imagine. Abu Dhabi, a city of about a million and a half people, was the capital of the United Arab Emirates and thus far one of the safest cities in the region, nearly untouched by the kind of terrorism that seemed to be plaguing everywhere else.

The prince picked up the narrative. "As soon as Paul gave me the details, I ordered our special forces into action. It got pretty messy—a nine-hour gun battle. All five jihadists were killed, but we lost two officers in the process."

"I'm sorry."

"So am I. These were very fine men—smart, experienced. A difficult loss. But the site itself was a gold mine. The cell consisted of four Saudis and one Syrian. They all lived in a small apartment just blocks from the Sheikh Zayed mosque. The Saudis, it turned out, were the muscle—bodyguards for the Syrian."

"And who was the Syrian?"

Pritchard took that one. "An aide to Abu Khalif, and pretty high up the food chain. We recovered his laptop, and once we cracked the hard drive, we discovered the guy reported to one of the Baqouba brothers—Faisal—but essentially he was a courier for Khalif. Specifically, it turned out, he was an emissary between Khalif and his wives. In other words, well vetted. Highly trusted. On the hard drive we found some of Khalif's correspondence with his wives over the last several years. We found digital photos of the wives' and kids' passports. We also found digital photos of the kids, names, dates of birth, all kinds of stuff. A real bonanza. At first we didn't even know what we'd found. Like I said, we didn't know he was married either. But the more we kept looking, the clearer it all became."

For the next hour, bin Zayed and Pritchard walked me through what they themselves were just learning, starting with the names of the four wives—Aisha, Fatima, Alia, and Hanan—and backgrounds on each.

"Here's something interesting," Pritchard said. "We've got medical records indicating that Aisha is barren. She was treated for several years but apparently never was able to bear children for Khalif. And yet Khalif never divorced her."

"That *is* interesting," I said. "They're in love."

"That was my take," he replied, "which is one

of the reasons I think she's with him. The Saudis insist she's not in the kingdom. Travel records say she flew to Islamabad four months ago, and from Pakistan to central Asia. But then the trail goes cold."

"Four months, you say?"

"Yes."

"That would have been about the time Khalif's men were planning to break him out of Abu Ghraib," I said.

"Exactly," the prince said. "My guess is they were moving her to safety, and specifically to a place he could see her after his escape and maybe even live with her."

"What about his other wives?" I asked.

Pritchard told me Fatima, who at twenty-seven was nearly a decade younger than Khalif's first wife, had a boy and two girls. Alia, only twenty-two, was the mother of two more Khalif boys and one girl. "We think Alia is the wife Khalif loves most," he said.

"Not his first wife, Aisha?" I asked.

"No."

"How can you be certain?"

"Most of the correspondence we've intercepted is to her," Pritchard said. "The language is flowery, passionate, laced with poetry, while letters and notes to the other wives are more newsy, more practical, less romantic."

The last of the four wives was Hanan, a Palestinian and a distant cousin to Khalif. Hanan had married the ISIS emir three years earlier when she was only fourteen. Now she was seventeen and the mother of a baby boy.

Bin Zayed then told me that Hanan's parents had just been found that morning—living on the outskirts of Dubai—and had been arrested and interrogated by the prince's men. They insisted they had no idea where their daughter was. They said they had not been to the wedding and swore they had never given their blessing to Khalif to marry their daughter. In fact, both the father and the mother—interrogated separately—went to great pains to renounce Khalif and ISIS.

"Do you believe them?" I asked.

"I'm not sure yet," the prince conceded. "We've just gotten started with them. Give me another few days."

"What did you find in the house?"

"Nothing that links the parents directly to Khalif or the Baqouba brothers, or even to ISIS," the prince replied. "But we're still looking."

"Okay," I said. "So this is a big breakthrough. Abu Khalif has four wives and at least seven children that we know of, right?"

"Right," Pritchard responded. "Four boys and three girls, ranging in age from two to twelve. And based on the correspondence we've captured, he seems to be very fond of the children. Remembers their birthdays. Sends them presents through the courier. Sends them cash. And keeps saying he misses them and wants them near him."

"So like you said, if we can find them, maybe we find him," I said.

"Exactly."

It made sense, but my head was still reeling.

"How come no one had this before?" I asked.

"Marriage? Kids? How do you keep these things secret from the world's greatest intelligence services?"

"Good question," Pritchard said. "Painful— but fair. To be blunt, the first answer is simple: I don't know. We missed it. Everybody missed it. That's on us. On me. But the second answer is, the guy lives in the shadows, right? I mean, until your profile of Jamal Ramzy and then Khalif himself, we hardly knew anything about these guys. There had always been bigger fish to catch before them—bin Laden, Zawahiri, KSM, Zarqawi, the list went on and on. So Khalif and Ramzy came up through the ranks. We knew some basics, but until you put a spotlight on them—and they let you—they had stayed off the radar. That's how they survived. That's how they climbed to the top of the greasy pole. They didn't want their names in the papers—they didn't want to draw the attention of foreign intelligence agencies—because they knew that those who did had a very short life span."

"But somehow the Iraqis captured Khalif," I said. "They knew he was a threat. They obviously went after him. They caught him. They put him in Abu Ghraib."

"I talked to the Iraqis specifically about this after your story was published," the prince said. "They say they caught Abu Khalif in a raid aimed at scooping up other bad guys. Khalif just happened to be in the room at the time. They weren't targeting him. In fact, at first they didn't know who they had or how big a deal he was. Obviously that changed over time, but the Iraqis insist they didn't even have a file on Abu Khalif when they caught him. It was sheer dumb luck, and since he refused to talk—except to you—they never got anything out of him when they interrogated him. They didn't really know who he was, or anything about his associates, much less his family members. They certainly didn't know he was married or that he had kids."

I sat back and thought for a moment. This *was* a big deal. It gave us eleven new trails to follow. Only one of them had to take us to Khalif. But it was a race against time, for new attacks were being planned and they could be unleashed at any moment.

80

★ ★ ★

It was almost midnight when I got back to my hotel room.

But it was clear that sleep wasn't anywhere on the horizon. Yael and the local Mossad team were hard at work on their laptops, sitting around the dining room table in the executive suite with stacks of dirty dinner dishes and used glasses and coffee cups all around them. I was eager to discuss the conversation I'd just had. The new intel on Khalif's wives and children was astonishing to me. I also wanted Yael's take on the aggressive effort Prince bin Zayed and his men were making to hunt down Khalif himself. I knew she'd been listening in on the conversation. But that wasn't all. I also needed to process everything I'd learned about Paul Pritchard.

First of all, not only was Paul Pritchard still alive and well, he was still unofficially working for the CIA. Yes, he'd been publicly "fired" by Khachigian, but that, he'd told me, was only so that he could be sent on assignments that could not be traced back to the U.S. government. For nearly a year, Pritchard had maintained his own identity, using his supposed firing as motivation for wanting revenge against the agency. He'd managed to convince several jihadist leaders in Syria and Iraq that he was a turncoat and an ally of theirs. When the usefulness of that technique had run its course, Pritchard got himself officially knocked off in an elaborately staged car bombing in Sudan. Then he'd gotten plastic surgery, changed his name, moved to the United Arab Emirates, set up a small private security firm, and begun working as an intelligence advisor to Prince bin Zayed. Only a handful of people on the entire planet knew his real identity. Robert Khachigian was one of them. And now so was I.

Particularly interesting to me was the fact that Paul Pritchard's real name was actually William Sullivan. To my astonishment, he was the son of Lincoln Sullivan and the father of Steve Sullivan, my new attorneys back in Maine. It turned out that Khachigian had known the family forever and had personally recruited William into the agency some twenty-five years earlier.

This finally explained something I hadn't understood about Khachigian's letter to me, the one I'd been given that fateful morning back in Portland. There was an odd line early in the letter that read, *If I know you, you're wondering about Steve's father . . . We'll get to that in a moment.* I had indeed been wondering about Steve's father. And yet Khachigian had never come back to that point, never finished the thought, never explained himself. Rather, on the back of the letter there were three names I was supposed to track down, with contact information for each. Now it made sense.

I was eager to talk about all this with Yael and the team. There was just one problem. Yael and her team had neither the time nor the interest for such a debriefing. They had news of their own.

"The PM made the call," Yael told me when the hotel room door was shut and locked behind me.

"When?" I asked, taking a seat at the table across from her.

"He and Mahfouz finally connected about an hour ago. Ari just called to brief us."

"And?"

"We're in business," she said, leaning back in her chair. "Mahfouz really appreciated the PM's call. The two agreed to swap intel on the hunt for Abu Khalif, provided there be absolutely no leaks. It all has to be hush-hush."

"Wow, that's great," I said.

"There's more. The attack near the palace wasn't ISIS, and it wasn't directed at you."

"What?"

"Mahfouz says his people just arrested a Muslim Brotherhood cell—four men and two women—earlier today. They were found with weapons that matched exactly those used in the attack. Their vehicle matches one seen on several surveillance cameras. And one of the suspects has confessed. He said they were targeting Walid Hussam for his role in arresting Brotherhood leaders when he served as the head of Egyptian intelligence. It had nothing to do with you. The palace is absolutely certain of it."

I closed my eyes and said a silent prayer of

thanks. It was my first prayer since getting off the plane, and I suddenly was overwhelmed by a desire to call Matt.

But Yael had more.

"Mahfouz didn't waste any time before sharing intelligence with us," she said. She explained that the Egyptians had an informant in Doha, the capital of the Gulf state of Qatar, 225 miles due west of where we were seated. The informant was the sister of three ISIS jihadists, one of whom was a bank manager in Doha. "But that's just a cover for his ISIS role," she insisted. "Turns out he's a key player in the ISIS courier system." She claimed that three times in the last eight months, video and audio recordings created by Abu Khalif, including the most recent, had been passed along to Al Jazeera through the bank manager.

"Why don't they just grab the bank manager?" I asked. "Interrogate him, put pressure on him, make him talk? We're running out of time."

"Because he doesn't know anything," she said. "Egyptian intelligence is waiting for another courier to make contact. It might be Faisal. Whoever it is, they could lead us to Khalif."

This was good news. Big news. A real lead.

Yael sent a flash message to Shalit via secure text outlining the basics of my conversation with bin Zayed and Pritchard. She promised a full report by daybreak. Then she recommended that he brief Prime Minister Eitan and that the PM brief President Mahfouz. The fact that Khalif had wives and children—and that they had been positively ID'd—was huge. We needed to get the

Mossad's best people working on this. But we needed the Egyptians' help too. They might be able to tap sources we didn't have. What's more, it would be an act of good faith for the PM to share sensitive information back to Mahfouz just hours after receiving it himself.

"We need to get the Jordanians in on this as well," I said.

"You're probably right," Yael said, yawning and rubbing her eyes.

"I'm definitely right, and I don't think we can wait anymore," I said. "The prime minister should call the king first thing in the morning, right after he talks to Mahfouz."

Just after 5 a.m., the guys went back to their rooms, and Yael and I were suddenly alone. I went into the bathroom, brushed my teeth, and changed into gym shorts and a T-shirt. When I came out, I grabbed a spare blanket and pillow from the closet and lay down on the huge couch, leaving the king-size bed to her. She nodded and disappeared into the bathroom for a few minutes. When she returned, she said good night and crawled into bed.

I forced myself to close my eyes, then pulled the blanket over my head and said a prayer as she turned off the light.

She fell asleep almost instantly. I, on the other hand, had no such luck.

81

★ ★ ★

J. B. Collins's life is in danger—we need to talk.

That was the urgent message we'd just received from Jordanian intelligence, and that was the totality of the message. We had no other details. We didn't know the specific nature of the threat or how the Jordanians knew it existed.

Yael and I had, however, been summoned to a private meeting with King Abdullah II at the royal palace in the port city of Aqaba. So suddenly we were back on the Learjet, racing from Dubai to the Hashemite Kingdom. Total flying time for the nearly 1,300-mile trip: just under three hours. A quick glance at my grandfather's pocket watch suggested that would put us on the tarmac by midnight.

To my surprise, despite the gravity of the threat, the truth was I wasn't particularly worried for myself. Not anymore. For the first time in my life, I was absolutely certain where I was going when I died, and while I didn't want to go prematurely, I felt ready for heaven. I wanted to see my mom.

I wanted to see Josh. I wanted to see my grandfather and Khachigian and his wife, Mary, and so many other believers who had gone on before me. But far more, I wanted to meet my Lord and Savior face-to-face. I was new to the team, and I had wasted so much of my life running from the truth. But I was done running. I was ready to go home, whenever that moment came.

What truly worried me now, however, was the thought that more harm might come to Matt, Annie, or Katie because of me. I couldn't bear the thought that Abu Khalif and ISIS might still be hunting them.

To her credit, Yael did her best to calm my mounting fears. She reminded me that my family was in hiding, under the protection of the U.S. government. She pointed out that the message from Amman indicated that I was in danger, not my family. Her words didn't do much to assuage my anxiety. But for the first time since we'd reconnected, she was acting like my friend and not my adversary.

After a while she switched tactics. She was, after all, a professional spy. She'd been trained in the art of misdirection. So rather than trying to convince me that my family wasn't in danger, she instead tried to keep me focused on the primary task at hand.

"What's your take on this new intel?" she asked. "Is it possible Abu Khalif is really in Turkey?"

Five days earlier, such a question would have seemed nonsensical. But no longer.

Following my meeting with Prince bin Zayed

and Pritchard, the Israeli security cabinet had met in emergency session to discuss the progress Yael's team was making and the need for the Israeli government to make direct contact with the leaders of not only Egypt and Jordan but now the United Arab Emirates, as well. The vote was unanimous— direct contact was authorized. By seven that morning, Ari Shalit had called and given me explicit permission to formally introduce Yael and her Mossad team to the prince and to Pritchard. I was to explain why and how I was working with the Mossad to bring Abu Khalif to justice and request permission for Shalit to call the prince directly and discuss how the two countries could work toward this common objective.

Once so authorized, I'd called the prince immediately, requested another face-to-face meeting, and been invited to meet with him in his palatial office.

To my surprise, the prince wasn't caught off guard in the slightest. In fact, he told me he'd been quite certain I was in some way connected to the Mossad and had simply wondered when I would come clean. He wasn't offended or upset, and he agreed to take Shalit's call at once. Ten minutes later, the two spy chiefs were on a secure line, briefing each other on developments and comparing notes on their latest theories. When the call was over and the prince explained those theories to Yael and me, we could hardly believe our ears.

As the prince explained to Shalit, his agency's hunt for Khalif's wives and children was pointing not toward Syria or Iraq but toward the Republic

of Turkey. Three of Khalif's wives, they had determined, had taken flights through Dubai, Abu
Dhabi, and Doha in late November and early
December. One had traveled to Beirut. Another
had flown to Cairo. The third had gone to Cyprus.
But none of them had stayed there. All of them—
and several of the children—had eventually wound
up flying to Istanbul.

These flights—the last ones Khalif's family
members had taken on commercial airlines—
raised all kinds of new questions. Were they still in
Istanbul? Had they all been given false documents
and flown on to Europe or some other destination?
Or had they been picked up by ISIS operatives and
driven someplace, perhaps deeper into the interior
of Turkey?

For his part, Shalit briefed the prince on the
latest from Egyptian intelligence. They'd struck
pay dirt in their surveillance operation of the bank
manager in Doha. By studying the usage of the
manager's mobile phone, home phone, and office
phone—along with e-mail traffic from several
accounts he was using simultaneously—a curious
picture was emerging.

The guy's tradecraft was stellar. Nothing
pointed directly to a specific location for the
Baqouba brothers or any other couriers. But the
patterns were intriguing. Over the last year, there
hadn't been a single call or e-mail originating from
a single city or town in Syria. Zero. Zip. Nada.
There had been many calls and e-mails to and
from the Gulf states, North Africa, and Europe, as
one would expect of a banker. But there were also

thirty-seven messages from Turkey—twenty-one from in or around the Istanbul metropolitan area, the nation's commercial capital, and the rest from in or around Ankara, the nation's political capital. And a good 80 percent of these messages had come in the last three months.

Of course, a Gulf banker receiving messages from Turkey wouldn't normally be cause for interest, much less concern. The Republic of Turkey was a country of nearly 80 million people, at least 96 percent of whom were Muslims, and the country had a gross domestic product of more than $1.5 trillion. Naturally Turkish citizens were doing business in Doha, arguably the epicenter of Islamic business activity in the region. However, what made these thirty-seven messages unique, the Egyptian intelligence analysts noted, was that they weren't returned. The bank manager—whom we now knew for certain was an ISIS operative—had received thirty-seven phone calls and e-mails from people in Turkey over the past eight months, most of them in the last ninety days, yet he had not replied to a single one of them.

This raised even more questions. Were these unreturned messages from Turkey instructions or directives of some kind? Was it possible Khalif and the Baqouba brothers weren't in Syria after all? Was it possible they were actually in Turkey? Turkey was a NATO ally. Turkey was ostensibly part of the regional Sunni alliance against ISIS. Turkey was supposedly bombing ISIS camps in northern Syria. Why, then, might Khalif and the Baqouba brothers be in Turkey?

As I listened to the prince's report on his conversation with Shalit, it dawned on me how enormously complicated our investigation had just become. If Khalif were somehow in Turkey, of all places, who was going to go get him? What country would dare send fighter jets equipped with laser-guided missiles to take him out? I couldn't think of one. What country was going to send in drones equipped with Hellfire missiles to end Khalif's reign of terror? Again, I didn't see it happening. Who was going to send in a team of special forces commandos, or a team of assassins, to bring Khalif to justice? Not the Egyptians. Not the emirates. Certainly not the Americans. Maybe not even the Israelis or the Jordanians, though they had suffered the most from Abu Khalif's actions.

Simply put, the notion of launching an attack deep inside a NATO ally was virtually unthinkable. An attack against one NATO country could trigger Article 5 of the alliance, requiring a collective response by all NATO countries against the aggressor.

For me, that fact alone dramatically increased the likelihood that Khalif had specifically *chosen* to hide in Turkey. That's what I told Yael en route to Jordan while we both tried not to think about the new unspecified but apparently authentic threat on my life.

And to my surprise, she agreed.

82

* * *

AQABA, JORDAN

We landed in Aqaba just after midnight in the middle of a brutal winter thunderstorm.

Gone was the gorgeous, balmy weather of the Gulf we'd had no time to enjoy. Now, as the sky flashed and rumbled and driving rain made visibility limited at best, we were met by officers of the Royal Court, carrying large umbrellas, who hustled us into a small motorcade consisting of three silver Toyota Land Cruisers and six heavily armed bodyguards and drivers.

Minutes later we were exiting the airport grounds and driving at high speed along deserted roads under the cover of darkness and fog. Eventually, though, we slowed down and turned a corner onto a narrow, secluded driveway, lined by long rows of palm trees on either side, bending in unison in the gale-force winds. Ahead of us were massive steel gates under a stone archway. Jordanian soldiers in full battle gear stood at attention beside two armored personnel carriers with .50-caliber machine guns aimed directly at us.

We did not come to a full stop, however. We did not show IDs or even have a conversation. The driver of the first Land Cruiser saluted the guards as we approached and slowed down, and the gates immediately opened before us. On either side of us I could see high, thick walls and several well-lit guard towers and the silhouettes of sentries and sharpshooters. But soon we were picking up speed again, snaking our way along the winding drive-way until we came to another set of steel gates and more armed soldiers. Again we slowed but did not stop. Again the driver saluted, and again the gates opened for us, and before I knew it, we had arrived at the palace.

The motorcade pulled up under an awning that gave us a bit of protection from the elements, though not nearly enough, and our doors were immediately opened by protocol officers who greeted us and whisked us into the vestibule. They showed us each to separate restrooms and gave us fresh towels and a few moments to dry off and gather ourselves.

As I shut and locked the door behind me, I closed my eyes for a moment. We'd been work-ing eighteen to twenty hours a day for much of the last week. Even when there'd been time to lie down, I hadn't been sleeping well. There were too many interruptions—calls and e-mails and emer-gency discussions about new information con-stantly flowing to us—and even when there was a momentary break in the intensity, I constantly felt the weight of what we were trying to do.

When I finally opened my eyes and stared into

the mirror, I winced at what I saw. My skin was pale. My eyes were red. Having not shaved my head since leaving Bar Harbor, I was no longer bald. Rather, my hair was growing quickly, though to my chagrin it was far more gray than the last time I'd let it grow out, maybe five or six years before. I hadn't shaved my face either since the funeral, and I no longer had a goatee but a rapidly thickening full beard, also far more gray than I'd expected or wanted. I was starting to look old and tired. I was starting to look my age—older, actually—and I wasn't a fan.

Tossing the towel into the sink, I opened the door and flicked off the light. A few moments later, Yael joined me, and the chief of protocol took us to the king's private study.

The room was empty. We were told the king was on a call but would be here momentarily. A steward brought in a large silver tray bearing a teapot and three teacups, each hand-painted with the royal coat of arms. The steward poured us each a cup of mint tea and then backed out of the room.

A moment later the king arrived with his several bodyguards, though they did not enter the study. Rather, the king entered alone and immediately closed the door behind him. He looked tired but greeted us warmly. "Welcome back to Jordan," His Majesty said with a broad smile and a firm handshake. "It's a joy to see you both again," he said in his flawless English with that trace of a British accent picked up from years of military schools and British special forces service in his youth. "Still, I do wish it were under more favorable circumstances."

"Thank you for having us to your home, Your Majesty," I said. "It is truly an honor to see you again—alive and well and victorious over such a cruel and heartless enemy."

"The fight is not yet over, I'm afraid," the king replied as he beckoned us all to take our seats.

He expressed his profound regrets for the attacks against my family and the loss of my mother and nephew, and as he spoke, it was quickly apparent he had tracked the news coverage and knew many of the details of what I had been through. He asked me how I was holding up, and then just as generously he asked Yael about her health and the status of her recovery. Even in the midst of a crisis, the monarch had a personal touch. It was one of the many qualities that impressed me.

We answered his questions and likewise shared our condolences for the tremendous loss of life he and his kingdom had experienced, especially for the deaths of Kamal Jeddah, the chief of Jordanian intelligence, and Ali Sa'id, the chief of security for the Royal Court, both of whom had died in the ISIS attacks during the peace summit in Amman, as well as our friend and comrade-in-arms Colonel Yusef Sharif, the king's senior advisor and personal spokesman, who had joined us on the mission to rescue President Taylor and had died in the firefight at the compound in Alqosh. Yael also asked how the queen and the children were doing. We hadn't seen the king since all these events had transpired, and we were both eager for an update on his family, the government, and all the reconstruction efforts that were under way.

It became immediately evident, however, that these were not the topics he wanted to discuss at present, as important as they were to him. He said his family was well and safe, and seemed to intimate—though he didn't say outright—that they were not currently in the country. But he turned quickly to the reason he had summoned us in the first place.

"J. B., I'm sorry to have to say this to you, but I'm afraid you're in grave danger," he said, looking straight into my eyes and ignoring his tea.

"Okay," I replied, trying to stay calm. "What exactly does that mean?"

"Over the last few weeks, we've been picking up a lot of chatter among ISIS operatives we're surveilling," he said, leaning forward in his chair. "They're furious that they weren't able to kill the president during the attack on the State of the Union. They're even more enraged that they didn't kill more members of Congress during the sarin gas attacks on the Capitol. They believe you're an easier target. They also believe you have a high enough profile—a high enough value—that they can score a major propaganda coup in the U.S. and perhaps globally if they can capture and behead you. From what we've been able to gather, they think you went into hiding after the funeral, and they've been pleading with Khalif to issue a fatwa authorizing them to find you and kill you posthaste."

83

★ ★ ★

"With all due respect, Your Majesty, this isn't really news," I said.

I explained that the FBI had expressed their concerns to me back in Bar Harbor, noting that they were particularly anxious about sleeper cells operating in New England.

"I know," the king said. "I've spoken directly to President Taylor and CIA Director Hughes—an old friend of yours, I understand. I also spoke to Director Beck at the FBI. Beck told me he personally gave Agent Harris the assignment to keep you and your brother and his family safe."

"Yes, he did, and that's very kind of you, Your Majesty, to discuss my safety with each of them," I said. "I'm touched—really—and I can tell you that Agent Harris has, in fact, gone to great lengths to make sure Matt, Annie, and Katie are secure and we're very grateful."

"Yet here you are, J. B. You're not in protective custody. You're not under the watchful care of Agent Harris and his team. You're jetting about the Middle East, hunting for the very man who is hunting you."

"I'm not worried," I said.

"You should be," the king retorted. "Really, J. B., this could not be more serious."

"Is there proof Abu Khalif has agreed to his men's wishes?" I asked. "Has he issued the fatwa?"

"He did," the king said. "Tonight, while you were flying here from Dubai."

At this, I set my cup down on the coffee table, sat back on the couch, and took a deep breath. This king had earned a special place in my heart. He was an Arab. He was a Muslim. He was a direct descendant of the founder of Islam. We didn't share the same background or ethnicity or theological views. But this was a good man. A man of peace. A man of tolerance and respect for Christians and Jews and those of a wide range of other backgrounds and beliefs. This was a man who had welcomed millions of refugees into his country, not because he had extra resources lying around to provide for their food, clothing, housing, medical care, and education, but because he felt it was the right thing to do—despite the potential risks. Because they were fleeing from Assad and the al-Nusra Front and from ISIS and from genocide.

In the face of extraordinary threats, this king had not surrendered or cowered in fear. To the contrary, he had courageously gone to war against the forces of evil and extremism. He was engaged in a winner-take-all civil war inside Islam, a war that pitted the forces of reform and modernity against the radicals and those pursuing the apocalypse.

His Majesty had aged considerably in the last few months. His hair was grayer. He had new lines etched in his face. Yet he was still in remarkably good shape for a monarch in his midfifties. I had to ascribe that to his lifelong discipline of being a soldier and even head of Jordanian special forces and to the singular commitment he had to protecting his people and his kingdom. But events were clearly taking their toll on him. He looked as tired as Yael and I did. Maybe more so.

"Look, J. B.," the king said since I had not replied, "the chatter about you was worrisome before the funeral in Maine. But it has spiked enormously since then. Now Khalif has issued this fatwa calling for your head with extreme urgency. Once it is announced publicly, probably in the next few hours—no more than a few days—your life is . . . Well, it's hard to explain just how serious this is. It won't just be active ISIS operatives who will be authorized to find and kill you. It will be any radicalized Muslim, anywhere in the world. That's why I asked you to come here. I wanted to tell you in person what we've learned and to impress upon you just how dire I view this. It's not safe for you to be out in the field. It's not safe to be here in the region like this. Not anymore. You were in Egypt—and were nearly killed there. You were just in Dubai. You're here now. The number of people who have seen you, who are talking to you, who are interacting with you—that number is growing by the day, by the hour. That's a problem, because it significantly raises the possibility that your presence in this region will be exposed and that the people who want to kill you will find you."

"So you want me to stop," I said.

"I want you to live."

"By stopping."

"By going home."

"Your Majesty, I don't have a home."

"Then going back to wherever Agent Harris put you, wherever he thinks you'll be safe."

"Or what?" I asked.

"Honestly, J. B.—if you remain here, I doubt you'll make it a month, if that. You're playing a very dangerous game, my friend, against very dangerous adversaries. You've beaten the odds so far, but now they're targeting you. It's time for you to stop. It's time for you to go back to your family and leave this game to us. We've been trained to play and win. And let's be honest, you have not."

84

* * *

"J. B., can I talk to you outside?" Yael asked.

We were back at the command center at the Ramat David Air Base and had been here for four days. So far the question of whether I was going to voluntarily choose to go home, as the king had suggested, or be sent home by Yael or even Ari Shalit, had gone unaddressed. But I feared the time had come.

In the past four days, the team and I had been following every lead imaginable related to the new information about Khalif's wives and children. But there still was absolutely no concrete evidence that could direct us to a specific, definable location. The only thing we knew for certain was that chatter was growing of another coming mass casualty event, inside the United States, against civilian targets, and soon.

On that front, Unit 8200 was working miracles. They had terrifying Skype call intercepts of terrorists talking about "devastating" and "catastrophic" and "imminent" operations inside the American homeland. The attacks would come "soon" and "without warning," the jihadists insisted. Yet there were no details, nothing definitive and actionable. And tensions were rising.

The intel and the accompanying analysis had been given to the prime minister, who passed it along to President Taylor and his national security team. The White House wasn't showing any new interest in hunting down Abu Khalif, but the Israelis were determined to be good allies, passing along what they had, and not just to the American intelligence community but to Jordanian, Egyptian, and the Gulf state intelligence agencies as well.

The team was spent. We were eating and sleeping in the bunker. People's nerves were raw. Tempers were short. Arguments were flaring. I hadn't been aboveground since we flew back from Jordan, and I'm not sure the rest of the team had seen the light of day since Yael and I had departed for Egypt.

Now, responding to Yael's request, I followed her into the corridor. Suddenly we were alone.

"Let's go for a walk," she said.

The rain had stopped, and the grounds were surprisingly dry. Spring seemed to have sprung across Israel's northern tier when we weren't looking. The clouds had parted. The temperature was in the low seventies. A lovely breeze was coming in from the sea. Grass was starting to grow. Flowers were starting to bloom. Trees were beginning to bud. It felt amazingly good to be out of the bunker, breathing fresh, clean air.

"So what can I do for you, boss?" I asked, happy to be stretching my legs and walking with my friend, even if I had no illusions the conversation was going to be anything but professional. "And make it snappy, if you don't mind. I've been chewing on a new theory I want to run past you."

She took a deep breath, then stopped and turned to me. "I'm afraid there's no easy way to say this. But I have to. It's my job."

"Why? What is it?" I asked.

"J. B. . . . Ari and I think it's time for you to go back to the States."

"What?"

"Don't get me wrong. You've been an enormous help, especially these last four days. But Ari and I have been discussing what King Abdullah said, and the bottom line is the king is right. The risks to you and your family by you staying here in the region are way too high. Ari and I have been reviewing the intel over the last few days. The king was spot-on. The ISIS guys are gunning for you, and Khalif really has issued a fatwa calling for Muslims everywhere to find you and your family and kill you on sight. A spokesman for ISIS just released it on the Internet about fifteen minutes ago. By tomorrow, every radical Muslim on the planet will be looking for you."

I didn't say anything. I was hurt. Angry. But I knew there wasn't anything I could say to change her mind, much less Shalit's.

We started walking again, tracing the perimeter of the base along the interior fence. A jeep patrol rode by. We nodded to the security team

JOEL C. ROSENBERG ★ 457

and kept going. The final rays of the sun were slipping below the Carmel Mountains. Dusk was falling. The lights of the base were flickering to life.

"You're not going to say anything?" she asked.

"What should I say?"

"I don't know. I thought you'd at least make an argument to stay."

"Would it help?"

"No."

"So what's the point?"

We kept walking.

"It's probably best you call the Learjet company tonight," she said after a while. "Let them know you'll be ready to fly back tomorrow to wherever you came from. I don't want to know, so please don't tell me."

I said nothing.

"We can chopper you out of here after ten tomorrow. You can say good-bye to the team. I think you can schedule a departure for noon or so out of Ben Gurion or Herzliya, whichever you'd prefer."

Another five minutes passed, and I realized what a sprawling base this really was. We'd barely covered half of the perimeter, if that, but it was growing dark and even a bit chilly.

"Listen," she said, "it's getting late and I'm getting hungry. Can I drive us someplace and buy you a farewell dinner?"

I just looked at her. She wasn't kidding. After all we'd been through together, this was really the end. I was going "home" to hide, without winning the heart of this girl, and Abu Khalif was still out there killing.

"Sure," I said.

What else could I say?

85

* * *

It was a Friday night in Israel.

The Sabbath had just arrived. That meant no Jewish-owned restaurants would be open. So we climbed into her bright-red Jeep Grand Cherokee and drove to a little Arab restaurant in Nazareth.

"You really do hate me, don't you?" I said as we parked and I realized where we were.

"What is that supposed to mean?" she asked, looking a bit hurt.

"The leader of ISIS just put out a fatwa on my head, and you're taking me to an Arab hot spot for dinner?"

She smiled and lowered her voice. "Don't let on that you know, but every diner in this place tonight is a Mossad agent. We'll be very safe."

"Seriously?" I said, looking out the window at the bistro and already enticed by the aromas wafting from the kitchen.

Yael shrugged.

"They're here to keep me safe?" I asked, impressed.

"Well, technically they're here to keep me safe,

but they're good guys—they'll take a bullet for you, too. At least for one more night."

We went in and were immediately shown to a table for two near the back by the kitchen.

The server was young and inexperienced and a bit harried and overwhelmed. But she brought us some water and finally came back to take our order. We didn't get fancy. We didn't have much of an appetite, so Yael simply ordered some plates of hummus and tehina and falafel and a couple of small salads and skipped the grilled lamb and chicken.

"So listen," she said after several minutes of awkward small talk. "I've been trying to find a good time to tell you this."

Every muscle in my body tightened. Now what?

"Yes?" I asked as calmly as I could.

"Well, the thing is, I . . ."

She couldn't get the words out. She asked a passing server for more water and more pita. She shifted in her seat. Clearly she was stalling. I couldn't decide if I wanted her to spit it out or change the subject. It turned out not to matter, because before she could continue, our meal came.

We waited until the waitress had served us everything and departed. Then Yael tried again.

"So, look, J. B. . . ."

"Just say it, Yael," I said quietly. "Whatever it is, I can take it. Just say it, please."

"Okay. What I'm trying to say is . . . I'm . . . well, anyway . . . I'm sort of . . ."

"Sort of what, Yael?"

"Well, I'm sort of . . . engaged."

The word just hung there in the air. I heard it. I just couldn't believe it. "Engaged?" I said, trying to force my brain to process the meaning of this perfectly simple English word.

"Yeah," she said, not meeting my eyes but staring at her food.

"To be married?" I asked like an idiot.

"Yeah."

"You're really engaged."

She finally looked up at me. "Yeah."

"To whom?"

"You don't know him."

I stared at her. "I don't understand."

"I know; it seems weird to me, too."

"Two months ago you weren't even dating anyone. In fact, I seem to recall you kissing me rather passionately in Istanbul."

"Yeah, I know."

"And I remember asking you out at the peace summit in Amman. And I seem to remember you saying—what did you say?—oh, that's right, you said yes."

"That's all true."

"So were you engaged then?"

"Of course not. Look, J. B., I'm sorry. I mean, I know this must seem kinda sudden—"

"Kinda?"

"Okay, very sudden, but I've actually known him a long time."

"How?"

"We dated in high school, before I went to the army, before I met Uri."

"Uri was your husband."

"Right."

"The one who was killed by Hezbollah."

She sighed and nodded. "What happened was that Moshe—his name is Moshe—anyway, he's a doctor. Specializes in physical rehab for trauma victims. I didn't know that. We broke up my senior year, and I lost track of him after high school. But it turns out he became a medic in the army and then he went to medical school, and the next thing I know, I'm lying there in the hospital after Alqosh and Moshe walks through the door."

"He was your doctor?"

"Yeah."

"And you thought, what a small world."

"Well . . . I guess, yeah."

"And you got chatting, and one thing led to another."

"When I was released, we went out a few times, nothing serious. I was still thinking about you."

"Oh, gee, thanks."

"But then I got offered the job in the PM's office, and I wrote to you, asking whether I should take it. I thought you would . . . I don't know. But you just wrote back saying I should take it and made a stupid joke about getting a raise, like you couldn't care less what I did. I was a little hurt, okay? And maybe a little angry."

"A little?"

"Okay, a lot. And I started thinking about my life, and what I really wanted, and it was a life here, in Israel, in my world. Then Moshe started getting more serious, and yes, one thing led to another. He asked me, and I said yes."

I stared at the untouched food before us, trying to process her words and silently berating myself for not coming clean about my feelings. For not bombarding her with flowers and letters and gifts. For not jumping on the first flight to Israel after being released from Walter Reed and tracking her down and telling her how much I liked her. I never imagined the window would close so fast. Now *I* was hurt and angry. But I forced myself to stay calm. There was nothing I could do to change any of this. She was engaged. In the movies, people try to break up engagements, but I couldn't do it. I wasn't going to fight for a girl to love me. Not after all I'd been through with Laura. If it didn't happen naturally, it wasn't meant to be. I wouldn't force it. I couldn't.

Finally I looked up. "I guess congratulations are in order. Mazel tov."

"Thanks," she said, her eyes moist and red.

Then we were silent again. I looked around the packed restaurant. Everyone was talking and laughing. It was so joyous and raucous and loud and festive, it almost made me forget for a moment that this was all fake. These weren't random residents of Nazareth. They were all Mossad agents. They were pretending to be unrelated to us. But we were—or more precisely Yael was—the entire reason they were in this place tonight.

"So," Yael said after a while, breaking the awkward silence. "You wanted to tell me something too, right?"

The last thing I wanted to do at this point was talk about my new theory of how to find Abu Khalif. I just wanted to pay the bill, excuse myself, and get out of there. I didn't want to be with her for another moment. I couldn't breathe. Not sitting here like this. I needed to be alone. I needed to think, to pray, to call my brother and see how he and Annie and Katie were doing. Talk about a fish out of water. I was a long way from home. I had no idea where home was. But it certainly wasn't here.

I loved this girl, I realized. If there had been any doubts in my mind, they were all gone the moment she told me she loved someone else. Now it felt as if someone had hit me in the chest with a two-by-four.

"Okay, fine, yes, there is something I'd like your take on," I said, forcing myself to go forward with the conversation, completely against my wishes, only because I knew it was the right thing to do for Matt and his family.

"Sure, what is it?" she asked.

There was no point waiting. I might as well get it out and get it over with. The sooner I did, the sooner we could head back to the base and the sooner I could go to my small apartment and be alone. "Khalif earned his doctorate in Islamic studies in Medina, right? That's when he fell in love. That's when he got married for the first time and all that, right?"

"Right."

"Well, for the past few days we've been looking at his wives and where they once lived, thinking

maybe if we could find them, that's where he probably is."

"And?"

"And that's bothering me—I think that's the
wrong premise."

"What's the right one?" she asked.

"We shouldn't be looking for the wives any
more than we should be looking for the couriers,"
I said.

"Then whom should we be looking for?"

"The mentor."

"The what?"

"Khalif's mentor—the professor that had the
most impact on him in Medina, the one who converted him from Palestinian nationalism to apocalyptic Islam."

"And who's that?"

"His first wife's father—Dr. Abdul Aziz
Al-Siddiq."

She wasn't following, so I explained that for the
past several days, I hadn't been looking at any of
the intel regarding Khalif's wives. Instead, I'd been
studying Aisha's father, Dr. Al-Siddiq. Aisha, it
turned out, was the man's youngest daughter. Now
seventy-one years old, Al-Siddiq was arguably one
of the most prominent scholars—and advocates—
of apocalyptic Islam in the entire Sunni Muslim
world. He'd written nine books on the topic, I told
Yael, including a textbook on eschatology that was
required reading in most of the world's Sunni colleges, universities, and seminaries.

What intrigued me was that Al-Siddiq had
overseen Abu Khalif while the future ISIS leader

was researching and writing his doctoral thesis in Medina. The thesis, a five-hundred-page treatise on why the Mahdi would come back to earth to establish the caliphate sometime in the period between 2007 and 2027 if Muslims were faithful to prepare the way—starting with genocide against Christians and Jews and "apostate" Shia Muslims—was as convoluted and downright bizarre as anything I'd ever read.

"You actually read it?" Yael asked.

"Every page—what do you think I've been up to the last few days?"

"Not that."

The thesis was the essence of everything Khalif believed, I explained, and Khalif believed it for one simple reason: because Dr. Al-Siddiq had convinced him of it. Just as Al-Siddiq had later convinced Khalif to marry his youngest daughter. What's more, it was under Al-Siddiq's influence that Khalif had returned to al Qaeda in Iraq and persuaded the AQI leadership to distance themselves from bin Laden and then change their name to the Islamic State of Iraq and al-Sham—ISIS.

"Forget the couriers and forget the wives," I argued. "The person we should be looking for is Abdul Aziz Al-Siddiq. He isn't just Abu Khalif's father-in-law. He's Khalif's spiritual, political, and strategic mentor. And as we move closer and closer to the final battle and the cataclysmic End of Days—at least in Khalif's mind—who would he want at his side more than his professor, his mentor, his father? Find Al-Siddiq, and I guarantee you'll find Abu Khalif."

PART
SIX

86

★ ★ ★

RAMAT DAVID AIR BASE, ISRAEL

To my surprise, I slept soundly for the first time in months.

When the alarm on my phone went off at 6 a.m., rather than roll over and rest for another thirty minutes or so, I got up, threw on a pair of jeans, a sweater, and some sneakers, and went for a long walk around the base.

Despite all that had happened the previous evening, despite all that Yael had said and how hurtful it had been, I wasn't angry or bitter. I felt oddly rested, strangely peaceful, and truly ready to get back to my family.

There was no need to pack my suitcase. I had never unpacked since arriving on the base. I couldn't watch television; the apartment I was using didn't have one. Nor a radio. Nor anything to read.

I guess I could have checked the headlines on my phone. That was certainly how I normally started my day, but on that morning I had no desire to hear more bad news. I knew what our entire team knew: more ISIS attacks inside the

U.S. were not only coming, they were imminent. The pope was still heading to the U.S. any day. Despite the credible warnings the Mossad and other intelligence agencies were picking up, the Vatican refused to call off or even postpone the recently planned trip.

Meanwhile, large numbers of college students were heading south for spring break, even as the chatter concerning impending attacks inside the homeland—and particularly against resorts and theme parks and amusement centers—was growing exponentially. For all I knew, the attacks had already begun. If not, they would likely commence over the next few days. What was the point of torturing myself by tracking every threat in real time on Twitter or other social media? There was nothing I could do to stop the attacks. I'd been summarily removed from any such role. It had been made abundantly clear my services were no longer needed, and thus I was heading back to St. Thomas.

Hoping to pass the time and enjoy a final view of the Israeli countryside—as this was very likely the last time I would be here—I strolled the grounds of the base in the morning dew and fog. I watched several F-16s take off and bank toward the Syrian border. A number of Sikorsky helicopters also lifted off and headed northeast as well. I couldn't help but wonder if their pilots were embarking on training missions or routine patrols, or heading into harm's way. But there was no one around to ask, and no one would have told me anyway. I didn't exist. No one on the base outside of Yael's team knew my name. I was just "the new guy," and by tomorrow I wouldn't even be that.

Eventually I returned to the apartment and took a long, hot shower. I thought about shaving my head and getting rid of my beard as well, but didn't feel up to it. I'd let Matt get a good laugh and then shave it off next week. Instead, I toweled off, dressed in some clean khakis and a black polo shirt, and slumped in a chair.

I pulled up a Bible app on my phone but found I had no idea what to read. I had raced my way through the New Testament in the last few weeks and found all of it fascinating. I especially loved the verses that made it clear I'd go to heaven when I died.

Like when Jesus said, "Truly, truly, I say to you, he who hears My word, and believes Him who sent Me, has eternal life, and does not come into judgment, but has passed out of death into life."

Or when the apostle Paul wrote, "For I am convinced that neither death, nor life, nor angels, nor principalities, nor things present, nor things to come, nor powers, nor height, nor depth, nor any other created thing, will be able to separate us from the love of God, which is in Christ Jesus our Lord."

Or when the apostle John wrote, "He who has the Son has the life; he who does not have the Son of God does not have the life. These things I have written to you who believe in the name of the Son of God, so that you may know that you have eternal life."

Such verses had spoken powerfully to me in recent days. But now that I had read the New

Testament, what was I supposed to do next? Plow my way through the Old Testament? That had little appeal. *The Garden? The Flood? The Law? Who begat whom?* I had no idea how any of that was relevant to me. But was I just going to skip it? Wasn't it important? Weren't there things in there God wanted me to know? I had so many questions, and I looked forward to sitting down with Matt. I knew he had answers, and I was fairly certain I wasn't likely to find them on my own.

In the end, I did finally dip into the Old Testament. After stumbling around for a while, I settled on the book of Psalms. I picked a random number and decided to read the ninth chapter. One passage particularly captured my attention.

> My enemies retreated;
>> they staggered and died when you
>>> appeared.
> For you have judged in my favor;
>> from your throne you have judged with
>>> fairness.
> You have rebuked the nations and destroyed
>> the wicked;
>> you have erased their names forever.
> The enemy is finished, in endless ruins;
>> the cities you uprooted are now forgotten.

How I wished this were true for me. It just wasn't. My enemies were not retreating. By all measures, they were advancing. They weren't staggering or dying. They weren't finished or in endless ruins. Abu Khalif and his men were still on a geno-cidal killing spree. And I was being kicked off the battlefield and sent into hiding. Where was the justice in that?

I glanced at my grandfather's pocket watch and realized it was time. So I grabbed my suitcase and briefcase, walked out of the room, and locked the apartment door behind me for the last time.

I suddenly found myself overwhelmed by a profound and pervasive sense of sadness. I was about to leave a team I had truly begun to respect and admire. I was leaving a job unfinished, and there were few things I hated more. And then there was Yael, who had tried to let me down gently but nonetheless had rejected me. I wasn't angry at her. To the contrary, I genuinely wanted her to be happy. But it stung, in part because of the suddenness of it all. I'd come to Israel imagining everything going so differently between us. It had never even occurred to me that she might be see-ing someone else, much less falling for him, much less agreeing to marry him. Last night I'd been in shock. This morning I felt like I was grieving the loss of another friend.

We would not write. We would not call. We would not keep in touch. There would be no point. She had a new love and a new life ahead of her.

What exactly did I have in front of me?

87

★ ★ ★

It was nine o'clock exactly when I knocked on the conference room door.

A moment later, I heard Yael's voice through the intercom telling me to come in, and the electronic locks opened. I entered and found the entire team assembled with Ari Shalit at the head of the table. It was immediately apparent by their disheveled appearances and the empty coffee mugs that they had not just arrived. They'd been there much, if not all, of the night.

"Please, J. B., take a seat," Yael said.

There was a spot available next to her, but I chose not to take it. Instead, I walked over to Shalit and took the empty chair next to him and prepared myself for what was coming. Yael would undoubtedly thank me for being on the team, however briefly. She'd say I'd been helpful, and Ari would agree, and the team would nod, and I would say thank you, and they would clap, and that would be that. I'd already decided I wanted to leave on a positive note. I was grateful for these specialists, a unique breed with a high calling, and I desperately wanted—no, *needed*—them to succeed, so there was no point saying anything sour or critical. The entire little ceremony would be mercifully quick, and soon I'd be on a chopper bound for Ben Gurion International Airport and then on a long flight back to the U.S. Virgin Islands.

Except the morning took an unexpected turn.

"The team and I have been here since just after midnight," Yael explained after I'd sat down.

"Why's that?" I asked. "What's wrong?"

"We've been testing your theory," she replied.

"What theory?"

"About Dr. Al-Siddiq."

"Okay," I said cautiously.

"The short version is that over the past few hours we've determined that Al-Siddiq hasn't left Saudi Arabia in four years," she continued. "He lectures. He writes. He's somewhat of a big shot. Runs seminars. Runs conferences. Islamic scholars from all over the world come to see him. But he doesn't travel."

"Go on." Did the team find my theory compelling or ridiculous? And if the latter, why bother telling me minutes before I departed?

"Two days ago, Al-Siddiq booked his first international flight in four years," Ari Shalit noted. "Want to take a guess where to?"

"I have no idea."

"Istanbul," Shalit said.

"Interesting."

"We thought so," Shalit added. "Is he going on vacation? Doing a little sightseeing for the first time in his life? Or is he going to meet with his daughter and with Khalif?"

"The fact is we don't know for certain," Yael said. "But everything you told me last night about Al-Siddiq checks out. We've been going over his life, his writings, his phone calls and e-mails, our databases—everything—double-checking your work. And you're right—he's a close friend and advisor to Khalif. He clearly loves his daughter, as does Khalif. Once we realized he'd just bought a ticket to Turkey, we found ourselves hoping this was the break we've needed."

Shalit noted that Al-Siddiq was booked on Turkish Airlines flight 109, which would depart Medina at 4:40 p.m. local time and land in Istanbul at 8:15 p.m. From there he had a connecting flight to Antalya, the Turkish resort city on the coast of the Mediterranean. Then came the kicker: Shalit was sending Yael, Dutch, and me to Istanbul.

"Me?"

"The mission is this: Find Al-Siddiq, follow him, and report back," Shalit said. "You leave in fifteen minutes. Any questions?"

Many, actually—but one thing was clear: I wasn't going home just yet after all.

★　★　★

We flew first to Rome on a Gulfstream IV.

I was excited, encouraged by the break. I had raised the question of why they were sending me back into the field now that Khalif had issued a fatwa calling for my murder. They'd made such a big deal about how I wasn't trained and it wouldn't be safe. Now their message seemed to have changed.

Shalit had simply responded that my instincts had consistently proven accurate. That was why he'd brought me onto the team in the first place, and they were too close to success to monkey with the formula. He needed me to help run Khalif to ground. With false documents and disguises and the like, they would do everything in their power to minimize the danger to me, but Shalit had certainly been honest and direct with me about the risks. "There is a very real chance you won't come back," he had said before I left.

I knew, and I said yes anyway. I wanted to see this thing done. Period. End of sentence.

Dutch, Yael, and I disembarked with our luggage and headed into the main terminal. There, we were to board a commercial flight to Istanbul. Turkish Airlines flight 1866 would be wheels up at 3:25 p.m. local time and wheels down in the one-time capital of the Ottoman Empire—the former seat of the caliphate—just after seven that evening. This would be cutting it close. It would give us barely an hour before Dr. Al-Siddiq landed and entered the same airport. But Dutch insisted that the somewhat-convoluted route was the right way in. He had the most field experience in this type of operation, so Yael had appointed him ops leader for this mission.

Given the deeply strained relations between the Israeli and Turkish governments at the moment, a Mossad team couldn't simply jet into Istanbul directly from Israel these days without drawing a high degree of attention from the Turkish police and intelligence agencies. That would not do, especially now with the fatwa out there. The last thing we wanted was Turkish authorities focusing their attention on me, much less my Mossad colleagues. Far better, Dutch said, would be for us to all enter Istanbul on a commercial flight—on the country's national airline—through a long line at passport control with thousands of other tourists and businessmen.

He and Yael weren't particularly worried about getting into Turkey with their false papers. They were pros and did it all the time. But they were a little concerned about me. It wasn't just the Turkish border police we had to worry about. It was any Muslim who might have seen the photo ISIS was using—the one they were now spreading across the globe using all manner of social media—and who might notice me as I walked by. The good news was that the photo ISIS was using was one they'd pulled off the *New York Times* website. It was, therefore, somewhat dated. In it, I was bald. I was clean-shaven. I was wearing a Western suit and even a tie. What's more, it had been taken five or six years earlier.

Now I had a full head of hair. It was short, but it was growing, and along with my full beard, this changed my look fairly dramatically. In addition, Dutch insisted that Yael and I once again pose as a married Muslim couple, as we had in Dubai. Yael, therefore, was again wearing a black silk *abaya* and *niqab*, covering her head to foot, including her entire face. I, on the other hand, was not wearing the Zegna suit, Italian shoes, or gold Rolex watch I had worn in Dubai. Rather, I was wearing a crisp white cotton *thawb*, the full-length, long-sleeved, traditional tunic worn by men from the Gulf region. Dutch had also asked me to wear a *taqiyah*, a short, rounded skullcap commonly worn by Muslim men.

Had I been flying into Israel in such garb, I could have expected to be asked many questions by the Israeli border police about who I was, where I was coming from, why I was coming to Israel, whom I knew in the country, what other Muslim countries I had visited, and so forth. But just the opposite would be true flying into Turkey, especially given that I spoke Arabic reasonably well. Rather than standing out, I should blend right in. True, what Yael and I were wearing was distinctive to the Gulf, not Turkey, but Turkish airports had a steady stream of Gulf visitors and welcomed them without hassle and even without visas.

There was just one problem, and it had nothing to do with my appearance or my fake passport or my fake marriage to Yael. This was far more serious.

The plane was late.

88

* * *

Our arrival was delayed by nearly forty minutes.

By the time we touched down in rain-drenched Istanbul, cleared passport control, and linked up with the Mossad's station chief—a Turkish Jew in his midfifties who asked us to call him Mustafa—it was already 8:06 p.m. That gave us less than ten minutes before Al-Siddiq's flight from Medina was supposed to land.

From there, the news got worse. A quick glance at the arrivals board indicated that Al-Siddiq's flight had landed early. In fact, it was already disembarking, and it was on the other end of the terminal.

Yael and Dutch were calm, cool, and collected. They had been doing this sort of thing for a long time. But I was new and I was freaking out. We had no margin for error. This was our only known link to Abu Khalif. There was a very high likelihood that Al-Siddiq had been summoned by Khalif and could take us right to the ISIS emir. Losing him would be catastrophic, and I feared that's what was about to happen.

Mustafa tried to calm me down. He explained that he and his team had arrived and entered the airport three hours ago. He had four agents—two men and two women—stationed near the gate where Al-Siddiq's plane had arrived. He had other agents positioned along the corridors through-out the airport, allowing him to track the Saudi theological professor no matter what direction he chose to go. Furthermore, Mustafa had two teams of agents outside the airport, waiting in SUVs, ready to follow Al-Siddiq if he surprised us by leaving the airport instead of making his connect-ing flight to Antalya. If all that weren't enough, he had three agents on motorcycles positioned near the exit ramps to the main roads near the airport so that even if those driving Al-Siddiq somehow managed to elude Mustafa's two SUVs, he would still have eyes on the target until the others could catch up.

Mustafa's recommendation was that we head directly to the gate where our flight to Antalya would soon be boarding, and let his team take care of the rest. They were trained, experienced professionals. They knew this airport inside and out. They knew what they were doing, and they knew the stakes. Still, he said he was fairly confi-dent that all these precautions weren't going to be needed anyway. His instincts told him Al-Siddiq was heading to Antalya.

"Get on the plane," he whispered. "And don't get caught."

Dutch agreed and we quickly split up and went our separate ways. Yael and I wheeled our luggage through the airport, then headed to a café across from our gate, purchased cups of Turkish coffee, found an empty table, and sat together, eyes peeled and hearts pounding. Dutch, meanwhile, disappeared for a while, then passed by without acknowledging us and headed for a newsstand not far from the gate. There he leafed through magazines and bought himself a pack of gum and a candy bar, occasionally checking his wristwatch and waiting for the announcement that it was time to board.

Mustafa was nowhere to be seen. Nor were any other Mossad agents—at least none that I could identify. No one I saw around me or near me looked Israeli. None even looked Jewish. But then again, Mustafa didn't either. His dark features and bushy mustache weren't tricks of the trade. He wasn't wearing a wig and makeup. He was the real deal. Yael said the Istanbul station chief and his family had made aliyah in 1982. They were all now true-blue Israeli citizens. They'd gone to Israeli schools and fought in the IDF and paid Israeli taxes and assimilated into Israeli society. But Mustafa still looked Turkish because he was Turkish. He spoke the language as a native and could read and write as a native and thus was ideally suited to serve the Israeli intelligence system in Turkey.

One of the curious and fascinating advantages the Mossad had gained from two thousand years of Jews living in exile was that with Jews coming back to the land of Israel from every nation on the earth, the intelligence agency had the unique ability to recruit Israeli citizens who looked, sounded, and acted like Arabs, Russians, Germans, Italians, Ethiopians, Yemenis, Brazilians, Koreans, and even Chinese. These agents didn't need to be taught how to blend into a foreign society. They didn't need to learn new languages or customs or idiosyncrasies before becoming spies. This thought should have calmed me somewhat, yet it did not.

Where was Al-Siddiq? Had he already deplaned? Was he really going to Antalya, or was that just a ruse? Who was traveling with him? How would we identify them? What if they identified us?

I grabbed my phone and opened the app that Dutch had briefed me on during the flight to Rome. Everyone on the team, myself included, was wearing glasses similar to the ones I'd been given in Dubai. But this version didn't simply have a built-in microphone. It also featured a high-resolution video camera. Every team member was thus transmitting to each other's smartphones live images of whatever we were seeing at the moment.

When the app loaded, my heart nearly stopped, for there, in front of me, was a real-time, if somewhat grainy, image of Abu Khalif's mentor. He was here. He was on the ground, in the airport, and on the move.

A text message now flashed across the bottom of the app. **No checked luggage. Just a carry-on. No companions. Seems to be alone.**

I didn't buy it. There was no way Al-Siddiq

was going to the emir unaccompanied. I could believe he thought he was traveling alone, at least for the first leg of the journey. But I had no doubt Abu Khalif had ISIS operatives on that flight from Medina. I had no doubt they were in this airport. Watching their mark. Tracking his every movement. Just as we were. *So who were they? And why hadn't the Mossad guys identified them already?*

Heading to men's room, the next text read. **Six breaking off.**

Three, follow him, read a text from Mustafa.

Then came another: **One and two, reposition along the corridor.**

And a third: **Six, hold back in case he turns around. All others, hold your positions.**

Then came a message from Dutch. **Where are the trackers?** he asked, voicing my concerns precisely. **Tell me we've spotted them.**

I've got one, Yael texted. **At the gate to Antalya. Female, jeans, veiled.**

Startled, I instinctively popped my head up to look. I immediately saw an attractive Muslim woman in her late twenties. She was wearing designer jeans, a brightly colored blouse, and a *hijab*. At first glance, I was sure Yael was wrong. The woman looked like a college student, not a spy. But Yael quickly tapped my leg under the table with her foot. Her message was clear and emphatic: *Don't look. Turn away. Don't risk making eye contact.*

She was right, of course. I wasn't trained for surveillance. I wasn't supposed to be doing what everyone else was doing. For now, my job was to monitor the video feeds while keeping my head down and staying out of trouble.

Looking back at the app on my phone, I tapped the feed coming from Yael's glasses and studied the young Muslim more carefully. Now I knew Yael was right. The woman was pretending to read a magazine but she wasn't really reading. She was scanning the faces of every passenger in the lounge, and she was texting something. *But what? And to whom?*

She wasn't alone. That much was clear.

89

* * *

By the time we boarded, the team had identified no fewer than four ISIS operatives shadowing Al-Siddiq.

Dutch was sitting in first class and was among the first to board. That would allow him to study each passenger coming onto the plane after him and give us the opportunity to see each of them via the live images he was webcasting from the camera in his glasses. It would also give him the chance to "accidentally" bump into Al-Siddiq when the Saudi professor was boarding, enabling Dutch to slip a tiny tracking beacon into his pocket or his carry-on suitcase. Once we were back on the ground, we would be able to follow Al-Siddiq wherever he went.

Yael and I had been assigned seats in the very back of the plane—in the last row, actually, near the galley and the bathrooms—so we were among the last to board. This was a problem. Everyone else got to study us as we moved down the aisle. And since the release of Abu Khalif's fatwa, I was growing increasingly anxious, though I fought hard not to show it. Still, my heart was pounding. My palms were perspiring. I suddenly felt incredibly awkward and conspicuous in the garb of a Gulf Arab.

I immediately noticed the young woman with the *hijab*. She was sitting in first class, to my left as I boarded, in a window seat two rows behind Dutch, and she was eyeing me suspiciously, making me even more nervous. Five rows behind her were two large, burly Arab men sitting in aisle seats across from each other. They, too, had been identified by the team as likely ISIS operatives, and their cold, blank, soulless eyes sent chills down my spine as I passed them.

Two rows behind them, on my left, I spotted Al-Siddiq. I'd been studying photographs of him for days, and in the terminal I'd seen him from afar or via the video stream on my app. But to see him up close, face-to-face, made my blood run cold. This was the theological and ideological mentor to the man who'd killed my family.

It was disorienting how normal he looked. Unlike Khalif, who bore more than a passing resemblance to Charles Manson, Al-Siddiq looked more like a distinguished professor of English literature than a genocidal End Times psychopath. He had a somewhat oval face, a closely trimmed mustache and beard, a long, patrician nose, and bifocals in rather dated gold wire frames. Dressed in a light-blue oxford button-down shirt, a tweed blazer, tan slacks, and loafers, he was also sitting in an aisle seat, and it struck me that he was doing the exact opposite of what I was doing. He, a fanatic

Muslim, was trying to look like a Westerner while I, a brand-new Christian, was trying to pass myself off as a devout Muslim. We were trying to fool each other and anyone else who was watching, trying not to be noticed until our missions were accomplished.

That said, Al-Siddiq didn't look any more comfortable in his disguise than I was in mine. He had a John le Carré spy thriller in his lap, but he wasn't reading it. Rather, he was nervously fidgeting with the air-conditioning system and mopping his brow with a handkerchief.

As I moved past him, he looked at me and our eyes locked for a moment. I forced a smile and nodded to him, then looked away. But as I did, I saw his eyes narrow and his brow furrow, and I suddenly realized that I was acting more like an American tourist than a fellow Sunni Muslim from the Gulf. Now I was truly worried. *Had he recognized me? Why had I been so foolish? Why had I let myself make eye contact?* Worse, everyone else on the team who was riveted to the images on the app on their phones had seen the mistake I'd just made, along with Al-Siddiq's uncomfortable reaction.

Still, there was nothing I could do about it now. I had to keep moving and keep praying. Coming up on my right, three rows into the economy cabin, was a handsome young Arab man that I surmised was in his midthirties. This was the fourth ISIS operative the team had identified, and I was careful not to look in his direction at all as I passed him. I already had his face tattooed in my mind's eye, and it was he who struck me as the most dangerous of all. He had dark, brooding eyes and a large, bushy black beard. His features suggested he was a Saudi. He was in excellent physical shape, and he looked smarter and far more cunning than the two heavies sitting several rows ahead. Mustafa had alerted us all by text message just before we'd boarded that this was likely the leader of the ISIS team shadowing Al-Siddiq. But he'd also reminded us that there could be other ISIS operatives on the flight that had not been identified, including one or more of the flight attendants.

As per the plan, Yael took her seat by the window in the final row on the right. I took my seat on the aisle. That made me more exposed to anyone coming back to use the bathroom, raising the risk that I could be seen and identified. But we didn't have a choice. A Muslim woman traveling with her husband, especially one wearing an *abaya*, would never be allowed to have the aisle seat. So I buckled up and said a silent prayer, and soon we were rumbling down the runway and up into the treacherous winter storm that was descending not just on Istanbul but on much of the northern Mediterranean region.

Twice during the short, bumpy flight, Al-Siddiq made his way down the aisle to the restroom. Both times he eyed me strangely, and as he did, my stress was off the charts. The first time, I buried my head in *Asharq Al-Awsat*, the London-based Arab daily newspaper. The second time, about thirty minutes later, the young Saudi followed him to the restroom. That time I pretended I was reading *Al-Hayat*, another Arab daily, as he stood directly at my side.

My imagination ran wild with what atrocities the ISIS killer beside me had committed and what atrocities he was preparing to commit next. Compounding those fears, Al-Siddiq was spending an unusually long time in the restroom. Why? Was the turbulence causing him airsickness? Was he ill for some other reason? Were his own anxieties causing him stomach problems? Or was he suspicious? Had the run-in with Dutch made him paranoid? Was he searching his clothing? Had he found the tracking beacon? Maybe he hadn't found it the first time, but could that be why he was back again?

As Al-Siddiq came out of the restroom the second time and prepared to pass the young Saudi, the plane was suddenly jolted by turbulence. Both men stumbled in the aisle. Al-Siddiq grabbed the headrest in front of me to stabilize himself. And in that moment, out of the corner of my eye, I saw the young Saudi slip a small note into the outside pocket of Al-Siddiq's blazer. It happened so fast, so smoothly, so professionally that for a few moments I doubted that I'd actually seen it. But as the young man stepped into the restroom and Al-Siddiq worked his way back up the aisle and took his seat, I saw him look around nervously to see if anyone was watching him. He even looked back down the aisle toward the rear of the plane. I made sure I was carefully hidden behind the newspaper. When I looked again, I saw him pull the note out of his pocket, read it, and then quickly put it away.

I immediately leaned over and whispered what I'd seen to Yael.

"So contact's been made," she whispered back. "Now let's see where they go."

90

* * *

No sooner had we landed in Antalya than it became clear we weren't staying long.

Yael immediately received a call from Trotsky, informing her that someone had purchased a ticket for Al-Siddiq from Antalya to the Turkish city of Gaziantep on SunExpress Airlines. Flight 7646 would depart at 6:45 a.m. local time and was expected to land precisely at 8:00. What's more, Trotsky indicated that there were newly purchased tickets to the same city in the names of four additional passengers who had been on our flight from Istanbul.

This was a significant break. We had video and still images of the four ISIS operatives, but until now we didn't have their names. To be sure, the names on the passenger manifest were unlikely to be their real ones. But they could be cross-checked against the Mossad's databases as well as with Jordanian, Egyptian, UAE, and Saudi intelligence to put together a travel profile. We would soon know what cities they had been to in the last twelve months using these particular aliases and who their travel partners had been.

"We're on it," Trotsky told Yael.

As soon as Yael briefed us, Dutch called Mustafa. The Turkish station chief had arrived in Antalya with his team on a Learjet a mere twenty minutes before us. They were waiting for us with six rented sedans and SUVs, ready for us to follow Al-Siddiq and his handlers wherever they went. But now, with Al-Siddiq's revised itinerary, Dutch issued new orders. Three of Mustafa's men and one woman needed to purchase tickets and take the SunExpress flight to Gaziantep. That would put fresh eyes and new faces on the plane to watch Al-Siddiq's every move. The rest of us, Dutch said, needed to rush to the Learjet. Together we would head to Gaziantep with all haste.

★ ★ ★

Gaziantep was the last major Turkish city before the border with Syria.

It was almost eighty miles—close to a two-hour drive—south to Aleppo. Nearly every foreign fighter who wanted to join ISIS or the al-Nusra Front or one of the other rebel or jihadist groups battling for control of Syria found his or her way to Gaziantep. There they would hole up in a cheap hotel, make contact with a smuggler, and pay big money for someone to get them safely across the border.

Why the Turkish government was letting this

happen was another matter altogether. The fact that a member of NATO—a longtime and stalwart ally of the United States—was now allowing bloodthirsty terrorists (aka "foreign fighters") to crisscross its territory and its borders absolutely infuriated me. But the geopolitics of the situation was another matter for another time.

As our Learjet touched down at Gaziantep Oğuzeli International Airport just before sunrise, it was easy to imagine that Al-Siddiq was, in fact, about to take such a journey into Syria and very possibly into Aleppo. Several members of Yael's team were now actively considering the theory that Khalif was hiding out in Aleppo. That would keep him inside the caliphate's territory, near his forces, in direct contact with his commanders throughout Syria, but not in Raqqa, where so many ISIS members were being targeted and killed in drone strikes.

If this were the case, Al-Siddiq wouldn't have to wait for days in a cheap hotel. He already had his contacts. He already had four ISIS operatives at his side. He had a deep and intimate and enduring friendship with Abu Khalif. Indeed, he was the father of Khalif's first wife. He had almost certainly been personally invited on this journey by Khalif. There seemed to be no other reason for Al-Siddiq to be traveling to Gaziantep when he hadn't traveled outside of Saudi Arabia for at least four years. Whether he was specifically heading toward Aleppo or not, I couldn't say. I still leaned toward Khalif being hunkered down in Turkey. But either way, something big was in motion. I could feel it. I just hoped nothing I did would blow it.

By the time Al-Siddiq and his entourage landed, we were all in position and ready for any move he might make. There was a fresh team inside the airport, ready to jump on a new connecting flight if Al-Siddiq and his men surprised us again. The rest of us, however, were positioned in various vehicles on or near the airport grounds. I was behind the wheel of a dark-blue Toyota RAV4 with Yael at my side. We were idling at a gas station on Highway D850, not far from the entrance to the airport parking lot. I'd changed into blue jeans, a black sweater, and my leather jacket, though I still had the traditional Muslim skullcap on. Yael, meanwhile, had changed out of the *abaya* and was wearing gray slacks, a maroon blouse, and a black fleece, though she was also wearing a headscarf. We now looked a bit more like Turkish Muslims than ones from the Gulf—all the better, we hoped, to blend in to our surroundings.

Suddenly Yael's satphone buzzed with a series of text messages from Dutch.

Al-Siddiq exiting airport.

With three men.

Woman has broken off from group.

Have separate team following her.

Al-Siddiq and group walking to parking lot.

Getting into van.

White.

VW Caravelle.

Pulling out.

Heading north.

I pulled onto the highway, gunning the engine and putting us a good distance ahead of the approaching VW van. I knew Dutch and the two agents with him would be tailing Al-Siddiq in a silver Audi. Mustafa and three more members of his team would bring up the rear in a black Ford Explorer.

Tracking system working, Dutch texted. **Signal five by five.**

That was a relief, since Al-Siddiq was heading into the heart of the largest city in Turkey's eastern provinces, a metropolis of some 1.5 million people. Without the tracker, the chance of losing the Caravelle in a dense, highly congested city few of us had any experience in—and in which Yael and I had *no* experience—was very high. Even with the tracker we needed to stay fairly close. The system had a range of up to five miles, and was accurate to within one hundred meters, but if Al-Siddiq or his men were to realize we were trailing them, they might just be good enough to escape and disappear into a city whose layout they knew well and we did not.

Suddenly Dutch's Audi surged past the Caravelle and then past me. Dutch instructed me to slow down a bit and let the Caravelle pass. I did as I was told—subtly, gradually—and a few minutes later the VW did roar past. A minute after that, the Explorer passed us too, and now Yael and I were the last in line, a good three to four miles behind the Caravelle and at least five to six miles behind the Audi, even as other cars on this busy highway wove in and out around us.

After another ten minutes, Dutch texted to say he was exiting off the main highway onto O-54. He wanted to give Al-Siddiq and his men a wide berth and no cause for concern.

The Caravelle did not exit. It stayed on D850 and thus so did Mustafa and I.

A moment later, however, Dutch told Mustafa to stop for gas at the next service station. Yael and I would then be tasked with following the Caravelle while Dutch found a road to intercept us and reenter the mix.

As we headed into the city, the morning rush hour was building. I had barely gotten through the last few yellow lights to keep up with Al-Siddiq and was worried he or the men with him would soon realize we were following them.

"We need someone to relieve us," I told Yael, who immediately agreed and texted Dutch.

A moment later, a motorcycle roared past us, followed by a message from Dutch ordering us to drop back.

"Is that guy with us?" I asked. "I didn't know we had someone on a motorcycle."

"Neither did I," Yael said. "Let me check."

She sent a text, and a few seconds later the phone buzzed in her hands. "You're not going to believe it," she said, reading the message.

"What?" I asked, coming to a stop at a red light.

"That's Pritchard," she said.

"Paul Pritchard?"

"Yeah."

"From Dubai?"

"The very same."

"What's he doing here?"

"Good question," she said. "Guess we're about to find out."

91

* * *

I never would have imagined Gaziantep had a Holiday Inn.

But it did. It was right downtown, it was cheap—a mere thirty-five dollars a night—and it had plenty of vacancies, and that's where Al-Siddiq and the ISIS thugs stayed, in a suite with an adjoining room on either side.

Dutch and Mustafa rented the rooms directly above and directly below the suite and the two additional rooms. In these, they proceeded to attach listening devices onto the respective floors and ceilings, hoping to eavesdrop on private conversations and gain useful intelligence. Other members of the team took rooms on the same floor as Al-Siddiq's suite, specifically at either end near the elevators and stairwells. They discreetly set up small video cameras and motion sensors with silent alarms that would vibrate when any of the ISIS team left their suite or when anyone entered or exited the hallway. At the same time, they hacked into the hotel's Wi-Fi system and the local wireless phone network, hoping to intercept any e-mails or text messages.

We also rented a suite on the ground floor, which became our war room. Yael and I and two other agents—one male and one female—set up a bank of laptop computers, digital recording equipment, and various other devices allowing us to monitor everything that was happening in the rooms upstairs. We were far enough away that we could hold meetings and make calls back to the team at the Ramat David base without any risk of being overheard by the terrorists.

With the surveillance operation set up, Dutch, Mustafa, Yael, and I gathered in the war room with Paul Pritchard. I was eager to hear why Pritchard was there. So was Yael. And we were about to find out. The former CIA operative brought news. He explained that two of the three men now watching over Al-Siddiq were operatives who had personally worked for Abu Khalif in the past and were likely still closely connected to him.

"How do you know?" I asked.

"They were former residents of Abu Dhabi," Pritchard replied. "The Baqouba brothers recruited them into ISIS a few years ago, and Prince bin Zayed and his men have been tracking them ever since."

He handed us dossiers on both men, and I was struck by the level of detail. There were photos of the men and their parents and siblings along with fairly extensive bios and lists of their known associates. Perhaps most interestingly, there were transcripts of intercepted e-mail conversations between the men and Ahmed Baqouba from when they were first being recruited and didn't know they were being monitored.

"Why didn't the prince snatch these guys at the beginning?" Yael asked as she scanned the transcripts.

"That's on me," said Pritchard. "I advised him not to move too quickly. I was sure we could keep close tabs on these guys and that hopefully they would take us to the Baqoubas and then to Khalif himself. I was wrong. Less than two weeks after these e-mails were intercepted, both men gave us the slip. We've been hunting them ever since. When Ari Shalit sent stills of your suspects from Istanbul, Prince bin Zayed and I instantly recognized two of them. So here I am."

"Guess you're about to get a second bite at the apple," I said.

"That's the plan," Pritchard said.

"What about the third guy?" I asked.

"Sorry; I'm afraid we don't have anything on him," Pritchard admitted.

"Actually, we do," Yael said. "I just got an e-mail from the king in Amman. The moment Ari sent him the images from Istanbul, His Majesty called him to say he recognized one of the faces. The guy's a Jordanian. He was with Zarqawi from the earliest days of AQI. When Zarqawi was killed, he became loyal to Khalif. According to His Majesty, the guy is one of Khalif's personal bodyguards."

These were promising leads indeed. If all this was true, the evidence suggested some of Khalif's most loyal aides had been dispatched to pick up one of Khalif's most trusted friends. The chances we were getting closer to the emir had just grown exponentially.

Suddenly Dutch's phone rang. It was Nadia, the leader of the Mossad unit Dutch had assigned to track the young woman who had broken off from the others. About twenty minutes after Al-Siddiq and the team had departed the airport, she'd walked out of the terminal and gotten into a dusty old Chevy with an older woman who appeared to be in her fifties. Rather than heading north on D850 into Gaziantep, however, they'd taken a right onto D400 and headed east until they'd reached Nizip, a city of about a hundred thousand located about fifty kilometers east of where we were.

"Nizip? Why Nizip?" Dutch asked.

"We have no idea," Nadia replied.

"What are they doing now?"

"They've arrived at some sort of estate. It's a huge, sprawling compound."

"Like a hotel?"

"No, it's some sort of private home, I'd guess. The weird thing is, there aren't any men—just women and children."

"Give me the coordinates—we'll task a satellite over it."

"Sending them now."

"Good. Keep me posted."

"Will do."

Al-Siddiq wasn't taken to Aleppo or anywhere else that night. Instead, he and his handlers hunkered down in the hotel and did nothing. In fact, they did nothing for the next four days. No calls. No text messages. No e-mails. They barely even had any conversations. Nor did they leave the suite. Not once. They didn't go out to eat. They didn't go buy a newspaper. They did open the door once to get more towels from housekeeping, but that was it.

We could hear them eating every few hours. They munched on apples and cracked nuts, and we could smell fresh oranges on our casual walks past their closed doors. This suggested their suitcases and backpacks had been filled more with food than with clothes and other personal effects. It also suggested they had been anticipating hiding out in these hotel rooms for the better part of a week.

We, on the other hand, had not been anticipating doing nothing for so many days. We had to send members of the team out to restaurants and grocery stores to get supplies, even though we knew Al-Siddiq and his band could bolt at any hour of the day and we could get caught short-handed. We also risked someone spotting us and getting suspicious, reporting us to the local police or to ISIS itself. Why were these guys—and the women in Nizip—sitting around doing nothing? Why weren't they moving? Why weren't they linking up with others? Why wasn't Al-Siddiq being taken to Khalif?

One possibility was that they were waiting to receive word that it was safe to take Al-Siddiq into Syria. That was quite plausible, we concluded.

Another possibility was that ISIS had a team in the hotel, possibly even among the hotel staff, watching to see if anyone was following Al-Siddiq. Pritchard even suggested there could be an ISIS team operating out of nearby hotels and apartment buildings, watching around the clock, trying to determine if there was anyone suspicious, anyone who might be a foreign agent. If this was true, the longer we stayed, the longer we left vehicles on nearby side streets ready to move at a moment's notice, the longer we sent people out to get take-out and groceries, the higher the risk we could be spotted and attacked.

The only reassuring news was that if we'd been spotted already, we would probably have already been attacked. The fact that we were still alive suggested we had not been spotted.

At least not yet.

92

* * *

At just after nine Thursday morning, one of our silent alarms went off.

It was our fifth day in Gaziantep. Someone had just opened the door of the suite and was headed down the hallway. Yael alerted the rest of the team. Mustafa was on duty on the first floor, buying a Pepsi from a machine in the lobby, when one of Al-Siddiq's men suddenly burst out of the stairwell, brushed by him, and headed to the parking lot behind the hotel. Mustafa immediately texted the team and our four drivers, all of whom were positioned on various streets many blocks away, having been ordered by Dutch to remain even farther away from the hotel after Pritchard had raised his concerns. Now they fired up their engines and prepared to roll.

Ten minutes later, Al-Siddiq and his two other men came down the elevator and bolted out the front door. When the VW Caravelle pulled up, they jumped in and roared off.

Dutch and his men went to work in the cars. Pritchard quickly caught up to them on his motorcycle. They were trailing the Caravelle visually and via the tracking beacon while carefully watching their backs to make sure they weren't being lured into a trap.

The team had briefly debated attaching an additional tracking beacon to the VW. In the end, however, Dutch had decided against it. He believed the van should be neither tampered with nor even approached, on the theory that it was likely being watched closely for just such a development. Pritchard agreed, and that was that.

Yael and I did not roll with the trackers. Rather, we joined Mustafa and two of his agents upstairs to break into the terrorists' suite and adjoining rooms before housekeeping could get to them. It was a risky move, especially if there were ISIS operatives still in the hotel watching the rooms. But Mustafa insisted it had to be done.

We spent the better part of an hour going over each room with a fine-tooth comb, but the men had left nothing useful behind. There was no luggage. No personal items. Not even any trash. If that weren't discouraging enough, the rooms had been wiped down so thoroughly that not a single fingerprint—even from previous guests—could be lifted. This suggested neither Al-Siddiq nor his handlers were planning on returning to the hotel. They were moving on. But where?

We went back downstairs to the war room and waited. We played cards and paced and drank instant coffee. We didn't hear from Dutch or his team for more than an hour, and with every minute that passed, Yael's and my anxiety grew.

We didn't dare call or text the guys. They were in the midst of a high-stakes operation, and the last thing we wanted to do was distract them, even for a moment.

Then, just before noon, Yael received a call. But it was not Dutch. It was Ari Shalit, and he had news. President Mahfouz had just called Prime Minister Eitan. The Egyptians had been carefully reviewing the photos Shalit had sent them of the young woman in the *hijab* who had been traveling with Al-Siddiq. It had taken several days, but they now had a positive ID.

She was an Egyptian, born and raised in Alexandria, the daughter of a prominent leader of the Muslim Brotherhood who had been jailed and later executed after Mahfouz came to power. At that point, she and her three brothers had all become radicalized. Two had gone to Iraq to join ISIS and had blown themselves up in a joint martyrdom operation that killed 179 people at a church in Baghdad. Her remaining brother had died during the battle of Dabiq back in December. Now she was the only one left. According to Mahfouz, the young woman had been with ISIS rebels on the outskirts of Aleppo as recently as four weeks ago.

As Yael related the details to the rest of us, I couldn't help but be intrigued. Did these new tidbits suggest we might soon, in fact, be heading into Aleppo, however chaotic and dangerous the situation on the border?

But Shalit wasn't done. According to Israeli intelligence, the paramilitary forces of the Syrian Kurds had been engaged in heavy fighting with

ISIS in recent days along the Syrian-Turkish border. By all accounts, the Kurds had gained the upper hand. They were taking significant swaths of territory from ISIS, and there were now only a few corridors between northwestern Syria and Turkey still under ISIS control. Shalit said his analysts were telling him it might no longer be possible for any ISIS personnel to get from Gaziantep into Syria or from Aleppo into Turkey. If Abu Khalif was in Aleppo, he might be stuck there.

Then, just as the sun was going down, Yael's satphone rang again. This time it was Dutch. He and his team had tracked the VW all day. There was no question Al-Siddiq's men were trying everything they could to spot and shake anyone trying to tail them. Their tradecraft was spectacular, he said, but with the tracking beacon in place, Dutch and Pritchard and the rest of the team had ultimately followed the men to a compound high up in a mountain range not far from Nizip.

"Is Khalif there?" Yael asked.

"I don't know," Dutch said. "Maybe."

"What do you mean, maybe?"

"We haven't seen him. But it's possible."

"Where are you guys exactly?"

"I'm hiding in a cave near the crest of a ridge. Pritchard is on another ridge, off to my right. The rest of the team is watching the cars and maintaining a perimeter."

"What can you see?"

"I'm looking down at a huge walled compound—huge. The whole thing is about the size of a soccer stadium. It looks like an ancient

Ottoman fortress of some kind. Pritchard thinks it's from the sixteenth century. The walls have got to be fifteen or twenty feet high, and thick—two or three feet thick at least. There's an enormous mosque in the back left corner with a big marble dome and a stone minaret probably thirty, thirty-five feet high."

"What else?"

"There's a two-story row of stone buildings along the left side of the compound. I can see through some of the windows. It looks like classrooms. Could be a madrassa, though there aren't any kids around. On the right side of the compound, there's a similar two-story wing. Pritchard says from his angle it looks like a dormitory—bunk beds, dressers, lavatories, that kind of thing. In the middle there's a giant courtyard."

"Security?" Yael asked.

"Airtight," Dutch replied.

"How many men?"

"There've got to be at least two hundred ISIS fighters down there, maybe more if some are inside or downstairs—we've seen stairwells that seem to go to an underground level."

"You're sure they're ISIS?"

"Absolutely—the black flag is flying from the top of the minaret."

"In the middle of Turkey?"

"Well, I'd hardly call it the middle. We're 1,200 kilometers from Istanbul by road and a good 750 kilometers from Ankara. Believe me, this is the frontier—rural, rugged, and only ten or twenty miles north of the Syrian border."

"Would you hide an ISIS emir there?" I asked.

"I might," Dutch said.

"What are the men doing now?" Mustafa asked.

"Several dozen are patrolling the perimeter or hunkered outside the gates in huge APCs with a lot of weaponry. The rest are sitting in the courtyard, eating dinner."

"Who else is there?" I asked.

"What do you mean?"

"Do you see any women?"

"No."

"And you said no children?"

"Not any that I can see."

"What about elderly?"

"Not from my vantage point."

"So it's just young men?" I pressed.

"I don't see anyone older than forty—most look like they're in their twenties. Big. Strong. Good shape. Fighters. And they're Arab, not Turkish."

"All armed, I presume?"

"Heavily."

"Okay, so what's your gut tell you?"

"Well, there's no question Al-Siddiq is there, along with the three ISIS operatives who brought him."

"You can see the van?" Yael asked.

"Affirmative," Dutch replied. "And the tracking signal from Al-Siddiq is still strong and clear, but . . ."

His voice trailed off.

I was about to ask him to finish his sentence, but Yael held up her hand, motioning me to be quiet. She knew Dutch better than any of the rest of us. She knew how he thought, how he operated. She knew he'd speak when he was ready and not a moment before. And sure enough, a few seconds later, he finished his thought.

"But *if* Khalif is in there or if he's coming," he said, "we're going to need a lot more men."

93

* * *

As evening fell, we headed for Nizip.

Mustafa and the rest of his team brought food, water, blankets, more weapons, and additional ammunition to Dutch and his team up in the mountains. Yael and I, on the other hand, checked into a dusty, grungy old hotel, once again posing as a Muslim husband and wife, she in her *abaya* and me in my skullcap. The moment we found our floor and our chambers, we locked the door behind us and slid the dresser in front of the door. It would hardly stop jihadists from bursting into the room if they found us, but it might slow them down enough to give us a fighting chance.

Using the small desk in the room and the two nightstands on either side of the small double bed, we again set up a mini war room with our laptops, digital recording equipment, state-of-the-art headphones, and a slew of satellite phones and chargers. We kept two MP5 submachines always within reach.

Meanwhile, up in the mountains, Mustafa would soon be giving Dutch and Pritchard cases of sophisticated directional microphones and video cameras equipped with high-powered zoom lenses, night vision, thermal-imaging technology, and the ability to broadcast encrypted signals back to us. Our job was to pinpoint Al-Siddiq and listen to his conversations in the hopes that this might lead us to our prey.

By one in the morning, Mustafa had delivered the equipment, and Dutch and Pritchard had it all up and running. The encrypted signals were coming in. Yael and I were recording everything, and we'd located Al-Siddiq in the compound. He was not in the dormitory. He was in the other wing, in one of the classrooms located on the second floor of the madrassa. The shades were drawn, so we could not see him, but we could hear him, and we were stunned by what we were listening to.

Rather than being welcomed, the Saudi professor was being grilled. The interrogators—two of them—sounded significantly younger than Al-Siddiq, and they were asking questions in rapid fire, barely giving him time to answer. *Whom had he told that he was leaving Medina? Who else? What did his wife know? Who had booked his tickets? Why hadn't he followed the precise instructions he'd been sent? Whom had he spoken to on his journey? Why had he worn Western clothes? Didn't he understand that was forbidden? Had he been followed? How could he be sure? What precautions had he taken? Why hadn't he brought his laptop? Where was his laptop? Was it secure? Did his wife have access to it? Didn't he know the risks?*

The interrogation continued until just before

3 a.m. Then the men left, slammed and locked the door behind them, and all we could hear was heavy breathing and sobs and the sound of clanking metal, like chains.

What in the world was going on? Why was Al-Siddiq being treated like a spy, a traitor, a mole, rather than a guest of honor? Yael and I sent urgent flash text messages to Dutch and Pritchard and back to Ari—all encrypted, of course—telling them what we were hearing. They didn't get it either. I looked at Yael, stricken with the rapidly rising fear that this was not only a mistake but very well could be a diversion. Had Al-Siddiq been bait? Had he been cleverly dangled in front of us to distract from Khalif's real movements? The very thought sickened me. But for the moment, I could think of nothing else.

Yael texted our concerns to Shalit, who urged us not to give up hope.

Take a break, he wrote. **Try to get some sleep— a few hours at least. And we'll go back at it when the sun comes up.**

Yael and I looked at each other and then around the small, musty room and at the creaky double bed. This was hardly the five-star accommodations we'd had in Cairo or in Dubai, and we were both exhausted. For much of the past few weeks, we'd been operating off of sheer adrenaline. I had, anyway, and now it all seemed to have drained out of my system.

"I'll be out in a minute," Yael said, breaking the silence as she grabbed her MP5 and ducked into the tiny bathroom to change and brush her teeth.

I sat down on the bed, holding my MP5 and praying I'd never have to use it. I also prayed for something else, something far more important—the strength to let Yael go. We'd been spending an awful lot of time together, and though we weren't talking about personal things—and though we were often with the rest of our team, completely focused on our work—I was simply intoxicated to be in her presence. I'd never met anyone as strong and yet as sensitive, as funny and yet as intellectually stimulating. I loved watching her mind work. I loved seeing her process information, seeing her direct the team. And I also loved how she looked in every piece of clothing she put on. It was killing me to be so physically close to her, all day, every day, knowing she was engaged. She wasn't available. She'd chosen someone else. I'd lost my chance, before I'd even realized I had a competitor, before I'd even known I needed to fight for her.

I fumbled through my carry-on bag until I found my toothbrush and paste. Then I turned off the overhead light and the room was illuminated merely by the greenish glow of our electronic gear.

Just then, the bathroom door opened and Yael came out. I slid past her into the bathroom and took a cold shower. When I finally came out of the bathroom and clicked off the light, Yael was already in bed and under the covers. She just looked back at me and shrugged.

The room was tiny. There was nowhere else to lie down. If there'd been a full bathtub instead of a mere shower stall, at least I could have slept in the tub. Without another option, however, I reluctantly climbed into the bed and thought the entire hotel must be able to hear it creak. If I could have, I would have moved myself over to the very edge of the mattress, but there was literally no room to move at all. And so I lay there, trying not to move, listening to her breathing.

Sometime later, she turned over, and the bed made a terrible racket. Once she'd settled, her mouth was right by my left ear. "I'm sorry, J. B.," she whispered.

"For what?" I whispered back, surprised.

"For the way I treated you at first. And for not telling you sooner."

"Don't worry about it," I said. "I'm a big boy. I'll be okay. I'm glad you're happy."

"I'm not sure I'm the kind of girl that can do happy," she said.

"What is that supposed to mean?"

"You know what I do. You know what I see, what I know, where I am, where my job takes me. Not exactly conducive to being a happy person."

"Maybe it's time to stop."

"Maybe it is."

"*I'm* going to stop," I said.

"What do you mean?"

"When this is done, I'm going to put in my letter of resignation at the *Times*."

"Why? You're such a great reporter."

I didn't reply. I just lay there, staring at the ceiling, straining with every ounce of my being not to turn and kiss this woman.

"I don't know," I said finally, deciding I was

better off talking than not. "I think I'm just through."

"Yeah," she said. "Maybe this is it for me, too."

"There's always the prime minister's office," I said, trying to be helpful.

"I can't," she whispered. "If I'm done, I need to be really done. I need to start a new life—a real life."

"Meaning what?"

"Being a wife. Being a mom. Taking my kids to the park, to the beach, to the mountains, teaching them to read, to write, to sing."

"You'll be good at that," I said.

"You think so?" she asked.

"I do."

And a few moments later, she nestled up next to me and fell sound asleep.

94

★ ★ ★

NIZIP, TURKEY

I didn't sleep that night.

I couldn't. For the next few hours, I just listened to the monotonous ticking of my grandfather's pocket watch on the nightstand beside me and prayed for strength and mercy. In my forty-some-odd years, I'd made a lot of mistakes, done a lot of things I wasn't proud of. But that was the past. That was behind me. I was on a new path now. I wanted to do the right thing. I wanted to honor my Lord. I just wasn't sure I was going to make it.

By God's grace, I made it through the night without kissing the beautiful and unavailable woman sleeping beside me. And in the morning, the new day brought very good news.

Yael grabbed the satphone off the floor on her side of the bed, beside her MP5, and took the call from Dutch. "You're kidding," she said. "That's incredible. Okay, we're on it."

"What?" I asked, suddenly feeling a jolt of adrenaline surge through my system.

"They think they may have found him."

"Who? Khalif?"

"They're not certain," she explained. "But a few minutes ago, Al-Siddiq was let out of his cell. Someone apologized to him, told him they had to make sure he hadn't been compromised. Then— well, here, let's take a look."

She jumped out of bed, grabbed her laptop, and powered it up. In a moment we had our headphones on and were watching video footage transmitted from the mountain. The time stamp read, *07:12:36.*

At first, I didn't recognize Al-Siddiq. He was no longer wearing an oxford shirt and tweed blazer. Rather, he had on a traditional white *thawb* similar to the one I had worn entering Turkey. His head was covered in a red- and white-checked headdress known as a *ghutra*, secured to his head with a classic *igal*, a thick black cord that was worn doubled. He was strolling across the courtyard with another man, about his same height, also dressed in traditional white robes, though this one was wearing a ceremonial outer cloak known as a *bisht*. This man's *ghutra* completely obscured his face from anything but a direct, eye-to-eye view.

"Thank you for coming, father," the shrouded man said, speaking so softly we had to play it back several times to be sure.

"It is my honor," Al-Siddiq said.

"Ahmed and Faisal explained their procedures?"

"They did, and of course I fully understand."

"I hope you know they meant you no harm."

"Yes, yes, of course."

"We cannot be too careful."

"I know," Al-Siddiq said.

"You are my guest of honor."

"No, Your Excellency; it is my honor completely."

"So would you like to see her?"

"Is that possible?"

"It is surely possible."

"Then, yes, absolutely, I would love that."

"Good—she will be here in a matter of moments."

"She is coming? Here? Now?" Al-Siddiq asked.

"They are bringing her even as we speak."

The satphone rang. Yael answered it and motioned me to patch in through the app on my phone. It was Ari Shalit.

"Have you seen it?" Shalit asked, urgency thick in his voice.

"We're watching it now," she said.

"Both of you?"

"Yes."

"J. B. is with you?"

"Yes, of course."

"I'm here," I said.

"Good—so is it him?"

"Maybe," I said tentatively.

"It looks like him," Shalit said.

"I can't see his face," I said.

"Can you tell by his walk, his gait?"

"No, I'm sorry."

"But does it sound like him?"

"Hard to say," I confessed. "He's speaking low, almost mumbling. That's not like him. That's not how he was with me."

"Maybe he's different with his father-in-law," Shalit said.

"Maybe."

"But of what you could hear, does it sound like him—the style, the cadence, the air of authority?" Shalit pressed.

"Maybe—it's possible—it's a start," I replied. "We'll need more, but—"

Shalit cut me off. "No, no, you're not understanding the situation," he said. "I need an answer. I need to know now. The prime minister needs to know—not later, not tomorrow—we need to know right now, this second."

"Why? What's the rush?" I pushed back.

"If it is Khalif, how long do you think he's going to stay in that compound?" Shalit asked. "A few hours? A day? This is Abu Khalif. This is the emir of the Islamic State. He could leave in the middle of the night. He could leave in the middle of this conversation. This is the most wanted man on the planet. Just because we've found him—*if* we've found him—that doesn't mean we'll know where he is tomorrow."

Yael looked at me. I could see strain and fatigue in her eyes.

"You're the expert, Mr. Collins," Shalit pressed. "This is why you're here. No one in the West—no one outside his inner circle—has spent as much time with Abu Khalif as you have."

"Right now I'm looking at a man in a robe, with a shroud over his face, mumbling, practically talking under his breath, and you want a 100 percent positive ID?"

"It's not what *I* want," he shot back. "The prime minister and the entire security cabinet are assembled. They're in the Kirya, in the war room. They're waiting for an answer. Are we go or no go?"

"I need a few minutes," I said.

"You don't have a few minutes," Shalit warned me. "Right now there's a caravan of women and children heading toward the compound. As best we can tell, all four of Khalif's wives and all of his children have been staying in Nizip, and now they're headed to see Khalif—if it's him— and they're almost there. Dutch has a sniper rifle out. He's in position. He has this guy in his sights. He's ready to take the shot—and risk the consequences of two hundred ISIS fighters going crazy and storming up the mountain—but we need an answer, and we need it now."

95

★ ★ ★

My mind was racing and the pressure was enormous.

It *did* seem like Khalif, but could I be certain? If I was wrong, I'd be condemning an innocent man to death. Well, maybe not innocent. This was clearly a senior ISIS commander. He was surrounded by two hundred or more ISIS fighters. But was he the emir or not? For that, I needed more data. I needed more time. But Shalit wasn't going to give it to me.

So far, all the pieces of the puzzle were consistent with this being Khalif. The shrouded man had called Al-Siddiq "father," a term of honor, affection, respect. He'd apologized to Al-Siddiq for having his men interrogate him. And he had used the names Ahmed and Faisal—the first names of two of the Baqouba brothers. It would make sense they would be with Khalif, helping to protect him and vet his guests. What's more, Al-Siddiq seemed excited to see someone, a woman, and the shrouded man seemed to have planned ahead for Al-Saddiq to see her. Could it be Aisha, the professor's daughter, the emir's wife?

In almost every way, it added up. But there was a real risk. What I was seeing wasn't hard evidence. There could be other Ahmeds. There could be other Faisals. Al-Siddiq was Khalif's father-in-law, but he was the theological mentor of the entire Islamic State movement. There could be any number of other senior leaders who revered him as "father." And we hadn't actually heard any mention of a wife or a daughter, much less the name Aisha.

"Collins," Shalit pushed, "I need an answer."

"I'm sorry," I said. "But I can't. I don't have enough data."

"You've got all you're going to get."

"Then my answer is no—I can't say beyond a doubt that this is Khalif. I'm sorry."

"Yael, what do you say?" Shalit demanded.

"Don't ask me that," she replied.

"I'm not asking," Shalit said. "I'm ordering you to give me your assessment."

"You heard the expert," she demurred. "He spent hours with Khalif. He wants this guy as badly as any of us. But even he can't say for certain."

"Can you?" he asked.

Silence.

"You're the head of the unit tracking him," Shalit continued. "Collins doesn't work for us. You do."

"But *you* pulled him onto this team over my objections," she argued. "You didn't do it out of pity. You did it because he knows what he's talking about. He knows this guy. He's seen his face. He's heard his voice. He's the expert, and if he's not sure, then I'm not sure."

Shalit cursed.

Then Yael nudged me. She was staring at the live video feeds from the mountaintop positions. The women and children had arrived. They were pouring into the compound. Whatever chance we might have had was now lost, and suddenly the line went dead. The call was over. Shalit had hung up.

Yael just stood there, staring at the monitor, the satphone in her hand, not sure what to say or do. I didn't know either, and I felt sick.

I excused myself and headed into the bathroom and took a shower. By the time I came out, Yael was dressed in faded jeans and a gray sweatshirt and was sitting at the same desk, still watching the real-time video feed of the courtyard. As hundreds of armed men milled about at the edges of the compound, the children all gravitated to the shrouded man sitting under an archway, in the shadows, partially obscured from our view. Meanwhile, Al-Siddiq sat on the other side of the courtyard, beside a woman wearing a headscarf who appeared to be in her late thirties. They spoke in whispers. Our microphones weren't picking up any of it, but it certainly looked like a man and his married daughter catching up on old times.

Yael looked at me. "It was the right call, J. B. It was. The case was circumstantial. Ari was pushing you too hard, probably because he was being pushed too hard. For what it's worth, I'm proud of you."

"Thanks," I said, but Yael's encouragement didn't erase the gnawing feeling in my gut that I'd just made a very serious error in judgment.

Over the course of the next few hours, we picked up bits of audio—little snatches of sound— that gave me more and more confidence the man we were staring at so intently was, in fact, Abu Khalif. He finally used the name Aisha and then used it several more times. What's more, he asked Al-Siddiq for an update on the death toll from the attacks in America.

What sealed it for me was when the shrouded man asked for an update on the fatwa. And then came the moment that made my blood run cold.

"Has anyone found him yet?" he asked.

"Who?" Al-Siddiq pressed.

"Collins. Have we tracked him down? Has anyone gotten a lead on his surviving family? If one of our people find them, I don't want them killed. I want them alive. Make sure all our people know that. Especially James Bradley. I want him captured and brought to the site. I will take my vengeance out on him myself."

With that, the man I was now certain was Abu Khalif disappeared. He got up, left the courtyard, entered the front door of the mosque, and was completely obscured from our view. For the next three days, while the women and children remained in the compound and Al-Siddiq took a morning and evening stroll, often with his daughter, we did not see Khalif again, nor did we hear his voice.

Shalit was furious, and I couldn't blame him.

The longer Dutch and Pritchard and the others were up on those mountains, the more likely they were going to get spotted and captured. If they were caught, they'd be beheaded, or burned alive, right before our eyes. We were out of options and out of time, and there was no way to sugarcoat it—this was my fault.

96

* * *

"What if the women and children leave?" I asked.

It was about three in the morning on the fourth day. Yael and I were drinking bad black coffee we'd heated in a tin pan on a small portable hot plate and watching the monitors so Dutch and Pritchard and the guys in the mountains could get a few hours of shut-eye.

"What do you mean?" she asked.

"I mean, let's say the wives and kids all get up and leave one morning; what's the plan? We haven't seen Khalif in days. We don't know where in the compound he actually is at this point. The last time we saw him, he went into the mosque. But he could be anywhere, underground or in one of the two wings. So what if Dutch or the other snipers never get another look at him?"

She looked at me, considering. Then she said, "Honestly? I don't think it matters whether we can see him or not. Khalif is never leaving that compound."

"What do you mean? Why do you say that?"

"Think about it. This is where Khalif has

chosen to settle himself, his wives, his kids, and his senior leadership. He's safe here. He's in a NATO country, safe from air strikes by the U.S. or Israel. The Turkish police aren't in sight. Neither is the military. He isn't going anywhere. He's essentially got carte blanche."

"Why?"

"Why is the president of Turkey—with his megalomaniacal dreams of becoming an all-powerful sultan and reviving the glories of the Ottoman Empire—allowing the emir of the Islamic State to reside in his territory? I have no idea."

"You think he knows?"

"Maybe yes, maybe no, but let's face it—the government in Ankara are a bunch of Islamists, and they're becoming more radicalized every day. Why else have they been letting foreign fighters cross their territory to go fight for ISIS? Should it really surprise us the head of ISIS is living right here?"

"So you guys have to storm the place, like how the Americans got bin Laden in that compound in Pakistan."

"With the force we've got?"

"Well, you'd obviously need more men."

"It's not going to happen."

"Why not?"

"Dutch has been begging for more man-power, heavier weapons—but the security cabinet says no."

"Because if a bunch of Israeli commandos get caught or killed on Turkish soil, you've just triggered a war with NATO?"

530 ★ WITHOUT WARNING

"Maybe," she said.

"What about the Jordanians? The Egyptians? The emirates? They all want to take out Khalif. They've all provided tremendous support. You've seen it. This is historic—Israelis and Arabs working so closely on a major intelligence and military operation? It might be unprecedented."

"But they're not going to risk being seen as invading a NATO ally either."

"So where does that leave us?" I asked.

"The Kurds," Yael replied.

"The Kurds?"

"The Syrian Kurdish rebels, to be precise. They now control most of the border with Turkey, and they hate ISIS with a passion. They also hate the Turks. They want their own country. They want to link up with the Turkish Kurds—between ten and twenty million people—and the Iraqi Kurds to create a unified Republic of Kurdistan."

"So how does that help us?"

"A few days ago, a squad of Syrian Kurdish rebels near Aleppo got into a firefight with Assad's forces. The Kurds won. The regime guys were slaughtered. In the process, the Kurds captured a Russian-made surface-to-surface missile launcher—the SS-21 Scarab C. It's got a range of about 115 miles, and it's equipped with a GPS-linked guidance system, so it's pretty accurate."

"And?"

"And let's just say the Mossad has pretty close ties to the Kurds. We don't see eye to eye on everything—don't get me wrong. But the enemy of my enemy is my friend, right? The Kurds are taking out ISIS forces. They're taking out Assad's forces. We try to help where we can. So Ari asked the security cabinet to authorize the Mossad to discreetly let the Kurdish rebel commanders know someone might have found Abu Khalif, and if that turns out to be true, would they be interested in taking him out. The cabinet agreed, and Ari set the plan into motion. Now everything's set. The moment the women and children leave the compound, Ari will give the Kurds the precise coordinates for the missiles, and three minutes later, it will all be over."

I was silent, processing this new information, as we kept our eyes on the monitors. All was quiet at the compound. Everyone except the guards on duty was sound asleep. Yael suggested that I try to get some sleep, after which she would do the same.

I tried, but I simply couldn't fall asleep. Too much was happening—or more precisely, not happening. We'd done it. We'd hunted down Abu Khalif. We'd actually found him. We had him surrounded. Yet we couldn't take him out.

Meanwhile, out there in the rest of the world, innocent people were dying. ISIS was butchering, enslaving, and raping men, women, and children. And why? To hasten the coming of their messiah, to fulfill their ancient prophecies, and maybe for sheer pleasure. Yet however ghastly their killing spree had been so far, they were just ramping up. They had already come after my country. They had already come after my family. Soon they would be coming after me. The stakes could not be higher.

Yet as I lay there, staring at the ceiling, thinking of my mother and my nephew now in heaven and

Matt and his family now in hiding, I was growing desperate. Our window to move was rapidly closing. Dutch and his men couldn't stay out there much longer. They were going to get noticed. They could very well get killed. We had to pinpoint Khalif's precise location and then we had to strike fast.

But how?

97

* * *

For well over an hour, I war-gamed every possible scenario I could think of.

I prayed for wisdom—no, actually, I begged God to show me what to do. But no answer seemed to come.

Then it was my turn to relieve Yael and let her close her eyes and get some rest. Bleary-eyed, I splashed cold water on my face. Then I made myself a fresh pot of bad coffee, sat down at the desk in front of our laptops, and donned my headphones while she collapsed in the bed and immediately fell asleep.

Just before dawn, the Muslim call to prayer rang out from the minaret. It wasn't a recording. Even through my headphones I could tell someone was actually in the tower, calling the faithful to their morning rituals. I remotely adjusted one of the cameras and zoomed in, hoping it might be the emir. But it was Al-Siddiq. Soon hundreds of foreign fighters came out of the dormitory and into the courtyard, each with a prayer rug. Then they all bowed down, facing Mecca, and began their prayers.

Before long, the sun began to rise, yet the compound—tucked into a small canyon and surrounded by mountain peaks—was still covered in long, dark shadows. The two dozen guards at the front gate were replaced by a new shift. Various other clumps of guards throughout the grounds were being relieved as well.

Eventually, as the first rays of sun splashed across the lawn in the courtyard, Al-Siddiq came out and went for a long, quiet, peaceful walk. No one was with him. Not his daughter. Not any of the fighters. He simply walked alone. And still, no sign of Khalif.

Why not? Where was he? Why wasn't he showing his face? He couldn't possibly sense we were watching him. If he had, his men would have attacked Dutch and Pritchard and their colleagues, and we'd be dealing with a bloodbath, not the prospect of another day of sitting around doing nothing.

At precisely eight o'clock, the courtyard was full of Arab fighters again. Now they were doing their morning exercises. By nine, I could see signs the wives and children were gathering in the various classrooms to begin their daily studies. All of this was pushing my frustration to the boiling point. I was watching a genocidal, apocalyptic terrorist community going about their day, business as usual, and I couldn't take much more of it.

When Yael eventually woke up, showered,

and dressed, we spent several hours brainstorming ways to break the stalemate—but yet again we came up with nothing. At one point in the early afternoon, we got a call from Shalit. He wanted an update. We had little to tell him. He had little to tell us. The security cabinet was becoming divided. Several members were suggesting it might be time to pull us all out of Turkey. They understandably feared sparking a major confrontation with Ankara if Turkish authorities found us here. One member of the cabinet was urging Prime Minister Eitan to authorize the Kurds to simply decimate the entire compound immediately, even with Khalif's wives and children there. He argued that in the end it would be the Kurds who would get credit for taking out the ISIS emir and several hundred ISIS fighters, and they would take any blame for collateral damage as well.

However, the prime minister had strenuously objected to the suggestion. "The government of Israel does not target innocent women and children—*ever*—period, end of discussion," he'd said, and that was that.

For this I was immensely grateful and relieved. I hadn't signed up to kill innocents. I'd signed up to bring Abu Khalif to justice. I would never be party to an operation that would countenance the targeting of the wives and children of terrorists, no matter what some politicians back home or anywhere else in the world might advocate. I hadn't always lived by the morals and the ethics that my grandfather and my mom had modeled for me, but I had no doubt what they would say about purposefully killing innocents in pursuit of taking out a terrorist.

Some might argue that Khalif's wives and children weren't innocent. But I didn't buy the argument. So far as I was concerned, they were effectively hostages of Khalif and the demonic system he had built around himself. Under the Islamic system, no woman could refuse a marriage proposal by him. And regardless of what the women thought about Khalif, they had absolutely no say in his day-to-day affairs. The children? What choice did they have in being born to a genocidal father and raised in this sinister family? None whatsoever. Might some of them one day join ISIS and devote themselves to a life of violent jihad? Yes, I knew they might. I wasn't blind. I could see the path they were on. But did this condemn them to death by a Syrian missile before reaching their teenage years? Not in my mind. Besides, might they not choose other lives, especially if their father met his demise and they were free from his slavery? I couldn't say for sure, but they might, and even that sliver of hope was enough for me.

"Have you gotten any rest?" Yael asked by midafternoon.

"No, but I'm fine," I said.

"You don't look fine. Your eyes are bloodshot. You're getting dark rings under them. Why don't you try to lie down for a while?"

"How can I?" I asked her. "How can I sleep while Khalif is up there in the mountains, free and clear, planning some new horrific attack? We can't sit here anymore. We need to do something."

"I agree," she said. "But we've been over and over it, and we've come up with nothing."

I was about to throw my hands up in despair when suddenly a thought occurred to me. "How precise are those Syrian missiles—the ones the Kurds captured?" I asked.

"Quite."

"I mean, could they take out the mosque but leave the classrooms unaffected?" I asked.

Khalif's wives and children were sleeping in the madrassa, while Al-Siddiq and all the male fighters were sleeping on the bunk beds in the dormitory.

"I don't know about *unaffected*," Yael replied. "Those missiles pack some pretty powerful explosives. But yeah, given the size of the compound, I doubt anyone in the classrooms or the dorms would be killed if the Kurds hit the mosque. Injured maybe, but not killed. But why do you ask? I mean, we don't really know Khalif is in the mosque."

I ignored her question and asked another of my own. "What if Khalif was actually in the dormitory? Could one of the missiles take out the dormitory and not destroy the classrooms or kill those inside?"

"I think so."

"Can you find out for sure?"

"I could," she said, "but why? What good does it do if we don't have precise intel on where Khalif is?"

"Just find out," I whispered. "I have an idea."

98

* * *

It was almost midnight when Yael finally gave me some answers.

Yes, according to Shalit, the Mossad analysts, and the chief of staff of the Israeli Defense Forces, the Russian-built missile was that precise. Given the size of the compound, *if* we could actually find Khalif, and *if* he was actually in a part of the compound that was far enough away from the women and children, then yes, the Kurds could hit that section, and the women and children should survive.

But that was a lot of ifs. The brutal fact remained—we had no idea precisely where Khalif was, and without that specificity, the prime minister and his security cabinet were not going to authorize a strike.

I pressed Yael on the specifics. I asked dozens of questions about the technical details of the missiles, their size, their range, their speed. I pressed her on the design of the guidance system and on why Shalit and the IDF were so confident. To her credit, she really had done her homework. She had answers to all the questions I was asking and then some. In the end, I was satisfied.

And then she asked a question of her own. "Why are you asking all this? What are you thinking?"

I had wondered how I'd feel when this moment came. I feared I might be jittery, tense, equivocating. But instead I found myself speaking in a calm, firm, but gentle voice. "Yael, I'm going to that compound," I said. "Tonight."

"What are you talking about?"

"Khalif wants to find me, wants to kill me—fine, he can have me. I'm going to surrender," I told her.

"Are you crazy?"

"Not at all. Listen—the moment I arrive, Khalif will think he's won. But I'll be wearing a tracking beacon. I'll be wearing the glasses you guys gave me. You'll know exactly where I am and thus exactly where he is. The moment I'm in his presence, you can tell the Kurds to take the shot, and in three minutes, it'll all be over."

"But how will you get out?"

"I won't."

Yael's eyes went wide. "J. B., that's lunacy—no—absolutely not," she shot back and launched into a desperate attempt to dissuade me.

But I cut her off. "Yael, stop," I insisted. "My mind's made up. This is the only way, and you know it. Dutch and Pritchard can't stay up there indefinitely. They're going to be caught. They're going to be killed. And you said it yourself—Khalif isn't leaving that compound, and why would he?

He's hiding behind the human shield of his wives and children. It's time to take him out. Tonight."

"J. B., come on. You're exhausted. You're not thinking rationally. There's another way, and we'll find it."

"No, there isn't. I wish there was—believe me—but there isn't, and you know it. I've been thinking and praying about this nonstop. And this is it. We're out of time. This is our only play."

"What about Matt? What about Annie and Katie?" she asked, a look of near panic in her eyes as she observed the resolution in mine.

"Why do you think I'm doing this?" I asked her. "Khalif has triggered a worldwide hunt for my family and me. The only way Matt and Annie and Katie come out of this alive, safe, and free to live without fear is if we take out Khalif right here, right now."

"So what are you going to do, walk up to the door and knock?"

"Why not?"

"Because it's *insane.*"

"No, what would be insane is to keep sitting here doing nothing, to let him keep hunting my family, to let him continue his genocide without stopping him if I can."

"But what if the moment you're caught, he puts you in a cage in the middle of the courtyard and gathers his wives and children all around him?"

"That's why I have to go now, in the middle of the night, while his wives and children are sleeping."

"But what if he's sleeping with them?"

"Then his men will wake him, and he'll come to me."

"How do you know?"

"Because he won't be able to help himself," I replied. "He's a fanatical, apocalyptic Muslim. He believes he's ushering in the End of Days. He believes he's preparing for the coming of the Mahdi and the establishment of the global caliphate. He'll want to gloat. He'll lecture me. He'll go off on a bloodthirsty, demon-possessed rant, and while he does, the Kurds will push the button, and boom. It'll all be over before he knows it."

"You're really serious?" she said quietly. The look in her eyes was shifting. Gone was the shock. Gone, too, was the defiance. Now all I saw was sadness.

"I am," I said.

"And you're not scared to die." Her eyes were filling with tears.

"I used to be, Yael, but I'm not anymore."

"Why not?"

"Because I know where I'm going," I said.

I told her what I'd done. I told her how Matt had been trying to convince me about Jesus Christ for years. I told her how I'd been angry, how I'd completely rejected my brother, how I hadn't even talked to him for nearly a decade. But then I told her what had happened on the plane on the way to Dubai, how I'd finally received Christ as my Savior. "Everything's changed, Yael. *I'm* changed. I've made enough bad choices in my life. It's time to make a good one."

"But how could this possibly be good?" she asked, tears running down her cheeks.

"Because it's one of the first things I've ever done that isn't about me," I replied. "It's for Matt and Annie. It's for Katie. And for everyone else facing death at the hands of Abu Khalif."

Until that moment, I'd basically lived my entire life in utter self-centeredness. I'd ruined a marriage, become an alcoholic, and put countless friends and colleagues in harm's way. And for what? To get a good story? To win a Pulitzer or some other award? Was that really worth it? I'd concluded it wasn't. Not for me. Not anymore. It was time to do something for others. It was time to follow the example of my Savior.

"I told you about the letter Khachigian left me. Did I ever read it to you?"

"No, you just summarized it—that he was urging you to go after Khalif with everything you had. I don't think this is what he meant."

"Maybe not, but he did urge me to listen to Matt and give my life to Christ, like he finally did."

"Okay, fine, and you did that. But—"

"I know this doesn't make sense to you, Yael. And I'm sorry. But just listen to me for a moment. Khachigian closed the letter with a verse of Scripture, something Jesus said to his disciples. 'Greater love has no one than this, that one lay down his life for his friends.' Honestly, I'd never even heard of that verse until a few weeks ago. Then the pastor quoted it during the memorial service. I've been chewing on it ever since, but until this afternoon I never really understood it."

"And you think you do now?" she asked.

"Yeah, I do. Sometimes you don't get to win like they do in the movies. Sometimes, if you really love someone, you just have to lay down your own life so they can live. I know you think that's crazy. And for most of my life I would have agreed with you. But now I finally know where I'm going when I die. The moment I draw my last breath here, I'll draw my first breath in heaven with Christ. I'll get to see my mom and Josh again and be with them forever. Death isn't the end for me. It's just the beginning. I'm ready. I wasn't before, but now I am. And at least my death will mean something."

I reached for my carry-on bag and pulled out a few folded pieces of paper and handed them to her.

"What's that, your suicide note?" she asked.

"I'm not committing suicide, Yael."

"Of course you are."

"No, it's not suicide; it's called sacrifice."

"Same thing."

"Look, I don't want to die. I don't. But I'm willing to—for the right reason, at the right moment, and this is it."

"Okay," she said, wiping the tears from her eyes, though they just kept coming. "So what's that?"

"It's for Matt," I said. "Would you make sure he gets it?"

"What is it?"

"It's a letter explaining everything I just told you, with more details on how I finally came to trust in Jesus and how I came to conclude that this is the only way to keep him and his family safe. Don't worry—I left out anything that might be classified. I didn't mention you or Ari or any of the others. You can read it if you want. But will you take it to him personally? Will you promise me that?"

She nodded, and then she put her arms around me and began to sob.

99

★ ★ ★

The night was cold and quiet as I drove eastward along Highway O-52 toward the mountains.

I could still feel the sting from the tiny tracking beacon Yael had injected under my right armpit. In a final conference call with Yael and Shalit, Dutch had explained that this device, though minuscule, was designed to emit as strong a GPS signal as possible, even if I was taken underground.

I was touched by the last words Shalit and Dutch had said to me. They'd both told me I didn't have to do this. But when I'd insisted one last time, they'd said how grateful they were for my sacrifice, especially knowing that the entire plan rested on the Kurds taking all the credit. My name, I knew, would never be associated with this operation at all. I thanked them and said the last thing in the world I wanted was credit. The only way Matt and his family would ever be safe was if no one ever knew of my association with the plan to take down Abu Khalif once and for all.

Yael had said little on the call. Rather, she had

just sat beside me, holding my hand and answering any logistical questions that came up. When the call was over, she'd given me a long hug. And then she'd watched me walk out of the hotel room for the last time.

Beside me, on the passenger seat, was a brand-new satellite phone. It had never been used before. It had no phone numbers for Shalit or Dutch or Yael or anyone else in the Mossad programmed into it. I was not expecting to receive any calls on the way to the compound, nor was I planning to make any. But Shalit had insisted that I take it. It would only ring, he said, if he believed there was a technical glitch that could prevent the Syrian Kurds from firing their missile at just the right moment.

I pulled off the main east-west highway onto a dirt road that headed up into the mountains. I was following coordinates Dutch had provided for the Toyota's GPS system, and with no traffic, I was making good time. I thought about the letter I'd written to Matt. I hoped I'd been clear enough about how grateful I was to him and how much I looked forward to seeing him on the other side. I thought, too, of the other thank-you notes I'd left in my carry-on bag—one for Yael, one for Ari, one for President Mahfouz, another for Prince bin Zayed, and the last one for King Abdullah II. Without this team and their courage, we would never have found the ISIS emir, and we could never have brought him to justice. I was sorry I'd never get to write the story of the unprecedented cooperation I'd witnessed between Israel and these

Sunni Arab leaders. But I was grateful for the time I'd gotten to spend with them, for the insights and access they'd given me and the personal kindness they had shown me.

Finally I turned up a small, one-lane road. According to the map on my dashboard, I was less than half a mile from the compound. But suddenly I found myself approaching a guard-house flying the black flag of ISIS and manned by armed fighters in black hoods. The guards, clearly stunned to see any unauthorized vehicle coming toward them, immediately pointed their AK-47s and began screaming at me in Arabic. I pulled to a stop, turned off the lights, and killed the engine. Then, as instructed, I got out of the car with my hands over my head. The screaming continued in full force. I was instructed to lie down on the ground, on my stomach, spread-eagle. Then I was promptly searched and then stripped. When I was pulled back to my feet, I was stark naked, surrounded by no fewer than six men pointing weapons at me.

"Who are you?" the leader shouted. "Why have you come?"

"My name is J. B. Collins," I said in Arabic. "I heard the emir was looking for me. I've come to talk to him. I work for the *New York Times*."

The expressions on their faces were priceless, and I hoped the video image being captured by my glasses was being transmitted back to Yael and the team crisp and clear. The men around me refused to believe me at first until they went through my wallet and found my driver's license.

"You're really J. B. Collins?" the leader said, astonished.

"I am," I said. "As I understand it, the emir has invited me to see him. I have a source that says he is staying in a mosque just up the road. Would you please take me there? I have a deadline."

Again, the men were nearly speechless.

"What source?" the leader finally asked.

"I really can't say."

"You must."

"I will tell the emir, but no one else. I'm sorry."

The next thing I knew, the leader was on a cell phone, presumably to his boss, and a few moments later, they ordered me to put my jeans and T-shirt back on. They did not return my shoes or socks, or my grandfather's watch or my leather jacket, and I was freezing in the night air.

It was barely three o'clock in the morning. The temperature was somewhere below fifty degrees. But this mattered little to me. So far, the plan was working. My hands and feet were bound tightly with rope, and I was shoved into the back of the Toyota. The leader and two of his henchmen drove me to the front gate.

By the time we arrived, so had a crowd of ISIS fighters. There had to have been forty or fifty. Word was spreading rapidly through the camp as I was hustled through the main gates, across the courtyard, and into the mosque.

The hatred in these men's eyes was unlike anything I had ever seen, yet it was mixed with a bizarre combination of curiosity and disbelief. I knew I should have been terrified. At any other time in my life, I would have been. But there was something surreal about the entire situation. It was almost as if I were outside my body, watching myself through the monitors back in the hotel in Nizip, as Yael was doing now.

And then, suddenly, I found myself standing face-to-face with Abu Khalif.

100

★ ★ ★

The predawn call to prayer wouldn't go forth for more than an hour.

It was obvious that Khalif had just been roused from sleep. His robe was rumpled and his eyes were bleary. I, on the other hand, was all too awake. I was seated, chained to a chair. I was cold. But I was not afraid.

At first Khalif did not say a word. He just walked around me and then stopped in front of me—maybe three or four feet away. He stared at me, completely baffled. The fact that I no longer looked like I did when he first saw me in Iraq—that I no longer looked like the photograph he'd released to the world, that I was no longer bald, that I was sporting a full beard—all of it confused him.

Ahmed Baqouba walked into the mosque with some two dozen fighters. I recognized him instantly, but he too looked baffled when he saw me. Baqouba had my wallet in his hands, and he looked down several times at my Virginia driver's license and then back at me. He handed the license to Khalif, who did the same. Finally

Faisal Baqouba entered the mosque with quite an entourage around him, and now all three men were standing directly in front of me.

By God's mercy, the plan had worked. All three men were in the same place. I prayed the missile was already in the air.

But suddenly Ahmed surged toward me. He was seething with rage and as he approached, he slammed his fist into my face. I could hear the cartilage in my nose shatter. I could feel the blood gushing down my face. My glasses were crushed against my cheek. The pain nearly made me black out.

"Who are you?" Ahmed demanded.

"Collins," I said, willing myself to stay conscious despite the fact that my face felt like it was on fire. "James Bradley Collins."

"That's impossible!" the Baqouba brother roared. *"Tell me the truth."*

"I heard the emir wanted to see me," I continued, unable to see because of all the blood in my eyes. "So I came to see him. Perhaps he has something to tell the world."

"You're lying!"

Someone had grabbed me by the shoulders and was shaking me violently. But the voice was not the same. This was not Ahmed. Nor was it Faisal. Khalif himself was now standing in front of me, shouting.

"Who sent you? How did you know I was here?"

I tried to speak, but the pain was rapidly becoming unbearable. So I just kept silent and tried to focus my thoughts on what was coming.

I could imagine the missile exploding from the mobile launcher near the Syrian border. I could picture it gaining altitude, stabilizing, arcing toward the compound.

I thought of Matt. I thought of Yael. I thought of the decision I'd made on the plane to finally accept what I already knew in my heart to be true. I thought of the verse about what true love looks like—laying down your life for others.

Khalif continued screaming at me. But I just kept imagining the inbound trajectory of the Syrian missile as it streaked across the Turkish plains at more than five times the speed of sound.

And then, suddenly, it arrived.

EPILOGUE

My cell phone rang just after noon local time.

I was at the hospital, visiting Annie and Katie, so I didn't answer it. Annie had just come out of a coma. She was groggy and in pain. She couldn't speak. But she recognized me. When I held her hand and asked her if I was a doctor or her husband, she squeezed my fingers twice. When I asked if I was her husband or J. B., she squeezed once. I was ecstatic. Katie had already been awake for several days. She was sitting up. She was talking— not much, but she was trying, and I was overjoyed.

So when my phone rang four more times in a row, I ignored it. There was no one I wanted to talk to right then, no one I was going to interrupt these moments of miracles for. But then I heard a commotion out in the hallway. And then a nurse burst in and told me in the accent of the islands to quickly turn on the television.

"No," I snapped. "Please, give us some privacy. We don't want to watch TV right now."

"But the news—it is so wonderful!"

"Why?" I asked. "What happened?"

"The leader of ISIS—they got him; they really got him!"

That, I admit, got my attention. I clicked on the television in Annie's room and found myself watching the breaking news coverage, spellbound. All the broadcast networks and cable news networks were covering the story. I kept flipping from channel to channel. Details were sketchy so far, but the basic narrative was clear enough. After a two-month-long manhunt, Kurdish rebels, operating out of northern Syria, had hunted down and found Abu Khalif, the leader of the Islamic State, in a compound in eastern Turkey.

The missile strike had killed not only Khalif but two of his top deputies and at least a hundred of his most trusted fighters. The Turkish government denied knowing Khalif had been hiding on their territory and said they had police and military crews on the scene and a full investigation was under way. An anchor said the president of the United States was preparing to address the nation soon. Congratulations for the Kurds were pouring in from the leaders of Israel, Jordan, Egypt, the United Arab Emirates, and Saudi Arabia.

My thoughts immediately shifted to my brother. I pulled out my mobile phone, suddenly hoping it was J. B. who had called. Surely he knew the details. Very likely, he'd been right in the middle of the operation. But the number showed it wasn't J. B. It was FBI agent Art Harris instead.

I called back and after a single ring heard his voice.

"Is it true?" I asked. "Did they get him?"

"They did, Matt," Harris said. "The president will officially confirm it when he speaks to the nation at the top of the hour, but I can tell you we are certain. Abu Khalif has been killed."

"That's amazing—I can hardly believe it," I said, flooded with emotion. "And what about J. B.—did he call you? Is he okay?"

"What do you mean?" Harris asked. "Isn't J. B. there with you?"

"No, of course not. I thought he was working with you—or maybe with the CIA."

"Matt, what are you talking about?" Harris pressed. "You're saying J. B. isn't with you on St. Thomas?"

"No. J. B. left the same day you dropped us off here."

"He left? Where?"

"He said he was going to hunt down Abu Khalif. I was against it—fought him tooth and nail on it. But in the end I figured you two had cooked up some plot together."

Harris eventually convinced me he had no idea what this was all about, but he promised to look into it and get back to me.

Two days later, just after breakfast, there was a knock at the door of our home overlooking Magens Bay. I was alone in the house, preparing to go see Annie and Katie again. I went to the door and opened it, fully expecting to see Harris. Who else could it be?

Instead, I found a beautiful young woman wearing a pale-blue sundress and flats. She had a cast on her left arm and a number of fresh-looking scars on her face.

"May I help you?" I asked.

"I hope so," she said. "Are you Matt Collins?"

I just stood there, mouth agape, so caught off guard to hear my real name that I had no idea how to respond.

"I'm so sorry to bother you at home," the woman said, removing her sunglasses. "I realize you don't know me, and this must seem very strange. But my name is Yael Katzir. I was a friend of your brother."

"You're Yael?" I said, even more stunned.

Then she reached into her purse, pulled out several pages of a handwritten letter, and handed the pages to me. "I have this letter for you, Matt," she said. "It's from J. B.—a letter and a story . . ."

TURN THE PAGE

for an excerpt from the next thrilling novel by

JOEL C. ROSENBERG

New York Times bestselling author

***

* * * THE * * *

KREMLIN
CONSPIRACY

A gripping tale ripped from future headlines!

PREORDER NOW!

Available in stores and online March 6, 2018.

JOIN THE CONVERSATION AT

www.tyndalefiction.com   CP1292

$\star \quad \star \quad \star$

MOSCOW, RUSSIA

Louisa Sherbatov had just turned six, but she would never turn seven.

The whirling dervish had finally fallen asleep on the couch just before midnight, crashed from a sugar high, still wearing her new magenta dress and matching ribbon in her blonde tresses. Snuggled up on her father's lap, she looked so peaceful, so content as she hugged her favorite stuffed bear and lay surrounded by the dolls and books and sweaters and other gifts she'd received from all her aunts and uncles and grandparents and cousins as well as her friends from the elementary school just down the block at the end of Guryanova Street.

Strewn about her were string and tape and wads of brightly colored wrapping paper. The kitchen sink was stacked high with dirty plates and cups and silverware. The dining room table was still littered with empty bottles of wine and vodka and scraps of leftover birthday pie—strawberry, Louisa's favorite.

The flat was a mess. But the guests were gone and it was Thursday night and the weekend was upon them and honestly, her parents, Feodor and Irina, couldn't have cared less. Their little girl, the

only child they had been able to bear after more than a decade and two heartbreaking miscarriages, was happy. Her friends were happy. Their parents were happy. They were happy. Everything else could wait.

Feodor stared down at the two precious women in his life and longed to stay. He had loved planning the party with them both, had loved helping shop for the food, loved helping Irina and her mother make all the preparations, loved seeing the sheer delight on Louisa's face when he'd given her a shiny blue bicycle, her first. But business was business. If he was going to make his flight to Tashkent, he had to leave quickly. So he gently kissed mother and daughter on their foreheads, picked up his suitcase, and slipped out as quietly as he could.

As he stepped out the front door of the apartment building, he was relieved to see the cab he'd ordered waiting for him as planned. He moved briskly to the car, shook hands with the driver, and gave the man his bag. The night air was crisp and fresh. The moon was full, and leaves were beginning to fall and swirl in the light breeze coming from the west. Summer was finally over, thought Feodor as he climbed into the backseat, and not a moment too soon. The sweltering heat. The stifling humidity. The gnawing guilt of not being able to afford even a simple air conditioner, much less a little dacha out in the country where he and Irina and Louisa and maybe his parents or hers could retreat now and again, somewhere in a forest

with lots of shade and a sparkling lake for swimming or fishing.

"Thank God, autumn has arrived," he half mumbled to himself as the driver slammed the trunk shut and got back behind the wheel. Growing up, Feodor had always loved the cooler weather. The shorter days. Going back to school. Making new friends. Meeting new teachers. Taking new classes. Fall meant change, and change had always been good to him. Perhaps one day, if he continued to work very hard, he could save enough money to move his family away from 19 Guryanova Street, away from this noisy, dirty, run-down, depressing hovel on the south side of the capital and find some place really lovely and quaint and quiet. Some place worthy of raising a family. Some place with a bit of grass, maybe even a garden where he could till the soil with his own hands and grow his own vegetables.

As the cab began to pull away from the curb, Feodor leaned back in his seat. He closed his eyes and folded his hands on his chest. Yes, autumn had always been a time of new beginnings, and he wondered what this one might bring. He was not rich. He was not successful. But he was content, even hopeful, perhaps for the first time in his life.

He found himself reminiscing about the first time he'd laid eyes on Irina—the first day of middle school, twenty-two years ago. He was so caught up in his memories that he did not notice the car parked just down the street, a white Lada with its headlights off but its engine running. He didn't notice that the front license plate was

covered with some sort of masking tape, revealing only the numbers 6 and 2. Nor did he notice the car's driver, nervously smoking a cigarette and tapping on the dashboard, or the two burly men, dressed in black leather jackets and black leather gloves, emerging from the basement of his own building. When the police would later ask about the men and the car, Feodor would be unable to provide any description at all.

What he did remember—what he could never possibly forget—was the deafening explosion behind him. He remembered the searing fireball. He remembered the taxi driver losing control and crashing into a lamppost not fifty meters up the street, and he remembered smashing his head against the plastic screen dividing the front seat from the back. He remembered the ghastly sensation of kicking open the back door of the cab, jumping out into the pavement, blood streaming down his face, heart pounding furiously, and looking up just in time to see his home, the twelve-story apartment building at 19 Guryanova Street, collapse in a blinding flash of fire and ash.

ACKNOWLEDGMENTS

One of the greatest joys of writing novels is seeing where they wind up being read and by whom.

Over the years, I have had the joy of meeting and hearing from readers of my books all over the world, from police officers to prisoners on death row, from rabbis and imams to pastors and priests, from students in high school and college to ministry and relief workers in remote tribal jungles, from senior government officials in world capitals to soldiers, sailors, airmen, and Marines on the front lines of the war on terror. I always love discovering how such varied people from such varied backgrounds hear about these books and what draws them to reading these stories when they have so many other matters pressing for their time and attention.

That said, however, I was in no way prepared for what happened last year. In January of 2016, my wife, Lynn, and I learned that Jordan's King Abdullah II had read *The First Hostage*, and rather than banning me from his kingdom, he invited Lynn and me to visit him in Amman. We had never met a king before, but we were both deeply grateful for the invitation and for the tremendous hospitality His Majesty showed us when we arrived. We had the honor of spending personal time with the king and a number of his generals and advisors. We observed a live-fire military exercise, visited a refugee camp, flew in the king's personal helicopter, visited several military bases and training centers, and saw some of the Hashemite Kingdom's most impressive archaeological treasures and biblical sites, from Mount Nebo to Petra.

Those five days in Jordan last spring were surreal, and they made me shake my head, yet again, that I really get to do what I do. Since I was eight years old, I have always had a passion to tell stories on paper and on film, to take people on adventures, to lead them on journeys and through experiences they otherwise would never go. What I hadn't understood when I was eight, however, was that as I wrote such stories I, too, would get to go on so many adventures and enter places previously inaccessible.

Along the way, I have had the great honor of meeting all kinds of readers, young and old, rich and poor, powerless and powerful. And I want to thank each and every one of you in the U.S., Canada, Israel, Jordan, and in dozens of countries all over the world where my books are translated and sold. Thank you for reading these thrillers. Thank you for all the kind and supportive messages you send me via e-mail, Facebook, Twitter, and good old-fashioned snail mail. Thank you for the constructive criticism and for reading my blog and for sharing it with others. Thanks, too, for constantly urging me to turn out these books faster and faster. Believe me, I'm doing my best!

I learned quickly in my writing career that dreaming up stories isn't enough. I knew I would need an extraordinary team of professionals to help me get these stories published, marketed, and publicized. By God's grace I have been blessed with just such a team and am deeply grateful for their passion for excellence and their personal kindness to me and my family.

Scott Miller is my literary agent, and he and his team at Trident Media Group have consistently proven to be the best in the business. Since my first novel, *The Last Jihad,* so many years ago, Scott has been a wise counselor and a true friend.

Mark Taylor, Jeff Johnson, Ron Beers, Karen Watson, and Jeremy Taylor at Tyndale House have been an absolutely first-rate publishing group. All but two of my books have been published by them and I count it a tremendous joy and honor to work with such hardworking, creative and fun people. They not only do their best to help me do my best, but they have built a great team around them, including Jan Stob, Cheryl Kerwin, Dean Renninger, the entire sales forces, and all the other dedicated professionals that make the Tyndale brand shine.

June Meyers and Nancy Pierce work with me at November Communications, Inc., and they are beyond fantastic! Year in and year out they do an outstanding job helping me keep my head above water with everything from schedules to flights to finances and so much more—and they do so with great kindness, precision, and class.

I owe so much to my family and to Lynn's and

am so thankful for their prayers, their patience, and their boundless encouragement.

I'm so thankful for the four wonderful sons the Lord has blessed us with: Caleb, Jacob, Jonah, and Noah—I love being on this remarkable journey with these boys, whatever the twists and turns and regardless of how much turbulence we encounter.

My parents, Leonard and Mary Jo Rosenberg, keep running the race with perseverance and for this I am so grateful.

Most of all I want to say thank you, thank you, thank you to my dear wife, Lynn. She continually blesses, inspires, and astounds me. She is such an amazing, creative, hardworking, and super encouraging friend and soul mate. I don't deserve you, Lynnie, but I will stick to you like glue!

ABOUT THE AUTHOR

* * *

Joel C. Rosenberg is a *New York Times* bestselling author with more than three million copies sold among his twelve novels (including *The Last Jihad*, *Damascus Countdown*, and *The Auschwitz Escape*), four nonfiction books (including *Epicenter* and *Inside the Revolution*), and a digital short (*Israel at War*). A front-page Sunday *New York Times* profile called him a "force in the capital." He has also been profiled by the *Washington Times* and the *Jerusalem Post* and has been interviewed on ABC's *Nightline*, CNN *Headline News*, FOX News Channel, The History Channel, MSNBC, *The Rush Limbaugh Show*, and *The Sean Hannity Show*.

You can follow him at www.joelrosenberg.com or on Twitter @joelcrosenberg and Facebook: www.facebook.com/JoelCRosenberg.

FROM *NEW YORK TIMES* BESTSELLING AUTHOR

JOEL C. ROSENBERG

"IF THERE WERE A *FORBES* 400 LIST OF GREAT CURRENT NOVELISTS, JOEL ROSENBERG WOULD BE AMONG THE TOP TEN. HIS NOVELS ARE UN-PUT-DOWNABLE."
STEVE FORBES, EDITOR IN CHIEF, *FORBES* MAGAZINE

FICTION

J. B. COLLINS NOVELS
THE THIRD TARGET
THE FIRST HOSTAGE
WITHOUT WARNING

THE TWELFTH IMAM COLLECTION
THE TWELFTH IMAM
THE TEHRAN INITIATIVE
DAMASCUS COUNTDOWN

THE LAST JIHAD COLLECTION
THE LAST JIHAD
THE LAST DAYS
THE EZEKIEL OPTION
THE COPPER SCROLL
DEAD HEAT

THE AUSCHWITZ ESCAPE

NONFICTION

ISRAEL AT WAR
IMPLOSION
THE INVESTED LIFE
INSIDE THE REVOLUTION
INSIDE THE REVIVAL
EPICENTER

CP1042

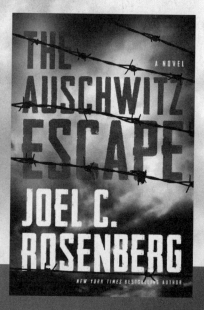

PRAISE FOR
JOEL C. ROSENBERG

"His penetrating knowledge of all things Mideastern—coupled with his intuitive knack for high-stakes intrigue—demand attention."

PORTER GOSS
Former director of the Central Intelligence Agency

"If there were a *Forbes* 400 list of great current novelists, Joel Rosenberg would be among the top ten. . . . One of the most entertaining and intriguing authors of international political thrillers in the country. . . . His novels are un-put-downable."

STEVE FORBES
Editor in chief, *Forbes* magazine

"One of my favorite things: An incredible thriller—it's called *The Third Target* by Joel C. Rosenberg. . . . He's amazing. . . . He writes the greatest thrillers set in the Middle East, with so much knowledge of that part of the world. . . . Fabulous! I've read every book he's ever written!"

KATHIE LEE GIFFORD
NBC's *Today Show*

"Fascinating and compelling . . . way too close to reality for a novel."

MIKE HUCKABEE
Former Arkansas governor

"[Joel Rosenberg] understands the grave dangers posed by Iran and Syria, and he's been a bold and courageous voice for true peace and security in the Middle East."

DANNY AYALON
Israeli deputy foreign minister

"Joel has a particularly clear understanding of what is going on in today's Iran and Syria and the grave threat these two countries pose to the rest of the world."

REZA KAHLILI
Former CIA operative in Iran and bestselling author of *A Time to Betray: The Astonishing Double Life of a CIA Agent Inside the Revolutionary Guards of Iran*

"Joel Rosenberg is unsurpassed as the writer of fiction thrillers! Sometimes I have to remind myself to breathe as I read one of his novels because I find myself holding my breath in suspense as I turn the pages."

ANNE GRAHAM LOTZ
Author and speaker

"Joel paints an eerie, terrifying, page-turning picture of a worst-case scenario coming to pass. You have to read [*Damascus Countdown*], and then pray it never happens."

RICK SANTORUM
Former U.S. senator

THE
THIRD
TARGET

TYNDALE HOUSE PUBLISHERS, INC., CAROL STREAM, ILLINOIS

JOEL C.
ROSENBERG

Visit Tyndale online at www.tyndale.com.

Visit Joel C. Rosenberg's website at www.joelrosenberg.com.

TYNDALE and Tyndale's quill logo are registered trademarks of Tyndale House Publishers, Inc.

The Third Target

Designed by Dean H. Renninger

The Third Target is a work of fiction. Where real people, events, establishments, organizations, or locales appear, they are used fictitiously. All other elements of the novel are drawn from the author's imagination.

For information about special discounts for bulk purchases, please contact Tyndale House Publishers at csresponse@tyndale.com, or call 1-800-323-9400.

ISBN 978-1-4143-3628-2 (sc)
ISBN 978-1-4964-2327-6 (mass paper)

Printed in the United States of America

23	22	21	20	19	18	17
7	6	5	4	3	2	1

To our son Jonah, whose very name reminds us each and every day that God not only loves Israel, but also greatly loves her neighbors and her enemies.

"You are a gracious and compassionate God, slow to anger and abundant in lovingkindness, and one who relents concerning calamity."

JONAH 4:2

CAST OF
CHARACTERS

JOURNALISTS

J. B. Collins—foreign correspondent for the *New York Times*

Allen MacDonald—foreign editor for the *New York Times*

Omar Fayez—Amman-based reporter for the *New York Times*

Abdel Hamid—Beirut-based photographer for the *New York Times*

Alex Brunnell—Jerusalem bureau chief for the *New York Times*

A. B. Collins—former Cairo bureau chief for the Associated Press, and J. B.'s grandfather

AMERICANS

Harrison Taylor—president of the United States

Jack Vaughn—director of the Central Intelligence Agency

Robert Khachigian—former director of the CIA

Arthur Harris—special agent with the Federal Bureau of Investigation

Matthew Collins—J. B.'s older brother

JORDANIANS

King Abdullah II—the monarch of the Hashemite Kingdom of Jordan

Prince Marwan Talal—uncle of the king of Jordan
and a senior advisor

Kamal Jeddeh—director of Jordanian intelligence
(Mukhabarat)

Ali Sa'id—chief of security for the Royal Court

TERRORISTS

Abu Khalif—leader of the Islamic State in Iraq and
al-Sham (ISIS)

Jamal Ramzy—commander of ISIS rebel forces in
Syria and cousin of Abu Khalif

Tariq Baqouba—deputy to Jamal Ramzy

Faisal Baqouba—ISIS terrorist and brother of Tariq

IRAQIS

Hassan Karbouli—Iraqi minister of the interior

Ismail Tikriti—deputy director of Iraqi intelligence

ISRAELIS

Daniel Lavi—Israeli prime minister

Ari Shalit—deputy director of the Mossad

Yael Katzir—Mossad agent

PALESTINIANS

Salim Mansour—president of the Palestinian
Authority

Youssef Kuttab—senior aide to President Mansour

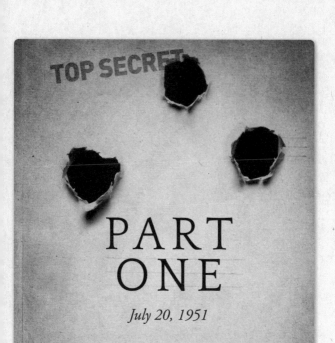

TOP SECRET

PART ONE

July 20, 1951

1

* * *

I had never met a king before.

Forty-eight hours earlier, I received a summons from the palace to meet with His Majesty at a certain time in a certain place for an exceedingly rare interview with a foreign journalist. But now I was late, and I was petrified.

Sweat dripped down my face and inside the back of my shirt. As the sun blazed in the eastern sky, the cool of the morning was a distant memory. My freshly starched white collar was rapidly wilting. My crisply knotted azure tie was starting to feel like a noose around my perspiring neck.

I glanced at my gold pocket watch, a graduation present from my father, and the knots in my stomach tightened further. I pulled an already-damp handkerchief from the pocket of my navy-blue pin-striped suit jacket, yet no matter how much I swiped at my brow, I knew it was a losing battle. It wasn't simply the sultry morning air that weighed heavy upon me. It was the nausea-inducing knowledge—indeed, the rapidly

3

increasing certainty—that I was going to be late for this appointment and blow the most important moment of my career.

I had been requesting this interview for the better part of a year and had been repeatedly rebuffed. Then, without warning, I received a telegram from the palace inviting me, A. B. Collins of the Associated Press, to come to Jerusalem and granting me an exclusive interview without limits or preconditions. I cabled my editors back in New York. They were ecstatic. I was ecstatic. For months I had been reading everything I could about this intriguing, if elusive, monarch. I watched every bit of newsreel footage I could scrounge up. I called or met with every expert I could find who knew him or had met him or could give me any tidbit of insight into who he really was, what he wanted, and where he was headed next.

Now the moment had come. I had been instructed to meet His Majesty King Abdullah bin al-Hussein, ruler of the Hashemite Kingdom of Jordan, at the entrance to the Dome of the Rock precisely at noon. That was in less than ten minutes, and at this rate I was never going to make it.

"*Faster, man*—can't you go any faster?" I yelled at my driver.

Leaning forward from the backseat, I pointed through the dust-smudged front window of the cramped little taxi that stank of stale cigarettes. It was an exercise in futility; the answer was pitifully obvious. No, he could not go any faster. It was a Friday. It was the holiest day of the week for the Moslems, and it was fast approaching high noon. Everyone and his cousin were heading to the Al-Aksa Mosque for prayer. It had been this way for twelve centuries, and it would always be thus. No one was going to make an exception—not for a foreigner, not for a Westerner, and certainly not for a reporter.

We were less than a hundred yards from the Damascus Gate, the nearest entrance into the Old City, but traffic was barely moving at all. I surveyed the scene before me and quickly considered my options. Ahead was a classic snapshot of the Orient I had come to know as a foreign correspondent for the Associated Press—a dizzying mélange of vibrant colors and pungent odors and exotic architecture and intriguing faces straight out of central casting. I had seen it in Cairo and Casablanca, in Baghdad and Beirut. Shopkeepers and street vendors who moments before had been brewing coffee and roasting peanuts and hawking everything from spices and kitchen supplies to bottles of Coca-Cola and religious trinkets for the pilgrims were now hurriedly shutting down for the day. Every taxi and truck and private car on the planet seemed to have converged on one traffic circle, their drivers honking their horns and yelling at one another, desperate to get home and then to the mosque. A siren wailed from the south—a police car perhaps, or maybe an ambulance—but it would never get through. A hapless constable sporting a dusty olive-green Royal Jordanian uniform was blowing on a whistle he held in one hand while pointing a wooden club with the other. He shouted commands, but no one paid him much mind.

Bearded, sun-drenched older men, their heads wrapped in white- and black-checkered kaffi-yehs, pushed carts of fresh fruits and vegetables as quickly as they could through the filthy, unswept streets while others led goats and camels through tiny gaps in the traffic, back to whatever barns or stables they were usually kept in. Boys in their late teens and young twenties with no jobs and nothing better to do and without fathers or grandfathers in sight seemed in no hurry to get to prayer, taking their last drags on their cigarettes. They stared at giggling packs of young schoolgirls scurrying past with eyes down while older women in long robes and headscarves scowled disapprovingly as they rushed home with boxes of food or pots of water on their heads.

Suddenly the muezzin's haunting call to prayer began to blare from the loudspeakers mounted high up on the minarets. My heart nearly stopped. I was out of time and out of options.

I was going to have to run for it. It was my only chance.

I shouted over the din for my driver to let me out, tossed a few dinars his way, grabbed my leather satchel, donned my black fedora, and raced down the stone steps toward the crush of people flooding through the gate, jostling past the faithful without shame, though I knew my prospects were grim.

I was supposed to meet His Majesty on the Temple Mount, what the Arabs called *"al-Haram ash-Sharif"*—the place of the Noble Sanctuary. After countless phone calls and telegrams from my office in Beirut to the press office in the palace in Amman, it had all been arranged. The most beleaguered and endangered monarch in the entire Moslem world would allow me to shadow him for the day and then sit down with him for his first interview with a Western journalist since a rash of assassinations had set the region on edge.

I couldn't be late. The chief of the Royal Court would never forgive me. He had insisted I get there early. He had promised one of his servants would be waiting. But now they all might be gone by the time I arrived.

I pushed my way through the crowd, a nearly impossible feat, but after considerable difficulty, I finally cleared through the massive stone archway and was inside the Old City. Still ahead of me, however, was a throng of people pressing forward to the mosque.

But I had been here numerous times as a war correspondent in '48 and '49, and I had actually come to know these streets well. I decided to gamble.

Rather than head straight into the *shuq* and up one of the two main streets toward the mosque, already clogged with thousands of worshipers, I moved left, stepped into a pharmacy, and before the owner could even yell at me, I was through the shop and out the back door. Breaking into a full run, I raced through a labyrinthine series of narrow side streets and alleyways, aiming for St. Stephen's Gate—also known as the Lions' Gate—and desperately trying to make up for lost time.

As I neared my destination, however, I found

that everything had come to a standstill. I could finally see the large green wooden doors that were the gateway to the epicenter of the epicenter, the entrance to the thirty-seven-acre plot upon which the third-holiest site in Islam was situated. I was so close now, but no one was moving forward. Not a soul. And soon I saw why.

A contingent of Jordanian soldiers blocked the way. People were yelling, demanding to be let in for prayer. But the grim-faced, heavily armed young men were having none of it. They had their orders, they shouted back. No one could enter until they received the "all clear" sign.

I was stuck, and like the crowd, I was furious. But I knew something they did not. The king was coming. He was heading to the Al-Aksa Mosque for the noon prayers, surrounded by bodyguards who feared for his life, and for good reason.

2

I set my jaw and pressed forward.

With my press credentials and telegram from the palace in hand, I was certain the soldiers would let me through. But first I had to get to them. The problem was that everyone was pushing forward. Everyone wanted to be at the head of the line. They were shouting at the soldiers to let them get to the mosque on time, and the more resistance they got from the guards, the more infuriated they became.

"Get back!" someone yelled at me.

"Who do you think you are?" another shouted.

Then a burly man with crooked teeth and hatred in his eyes screamed at me, *"Kafir!"*

I recoiled in shock. *Kafir* was an incendiary word. In colloquial Arabic, it technically meant "unbeliever" or "unclean." But on the street it meant "infidel." There were few things worse you could call a man in this part of the world—especially a foreigner—and upon hearing it, I instinctively took several steps back. To be branded a *kafir* was a worst-case scenario. In

9

a crowd already on edge, the term could spark a full-fledged riot, one I would not likely survive. I doubted even the soldiers could guarantee my safety if this crowd turned on me.

There had to be another way. I glanced at my pocket watch again and cursed myself for not having thought my plan through more carefully.

Moving away from the thick of the crowd, I backed into a corner and leaned against a stone wall, watching the raw emotions spiking around me. I could see the young soldiers growing edgy. This had all the makings of a mob. It wouldn't take much for the situation to devolve into violence. The armed military men—the oldest of them no more than nineteen or twenty, I would guess—braced themselves for a fight while I wiped perspiration from my brow. The scorching sun overhead was beating down on us all. The crush of people and the brutal heat began to conspire to make me feel claustrophobic. I couldn't believe what was happening. I wasn't just going to be late; I was actually going to miss this meeting altogether. My career was about to go into the tank. I was beside myself. I had to get out. I had to get some air, something to drink. But there was nothing I could do. Not yet. Not here. All I could do was wait and pray for the winds to shift and my luck to change.

Why hadn't I simply flown to Amman? Why hadn't I met the king's entourage at the palace and traveled with them across the Allenby Bridge, to the meetings they were scheduled to have in Ramallah and Jericho and then on up to Jerusalem? That was their plan. Why hadn't I asked to be part of it?

The reason was simple, though it did me no good now. I had flown from Beirut to Cyprus, and from Cyprus to Tel Aviv, for one simple reason: before I interviewed the king, I wanted to meet with the head of the Mossad.

I had known Reuven Shiloah, the director of Israel's nascent intelligence service, for several years—since before the Mossad had even been created, in fact. I had learned to trust him, and over the years, Reuven had come to trust me, too. Not fully, of course. He was a spy, after all. But he had seen firsthand that I would carefully use his insights but never quote him directly. His perspective was unique and useful for my readers, though I didn't use him as a source often. And I had been helpful to him on numerous occasions as well. He had leaked several important stories to me. I had handled them sensitively, and he had been as pleased as my editors. I was, in effect, a direct pipeline for him to the White House and to members of Congress and, by extension, to other leaders. He had his reasons for feeding me information, and I had mine for accepting it. So over breakfast that morning at a little café in Tel Aviv near the bus station, I asked the Mossad director about the Jordanian king and his situation. The chain-smoking Israeli spy chief had stared at me through his round, gold-rimmed glasses and in hushed tones in a back corner booth confided to me his serious and growing concerns.

"This is a terrible mistake," Reuven said. "He should not be coming."

"Who, the king?" I asked, astonished. "Not come to Jerusalem? Why not?"

"Is it not obvious, Collins?" he asked. "His Majesty is a marked man."

"You're saying he's not safe in Jerusalem, in his own city?" I pressed. "He's not safe anywhere," Reuven replied.

"Do you know of a specific threat?" It's not that I thought he was wrong, but hearing him say it left me deeply unsettled.

"No."

"Then what?"

"I have my gut, my instincts," he said. "The mood is dark, full of rumors and danger. What has happened elsewhere can happen here. As you know, the prime minister of Iran was assassinated just a few months ago."

I nodded. Ali Razmara, Persia's fifty-eighth prime minister, was only forty-nine years old when he was killed. He was the third to have been murdered while in office in recent years.

I pulled a pad out of my bag and began to take notes.

"There were several things notable about Razmara's death," Reuven continued. "He was slain in broad daylight. He was gunned down not by a foreigner but by a fellow Iranian. Indeed, the assailant was a fellow Moslem. And Razmara was walking into a mosque to pray. And Razmara's death was not an isolated incident. Less than two weeks later, Zanganeh was assassinated as well."

He was referring now to Abdol-Hamid Zanganeh, Iran's minister of education.

"Zanganeh was also hit in broad daylight, in this case on the campus of Tehran University," the Mossad director explained. "Very open. Very public. Lots of people. Hard to secure. The weapon was also a pistol. Small. Easily concealed. And who did it? A foreign spy agency? The Brits? The Americans? Us? No. In both cases, the assassins were Moslems, extremists, and locals."

Reuven went on to note that two years earlier someone had tried to assassinate the king of Iran, Shah Mohammad Reza Pahlavi. This too, he reminded me, had happened in broad daylight. In fact, it had happened on the campus of Tehran University, and it too had been the work of an Iranian—not a foreign agent—an Islamic extremist using a pistol. Five bullets had been fired. Four missed their mark. But the fifth did not. Miraculously, it only grazed the king's face, slightly wounding him. But a millimeter's difference would have killed him instantly.

"The assassin posed as a photographer— a member of the press—to get close to the king," the Mossad chief added.

"But that's Iran, not Jordan," I finally said, looking up from my notes. "The situation here is completely different."

"Is it?" he asked. "Certainly there are differences; I grant you that. Iran is ethnically Persian, and Jordan is ethnically Arab. Iran is largely a Shia Moslem nation, while Jordan is predominately Sunni. Iran has oil; Jordan does not. Iran is large and populous, and Jordan is not. But those differences are immaterial. What is important is the pattern."

"What pattern?"

"Iran is a monarchy," Reuven explained. "So is Jordan. The Pahlavi regime is moderate. So are the Hashemites. Iran is pro-British. So is Jordan. Indeed, it was a British colony. What's more, Iran is pro-American. So is Jordan. And though they are quiet about it, Iran under the shah is one of two countries in the region that are on relatively friendly terms with Israel and the Jews. The other is Jordan."

At that, I had to push back. "Now wait a minute—Jordan just fought a war with you. That was only three years ago."

"Things are changing," he said, opening another pack of cigarettes.

"How so?"

There was a long, awkward silence.

"Reuven?"

The Mossad chief glanced around the café. The regulars were starting to fill the place up.

"This is totally off the record," he said finally. "Really, A. B., you cannot use this—agreed?"

"Agreed."

"I have your word?"

"You do," I said.

"I'm serious. You cannot print it under any circumstances. But I'm going to tell you because it's important for you to have some context of who King Abdullah is and what he really wants."

I nodded.

"When I can give you this story, I will," the Mossad chief added. "But we're not there. Not yet."

"I understand, Reuven," I replied. "Really, you have my word. You know me. I won't burn you."

He lit his cigarette and scanned the room again. Then he lowered his voice and leaned toward me. "The king is quietly reaching out."

"To the Mossad?"

"Through us, not to us."

"To whom, then?"

"David Ben-Gurion," he said.

I was stunned. The king of Jordan was reaching out to Israel's aging prime minister?

"Why?" I asked, immediately intrigued.

Again the director scanned the room, making sure no one was listening in on our conversation. Again he lowered his voice, so much so that I could barely hear him and had to lean forward even farther to catch every word over the din of the café.

"His Majesty is probing the possibility of secret peace talks," Reuven confided. "It seems he wants to meet with the PM personally. It's very premature, of course, and all very deniable. But the king seems to be intimating that he wants to make peace with Israel."

I could not hold back my astonishment. "A treaty?"

Reuven shifted in his seat. "Not exactly," he said.

"Too public?" I asked.

He nodded.

"A private 'understanding,' then?" I asked.

"Perhaps," Reuven said, exhaling a lungful of blue smoke. "But even that brings with it great risks. The king knows he's a marked man.

Not by us. We don't have a problem with him. He went to war with us in '48. But we stopped him. We fought him to a standoff, and as far as we're concerned, it's over now. His real problem is the Egyptians and the Syrians and the Iraqis and the Saudis. They hate him. Hate doesn't even begin to describe it. They don't think he's one of them. They don't think he's a team player. They don't think the Hashemite Kingdom is going to be around for long anyway, so they're all gunning for him. They all want him dead, and they're all angling to seize his territory when he collapses."

"So if he opens a back channel with you and comes to an understanding, then maybe it's 'all quiet on the western front' and he can focus his intelligence and security forces elsewhere?" I asked.

"Something like that," Reuven said with a shrug. "Anyway, I don't believe the king wants war with Israel. He certainly doesn't want to annihilate us like the others do. All the evidence says he's not a fanatic. He's a pragmatist. He's someone we can work with. Like the shah."

"But the fanatics want the shah dead," I noted.

Reuven nodded.

"Which is why you're worried someone might try to kill the king—because you think he and the shah are cut from the same cloth," I added.

"It doesn't matter what I think," Reuven demurred. "What matters is what the fanatics think. Which brings us to Monday."

"You mean Riad el-Solh."

"Of course."

I was starting to understand Reuven's concern

now. On Monday, July 16, 1951—just four days earlier—Riad el-Solh, the former prime minister of Lebanon, had been assassinated. Like the shah and the king, el-Solh was a moderate, a pragmatist, and a much-respected regional statesman. His death would have been tragic enough, but he was not murdered in Beirut or in Tehran.

"As you well know, the man was murdered in Amman," Reuven said soberly, his piercing blue eyes flashing with anger. "He was gunned down at Marka Airport, just three kilometers from the palace. He'd been in Jordan visiting with the king, his longtime friend and political ally. Yet he was ruthlessly taken down by a three-man hit team. And I'll give you a scoop. Nobody has this yet. One of the assailants was shot by the police. One committed suicide. But one is still at large."

The implications of that last sentence hit me hard. I just sat there, staring at my cold cup of coffee and untouched plate of eggs and dry toast, trying to make sense of it all. Then Reuven dug in his pocket, plunked down enough lirot to pay for both of our meals, and slipped out the side door without saying another word.

3

★ ★ ★

The crowd around me grew more frantic by the minute.

The time had come. The muezzin's call was over. The faithful were supposed to be in the mosque by now, washed and purified and ready for their noon prayers. But still the soldiers held their ground.

I looked at these young men, barely out of high school, and wondered what they were made of. If they were rushed by this crowd, would they really fire? I wondered. If a disturbance erupted, how quickly would they respond? If someone threatened their ruler, would they really sacrifice their lives to protect him? How well trained, how disciplined were they? How deep did their loyalties to the throne truly run?

We were about to find out.

In mere moments, King Abdullah bin al-Hussein would be arriving just a few hundred steps from where I was standing. Could these young men really protect him? Or was the sixty-nine-year-old monarch truly in grave danger?

Might extremists—perhaps someone in this very crowd—be plotting against him? Abdullah had only formally been on the throne for five years, since May 25, 1946, when the League of Nations granted Jordan its independence at the end of the British Mandate. Was it really possible that someone—or some group—was plotting to take him down and topple his entire kingdom?

I knew from my conversation with Reuven Shiloah that morning that the Israelis were worried for the king's safety. Surely they were not the only ones. Reuven had said that His Majesty had been strongly urged by his own Jordanian intelligence service not to make this trip to Jerusalem. At the very least, they had urged him to reschedule it. But he was not listening. He was his own man. He had business in the Holy City, a city he considered himself personally responsible for, and he would not be deterred. He was, after all, a direct descendant of the prophet Muhammad. His forebearers had been responsible for governing Mecca and Medina for centuries. Now he was the guardian of some of Islam's most revered landmarks. He simply would not cower or shrink away in the face of personal threats, however serious.

That was the king's way. I wasn't sure it was wise, but I had to admit, privately at least, that I wasn't protesting. After all, His Majesty was also being urged by his closest counselors not to speak to the Western press at all—and certainly not to agree to an interview with an American—but he was ignoring this advice too. Clearly he had something to say to the world and had decided to use me to say it, and for this I felt enormously grateful.

I had worked for United Press International and the Associated Press for nearly ten years. I'd interviewed generals and commanders and local officials of all kinds. I had been posted in London, Paris, Bombay, and most recently Beirut. I'd met presidents and prime ministers and heads of state. But I had never even seen a king in the flesh, much less interviewed one, and I confess that the very notion of conversing with a monarch held for me a certain mystique that I cannot put into words.

So this was it. If I didn't do something quickly to get through this crowd and past these guards, I knew I would regret it for the rest of my life.

I scanned the crowd, picked my target, and took my fate into my own hands. Wiping my palms on my trousers, I set my plan into motion. I began pushing aside several old men, then shoved a few teenage boys out of my way, working along the stone wall to my right, toward the soldiers. Immediately, curses came flying back at me thick and fierce, but those I had moved past didn't have a chance. I was over six feet tall and nearly two hundred pounds. So I kept moving toward my target, and with a few more steps I was there. Without warning, I drove my elbow hard into the ribs of the burly young man with crooked teeth who minutes before had called me an infidel. He was probably about twenty-four or twenty-five years old, and I suspected he had far more experience street fighting than I did. But for the moment, at least, I had the advantage. I had a plan, and he was being blindsided.

Infuriated, his eyes flashing with the same rage I had seen before, he took a swing at me with all his might. I knew it was coming, and I ducked in time, so his fist slammed into the stone wall behind me. At that moment, I embedded my right fist in his stomach. He doubled over, and I lunged at his waist, toppling him to the ground, whipping the bloodthirsty crowd around us into a frenzy. It didn't take long for him to recover his wits and flip me over, but as he did, the whistles of the soldiers started blowing. I covered my face with my arms as he landed several blows. But before he could do any real damage, a half-dozen Jordanian guards descended upon us. They beat back the crowd with wooden clubs and soon were beating him, too, until they could pull him off me and clamp handcuffs on him. I received several kicks, one to my back and one to my stomach, and then I too was cuffed. But in the grand scheme, since I was on the bottom of the pile, I actually got the least of it, and when they realized I was not a Jordanian or a Moslem but a Westerner, the captain of the unit—a Captain Rajoub, according to the name on his uniform—looked horrified.

"Who are you?" he demanded while his colleagues aimed their rifles at me.

"I am a reporter," I said in English, scooping my hat off the ground, dusting it off, and replacing it on my perspiration-soaked head as two soldiers rifled through my leather satchel.

"From where?"

"America," I replied.

There was no point in saying I was actually based in Beirut. It would just confuse the matter. And although I was fluent in Arabic, I spoke only in English since the whole point was to distinguish myself from the locals, to be as foreign as possible. *America* was a word I was sure these men knew. They didn't love us. But they had the decency to fear us.

"Papers!" the young captain insisted, bristling.

I slowly reached into my suit pocket, careful not to make the boys with the rifles any more nervous than they already were. I pulled out my American passport and my AP credentials and handed them to him. The man opened the passport first, looked at the photo, then looked back at me.

"Andrew?" he asked, his accent thick but his English passable, to my surprise. "Is that your name?"

I nodded.

"Andrew Bradley Collins?"

I nodded again.

"Born September 9, 1920?"

"Yes."

"In Bar . . . Bar . . ."

"Bar Harbor," I said.

"What's that?"

It seemed ridiculous to be discussing my hometown. "It's a little town in Maine."

The man just looked at me. Indeed, the whole crowd was staring at me, and many seemed ready to tear me limb from limb.

"Why are you here?" Captain Rajoub asked.

"I have a telegram," I said, slowly reaching back into my breast pocket and pulling out the crumpled yellow sheet from Western Union. I handed it to the captain and watched as he read it.

Then I saw his eyes widen.

"You are supposed to meet His Majesty?" he asked, incredulous. "You're meeting him here?"

"I'm supposed to—I was trying to get this message to you, sir, but that lunatic there tried to kill me," I said, pointing at the burly man being forcibly restrained by several soldiers from trying to attack me again.

"You're supposed to meet him now?"

"Yes—if you and your boys will let me through."

Genuine fear flashed in the captain's eyes. He and his men had arrested and very nearly shot a man who was supposed to be meeting with the king. For a moment, he was speechless. But only for a moment.

"Right this way, sir," he said at last. "Please, my friend, come—I will take you to His Majesty."

He turned to his dumbfounded men and barked a command in Arabic. Stunned by all that had just occurred, the soldiers immediately cleared a path. Then the captain beckoned me to follow him. I grabbed my satchel from the soldier holding it, straightened my tie, brushed myself off as best I could, and followed the captain onto the Temple Mount.

My desperate plan had worked, and I could hardly believe my eyes.

I was late, but I was in.

4

* * *

I desperately scanned the plaza but did not see him.

Had I missed my chance?

Captain Rajoub told me to follow him closely and not to say a word, and then he set across the plaza at a rather brisk pace. I did what he said, amazed that I was really on the Temple Mount for the first time in my life.

Rising before me was the stunningly beautiful Dome of the Rock. Built in the seventh century and completed around AD 691, it was larger than I'd expected, rising several stories from its stone base. The octagonal structure of the building, covered in exquisite blue-and-green tile work with Islamic decor, was spectacular. And of course the expansive wooden dome, gilded in pure gold, was even more spectacular—and very nearly blinding as well—gleaming majestically in the noonday sun.

Captain Rajoub and I turned the corner and headed for the front door of the mosque, on the south side of the complex, but there was still no sign of the king. I saw several soldiers patrolling the grounds, but not the royal entourage. I was tempted to despair, I'll admit, but I wouldn't allow it—not yet, anyway. Rather, I started asking questions.

"Excuse me," I said in Arabic to a pair of soldiers walking nearby. "I was told to wait here to conduct an interview with His Majesty. Have I missed him?"

Both men looked at me suspiciously, but the captain assured them my story was true and showed them the telegram. What's more, the captain promised them he would stay at my side and make certain I caused no trouble. They glanced at the pistol strapped to the captain's belt and then looked back at me, apparently satisfied.

"No, you have not missed him," the older one replied in reasonably good English. "His Majesty is on his way. Wait over there."

"*Shukran,*" I replied, thanking the men, amazed at my good fortune.

I did my best to look calm, but my heart was racing. *The angels must be looking out for me,* I thought. Somebody up there was.

Perhaps there really was something mystical, even magical, about this spot, I mused while I waited. It was here, the Jews said, that the biblical Abraham nearly sacrificed his son Isaac, until God intervened and saved the day. It was here—on this very spot—that not one but two Jewish Temples had once stood, and where the Jews believed a third Temple would one day be built. That certainly seemed implausible, given that the

Jews hadn't controlled the Old City, let alone the Temple Mount, for more than two thousand years.

Besides, the Moslems would never allow the Jews to build here. After all, they too considered the site sacred. They believed that Muhammad, their Prophet, had arrived here after taking his famed night flight from Mecca on a winged, white horselike creature. Furthermore, they claimed that from this very spot he had been taken up to heaven.

The Christians, meanwhile, believed that not far from here Jesus of Nazareth had been crucified, buried, and resurrected—and that he would return to this very spot at the End of Days to judge his enemies and set up his eternal Kingdom.

I had no idea who was right. I'd never been religious growing up—never cared much about it, I must say. But if there was a God, he had certainly shown me kindness this day.

While I waited, and the soldiers eyed me warily, I tried to get my thoughts in order. What was I supposed to do first when I met the king? Did one shake his hand? Bow down? Kiss his feet? I suddenly realized that I had no idea what the protocol was. No one had told me, and foolishly I had not asked.

I brushed such thoughts aside. There was no reason to be anxious. This man had agreed to meet with me because I had something he wanted: a worldwide audience. He and his advisors had obviously vetted me. They surely had read my dispatches from the region. They must have concluded I was a fair-minded reporter who strove for balance and accuracy. More important, His Majesty clearly had something he wanted to say through me to my readers, to the nations, and to the men who ruled them. But what?

There was something about this particular monarch that intrigued me a great deal. On the face of it, one could argue that King Abdullah didn't matter much to my American readers or even to most Europeans. His kingdom possessed no oil, no gold, no silver, no diamonds or precious minerals. It had no real natural resources to speak of at all, in fact. It had no heavy industry, nothing of substance to export. It had far too little water and precious little arable land. The king ran a tiny, tribal nation of bedouin Arabs who had not exactly distinguished themselves by splitting the atom or curing polio or inventing the wireless or creating the world's tastiest breakfast cereal. This wasn't a nation abounding in Pulitzers or Nobel Prizes. If Jordan was known for anything, it was instability and shifting sands. The nation had gained its independence amid the collapse of the Ottoman Empire. It was first governed by a man who wasn't even born there but rather in Mecca. Then it was overrun in 1948 by hundreds of thousands of Palestinian refugees, most of whom had fled the war with the new state of Israel, though some had been driven out of their homes by the Jews. The Palestinians called the war *"al-Nakbah"*—the "catastrophe," the "disaster"—and they were deeply embittered. How loyal were they to the current king? I couldn't say. But my sources told me officials in London worried about the stability of the throne in Amman. So did officials in Washington.

So beyond a few government officials, who in the U.S. or Great Britain really cared about the fate of Jordan? The AP didn't even have a bureau in Amman. Neither did UPI or the *New York Times* or Reuters. Cairo? Yes. Jerusalem? Of course. Damascus and Beirut? Without question. But not Amman. Didn't that say something? Nevertheless, there was a story here—I was sure of it—and Abdullah was the key.

Suddenly I saw him.

He was approaching from the east, through a grove of trees and an ancient stone archway, flanked by a handful of bodyguards in plainclothes—I counted six—several aides, and a dozen uniformed soldiers, each carrying a submachine gun. The king was dressed entirely in white cotton robes that shimmered in the sunshine, and he wore a white turban. He appeared to be bald, but he sported a well-groomed mustache that connected with a full goatee. As he drew closer, he struck me as more diminutive in stature than I had expected, no more than four or five inches over five feet, if that. But he strode purposefully across the warm stones with a regal bearing, commanding and self-assured. His skin was the color of hot tea with a splash of milk. His eyes were bright and intense, though they never looked at me.

Several minutes behind schedule now, the king headed straight for the ancient mosque. The captain beside me stood ramrod straight and saluted, as did the soldiers nearby. Then I noticed a young boy, no more than fifteen or sixteen years old, dressed in full ceremonial military garb, walking a stride or two behind the king.

"Who is that?" I whispered to the captain.

"That is Prince Hussein, of course," the captain whispered back.

"The king's grandson?" I asked, startled because no one had told me he was coming.

"Who else?"

As the entourage rushed past me, I feared the deal was off and the interview had been forgotten or ignored. But then one of the king's aides caught my eye and motioned me to follow. I quickly complied. As we headed down a flight of steps toward a small crowd of worshipers and well-wishers, the aide moved to my side.

"Mr. Collins, I am Mansour, His Majesty's spokesman," he said in a hushed tone as we walked. "Please forgive us for being late."

"Don't mention it," I said, breathing a sigh of relief. "Is everything okay?"

"Yes, yes—well, it is now," he said. "I confess we had a bit of a scare as the motorcade came over the Mount of Olives. There was a demonstration of some kind—a roadblock, quite unexpected. And as you can imagine, our security detail is on heightened alert."

"Yes, of course," I said, trying to keep pace with him and the others.

"At any rate, our security men were worried for a few minutes, but it all worked out. Everything is all right. I think we should have a good day, and then we will find a time for you and His Majesty to sit down and speak together. He is looking forward to meeting you, and he has confided in me his desire to give you quite a . . . scoop, I believe you call it."

I was elated. This was really happening. Here I was, being escorted into the Al-Aksa Mosque, the third-holiest site in the Islamic religion, right behind one of the descendants of the prophet Muhammad, and I was soon going to speak with him as well.

Ever since my days as a young boy at Phillips Academy in Andover, I'd wanted to be a news correspondent in foreign lands. I cannot explain the obsession. There was no obvious rationale. My classmates certainly did not aspire to be journalists. They wanted to be baseball players and bankers, congressmen and corporate titans. There were no journalists in my family. My father was a tax attorney. My mother was a piano teacher. My father was a good man, kind and generous, but he never traveled outside the United States. He didn't even own a passport. Yet since childhood I harbored an insatiable desire to explore deep jungles and vast deserts and exotic locales of all kinds. My father couldn't stand meeting new people; I lived for it. At Princeton, my father immersed himself in numbers. At Columbia, I immersed myself in history. My father read the King James Bible and the *Wall Street Journal*. I'd had my own subscriptions to *Life* magazine and *National Geographic* since I was eight years old and used to sneak a small transistor radio into my bed at night to listen to the reports of Edward R. Murrow. And here I was, in

Jerusalem—at the Dome of the Rock itself—in the presence of royalty.

A thousand questions flooded my head. Where would I possibly begin? Here was a man who was already eighteen years old when the twentieth century began. Here was a member of the Great Hashemite Dynasty, the son of Sharif Hussein bin Ali, onetime ruler of Mecca of the Hejaz. This king had been schooled in Istanbul at the peak of Turkish power. Later, he had gone back to Arabia and emerged as the esteemed commander of the Great Arab Revolt against the Ottomans. He had been personal friends with T. E. Lawrence, the legendary British colonel who became known as Lawrence of Arabia. Together they had taken the region by storm, organizing the Arab tribes to fight against the Ottomans. And when it was all over and the dust had settled, the Turkish empire had collapsed, and the Hashemite family had been amply rewarded. The Brits carved up the remains of the Turkish fiefdom and gave the Hashemites three territorial gifts: the desert region known as the Arabian Peninsula, the fertile Mesopotamian region that became known as Iraq, and the land on the eastern side of the Jordan River that became known as Transjordan. It was over this last swath of territory that Abdullah now ruled, and as the door to the mosque was opened for us, it finally dawned on me which question I had to ask him first.

5

As the king neared the doorway of the mosque, I saw a flicker of movement.

It happened fast, but it seemed odd—out of place.

I looked to my right and saw a man bolt from behind the door and jump from the shadows. He pulled out a small pistol. He aimed it at the monarch's head. The guards didn't react at first. Neither did the king. They were all too stunned, as was I. Then I saw a flash from the barrel and heard the boom—then another—and a third.

Horrified, I watched the entire scene unfold before me as if in slow motion. The king jerked back again and again and finally collapsed to the ground. I turned and saw his grandson lunge forward without a second thought, attacking the shooter. The two men struggled for a moment before I heard another shot. And then the young prince crumpled to the ground, writhing in pain.

A flutter of birds raced for the sky. People screamed and ran for cover. But the shooting didn't stop. For several seconds, the man kept firing, and then he began to run. He was coming straight for me. The king's guards pivoted now and began to return fire. I dropped to the ground and covered my head and face. The Temple Mount had erupted in gunfire at this point. Bullets were whizzing past my head and I was certain these moments were my last.

But a split second later, the assailant crashed to the ground not far from where I was. I didn't know if he had been shot or had simply stumbled. Without thinking, I sprang up and jumped on him. Before I realized what I was doing, I was beating him about the face and head. Soon I could see that he had been shot in multiple places. He was bleeding profusely. But he was not dead—not yet—and I was determined he was not going to run. For the moment I had forgotten I was a journalist. I had forgotten, too, that I was now in the line of fire. I was enraged, and my fists kept raining blows down upon him.

Seconds later, soldiers surrounded us, guns locked and loaded and pointed at both of us.

"Stop—don't move any farther!" they shouted.

Immediately I stopped beating the man. The soldiers yelled at me to put my hands above my head, where they could see them. Then they ordered me to slowly get off the man and step away. I did as I was told and saw two of the king's personal guards running toward us. Before I realized what was happening, someone behind me smashed the back of my skull with what must have been the butt of a rifle. I collapsed to the ground, not far from the assailant. I could feel blood running down the back of my scalp. My eyes were tearing, and I was in intense pain. But I did not black out, and as I lay there, I watched a soldier scoop up the still-smoking pistol lying by the assassin's side. They checked the man for more weapons but found none. Then they checked his pulse.

"He's done for," one of the guards said.

I could hardly believe it was true. Dead? Already? But who was he? What was his story? Who had sent him? I was seething. This man had tried to kill a king. He had tried to kill a prince. He had done so on sacred, holy ground. Why had he done it? I wanted answers.

A soldier grabbed my arms and tied them behind my back. Another took my satchel and patted me down for weapons. As he did, one of the king's guards was rifling through the assassin's identification papers and personal effects.

"What's his name?" his partner asked.

"Mustafa," the guard replied. "Mustafa Shukri Ashshu."

"He's not a Jew?"

"No, his papers say he's a Moslem, sir, a Palestinian."

"You cannot be serious."

"I am, sir."

"Are they forgeries?"

"No, they look real."

"Let me see them."

The guard handed the papers over to his partner.

"They are real," he said in disbelief. "He lives right here in the Old City. He's a tailor."

"How old was he, sir?"

"Just twenty-one."

The older guard let fly a slew of obscenities.

"How in the world did he get by all of us?" he fumed.

That, of course, was a question the papers did not shed light on.

Suddenly the two bodyguards turned to me.

"Who are you?" they shouted. *"Where did you come from?"*

Their questions came fast and furious. I explained I was an American, there to meet the king. They pressed for details, and that's when Captain Rajoub came running up, gun in one hand, the telegram from the palace in the other. The guards read the telegram, checked my papers, and conferred with one another. Rajoub confirmed I was telling the truth, and finally the men untied me, pulled me to my feet, gave me my bag and hat, and ordered me to leave.

"But I was expecting to interview His Majesty," I protested.

"You must go. There is nothing for you here," the older guard said. "His Majesty is dead."

I just stared at him, unable to speak. The king was dead? They were confirming this? I don't know why I thought it would be otherwise. I had seen the entire event unfold before me. His Majesty had been shot in the face and chest at point-blank range. But with all that had just happened, it had not yet occurred to me he might actually be dead. Call it denial. Call it the fog of war. Or perhaps I simply still wanted the interview I had been promised. I'd had an appointment. I had made it on time. He was the one who was late. I had been there. I was ready. I had my questions. And now I was being ordered to leave.

A chill rippled through my body. Despite the intense noontime heat, I suddenly felt cold. I was lonely and intensely tired. I knew I was in danger of slipping into shock, and there was a part of me that wanted to succumb to it. I could hear the sirens. Within minutes, doctors and nurses would be arriving. They would take care of me. They would whisk me off to a hospital and pump my body full of drugs and I could sleep and try to forget all this had ever happened. But there was another part of me that forced my legs to straighten, forced myself to stand, and before I realized what was happening, I was walking straight toward the lifeless body of the king, my right hand instinctively pulling a notebook out of the leather satchel hanging from my shoulder.

A crowd of guards and soldiers had surrounded His Majesty, guns drawn, as the young Prince Hussein, weeping over his grandfather, knelt at his side. But it was instantly clear the soldier had been right. The king was dead. His skin was white. His eyes were closed. His white cotton robes were smeared and stained with blood.

I turned to a Moslem cleric of some sort standing nearby, his mouth agape, tears in his eyes, saying nothing.

"Do you have a telephone?" I asked in Arabic, handing him my damp handkerchief. I was surprised by how calm my voice sounded.

"No, no, not in the mosque," he stuttered, accepting my gift and wiping his eyes. "But there is one in the office."

"I must use it to call the palace," I said, choosing for the moment not to identify myself.

"Yes, of course," he said, obviously not thinking about my request clearly or questioning who I was.

As if in a stupor, he led me to a squat outbuilding nearby that housed the administrative offices of the Waqf, the religious institution charged with protecting and maintaining the Islamic holy sites on the Temple Mount. Fumbling with his keys, the cleric opened the door. He led me to his office, showed me the telephone, and explained how to get an operator to place the call to Amman. Then he left me in peace and shut the door behind him.

I picked up the receiver and felt my hand trembling. I took a deep breath and tried in vain to steady my nerves.

"May I help you?" a woman asked at the other end of the scratchy line.

"Operator, I need to make a call to the United States," I said as calmly as I could. "Can you help me with that?"

"Yes, sir, I can," she replied.

I gave her the number and waited for the call to be put through. Finally I was connected to a young woman at the assignment desk in New York. Unwilling to entrust this breaking news to whatever fresh-faced college grad had just answered the phone, I demanded to speak to the international editor, a longtime personal friend, and said it was an emergency.

The woman, however, replied that he was not in, and asked to take a message. *Not in?* I thought. *Why the blast not?* Then I glanced at my pocket watch, and it dawned on me that it was only 12:25 p.m. local time, which meant it was not yet 5:30 in the morning in New York.

"Who's the editor on duty?" I asked.

"Mr. Briggs, sir," the young lady replied.

"Roger Briggs?" I asked, the strain on me beginning to show itself in my speech.

"Yes, sir."

"Well, I need him immediately. Tell him I'm calling from Jerusalem with an urgent exclusive, but it won't hold long."

The wait that followed seemed like an eternity, and the longer it took, the more terrified I became that UPI or the *New York Times* or the *Jerusalem Post* or some Arab paper would scoop me. Surely many had heard the gunshots, and now everyone in Jerusalem was hearing the sirens coming from all directions. I had no idea who was out there in that group of well-wishers. Maybe there had been another reporter. Maybe there had been more than one.

"This is Briggs. Who's this, and what's all the hubbub about? For heaven's sakes, man, you know what time it is?"

"Roger, this is A. B. Collins in Jerusalem."

"A. B., is that really you?"

We had known each other for years.

"Yes, yes, now take this down immediately."

"What did you say?" Briggs asked. The line crackled with static. "Repeat. Say again."

"I said this is A. B. Collins in Jerusalem. Take this down. 'King Abdullah bin al-Hussein of the Hashemite Kingdom of Jordan . . . is dead.'"

PART TWO

Present Day

6

* * *

I had done a lot of crazy things in my life, but nothing as stupid as this.

As I stared out over the roiling waves and countless whitecaps of the Mediterranean below, I couldn't help but think about my grandfather. A. B. Collins was once the Beirut bureau chief for the Associated Press. Long before I was born, he flew this exact route as an American foreign correspondent in the war-torn Middle East. His career was legendary. As a young boy I dreamed of following in his footsteps. As a teenager, I read all his journals. In college I spent hours in the library reading his old dispatches on microfiche. Now here I was, a foreign correspondent for the *New York Times*, wondering if, given all the risks my grandfather had taken, he'd ever done anything quite this foolhardy.

There was still a way out, of course. I could still change my plans. But the truth was I didn't want to. I may never have interviewed a king or witnessed the assassination of a monarch. But I was just as committed to my craft, and I was going in, come what may. That's all there was to it. In six minutes, my Air France flight would touch down in the Lebanese capital. In nineteen minutes, I'd link up with my colleagues. Together we'd drive ninety miles to the border of Syria. And if all went well, by nightfall we'd slip across the border unnoticed and eventually locate one of the world's most feared jihadi commanders.

Jack Vaughn, director of the Central Intelligence Agency, had personally warned me not to do this. So had the head of the Mossad and the chief of Jordanian intelligence, not to mention my mother. My editor, Allen MacDonald, had expressly forbidden me to go. Their rationale was as simple as it was compelling: Jamal Ramzy was a killer.

Born in Jordan. Raised in the Gulf. Went to Afghanistan. Joined the mujahideen. Killed more Russians than any other Arab fighter. Met bin Laden. Became his chief bodyguard. Was in the room when bin Laden created al Qaeda in 1988. Sent to fight in Somalia. Became a top aide to Khalid Sheikh Mohammed, the mastermind of the 9/11 attacks. Personally trained the 9/11 hijackers. Helped plan the bombings of two American embassies in Africa. Helped behead a *Wall Street Journal* reporter in Pakistan. Became a top aide to Ayman al-Zawahiri, the head of al Qaeda after bin Laden was killed, but had a severe falling-out with him over the future of the organization. Teamed up with his barbaric younger cousin Abu Khalif, the head of "al Qaeda in Iraq and the Levant," an ultra-violent breakaway faction of the mother ship. Sent to command a force of rebel fighters in Syria. Ordered to bring back Assad's head on a platter. Literally.

This was the guy I was trying to locate. I knew it was crazy. But I was going anyway.

To my knowledge, Jamal Ramzy had never been photographed or interviewed by a Western reporter. But after nearly a year of my constant e-mails to someone I believed to be Ramzy's lieutenant, he had finally said yes—to the interview, anyway, if not the photograph. If I was communicating with the right person, and if he was being truthful—neither of which, at the moment, I was able to fully verify—the big questions were these: Why would Ramzy talk to anyone? Why now? And why me?

The answers, I believed, were simple: He wanted to be on the front page, top of the fold. He wanted to be the new face of the Radicals for all the world to see. And he knew full well that there was no bigger venue than the *New York Times*, the world's newspaper of record, for which I had been a foreign correspondent for nearly a decade.

As far as timing went, my operating theory was that it was not vanity that was persuading Ramzy to finally respond to my repeated overtures. After all, the Jordanian-born terrorist had lived in the shadows for decades. He had survived all this time by living off the grid, and I suspect he would have been content to remain there if possible rather than risk being obliterated without warning one day by a drone strike, like most of his comrades-in-arms. No, it was unlikely that vanity was driving Ramzy. Rather, I was fairly certain he had something to say at this moment, something he had never said before, and that he was planning on using me to say it.

For the past several weeks, I had been picking up rumors that Ramzy and his rebel forces had captured a cache of chemical weapons in Syria. The Assad regime had supposedly allowed international forces to destroy its remaining weapons of mass destruction, but it was widely believed that at least some stockpiles had been hidden. Now one well-placed American intelligence source told me his agency had picked up frantic radio traffic three weeks earlier between Syrian army forces loyal to Assad saying one of their WMD storage facilities not far from Aleppo had just been overrun. The Syrian forces were desperately calling for air strikes, but while the air support had come, it was too late. Quite separately, another source, this one in a foreign intelligence service, confided to me that a high-ranking Syrian general had just defected to either Turkey or Jordan (he wouldn't say which) and claimed some al Qaeda breakaway faction had seized several tons of chemical weapons south of Aleppo within the last few weeks.

Was it true? I had no idea. All I knew for certain was that nothing of the sort had yet been reported in the Arab press or anywhere in the West. No one at the White House, State, or the Pentagon would confirm or deny my discreet inquiries. Part of this, I suspected, was to prevent the widespread panic that was sure to break out if it became known that one of the world's most dangerous terrorist organizations now had control of some of the world's most dangerous weapons.

Of course, I hadn't raised any of this in my e-mails to my source in Syria. I'd simply repeated my long-standing requests for an interview. But I was increasingly certain this was why Ramzy wanted to talk now, when he had never talked publicly before. He wanted the world to know what he had. He wanted the American people and their president to know. What's more, I had to believe he savored the irony of Ayman al-Zawahiri hearing through an American newspaper that one of his former advisors had hit the mother lode—that an al Qaeda offshoot finally had possession of the very weapons al Qaeda itself had been desperately seeking for nearly two decades.

I hoped I was right. Not that Ramzy had the WMD, mind you, but that he had a story—an important story—he wanted to communicate through me. It was, I suspected, my only hope of survival. After all, this was a man who cut people's throats for sport, Americans' most of all. Only if he really did want to use me to communicate a big story would my colleagues and I be safe.

It was no wonder no one I knew wanted me to head into Syria to track this man down and speak with him face-to-face. Even the colleagues I was about to meet were deeply uncomfortable. I certainly understood why. And I didn't blame them. What we were about to do wasn't normal. But I—and they—were part of "the tribe," part of an elite group, a small cadre of foreign correspondents whose lives were devoted to covering wars and rumors of war, revolutions, chaos, and bloodshed of all kinds. It's what I'd gone to school for, nearly twenty years earlier. It's what I'd been doing for the *New York Daily News* and the Associated Press and the *Times* ever since. I loved it. I lived for it.

Some said it was an addiction. They said people like me were adrenaline junkies. Maybe I was. But that's not the way I thought of it. To me, risk was part of my job, and it was a job my colleagues told me I wasn't half-bad at. I had won an award for covering a Delta Force firefight in Kandahar, Afghanistan, with another *Times* reporter in 2001. And I had even won a Pulitzer for a series of articles I wrote in 2003 when I was embedded with the First Brigade of the U.S. Army's Third Infantry Division as they stormed Baghdad. The awards were gratifying. But I didn't do this to win awards. I did it because I loved it. I did it because I couldn't imagine doing anything else.

Most reporters couldn't wait to get out of Afghanistan or Iraq after the initial invasions and the establishment of the new governments. But I repeatedly requested longer tours. I loved getting to know our boys who suited up for battle every day. I loved interviewing the Iraqis our troops were training and taking into battle. I also loved having beers and trading gossip with the spooks from Langley and MI6 and every other intelligence agency on the planet who had come to play in the Big Game. Most of all, though, I found it absolutely fascinating to slip away from the Green Zone and get out in the hinterland and risk life and limb trying to hook up with one insurgent commander or another to get his story. *All* the news that's fit to print, right? I wasn't there to regurgitate whatever the flacks at State or the Pentagon tried to spoon-feed me. I was there to find the real stories.

So whatever lay ahead, I was absolutely determined to head into Syria. I was going after the story. Not a single person I had confided in approved of what I was doing. But I wanted to think that one would have. I wanted to believe my grandfather would have been proud of me. At least he would have understood what I was doing and why.

A. B. Collins covered the Second World War for United Press International. Then he worked for the Associated Press all over the globe. To be perfectly honest, he was my idol. Maybe it was because of all the stories he used to tell me when I was growing up. That man could really spin a good yarn. I was in awe of the way he had seemed to have met everyone and seen everything. Then again, maybe I simply loved him because of all the ice cream Pop-Pop used to buy my older brother and me whenever he and Grammie Collins came to visit. Or maybe it was because my father had left us when I was only twelve, and I never saw him again—none of us did—and Pop-Pop was the only man I really had in my life growing up. It was he who took me fishing on Eagle Lake and hiking in Acadia National Park. It was he who taught me how to use his collection of rifles and took me on hunting trips all over Maine and even up in Canada. Whatever the reason, I loved the man with every fiber of my being, and for as long as I could remember, I wanted to do what he did, to be what he was. Now here I was, about to touch down in Beirut, a city he had worked in and lived in and loved dearly.

Maybe the olive didn't fall far from the tree.

Then again, my grandfather had lived a long and fruitful life and despite his many adventures had died in his bed, in his sleep, in his old age. At the moment, I had no presumption of meeting such a quiet and peaceful fate.

7

BEIRUT, LEBANON

I stared at my hands.

They were trembling. Not much. Not so that anyone else would necessarily notice. But I noticed. It had never happened before.

I unscrewed the top from a bottle of Evian and took several gulps. A flight attendant announced the local time of 6:54 p.m. We had lifted off from Heathrow in London at 10:05 that morning. Air France flight 568 was touching down a minute early. I pulled out my grandfather's gold pocket watch, the one he gave me just before he died. I wound it up and set it. Then I pulled out a pen and my dog-eared passport and began filling out the Lebanese immigration and customs form.

Name: James Bradley Collins
Date of birth: May 3, 1975
City of birth: Bar Harbor, Maine
Nationality: American
Country of residence: United States

City passport was issued: Washington, D.C.
Countries visited before landing in Lebanon:
   Turkey, France, Germany, U.K.
Purpose for visit: Business

I filled in my passport number and marked that I had nothing to declare. Then I flipped through the pages of my well-traveled passport from back to front, reading through all the stamps I had acquired over the years—every European capital, every Asian capital, and every capital in the Middle East and North Africa. Except Israel's. I had been in and out of Ben Gurion International Airport near Tel Aviv more times than I could count, of course, but I had always been careful to ask the authorities there to stamp my visa, not my passport, so it didn't prevent me from entering certain Arab countries that would refuse a traveler entry if he had an Israeli stamp in his travel documents.

Before I realized it, I was wincing at the terrible photo of me taken nearly a decade earlier. I was reminded of the old adage: "If you really look as bad as your passport picture, you're too ill to travel." Then again, in some ways the photo was better than the current reality. My eyes were green back then. Now they seemed permanently bloodshot. I'd had twenty-twenty vision then. Today I sported prescription eyeglasses in black, semirimless designer frames for which I'd paid more than I care to mention. In the photo, my muddybrown hair was hideously long and badly in need of a cut. But then again, I actually *had* hair—on my head, at least, though not on my face. Ten years later, I was completely bald (by choice, thank you very much) and sporting a salt-and-pepper mustache and goatee.

As we taxied to the gate, I powered up my phone and checked my e-mails. The first that came up was from my brother. I skipped it and moved on. Most of the rest were a potpourri of updates and questions from colleagues in D.C. and sources I was working around the world, as well as RSS feeds of the latest stories published by the *Times* on the Middle East, national security issues, intelligence matters, and other issues pertaining to my beat. One story was by Alex Brunnell, the *Times* bureau chief in Jerusalem. I scanned it quickly. It was a ridiculously pedestrian piece that focused on why the peace talks between the Israelis and Palestinians had bogged down again and why the White House might soon abandon its effort to strike a comprehensive deal and shift its attention from the Middle East to the Pacific Rim. It was badly sourced and poorly written and contained nothing but conventional wisdom. Everyone knew the talks were going nowhere. Everyone knew President Taylor and his secretary of state had bitten off more than they could chew. This was hardly news. The *Wall Street Journal* had done the same story a month earlier. Everyone else had done it since then. But this was typical of Brunnell. He never seemed to break news, just chase it. Why the suits in Manhattan had given a third-rate hack a byline in the world's most respected newspaper, I would never understand.

The next e-mail, however, sucked the wind out of me.

It was from our publisher, addressed to all of the paper's staff around the world.

> It is with a heavy heart that I write to inform you of the tragic death of Janet Fiorelli, *New York Times* Cairo bureau chief. Janet was working on a story detailing the lingering effects of the Arab Spring in Egypt when she was killed yesterday in a suicide bombing in Cairo. The U.S. State Department is investigating the attack. Janet was a top-rate journalist who was respected and beloved by colleagues and readers alike for her professionalism and kindness, and . . .

I stopped reading. I couldn't believe it. I knew Janet. We were friends. We'd worked together on countless stories. I knew her husband, Tom, and her twins, Michael and Peter. I'd been to their home in Heliopolis a dozen times or more. I read the first sentence of the e-mail again and again. It couldn't be true.

Suddenly we were at the gate. Everyone else got off the plane, but I just sat there, staring out the window.

"Sir, is everything okay?" asked an attractive young flight attendant, trying to be helpful.

No, it wasn't, I wanted to say. But I just nodded and stood, trying to get my bearings.

"Is there anything I can do for you, sir?" she asked.

She had a lovely smile and gentle eyes. I found myself looking at her for a moment too long, then caught myself.

"Sorry; no, I'm good," I said.

I felt numb. I'd had dinner with Tom and Janet in Alexandria only a few weeks earlier. Now she was gone. It seemed impossible.

The flight attendant handed me my black leather jacket and backpack from the overhead bin. I thanked her and deplaned and made my way through the crowds to the baggage claim. I never checked any bags, not anymore, not since Lufthansa lost my luggage back in 2007 while I was on the way to interview the German chancellor. Nevertheless, my editor had told me to meet my colleagues at baggage carousel number three, so that's where I went.

"J. B., my friend, welcome back to Beirut—you look terrible!"

A gargantuan man, swarthy and unshaven, laughed from his belly, his booming voice turning heads in the terminal—not exactly the low profile I was looking for. Then he gave me a bear hug that nearly crushed my spine. I'd told him a hundred times to go a tad lighter, but it was always the same thing.

"Good to see you, too, Omar," I replied, so not in the mood for all his energy. "You ready for this?"

"Ready?" he shot back. "Have you completely

lost your mind? You're a fool, a complete lunatic. You're going to get us all killed one day. You know that, don't you?"

I just stared at him.

"What?" he asked. "What's the matter?"

"You haven't read your e-mails," I said.

"No, what e-mails?"

"You haven't heard about Janet Fiorelli."

His expression changed immediately. "No, why? What has happened?"

I nodded toward the smartphone in his hand. He read the e-mail and I watched as the enthusiasm drained from his face.

Omar Fayez and I had been through a great deal together, and we had lost more than our share of friends and colleagues over the years. Though he was only thirty-two, he had always treated me like I was his younger brother, looking out for me, watching my back. Six feet five inches tall, at least 275 pounds, and in remarkably good shape for his size, Omar looked like an NFL linebacker. But he had a master's from Harvard and a PhD from Oxford in Middle Eastern studies and spoke four languages—Arabic, French, Farsi, and English. Born and raised in Jordan, he'd been a reporter, interpreter, and "fixer" for the *Times* in Jordan and Baghdad for the last six years, much of that time working at my side.

"Let's talk about something else," I said. "I can't process this right now."

Omar nodded.

"How's Hadiya?" I asked, going straight to his favorite topic.

"Like always, my friend, a gift from heaven," Omar replied, his voice now more subdued.

"Glad to hear it."

"She sends you a kiss," he said.

"Give her my love."

"I will."

Then he paused.

"What is it?" I asked.

"Well, I was going to save this for later, but maybe you need to hear it now."

"I can't handle any more bad news just yet," I said.

"No, no, it's good news."

"Oh?"

"Hadiya and I are expecting in March."

I couldn't help but grin. This *was* good news. They had been trying to have children for years without any success, and their marriage had struggled for a time because of it. I gave him a hug and congratulated him. "Good for you, Omar—when we get back, we must celebrate."

"We would like that very much," Omar replied. "God has been so good to us. Hadiya is happier than I have ever seen her."

I had no doubt. But I couldn't help but notice that as he said this, the tone of Omar's voice and his body language changed ever so slightly. He was worried about the task ahead of us, and for the first time, I felt a pang of guilt for taking him into harm's way.

8

* * *

"Where's Abdel?" I asked as I scanned the faces in the crowd.

"He's bringing the car," Omar said. "Come; we must hurry. A storm is rolling in. We need to get moving. We don't have any time to spare."

As we exited the airport, what struck me first was the chill in the air. The sun had long since set. It was mid-November. The winter rains were coming. Dark thunderheads were rolling in over the city. The winds were picking up. Omar was right—a storm was coming, and I needed something warmer than a T-shirt and khakis. I stopped for a moment, dug out a black wool crewneck sweater from my backpack, and put it on along with my leather jacket.

Just then, a silver four-door Renault pulled up to the curb and stopped in front of us. As the trunk popped up, the driver's door opened too, and out jumped a lanky young man with a touch of acne and long, curly, unkempt hair. He wore tattered blue jeans, a dark-green hoodie, and black running shoes. "Mr. Collins, I'm so sorry I'm late," he said with a genuine air of anxiety in his voice. "Please forgive me, sir."

"Don't worry, Abdel; you're not late," I assured him, shaking his hand. "We're a bit early. My flight was on time for once, and I didn't check any bags."

"You are very kind, sir, very kind," he said as he took my backpack and put it in the trunk alongside Omar's luggage and his own. "Please, get inside and get warm, Mr. Collins. I have the heat on for you, plus hot coffee and baklava."

I didn't know Abdel Hamid particularly well. We had worked together just one time, and only briefly at that, but everyone said he was a good kid. I knew for certain he was a phenomenal photographer, and I had asked for him by name to be assigned to me on this project. A Palestinian by birth, he'd grown up in a refugee camp on the outskirts of Beirut. He had no college degree and no formal training as a photographer, but prior to being hired by the *Times*, he had made a name for himself as a freelancer for the work he'd done in Syria, producing some of the most heart-wrenching images of the civil war of anyone in the business. As I got into the backseat, Omar headed around to the other side of the car and got in beside me so we could talk more easily on the three-hour drive ahead of us. And sure enough, waiting for us were two cups of steaming hot coffee.

"Cream and three sugars for you; is that right, Mr. Fayez?" Abdel asked as he got behind the wheel and checked his mirrors.

"It is indeed, Abdel."

"And black for you, Mr. Collins?"

"You got it," I replied. "You're fast becoming my new best friend, Abdel."

"I'm only too happy to help, Mr. Collins."

"Abdel, please, call me J. B.," I told him, patting him on the back. "You say Mr. Collins and I think my grandfather just showed up."

"I would have loved to have met him," Abdel said. "From all I have read, he was a remarkable man and a tremendous journalist."

"That's very kind of you to say, Abdel," I said, touched that he knew anything about my grandfather.

"It is my pleasure, Mr. Collins; thank *you*, sir— you are very kind."

He had completely missed the request that he call me by my first name, but I didn't have the heart to correct him again, so I moved on.

"So look, Abdel, last time I was here was what, July?"

"Yes, late July, Mr. Collins."

"Right, and wasn't there a young lady in your life at the time?"

"Oh yes, Mr. Collins, that's true," he said, clearly surprised. "You mean Fatima. You have a good memory."

"How's that going?" I asked. "As I recall, you were quite taken with her."

"Yes, yes. I was—I *am*."

"How is she these days?"

"Ah yes, she is very well, Mr. Collins," Abdel told me as he wove through evening traffic, heading east toward the city of Zahle. "Thank you for asking. We are very much in love."

"And I understand you have a little news," I said. "Is that right?"

Abdel looked at me in the rearview mirror, startled but not unhappy. "Well, yes, how did you know?"

"I have my sources, Abdel." I smiled. "That is my job, after all, right?"

"Yes, you have always had very good sources," he said, beaming, but then realized that Omar had no idea what we were talking about. "Fatima and I got engaged last week."

"Oh, wow, congratulations!" Omar exclaimed.

"Yes, that's very exciting, Abdel," I added.

"Yes, it is. Thank you both. We are very happy."

"When is the big day?" I asked.

"In a few months—January, probably."

"Very good. And Fatima is still in school, is she not?"

"Yes, she's in her last year."

"At A.U.?"

"Yes, sir."

"What is she studying?"

"Journalism."

"How can you go wrong? Well, bravo, Abdel. I'd love to meet her, and maybe someday she'll end up working for the Gray Lady."

"Oh, she would love that, Mr. Collins. She would love that very much."

Omar turned to me, took a sip of coffee, and asked me about my mom. I knew he was sincere. He was a decent, caring soul, and I loved that about him. But I also knew he was just warming up to the topic he really wanted to discuss: why in the world were we trying to meet Jamal Ramzy?

"Mom's hanging in there," I said, trying my best to be polite.

"And that old house you grew up in—does she still live there?"

"She does, though for the life of me I don't know why."

"Too expensive?"

"Not really. The mortgage is all paid off. But you know, it's big and empty and it's just her. Takes a lot of work to maintain that old place, and with her knee and back trouble . . . Well, anyway, it is what it is."

"And your suggestion that she sell it and move to Florida?"

"Going nowhere, I'm afraid," I conceded. "Doesn't even want to talk about it."

"How is Matthew doing?"

"No comment," I said. "Next question."

Omar looked surprised by my clipped answer. He had once met my older brother at the airport in Amman and seemed to take a liking to him. But to his credit, he quickly shifted gears. "And Laura? How's that all going?"

That wasn't a topic I wanted to discuss either. There was a long, awkward silence as I stared out the window, trying to come up with a suitable yet honest answer as I watched row after row of newly built apartment buildings blur past. "About the same," I said at last, then changed the subject again. "So look, were you able to get anything from the Mukhabarat?"

A few days earlier, as we made plans for this trip, I'd asked Omar to work his sources in the Jordanian intelligence service to see if they would give us anything on Ramzy.

"A little," he said, accepting my discomfort in talking about personal matters and getting to the main topic. "I had coffee with Amir last night. He wouldn't give me much. Told me we were crazy to do this thing, said it simply wasn't worth it."

"He doesn't believe we're going to get to meet with Ramzy."

"No, that's not it," Omar said. "He told me he absolutely thinks we are going to find and meet Ramzy. And that's precisely what worries him."

"What exactly?" I pressed.

"He doesn't want to get on YouTube tomorrow and see the three of us being beheaded."

9

HOMS, SYRIA

Omar, Abdel, and I stashed our rental car in some bushes.

Then we slipped across the border into Syria and hiked for several hours. As we approached the city, we inched our way forward under the cover of predawn darkness. Finally, the three of us lay on our stomachs in the mud in a grassy field trying to figure out our next move.

The crackle of machine-gun fire had grown louder over the past several minutes. Artillery shells were now screaming over our heads. The ear-splitting explosions were becoming more intense. The earth shook violently beneath us, and I realized I was shaking too.

To my left I could see the torched wreckage of a Russian-built T-72 battle tank. To my right, about fifty yards away, was the charred hulk of a school bus. Beyond that, about a hundred yards away, stood the carcass of an old VW van. Behind us lay a deserted playground, complete with slides and balance beams and swings swaying in the bitter winter wind. But there were no children—no human presence of any kind, so long as you ignored the dozens of shallow graves that seemed to have been dug quite recently.

Clouds scattered and then regathered overhead, and in the intermittent moonlight I could see row upon row of bombed-out apartment buildings ahead of us. There were no lights on in any of them. No sounds of music or talking or laughter emanated from their midst. Indeed, there were no signs of normal life at all as far as the eye could see.

Welcome to Homs.

Once a thriving metropolis, Homs had been the third-largest city in Syria after Damascus and Aleppo. More than six hundred thousand people had, until recently, called this their home. Now it was fast becoming a ghost town. Most of the residents had fled for their lives over the past few years. Some neighborhoods were nearly empty of living souls. If a ferocious battle between government and rebel forces hadn't just erupted nearby, I would have had no idea anyone was still left in the area.

Just why anyone was still fighting over this wasteland was beyond me. What was the point? What was left to fight over? Most of the factories had been blown up. Most of the schools had been burned down, the Catholic and Orthodox churches and the mosques, too. The banks had been looted. All but a handful of stores were shuttered. There was barely anything to eat. No running water. No working sewage system. The airport had been obliterated. Even if you had a functioning car or truck, you couldn't use it. The gas stations had no petrol. The roads were ripped up or blocked by soldiers or rebels. There was no legitimate way into the city, and only a fool would try to enter. Yet there we were, watching the blaze of rockets and mortars streaking through the sky. We could see tracer bullets slicing through the night.

We couldn't stay put. Forces from one side or the other would be coming soon. We had to keep moving.

Though I tried not to, I couldn't help but think about all my friends who had died covering this miserable war. My *Times* colleague and fellow Pulitzer Prize winner Anthony Shadid had died in Syria. So had Gilles Jacquier, a photojournalist with France Télévisions. And Marie Colvin with the *Sunday Times* of London. The list went on and on. Well over two hundred reporters and photographers had been killed in Syria alone since the start of the civil war. And that didn't even count Janet Fiorelli and all the other journalists who had died covering the Arab Spring or the wars in Afghanistan and Iraq.

I didn't want to be one of them, but I did want this interview. I wanted this exclusive, and I was determined to get it—or get shipped home in a body bag.

I whispered a plan to Omar. He quickly relayed it to Abdel. Then, looking into each man's eyes and making sure we were on the same page, I grabbed my backpack, put it once again over my shoulders, and jumped to my feet and began sprinting toward one of the bombed-out apartment buildings. As soon as I did, however, a machine-gun nest to our right suddenly roared to life. I didn't dare stop. I didn't even dare slow down. If I was going to die, I decided, so be it. I would die on the move, on the hunt for this story, not pinned down in the mud, not cowering in fear or groveling for mercy. I wasn't as fast as I'd been in college. I wasn't as fast as I'd been when this war began. Hate it though I might, I wasn't young anymore, and war correspondence was a young man's game. But I kept moving.

My heart pounded. My lungs desperately sucked in air. My legs burned, but I kept going. As I roared past the back of the bus, I could hear .50-caliber rounds tearing through, but I kept moving. I was terrified—far more so for Omar and Abdel than even for myself, if that were possible—but I didn't dare look back. I had no idea if the guys were still behind me. I hadn't heard any screams or cries, though I'm not sure I would have. My ears were filled with the excruciating roar of explosions and automatic-weapons fire. For all I knew, I was alone. I just hoped it wasn't their time or mine yet.

I broke left and headed for the back door of one of the tenements. As I drew closer, I could see bullets ricocheting off the cinder blocks. The intense roar of the machine-gun fire seemed to increase exponentially. I wondered if two people were firing at us instead of one. Instinctively, I changed direction. Breaking to my right, I could see the VW van just ahead. It had been burnt to a crisp. It had no tires, no windows. It was nothing but a bullet-ridden shell, but it was my only chance, so that's where I headed. As I finally reached it, I wasn't sure I'd stop in time, so I did a Pete Rose, diving headfirst behind the chassis as a hailstorm of bullets slammed into the engine block.

The withering gunfire didn't stop or slow. Dozens of rounds pelted the side of the van. I could hear many more whizzing over my head. I pressed myself as low to the ground as I possibly could and covered my head with my arms. I'd never experienced anything like this. Not in Afghanistan. Not in Iraq. Not covering the revolutions in Egypt or Libya. In the past, I'd usually been on the move with soldiers. I often stuck close to professionals who were heavily armed and trained for battle. On rare occasions, I even traveled with a group of insurgents, but I'd never been alone, in the open, being shot at with no one around me who could shoot back, no weapons, and no way to defend myself.

Almost before I had time to think, Abdel dove in beside me, and Omar right behind him. Abdel was shouting something in Arabic I couldn't quite make out in the cacophony. Omar was breathing as hard as I was. By the way he was shaking, I guessed he was probably just as afraid as I was that his heart was going to explode out of his chest even before he was shredded by bullets and left to bleed to death in an open field. But there was no time to commiserate.

"We can't stay here!" I shouted.

"Well, we can't keep going," Omar shouted back. *"They'll kill us all."*

"We should just stay," Abdel yelled. *"They have to reload eventually."*

"But when they do, we need to move fast," I yelled back. *"I'll go first, but don't follow me. We need to break up. Head out in three different directions. Pick a building, each a different one. Then we'll regroup on the front side. Hopefully it will be quieter over there."*

"No, no, we need to stay here," Abdel shouted at me.

I shook my head vigorously and tried to rally my men. *"If we do, we're dead!"*

No sooner had I spoken the words than there was an ever-so-brief lull. This was it, I thought. We had to move now.

"Go, go, go!" I shouted, springing to my feet and running again.

I didn't look back. I couldn't. But sure enough, moments later, the machine-gun nest roared back into business. Bullets pulverized the walls all around me, but somehow I burst through the rear entrance of the building, out of the line of fire, unscathed.

Now, however, I really was alone. I could hear mortars and artillery shells landing close by and moving closer. The explosions grew louder, and I both sensed and felt the already-pummeled and fragile building above me rocking and swaying with every concussion. I began to wonder how much more the structure could take. There was no reason I could think of for anyone to be firing directly at it. But what if a shell or two went astray? What if the building were hit? Might the whole thing come toppling down?

It occurred to me that no one back home had any idea where I was. Allen MacDonald, my editor in Washington, thought I was merely heading up to the Lebanese–Syrian border to interview refugees about the latest battles in the village of Al-Qusayr, since that's all I had told him after he shot down my Ramzy pitch. My mother thought I was going to Beirut to interview a Hezbollah commander. My brother? I hadn't talked to him in years.

Standing in a long, dark hallway, the floor rumbling beneath me, I had absolutely no idea what was in front of me. But I couldn't turn back now. So I stumbled my way down the hallway, groping in the near pitch-dark with one hand, my other hand touching the wall, as shards of broken glass crunched beneath me.

I felt something run across my feet and then something else. I immediately kicked the second one away, but a shudder ran down my spine. What were they? Rats? What exactly was I heading into? My imagination kicked into overdrive.

Just then, in darkness so complete I could no longer see my hand in front of my face, I stumbled over something and crashed to the floor. I had no idea what it was, but it was large and yielding and my hands slid along the floor tiles into something wet and sticky and cold. Repulsed, I wiped my hands on my khakis and felt around for the iPhone in my jacket. I pulled it out, punched in the security code, and clicked on the flashlight app. Instantly, I realized I had landed in a pool of coagulating blood. The fact that it was not yet completely dry made me shudder all over again. I turned and pointed the camera behind me and froze as I stared down into the lifeless eyes of a young boy, no older than fourteen or fifteen, shot at least a dozen times, his white, stiff hands in a death grip around an AK-47.

Click. Click. Click. My journalistic instincts kicked in and I snapped three pictures, then turned away in horror, wondering anew when the senseless killing in this godforsaken country would ever stop.

I pointed the light of the phone toward the end of the hallway and made my way to the front door. But as I reached for the doorknob, I hesitated. I needed to find my colleagues, to be sure. I certainly didn't want to be in this city alone. Nor, I had to imagine, did they. But then again, I had no idea what lay ahead. How in the world were we going to find Jamal Ramzy? For all we knew, he was leading this battle.

Pulse pounding, I again wiped my hands on my pants, then slowly opened the door. What lay before me was a scene from the apocalypse. But Omar and Abdel were nowhere to be found.

10

★ ★ ★

The stench of death was thick, revolting, and inescapable.

Everywhere I looked—up and down the street in both directions—I saw mountains of rubble and twisted rebar from half-collapsed buildings, the scorched remains of tanks and trucks and cars and motorcycles, and the ghastly sight of decomposing bodies that even the vultures had rejected. All of it was shrouded in an eerie fog of smoke and ash, bathed in the bluish-silver tint of the moon.

I didn't dare step out of the doorway. I wanted to call out to Omar and Abdel, but I kept my mouth shut. I pressed myself back into the shadows and all but closed the door to the apartment building, keeping it open barely a crack. Then I peered out into the night, scanning for any movement, any signs of friends or enemies. But nothing was moving save the smoke and ash in the winter winds that were now picking up and bringing a frightful chill. As slowly and quietly as I could, I zipped up my jacket and turned the collar up to protect my neck. Then the light began to dim as a curtain of clouds descended upon the moon.

What now? We were not yet at our rendezvous point, though as best I could tell we were getting close. To get to Ramzy, we were supposed to meet up with Tariq Baqouba, one of Ramzy's top lieutenants. Born in the Decapolis region of northern Jordan, Baqouba was, by all accounts, a young but battle-hardened fighter who had distinguished himself killing American Marines and Army Rangers in Iraq before turning his "talents" to the killing fields of Syria. It was his younger brother, Faisal, a former technician for Al Jazeera television, who was my e-mail contact.

Faisal's instructions had been simple: My team and I were to meet him in the remains of the Khaled bin Walid Mosque in a neighborhood several blocks away called al-Khalidiyah. Faisal would then take us to his brother Tariq, who would take us to Jamal Ramzy. I checked my pocket watch. The rendezvous time was just twenty-three minutes away. Yet how could I continue on without Omar and Abdel?

My fears were getting the best of me. Had the fighters manning the machine-gun nests cut my friends down before they had reached safety? Had the jihadists come after them? Had they reached a "safe" building, only to stumble upon armed men inside? Mortar rounds kept exploding. The building kept shaking. I knew it wasn't safe to stay. But I had no idea where to go, unless I headed to the mosque alone. The longer I stayed put, the more questions raced through my thoughts. What if they were injured? What if they were bleeding, dying? Should I go back for them? Of course, I had no idea which buildings they had gone to. Had they split up as I'd told them, or had they stayed together after all?

Feeling dehydrated, I grabbed the water bottle out of the side of my backpack and took a swig. Then, oddly enough, the explosions outside stopped. I had no idea why. Perhaps it was just a lull, but for a few unexpected minutes, there was near silence, broken only by the sporadic crackle of machine-gun fire in the distance . . . and by the ringing in my ears. I began to breathe normally again, but just then I heard a noise behind me. I turned quickly and saw a flash of moonlight pour through the doorway at the other end of a long hallway, though only for a moment. Someone had opened and closed the door. Someone had entered the building. The hair on the back of my neck stood erect. My heart started racing again. Who was it? Was it one of my men? Or someone about to kill me?

I closed the door behind me all the way, careful not to make a sound. I didn't want even the slightest ray of light to fall upon me or make me a target.

Now, however, the hallway was completely black. I was stuck. There was no way forward, and I didn't dare go back.

And now shards of glass were crackling under someone else's feet. Whoever it was, he was moving toward me. Slowly. Step by step. Inching his way forward.

Trying not to panic, I slowly lowered myself

to my knees. Whoever was coming, if they were armed and started firing, I was determined to present as small a target as possible. Then I remembered the AK-47. It was just a few yards away, in the hands of the young boy who likely had been killed merely a few hours earlier at most. I had noticed that the magazine was still in the weapon. I had no idea if there was any ammunition left, but what choice did I have? I did not want to die. Not here. Not yet. On my hands and knees now, I felt around in the dark until I found the cold, stiff corpse. I kept feeling around until my hands came upon the gun.

The crunching of boots on broken glass was getting louder. Whoever was out there, they were getting closer. I was running out of time. Desperate, I pried the boy's stiff fingers from the weapon and pulled it to my side.

Feeling every part of the machine gun in the dark, I tried to make sense of it. I'd never held a Kalashnikov. It wasn't like the shotguns or rifles my grandfather had taught me to use back in Maine. Then again, how different could it really be? The key, I decided, was the safety. It was clear the weapon had one. I could feel the switch. I toggled it up and down. But in the dark I couldn't be sure whether the safety was engaged when the lever was up, or whether it had to be down. There was only one way to find out, of course—aim, squeeze the trigger, and see what happened.

But I hesitated. *I'm a reporter, not a combatant,* I told myself. *I'm not here to kill, but to cover.* This had been my mantra in every conflict I'd ever reported on. Now, however, everything seemed different. Suddenly I wasn't so sure of my ethics. But this was it. I had only a moment. If I didn't shoot now, I might never have the chance. The closer he got, the more likely he was to shoot if I didn't. I crouched down and aimed. I knew if I pulled the trigger and the gun didn't fire, I'd still have time to flick the safety the other direction and pull the trigger again. With the element of surprise, I had the chance to live. But should I take it? What if I was wrong? What if he wasn't alone? What if other armed men were prepared to rush into this hallway and gun me down the moment I fired? If I set down the gun, yes, I might be caught. But in that case, as a journalist, I still might be able to talk my way out. I might be able to persuade this person I was there to help them, to give them a voice to the outside world, and wasn't that my job? If I was caught with a smoking gun in my hand, there would be no mercy. I was sure to be butchered like an animal, whether the footage wound up on YouTube or not.

I heard a rattling behind me, and the door to the street swung open. Instantly the hallway was flooded with moonlight. I pivoted hard, gun in hand, and found myself staring at two silhouettes. I was about to pull the trigger but could barely see. My eyes were desperately trying to adjust, and as they did, I found myself wondering if this was Omar and Abdel. Were they alive? Had they found me? My whole perspective started shifting. But before I could react, a burst of gunfire erupted from over my left shoulder. Stunned, I yelled out but it was too late. The two men standing in the doorway had been hit. They fell to the ground outside, screaming in agony. Horrified, and without thinking, I dropped the gun, jumped to my feet, and ran through the open door to their side. But they were not Omar or Abdel. They weren't anyone I knew. To the contrary, both were in uniform. They were soldiers in the Syrian army. Both held machine guns in their hands. The safeties were off. They had been about to kill me.

One of the men was writhing on the pavement, choking on his own blood. Seconds later, he went limp. The rifle dropped away. He was gone.

The other man had been shot in the face and chest. He was dying a slow, cruel death, and worst of all, he knew it. I stared down at him in the moonlight, sickened but unable to look away. He stared back at me, his eyes wide and filled with terror.

"Help me," he groaned in Arabic.

I stood there for a moment, not knowing what to say.

"Please," he said, his voice barely a whisper.

"I'm so sorry," I said finally.

"I don't want to die. Please, do something."

But I just stood there, frozen. I wanted to help. I really did. But how? I had no medical supplies with me. I wasn't a doctor. I had no training. There was literally nothing I could do, and as soon as he understood, his fear grew all the more.

In all my years covering wars, I had seen my share of battlefield deaths. I'd seen men die in drone strikes and by Hellfire missiles. I'd seen suicide bombers and carpet bombings and sniper shootings. I had seen men die instantly and unaware. One moment they were full of bravado and testosterone, and the next they were gone.

I'd also seen men die in the hands of professionals. I'd seen medics and fellow soldiers fight valiantly to save their friends, racing against time, doing everything humanly possible to save their lives.

But I'd never seen anything like this. This man was about to leave this world and enter the next. He was begging me for help, desperately clinging to life, even as it slipped away. Then his eyes unlocked from mine. He was staring up at the sky now. He had forgotten about me. He seemed to be able to see something I couldn't. He was riveted on it, and it filled him with panic.

"No!" he shrieked. *"No—!"*

Another deafening gunshot pierced the night sky. Then all was quiet. I turned and saw a young boy standing next to me. At least, I assumed he was a boy because of the way he was dressed. But I couldn't actually see his face. He was wearing a black hood, and he was aiming a pistol at the soldier's head. Smoke curled out of the barrel.

And then he turned the pistol on me.

11

★ ★ ★

"Who are you?" he demanded in Arabic, his voice cold and detached.

For a second I was too startled to answer. His head and face were covered by a black hood, but I could see his eyes, and that's what chilled me. They were dark and soulless. There was not a spark of life or hope in them. He had gunned these men down without giving it a thought. He had clearly killed others. Probably many others. And I knew at that moment he would not hesitate to kill me.

"I'm a reporter," I replied in Arabic, my mouth bone-dry.

He said nothing.

"I'm supposed to interview someone."

Still nothing.

"Soon," I added.

The boy just stared through me, this haunted, hunted look in his eyes.

"At the Khaled bin Walid Mosque," I mumbled, not sure why I was still talking.

He obviously couldn't have cared less, and I wondered if he was going to shoot me now.

There was a long stretch of silence. Well, silence in the sense that neither of us was talking. The winds were howling through the concrete canyons and across the barren wasteland of the streets of Homs. A fresh round of gunfire could be heard several streets to the east, the *rat-a-tat-tat* staccato of automatic weapons being fired in short bursts. I heard a stray mortar round or two, but the pitched battle of the last hour appeared to be dying down. Then again, maybe that was wishful thinking.

"The bag—what's in it?" the boy asked at long last, pointing the pistol at my backpack.

Startled, scared, not sure how much to say, I stammered, "Oh, uh, you know, just some stuff. Notebooks, pens, whatever."

"Food?" he asked in a barely audible voice.

"I'm sorry?" I replied, not sure I'd heard him right.

"Do you have any food?" he repeated, only marginally louder now.

"Oh yeah, well, a little—not much—just some apples, some PowerBars, that kind of thing."

"Give it to me," he said.

"Which?"

"All of it—whatever you have."

Was he serious? Didn't he want my wallet, my cash, my credit cards? Then it dawned on me these would do this boy no good. There was no place for him to buy food no matter how much money he had. I took the pack off, set it on the ground, and unzipped the top.

"I haven't eaten anything but a few olives in the past three days," he said as if reading my thoughts.

I stopped what I was doing and looked up. What he said stunned me—not his words but the way he said them. There was no emotion in his voice. None. He wasn't complaining. He wasn't a little kid whining or moaning or asking for sympathy. He was just stating a fact, and come to think of it, I don't think he was even saying it to me. It was almost as if he were saying it to himself. I just happened to be standing there.

As I looked more closely, I saw how loose his trousers were, how they barely hung on his emaciated frame. His gloveless hands, gaunt and bony, looked cold and raw.

Who was this boy? I wondered. What was his name? Where did he live? How did he spend his days? Who looked after him? Did anyone, or was he just roaming the streets at night, gunning down strangers in hopes of finding a little food? I wanted to ask him so many questions. I wanted to write a story about him, put him on the front page of the *Times*.

But he waved the gun at me, hurrying me along. He was growing impatient, and I could sense how dangerous it would be to try to engage in conversation. Whoever he was, he had long since lost his innocence. He had seen too much, done too much, and he didn't want the world to know. His world had contracted. His only aspiration was to survive the night, not tell his story, yet in that cold, dark street I wondered if even his will to live would last much longer.

"Never mind," he said with a sudden urgency. "Just give me the bag."

Again I looked up at him. I could see in his eyes that he meant it. There would be no arguing. No negotiating. And he wasn't going to ask twice. I zipped up the backpack. It wasn't simply filled with notebooks and pens and a bit of food. It also held a brand-new digital camera and telephoto lens and a digital audio recorder, all property of the *Times*. I cautiously took a few steps forward and held it out to the boy. For a moment I wondered if he would look inside and then shoot me for not telling him the full contents. But then I saw he was getting edgy, anxious to get moving, off this street, back into the shadows. I set down the pack and carefully backed up to where I had stood before.

Glancing around in every direction to see if the coast was clear, he reached down, stripped the dead soldiers of their ammo, stuffed the magazines into one of the side pockets of the backpack, slung it over his shoulder, and ran back into the long, dark hallway.

Before I knew it, I was standing all alone in the middle of the rubble-strewn street, just me and two new corpses. I knew I should run. To stand there was to be a target. But I just stared at the two soldiers and the sheer terror in their eyes.

My brother liked to talk about heaven and hell. That's what he'd been trained for. That's what interested him. Until now, I'd honestly never thought much about one or the other. But at that moment, I realized I could not say these men were in a better place. As cruel as their last moments were, was it possible they still existed but now in someplace worse? I didn't want to think this way, and I never had before. I'd never thought much about the afterlife, but to the extent I'd pondered it at all, I had just assumed that when we died, we were all simply snuffed out like a candle. That was it. That's all there was. But now I was haunted by this Syrian's last words. As he was slipping away from this world, he had clearly seen another, and it had terrified him. I'd seen it in his eyes. I'd heard it in his voice. And all of it rattled me.

Forcing myself to turn away, to think about something else, I looked around me. All I saw was carnage and ruin. Ten-, twelve-, fifteen-story apartment buildings were partially collapsed, riddled with bullet holes, devoid of windows, blackened and charred by fire. Not one or two buildings looked this way. They all did. Everything was devastated and abandoned.

This was Syria. This was what the Arab Republic of the Assad years had degenerated into—a concrete jungle of Syrian soldiers and starving, suffering, soul-scarred children rooting around for bits of food, and the decomposing bodies of those who got in their way. Did the world really understand what was happening here? Did it care? Did I? How long had I covered the war like a football match, chalking up wins and losses, with play-by-play and color analysis? How many peace conferences and diplomatic initiatives had I written about from swank five-star hotels in Geneva and Paris, wining and dining with foreign ministers and secretaries of state and defense, all pontificating about the tragedy but never actually doing anything about it? Year after year this nightmare was unfolding, and still the world did nothing definitive to stop it. In Washington, the politicians talked tough. In London and Paris and Berlin and Geneva, it was all the same. But nothing changed. Nothing got better. Not for these two men. Not for this little boy. Not for anyone who had once lived on this street in Homs.

I was witnessing the implosion of an entire country, and for the first time it began to truly dawn on me that if no one stepped in, there might not be a country left in another year or two. Was that really possible? Were we witnessing the utter disintegration of a modern Arab state? Might this nation actually never be put together again?

I'd never thought like this before. I'd certainly never written anything of the sort. But suddenly, standing alone on this street, seeing what I had just seen, I realized I had absolutely no idea what would become of Syria. Perhaps Hezbollah and the Iranian Revolutionary Guards would take it over and turn it into another province of the mullahs in Tehran. Or maybe al Qaeda and the other Sunni rebels would win the day and create a new Afghanistan or Somalia on the borders of Israel, Lebanon, and Jordan. Either way, I couldn't see President Assad and his forces lasting much longer. Honestly, I was stunned that he was still alive after all that had happened so far.

I heard a roar overhead and looked up to see two F-4 Phantoms streaking past. Moments later, two more shot by. Then the bombs started falling. It was the thunderous explosions and massive balls of fire, all just a few blocks to the north, that snapped me out of my foolish introspection. This was neither the time nor the place to muse over the future of Syria. There were far more urgent questions facing me. What was I going to do now? Where was I going to go? Time was fleeting. Faisal Baqouba wasn't going to sit around in that mosque all night. Unless I got moving, I was going to miss him and miss his brother Tariq, and with them the interview that could make my career.

Then again, if I started moving toward the mosque alone, there was a very real chance I wasn't going to make it home alive.

A new round of machine-gun fire erupted, and then sniper fire too. Someone was squeezing off single rounds from a high-caliber rifle. I'd heard it before, but never so close. If I had to guess, I'd have said it was just up the street and around the corner to the north.

I was out of time. I had to get out of there. Stepping over mounds of broken, crumbled concrete blocks, I moved off the street and ducked into the shadows of a doorway.

Someone grabbed me from behind. Before I realized what was happening, he clamped a hand over my mouth. Someone else grabbed my arms and pinned them behind me. I couldn't move, could hardly breathe. They dragged me into a windowless, putrid building. I couldn't see a thing. A surge of adrenaline shot through my system. I wanted to fight back, but I knew someone would slash my throat or put a bullet through my head before I got in my first good hit, so instead I went limp and crashed to the floor.

Immediately I felt the cold steel barrel of a gun jammed into the base of my skull. Someone's boot thrust down hard on my back. Another came down on my neck. My hands were wrenched behind me again. In short order they were bound with rope so tight it cut into my wrists. I felt them start to bleed.

Then someone threw a bag over my head. It was plastic and opaque, a garbage bag probably. It was tied snug around my face and neck. I began to hyperventilate. I kept telling myself to calm down, not to panic, but to no avail. The walls were closing in. I felt claustrophobic. I decided they weren't going to shoot me or they would have done it already. But that could only mean one thing: they were going to behead me. The very thought nearly made my heart stop. Then I felt a needle being jammed into my arm, and time stood still.

12

* * *

When I woke up, I had no idea where I was.

I had no idea how long I'd been unconscious. There was still a garbage bag over my head and tied around my neck, but it had been loosened enough that I could breathe. I was achy and stiff and freezing. My jacket was gone. So was my sweater. All I had on were my T-shirt and boxers.

My arms were still tied behind me. My feet were now bound as well, but my shoes were gone and so were my socks. As best I could tell, I was sitting on a frigid concrete floor, leaning against cold cinder blocks, and I could hear a driving rainstorm and the most intense booms of thunder I had ever experienced.

In the distance, I could also still hear the occasional burst of automatic-weapons fire. I strained to hear anything else, something that might tell me where I was. Soon I heard what sounded like two fighter jets roaring overhead. After a moment, another two flew past, and then I heard repeated explosions. They weren't loud or close—certainly not as close as when we'd first entered the city. But the activity suggested a government offensive was still being waged against a rebel enclave.

I could also hear something flapping in the breeze. At first it sounded like a flag. But then it sounded like sheets of plastic. A terrible draft was coming into whatever room I was in, and occasionally a spray of bitterly cold rain. I didn't hear any windows rattling. Indeed, I hadn't seen much evidence that there was any unshattered glass left in the city. So I concluded I was in a place where plastic bags or sheets of plastic had been fastened over the blown-out windows in a semi-futile effort to keep out the worst of the wind and the rain.

Then I heard heavy footsteps. I don't know how to describe it precisely, but there was something about the tone and pitch of the sounds that made me think someone—or actually several people—were ascending a nearby concrete stairwell. Whoever they were, they clearly wore boots, and the weight suggested they were men. Whether they were regular soldiers or jihadist rebels I had no idea, but I was sure I was not in a bunker or a basement. I was several flights up at least, perhaps in a top-floor apartment or office, doubtless stripped of all carpets and furniture and other amenities.

No one was saying anything, but they were getting closer, and with each step I feared my end was drawing near.

There was so much at that moment that I didn't know. All I knew for sure was that I was not ready to die. There's no other way to put it. I could tell you I was bravely ready to meet my Maker, but that would be a lie. I was petrified.

The footsteps stopped right in front of me.

"What is your name?" a man asked me in English, though his voice bore a thick Arab accent.

I tried to swallow but had no saliva. Suddenly I felt the edge of a blade against my throat, just below my Adam's apple.

"James," I replied, trying to steady my voice. "James Bradley Collins."

"Where are you from?"

The very question struck terror in my heart, but what choice did I have? Would they really hesitate to kill me if I acted Canadian, British, or Australian? Maybe, for a while. But what would happen when they found I was lying to them?

"America."

"What city?"

"Washington."

"What do you do?"

"I'm a reporter."

"For what paper?"

"The *Times*."

"Which one?"

"The *New York Times*."

"Why did you come to Syria?"

Here I hesitated. What was the right answer? Who was holding me? What did they want to hear? My mind rapidly considered a wide range of options. But in my situation, none seemed viable. I didn't have the energy and mental wherewithal to construct a cover story and stick with it through days or weeks of starvation, sleep deprivation, beatings, and whippings. I wasn't in the CIA. I wasn't trained for this.

A simple thought then crossed my mind: *Just tell them the truth—there's nothing to be gained by lying.* But that wasn't necessarily true, I told myself. Lying might buy me time until I could figure a way out of here or until someone could come rescue me, maybe Omar, maybe Abdel. Lying, I thought, just might save me. But before I knew what I was doing, I heard myself saying I had come to do an interview.

"With whom?"

"Ramzy," I said without thinking.

"Jamal Ramzy?" came the reply.

"Yes."

"Why?"

"He invited me."

No one said a word.

"Look in my pocket," I said quickly. "The pocket of my trousers. You'll find a printout of the e-mail."

Did they believe me? Did they care? Were they part of Assad's forces or rebels? And where were Omar and Abdel? Had they already been killed? Had they been captured? Were they being interrogated? All the more reason to tell the truth, I decided. My captors very well might know the answer to every question they were asking me.

Thunder crashed around us. The winter rains were coming down even harder now. I thought I heard the rustling of a piece of paper but couldn't be sure. Then the blade was removed from my throat, though I felt it nick me and draw blood. A moment later, the plastic bag was ripped off my head. A flash of lightning momentarily blinded me, but as I got my bearings, I found myself staring up at three men.

Each was well built, muscular, armed to the hilt, and covered in a black wool hood. The one on the left wore a dark-blue sweatshirt, faded blue jeans, and black combat boots. He held a machine gun pointed at me. The one on the right wore a winter parka, green fatigues, and brown boots. He was brandishing a sword, which shimmered in the moonlight. I thought I detected a drop of my blood on its tip. The one in the center seemed the youngest. He wore sneakers, black jeans, and my leather coat. He already had the e-mail in his hand, and when our eyes met, it was he who spoke.

"*As-salamu alaykum*, Mr. Collins. I am Tariq Baqouba. These are Faisal and Ahmed. They are my brothers. Welcome to Homs."

I was stunned yet relieved. I know it sounds strange to say, and I admit that before that night it would never have occurred to me to breathe a sigh of relief in the presence of three proven al Qaeda killers. But I was relieved. Maybe *relieved* isn't the right word, but I cannot think of another. The simple fact was I was glad to still be alive and off the streets. I had not yet missed my appointment, and I was now heading—I hoped—to meet the man for whom I'd come all this way.

"Now, come with me," Tariq ordered.

The man on the right quickly put his sword in its sheath. He untied my feet, pulled me up, and produced a bag that turned out to be filled with my clothes. While his brothers held their weapons on me, he set my hands free long enough for me to put my clothes and shoes back on. They were cold and a bit damp, but under the circumstances I was grateful, especially when I felt my grandfather's watch ticking away in my right front pocket.

I had a thousand questions, starting with where my colleagues were. But I said nothing. My hands were tied again. A machine gun was thrust into my back, and we proceeded down the concrete steps, down five floors to the ground level. Along the way I came to realize we were, in fact, in what was left of the Khaled bin Walid Mosque. It had been shelled and shot up pretty good. But it had not yet collapsed, and I saw signs that people had been here recently. A few sleeping bags in one place. The remains of a campfire in another. Shell casings and cigarette butts were everywhere. It seemed to be a safe house of sorts. I made a mental note of it in case I ever got out of this country alive.

We didn't stay for long. When we reached the ground floor, they led me through the charred remains of the main hall. Then we stepped into another stairwell, where we descended to the basement. They turned on flashlights as we walked down a labyrinth of damp, dripping hallways until we reached a mechanical room of some kind. We entered and they led me past the boiler and some new-looking electrical panels. I couldn't fathom their purpose. The room wasn't that big. What could the panels possibly be powering? But as we turned a corner, I saw an opening in the rear wall.

Feeling the barrel of the machine gun being prodded into my back, urging me to go through the opening, I ducked down and, trying not to lose my balance, crawled through the hole. I found myself crouched in a makeshift tunnel that had been dug under the city. Strangely, though most if not all of the city of Homs was blacked out, the tunnel had power and was reasonably well lit. It was no more than five and a half feet high and at best four feet wide, but it was long. It seemed to go on forever. It reminded me of the smuggling tunnels I'd seen on the Sinai border with Gaza and on the U.S. border with Mexico.

The rebel with the machine gun told me to move faster, and I did as I was told. I hunched over and began to walk. After what I guessed was a good ten or fifteen minutes, we finally reached a ladder and a hole in the ceiling. The tunnel didn't stop there. It kept going and broke off in two directions. But I was directed up the ladder, and with some difficulty since I couldn't use my hands, I eventually made it to the top, where two more hooded thugs, both well armed, grabbed me, pulled me through the hole in the floor, and threw another bag over my head. We walked for another long stretch, down hallways, up and down flights of stairs, and through another tunnel, until finally I was told to stop, sit down on a cold metal stool, and keep my mouth shut. When the bag came off my head, I could barely see at all.

Enormous klieg lights were shining in my face. I was sitting at an old metal table. It reminded me of the kitchen table I'd grown up with. As I squinted, I could see a giant figure sitting across from me.

"Welcome to *ad-Dawla al-Islāmiyya fi al-'Irāq wa-al-Shām*, Mr. Collins," he said in a throaty, almost-gravelly voice, like someone with emphysema or throat cancer. "I am Jamal Ramzy."

13

* * *

The instant Ramzy said his name, the klieg lights shut down.

It took a few moments for my eyes to adjust, but when they did, I saw a gargantuan man—six foot five, three hundred pounds at least, dark-skinned, and masked only by a thick, full, black beard without a touch of gray. He wore a black robe and a black skullcap and had a Kalashnikov and an ammo belt slung over his shoulder. He had small, suspicious brown eyes, which immediately locked onto my own and never wandered, making me even more uncomfortable than I already felt, surrounded as we were by armed men in the signature al Qaeda black hoods. Everyone stared at me as my feet were promptly chained to enormous metal spikes driven into the concrete floor.

We were in a cavernous bunker of some kind. It was as big as a football field, and tall and wide enough to park a jet plane or a few dozen tanks, though at the moment it was empty but for a couple dozen large wooden crates, a few pickup trucks, and some cots. On the metal table before us sat a notebook, several pens, and a digital recorder. I immediately recognized them as my own. Taken aback, I was about to say something when I noticed a smudge on the side of the recorder. It looked like blood. I said nothing. I didn't want to know how they had retrieved my backpack. I didn't want to know what had happened to the boy who had taken it from me.

Even as I looked at him, and he stared back at me, it was still difficult to fully process that I was sitting across from the commander of the Syrian forces of the Islamic State of Iraq and al-Sham, commonly referred to in Western intelligence agencies as ISIS, pronounced "eye-sis." Others called it ISIL—the Islamic State of Iraq and the Levant—while many in the media called it simply the Islamic State. But whatever you called his terrorist organization, Jamal Ramzy was fast becoming one of the most wanted men in the world. The American government had recently marked him a specially designated global terrorist under Executive Order 13224. The State Department had put a $5 million bounty on his head. Yet to my knowledge, no reporter had ever spoken with Ramzy, much less seen him face-to-face. Though he had been mentioned in a handful of articles over the past year, not a single profile had been written on him. Mine, I hoped, would be the first.

"Mr. Collins, you're thinking about the reward," he began, his face expressionless. "I can see it in your eyes. Let me give you a piece of advice. Stop."

I wasn't actually, not really, but just the way he said it made my blood run cold.

"You have thirty minutes," he said after a long pause. "Shall we begin?"

Someone came up behind me and cut the ropes that bound my hands. My wrists were bleeding, but not terribly. They were aching, but I didn't allow that to distract me. I pulled the pocket watch out and set it on the table. Then I reached for the recorder, started it, picked up a pen, and asked my first question.

"Is Jamal Ramzy your real name?"

"Yes."

"When were you born?"

"January 6, 1962."

"Where?"

"Irbid, Jordan."

"Are you Palestinian?"

"You know I am."

I looked up from the notepad. "I don't want to make any assumptions," I said carefully. "I want the facts straight from you."

He just stared at me without blinking. "Yes," he said at last.

"Where is your family originally from?"

"Hebron."

"Was your grandfather killed in the 1948 war?"

"Yes, the Zionists killed him and all my uncles."

"Then your family fled to Jordan?"

"They were ordered to leave."

"By the Jews?"

"No, by the coward Arab leaders who chose to run rather than fight."

This caught me off guard. I suspected it partially explained his apparent preference to spend more time fighting his fellow Arabs than the Jews. It was a thread I wanted to pull on, but there was no time. This was all background information. I needed to get to the real issues, and quickly.

"After high school, your family moved to the Gulf, correct?"

"Yes."

"Bahrain first and Dubai?"

"Yes."

"When were you in Afghanistan?"

"March 1980 to August 1983."

"You were young."

"I serve at the pleasure of Allah."

Now I changed directions. "Why did you change the name of your organization to ISIS?"

"The Islamic State is not my organization," he said. "Allah is our leader. Islam is our path. Jihad is our way. Abu Khalif is our caliph. I am but a servant."

There he was: Abu Khalif, Ramzy's younger cousin, the true leader of ISIS. I had been told by reliable sources that Khalif—not Ramzy—should be my real target. But I was not ready. Not yet. I would have to come back to this.

"Your faction was called al Qaeda in Iraq," I noted. "Now it's the Islamic State of Iraq and al-Sham. Why the change?"

"Again, it is not my faction, Mr. Collins," he said calmly. "Abu Khalif is our leader. And it is the movement of Allah, not our own. At any rate, the original name was given by Ayman al-Zawahiri.

But we no longer serve him. He is a traitor to Islam. Abu Khalif told him to repent. He chose not to. We are no longer responsible for what happens to him. We do not wish to be identified with anything connected to a traitor."

I was about to ask another question, but Ramzy continued.

"Let me be perfectly clear, Mr. Collins. We do not serve al Qaeda. There is no reason to have this in our name. We serve Allah only, and Allah has given us a simple mandate: reestablish the caliphate. We have started in Iraq to bring down the apostate leadership there. But this is about more than just Iraq. Al-Sham, as you must know, is the Levant, the East, the place of the rising sun. This is our focus."

"Beginning with Syria?" I asked.

"Of course," he said. "Assad is a criminal. He has never been a true Muslim. He must be dispatched to the fires of judgment, with his family and all those loyal to him. Assad is a doomed man. But he is just a piece in the puzzle, you might say."

"What are the other pieces?"

"The entire Levant," he said matter-of-factly.

"Again, I don't want to assume anything, and I don't want my readers to assume either," I said. "You've mentioned Iraq and Syria. Do you also plan to take over Lebanon?"

"Of course."

"Turkey?"

"Yes."

"Cyprus?"

"Yes."

"Palestine?"

"Of course."

"Israel?"

"Palestine," he replied.

"I mean the Jewish State of Israel proper," I clarified, adding, "inside the pre-1967 lines."

He stared at me. "*All* of Palestine," he said, his voice rising for the first time.

"Yes, of course," I said. "Just trying to be clear. What about Jordan?"

His eyes narrowed. "How many times must I say it, Mr. Collins?" he said, barely restraining the anger in his voice. "*All* of Palestine."

"Very well," I said. "These are the boundaries of the Islamic kingdom your leadership envisions?"

"The initial boundaries, yes."

I raised my eyebrows. "There's more?"

"This is enough for now."

"So this is a multistage plan?"

"Yes," he said. "We have declared jihad to bring down the blasphemous regime in Baghdad and the equally apostate regime in Damascus. But we will not rest until we bring down every leader, every government, until every man, woman, and child is governed by Sharia law, by the will of the Prophet, peace be upon him."

"At the moment, you are waging war on two fronts—Syria and Iraq. Will there be a third?"

Ramzy paused. I doubted he was authorized to go that far. After all, *that* would be news—ISIS declaring war on a third front.

"Yes," he said at last.

Surprised he was being so candid, I immediately

sought to clarify. "You're going to open a third front?"

"Yes."

"When?"

"Soon."

"How soon?"

"Very."

"Against whom?" I pressed, assuming it was Israel but not wanting to put the words in his mouth. "Who is the third target?"

Ramzy leaned forward in his seat, his eyes dancing. "Anyone who betrays the Palestinian cause, anyone who helps the racist Zionist regime," he said with real emotion in his voice.

"Do you mean the United States?" I asked.

"Anyone who betrays the Palestinian cause will pay dearly," Ramzy replied.

He wasn't being precise, but he wasn't denying that it was the U.S. either, I noted.

"Are you saying ISIS is planning to strike inside the U.S.—on the homeland—at American citizens traveling abroad, at military bases, companies, et cetera?"

"We are about to launch a Third Intifada, Mr. Collins," he said flatly. "But this will be unlike any that has gone before—the scale, the magnitude. You have not seen anything like this. Those who betray the cause of Islam to obtain a false peace with murderers and criminals—they will burn. All of them will burn."

So it was true. I furiously scribbled down every word, terrified the digital recorder might fail. Abu Khalif and Jamal Ramzy and this breakaway al Qaeda faction were about to target the U.S. and Israel, and with them the latest peace process that was reportedly sputtering to a failure like all the others before it.

He was saying ISIS would target those who supported Israel—and no nation was a bigger ally of the Jewish state than the U.S.—but he was also using the term *intifada*. This was an Arab word for "uprising" or "revolution." It literally meant a "shaking off."

The First Intifada had erupted in the West Bank and Gaza in December of 1987. Though it had largely been a popular rebellion using stones and slingshots, burning tires, and Molotov cocktails, the uprising had prompted Israel to respond with mass arrests, tear gas, and shooting at crowds with live ammunition, and later with rubber bullets, all captured by TV crews who broadcast the images into people's homes every night at dinnertime, in the U.S. and around the world. That intifada hadn't won the Palestinians any new rights or freedoms. But it had created a public relations disaster for Israel, making the Jewish State look like the big, bad Goliath staring down the helpless, underdog Palestinian David. That had been the narrative of the international media, anyway, including the *Times*.

The Second Intifada had erupted in September of 2000 after the breakdown of Mideast peace talks at Camp David between President Clinton, Israeli prime minister Ehud Barak, and PLO chairman Yasser Arafat. That time, the Palestinian extremists had unleashed a wave of suicide bombers that struck Israeli buses, cafés, and elementary schools, followed by a barrage of rockets and mortars fired from Gaza at innocent civilians living in southern Israeli towns and villages. The Palestinians had vented their rage at the "Zionist occupation" but this time won little sympathy in the West from mothers and fathers who were horrified by the sight of Jewish children and their parents being blown up by Palestinian bombs and rockets.

"What will this Third Intifada entail?" I asked. "Are we talking about suicide bombers, rockets, IEDs, snipers, kidnappings?"

"I will not say more about this," he said sharply, though I noted he did nothing to deny these were all options. "You will see when it happens."

"Fine, I understand; but just to be clear, are you declaring war on Israel and the United States?"

"No traitor is safe. Allah is watching. Judgment is coming."

14

* * *

"Mr. Ramzy, I have just a few more questions,"
I said.

I was still writing as fast as I could, trying to
ignore the cramping in my hand.

"Be my guest," he said, leaning back in his
chair, suddenly seeming relaxed as if pleased with
himself for what he had just told me.

I glanced at the pocket watch and winced. The
time was going so quickly. Then I checked the
digital recorder. It was still running. Hopefully it
was really recording. I took a deep breath, sat up
straight, and then leaned forward.

"I have two sources who tell me ISIS now has
chemical weapons."

For a moment, Ramzy looked taken aback, but
he quickly composed himself. He said nothing.

"My sources say you're planning to use them
against Israeli and American targets during
Hanukkah and Christmas."

Jamal Ramzy didn't blink. He just stared at me
and remained silent.

I stared back, waiting. The man certainly had

a flair for drama, but I had little doubt this was really the news he wanted to make.

"Is there a question there?" he asked finally.

"Are my sources accurate?" I asked point-blank.

"No," he replied. "They are liars."

I was floored. "Liars?"

"You heard me."

I had, but I was not convinced. "Now wait a minute, Mr. Ramzy. Let me be clear about this. I have a very high-ranking source in a Western intelligence agency who has clear proof that you and your forces captured a cache of chemical weapons in north-central Syria three weeks ago, in late October, and that you have transferred these weapons to sites in Lebanon, western Iraq, and the Sinai in preparation for a major attack on Israel, and to sleeper cells in Canada and Mexico in preparation for attacks on the U.S."

"These are all lies."

I pressed on, undeterred. "This source tells me he has personally listened to audio recordings of radio traffic between two Syrian generals. One of them is frantically telling the other that one of their chemical-weapons storage facilities not far from Aleppo had just been overrun. The other is desperately calling for air strikes and ground-troop reinforcements, but the evidence indicates they were too late. Your men got there first and left with truckloads of warheads filled with chemical agents. There is further signals intelligence that your men are developing plans to hit New York, Washington, Los Angeles, and Tel Aviv."

"Your source is misleading you. You should get another."

I had no idea why Ramzy was denying all this, but I forged ahead. "I have another, a source in a different intelligence service in an entirely different country with no connection to the first source," I continued. "He told me that a three-star Syrian general defected to a Muslim country at the end of October. He claimed an al Qaeda faction seized several tons of chemical weapons south of Aleppo within the last few weeks. He gave this Muslim country hard intel—in terms of satellite phone intercepts—indicating this al Qaeda faction is planning to use the chemical weapons against U.S. and Israeli targets during the Christmas holidays."

Now Ramzy leaned forward and smiled. "What can I tell you, Mr. Collins? These are fanciful tales. I wish they were true. I do. But you've been fed a pack of innuendos, deceptions, and disinformation."

"You're denying ISIS has captured chemical weapons?"

"Yes."

"You're denying that you're developing plans to use them in the next few weeks against the U.S. and Israel?"

"You read too many spy thrillers, Mr. Collins."

I was getting exasperated and had to fight to keep my cool. "You just told me you're going to launch a Third Intifada," I reminded him. "You just told me it was going to be unlike any uprising we've seen before. You just told me the Zionists and those who support them will burn."

"That I stand by," he replied.

"Then why not just tell the world the magnitude of the operation you're planning? It'll be front-page tomorrow morning on the biggest newspaper in the world. It'll be picked up by every other news outlet on the planet."

"What I gave you already will be front-page news, will it not, Mr. Collins?" Ramzy pushed back. "ISIS announces a third front, a Third Intifada—won't that be picked up by every media outlet in the world?"

He was right, of course, but I had no intention of giving him the satisfaction of hearing it from me; not before I tried again to get an even bigger story out of him. "It's news," I told him. "But I doubt it will go viral. Not like it would if you confirm ISIS has chemical weapons."

"Sorry to disappoint you, Mr. Collins," Ramzy replied. "And we were getting along so well."

I was baffled. My sources were solid. Unbeknownst to each other, both had let me listen to the tapes in question and had even given me transcripts for my story. Neither source knew I was going to Syria to try to confirm what I had been told. I hadn't even made my plans until after I'd spoken to each of them and had suddenly received the e-mail from Faisal Baqouba about coming to meet Ramzy. This was a major exclusive. I had been sitting on it for more than ten days. It wasn't going to hold much longer.

"Isn't this the story you invited me here to confirm, the chemical weapons?" I pressed.

"No."

"Then why have me come all this way and go through all this trouble, just to tell me what you could have announced in a press release?" I asked again. "Why stop short of giving me the story that would be the shot heard around the world?"

"Time's up," Ramzy said.

That wasn't possible. It couldn't have been thirty minutes. Ramzy was playing with me. But I had to keep my cool as I continued writing out my notes and flexing my aching fingers.

Suddenly he said, "Time to take some pictures."

My pen stopped writing. I looked at him in disbelief, then watched as he snapped his fingers. I turned my head, and in through a side door came Omar and Abdel, surrounded by more men with machine guns.

I couldn't believe it. They were alive. They were safe. They were here. Without thinking, I jumped up from my seat and tried to move toward them but realized—almost too late—that my feet were still chained to the floor. When I noticed several of the guards around us moving their fingers to the triggers of their weapons, I quickly sat down.

My colleagues were brought closer, and I noticed they were in shackles too. They were kept a good ten yards from each other and had a guard on each side. Still, they were smiling and looked no worse for the wear.

One of the guards handed Abdel his Nikon and gave him a few instructions. Then the klieg lights powered back on, creating stunning conditions for a one-of-a-kind portrait of a key terrorist figure the world knew very little about so far.

When all the preparations were complete, Ramzy nodded, and Abdel began snapping away.

Barely a minute later, Ramzy held up his hand and a guard grabbed the camera out of Abdel's hands. The photo shoot was over.

Ramzy walked over to me and handed me my backpack. I wasn't sure I wanted it but knew there was no point in saying so.

"One more thing, if I may?" I asked.

"What is it, Mr. Collins?" Ramzy replied, beginning to sound annoyed.

"I would like to meet Abu Khalif," I said. "Would you introduce me?"

Ramzy didn't bat an eye. "That's not possible."

"Why not?"

"He doesn't speak to reporters."

"Neither do you."

"I made an exception."

"Maybe he will too."

"He won't."

"Is he still in prison in Iraq?"

"This is none of your concern."

"Which prison?"

"You are treading on thin ice here, Mr. Collins."

"But he still runs ISIS, doesn't he?"

"Of course."

"So he's the one who gave the order to launch the Third Intifada, correct?"

"Abu Khalif is our leader."

"So he makes the decisions?"

"That's what leaders do."

"Then why can't I meet him? Why can't I talk to him and get his take on where this region is heading, where ISIS is heading? Just like you, he's got a story to tell, Mr. Ramzy. Let me tell it."

"You do not understand what you're asking," he replied, his eyes narrowing.

"I think I do."

"Oh, but you don't, or you would never have brought it up."

Risking everything, perhaps including my life, I stood and stepped as close to Jamal Ramzy as my shackles would allow. He stiffened but held his ground. In my peripheral vision I could see his guards grow tense. But I didn't care. I leaned in to Ramzy's face and spoke to him man to man.

"Look," I said, "you knew Abu Musab al-Zarqawi. You and Abu Khalif were sent to Iraq by bin Laden and Khalid Sheikh Mohammed to help him establish al Qaeda in Iraq. Zarqawi was the face, but you and Abu Khalif were the brains. It was your ideas, your strategy, your tactics, your money, and your weapons that put Zarqawi on the map, right?"

Ramzy said nothing, but I went on.

"When Zarqawi was killed by that air strike in '06, you and Abu Khalif wanted to take the organization in one direction. Abu Ayyub al-Masri and his forces wanted to go in another. For a time, Masri prevailed. But in the end, you and Abu Khalif outlasted him. Abu Khalif became head of AQI. It was he who brought you in as his chief of operations. It was he who decided to expand the mission, change the name, raise the stakes. It was he who ordered you to build an army strong enough to storm Syria and bring Assad's head back on a platter. And in the end, it was he who broke with bin Laden and later with Zawahiri, and you supported him every step of the way. Am I right?"

Ramzy said nothing, but his eyes told me I was right.

"That must mean Abu Khalif told you to talk to me," I continued. "Why? Because he's about to start a new war, a war that's going to set this region on fire. You don't want to talk to me about the chemical weapons? Fine. I've got two sources. I'll run the story with or without your comment or his. But I'm giving you something no one else can, something money can't buy. I'm giving you and your boss the opportunity of a lifetime, the opportunity to be the new face of al Qaeda, to be the new face of global jihad. Forget your blood feud with Zawahiri. Forget all the men in the caves. Their time has come and gone. Your day has arrived. But I can't do it just by profiling the number two guy. I'm sorry. I can't. I need to talk to the emir. I need to get him on the record. You know it. He knows it. So give me access—exclusive access—before the war begins, before—"

I caught myself just in time. I was about to say, "Before you're both dead." But at the last moment I said, "Before you both go underground forever."

When I was finished, I gave him a little space, a little time, to take the bait. But Jamal Ramzy did not bite.

"We're done here, Mr. Collins," he said through gritted teeth. "But know this: you have made a terrible mistake. You will not write one word about chemical weapons, or you will not live to see it printed. You certainly will not meet Abu Khalif. And you will never presume to lecture me again about what is best for our cause. You are an infidel, Mr. Collins. You and your friends are alive because Abu Khalif chose to keep you alive. You will continue to live until he decides your usefulness to him is over. And when that day comes, he will give me the order, and I *will* kill you—all of you—and believe me, I will take my time and make you suffer."

15

Ramzy's men led us back through the tunnels.

When we emerged aboveground, they put black plastic bags over our heads and led us through the driving rains across one neighborhood after another until they told us to stop.

"Count to one hundred," one of them ordered, his voice seeming to echo a bit.

"Why?" I asked, worried.

"Just do it, and don't ask questions."

I had a lot of questions. Omar, Abdel, and I hadn't been permitted to talk since we left Ramzy's lair, and I was eager to know what my colleagues were thinking. How had they wound up with Tariq Baqouba? What did they make of the ISIS commander? Why did they think he wasn't willing to talk about the chemical weapons? Was he really lying, or was I being misled by more faulty Western intelligence? And what was the deal with Ramzy clamming up about Abu Khalif? Something wasn't right about that, but at the moment I was too scared to figure out what.

The good news was we weren't dead. That

much was clear, but not much else. I was freezing. I was dripping wet. I was eager to get out of Syria and back to Beirut. I needed someplace warm and dry and equipped with Wi-Fi so I could write my story and get it filed.

So I started counting. Out loud.

I could hear men breathing near me. I assumed these were Omar and Abdel. I wanted to be certain. I wanted to know they were okay. But we were not supposed to ask any questions. So I didn't. I just counted.

When I reached one hundred, I stood there in silence, the bag still over my head, having no idea where we were and no idea what to do next.

Finally I tore the bag off my head and held my breath. No one shot me. No one beat me. We were alone. Or at least we seemed to be.

We were standing in the stairwell of some building, and Ramzy's men were gone. Relieved, I exhaled and tried to start breathing normally. Then I leaned in and whispered to Omar and Abdel that they could both take the bags off their heads but that they should keep quiet and follow me. They quickly complied and I led them up five flights of stairs.

As we stepped out onto the roof, we were immediately greeted by multiple flashes of lightning. We could see jagged, crackling sticks of lightning hitting a nearby radio antenna and then felt the *boom, boom, boom* of the thunder rattling our bones.

"What time is it?" Omar asked.

I pulled out my grandfather's pocket watch,

unsure why Ramzy and his thugs had not kept it but grateful nonetheless.

"It's late," I replied. "We'd better keep moving."

The sun would be coming up soon—if it wasn't up already. We wouldn't see it, of course. The ferocious storm slamming western Syria was likely to last for some time. But as dangerous as it was to be caught out on a night like this—in a civil war zone, no less—I knew the only thing worse would be to try to traverse these streets and fields in the full light of day, even a stormy one.

A quick look around revealed we were standing atop one of the least damaged high-rises in the city. It had been hit numerous times, to be sure. There was an enormous crater in the center of the roof, no doubt a direct hit by one of Assad's fighter jets. But overall, the structure seemed sound. We spread out in three directions, looking over the edges and trying to get our bearings. Then we regrouped inside the stairwell.

"I saw the playground we came across last night," Abdel said.

"What about the machine-gun nests?" Omar asked.

"From this height, I could see them too, both of them—they're empty."

"Snipers?"

"I saw no signs of movement," he replied. "Can't make any promises. But with this weather, and with the sun about to come up, I'm guessing they're all gone for the night."

"Would you bet your life on it?" I asked.

"What choice do we have?" he responded.

We all stood there contemplating the question. We weren't out of this thing yet. We had the story—part of it, anyway—but a lot could still go wrong before we were in the clear. Snipers were one concern, but there were others. Mines. Booby traps. Night patrols. Drones. Random twelve-year-olds bearing Kalashnikovs.

"Look, the only question that really matters right now is this: Do you know how to get back to the border?" I asked.

"I think so," Abdel said.

"Good," I said. "Then I want you to lead the way."

Abdel nodded.

"But I want you to do something for me first," I said.

"What's that?"

"Take a picture of my buddy Omar and me on this roof," I explained.

"Sure thing, Mr. Collins," Abdel said. "I'll call it 'The Survivors.'"

Omar put his massive arm around me and chuckled. "I'll call it 'The Lunatics.'"

Abdel snapped a few pictures, then asked if he could take one with me too.

"Of course," I said, and Omar did the honors.

Then I instructed Abdel to use my satellite phone and transmit all his pictures back to the bureau.

Abdel nodded, fished my satphone out of my backpack, grabbed a cord from his own backpack, and digitally transmitted more than a hundred photos he had taken in the past twenty-four hours, including all the ones of Jamal Ramzy. I texted Allen MacDonald, my editor in Washington, telling him that we'd found Ramzy and gotten the interview and were heading back to safety. I knew he would be simultaneously furious with me for going into harm's way without his permission and ecstatic to get the story. But I would have to deal with all that later. Right now, we just needed to get out of there.

We headed down to the first floor, using our cell phones to light the way. When we got to the main level, Abdel motioned for us to follow him down a long hallway, but I grabbed his shirt and held him back.

"Maybe we should . . ." I stopped midsentence.

"Should what?" Abdel asked.

"Find another way," I said.

"Why?" Omar asked. "What other way?"

"I don't know," I confessed. "There's got to be another way out."

"So what?" Omar said. "Let's just go. It's going to be light out there soon."

"No," I said.

"What in the world are you talking about?"

"What can I say?" I half mumbled. "I just have a bad feeling about this."

They looked at me like I was crazy. Both of them. Maybe I was. I couldn't explain it then. I can't explain it now. But I didn't want to go down that hallway. Something wasn't right. I didn't have anything to back it up. It was just a gut feeling, but they were every bit as cold and tired as I was, and they had had enough.

"I mean no disrespect, Mr. Collins; I just want to get home," Abdel said. "I need to call Fatima. She worries about me. You go any way you like. But if it's all the same to you, I'm going this way."

It wasn't all the same to me. Still, I appreciated his humility. Abdel had a kind and decent heart. I knew he wasn't trying to be contrarian or disrespectful. He loved his girl. I got it. I could still remember feeling that way. I'd been married once. It had been a disaster. But even with all the pain, I hadn't forgotten what a good romance felt like. So I nodded, and Abdel left. But I wasn't going to follow him. I poked my head into another room, shining the flashlight on my phone from right to left and back again. It was a large, empty hall that had probably been used as a dining room, I figured, though it had long ago been looted of every furnishing and anything else that was valuable, from the light fixtures to the copper wires and pipes in the walls. Everything had been ripped out. It was all gone.

"You coming with me?" I asked Omar.

"Allen says I have to," he replied.

"What do you mean?"

"He told me to watch your back," Omar replied. "I'm already feeling guilty for having gotten separated from you last night. I don't plan to let that happen again."

"You're a good man, Omar," I told him. "Come on. Let's get out of here."

16

★ ★ ★

Omar and I moved through the cavernous hall.

Then we made our way through the gutted kitchen right behind it and then a large but completely empty pantry before we found a back door. It was unsettling to walk through a totally abandoned building knowing it had once—not so long ago—been teeming with boys and girls and women and men trying to make a life in this little corner of the world. Once families had eaten breakfasts, lunches, and dinners here, held birthday parties and wedding receptions, graduation parties and anniversary celebrations here. Once these walls had echoed with laughter and inside jokes and gossip and fights and tears and memories, but now the place was hollow and empty, silent and dark. It was eerie. It felt like one of those early scenes in *Titanic* when Bill Paxton's character—you know, the Jacques Cousteau meets Indiana Jones character who's hunting for the blue diamond—directs that robotic camera through the underwater passageways of the great, sad ship, down long, dark hallways and through ballrooms and stairwells long forgotten, haunted by memories so joyous and so tragic. It was as if Homs had sunk to the bottom of the ocean, and Omar and I had come to navigate our way through its dark and forlorn rooms.

When we got to the back door, we were careful not to go bursting through it. We peered through the jagged shards of what remained of the window, out to the rain and fog. Ahead of us was the large field we had come across the night before—the old VW van, the broken-down school bus, the deserted playground, the charred Russian tank, and all the rest. Ringing the field were dozens of ruined apartment buildings. We looked for Abdel and for any other signs of life, but we saw nothing and no one moving.

"He's probably already made a run for it," Omar said.

"Hope so," I said. "Come on—let's go this way. Stay close, and keep an eye behind us as well."

Omar nodded, and we began. There was no way I was heading across that field again. Maybe the snipers had gone home. Maybe they hadn't. I wasn't taking that chance. Instead, I decided we should work our way around the perimeter. By moving fast and sticking close to the walls of the surrounding buildings, under the cantilevers that jutted out from most of them over a wide side-walk that encircled the park, I hoped we could stay out of the rain and out of the view of any gunmen operating from the buildings on the south side. That's where they had been the night before. We had taken no shots from anyone in the buildings on the north side. If there were snipers in the south-side buildings, we would essentially be underneath them for most of our run, almost impossible to see. If someone did start shooting from the other side of the field, unless they took us out on the first shot, we should be able to quickly duck through doors into abandoned apartments that would hopefully provide us some measure of protection.

It wasn't a great plan, but it was the best I could do on short notice, and once we started running, I was convinced we were home free. But when we were about halfway to our objective, we suddenly caught a glimpse of Abdel. He was running out of one of the buildings on the other side, across the field, toward us. I stopped dead in my tracks. Omar nearly ran me over. We looked at each other and then back at Abdel. It was clear that he hadn't gone ahead of us to the rendezvous point at the border. Rather, he had been waiting for us all along. Now that he saw us, he was apparently afraid of being left behind. But why he would run out into the open was beyond me. Worse, he was yelling for us to stop and waving his arms frantically so that we would see him. My heart almost stopped.

"What in the world is he doing?" Omar whispered. "He's going to get us all killed."

I was glad Omar had said it first. Honestly, I'd have felt guilty saying it out loud. But he was right.

Then it was as if Abdel realized what he was doing. When he had nearly reached the wreckage of the Russian tank, he abruptly stopped running, stopped yelling, stopped waving his arms. He just froze and stood motionless, his hands in the air like he was being robbed.

Lightning flashed. More thunder boomed overhead.

"Now what's he doing?" Omar asked.

I had no idea. I scanned the perimeter and found myself backing slowly into one of the buildings. Omar noticed what I was doing and followed suit. He didn't want to get picked off by a sniper any more than I did. We scanned the room behind us. No one was in there. There were no signs that anyone had been recently. We crouched down and watched to see what Abdel would do next.

More than a minute passed, but Abdel kept standing there.

Why?

Didn't he understand the danger he was in?

Come on, Abdel. Move.

Didn't he remember what we had been through the night before?

You can do it. Just start walking.

I wasn't making a sound, but in my mind I was screaming at him, trying to will him to get going with all the mental energy I could muster. But with every second that passed, I grew more scared. I could barely look.

Come on, Abdel; come on. Think of Fatima. She's counting on you, buddy. She's waiting for you. Come on, just one foot in front of the other.

But Abdel just stood there, looking terrified and confused. My hands were trembling again. I desperately needed something to drink. I reached for my water bottle, but it was gone. I dug through my backpack, but it was not there. Another full minute went by. I couldn't bear it. I actually put my hands over my eyes. I had this palpable fear that a sniper was going to blow Abdel's head off and that would be my last memory of him.

Finally Omar nudged me.

"Maybe we should go out there and get him," he said.

I opened my eyes. "Are you crazy? You want to get killed?"

But Omar persisted. "Something's wrong. Something's out there. Maybe he's found something."

"Then he should bring it here."

"I'll go," Omar said and moved toward the door.

"No way," I responded, grabbing his arm. "You're not going anywhere."

I turned and shouted out the window. *"Abdel! Come on! We can't wait any longer!"*

But Abdel didn't move. I yelled again. I knew I was giving away our position. But I also knew if I didn't, Omar would go racing out there like a fool.

"Abdel!" I yelled again through the thunder and the rain. *"It'll be okay. Come on. Let's go home!"*

Even from such a distance it was clear how scared he was. He still held his arms high over his head. I had to assume he could see a sniper and was wondering why the guy wasn't pulling the trigger. I was wondering the same thing.

Abdel was soaked to the bone by now. But he still didn't move. And he still hadn't been shot. I had no idea what to do. So I just stared at him and did nothing. Then I saw Abdel's hands slowly beginning to lower. His head began to droop as well. His shoulders slumped forward. He hadn't started walking yet, but something was changing. I could only guess that he knew he had done something terribly foolish, but he also had to know there was no turning back now. If he didn't start walking, he'd never get to us, never get home, never see Fatima. Maybe the sniper was going to let him go.

"That's right, Abdel!" I shouted. *"You can do it!"*

My heart started beating again. Clearly Abdel was steeling himself for what was ahead. I found myself praying God would somehow help him make it across the field without getting shot. I just couldn't bear the thought. There had been too much sadness already.

But then the entire park was rocked by an enormous explosion.

Abdel Mahmoud Hamid disintegrated before our eyes.

He had stepped on a land mine. Now he had just stepped off it. And just like that, he was gone.

TOP SECRET

PART THREE

17

* * *

Omar battled his way through rush-hour traffic.

Finally we reached downtown Beirut. Omar took a left past the promenade along St. George Bay. Then he worked his way around the beautiful tree-lined campus of the American University before pulling up to the main entrance of the Mayflower Hotel.

We had driven the entire way from the Syrian border in silence but for the high-speed *whoosh-whoosh* of the windshield wipers, the crackle of lightning, and the bone-rattling claps of thunder in a storm that was only getting worse. Now, as we arrived at the hotel where Abdel had reserved a room for me to do my writing, Omar insisted I go upstairs and get started on my story while he went and broke the terrible news to Abdel's family and to Fatima.

"Absolutely not," I said. "I'm going too."

But Omar would not hear of it. He said he knew I was racked with guilt. He knew I thought it was my fault since I'd taken Abdel into Syria

127

without authorization. But Abdel was a professional, he said. He knew the risks. He could have
said no, but he didn't. Abdel loved what he did,
and he'd loved being with us.

"Abdel was my responsibility," I protested.
"I need to tell the family myself."

But Omar was adamant. "For crying out loud,
J. B.," he nearly yelled at me. "You've got a major
article to write. ISIS is about to launch a new war
against the U.S. and Israel. You have two sources
indicating they have chemical weapons. You don't
know when the attacks are coming, but the main
commander on the ground in Syria says it's soon.
That's it. That's all you ought to be thinking
about right now. You have to tell the world what
you know. Lives are at stake. Hundreds, maybe
thousands, of innocent lives. That's why we went
there, because you smelled this story, and you were
right. Now get it written and get it out. Because
if the Ramzy story isn't on the *Times* website by
tonight, and isn't on the front page of tomorrow's
paper, then Abdel Hamid died in vain. Is that what
you want?"

It wasn't, of course.

Omar grabbed my shoulders and looked me
in the eye. "I'll be back in a few hours," he said.
"Don't do anything stupid while I'm gone."

I knew exactly what he meant. I nodded dutifully. But as he pulled away from the hotel, I had
no illusions I was going to be able to keep my
promise.

The Mayflower had been a favorite of the international jet-setter crowd since the early 1960s, but

this was my first time at the iconic hotel. Heading into the lobby, I checked in at the front desk. As the clerk made a photocopy of my passport and ran my credit card, I picked up one of the hotel's brochures and began leafing through it. I had no desire to think about the story I had to write or any of what we had just been through. All I wanted at that moment was a hot shower, a hearty breakfast, and a large bottle of anything alcoholic. Preferably two. I knew I shouldn't. I knew it was wrong. It had been exactly two years, three months, and four days since I'd had my last drink. But my willpower was shot. I was losing emotional altitude. What I needed just then was to drink heavily and without interruption.

Scanning the brochure, my eye was drawn to the picture of a beautifully appointed British watering hole. *As the quintessential London pub, the Duke of Wellington conveys an air of timelessness,* it read. *Built in 1960, it has not changed over the decades. It is a treasure cave of obscure and amusing artifacts where you can genuinely enjoy a good pint with friends. Named after the first Duke of Wellington (1769–1852), the pub boasts a relaxed and cozy atmosphere. Every night, a happy mixture of local characters and loyal crowd comes to enjoy the friendly ambience, savory snacks, and fine spirits.*

Perfect, I thought.

The problem was, the pub was closed. It might not open for hours. I didn't have that long.

Bursting into my room, I threw my backpack on the queen-size four-poster bed and headed straight for the minibar. My hands quivered, and

I fumbled with the keys, so it took me a moment to get the blasted thing open.

It was empty. I picked up the phone.

"Room service," a young man at the other end of the line said with a slight British accent. "Would you like some breakfast this morning, Mr. Collins?"

"No; well, yes, but—never mind," I said, practically tripping over my words. "Look, what I need right now is a bottle of Jack Daniel's."

"I'm sorry, sir, but the bar is closed until happy hour."

"Can't you at least fill up my minibar?"

"I'm sorry, sir. We cannot do that until five o'clock."

"But there's nothing in there," I protested. "No Cokes, no water, no candy bars, and certainly no alcohol."

"I'm so sorry, sir. That is our policy."

"Look, I'm paying good money for this room, and I'd like my minibar restocked immediately."

"I do apologize. There's nothing I can do."

I slammed the phone down, then picked it up again and called the front desk. I demanded to speak to the manager. When he came on the line, I let fly like Mussolini from the balcony. After riding out my brief tirade, he told me there was nothing he could do. It was hotel policy not to serve alcohol until five in the afternoon.

"And frankly, sir, even if that were not the case, my staff and I are under strict orders not to serve you any drinks at all, Mr. Collins."

I was rendered speechless for a moment. *Strict orders?*

"Why not?" I finally bellowed. *"Orders from whom?"*

"I'm afraid that is a matter for you and your company, sir," the manager said. "Is there anything else I can help you with today?"

"You're saying the *New York Times* won't let me drink?"

"I'm saying they won't pay for it."

"Fine," I said, finding the loophole. "Then I'll pay for it all personally."

But the manager would not budge. "Again, I'm sorry, sir," he said calmly. "We do a lot of business with the *Times*. Many of your correspondents stay with us. I cannot risk our relationship with this fine client just for you, sir. Now, is there anything else I can do for you?"

I slammed down the phone again. I was seething, and I was more desperate for a drink than any time I could remember.

Then my phone beeped. I had received a text.

It was Omar. **Take a shower. Get writing. And stop harassing the manager.**

Omar knew me far too well.

18

* * *

Two hours later, Omar was still not back.

Avoiding the hotel's public Wi-Fi, I plugged my satphone into my laptop and transmitted my two stories to Allen MacDonald. The first focused on the imminent threat of an ISIS attack against the U.S. and Israel and included the fact that sources in two intelligence services—one Western and one Arab—had evidence that ISIS had recently captured chemical weapons. It occurred to me that Ramzy had threatened my life if I wrote about the chemical weapons, but I dismissed the thought. This story was too important. For balance, I included Ramzy's denial but incorporated extensive details from the material I'd been given on the ISIS coup near Aleppo. The second piece was a full profile of Ramzy, with biographical material and long excerpts from our interview. I also transmitted the digital recording of the interview so Allen could get it transcribed. He would likely run that, too, on one of the jump pages.

I caught a cab for the ten-minute ride to Beirut's Rafic Hariri International Airport, named after the former Lebanese prime minister who was assassinated by a car bomb in 2005, allegedly by Hezbollah operatives who some believed were working at the behest of the Syrian government. It was yet another reminder of the cruel and wanton violence of this crazy part of the world.

On the way, I checked my phone for the latest headlines. One in the *Wall Street Journal* particularly caught my eye:

**Palestinian Leaders Warn Israel
Must Agree to Divide Jerusalem or
Peace Talks "As Good As Dead"**

I also sent four texts. The first was to my mom. I let her know I was doing fine and heading back to the States. There was no reason to tell her anything else. She was an avid reader of everything I wrote for the *Times*. She'd know where I'd been soon enough.

The second text was to Robert Khachigian, former director of the Central Intelligence Agency. It was Khachigian, now retired at seventy-three but still very much engaged with the intelligence world, who had first tipped me off that ISIS had captured a cache of chemical weapons. He had pointed me to one source. I had found the other. Khachigian had always been a straight shooter with me, and I had come to trust him implicitly. Indeed, I had just included a quote from him in one of my articles, though not by name. I'd simply referred to "a former senior American intelligence

official" who warned that "it would be a nightmare scenario if ISIS has acquired weapons of mass
destruction, perhaps the most dangerous development of our age." That said, I needed to look him
in the eye and get his take on why Ramzy had
flatly denied it all.

Need 2 talk ASAP, my text said.

The third message was to Ari Shalit, deputy
director of the Mossad. At fifty-seven, Shalit was
one of the most interesting operatives I'd ever met
in the Middle East. Born and raised in Morocco,
he looked and sounded like a full-blooded Arab to
me, though he was actually fully Jewish on both
his mother's and father's sides. He emigrated to
Israel with his family when he was only fourteen,
then joined the IDF and rose to become the commander of Israel's most elite and secretive commando team, known collectively only as the Unit.
Fluent in Hebrew, Arabic, French, and English,
and not bad at Russian, he was quickly snatched up
from the IDF by the Mossad and sent on some of
the most dangerous and highly classified missions
behind enemy lines in the history of the Israeli spy
agency. I had met Shalit quite a few years earlier
when I was trying to track down how the CIA and
Western intel agencies had gone wrong on the Iraq
WMD assessment. I'd used him as an unnamed
source on a few stories about Iran's nuclear program over the years. We'd stayed in touch on and
off, but now I urgently needed his help.

Hearing ISIS has CW, I wrote. **Want to compare notes. Can we talk?**

The fourth text was for Ismail Tikriti, the

forty-seven-year-old deputy director of Iraqi intelligence who, interestingly enough, was neither a Sunni nor Shia Muslim, and not an Arab either. Ethnically he was Chaldean. Religiously he was a Christian. Born and raised in Tikrit, the same town as Saddam Hussein, Ismail came from a military family that had been loyal to Saddam. But after the war, he had been recruited first by the Americans as a translator, then by the newly restructured Ministry of Defense as an operations specialist. He had impressed one supervisor after another and risen through the ranks. We had met while I'd been covering U.S. military operations in his country, beginning with the March 2003 invasion through the insurgency and the withdrawal of all American armed forces from Iraq in December 2011. A brilliant guy who spoke remarkably good English given that he'd never studied outside the country, Ismail Tikriti had his eyes and ears on everything that was happening. More important, he owed me a favor, and I was calling it in.

Found holy grail. Will trade for mtg w/ AK, I wrote, certain he would know I meant Abu Khalif.

With Shalit and Tikriti, I was chumming the waters. I needed both of them to bite to move the story forward. But I had no guarantees.

Once through airport security, I headed up to the terminal's third level, where there was a Japanese seafood restaurant. I'd been there several times. But it was crowded. And I was alone. They said they didn't have a table for one. But after slipping a twenty to one of the waitresses, I finally was offered a seat at the bar.

I hesitated. I was famished and still craved a round of good, stiff drinks. But Omar had been right. I needed to stay sober. I'd made it this far, more than two years without a drink, and I was scared how far I might fall if I didn't stay on the wagon.

"Do you want the seat or not?" the waitress asked when she saw I wasn't following her.

"Sure." I shrugged. "Whatever's available."

The moment I said yes, I knew it was a mistake. Soon I was staring at shelves full of vodka and bourbon and rum and whiskey and all manner of spirits. The aroma of any one of them would have made my mouth water, but with the combination, I was in serious trouble. I felt my forehead break into a light sweat. Not enough that anyone would have noticed unless they were looking carefully. But I knew and winced. I also knew I should get out of there immediately, but I was so hungry, and my flight was leaving soon. If I was going to eat anything, it was going to be here. What choice did I have?

"What'll it be?" said the young bartender, who looked like he was barely out of college, if he had even gone at all.

My name is James Bradley Collins—I'm an alcoholic, I said to myself.

I am powerless over alcohol—my life has become unmanageable.

Only a power greater than myself can restore me to sanity.

"Perrier," I said with all the discipline I could muster, "and some sushi, as quick as you can."

The kid raised his eyebrows as if to ask, *That's it?* But a moment later, he brought back a sushi menu and set a distinctive green bottle of French sparkling water in front of me with a clean glass, a slice of lemon, and a few cubes of ice. I poured half a glass and watched it bubble and fizz. Then I took a long, slow drink and closed my eyes.

One day at a time. One step at a time.

When I opened my eyes, Omar Fayez plunked down in the seat on my right.

"Looks like I found you just in time," he said.

"What are you doing here?" I asked, startled by his presence.

"I'm going back with you," he said, smelling my glass to make sure I had truly ordered Perrier.

"Absolutely not," I protested. "You need to get back to your wife."

"Who do you think told me to fly back with you?" he replied, pulling out his own satphone and hitting speed dial.

"What about Abdel's family?" I pressed.

"All taken care of," he replied. "I can tell you about it on the flight. But right now you've got a call to make."

As soon as he handed me the phone, I winced. I knew full well he had dialed my editor, Allen MacDonald, at his home in McLean, Virginia. It wasn't a call I was planning to make until I was out of Lebanon.

"You haven't talked to him yet, have you?" he said.

"No."

"You have to."

"Not yet."

"Now."

Suddenly Allen was on the line. I sighed and began talking. He was not happy to hear from me for a host of reasons, not the least of which was because it was only five in the morning in the D.C. area.

"You're going to need to rewrite your story," he began.

"Why?"

"You need to take out the references to the WMD."

"Why?" I asked, taken aback. "It's a solid piece."

"But Ramzy denied everything."

"I quoted him," I replied, a bit defensively.

"Why do you think he did that?"

"I'm not entirely sure."

"Did you push him?"

"You heard the interview."

"I did."

"He must not have authorization from Khalif."

"Or maybe ISIS really doesn't have the stuff."

"They do, Allen," I replied. "The story is solid."

"But you wanted him to confirm it. You risked your life, and cost Abdel his, on the premise that he would confirm it."

"I was wrong on that, but—"

He cut me off. "What if you're being set up?"

"By Ramzy?"

"No, by your intel sources."

"I saw the documents, Allen," I protested. "I heard the tapes for myself. I have the transcripts."

"Maybe you saw what someone wanted you to see."

"I have two completely different sources—neither have ever steered me wrong."

"What's to say they weren't coordinating with each other, planting the bait, hoping you'd be hooked by the prospect of a big scoop?"

"These two guys don't even know each other—two different men, two different countries, two different agencies."

"It's not enough," he said. "You need another source, from a third different country."

"Allen, come on," I said. "That's impossible. I'm telling you, the story is solid. It's a huge scoop. And we need to move on it before the *Post* or someone else gets it."

"Forget it, Collins—I'm not going to be set up with another WMD story that turns out to be bogus," he pushed back. "And don't tell me this thing is a 'slam dunk.' Been there, done that. Get a third source and we'll talk. In the meantime, rewrite both pieces ASAP. Take out the references to WMD in the Ramzy profile, and focus on the 'new attacks coming' angle in the ISIS story. That's big enough news for now."

"I'm about to catch a flight home."

"Nonstop?"

"No, I have a layover in Istanbul."

"Rewrite it on the first leg. Retransmit from Istanbul. And I'll need an obit for Abdel by the time you touch down in D.C."

I started to protest that I didn't have the time, that it would be impossible to do the piece justice when I was flying across the Atlantic, but again MacDonald cut me off. He was in no mood for attitude. He said I owed it to Abdel and his family. He was right, of course, which made it all the more painful to hear. I said I'd call him again from Turkey, but I was fuming. I hung up and handed the phone back to Omar.

"I'll do it," Omar said without hesitation as he put the phone back in his briefcase.

"Do what?"

"Abdel's obit," Omar repeated. "I'll write it on the way to Istanbul."

"No, Allen's right," I conceded, ashamed at myself for having resisted the assignment even for a moment.

"Of course he's right that we owe it to Abdel, but he's not right that you can do all this on your own," Omar insisted. "You rewrite the Ramzy piece. I'll write the obit. Now let's order before we run out of time."

"Thanks," I said quietly, unable to look Omar in the eye just then.

"Don't mention it," said the bear of a man sitting beside me. "I've got your back, J. B. Always have."

19

★ ★ ★

ISTANBUL, TURKEY

Turkish Airlines flight 825 landed in Istanbul at
5:35 p.m. local time.

The moment the flight attendants would let
me, I powered up my laptop and satellite phone
and transmitted revised copies of the ISIS story
and my profile of Jamal Ramzy to D.C. I was still
opposed to Allen's decision, but I had no choice.
If I didn't do the rewrite, he'd chop up the piece
himself, and I definitely didn't want that. At least
this way I still had some degree of control over
how the piece was phrased.

Then Omar showed me his story on Abdel.

"This is good," I whispered as we taxied to
the gate.

Omar said nothing. I quickly glanced at him,
sitting next to me in business class. The expression on his face looked as pained as I'd ever seen
him. He was a good writer, but this one had clearly
taken its toll.

"Really, it's very good," I said. "I'm sending it
as is."

With that, I immediately e-mailed the obituary to Allen, then powered up my iPhone and began figuring out how to get us home. After a frustrating fifteen minutes or so on multiple travel websites, I finally came to the annoying realization that there were no direct flights back to Washington that evening from Istanbul. When I tried to route us through Brussels or London or Paris or Frankfurt, I found that there were no late-evening flights to D.C. from any of those hub cities either. Any way we sliced it, we were going to have to spend the night in a hotel and fly out the next day. The best I could do was book us tickets on a Turkish Airlines flight that would depart at 8:10 the following morning for Brussels. We would then change planes and fly United across the Atlantic, touching down at Dulles at 2:45 in the afternoon.

With no other options, I booked the flights, then scanned my e-mails and text messages. There was only one that stood out. It was from Ari Shalit, deputy director of the Mossad, whom I had texted earlier that afternoon. As luck would have it, Shalit would be arriving later that night in Istanbul and was asking me to meet him at midnight in front of the famed Blue Mosque. My mood suddenly improved. The night might not be a complete waste after all.

Omar rented a car and we drove for the Ibrahim Pasha, a four-story hotel in the historic Sultanahmet neighborhood, not far from the Blue Mosque. While I paced in front of a roaring fireplace in the lobby, returning e-mails and scanning headlines, Omar secured two adjoining rooms.

I asked him to clear my minibar of all alcohol. He gave me an "attaboy" slap on the back and took care of it immediately.

We met later in the hotel restaurant, and over a meal of lamb kebabs and rice we speculated about what kind of splash the Ramzy profile and interview would make when it went public in a few hours. We talked about how hard Abdel's fiancée had taken the news of his death and discussed how we could send her some money discreetly, perhaps even anonymously. It seemed the least we could do.

At one point during our meal, Omar asked me why I thought Shalit would want to meet so late, and why in front of the mosque.

"I have no idea," I said. "Why do you ask?"

"I don't know," Omar replied. "Just seems odd. I mean, how did he know we'd even be in Istanbul tonight?"

"Good question."

"Did you say anything in your text?"

"No."

"What did you say?"

"I just asked if we could talk."

"You think he was already planning a trip here, or is he coming just to see you?"

"Does it matter?"

Omar shrugged. "I don't know."

I noticed he wasn't really eating, which wasn't like him. "What is it, Omar?" I asked. "What are you thinking?"

He shook his head. "I'm not really sure," he replied. "Maybe it's nothing. I just . . ."

"What?"

"I just have a strange feeling. But I can't really say why."

We finished dinner feeling a bit unsettled. But then again, we were both exhausted and traumatized by Abdel's death and all we'd experienced in Homs. I decided to go upstairs and take a nap for a few hours. Omar went out jogging.

At precisely 11:30 p.m., the alarm on my iPhone went off. I got up, took a quick shower, and met Omar downstairs. Together we finalized our plan and then headed out to the Blue Mosque.

I went on foot, and Omar shadowed me in the little silver Hyundai compact he'd rented at the airport, keeping a good block or so behind me—close enough to make sure I was okay but not so close that he'd be immediately spotted. It was raining, though not nearly as hard as in Homs. The streets were slick. The air was foggy.

Soon I came to the Sultan Ahmed Mosque, commonly known as the Blue Mosque for the twenty thousand exquisite hand-painted blue ceramic tiles lining its interior walls. It was, of course, locked and closed for the night. But with each of its six minarets and the main dome and its eight secondary domes bathed in the yellow light of high-powered lamps and set against the backdrop of such a stormy night, the entire seventeenth-century structure looked spectacular in the mist, and even with the rain, the dappled reflection in the nearby pool was spectacular as well.

Few people were crazy enough to be out in such weather, but there was a young couple in love making out near the fountain, and a few police officers strolled the grounds. Ari Shalit was nowhere in sight, so I was startled when I heard someone saying my name from the shadows of a small grove of palm trees and even more startled when I realized it was a woman's voice, not that of the man I thought I was to meet.

"Mr. Collins, over here," said the woman, a slim, striking brunette wearing a black faux-silk London Fog trench coat and holding a polka-dot umbrella. "My, my, you're getting soaked. Please, won't you join me?"

"I'm sorry; do I know you?" I asked, genuinely puzzled.

"No, I'm afraid we have not had the pleasure," she said with a warm, alluring smile as she removed a leather glove to shake my hand.

In so doing, she slipped a note into mine and whispered, "Ari sent me."

I looked at her, wondering if that could possibly be true. Did she really know Ari Shalit? Had the Mossad's deputy director really sent her? Why? Why hadn't he come himself? These and a dozen other questions raced through my mind, but before I started asking, I looked down at the note.

J. B.—Sorry I couldn't come in person. The Old Man needed me. Meet Yael Katzir. Works on my staff. Expert in CW. Fully briefed on our conversations. She can help you.—A. S.

I stared at the note, trying to make sense of it. It certainly sounded like Ari. It was concise, to the point, and consistent with the text message Ari had sent while Omar and I were flying to Istanbul from Beirut.

Meet in front of SAM in I, he'd written. **Midnight. Will carry PDU.—A. S.**

SAM was the Sultan Ahmed Mosque, aka the Blue Mosque.

Did *PDU* mean "polka-dot umbrella"?

The "Old Man" was the nickname Ari called his boss, the Mossad director. Whoever had written the text had certainly known about the chemical weapons angle I'd wanted to discuss. But was all this legit? Had someone hacked his account or accessed his phone somehow? Was this a setup?

I looked at this woman, trying to make sense of her. She was lovely, that was for certain, with a natural, unpretentious beauty that I found instantly attractive. She wore no eye shadow or lipstick or makeup of any kind. She wore no earrings or necklace or bracelets, and her short, well-trimmed nails were not painted. She looked more Arab than Jewish, but then again, so did Ari. Her large brown eyes seemed gentle and relaxed, and they twinkled in the streetlights. Despite the raincoat, I could see she was wearing a black cashmere sweater, well-worn denim jeans, and stylish brown leather boots that went up to her knees. These added a couple of inches to her height, but she was still quite a bit shorter than me. I'm six foot one, so I pegged her at about five-five or five-six. She carried no purse or handbag, just the umbrella, which she kept propped up over our heads to shield us from the drizzle.

She didn't look like an assassin. Then again, no one involved in a honey trap would. But did she really work for the Mossad? Or had she been sent by ISIS? It seemed unlikely that Abu Khalif and Jamal Ramzy were ready to kill me. The story they wanted the world to read hadn't even been published yet. If anyone wanted me dead just now, it would be Khalif's rivals in al Qaeda, not ISIS. But before I could process the questions any further, she leaned toward me, put her warm, soft hands on my face, and kissed me on the lips. I was so caught off guard that I immediately pulled away, but she leaned closer and whispered in my ear.

"You and I are either brother and sister, or we're lovers, Mr. Collins," she explained matter-of-factly. "At this hour, there's no other reason for the police to think we'd be together . . . unless, of course, you want them to think I'm a prostitute . . ."

Her voice trailed off, but she didn't need to finish her point. While prostitution was legal in Turkey, being seen by the police with a *fahişe* could raise all sorts of problems I didn't want to deal with. So I put my arms around her waist, and she pulled me toward her, kissing me even more convincingly this time.

"Nice to meet you, Miss Katzir," I whispered.

"Likewise," she said, raising her eyebrows and seeming to enjoy the game. "Now let's start walking arm in arm, like true lovers."

I did as I was told, still trying to size up the situation.

"Call me Yael," she said quietly.

"Fair enough—call me James," I said, though I had no idea why. Hardly anyone called me James except my mother. Everyone else called me J. B. The guys at the *Times* did. Omar did. Laura had. Everyone did. Why in the world had I just asked her to call me James?

"Very well, James." She smiled. "Is there a place we can talk, you know, privately?"

20

* * *

I had no idea where to take this woman.

Over the years I had been in and out of Istanbul many times, but I didn't really know the city well. I couldn't very well take her back to the hotel, and I could only imagine what Omar must be thinking at the moment. So I suggested we go find an all-night café and get some coffee. She agreed.

That was easier said than done, however. Istanbul, the ancient metropolis straddling the Bosphorus, once named Constantinople, had served as the eastern capital of the Roman Empire, but it wasn't exactly New York or London or even Tel Aviv. It didn't abound with late-night watering holes and all-night restaurants and entertainment. But off we went, looking for one anyway.

We held hands as we walked through the rainy streets. She nestled close to me and laughed and twirled her umbrella and acted like we had been dating for years. It was, I hoped, a solid performance for anyone who didn't know us. But I needed more convincing that she really was who she said she was, so as we walked, I plied her with questions. Her answers were spot-on. She knew detailed elements of my past meetings and conversations with Ari that no one else could have known unless they'd been told by one of the two of us. She was trying to convince me that the deputy director of the Mossad really had sent her, that I really could trust her, that I really could confide in her whatever I had texted Ari was so urgent about my brief trip into Homs, and it was beginning to work.

"Ari says you went into journalism because of your grandfather. Is that true?" she asked as we found ourselves walking along the Sea of Marmara toward the grand Topkapi Palace, once the seat of the sultans who ruled the Ottoman Empire for over four hundred years.

"Actually, it is," I replied.

"A. B. Collins?"

"Right again."

"What did that stand for?"

"Andrew Bradley," I said.

"So you were named after him, right—James Bradley?" she asked.

"As a matter of fact, I was."

"Ari said your grandfather was really rattled when his wife—your grandmother, Betty—passed away in 1980. He never remarried?"

"No."

"They were close."

"Soul mates."

"How long were they married?"

"Thirty-eight years."

"Wow."

"I know."

"Who does that anymore?"

"No one I know."

"My parents divorced when I was fourteen," she said.

"I was twelve."

"Did you live with your mom or dad?"

"My mom."

"In Bar Harbor?"

I nodded.

"And your dad went to Miami Beach?"

I heard the question, but I didn't answer. We kept walking. Suddenly this wasn't so fun anymore. I got it. She knew everything about me. Was she showing off?

"I'm sorry," Yael said after a few moments. "Bad choice of topics."

I shrugged.

"And Ari says Matt is off-limits."

"He is."

"Why?"

"Look, Matt's a good guy, and he's my brother," I said. "We were close when we were young. Not so much anymore."

"Where is he these days?"

"Amman."

"Jordan?"

"Is there another?"

"What's he doing there?"

"I don't know—a sabbatical of some kind."

"What does he do when he's not in Amman?"

"Does it really matter?"

Yael shrugged. "Sorry; I'm not trying to pry."

I sighed and kept walking. "He's a professor," I said at last.

"Where?"

"At a seminary near Boston," I replied. "Can we talk about something else?"

My relationship with Matt was a long story and not one I wanted to get into now.

"How about Laura?" she said.

I stopped dead in my tracks. "You've got to be kidding me."

"Ari said that didn't go well."

"That's none of your business," I said, more coldly than I intended.

Whoever this woman was, I had no intention of talking with her about my ex-wife. It was true Shalit and I had talked about my divorce some at the time. He'd been going through a breakup of his own marriage. I guess we'd sort of compared notes. But this wasn't anything I wanted to discuss now, and certainly not with Yael.

"I'm sorry," she said. "I didn't mean to—"

"It's fine," I lied. "Let's just . . . you know."

Yael had certainly gotten the picture. She took my arm again to maintain our cover, and we kept walking. "Should we talk about Fordow?" she said.

I knew she was referring to the previously secret Iranian nuclear facility near the holy city of Qom that was revealed by Western intelligence agencies to the *Times* and other media in the fall of 2009.

"Ari says you were very helpful when he wanted to leak some details and get world leaders focused on just how much of their nuclear program Iran was hiding."

My mind raced. Was she saying Ari had told her I contributed to the *Times* article on the Fordow facility? Why else would she be mentioning it?

As if answering my unspoken question, Yael surprised me yet again. "'A senior intelligence official said Friday that Western spy agencies had "excellent access" to the site, suggesting human spies had penetrated it,'" she said, looking at me.

She was quoting from the story, from memory. I said nothing.

She continued. "'The official said that "multiple independent sources" had confirmed that it was intended for nuclear use. The intelligence official and other officials declined to be named because they were discussing intelligence matters.'"

Then she added, "Ari said he was one of the 'multiple independent sources' you used to back up the story."

"Why would you think I worked on that story?" I asked. "My byline isn't even on it."

"Ari told me all about it," Yael explained. "He told me how he brought you to Mossad headquarters in Tel Aviv, took you to room E-38, and gave you an ice-cold Mr. Pibb and a plate of hummus and some fresh pita from your favorite restaurant in Abu Ghosh. He showed you satellite photos and let you listen to telephone intercepts and read highly classified reports from agents in the field. And he told me why—so the *Times* would run the story and so the world would know that Iran was hiding key elements of its nuclear program."

Again I stopped dead in my tracks, just a few hundred yards from the palace, and stared into her eyes. She was exactly right, yet I had never told a soul all of these details. I hadn't written these things into my notes. I didn't keep a journal. There was no way she could know any of it—much less all of it—unless Ari Shalit had told her.

I began to breathe easier. She was the real deal. She really did work for the Mossad. She really had been sent to help me. And I guess I had to trust her, as much as I could trust any foreign intelligence agent.

A pair of policemen came walking around the corner. They were on the other side of the boulevard, but when they seemed to take an inordinate interest in the two of us, I leaned forward, put my arms around Yael again, and kissed her on the lips.

For a moment, it seemed as if she had lost her breath. But so had I. Our kiss became so passionate that the policemen kept walking and didn't give us another thought. Yael's plan had worked. We looked like lovers. But it felt so good I wasn't sure if she was still playing a game.

Then again, I wasn't sure I was either.

21

We finally found a restaurant that was still open.

The owner graciously offered to take our soaking-wet coats and hang them up to dry. Then he showed us to a table in a back corner near the crackling fireplace. A waiter quickly brought us piping-hot chai and some warm bread, and we both began to settle in.

It was a cozy little dive. The place was about half-full, all foreigners. Most were young couples in their twenties and thirties. The problem was they were all drinking beer or cocktails, not tea or coffee. Immediately I felt the cravings I was already battling intensify. Everything in me wanted to begin drinking heavily. The ambience. The aromas. The company, to be sure. And the immense grief that was weighing so heavily upon me.

Yael quickly ordered a glass of a French cabernet, then asked if I'd like to share a bottle. It was tempting beyond measure to say yes. The only reason I could think of to decline was because I wanted something stronger. Over her shoulder I could see shelves behind the bar filled with bottles of Johnnie Walker, Jim Beam, Absolut, and Stolichnaya. All my old friends were whispering my name.

"I'll stick with the tea," I said.

I glanced at Yael to gauge her level of disappointment. Instead, she canceled her cabernet and said she'd stick with the tea as well.

The waiter shrugged and walked away.

"A *tea*-totaler?" Yael asked with a wry grin.

"Recovering alcoholic," I admitted. "If Ari told you anything, he surely told you that."

"He did," she said. "I just wanted to see if it was true."

"Two years, three months, and five days."

"One day at a time." She smiled.

"One day at a time," I sighed.

Just then, I saw Omar walk in, scan the room, and spot me. In another context, I might have cursed him under my breath and found a way to get rid of him. Instead, I stood, introduced him to Yael, and asked him to join us. The fact was I needed a chaperone—and not just to keep me from drinking. It had been a long while since I'd been around anyone as alluring as Yael, and I honestly couldn't remember the last time I'd kissed someone the way she and I had just kissed. I'm not sure I'd realized before that moment how lonely I really was, and it scared me to see how willing I now felt to be swept off my feet by the first beautiful woman who showed me some attention.

"Omar is a good man," I told Yael as we got settled again. "We go way back."

"So I hear," she said, turning to him. "Ari speaks very highly of you."

"Please give him my regards," Omar said.

"I will indeed," she replied.

I tried to take a sip of tea but it needed to cool a bit. So I took a deep breath and got down to business.

"Look, Yael, in a few hours, the *Times* will run a front-page profile of Jamal Ramzy, based in part on the interview I did with him in Homs," I began.

"So your plan worked?" she asked, clearly up to speed.

"It did."

"You were crazy to go there."

"Tell me about it."

"Ari specifically told you not to go," she said.

"Everyone told me not to go."

"But you just couldn't help yourself?"

"A bit of a contrarian, this one," Omar quipped.

"Can only imagine him as a kid," Yael said.

Omar shook his head. "You have no idea."

I didn't play along. "The short version is that Ramzy and Abu Khalif are about to launch a massive series of terrorist attacks," I continued.

"When?" she asked.

"Very soon—that's all he would say."

"Where?"

"All signs point to attacks against my country and yours."

"I'm guessing he didn't draw you a map."

"I'm afraid not."

"What's his plan?"

"He said this was the beginning of a Third

Intifada. He said anyone who helped the Zionists were traitors and would be punished by Allah."

"That's standard jihadist rhetoric," she said. "Why take it seriously?"

"Two reasons," I said. "First, because Ramzy wanted to go on the record and because he wanted to do so with the *Times*. He's never talked to a Western reporter before, certainly not to an American. But he wants people to know. He wants Washington to know. Something big is coming—very big—and when it does, he wants to make sure ISIS gets credit, not Zawahiri and al Qaeda. Now, I realize not every terrorist group signals its intentions ahead of time. But some do. Bin Laden declared war on the U.S. ahead of the 9/11 attacks."

"And the second reason?" Yael asked.

"I believe ISIS has chemical weapons. Ramzy denies it. But I've got two sources from two different intelligence agencies, from two different countries. They're both solid. I'll follow up with both in short order and go back over everything they told me, point by point, to make sure I didn't miss anything. But my editor is feeling edgy. The *Times* has been burned on stuff like this before. He wants me to get a third source—different intel agency, different country. That's why I wanted to meet with Ari. I need to know what you guys know, and I need to know fast. Imagine ISIS with chemical weapons. Imagine how many Israelis and Americans they could kill. And what if they gave this stuff to Hamas and Hezbollah? What if all the rockets you guys have been hit with in recent years were filled with sarin gas? The story that comes out tomorrow doesn't mention chemical weapons. But I need to do a follow-up story immediately."

"And you need our help?"

"Exactly."

It was clear I had her interest, but Yael was keeping her cards close.

"Tell me about Jamal Ramzy," she said. "I'll admit, our files on him are pretty thin. Then I'll help you if I can."

I hesitated, but only for a moment. By this time I was convinced Yael was who she said she was. Talking to her might be as close to talking with Ari Shalit as I was going to get for now. So I dove in.

"The first thing that struck me was how old Jamal is," I began. "I mean, he was born in 1962. That makes him one of the longest-surviving jihadist leaders around. Bin Laden, of course, was born in '57, but he's dead. Zawahiri was born in '51, and he's still kicking, so that makes him the elder statesman within the al Qaeda world. But then Zawahiri isn't in a front-line combat position. Jamal is."

"Another thing that's key is that Jamal and Abu Khalif are related," Omar added. "Jamal is the older cousin by a good seven years. So they're family, but not just any family. A source of mine in Amman told me the family traces its lineage back to Grand Mufti Mohammed Amin al-Husseini."

Yael looked surprised. "The Grand Mufti of Jerusalem?" she asked.

"Exactly," Omar said.

"The one who allied with Hitler and the Nazis during the war?"

"That's the one," Omar confirmed. "These guys aren't simply run-of-the-mill jihadists. They're cut from a certain bolt of cloth. Their hatred of Jews in particular runs exceptionally deep."

"So Jamal decided to follow in the footsteps of Great-Grandpa and went off to fight in Afghanistan?"

"Right—from '80 to '83," I explained. "Then Jamal recruited his younger cousin Abu Khalif to join the mujahideen as a teenager and come fight in Afghanistan from '84 to '86. When the Russians were on the road to defeat, Abu Khalif left the battlefield. He decided to go make some money in the Gulf to support his mother. But Jamal stayed with bin Laden. Jamal was in the room when al Qaeda was born in 1988. In time, he began working with Khalid Sheikh Mohammed, helping to plan terrorist operations. And when Abu Khalif's mother passed away in 1994, Jamal persuaded his cousin to join al Qaeda and serve under KSM."

"Are they headquarters people or field people at this point?" Yael asked.

"Both, and that's what makes them unique— and so dangerous," Omar replied. "They were close to UBL and KSM. They knew the inner workings of al Qaeda. They knew all the top people. But they were also exceptionally proficient both in developing and executing the organization's trade craft. They helped bomb the two American embassies in Tanzania and Nairobi in '98. They were directly involved in training the 9/11 hijackers. In fact, Abu Khalif volunteered to be one of the hijackers, and Jamal supported him, but KSM said no, Khalif was too valuable to him personally. Then, when KSM was captured in Pakistan in '03 and several of his successors were killed in drone strikes, Jamal started working directly for al-Zawahiri as chief of operations."

"How come we've heard so little about Jamal?" Yael asked.

"The Jordanians suggest he kept a very low profile precisely because so many of his predecessors were killed in such short order," Omar said.

"And this is the turning point," I noted. "In 2004, at Jamal's recommendation, UBL and Zawahiri personally met with Abu Khalif. They sent him into Iraq. They told him to create a suicide bombing and kidnapping campaign. They told him to help build al Qaeda in Iraq. Khalif agreed. With Jamal's help, Khalif became a top deputy to Zarqawi. Of course, Zarqawi didn't last long. On June 7, 2006, Zarqawi was killed, and that's when a brutal and bloody internal power struggle began. Abu Khalif wasn't the first choice of bin Laden or Zawahiri to run AQI, but after several other leaders were killed or captured, he emerged as the top dog. He also had the full support of Jamal, who saw his cousin as the better strategist."

"But Abu Khalif wasn't content simply to rape and pillage Iraq," Yael said.

"Hardly," I agreed. "Khalif wanted to expand the mission into Syria. He wanted to topple Assad.

So he renamed his group ISIS, the Islamic State of Iraq and al-Sham. Again, Jamal fully supported his cousin, but bin Laden and Zawahiri were furious. They wanted Khalif to stay focused on Iraq, not get spread too thin. Tensions built within al Qaeda. After U.S. Special Forces took out bin Laden on May 2, 2011, the infighting intensified. Khalif asked Jamal to come with him and command ISIS forces in Syria. Zawahiri went ballistic, but Jamal did it anyway. Zawahiri rebuked the cousins, told them to get out of Syria and change ISIS back to 'al Qaeda in Iraq.'"

"That's when the cousins broke away from Zawahiri once and for all?" Yael asked.

"Exactly," I confirmed. "They think the old man has gone soft. They claim they are the true warriors for Allah. And ISIS is becoming hugely powerful. By early 2012, they had essentially driven U.S. forces out of Iraq. Now they've seized Fallujah. They've seized Mosul. And they've won major battles against Assad's forces in Syria. They've recruited and introduced upwards of thirty thousand foreign fighters into the Syrian theater. They're raising millions from key donors in Saudi Arabia and the Gulf. They're involved in kidnapping, blackmail, extortion, drug smuggling, and drug sales. They see Zawahiri as old news and themselves as the vanguard of the Salafi movement, which they believe is the epitome of true Islam."

"And now?" Yael asked.

"Now, according to Ramzy, they want to open up a new front against the U.S. and Israel, and they want the world to see them eclipsing the old al Qaeda."

"And you think Jamal Ramzy wouldn't have gone on the record with you unless he and his men actually had chemical weapons in their possession?"

"Why else?" I said. "He's never spoken to the media before, never let his photo be taken before."

"You asked him specifically whether ISIS had chemical weapons?"

"I did. I told him I had two sources, from two different intelligence agencies in two different countries. I explained the intel I had personally seen with my own eyes and heard with my own ears."

"And he told you that you don't know what you're talking about."

"Basically, yes," I confirmed.

"He's a liar," Yael said coldly.

I looked at her, then at Omar, then back at Yael.

"You're sure?"

"Absolutely."

"ISIS has chemical weapons?"

"Are we off the record?" she asked.

"Do we have to be?"

"I'm afraid so."

"Then we're off the record," I conceded.

"Then, yes, ISIS has chemical weapons."

"And you can prove it?"

"Of course."

She looked around the room and lowered her voice. "Look, these are the ground rules, and they are sacrosanct," she whispered. "Ari sent me because he wants you to tell the world what ISIS has and how dangerous they've become. They're rapidly eclipsing al Qaeda as the most dangerous terror group on the planet, yet most of the world doesn't really get it. So I can help. But only on the condition that you don't mention the Mossad or any Israeli intelligence agency or operative—not in your article and not to anyone else with whom you discuss what I'm about to tell you. We're clear?"

"Crystal."

She looked at me for a while and then at Omar, who nodded his assent as well.

"We're completely off the record here, and you give me your word?" she pressed. "Both of you?"

We both said yes.

Then she sipped her chai. I sipped mine.

"I don't know who your other sources are, and I won't ask—I don't want to know," Yael began. "But I can tell you for certain that ISIS has captured chemical weapons."

"From where?" I asked, curious to see if her story matched what I had learned.

"A few weeks ago," she began, "Jamal Ramzy's top deputy—a guy named Tariq Baqouba, a real thug, by the way—"

"Yeah, we met him," I broke in. "His brothers, too."

Yael looked surprised but continued. "Anyway, Baqouba and his forces attacked a Syrian military base a few klicks south of Aleppo. At the time, I honestly don't think Baqouba knew it was a storage facility for chemical weapons. After all, it had been widely reported that the U.N. had removed all of Syria's WMD out of the country. But of course that was a lie. The regime had given up a lot, but it was still hoarding plenty. At any rate, radio intercepts suggest the ISIS forces were running low on ammunition. They seemed to have hit this particular base because it had a large ammo storehouse. The firefight that ensued was brutal, one of the fiercest to date. Baqouba's forces seemed taken aback by the strength of the resistance they faced, but rather than back off, they doubled down, probably because they realized they had obviously stumbled onto something valuable. Anyway, they killed off most of the Syrian regulars, and before reinforcements could arrive, Baqouba and his men entered the base and found the WMD stockpiles—sarin nerve gas, to be precise—and the bombs and artillery shells to deliver them."

"How can you be so sure?"

"Drones," she said. "We've been monitoring each of the sites where the Assad regime kept chemical weapons. Again, most of the stockpiles, as you know, were removed under U.N. supervision. But we suspected all along that Assad's people were holding back, not giving the U.N. all they had. So we kept an especially close eye on several of those sites, including the one near Aleppo. We've also been monitoring all radio, phone, and e-mail traffic in the area around these bases. And of course, we have people on the ground, paid informants, and other sources."

So far, everything she said matched precisely what I had learned from the other sources, but it wasn't enough. It was tantalizingly close, but I had to be certain.

"You've personally reviewed all the data?" I asked.

"Yes."

"And?"

"Look," she said, "I was a chemical weapons specialist when I served in the IDF. When Ari recruited me, he put me in a special unit to track chemical WMD in the region. This is what I do."

"And you're certain Jamal's men have these weapons now?"

"There's no question about it," Yael said. "They have them, and they're going to use them. It's a matter of when, not if. And when that happens, it's going to be very, very ugly. Have you ever seen what sarin gas can do?"

22

* * *

I knew that sarin nerve gas had been developed by the Nazis.

What's more, I knew Saddam Hussein had used the stuff against the Kurds in the late eighties, killing some five thousand men, women, and children.

I also remembered that a Japanese cult had used sarin gas in the Tokyo subway system back in the midnineties, killing at least a dozen people and wounding nearly a thousand more.

And Omar and I had covered the sarin attacks on rebel forces by the Syrian regime in the summer of 2013 that had killed more than a thousand people—mostly women and children—and nearly led to military strikes by the U.S., British, and French until all three governments backed out at the last moment. That said, we were both novices on the technicalities of sarin gas, as we readily conceded.

"You have to understand how serious this stuff is," Yael said. "Sarin is among the most toxic and deadly nerve agents. But you can't smell it. You can't taste it. You can't even see it, which makes it all the more dangerous."

She explained that sarin was not a natural substance, but rather a man-made chemical compound, an organophosphate that was similar in many ways to insecticides but, she said, far more lethal.

"Sure, you can fire rockets and mortars and missiles with sarin-filled warheads at an enemy, and you can kill a lot of people," she told us. "You could release it in an aerosol form in a room or in a subway or a mall or a school and kill hundreds or thousands. But it's not just a gas. It can also be a liquid. You could dump barrels of sarin into the water supply—or lace it into the food supply—and you'd kill millions. That's what I worry about. And it's a hideous way to die."

"What happens?" I asked.

"It starts off simple. You get a runny nose. Your eyes start watering and hurting and your vision blurs. But that could be anything. You might not realize how serious it is at first. But then your eyes start dilating. You begin sweating profusely. Soon you're coughing uncontrollably, choking, drooling, possibly foaming at the mouth. You're having trouble breathing. You feel dizzy and nauseated, and then you start vomiting—a little at first, but then again and again until you have nothing left in your system. Then your stomach begins cramping. You have intense abdominal pains. You can't think straight. You're confused and disoriented. Then the convulsions start. If you're lucky, you black out. But more

likely you're fully lucid—and filled with terror—
as your bodily functions shut down and paraly-
sis sets in, and then you can't breathe, and then
you're dead."

I sat there for a few moments, trying to take in
what she was saying.

"ISIS with sarin is a worst-case scenario,"
she said, seeing me process the unthinkable. "An
attack like this in my country—or yours—would
be catastrophic. You need to write about this. You
need to warn people, and fast."

"I agree," I said. "But like I told you, my editor insists I get another source. Will Ari show me
what you have?"

"How soon can you come?" she asked.

"To Tel Aviv?"

"Yes," she said. "You wouldn't be allowed to
take notes or pictures. You couldn't make copies,
and you wouldn't be able to quote anything you
hear in your articles or to anyone else you speak
with. But since you've already got two other
sources, Ari is prepared to show you what we've got
and confirm your story based on the intel we've
developed."

"Why?"

Yael leaned across the table. "The prime minister has decided Israel needs the world to know
who ISIS really is and what they now have," she
whispered.

"Yes, but why now?"

"He's concerned the White House isn't taking
the ISIS threat seriously enough."

"But if the public knows, maybe they'll light a

fire under Congress, and Congress can light a fire under the president?"

"Something like that."

"So why give the story to me?" I asked.

"Honestly?" she asked as she finished her tea. "Because you already have it, and as you say, time is of the essence. Of course Jamal Ramzy doesn't want to say he's got WMD because that will put every government in the world on heightened alert. But that's exactly why two other governments—and now ours—are giving you the story. We need to make sure everyone knows who ISIS is. We need to make it that much harder for them to operate freely. We have no choice. The attacks could start any day. They've already had the stuff for nearly a month."

"So who do you think is the main target, you or us?" I asked.

"I have no idea, but it's probably us."

"Because you're closer?"

"That, and because of the timing."

"What do you mean?"

"Because the peace process is coming to a head."

"*What?*"

"I mean if we actually strike a final deal with the Palestinians in the next few days, ISIS is going to go ballistic."

I wasn't sure I'd heard her right.

"What are you talking about?" I asked. "I thought the peace process was going nowhere."

"You thought wrong."

"Wait, I don't understand—your prime minister keeps saying the talks are going nowhere, and President Mansour says he's going to walk out of the talks by the end of the month if no progress is made," Omar said, referring to Salim Mansour, the president of the Palestinian Authority. "King Abdullah keeps warning the parties to get serious or a new regional war will break out. If that's all true, it wouldn't seem like Jamal Ramzy and his brethren have much to worry about."

"Actually none of that is true—it's all spin," she said, leaning back in her seat.

"What do you mean by that?" Omar asked.

"Spin," she repeated. "Dissembling. Sleight of hand."

"You're saying the peace talks are moving forward?" he asked.

Yael looked disappointed. "Don't tell me you two have really been buying all this nonsense in the press."

"It comes from the highest officials," I said. "Of course we have."

"Well, stop," she said. "The deal is done."

"What deal?" Omar asked.

"The peace deal," Yael said.

"A full treaty?" I asked.

"Yes."

"How is that possible?"

"Your guess is as good as mine," Yael said. "I'm just telling you what I know. My PM has made major concessions—more than I'm comfortable with, frankly, but that's another story. They don't ask for my opinions on such matters. Anyway, I can't say more about this. I'm definitely not authorized to speak about any of these things. And you can't write about this. Seriously. Nobody knows what I'm telling you right now. But it's important you understand what's motivating Abu Khalif. We don't know where he is—somewhere in Iraq, we think—but we're guessing he knows more about the true state of the peace talks than the *New York Times*. We're also guessing he's about to give orders to kill a whole lot of people to keep this peace treaty from being finalized. Look, James, I'm glad you got your interview with Ramzy. I'm sure it'll be an important story. But don't get distracted. Jamal Ramzy is a supporting character. Abu Khalif is the lead actor. He's the big story. He's the guy you need to talk to, ideally before all hell breaks loose."

"I'm trying," I said. "But I can't find him. No one will tell me where he is. All I know is he's in prison in Iraq. Can you guys help?"

"We don't know any more than you," she said. "If we knew where he was, believe me, he'd be a corpse."

"I assume that's off the record as well." I smiled.

Yael smiled back. "Look, I wish I could give you more specifics, but I can't. But you should hunt him down like you did Ramzy. Find him. Talk to him. See what he says. Then brace yourself for some serious blowback. Because I'm telling you, this is why Abu Khalif is getting ready to strike. He's a barbarian. He's livid at the prospect of the Palestinians cutting a deal with the 'dirty Zionists.' He's enraged that President Mansour is about to legitimize the presence of a single Jew in

'Palestine.' He's hell-bent on doing everything he can to disrupt the peace process, and if that means killing a whole lot of innocent people, then he figures, so be it."

At that, she looked at her watch and stood. "Well, gentlemen, it's been a pleasure, but it's late, and I'm afraid I've got to go," she said. "I fly back to Tel Aviv around noon. If you're smart, you'll come with me."

Omar and I stood as well.

"Thank you, Yael," I said, taking her hand in mine. "It's been a lovely evening."

"Let's do it again soon," she said and then winked at me.

"I'd like that," I replied.

We exchanged numbers. I said I'd call my editor and get back to her as quickly as possible. Then I offered to give her a ride back to the hotel. Given how hard it was now raining, she readily accepted.

"Where's the car?" I asked Omar.

"Just up the street a bit," he said.

"Fine, I'll pay our tab and meet you there," I said, trying to get our waiter's attention to bring the bill.

"And I'll get our coats," Yael said.

As she went to find them and Omar headed out into the pouring rain, I gave the waiter my credit card and pulled out my iPhone. There were twenty-seven new e-mails, none of which were useful, so I sent three of my own.

First, I wrote to Youssef Kuttab, a senior advisor to Palestinian president Salim Mansour.

Y—We need to talk. Hearing rumors
a deal is almost done. Eager to know
more. Can I come see you?—JB

If I was going to Tel Aviv, I figured, I might as
well start working on the next story too.

Next, I wrote to Hassan Karbouli, Iraq's minister of the interior. We'd known each other for
years, and typically he'd been quite helpful, so
long as he wasn't quoted. But he'd gone dark for
the last few weeks, and I was getting desperate. If
anyone could help me track down Abu Khalif, it
was Karbouli.

Hassan—This is my fifth e-mail. Where
are you? Running out of time. Must
ask you directly: where is AK being
held? Just interviewed Jamal Ramzy.
Story to run in tomorrow's paper.
Now need to follow up with AK. Have
gone through all the proper channels,
but no one will help me. Know you're
swamped, but asking for your help.
Thanks.—JB

Finally, I sent a quick note to Prince Marwan
Talal in Amman, an uncle of the Jordanian king
and one of His Majesty's most trusted advisors.
Marwan was getting up in years, but because he
had been around so long, he knew everyone in the
region and had his finger on the pulse of all that
was happening.

Your Royal Highness—I need your help.
Trying to track down AK. Planning a
major attack. Solid sources say he has
WMD. Can we talk soon?—JB

A moment later, Yael came back with our coats.
I finished paying the bill and helped her with her
coat, then put mine on as well. We were about
to leave when she realized she had forgotten her
umbrella.

"I'll be right back," she said.

I offered to get it for her, but she insisted it
was no problem. *So much for chivalry,* I thought.
I waited for her by the front door.

Outside, I could see Omar climbing into the
driver's seat of the rental car up the street. But I
wasn't thinking about Omar. My thoughts were
consumed with Yael Katzir. I could still smell her
perfume. I could still feel her lips on my own.
I pulled her business card out of my pocket and
looked it over. It was a simple card, black and
white, bearing only the initials *YK* and a European
mobile number. No Mossad logo. No mention of
the intelligence agency at all. No address or even
post office box number. For a moment, I wondered if the phone number was even real. Then I
started asking myself whether she was at all interested in me or if she had just been doing her job. If
I asked her to dinner in Tel Aviv, might she accept?
If I asked her to join me for a movie, what would
she say? Omar and Hadiya kept telling me it was
time. I kept telling them I wasn't ready. But maybe

they were right. All I knew for certain was I liked this girl. I wanted to see more of her. The moment wasn't convenient. But when would it ever be?

Yael sidled up beside me with her polka-dot umbrella. She slipped her arm through mine and smiled.

"Ready when you are," she said.

"After you," I replied.

As I opened the door for her, I could hear Omar trying to start the car. He turned the engine over several more times, but to no avail. Suddenly a wave of physical and emotional exhaustion washed over me. Frustration, too. I had neither the time nor the energy to hang out while Omar waited for a tow truck, if that's really what was needed. I wanted to get back to the hotel, type up my notes, take a hot shower, and get to bed.

As we stepped out of the café, I glanced to my left to see if any cabs were coming. Unfortunately, it was now almost three in the morning. The streets were empty. There were no cabs to be found. So I looked back at Omar trying to get the thing started and began wondering how long it would take to call for a taxi.

And that's when the Hyundai erupted in a massive explosion.

TOP SECRET

PART
FOUR

23

* * *

I woke up screaming, but this was not a nightmare.

Soaked in sweat, my whole body was shivering. I could see Omar inside the car, trying to start the engine. I could feel Yael at my side, her arm in mine. I could feel the heat and force of the massive explosion, the flames shooting into the sky, glass and shards of metal flying in all directions. I could smell burning gasoline, burning flesh. I could hear the ear-piercing boom. It wasn't distant or hazy or detached. It was as if I were still standing on that street, walking out that doorway. It was real, and it was happening again and again and again.

I sat bolt upright in some bed in some dark room illuminated only by the red numbers of a digital alarm clock that read 2:14 a.m. I looked down and found myself dressed only in my underwear. Disoriented, my heart racing, I had no idea where I was or how I'd gotten there. I was breathing so hard I was in danger of hyperventilating.

Dizzy and nauseated, about to vomit, I lay back down in the bed. The pillow was damp with perspiration, so I turned it over and was relieved to find the other side cooler and dry. I kicked off the covers and tried to get comfortable.

Exhausted, I closed my eyes, desperate to regain a sense of equilibrium. But as soon as I tried to fall back asleep, the explosion replayed all over again.

★   ★   ★

"Good morning, James. Are you awake?"

I heard the voice but could not place it. It was a woman's voice, gentle and comforting, but it also seemed distant and far away. Was it Yael's? Had she survived? Had she found me, come back to rescue me?

Foggy and confused, I tried to open my eyes but my head was pounding terribly. My limbs ached and my breathing was labored.

The woman I saw in the morning light was not Yael. It was a nurse, checking my vital signs and giving me a shot in my left arm.

"Hush," she said. "Don't move. Don't try to get up. It's okay. You're going to be fine."

I passed out again.

★   ★   ★

The next time I opened my eyes, the digital clock said it was 8:56 p.m.

I squinted through the darkness and then noticed the date in a corner of the display as well. I blinked hard and looked again. That couldn't be right, I thought. But sure enough, the date read November 27.

A shot of adrenaline coursed through my system, and once again I sat straight up in bed in the pitch-black of night. *Four days?* It couldn't be. Or was it five? How had so much time gone by so quickly? Where was Omar? I had a story to file. The deadline had long since passed. Allen had to be furious. I had work to do. Where was my laptop? Where were my notes?

My head still ached, but it no longer felt like it was clamped into a vise, being squeezed without mercy. That was progress, and I would take it.

"Good morning, Mr. Collins," a voice off to my left said.

I turned my head and saw three men standing in my hospital room. One was Turkish, probably in his early thirties, medium height, medium build, jet-black hair, spectacles—a physician of some kind, judging from his white lab coat and the stethoscope around his neck. The other two wore suits. They certainly weren't Turkish. From their manner and their wing-tip shoes, they struck me as Americans, probably from the American embassy or consulate. The younger of these two appeared to be in his late twenties, and it was obvious he was packing heat. He stood near the door. He was security. But it was the older of the two—in his midfifties, I guessed—who was talking.

"You're lucky to be alive," he said.

I wasn't sure that was true, but I said nothing.

"I'm Art Harris," he continued. "I'm a special agent with the FBI."

I nodded.

"Do you know what day it is?"

"The twenty-seventh."

"Do you know the month?"

"November."

"But you read that off the clock radio, correct?"

I nodded again.

"Do you know where you are?"

"Looks like a hospital," I said. "Am I still in Istanbul?"

"You are indeed," Harris said.

But now it was the doctor who spoke as he stepped forward and checked my pulse. "How do you feel, Mr. Collins?"

"I'm fine," I lied. "How soon can I leave?"

"In a few days probably," the doctor said.

"Do I have any broken bones?"

"No," he said. "Fortunately you do not."

"Did I require surgery?"

"Some stitches here and there, but no, surgery wasn't necessary."

"Did I require a blood transfusion?"

"No, nothing like that," he said.

"Then I want to leave today," I said.

"Not quite yet," he replied. "We want to keep you a bit longer for observation. You've been through quite a trauma."

"Perhaps I could have a few minutes alone with Mr. Collins," the man named Harris said.

There was an awkward silence, and then the doctor stepped out of the room, followed by the other FBI agent, who was apparently not there in an investigative capacity. As the door swung open, I noticed two other agents just like him in the hallway.

"Am I under arrest?" I asked.

"Of course not."

"Do you think I did this?"

"No."

"Then why all the suits and guns?"

"Someone's trying to kill you, Mr. Collins," he replied. "My job is to figure out who, and these men have been assigned to protect you."

He handed me a business card. It bore the FBI logo, a local office address, an e-mail address and phone number, and the words *Arthur M. Harris, Special Agent in Charge*.

"What do you remember about the other night?" Harris asked.

I did my best to describe the final moments of watching Omar get into the Hyundai, his efforts to start the car, and the enormous explosion.

"Do you remember being thrown through the plate-glass window of the café?"

I didn't.

"How about the local ambulance crew giving you first aid?"

I shook my head. "I don't remember anything after the explosion until I woke up here."

"What about the woman?" he asked.

"What woman?"

"The woman you and Mr. Fayez were having tea with," Harris said. "The owner says you were leaving the café with her when the bomb went off. We have a description. We have a sketch artist working with several of the witnesses right now. But in all the commotion, she disappeared. I'm hoping you can help us identify her."

My pulse quickened. I wasn't sure what to say.

Was Yael okay? Was she safe? Why had she fled the scene? Didn't she know that would raise suspicions? I supposed she must not have been seriously harmed if she'd had the wherewithal to slip away. Apparently she hadn't turned up in any hospitals or medical clinics in Istanbul, or Harris would have known about it by now. Surely he and his team were canvassing every location. Yael, after all, was either a material witness to a serious crime or a suspect.

Now that I'd had two seconds to think about it, it was clear why she'd fled. She was a senior intelligence agent for the Israeli government, operating in Turkey, which didn't exactly have close working relations with the Israelis at the present time. She didn't want to be interviewed by local Turkish authorities or by the FBI. She didn't want there to be any traces back to the Mossad; that was for sure. So she'd bailed before emergency crews had arrived on the scene. Which meant she didn't want me talking about her.

Still, Harris was a federal agent. I couldn't lie to him. That would be a felony.

"I'm afraid I can't help you," I replied.

"Can't or won't?" Harris asked.

"Look, she's a source—and a confidential one at that," I explained. "She made me promise I wouldn't reveal her identity. I'm sorry."

"Is she American?"

"I really can't say."

"Turkish?"

"Sorry."

"Is she an Arab, Mr. Collins?" Harris pressed. "Someone connected to your trip to Syria?"

"How do you know about that?"

Harris looked confused. "The whole world knows you went to Syria, Mr. Collins," he replied. "You wrote about it on the front page of the *New York Times*."

"The story is already out?"

"What do you mean?" he asked. "Of course it is. It ran several days ago."

Of course it had. I'd been in the hospital four days, which meant the stories on ISIS and Ramzy had already been read by millions around the globe.

I apologized. I was still trying to clear my head and orient myself to all that had happened. But Harris kept pressing.

"What do the initials YK stand for?" he asked.

I was startled but said nothing.

"They were on the business card in your pocket," he explained. "We've tried the phone number. It's local, but it's been disconnected. Imagine that."

"You think my source is trying to kill me?" I asked.

"You tell me."

"It's not possible."

"No?"

"No. She's trying to help me on a very important story."

"About Jamal Ramzy and Abu Khalif?"

"I can't say."

"About ISIS?"

"I told you, I'm not at liberty to tell you anything about her."

"You understand why I'm asking."

"Of course."

"Someone just murdered your colleague," Harris said. "And they were trying to take you out as well."

"And you think she's connected?"

"I don't know what to think, but it's my job to track down every lead," Harris said. "Right now I have a car bombing in Istanbul in front of an all-night café frequented by foreign nationals. I've got a Jordanian reporter for the *New York Times* dead. I've got an American correspondent for the same newspaper who should be dead but isn't and a mysterious woman who has vanished off the face of the earth. No name. No address. No working phone number. Just the initials YK. See what I'm saying?"

"I do, but I can assure you she's trying to help me, not kill me."

"You've known her a long time?"

"No."

"Months, years?"

"No, we just met here in Istanbul."

"But you're vouching for her?"

"I know her boss. He sent her to meet with me."

"You trust him?"

"I do."

Harris said nothing. He just looked at me, and I could see him trying to decide whether I was telling the truth.

"I'm not the kind of person to go around lying to the FBI," I said in my defense.

"I don't know what kind of person you are," Harris replied.

"I tell the truth for a living," I explained. "All I have in this world is my reputation for explaining events to my readers as accurately as I possibly can. That's something I guard very jealously, Mr. Harris."

He nodded, then pulled out a small notebook and a pen and began jotting something down.

"The reason I'm so concerned, Mr. Collins—the reason I'm asking so many questions—is we have evidence that suggests the bombing was the work of an al Qaeda cell."

"Al Qaeda?"

"Yes."

"Not ISIS."

"No."

"What evidence?" I asked.

"The design of the car bomb was distinctive—very similar to those used by al Qaeda in Afghanistan," Harris said. "The explosives used in the bomb have the exact same chemical composition of a bomb used three weeks ago to kill an American diplomat in Kabul—a case that led to the capture of three al Qaeda operatives, all of whom have since confessed."

"But why would al Qaeda want to kill me?" I asked.

"I was going to ask you the same question."

24

★ ★ ★

The moment Harris left, I powered up my iPhone and called Allen MacDonald.

"Thank God," he said when he heard my voice. "How are you feeling?"

"Fine—just a little shaken up," I said. It wasn't exactly true, but I was feeling increasingly desperate to get back in the game. "But I'm devastated by Omar."

"I know," Allen said. "We're all in shock. First Abdel, and now this. It's hitting everyone hard."

"I'd like to go to the funeral," I said.

"For Omar?"

"Of course."

"In Jordan?"

"Where else?"

"I don't think that's a good idea, J. B."

"Why not?"

"Because the FBI thinks al Qaeda is gunning for you."

"They told you that?"

"Told me, and then demanded I not print it," my editor replied.

"Why not?"

"Obviously they're afraid AQ is going to try again," Allen said. "Didn't they send an agent to talk with you? They said they would."

"Yeah, he just left."

"They think someone working for al Qaeda might have spotted you in the airport in Beirut and tipped off the leadership. They say it's not uncommon."

"But why me?"

"Their working theory at the moment is that AQ got wind of your meeting with Ramzy somehow and wanted to stop you from writing your story elevating ISIS," Allen explained.

"Seems a little petty."

"Maybe," Allen said. "But I don't like the idea of you making yourself a target in Amman. I want you on the next plane back to D.C., first thing tomorrow morning."

"They won't let me leave," I said. "The doctor says he wants to keep me for observation."

"I've already spoken to the chief administrator at the hospital. He'll clear your release so long as I promise to put you in an American hospital for a few more days when you get back."

"No, Allen, I need to go meet another source."

"Where?"

"I can't say—but in the Middle East."

"Absolutely not," he shot back. "Are you crazy?"

"I found another source," I explained. "They're going to confirm the WMD story. It's solid. They have proof. But I need to see it in person."

"You're out of your mind. You know that, don't you?"

"Look, I just need twenty-four hours," I insisted. "I'll turn in this story, and then I'll come back."

"No. I've booked you on a flight back to D.C. that leaves in the morning."

"Allen, all I'm asking for is twenty-four hours."

"The answer is no."

"This story is going to win the Pulitzer."

"Not if you're dead."

"I'll be fine."

"Fine like Abdel? Fine like Omar? Nice try. Get on the plane. Then come straight to the office. We'll regroup. I'll go over your notes and we'll figure out our next moves. End of discussion. And don't try to do an end run around me again, J. B. You went into Syria in direct defiance of my orders. You've gotten two of our guys killed. You make one more move like that, and you're fired. Got it?"

Stung by his vehemence, I said nothing.

"Good," he concluded. "See you tomorrow."

I was angry as I hung up the phone. I didn't need a lecture from my editor on how much danger I was in, but to my way of thinking, the very fact people were trying to kill me only reinforced how important these stories were. There was no way I was going to give up, but at that moment I wasn't sure I was in a position to disregard Allen's explicit directive to come back to D.C. And if I was honest, I had to admit that nothing he had said indicated he was trying to stop me from doing the WMD story. He'd said he was willing to review the evidence I'd gathered and figure out what to do next. But for the moment, he was simply trying to save my life. I appreciated that, and there was a part of me that was grateful. But in the end, what did my life matter when tens or hundreds of thousands of other lives—American and Israeli—hung in the balance?

Looking down at my phone, I was amazed to see there were more than twelve hundred e-mails and two hundred text messages waiting for me, along with a few dozen voice messages. The first wave was from colleagues and friends calling to congratulate me on the Ramzy stories, and TV producers inviting me on their weekend talk shows to discuss Ramzy and the rising threat of al Qaeda and ISIS.

The second wave of messages—and the overwhelming majority, by far—were people checking on me after reading the front-page *Times* story that ran the day after the Ramzy piece, describing the car bombing in Istanbul. There were messages from correspondents and bureau chiefs all over the world. The White House press secretary had called. So had several members of Congress, including the chairmen of both the House and Senate select intelligence committees. There were also messages from a wide range of sources at the Pentagon and the CIA, including Jack Vaughn, the current CIA director, even though he'd specifically warned me not to go. Again, I was grateful and touched by the messages I read and listened to. But I couldn't let myself get bogged down in it all.

I needed time to think, not type e-mails and write thank-you notes and chitchat on the phone.

I sent a quick text message to my mom, letting her know I was all right and that I'd call her when I got back to the States. I deleted a voice-mail message from Matt and an e-mail from Laura. Then I tapped out a generic e-mail thanking everyone for their kind words and assuring them I was okay and would be back on the beat soon. I BCC'd my entire contact list and hit Send, then copied the message and pasted it into all the text messages and hit Send over and over again.

Noticeably absent were any messages from Prince Marwan Talal in Amman or Ismail Tikriti in Baghdad. That bothered me. I'd always been good to both men. We'd helped each other in the past. Why were they ducking me now?

Eventually I came across a text from Robert Khachigian. The onetime director of Central Intelligence had responded to my urgent request for a meeting by saying he'd be happy to meet but was leaving for Asia on Monday.

That was only two days away. **Can we talk by phone?** I wrote back to him. **When's best for you?**

Next I found three e-mails from Youssef Kuttab, senior advisor to the Palestinian chairman. I had e-mailed him about the peace process from the café here in Istanbul just before the explosion. *It is always a pleasure to have coffee with you, my friend,* he wrote in his first response to my inquiry. *Call me when you get into town.* The second was more urgent. *I thought you were coming to Ramallah. Things are getting complicated. We need to sit down in person. Where are you?* The third read simply: *Just heard the news. No words—are you okay?*

"Getting complicated"? What did that mean? I had no idea, but whatever it was, one thing was clear: I wasn't going to find out by e-mail or phone. I was going to have to go to Ramallah and sit with Kuttab personally, or I wasn't going to hear it at all.

Not sure how to thread that needle just yet, I focused on two text messages from Hassan Karbouli, whom I'd been trying to contact about finding Abu Khalif. His first message, written the day the Ramzy story was published, read, **Good to hear from you, my friend. Wish I could help. Sorry.** I wasn't sure whether to laugh or throw the phone across the room. Karbouli was the Iraqi interior minister, for crying out loud. He oversaw the country's bureau of prisons. If he wanted to help me, he certainly could. He answered only to the prime minister and Allah.

If Karbouli's first text message was infuriating, however, the second was ominous. Dated the day the car bombing story was reported, it was brief: **Drop AK story. Not safe.**

"Not safe"? I wondered. *For whom—for me or for him?*

Perhaps both.

To be sure, Karbouli had always struck me as a good man in a tough spot. Born and raised near Mosul, he was one of the few Sunni Muslims serving in a predominantly Shia government in Baghdad. In the past I had always felt I could trust him. But now I wasn't sure. Was this a warning or a threat?

Either way, the two messages in combination had me firing on all cylinders. This guy knew exactly where the emir of ISIS was, I realized, and if I could get to Hassan Karbouli, I just might be able to get to Abu Khalif.

25

* * *

My flight out of Istanbul departed at 8:15 in the morning.

Which meant I had to be at the airport by six.

Which meant I had to be up, showered, and dressed by four thirty.

The three agents Special Agent in Charge Harris had assigned to keep me safe at the hospital graciously offered to drive me to the airport and take me to my gate out of an abundance of caution. They also returned my luggage and briefcase, which I'd left at the Hotel Ibrahim Pasha.

After a grueling mechanical delay, I was finally hurtling down the runway on an Airbus A320 headed for Frankfurt. From there, I'd have a tight connection to catch my flight to Washington Dulles. If all went well, I'd be back on American soil by four o'clock that afternoon, local time.

Then what? I had no idea.

* * *

There were storms over Frankfurt.

My flight was late and I had to run to get to

my gate on time. But that's when I got an urgent text from Khachigian.

Grave development. Need to meet ASAP.

I wondered if I should stop running and text him back immediately. But I could hear the last call going out for passengers on Lufthansa flight 418 to Washington Dulles International Airport. I was in danger of missing my connection, so I kept running. A few minutes later, I finally made it to the gate and was the last person to board the plane. The moment I found my seat and buckled in, I immediately texted him back.

What's happening?

Five seconds later I got his reply. **Can't explain by text.**

Call?

Too sensitive.

Soon, the text messages between us were flying back and forth.

Topic?

ISIS.

Listening.

Need to meet tonight.

Can't—in Germany, but heading back shortly.

Fine, I'll go to the Post.

What??? Absolutely not.

Can't wait. Story won't hold. I have to get it out. And my trip to Asia has been bumped up. I leave tonight.

Then let's talk now by phone.

No. I can't.

I touch down at Dulles at four. How about dinner?

Sorry. Too late. I'm going to the Post.

Robert, you owe me this.

I don't.

I've done everything you asked. Nearly got myself killed on this story you told me to pursue. Lost two colleagues. Now you're going to the Post???

Suddenly Khachigian wasn't writing back. A minute went by. Then two. I was dying. They were closing the cabin door. A flight attendant was asking me to power down my phone.

You still there? I wrote.

Another minute went by.

Yes, he finally replied.

And?

Thinking.

Hold on the story, please, I insisted. **Meet me at Union Station.**

There was another long pause. A minute. Two. We were beginning to taxi. A second flight attendant was insisting I shut off my phone. Three minutes. Finally, after four minutes my phone chirped with a new incoming text.

Fine. Union Station. Center Café. 7:30 p.m. Don't be late.

26

* * *

After repeated weather delays, Lufthansa flight 418 finally landed at Dulles.

As we taxied to the terminal, I pulled out my grandfather's pocket watch. It was now 5:35 Sunday afternoon, a full ninety minutes after our scheduled arrival time.

My nerves were a wreck. I still needed to clear passport control and customs, race home to shower and change before making it to the *Times* bureau at 1627 I Street downtown to meet with Allen for who knew how long, then arrive at Union Station by seven thirty. Otherwise whatever scoop Khachigian was saving for me was going to the *Washington Post*.

With a full flight out of Istanbul, my protective detail hadn't been able to travel with me. But they'd assured me that I'd be met by agents from the D.C. bureau the moment I arrived. As I stepped off the plane, however, there was no one waiting for me. I had no intention of staying around.

Already I was checking flights to Tel Aviv later

that night or the next day at the latest on the working assumption that Allen would see the light and let me go once we'd talked through the evidence I'd gathered so far. At the same time, I knew I needed to call my mom. I needed to let her hear my voice and know for sure I was really okay. She would insist I come up to Maine, but that wasn't going to happen. Not for a while. At least not until I got back from Tel Aviv and Amman. After all, I had to visit with Omar's widow. I had to give her my condolences and tell her what an amazing friend her husband had been to me.

But the truth was, at that moment my thoughts were mostly on Yael. Where was she? Was she safe? Was she okay? I'd already tried the number on her card. Harris was right. It was no longer working. I'd also sent a text message to Ari Shalit asking about her and asking for permission to come see him as soon as possible. So far, I'd heard nothing back.

As I worked my way through the airport, I noticed a crowd gathering around a TV set. When I heard the trademark voice of James Earl Jones saying, "This is CNN Breaking News," I stopped immediately to see what was happening.

"CNN has just learned that Ayman al-Zawahiri, the head of al Qaeda since 2011, is dead," said a female anchor in the Atlanta studios while raw, unedited video of a smoldering crater on a crowded street and the burning wreckage of what appeared to be an SUV played on the screen. "Several sources are telling CNN the al Qaeda leader was killed in a drone strike, but at least one former CIA analyst says the images are more consistent with a car bombing."

I quickly checked the headlines on my phone. Agence France-Presse was quoting an unnamed source inside Pakistani intelligence confirming that Zawahiri and two of his bodyguards had been killed less than an hour earlier as a result of an explosion, but the story offered no further details on how the al Qaeda leader's car had exploded. A quick check of the AP and Reuters wires indicated that neither the Pentagon nor the State Department was commenting, but an unnamed White House source—cited only as a senior aide to President Taylor—said that while U.S. officials were awaiting confirmation from the Pakistani government, they were "cautiously optimistic" that "a great victory over terrorism has been achieved."

Meanwhile, I could hear an analyst on CNN saying, "This could prove to be the beginning of the end of al Qaeda," and adding that under President Taylor's leadership, al Qaeda was being "systematically dismantled."

I hoped it was true. I feared it was not.

Grabbing my briefcase and carry-on luggage, I bought a cup of coffee and a copy of the Sunday editions of both the *New York Times* and the *Washington Post*, hailed a taxi, and gave the driver the address of my apartment in Arlington. As we pulled out of the airport and headed southeast on the toll road toward D.C., the lead headline from the *Post* caught my eye.

**President Warns Israelis, Palestinians
of "Catastrophic Consequences"
if Peace Talks Fail: Aides Say
Administration Will Reconsider
Aid Levels if Deal Not Struck Soon**

Written by the *Post*'s top White House and
State Department correspondents, the article was
the latest installment in the ongoing media narrative over the past month or so that the Mideast
peace talks were floundering, that the parties were
not taking the process seriously, and that both
sides seemed to be trying to paint the other as
the intransigent and irresponsible one. This version added a bit of spice to the stew with the
idea that the White House might actually reduce
U.S. military aid to Israel, which averaged over
$3 billion a year, and might also cut aid to the
Palestinians, which averaged about a half billion
dollars annually.

The story certainly fit the conventional wisdom inside the Beltway, but was it true? I was
now starting to wonder whether just the opposite
dynamic was in motion. Yael had insisted that the
parties were, in fact, incredibly close to a deal and
that the consummation of a comprehensive peace
treaty actually made the prospect of a major series
of terrorist attacks more likely, not less so. Who
was right?

The peace talks were not my beat, per se.
I focused primarily on national security and terrorism stories, but obviously the two were related,

and the deeper I read into the *Post* story, the more curious, and perhaps more cynical, I became. Was the White House trying to pull off the head fake of the century? With all the carefully timed leaks about how badly things were going, was the administration driving down expectations so that the announcement by the president of a final, comprehensive peace treaty between the Israelis and Palestinians would give him a political bounce of epic proportions?

A text message came in. It was from the senior producer at the *Today Show*. She wanted me on the following morning to discuss my Jamal Ramzy article and the terror attack that had nearly taken my life in Istanbul. She was also interested to know whether I thought the president had ordered the hit on Zawahiri as retaliation for what had happened to Omar and me.

As I checked my other messages, I found interview requests from a dozen other media outlets, from *Good Morning America* to *60 Minutes*. I had no interest in going on any of them. I wasn't a pundit. I was a foreign correspondent. And I didn't plan to spend a second longer on American soil than I absolutely had to.

I dialed my mom. She picked up on the fourth ring. She was ecstatic to hear from me and wanted every detail. I was guarded, not wanting to worry her any further than she must already be, even though I knew she'd been reading all the coverage of the attack on me that she possibly could. She asked me, of course, to come up to Maine that night. I said, of course, that I couldn't.

"When can you get here, honey? You missed Thanksgiving. I didn't celebrate it either. I was too worried about you. But we could celebrate together. I'll make you a big feast."

"Thanks, Mom, but I'm not sure how soon I can get up there. There's an awful lot going on."

"I know, but sweetheart, it's been so long, and I . . . well . . . you know, I miss you."

She sounded so deflated.

"I know, Mom, and I miss you. I'll come visit. I promise. But it looks like I need to go to Tel Aviv and Amman first."

"You're going to Amman?" she asked, seeming to brighten.

"I hope so," I said.

"When?"

"In the next few days."

"Great," she said. "You can see Matty!"

I took a deep breath. "I don't know if I'll have time, Mom. It's not going to be a pleasure trip. It's for work."

"But, James, obviously you can make some time to see your only brother."

"I'll try."

"Good. He wrote to you recently, right?"

"I don't know. Did he?"

"He told me he was going to."

"Maybe he's been busy."

"Maybe you're not reading your mail."

"I was in Syria, Mom, and then someone tried to kill me."

"That's no excuse," she said without a hint of

irony. "You really ought to talk to your brother. You two need each other."

"I'm sure he and Annie are doing just fine without me."

"They are fine, but the fact is they miss you, young man."

"Okay, Mom."

"Really, James, would it kill you to return his notes or to call him now and again? He's your older brother. He loves you and he's worried about you."

"I'd really rather not talk about it."

"That's the understatement of the year."

"Nevertheless . . ." I glanced out the window of the cab. Route 267, the toll road, was now merging with 66. We'd be in Arlington any moment. Which was good. I desperately needed a shower and a change of clothes.

"So, any word from Laura?" my mom suddenly asked.

Every muscle in my body tensed at the very name. "No," I said.

We drove a bit longer.

"Nothing at all?"

"No."

There was no way I was going to tell her I'd just deleted an e-mail from my ex-wife and had no idea what it said.

"I'm sorry, Mom. That chapter is over."

"I'm so sorry, too, Son. Guess I always thought she was the one."

I didn't respond. What was there to say?

"Listen, Mom, I gotta go," I said instead. "I'll call you again tomorrow."

"You promise?"

"I promise."

"Okay. Bye."

She didn't sound like she believed me. I couldn't really blame her. Nevertheless, I said good-bye and hung up. At that moment, though, I realized that rather than exiting into the city of Arlington—toward my apartment—as I'd instructed, the driver was staying on 66. In a moment, we'd be heading out of Virginia and into the District of Columbia. It was not only the exact opposite of where I wanted to go, but given the challenges of D.C. traffic, the error was going to take forever to correct. I was as annoyed as I was confused. I leaned forward and told the driver he was making a mistake.

"I have my orders," he replied.

"What orders?" I asked. "What are you talking about?"

But the driver didn't answer. The car accelerated. The doors of the car abruptly locked as the Plexiglas screen between the front and back seats suddenly closed.

"What in the world are you doing?" I yelled, but still the driver did not answer.

I demanded he turn the car around, but he ignored me. I pulled out my phone to call 911, but now there was no signal. That was impossible, of course. We were heading into the epicenter of the American government. There was plenty of cell coverage to be had. The only possible explanation was that the driver had a device that was jamming my phone. He must have turned it on right after I hung up with my mom.

I looked at him. He briefly glanced at me in the rearview mirror. Furious and becoming frightened now, I demanded he take me home, but even if he could hear me through the Plexiglas, he did not alter his course.

We were not going to Arlington. That much was clear. I had no idea where we were going instead, but given all that had happened in recent days, I found myself fighting panic.

Who was this guy? Who was he working for? And what did they want with me?

Before I knew it, we'd passed the Lincoln Memorial.

We headed east on Constitution Avenue. Then we took a sharp left on Eighteenth Street and started zigzagging through a series of side streets before barreling down a ramp into a dark parking garage, tires squealing like a stunt car's in a movie. Down, down we went, lower and lower into the bowels of the garage, and this guy was driving far faster than was either normal or safe. I was certain we were going to plow into a car coming up in the opposite direction, but no sooner had the thought crossed my mind than he hit the brakes and brought us to an abrupt halt on a deserted level.

The doors automatically unlocked. Immediately both rear passenger doors opened and I became aware that a half-dozen men in dark suits were standing around the taxi. They looked and acted like federal agents, but we were a long way from the Treasury Department and even farther from the Hoover Building.

"Mr. Collins, please step out of the vehicle," one of them said.

"Who are you?" I asked. "What's going on here?"

"Please step out, sir. And follow me."

"Why? To where?"

"Just follow me."

I couldn't decide if I was really in danger. This was Washington, after all, not Syria. In any case, it was clear I didn't have a choice, and by nature I was insatiably curious. They hadn't killed me yet. The deserted level of a downtown parking garage on a Sunday evening seemed as good a place to do it as any. But if that wasn't the objective, what was? It seemed unlikely that Abu Khalif or Jamal Ramzy had an entire group of American-looking thugs operating out of central Washington.

I got out of the cab and followed the agent who was doing all the talking. As I did, the rest stepped behind and around me. We entered a stairwell, but rather than ascend to street level, we went down a flight of stairs. The leader unlocked what appeared at first to be a utility closet but actually led to a tunnel. We stepped through the doorway into the tunnel and proceeded on our way. As we walked, I had a flashback to being taken to see Ramzy, and the farther we went, the more curious I got.

A few minutes later, the point man unlocked and opened another door, and then we were standing in a nondescript vestibule of some sort— white walls, black marble floors, a high ceiling, and a small surveillance camera mounted over the entrance to an elevator, whose door was already open as if waiting for us to arrive. One of the men patted me down and then four of them escorted me into the elevator, and soon we were ascending.

When the door finally opened, I stepped out and couldn't believe where I was.

I was standing in the second-floor private residence of the White House.

27

The president of the United States stepped forward.

"Welcome to the people's house, Mr. Collins. I'm Harrison Taylor. It's an honor to meet you."

"It's an honor to meet you as well, Mr. President," I said, shaking his hand.

For all my years working in the media, I had never actually met this president. Years before, I had interviewed several of his predecessors, but as a foreign correspondent for the *Times* who spent most of my time abroad, there was no particular reason for me to have met this one. At six feet four inches, he appeared even taller in person than he did on television, and he was certainly a distinguished-looking Southern gentleman. Slender, even lanky, with jet-black hair graying at the temples, a firm jaw, and piercing blue inquisitive eyes, Harrison Taylor was the great-grandson of a famous governor of North Carolina. He himself had made a fortune building a software company in the Research Triangle just outside of Raleigh before selling the company for a half-billion dollars, winning a

Senate seat, and later winning the governorship in a landslide. Now this policy maverick—a fiscal conservative but social liberal—was president of the United States.

But he was in serious political trouble. The U.S. economy was stalled. His immigration reform agenda had likewise stalled in Congress. His foreign policy was in disarray. And his approval ratings were drifting ever downward and were currently in the dangerous midthirties. He had ridden into the Oval Office on a wave of populist sentiment and had benefited from a late-breaking scandal in the Republican nominee's campaign, but more recently he had struggled to find his political sea legs, and I found it striking to see up close how much the last several years in office had worn him.

"Of course, you know Jack here quite well," the president said, turning to Jack Vaughn, the former chairman of the Senate intelligence committee who was now director of the Central Intelligence Agency.

"I do, indeed, Mr. President," I said, shaking Vaughn's hand. "Good to see you, Jack."

"Good to see you, too, J. B.," Vaughn replied. "So glad you're okay."

"Thank you, sir."

"Bet you're wishing now you'd followed my advice, eh?"

"Now, now," the president interjected. "There'll be no 'See, I told you so' speeches in this house, Jack. Not today. This is going to be a friendly conversation. Mr. Collins wasn't exactly expecting this meeting, but I'm grateful he's here. So let's be on our best behavior. Fair enough?"

Jack smiled. We both nodded.

The president led us from the foyer by the elevator to the Yellow Oval Room. I had seen pictures but had never had the privilege of actually standing in the distinctive room before. It was here that Franklin Delano Roosevelt had famously been relaxing when he was told by aides that the Japanese had bombed Pearl Harbor on December 7, 1941. Most of the chief executives who followed Roosevelt tended to allow their First Ladies to use the parlor for their own meetings, but I had read somewhere not long ago that President Taylor liked to use it for more personal and in-depth conversations with visiting heads of state.

The room was certainly less formal, and thus perhaps less intimidating, than the Oval Office. But it was still more exquisite in real life than in any of the pictures I'd seen. The walls were painted a lovely pale yellow, and the couches and chairs were all upholstered with a fabric that was paler still. The room featured a high ceiling, a marble fireplace on the east wall, and two candelabras, one on each end of the mantel. Two large couches faced each other perpendicular to the fireplace. Below our feet was a thick, rich carpet—pale yellow, of course—with an intricate design of flowers and swirls of red and blue and green and a half-dozen other colors.

But what really caught my eye was the door to the Truman Balcony. Ever the politician, as soon as the president saw me admiring it, he marched right over, opened the door, and invited Jack and me to step outside.

A bit embarrassed that I was acting more like a tourist than a hardened, grizzled foreign correspondent, I nevertheless accepted the invitation. I'd seen this view in movies, of course, but it was quite something to be overlooking the South Lawn of the White House, the Washington Monument in the distance, the Potomac River beyond that. It was a stunningly beautiful sight, surely the most beautiful in Washington. What's more, the gleaming green-and-white Marine One helicopter was idling outside.

"We just got back from meetings at Camp David," Jack noted.

"Discussing what?" I asked, fishing for a story.

"You," the president said.

I couldn't help but chuckle, sure he was kidding.

He was not.

"Look, J. B., we need to talk candidly," the president said.

"What about?" I asked warily.

"Your stories on Jamal Ramzy and ISIS," he replied. "They've made a lot of waves in this city. They've got European leaders on edge. I've gotten two calls from Lavi in Jerusalem. He's getting heat from his cabinet. You've created a firestorm."

Vaughn added, "Everyone's trying to figure out what ISIS is up to, what their next moves are, what their next target is."

"Especially now that you've taken out Abu Khalif's chief rival," I noted, hoping to get some insight into the president's decision to assassinate Zawahiri.

"Everything we say here this evening is off the record," the president said. "Is that understood?"

"That would be a shame," I replied. "People are eager for your thoughts on the strike on Zawahiri. Why not go on the record with me right now?"

The president smiled one of those pitifully fake political smiles. "I'm afraid I can't make any news for you on that, Mr. Collins," he said. "I'll make my thoughts known to the American people at the appropriate time. But this is a very delicate moment. And that's why I've asked you here today. So are we agreed all this is off the record?"

What choice did I have? "Of course, Mr. President."

"I have your word?"

"You do."

"Good, now let's go back inside. You survived Homs and Istanbul. I don't want you catching pneumonia outside the White House."

We went back in. The president sat in an ornate wooden armchair near the fireplace. When Jack retired to one of the couches, I took my place on the other, directly across from him. A steward served us all coffee and then stepped out of the room. Two Secret Service agents took up their posts by the doors, but other than that we were alone, and the president turned his attention to me.

"Look, Mr. Collins, things are very sensitive at the moment because . . . well . . . because the Israelis and Palestinians are about to sign a final, comprehensive peace treaty and create a Palestinian state once and for all."

"Good—my sources are telling me the truth," I said, moving quickly, not wanting to let the president box me in. "That's a story I'll be happy to print."

"You already have this?" the president asked, his face not quite incredulous but trending in that direction.

"There are a few more people to talk to, but yes, I'm getting close to running with it," I replied. It wasn't entirely true, but I rationalized that it wasn't a complete lie, either.

"No. You cannot print that yet," the president stated. "The key to success is absolute secrecy."

"I'm sorry, sir; I can't promise that," I noted calmly.

"You have to," he replied. "We agreed this conversation is off the record."

"And it is," I said. "But that doesn't apply to original reporting I'm already doing."

"It absolutely does," the president insisted. "This is a matter of national security."

"And a matter of enormous public interest," I countered.

"Mr. Collins," Vaughn interjected, "you just gave the president of the United States your word that nothing that was said in this conversation was on the record."

"And I will honor my word," I said, doing my best to stay calm. "But I walked in here with sources already telling me the deal was done and the treaty was about to be announced, and I'm sorry—I'm not obligated to ignore information I had before I walked into this room."

The president and CIA director looked like they'd just been hit with a two-by-four.

"J. B., listen to me. A leak at this moment would be devastating," Vaughn said, clearly looking for a way out of the impasse. "But I'll make you a deal."

He glanced at the president, then looked back at me. "We'll leak the final details of the treaty and the behind-the-scenes story of how it came together once everything is ready. We'll give you an exclusive one-day jump on your competitors. You have my word. But you need to sit on this for the moment. The secretary of state is just crossing the t's and dotting the i's with leaders on both sides and with King Abdullah of Jordan. But we need a little more time. A leak, especially right now, could destroy everything."

"How much time do you need?" I asked.

It was a good offer—an excellent one, actually, especially since I was bluffing. I'd gotten a lead on the treaty story from Yael, and I was fairly certain I could get more out of Ari Shalit in the next few days in exchange for doing him the favor of getting the WMD story out. But I didn't have anything else at the moment, and the president and CIA director were offering me an exquisite gift on a silver platter. Why not take it, especially since the peace process was neither my beat nor even of particular interest to me. I wanted the chemical weapons story. I wanted an interview with Abu

Khalif. And to get either or both, I was going to need to stay focused.

Vaughn again looked at the president. "Two weeks, maybe three, tops," he said at last. "Like I said, the negotiators are ironing out final details. But I think we could see a White House signing ceremony before Christmas."

"That's less than a month," I said.

"Exactly. That's why we have to keep a lid on this thing," the president said. "We are engaged in the most delicate, high-stakes high-wire act in the history of modern diplomacy. My predecessors haven't been able to get it done. There was many a night I didn't think I could get it done either. But we're there. So do we have a deal?"

I looked into the president's eyes and then into Vaughn's. Why was this so easy? Why were they giving me so much, so fast? They wanted something else. I decided I'd pocket one story and brace myself for whatever was coming next. "Yes, sir, Mr. President."

"You won't write any stories on the peace treaty until we give you the go-ahead?"

"You'll give me a true exclusive, including the first journalist's look at the treaty itself, and no one else gets the story before me?"

"Yes," the president said.

"Then yes."

We shook hands, and then the president dropped the hammer. "Now, we need to talk about your other story."

"Which one?"

"I understand you're about to run a story that

al Qaeda has captured a cache of Syrian chemical weapons."

"Well, ISIS—not al Qaeda—but yes," I said.

"That's a problem as well."

"How so?"

"It could trigger a wave of panic right at the moment when we're trying to help Arabs and Jews make some very hard, very painful concessions," Vaughn said.

"I'm asking you not to print it," the president said. "Not yet. Not until after the peace treaty is signed, sealed, and delivered. I'm willing to make a deal on that as well, but I really have to insist you not publish anything before the end of the year."

I was floored. The story was basically finished. In less than forty-eight hours, possibly sooner, I'd have my third confirmation. The story was ready to go, and it was going to be huge.

"Well, gentlemen, I appreciate your concerns, but I'm afraid we're going to move forward."

"And risk blowing up this peace deal?"

"Sir, if this deal is the real thing, surely it will have to be strong enough to survive a newspaper story that doesn't fit your 'peace in our times' narrative," I replied. "And anyway, it's ISIS that's going to try to blow up your peace deal, not me."

"It's not just about public relations," the president said. "The larger problem is that the facts aren't there."

"Actually, yes, they are, sir," I responded. "I have confirmation from high-ranking officials in three different governments, including your own."

"It's a mirage."

"With all due respect, it isn't. I've personally seen satellite photos, drone video, listened to phone intercepts, read intercepted e-mails. Believe me, Mr. President, the story is solid."

"I'm afraid that's where you're wrong," the president said. "Jack?"

I looked into President Taylor's eyes. He didn't look angry. He didn't look frustrated with me. Nor did I feel like he was necessarily trying to spin me. In fact, he genuinely looked like he was trying to help me. But the man was a politician and thus, by practice if not by definition, an actor. He knew how to persuade people, and I'd been "handled" by enough people in Washington over the years to have become even more cynical than I was already naturally inclined to be. I turned to Vaughn and braced myself for the pitch.

"Look, J. B., you can't quote either of us on this, but the intel you've been given is, in fact, solid," the CIA director began.

"Solid?" I asked, wondering if I could possibly have just heard him correctly.

"That's right; it's solid."

"Well, isn't that what I just said?"

"Hold on; just listen to me," Vaughn continued. "What you've seen and heard is accurate. I'm sure of that. That's not the problem."

"What is?"

"It's incomplete."

"Meaning what?" I asked, wishing I had a notepad with me.

"Meaning the president and I have seen a lot more intel than you have, and we're not convinced."

"Why not?"

"Because the data doesn't add up."

"Okay, I'm sorry, but I'm not following you, Jack. Stipulate the facts we're talking about so I know we're on the same page." I was sure Vaughn wouldn't take the bait, but I was certainly willing to go fishing anyway.

Vaughn looked at the president, who, to my shock, nodded his assent.

"When you're making sarin gas, you're combining two different chemical precursors," the CIA director explained. "The first is isopropanol. The second is methylphosphonyl difluoride. You don't mix them together until you're ready to kill people. Why?"

"Because you don't want to take an unnecessary risk."

"Exactly. You don't want the whole thing to blow up in your face. So you store the two different chemicals separately—on the same base, but in different buildings. Okay?"

"Okay."

"Now, we know the ISIS rebels hit the Syrian base near Aleppo. We know that historically the base was a storage site for WMD, among other types of weapons. We know that for many years, both chemicals were stored on the base. But that was years ago. We know the rebels removed several hundred crates on trucks and that they sent those trucks to at least five different locations, maybe more. What we don't know is what exactly was in those crates and on those trucks."

I was surprised but pleased to hear Vaughn

confirm this much. I couldn't quote him, of course. But now I knew with even greater certainty that my story—nearly entirely written and waiting on my hard drive—was accurate.

"You think the rebels were carting away office equipment and linens?" I asked.

"I don't know what they were carting away, and neither do you."

"What about all the phone intercepts after the rebels seized the base?"

"What do they actually say?" Vaughn asked. "One rebel tells his commander his men have captured the 'crown jewels.' Another boasts, 'Allah will be most praised.' A third e-mails Jamal Ramzy and says, 'Zionists will suffer.'"

"Right. So why do you think they're so happy?"

"Again, we can't know for sure. The intercepts are intriguing, but they're not proof," Vaughn continued. "And remember, while it's theoretically possible that the Assad regime hid a cache of chemical weapons at that base, the Syrians say they haven't had any WMD in more than a decade. The U.N. inspectors went there. They searched the place, and they certified that there were no chemical weapons. The Syrians claim they gave up all of their stockpiles to the U.N. to be removed from the country and destroyed, and the U.N. weapons inspectors say they feel reasonably confident that the Syrians did exactly that."

"You're going to rest your case on 'reasonably confident'?" I asked.

"You're going to rest *your* case on nothing

but circumstantial evidence that's weak at best?" Vaughn countered.

"Look," I said, "the agency is gun-shy after the blown call in Iraq. I get it. But here you have jihadists seizing a known WMD base in Syria and boasting they have the 'crown jewels' and saying they are going to annihilate the Jews, and you want the *New York Times* to back off the story?"

"You're not listening to me, J. B.," Vaughn protested. "I'm telling you the case is circumstantial at best. Might ISIS have chemical WMD? Yes. I grant you that. And it scares the daylights out of the president and me. Believe me. We can't sleep at night. We're doing everything we can to confirm this story, but so far all we have are a bunch of dots. In my position, I can't connect them based on gut instinct. I have to have ironclad proof. I can't tell the president of the United States that my circumstantial evidence is a slam dunk. And I don't want the American people—or the Israelis and Palestinians—to live in sudden fear that we, or they, are about to get hit by chemical weapons of mass destruction unless I know that for certain. I don't think that's right. I don't think that's moral. And deep down, I don't think you do either. Am I wrong?"

28

★ ★ ★

I checked my grandfather's pocket watch again.

The meeting at the White House was finally over. But it was now 7:43 p.m. The former CIA director had already been waiting for thirteen minutes, and I was mortified.

Even in retirement, Robert Khachigian was an important and powerful man. He certainly had a far tighter schedule than mine. He was leaving the country in just a few hours. What's more, he had been a friend of my family's for years, and I had given him my word I would not be late. Twice I had called his mobile phone from the car to tell him what was happening, but he hadn't picked up either time. Now my guilt was spiking along with my heart rate.

A cold late-November drizzle had descended upon Washington. I had neither a warm coat nor an umbrella. I was reminded of meeting Yael in Istanbul just a few nights before, and the very thought made me feel even worse. I wanted to see her again. But how?

The black armored Chevy Suburban I was

riding in pulled to a stop. Four FBI agents newly assigned to me jumped out first, scanned the area, and then gave me the green light. I grabbed my briefcase and dashed into Union Station, the mammoth train depot located just a few blocks from the Capitol building. I raced to the Center Café, a restaurant appropriately positioned in the bull's-eye of the gargantuan Main Hall, and prayed Khachigian was still there.

"Yes, he's waiting for you upstairs," the maître d' said. "Right this way, Mr. Collins."

Every table on the ground level was taken, and there was a line of tourists waiting to be seated as we headed upstairs. One of the agents assigned to me took up a position at the base of the winding staircase. The other three followed me to the second level.

Khachigian was sitting alone at a table for two on the far side of the restaurant. He did not look happy, though as a rule he was a fairly serious guy anyway. As I greeted him, I apologized profusely for my tardiness, but he waved it all off and told me to have a seat.

"You're mad at me," I said.

"No," he demurred.

"You look mad," I insisted.

"I'm not mad, but we don't have much time," he said. "We have a real nightmare developing. But how are you?"

A consummate professional, but always the gentleman.

The graying, bespectacled man before me was the elder statesman of the Washington intelligence community, and he was dressed to the nines. He wore a dark-blue suit, a light-blue monogrammed dress shirt with gold cuff links, suspenders, and a snappy lavender bow tie, which seemed to me a relic of an earlier age. At his feet stood a small suitcase. Clearly he was heading to the airport straight from this meeting.

"I've been better," I said, not sure how much detail he wanted.

"Secret Service?" he asked, referring to the two agents who were now sitting at a table directly behind him and the third standing by the top of the stairs.

"FBI," I replied. "To be honest, I'm not exactly sure if they're protecting me or keeping tabs on me."

"Both," he said without hesitation. "Pain?"

"Sorry?"

"Are you in pain?"

"Oh, well, a little."

"Percocet?"

"A lot."

"Be careful."

"I will."

"I mean it."

"I got it."

"Addictive personality and all."

"Yeah, thanks. Really, I'm fine."

Khachigian and my family went way back, and he'd always seemed to take a liking to me. Almost like a surrogate grandfather, he'd kept an eye on me. In his youth he was a nonofficial cover operative for the Central Intelligence Agency. He was based primarily in Eastern Europe and traveled in and out of the Soviet Union during the Cold War. When he retired from the intelligence business, he returned to Maine, the state where he had been born and raised. He and his wife, Mary, were from Bangor, a bit to the northwest of us in Bar Harbor. They had known my grandparents and later my parents and had become fairly close family friends. After practicing law for a few years, Khachigian ran for office and won the seat serving the Second Congressional District. Later he went on to win a Senate seat and wound up chairman of the Senate Select Committee on Intelligence. Eventually, he was appointed to the top spot at the CIA and served for almost three years before retiring for real.

Over the years, my grandparents—and my mom—contributed to his various political campaigns. In college, I did an internship in his Senate office. During election cycles, my mom often volunteered to put up signs and answer phones and go door to door leafleting for him. She and Mary Khachigian became quite close. They were pen pals and loved to host an annual Christmas tea together for friends and political supporters—that is, until Mary passed away of ovarian cancer three years ago.

Interestingly enough, Robert—called Bob by his friends but always "Mr. Khachigian" by me—had never been a source of mine for all those years. He probably would have agreed if I had asked, but I never had. There was no question he was a treasure trove. He obviously had a great deal of insider details from his various government positions, and I certainly would have benefited from access to all that behind-the-scenes information, especially in the early years when I was building my career. But it never seemed right. I never wanted to cross the line, never wanted to make him think I would trade on a personal relationship. I actually felt uncomfortable even when my mother asked Mary to get me the internship way back when.

I'll never forget the day Khachigian called me out of the blue and asked me to meet him in London, where he was giving a lecture the next evening. At the time I was still a young reporter, and the timing was hardly ideal, and he refused to give me even a hint as to what he was thinking or why he wanted me to come. Nevertheless, I found myself so intrigued that I immediately booked the flight.

Upon my arrival, Khachigian picked me up at Heathrow, alone, and drove me to the Dorchester, one of the swankiest hotels in London. There we had a private, intimate dinner with the up-and-coming leader of the Israeli opposition at the time, a man by the name of Daniel Lavi.

"James, this man is going to be the prime minister of Israel soon," Khachigian told me the moment Lavi and I shook hands. "The polls don't show it. Most analysts don't believe it. But I'm telling you right now it's going to happen. And Daniel here specifically asked me to arrange a meeting with you. He's an admirer of your work. Has read it all. Says you're one of the most trustworthy reporters in the biz. I agree. So I decided to introduce you before Daniel's life gets much busier."

The following morning, Khachigian and I drove to the Ritz in the Piccadilly section of London. There he led me up to the Prince of Wales suite (which I later learned went for a jaw-dropping 4,500 pounds per night) and introduced me to an older gentleman who turned out to be Prince Marwan Talal. At the age of seventy-eight, he was an uncle of Jordan's King Abdullah II and a trusted senior advisor to His Majesty. Khachigian seemed unusually pleased by bringing the two of us together.

"James, His Royal Highness is a dear friend and a most faithful, stalwart ally in the fight against the extremists in the epicenter," he told me as the three of us talked over brunch. "He is not a public man. He lives in the shadows, and he prefers it that way. Few people outside His Majesty's inner circle even know his name. But he knows theirs. He knows where all the bodies are buried. And I mean that literally. He has seen all there is in the region—the good, the bad, and the ugly. Confidentially, I will tell you that Prince Marwan is the king's consigliere when it comes to the peace process. He was an advisor to the late King Hussein, God rest his soul, and upon taking the throne, King Abdullah began leaning on this man—his uncle—for counsel. He's a devout Muslim. He is worried for the future of his country and region. And whenever I find myself growing pessimistic about the prospects for peace in the Middle East, I sit with Marwan and drink coffee and eat hummus and become hopeful once again. I don't know why, but I have a feeling that one day—perhaps not too long from now—you two will find it useful to know each other. This is why I wanted to bring you both together now, before the maelstrom comes."

Khachigian's instincts had been remarkable. Daniel Lavi was now not only the head of Israel's Labor Party; he was also the Jewish State's prime minister. He had recently toppled the right-wing government of his predecessor and cobbled together a center-left coalition most political analysts had believed to be unlikely at best just a few short years earlier.

And now, if my sources were to be believed, Lavi was on the phone almost every day with the prince. Together they were trying to fashion a peace deal that the world said was impossible. I too had thought it impossible. But finally, it seemed, it might actually be coming to pass—unless Abu Khalif and Jamal Ramzy had their way.

I trusted this man implicitly. So what was so important that Khachigian had to tell me tonight or tell the *Post* if I didn't show up in time?

29

* * *

"Omar?" Khachigian asked after a long silence.

Every muscle in me tensed. This wasn't a topic I could afford to discuss just then. Too much else was happening. The clock was ticking—for both of us—and I knew if I let myself dwell on the bombing, I wasn't going to make it through the rest of the day. But I didn't want to be rude. Nor did I want to dishonor my friend's memory by brushing off the question or seeming like I didn't care. I did, and it was the very thought of avenging Omar's death somehow that was keeping me going.

"God rest his soul," I managed, though even as the words came out of my mouth, I wasn't sure why I'd put it quite that way. It sounded more like something my mother would say, or more precisely, my brother.

"You two were close?"

"Yeah," I said, though inside I was pleading with him to change the subject. He had to know me better than this.

Then it was quiet again. But instead of spilling

his secrets, the man opened his menu and studied it carefully. I wasn't sure I could wait any longer. He had a plane to catch. I had an editor to meet. Why was he taking so long?

"Can't decide," he finally mumbled.

"On what?" I asked.

"Ordering."

"Really?"

"Yes."

"Get the salmon."

"What?"

"The salmon—it's excellent."

"You're sure?" he asked, the skepticism in his voice palpable.

"Trust me," I said. "It's delicious. You'll love it."

"Cedar plank roasted salmon?" he asked, reading off the menu.

"Right, with the steamed snow peas."

"Really?"

"Positive—I've had it before."

And then it was quiet again.

A waiter filled our glasses with water. My old friend and mentor wasn't talking. I didn't want to think about Omar. I didn't want to think about salmon. I had no appetite. So I just twiddled my thumbs and tried to stay patient. The last thing I needed to do was pressure this man. He would tell me whatever he had to say when he was good and ready.

Finally a waitress came to take our order. Khachigian handed his menu to her, leaned back, and folded his hands. "Lobster ravioli," he said.

I just looked at him and shook my head. Some

things never changed. "Salmon," I told the woman as I handed over my menu.

"So . . . ," he began.

"So," I replied.

Finally this was it. But I was wrong.

"How's Laura?" he asked quietly.

He had to be kidding.

"Listen, I know you're rushed for time," I said. "So maybe the best thing is—"

But Khachigian cut me off midsentence. "How . . . is . . . Laura?"

I just stared at him.

"It's not a trick question," he said calmly, though I wasn't sure I believed him.

"Why would you even ask?"

"Simple," he replied. "I'd like to know."

"Well, I have no idea."

"You haven't talked to her?"

"No."

"Haven't written?"

"Of course not."

"Has she written to you?"

"No."

He paused. He looked at me like he knew something.

"Has . . . she . . . written to you?"

It dawned on me that Khachigian was not only a lawyer by training but also a spook. This wasn't a conversation. It was a deposition, an interrogation, and he already knew the answers.

"I got an e-mail from her the other day."

"When?"

"Sometime after the explosion, I guess."

"You guess?"

"I didn't read it."

"Why not?"

"I deleted it."

"Why?"

"I don't know."

"Of course you do."

"I really don't know, sir."

"Come on, James."

"Look, I don't want to hear from her, okay? I want nothing to do with her. She's a horrible, spiteful, vindictive person, and—with all due respect—I wish you'd never introduced the two of us."

Khachigian leaned forward. "You don't mean that," he said.

"Actually, sir, I do."

"You were in love."

"That was a long time ago."

"Not that long."

"What do you want from me?"

He sighed. "Nothing," he said at last.

There was a long pause. I had nothing to say, and he seemed to be trying to formulate the right words.

"The truth is I haven't seen my niece much since your divorce was finalized," he said at last. "We talk from time to time by phone. We e-mail occasionally. But I want to tell you something I never told you before."

I sat there and waited, my stomach in knots.

"After she left you, after she moved in with . . . Well, anyway, after it all happened, I went to see her on the Upper East Side. I took her out to dinner—just the two of us—and I asked her what went wrong. You two seemed so happy. And she . . ."

The words just trailed away.

"What?" I asked.

"I asked her about that summer when you both interned in my office. If there were still any embers of the love that caught fire that summer."

"And?"

"She said yes."

"I'm not sure I can put into words how much I don't want to have this conversation."

"Well, I thought you should know—she's not with that guy anymore, and she doesn't hate you. I think she feels quite guilty."

"Good."

"And she's moving back to Maine to start her own practice. That's all I wanted to say. Now, tell me about the president."

"You knew I met with him?"

"Of course I knew."

"How?"

"I'm still reasonably well connected in this town, James."

"Did you know Jack was there?"

He nodded.

"So you knew we were talking about the status of the peace process?"

"The peace process is a done deal," Khachigian replied.

"I'd been hearing rumors, but that meeting

confirmed it. Until the last few days, I'd have thought the whole process was going nowhere."

"It's not going nowhere. That's why ISIS is getting ready to strike."

"How much do you know?"

"A lot."

"How much can you tell me?"

"Not much. And you can't print any of this. Not yet. But soon."

"I understand," I replied. "Just cut to the chase."

"I have a good friend, still at the Agency. He left yesterday to visit Jerusalem to do advance for a possible presidential visit."

"Jack said he expected a signing event at the White House just before Christmas."

"I have no doubt," Khachigian said. "But that doesn't preclude a presidential visit to the region. Based on what I'm hearing from old friends here and over there, the White House is planning a surprise trip to Jerusalem in the next week or so. Big photo op. Great optics. Huge international headlines. Signing a 'declaration of principles' or something like that. Then they'll come back and do a big signing ceremony of the final peace treaty in late December, or better yet, in early January as a lead-in to the State of the Union."

"Have you talked to Danny?" I asked, referring to the Israeli premier.

"Among others."

"And he's confirming this?"

"You can't write this," Khachigian said. "That's not why I'm telling you."

"Don't worry; I've got a deal with the president

on an exclusive when they're ready. But as you just said, this is tied into why ISIS is preparing a strike."

"Exactly."

"Which is why you wanted to talk so urgently," I said. "What do you have?"

Khachigian looked around to make sure no one was listening in on our conversation.

"ISIS has loaded sarin nerve agents into artillery shells and missile warheads," he whispered. "My sources say they've moved their men and launchers into position. All they're waiting for now is a final authorization from Abu Khalif."

30

★ ★ ★

"How soon?" I asked.

"That I don't know. But I suspect it's very soon, possibly before this peace deal gets done. That's why you have to finish this story and get it out there fast."

"Jack Vaughn says ISIS doesn't have WMD."

"He told you that?"

"Yes."

"He said those exact words, that ISIS categorically does not have chemical weapons?"

"Well, no," I clarified. "He said it couldn't be confirmed what was in those crates the rebels were taking out of the Aleppo base."

"Jack's wrong."

"You're certain?"

"I am," he replied. "But it doesn't matter what I think. I'm not the director of Central Intelligence. Not anymore. I don't have the ear of this president. And I'm not the *New York Times*. I don't have the ear of the public. But you do. So it's you who has to be sure."

"But how can I be sure?" I asked. "Sure enough to go public with the story?"

"Isn't Ari Shalit going to help you?"

"Maybe. But maybe that's not enough."

"Then talk to the prime minister. Talk to Danny. Ask him to show you what the Mossad has."

"I'm already authorized to see all they have," I said, growing anxious. "Who do you think was with Omar and me in Istanbul? It was a woman from the Mossad. She invited me to Tel Aviv to see what they have. But Jack says that while what I've seen so far is solid, it's also circumstantial. He says it's not proof. He says I need more or I risk panicking a whole lot of people and possibly blowing up the peace process."

"It's spin," Khachigian said. "The president doesn't want you to rain on his signing ceremony."

"I'm sure he doesn't, but that doesn't mean they're wrong. The case *is* circumstantial. Don't get me wrong—it's still a hot story. I can fly to Tel Aviv tonight. I can see what they've got tomorrow afternoon. I can go back to my hotel room and finish my story tomorrow night, and the whole world will read it on Tuesday morning. But it's incomplete. I don't have the whole story. Just because the ISIS rebels captured that base and carted away a bunch of boxes, that doesn't prove they have WMD."

"Then just say that in the story," Khachigian insisted. "You're not writing a book. You're not making a documentary film. You're writing a newspaper story. You have a piece of the puzzle that no one else has. It's important. It's relevant. It's not complete—I grant you that. But what you have *is* news. ISIS rebels under Jamal Ramzy's authority captured a known Syrian chemical-weapons base. They carted away hundreds of crates. They claim to have captured the 'crown jewels' of the Syrian regime. And they're threatening not just to attack but to *annihilate* the United States and Israel with a Third Intifada. Some senior intelligence experts inside the U.S. and two foreign governments believe ISIS now has sarin gas. Ramzy denies it. Senior White House officials downplay the threat. But if ISIS really does now have the very weapons Osama bin Laden only dreamed of obtaining, we are rapidly approaching the most dangerous moment in the history of the War on Terror. There. I just wrote the story for you. That's news, my friend. Game changing. So get it out there, and then go get more."

"More?"

"Go find the source."

"You mean Abu Khalif."

"Absolutely," Khachigian said, leaning toward me. "He's the big story."

"What if Khalif was behind the Istanbul bombing?"

"He wasn't. That was al Qaeda."

"How can you be so sure?"

"I can't," Khachigian admitted. "I'm guessing. But I don't think ISIS is finished with you yet. You're useful to them."

"So you want me to go track him down, even though ISIS is beheading people, crucifying people, blowing them to kingdom come?"

"Look, James, it's a very simple equation," Khachigan said, looking me straight in the eye. "Abu Khalif wants the world to know that ISIS—not al Qaeda—is the most dangerous force on the planet. Now that Zawahiri is dead, he may very well be right. But make no mistake: ISIS doesn't want the world to know they have chemical weapons. Not yet. They want the element of surprise. That's what they have at the moment, and they're going to do everything they can to keep it. That's why you have to get this story out there. You don't work for the president. You don't work for Jack Vaughn or any of the rest of them. You work for the American people. And the American people—not to mention the Israelis, the Palestinians, the Europeans, and the whole world—they all have the right to know just how dangerous this moment is. They have a right to know the president is pushing, pushing, pushing for this deal that is supposed to bring peace but might actually lead to the most catastrophic chemical weapons attack in human history. What people do with that information, what governments do, that's not your business. Your business, like mine, is obtaining intelligence and passing it on to your boss. My boss was the president. Your boss is your readers. Solid, actionable intelligence is worthless unless the people who need it actually have it, know it, and can make decisions based on it. You follow?"

"I do," I said, then paused as the waitress brought out our meals and set them before us. When she had departed again, I said, "But you're not just asking me to publish a story. You're asking me to publish a story Abu Khalif doesn't want out there—a story Jamal Ramzy specifically said he would personally kill me if I published—and then go to Iraq and meet with these guys."

"You think I'm wrong?" Khachigian asked.

"I think you're crazy."

"Maybe, but am I wrong?" Khachigian pressed.

"I don't know."

"Yes, you do. I told you weeks ago the real story wasn't Ramzy. It's Abu Khalif. You agreed. Why?"

"You made a persuasive case—Ramzy is the muscle; Khalif is the brains."

"And what did Sun Tzu say?"

"I know, I know," I said.

"So say it."

Back when Khachigian was the chairman of the Senate intelligence committee, he used to make all of his staff interns learn a few lines from *The Art of War*. He'd made me memorize them too.

"'The reason the enlightened prince and the wise general conquer the enemy whenever they move—and their achievements surpass those of ordinary men—is foreknowledge.'"

"Keep going," he prompted.

Reluctantly I continued. "'What is called foreknowledge cannot be elicited from spirits, nor by analogy from past events, nor from calculation. It must be obtained from men with knowledge of the enemy situation.'"

"Exactly," Khachigian said. "The only way to really know for sure what ISIS has and what they're going to do with it is to go talk to their leader. That means talking to Abu Khalif."

"Even if he kills me."

"He won't kill you."

"Yeah, well, with all due respect, isn't that easy for you to say?"

"Yeah, well, with all due respect, don't think of yourself more highly than you ought."

"What's that supposed to mean?"

"It means every single one us—this tiny group of us who are trying to get this information out to the American people—we're all in danger. You have friends who have already died because of this story. You of all people should know how very high the stakes are. But, James, many, many more Americans—and Israelis, too—are going to die very soon if Abu Khalif has his way. He needs to be stopped. And the only way he's going to be stopped is if he is exposed. Vaughn isn't going to do it. The president isn't going to do it. The Israelis want to be able to react to the story, not put it out there themselves. So that leaves you . . . or the *Post*. Which is it going to be?"

31

Our food was sitting in front of us getting cold.

But I couldn't eat. I just sat there and said nothing. There was no question I wanted to find Abu Khalif and expose him. I'd even been actively pursuing leads as to his whereabouts. I just didn't want to die.

For most of my life—and certainly for most of my career—I'd never really thought much about dying. There was something thrilling, even addictive, about going into dangerous places as a foreign correspondent. I'd always loved taking risks, living on the edge, cheating death, and the exhilaration of coming home alive. But now something was different. Something was changing. *I* was changing. For the first time in my life, I found myself thinking about what was on the other side, about where I was going when I breathed my last, and whether I was really ready for it.

And I knew I wasn't.

I was haunted by the images of Abdel's and Omar's last moments. I was haunted by that soldier dying on the street in Homs, the one who had begged me for help, desperately clinging to life. I couldn't shake the terrified look I had seen in his eyes as the life drained out of him. The sound of his voice was tattooed in my brain.

"James?"

I realized Khachigian was trying to get my attention. I had completely zoned out. "Sorry."

"You okay?" he asked.

"I will be."

"It's okay, son. I know what you're going through. Believe me, I do," Khachigian said, the tone of his voice changing ever so slightly. "You have to do what you think is right. But may I make a suggestion?"

"Uh, yeah, sure," I stammered. "Go right ahead."

"Get on a plane to Israel tonight," he said quietly, almost whispering. "Meet with the Mossad tomorrow. Get that story finished. Get it out there. Make a big international splash with it. And then make a decision about Abu Khalif. But let me suggest that after the *Times* publishes your story on the chemical weapons, there'll be no more reason for Khalif to kill you."

"Why not?"

"Because the reason Jamal Ramzy threatened you was to keep the story from coming out. Once it's out, then the damage is done. Once it's out, I think Khalif would want to talk to you specifically to spin the story, not to deny it. What he wants most is the element of surprise, clearly. But he'll settle for the mystique of being the world's most dangerous terrorist in possession of the world's most dangerous weapons. If anything, publishing that story will be your 'get out of jail free' card."

"That's your theory?" I asked.

"That's my theory," he replied.

I shrugged. Maybe the man was right. I wasn't sure I was ready to find out.

"Aren't you forgetting one thing?" I asked after a few moments.

"What?"

"How exactly am I supposed to hunt down Abu Khalif with five FBI agents connected to my hip?"

"I thought you only had four."

"One is sitting out front in the driver's seat of an armored Chevy Suburban."

Khachigian pulled an envelope out of the breast pocket of his finely tailored suit. He glanced around the restaurant and discreetly slid it across the table.

"What's this?" I asked.

"Don't open it," he said.

"Why not?"

"Just put it in your pocket."

"What is it?"

"Just put it away now," he insisted.

I picked up the envelope and slipped it into my pocket.

"It's a new identity for you," he whispered.

"What?" I asked, completely confused.

"New name," he continued. "New passport. New driver's license. Two new credit cards. And a ticket to Tel Aviv tonight in this new name, not yours."

"Why?" I asked, intrigued.

"Because you're right," he said. "You're going to need to give your new friends from the bureau the slip."

Then he pulled out his smartphone and sent a text. "There."

"There what?" I asked.

"I just told my assistant to book you—the real you—on a series of flights tonight from BWI to Bar Harbor, via Boston and Portland," Khachigian said. "That should provide you with some cover. She's been waiting for my authorization. I just gave it. Now, in a few minutes, I'm going to order dessert. When I do, I want you to go to the restroom—the one over by the Amtrak waiting area near gate A. You know it?"

"Sure."

"Good. Several of your security team, maybe all of them, will follow you. Ask them to check the restroom and make sure it's secure. They will. Then ask them for a moment of privacy and go into the last stall along the far wall. They will step outside and give you some space. That's your moment."

"Why?"

"Because there's a ceiling panel there. Stand on the toilet seat, pop out the panel, pull yourself up, and replace the panel below you."

"You're kidding, right?" I asked.

But Khachigian kept talking, low and fast. "You'll find yourself in an air-conditioning shaft. Go to your left. In about twenty yards, you'll find an opening. Drop down. You'll be in a narrow tunnel that eventually leads to another door. Go through that and you'll end up in an Amtrak storage facility. At this time of night, there won't be anyone there. Exit on the far side, and you'll be on First Street, across from the National Postal Museum. Can you picture that?"

"Yes," I said, a bit mesmerized by the tradecraft and trying to remember every detail.

"It's getting a bit late, but there should still be plenty of cabs. Grab one and head straight for Dulles. By the time the FBI boys figure out you're gone and start to hunt for you, you'll be well on your way. They'll quickly pick up on the reservations from Baltimore back to Maine. Eventually they'll realize it's a ruse, but that should buy you enough time to be on your way to Tel Aviv. And since you'll be using an alias they're completely unaware of, you should make it to Israel with no problems. That ought to give you plenty of time to do your story and make a decision whether to head to Iraq or not."

"You've thought of everything," I said.

"This is what I do," he said. "Well, what I used to do."

I was impressed.

"There's just one thing," he added.

"What's that?"

"You need to turn off your phone right now and remove the battery."

"Okay."

"Don't turn it on for any reason until after you file your story from Tel Aviv."

"Or they'll find me?"

"Exactly."

Then he took a smartphone out of the pocket of his trousers, slid it across the table, and told me to quickly slip it into my pocket.

"What's this for?" I asked, putting it in my pocket.

"You're going to need a phone."

"But they'll know it's yours."

"No, it's totally new. It's not connected to me. It's not even connected to your alias. But it does have all your contact information on it."

"How . . . ?"

"Don't ask," he said. "Use it sparingly, only for emergencies. And whatever you do, don't call your mother."

I nodded, though somewhat reluctantly. This was not a plan I felt comfortable with. I wasn't even sure it was going to work. Still, I was grateful for all the thought and planning he had put into this, and I certainly didn't have a better idea. It wasn't clear to me at that moment that the men from the bureau would prevent me from flying to Tel Aviv that evening if I just decided to head to Dulles and try to book a ticket. But they might. The president didn't want the story out there. Neither did Vaughn. Who knew what excuse they might come up with to keep me in the country. It was not a risk I was willing to take.

Khachigian began to eat his lobster ravioli. I, on the other hand, had no appetite whatsoever.

"Listen," I said, gathering my thoughts, "you said earlier that your sources are telling you that ISIS has mixed the precursors, that they've loaded sarin nerve agents into artillery shells and missile warheads, that they've moved their men into position, and all they are waiting for now is authorization. Right?"

Khachigian nodded as he washed down his pasta with a sip of water.

"So where do your sources say ISIS is going to strike?" I asked. "Here in D.C.? New York? Tel Aviv? Where, and how soon?"

That's when the first gunshot rang out.

32

More gunfire came in rapid succession.

It sounded like it was coming from below us, but with the explosions echoing throughout the main hall of Union Station, I couldn't be certain. People began screaming and running in all directions. Under different circumstances, I might have assumed a random shooting spree was under way. But I knew instantly someone was coming for me, and for a moment I was paralyzed with fear.

The first line of defense was the FBI agent standing post at the bottom of the stairs. Had he been hit? Was he returning fire? The agents at the top of the stairs and the table next to us had already drawn their weapons and were preparing for the possibility of a gunman—or several—charging up those stairs. But as I watched, each of them—one by one—was shot in the back before any of them realized what was happening. Someone was now firing from a position above us.

Khachigian reacted instantly. *"Get down, get down!"* he shouted, reaching across the table and trying to pull me to the floor.

But it was too late. Just then, Khachigian was hit directly in the forehead, right in front of me. His whole upper body snapped backward. The back of his head exploded. It all seemed to happen in slow motion. And yet, somehow, rather than remain frozen in horror, my brain and nervous system reacted to his last words. I immediately dove to the floor, knocking over chairs and crashing into other patrons who were doing the same thing, all of us scrambling for cover.

There had to be at least two shooters, I concluded—one on the main level, creating a distraction, and a sniper firing from the floor above me.

Crack, crack, crack.

Each shot echoed through the hall. I could hear wineglasses and china shattering all around me. People were being hit. They were writhing on the floor, covered in blood, screaming in pain, but there was nothing I could do to help them. Not yet. Not now. Not while I was so exposed.

The sniper, I realized, had to be in one of the arched alcoves ringing the upper level. I desperately scrambled past several tables, trying to get behind the bar, which I hoped might keep me safe. But then I saw one of the agents, a pool of blood all around him. To my astonishment he was still alive, though he wouldn't be for long. His face was a ghostly white, but there was still fire in his eyes.

"Get down!" he yelled, then aimed his government-issued sidearm at one of the alcoves over my right shoulder and unloaded an entire magazine.

My instinct was to flatten myself to the ground

and cover my head, but I was still too exposed. The only chance I had to make it through this was to use this agent's covering fire to get to a safer position. So as he pulled the trigger again and again, I climbed over broken glass and bleeding bodies to one of the other agents lying motionless next to the bar. As I reached him, I heard more gunfire erupt from the alcove behind me. A split second later, the agent I had just left was dead. But I kept moving.

Lunging forward, I grabbed the Glock handgun lying beside the nearest agent and quickly found his spare clip. Then I rolled behind the bar just as the shooter in the alcove turned his fire on me. I could hear bullets whizzing over my head. I could hear more bottles exploding and the wood counters being shredded. I was pinned down, and I was terrified. I knew full well the FBI agents and tourists sprawled all around me were not the targets. Khachigian had been, and so was I. This was not another mass shooting event like the ones Americans were becoming all too used to in schools and movie theaters and churches all across the country. It might seem that way. It might even get reported that way at first. But this wasn't random. The shooters weren't going to turn out to be a few drugged-out high school kids overly influenced by violent video games. This was terrorism. This was a professional hit. This was al Qaeda—or more likely ISIS—and Khachigian was right; they weren't going to stop until anyone trying to break the story about the chemical weapons was dead.

Pressing myself as far under the counter as I

could, out of the line of sight of the shooter in the alcove, I aimed the gun at the end of the bar, fearing that the second shooter—if there really was a second shooter—would be coming around the corner at any moment. In all the chaos and confusion, I couldn't be sure exactly what was happening. Nor did I see any way out. If there were multiple assailants, what exactly was I supposed to do? Even if I could take out one of them, how could I stop the rest of them from sending me to the afterlife?

In that moment, I suddenly thought of my brother. Of the two of us, it was Matt who had become religious. It was Matt who had married the daughter of an Anglican priest and then become a seminary professor. Though I'd ridiculed and mocked him for it all through high school and college, it was he who was always talking about the Bible and urging me to "get right with God." What if he was right and I was wrong? What if he was going to heaven and I was about to go to hell?

I felt my fear shift to rage. I wasn't ready to die. But if I did, it wouldn't be cowering under a counter. I determined I would fight back. I was not going to surrender to these bloodthirsty barbarians. I was going to do everything in my power to expose them to the world.

A surge of adrenaline shot through my body. All my senses seemed to go to a higher level of alertness. I began to move, crawling over the lifeless body of the bartender until I came around the corner and saw an opening to the stairs.

This was the only way out. I had no other choice. The shooter behind me knew it, and he had the advantage. But I knew I could not wait. If I didn't go now, I might never get out. Above all the screaming and cacophony down below, I could hear sirens coming from all directions. Within moments, the place was going to be swarming with D.C. Metro police, SWAT teams, and the FBI. They would find the shooters. They would kill them, and then they'd lock the place down. I'd be a witness to yet another crime scene. They'd never let me out of the country.

I checked the pistol to make sure it was ready to fire. It was. I waited for the shooter above me to fire more rounds. When he paused to reload, I popped my head up, aimed for the alcove, and fired off three rounds. Then I jumped to my feet and ran for the stairwell.

As I did, though, I heard more gunfire erupt from down below. I saw a policewoman drop to the floor, blood spraying from her neck. I'd been right. There *were* two shooters. One was firing from above. The second was on the main level, and he was firing at police now arriving on the scene. It was a suicide mission. Both shooters would be dead within minutes. They certainly weren't going to outlast all the layers of police on Capitol Hill. But obviously they knew that, and obviously they didn't care.

My heart was pounding. My adrenaline was surging. I was going on instinct, and my instinct was to move. I raced down the curved stairway— my white knuckles gripping the pistol in front of me for dear life—even as both shooters kept firing on everyone in their path.

As I neared the bottom, I was surprised to see that the first shooter was a woman. She was dressed in dark-blue sportswear as if she'd just come from a gym. She was wearing a black ski mask, holding an AK-47, and spraying anyone and everyone she could. At the moment, her back was to me. But as she started to turn, I pulled the trigger. Again and again I fired. Though several shots went wild, I hit her once in the shoulder and once in the neck. She went sprawling across the blood-spattered marble floor. Then I aimed up to the alcove, emptied the rest of the magazine, and began to sprint.

I couldn't tell for sure if I had killed the first shooter, but I thought I had. I couldn't allow myself to think about it now. I'd never killed anyone before, but for now I just had to keep going.

I had no illusions that I had taken out the upstairs shooter, but I figured I'd at least bought a few precious seconds of cover, and I wasted none of them. I ran across the main terminal and deeper into the station, past the Amtrak ticket counter, past shops and boutiques, and headed for the men's room in the back by gate A. I was following Khachigian's plan. I would use the utility door and the escape tunnel, just as he'd told me to. But when I got there, I found the door barricaded shut by people huddled inside, desperate to protect themselves. I pounded and yelled and begged for them to let me in, but all I got was an earful of curses in return.

I froze with panic. I hadn't anticipated this, and I had no idea what to do next. I couldn't just stand there, vulnerable and exposed. No one was left in this section. It was completely deserted. But it wouldn't take long. Someone would see me. Someone would find me, either the second shooter or someone in law enforcement, and I didn't dare be caught by either.

I glanced to my right and saw glass doors. Beyond them were row upon row of railroad tracks. There were no trains coming or going at the moment—it was clear this was my only way out. Hopping over a barricade, I tried to burst through the doors, but they were locked. I moved right and tried to exit through gates B and C, but they were locked as well. Perhaps they had been automatically locked once the shooting started. I had no idea. But I had a pistol in my hands and didn't think twice. Backing up, I ejected the empty magazine and loaded the spare. Then I fired away until the glass shattered and I could crawl through. Ditching the pistol in a nearby trash can, I sprinted down the tracks. I ran as fast as I could until the sounds of the sirens began to fade. Only then did I dare leave the tracks.

As I climbed up an embankment, I spotted a gas station. I ran to it, found the men's room, and locked myself inside for a few minutes to wash up and catch my breath.

I could still hear sirens screaming toward Union Station. I knew I had to keep moving. I slipped out of the men's room and jogged several more blocks to the north. There I found a cab. I thrust a wad of cash in the driver's face. Fifteen minutes later, I was back at my apartment.

I took a quick shower, changed clothes, packed a bag, and drove my own car to Dulles airport. I was going to Tel Aviv and then on to Iraq. I was going to finish this story. I'd come this far. I couldn't stop now.

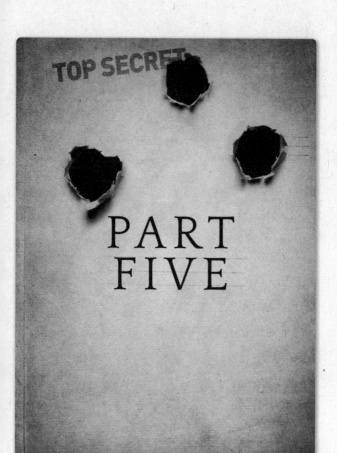

TOP SECRET

PART
FIVE

33

* * *

I landed at Ben Gurion International Airport just after 4 p.m. local time.

Fortunately, I'd fallen sound asleep even before taking off from Washington. I'd woken up only on hearing the pilot say we were on final approach into Tel Aviv. But I hardly felt rested, and I was starving. I'd missed both meals and the snacks.

Then again, I'd missed the chance to buy alcohol too.

Low blood sugar was not helping me. The challenges ahead were daunting. I was about to go through Israeli passport control using a fake passport. For all I knew, I would then be arrested for traveling with false papers. I'd never done this before. I wasn't a trained CIA operative. I had no idea whether I could bluff my way through Israeli security. Even if I could, I still had to get myself to Mossad headquarters, where I had no idea if Ari Shalit would receive me. But I didn't dare contact him yet, lest the FBI pick up my trail.

And these were just my immediate problems. The next set—getting to Iraq and tracking down Abu Khalif—was more daunting by far. Yet I didn't feel scared. At the moment, I just felt numb.

The lines to go through passport control were crazy long. Four international flights had arrived within minutes of each other, and the arrival hall was mobbed. The good news was that the Israeli border control officials were in a hurry to get people processed and through. When it was my turn, I handed over my fake passport and tried to act natural. I waited for the questions, but they didn't come. I waited to be pulled aside, but it didn't happen. Moments later, I was through without a problem. But I was hardly relieved. I was still battling shock.

I headed out into the chilly winter rains to grab a cab when someone suddenly came up behind me. I turned, and to my astonishment, it was Yael Katzir.

"James, thank God you're safe," she said, giving me a hug. "Welcome to Israel."

She had scrapes and contusions all over her face and neck. She had burns and bandages on her hands and arms. But she was alive and holding me.

"Yael," I stammered, "how . . . ? What . . . ? I don't understand."

"Didn't you come to Israel to see me?" she asked.

"Well, I . . ."

"You didn't really think we'd be fooled by your new passport, did you?" she said with a wink.

I just stared at her blankly as a jet-black, four-door BMW pulled up. Yael opened the back door for me.

"Come on; we can talk on the way," she said, her eyes sober but warm.

Rattled by all that had happened in the last twenty-four hours but grateful to see her, I said nothing, just got into the car. Yael got in the other side and gave the driver orders in Hebrew. Then we were off, presumably to Mossad headquarters in Tel Aviv.

"I'm so sorry about Omar," she said, taking my left hand and squeezing it gently. "I know you two were close."

I nodded, still numb.

"And I'm sorry for taking off after the explosion," she continued as we got onto Highway 1, headed west through the increasing rain. "I wanted to see you. I wanted to make sure you were okay. But I was under orders not to draw the attention of the Turks under any circumstances. I hope you understand."

I nodded again. "But you're okay?" I asked.

"I'll live," she replied.

It was a professional answer, polite and succinct and completely expected, but it wasn't enough. I wanted more. I wanted the truth. I wanted to know how she was really doing. Yet what was I supposed to do? I wasn't entitled to anything. She didn't owe me anything. We weren't a couple. We weren't even friends. Not really. After all, we had only just met.

Yael, I was certain, could see the struggle in my eyes. So she changed the subject and offered her condolences for the death of Robert Khachigian. She said she and her colleagues had known Khachigian quite well and had admired him greatly over the years. "We worked together on several operations," she confided. "He was a class act."

"He was," I said, wanting to say more and embarrassed that the words would not form.

The car was silent for several miles. It was awkward, but not just for me. Yael seemed uncomfortable as well. She turned away and looked out the rain-streaked window. I turned and looked out mine. A hundred questions rushed through my mind, but I didn't ask a one.

"Can you tell me what happened in Union Station?" she said after several kilometers. "Ari's going to want details."

It was hardly a topic I wanted to discuss. I still hadn't fully processed the fact that I had very probably killed someone during my escape. Nevertheless, I shared as much about the attack as I could remember, though I left out the details of Khachigian's and my conversation. Some things were private. But there was no good reason not to tell her the rest, and in the end it was helpful to have someone I could talk to, someone who understood the enormous trauma I was going through.

"The media in the States are reporting this as a 'mass-casualty event,'" she said, handing me several printouts of articles off the websites of my own paper and the *Washington Post*. "The FBI is telling the media that one suspect was shot dead at the scene. That's the female shooter you brought down. But a second suspect is on the run. They're not releasing any names or descriptions or any details at all. There are just a few leaks from 'unnamed senior law enforcement sources' hinting that right-wing white supremacists may be responsible."

"Tell me you're kidding."

"I'm not," Yael said. "And the FBI hasn't released the names of the dead. The director is saying not all of the next of kin have been notified."

"You don't believe him," I said. It was an observation, not a question.

Yael shook her head. "Do you?"

I turned and looked out the window again. Why weren't they officially releasing the names, at least some of them? At the very least, why hadn't someone leaked Khachigian's name to the media?

"It's political," I said, almost to myself, as I stared out the increasingly fogged-up window and the driving rains pelting Israel's second-largest city. "They don't want to say a former CIA director was assassinated in broad daylight. They don't want to say it's an act of Middle Eastern terrorism, in the heart of Washington, on the eve of announcing a Middle East peace deal."

"You may be right," Yael said. "But I think there's more."

"What do you mean?" I asked, turning back to her.

"It's not just Khachigian," she said. "I think they don't want your name out there either. They don't know what's happened to you. They don't know why you left the scene. Maybe you were kidnapped. Maybe you were complicit. Either way, they don't want the media to report that you were there."

"Because that would put focus on the threat ISIS just issued."

"That would be my guess," she agreed. "You're a big deal now. You broke the story on how serious a threat ISIS really is and that they are planning a series of imminent attacks on Israel and allies of Israel. But you're also a big deal because you were just nearly killed in Turkey. Can you imagine how big a story it would be if people knew you were almost assassinated in D.C. as well?"

"You don't think they really believe I'm involved, do you?" I asked. The thought hadn't even crossed my mind. Nor had the implications.

"No, but I think you need to contact the FBI immediately. Have you even touched base with your editor yet?"

"No, but I have to get this WMD story done first—tonight," I said, now looking her in the eye. "People need to know about the ISIS attack on that base in Syria. They need to know it's possible that ISIS now has chemical weapons, and that they may be planning an attack on the U.S. or Israel at any moment. I can't do anything else until I get that done."

"I agree, and so does Ari," she assured me. "And as I told you before, the prime minister has given us full authorization to help you, so long as you don't quote us or cite any Israeli sources. Deal?"

"Deal."

"You understand that means you can't have a dateline on your story tomorrow from Tel Aviv or Jerusalem or anywhere in Israel, right?"

"I can live with that," I said.

It wasn't ideal, but it was certainly a small price to pay for a scoop like this.

"Good," Yael said. "We're only about ten minutes out. When we get to HQ, I will take you into the vault, as we call it, and show you everything about the ISIS offensive near Aleppo. But there's something else you should know."

She set the latest edition of the *Jerusalem Post* in my lap. The Union Station attacks in Washington had made the front page. But the lead headline read, **ISIS Forces Continue in Race toward Baghdad.**

I quickly scanned the first few paragraphs. A few thousand Sunni jihadists had already captured control of Mosul, Iraq's second-largest city, and driven off two U.S.-trained Iraqi army divisions. Now the *Post* was reporting that ISIS forces had seized the central bank of Mosul, making off with the equivalent of nearly a half-billion dollars in cash, and were continuing to threaten the capital.

"So Baghdad is about to be attacked by what is now the richest terror group on the planet," I said.

"There's more."

"What?"

"The Iraqi government is in full panic mode. Their army is in retreat. Their capital is in jeopardy. The top Shia cleric is calling on fellow Shias to wage jihad against the Sunnis. Tehran—of all places—is offering to help, even offering to

send in Iranian military and paramilitary forces
to fight ISIS. But President Taylor is doing nothing. The Iraqis are asking for U.S. air strikes, but
the president says no. They're asking for a massive
new infusion of military aid. The president says
he'll think about it. *Think about it?* We could lose
Iraq to a bloodthirsty jihadi force. Do you realize what that means? You guys lost four thousand
soldiers and Marines fighting to liberate Iraq, and
now you're going to effectively hand it over to
ISIS? A group so crazy they were thrown out of
al Qaeda for being too extreme? A group that now
has chemical weapons and is getting ready to use
them at any moment? This isn't leadership, James.
It's surrender. But your president doesn't seem to
get it. Or maybe he just doesn't care. Instead of
taking action in Iraq, he's obsessed with carving
up the Holy Land. He's offering all kinds of incen-
tives to my country to sign a deeply flawed peace
treaty with the Palestinians, and my prime minister is buying it hook, line, and sinker. It's absolute
lunacy."

"I'm guessing that's off the record?" I quipped
as we slowed to a crawl and wove through late-
afternoon rush-hour traffic.

She didn't respond.

Changing topics, I asked if she thought the
military offensive Jamal Ramzy had promised in
his interview with me might actually be against
Iraq.

"No, I don't think so," Yael said. "Iraq isn't the
third target. It's the primary target. Syria is second. I'm guessing Israel is third, though it could

be you guys. Khalif and Ramzy aren't idiots. They see the U.S. retreating from the region. They've seen their successes in Syria. And they obviously saw an opening, a growing weakness in the heart of the Iraqi regime, and they decided to strike and exploit it for all it's worth."

"Heck of a gamble."

"They don't call themselves the Islamic State of Iraq and al-Sham for nothing. Controlling Iraq, imposing full-blown Sharia law there, and establishing a caliphate in Baghdad is the ultimate objective. It's the main course. Everything else is dessert."

"Could Baghdad really fall to ISIS?" I asked. "Are they that strong?"

"I don't know if they could seize the capital, but they are definitely getting stronger, especially now that they have WMD," she replied. "And I'm sorry; they're not just an extra-radical faction of al Qaeda, as you wrote in your profile on Ramzy. They're actually becoming a very sophisticated army—highly motivated, well-trained, increasingly experienced, incredibly rich, and very, very dangerous. Imagine what would happen if they truly gained control of all of Iraq. They'd create a base camp from which they could export terrorism, attack American citizens, destabilize moderate Arab nations, terrorize the Iraqi people, drive up the price of oil, and seriously harm the global economy."

"And attack Israel," I added.

"And attack Israel," she agreed. "Wouldn't that be the ultimate irony?"

"What?" I asked.

"If the U.S. invaded Iraq to protect itself and Israel from weapons of mass destruction—which it turned out the Iraqis didn't really have or have many of—only to set into motion the conditions that would leave the rulers of Iraq in a position to threaten both of us . . . with weapons of mass destruction."

Irony didn't begin to describe it.

34

* * *

The next twenty-four hours were a whirlwind.

Yael and Ari were true to their word. They gave me everything I needed and then some.

As I was preparing to leave, Ari explained why he hadn't personally come to meet me in Turkey. He told me—completely off the record, of course—that the prime minister had sent him on a secret mission to Jordan.

"Lavi is determined to be remembered by history as the leader who nailed down a final peace accord with the Palestinians," he whispered. "I told him the timing was wrong. I'm not opposed to a two-state solution. Not at all. But to make a deal right when ISIS is about to hit us with chemical weapons? It's foolish. But he doesn't agree, and he's the boss. So I went. I'm sorry I wasn't with you."

I thanked him for his candor and all his help and Yael's. I apologized for putting Yael in harm's way, but he wouldn't hear of it.

"That's what I pay her for," the Mossad chief said.

"It can't possibly be enough," I said.

Yael sighed. "You've got that right."

Ari and I shook hands. Then Yael drove me to a private airfield. On the way, she gave me her real mobile number and asked me to call her when I arrived in Amman. Then she put me on a Learjet and instructed the pilot to fly me to Cairo. She said I could write my story there in peace and quiet and have it datelined from an Arab capital, not from Israel.

It was a good idea, and I was grateful. I would be safe there. No one would suspect me of being in Egypt. I didn't want to leave Tel Aviv. I wanted to spend more time with Yael. But the clock was ticking. She wished me well, shook my hand, and said good-bye, and with that, she was gone.

Once on the ground in Cairo, I took a cab downtown. I used the phone Khachigian had given me to scan through the headlines back in the States. The nation was riveted on the events at Union Station. The president had called it a tragedy. The mayor of D.C. called it another senseless slaughter. The head of the FBI called it a cold-blooded homicide without rhyme or reason. But that was all spin. The FBI knew there was a reason for the attack. They knew it was terrorism, and they had to suspect it was either al Qaeda or ISIS. But they were still treating the case like another Columbine massacre or the shootings at Sandy Hook, not like a national security emergency.

What's more, the bureau was keeping what cards it had closer than usual. They still weren't releasing the names of any of those who had been killed. Nor were they releasing the name of the female shooter who had been pronounced dead at the scene. At least they were no longer sticking to the "right-wing white supremacist" nonsense.

The Feds had now confirmed there had been a second shooter. MSNBC was running grainy video footage from someone's smartphone showing a sniper on the second floor, back in the corner. An intrepid *Washington Post* reporter had even gotten a detailed description of the sniper and his weapon from an off-duty D.C. police officer who happened to be eating at the Pizzeria Uno on the second floor at the time of the shooting. The officer had tried to chase the sniper but had been shot twice and was now in guarded condition at a local hospital. The Associated Press, meanwhile, was quoting several witnesses who said there was a third shooter as well. That, I assumed, was me, and I knew I would have to talk to the FBI soon lest I become an active suspect.

I directed the cab to a Hilton I had once stayed in near the American embassy. There were few tourists, few business guests, and plenty of rooms available. I took a spacious suite overlooking the Nile, pulled out my laptop and notes, and set to work.

The process didn't take long, given that I had already written several drafts over the past few weeks. Essentially, all I needed to do now was add in the new material I had gathered over the past forty-eight hours, including several quotes from Khachigian. I decided to break the story of how deeply involved in this process Khachigian had been, along with the fact that he'd been killed at

Union Station. I didn't connect all the dots about why he'd been killed. I didn't need to. I just wanted to stick to the facts that I could prove, and I had plenty.

When I was finished, I debated calling Allen and personally updating him on all that had happened. In the end, however, I opted against it. I simply sent him the story by e-mail with a single sentence that I was safe and coming home soon. I didn't want an argument. I didn't want a dressing-down. I just wanted to file and keep moving. If he was going to fire me, so be it. I wasn't going to fight for my job. I was just going to keep doing it until I was either broke or dead.

The moment the e-mail went through, I jumped in a cab, raced back to the airport, and bought the last seat on the last flight to Amman, Jordan, that night. I didn't want to be in Cairo when my story hit the newsstands. Besides, from Amman I could get a direct flight to Baghdad.

In the meantime, now that my story had been filed, it was time to put the battery back in my iPhone and go to work. I e-mailed and texted every contact I knew in the Iraqi government. Yet again I pleaded for their help to locate and then secure an interview with Abu Khalif. I also said I was coming to Baghdad in the next twenty-four to forty-eight hours and would be deeply grateful for their assistance. It was an enormous risk, especially after filing a story about chemical weapons and ISIS. Jamal Ramzy had been crystal clear that I was to go nowhere near that story. But I was going anyway. I had to.

Live or die, I was going to hunt down this story to the end.

★   ★   ★

The next morning, I woke up at Le Méridien, an upscale hotel in downtown Amman.

I glanced at the alarm clock on the nightstand beside me. It was 7:23 a.m. I got out of bed, rubbed the sleep from my eyes, and powered up my laptop. As I ordered room service for breakfast, I wondered what Allen had done with the story I'd sent him. Had he run it or buried it? I didn't dare guess. I'd defied his direct orders. He had insisted that I come meet with him in Washington, and I'd planned to, of course. But events had taken a turn I could never have expected. In any case, I had gotten him the third source he'd insisted upon with regard to the WMD story. The final draft I'd sent him was written with significantly more care and precision than the previous versions. But it was still an explosive piece.

If Allen had signed off on it and it was really going to be published soon, it was going to create an international firestorm. Just a few months earlier, few people outside the intelligence community had ever even heard of ISIS. Now the jihadist movement had captured half of Iraq and much of Syria and could very well be in possession of large amounts of sarin gas. Not only that, they were threatening to hit a third target beyond Iraq and Syria. The implications for U.S. and Israeli national security were chilling, to say the least. But would Allen really run with it? I hoped so, but I didn't know.

I pulled up the *New York Times* home page and held my breath.

There it was, on the front page.

ISIS Forces Seize Syrian Base Where Chemical Weapons Stored, read the enormous banner headline, with a subhead that read, *"Intelligence experts warn al Qaeda faction, now signaling new terror attacks, may have WMD."*

My body tensed. I thought I'd be excited. But as I scanned the story, I actually felt full of dread. The weight of what this all meant began to come down on me. I read through it quickly. It was all there. Allen had made only minor edits. Now the story was available for the whole world to see. There was no turning back. The president was going to wake up to it. So was the director of the CIA. And Prime Minister Lavi. And Jamal Ramzy. And, I had to assume, Abu Khalif. What would they say? What would they do?

I had included all the caveats the president and CIA director had warned me about—though not citing them, of course. I had carefully noted that while three different intelligence agencies had clear proof of ISIS seizing the base and carrying off hundreds of crates, none of them could give definitive evidence that ISIS now actually possessed WMD. The *Times* didn't want to get burned on another bogus Mideast WMD story. Neither did I. It was my reputation on the line, and I guarded it jealously.

I had woken up hungry. Now I had lost all interest in food. Instead, I pulled up airline schedules online and considered my meager options. I was going to Baghdad. ISIS could kill me, but they couldn't stop me from letting the world know what they were up to. I had Ramzy's interview. I had the WMD angle. Now I wanted Abu Khalif, and the only way to get him was to get to the Iraqi capital and hunt him down.

I booked a seat on Royal Jordanian Airlines flight 810, departing at 5:30 that evening and landing at about 8 p.m. local time. From the airport, I would head straight for a hotel in the Green Zone where I had stayed in the past.

It would be a return to familiar but dangerous territory: the hotel had a well-trafficked bar. During the second Iraq war, I'd spent countless nights there. I'm guessing that's where I officially became an alcoholic. Everyone who was anyone hung out there in the evenings, after the Western submission deadlines had passed. It was the kind of place I could pick up leads and get the lay of the land. But it was all done over whiskey and bourbon and an occasional bottle of vodka. For that reason alone, it was probably suicide to go back. But that's where the sources were, so that's where I had to be too.

I opened the door to the hallway, picked up my complimentary copy of the *Jordan Times* from the carpet, and brought it into the room. Pulling back the drapes to let in some light, I looked out over the sprawling skyline of the Jordanian capital and thought about Yael. I debated calling her, but what was there to say? We couldn't have a personal conversation on the phone. She had work to do, and so did I. She had probably given me her real number in case I had a follow-up question. She was a professional. She was a spy. She hadn't suggested I ask her out. Even if I did, when was I going to be back in Israel? The whole thing suddenly seemed ridiculous and awkward. Here I was, a grown man. Divorced. Single. Not seeing anyone. Yet I felt like a boy trying to get up the nerve to ask a girl to the junior high dance.

I grabbed my phone off the desk. It had finished charging overnight. Yet instead of calling Yael or even texting her, I found myself sending an SMS message to my brother. He was in Amman. Maybe I should say hi. Seemed like the decent thing to do. I couldn't avoid him forever, and it would make my mom happy.

Matt—hey, in town for a few hours. You free?—JB

I debated calling Hadiya, Omar's wife, but I wasn't sure she would be happy to hear from me. Instead I sent her an e-mail telling her how much her husband had meant to me and how sorry I was for her loss. Perhaps in time I could express my sorrow and regret to her in person. For now, I decided, she probably needed some space.

With no one else to contact at the moment, I scanned the local headlines. None were what I expected.

**King Says 'Historic Breakthrough'
Possible in Palestinian Peace Talks
with Israel**

**Prime Minister Says 'Peace to
Our West' Would Help Calm
'Storm to Our East'**

**Palestinian President Mansour to
Meet with King in Aqaba**

**Gas Prices Climb, but Food Prices
Stable in November**

To my astonishment, there was nothing about ISIS on the front page, only an allusion to the implosion of Jordan's next-door neighbor. I knew the palace kept a pretty tight grip on news coverage, but were they really going to try to act like ISIS wasn't on the move? I quickly flipped through the pages, but there was little mention of the Islamic State inside the paper either. One story focused on a new refugee camp Jordan and the U.N. were building in the north. Another noted that the U.S. had just authorized the sale of new Hellfire missiles and other arms to the Iraqi government. Only deep inside did I find this headline: **Jordan Does Not Fear ISIS Rebels, Says Interior Minister.** But the accompanying article was only six paragraphs long.

Why?

This was Jordan's largest English-language daily newspaper. The palace was clearly using it to lay the groundwork for the peace talks "to the west," but why were they not making it clear how serious was the "storm to the east"?

I did a quick Google search to see how much coverage of ISIS this and other Jordanian papers had published in recent weeks. Some, but not much. Again, why? To be sure, well over half of Jordan's population was of Palestinian origin. Some said the number was as high as 70 percent. Most held Jordanian citizenship. They were certainly deeply concerned about the future of their Arab brothers and sisters on the west side of the Jordan River. They strongly supported the creation of a Palestinian state. Most believed it was a terrible injustice of the West not to have helped create a Palestinian state sooner. But ISIS posed a clear and present danger to the region.

The Hashemite Kingdom of Jordan sat wedged between Iraq, Syria, the Palestinians, and Israel.

A threat to the others surely posed a threat to Jordan, too.

35

★ ★ ★

The phone rang.

Not the room phone but my mobile. I glanced at the caller ID to see who in the world it could be. The screen read simply, *Unknown caller*.

My pulse quickened. Maybe it was Yael. Then again, maybe it was my brother.

"Hello?"

"Mr. Collins?" asked the voice at the other end. "Is that you?"

"Who's asking?" I replied, now somewhat guarded.

"Good, it is you," he said. "I've been worried about you. Are you all right?"

"I'm sorry; who is this?" I asked.

"Come now, my friend, you don't recognize my voice?"

"No, I'm sorry. I don't."

"It's Marwan. Are you dressed?"

Startled, I suddenly found myself rising to my feet. I had not expected a call from Prince Marwan Talal.

"Your Royal Highness, forgive me," I said. "No, I'm sorry. I just woke up."

"I have sent you a car and driver—they are waiting in front of your hotel," he said. "Take a quick shower. Get dressed. And meet the driver in ten minutes. We need to talk."

★ ★ ★

I had met with Marwan Talal many times over the years, but never at his home.

But the farther we drove from the hotel and veered away from any of the main government buildings with which I was familiar, the more I became convinced that's where I was being taken.

Though we e-mailed occasionally, it had been quite some time since I had actually seen the king's eldest uncle. He was now in his eighties, and I'd heard rumors his health was not so good. But as the Mercedes pulled through the security gates of a palatial home on the outskirts of Amman—past the Humvee out front with the soldier manning a .50-caliber machine gun, past at least a dozen other heavily armed guards, and up the long, winding palm tree–lined driveway—I was not prepared for the man who awaited me.

The prince was confined to a wheelchair now. His gray hair had thinned considerably. His face looked gaunt, and I wondered if I was detecting a bit of jaundice as well. But when I stepped out of the car and came over to him, he greeted me with the same warm smile and twinkle in his eye for which I had come to know him. And though his hands trembled slightly as he took both of mine, and though his voice was somewhat raspier than I remembered, there was also an indescribable air of confidence about him that gave me the sense he was still in command of his faculties. That was reassuring, I thought. But that was pretty much the only thing about our time together that was.

We gave each other a traditional Arab kiss on both cheeks, and then I followed as a steward wheeled the prince through the handsomely appointed entry hall to a veranda overlooking the capital. Soon we were served the best Turkish coffee I think I've ever had, and then we were left alone to chat.

"You are a survivor, Mr. Collins," Marwan said to begin our conversation.

"I've been lucky."

"No," he said, wagging his finger at me. "Your protection is Allah's doing. Your enemies have tried to kill you twice. But clearly Allah is not done with you."

"Not yet," I quipped.

"Indeed," he said. "Not yet. Are you okay?"

"I'm fine."

"You look terrible."

"Thanks a lot."

"I just mean all the cuts and bruises and bandages. And you're as pale as a ghost."

"Yet I'm sitting in Amman with an old friend."

"That you are. But you were sitting with an old friend at Union Station when all the shooting broke out."

"Are you saying I'm in danger here?"

"I'm saying one never knows where danger lurks."

"True," I said. "One never knows."

The prince did not touch his coffee. He just sat there and looked at me as if he were studying me, as if he were trying to make sense of who I was despite the many years we had known each other.

"Mr. Collins . . . ," the prince began, and then his voice trailed off for a moment.

He was not the only prince in the royal family. Indeed, there were many, and some of them were very close to the king. But Marwan Talal was the most senior of the princes. Perhaps it was because of his age and insistence on tradition and protocol that he persisted in calling me Mr. Collins. I had long since given up on persuading him to call me James—much less J. B.

"Yes, Your Royal Highness?" I prompted.

"Mr. Collins, are you ready to become a follower of the Prophet, peace be upon him?"

I wasn't sure what to say to that. He knew I wasn't a religious man. But then again, there were few if any Muslims in the royal court as devout as Marwan Talal. He was a direct descendant of the prophet Muhammad. He had been trained as a Sunni cleric and for years had taught Sharia law in Jordan's most prestigious seminary. And honestly, I think he'd been trying to convert me—at least to deism, if not Islam—since the day I'd met him. I appreciated the gesture, but this question still made me uncomfortable.

I briefly considered telling him that my days of atheism and agnosticism had apparently passed.

I did, in fact, believe in God. I just didn't know how to find him, though I was becoming increasingly convinced I had to try. But not here. Not today. And with all respect to Marwan and his impressive family, I was not about to become a Muslim. I'd been raised in a Christian home by a very devout mother. I wasn't exactly ready to embrace my mother's beliefs. I wasn't really sure where I stood with Jesus at this point in my life. But I certainly wasn't about to give my mother a stroke by asking her to come down to the local mosque to pray with me five times a day.

"I am still finding my way, my friend," I said.

"There is only one Prophet," he replied. "There is only one path. There is only one guide, the Qur'an."

"You're starting to sound like a member of the Brotherhood," I said, trying to lighten the mood.

"Why would you say such a thing?" he asked, sounding a bit defensive.

"Didn't you just recite the slogan of the Muslim Brotherhood?"

"Certainly not," he replied. "The Muslim Brotherhood's mantra is: 'Allah is our objective. The Prophet is our leader. Qur'an is our law. Jihad is our way. Dying in the way of Allah is our highest hope.'"

"Close."

"A man can be a faithful Muslim and not be a member of the Brotherhood, can he not?"

"Of course."

"Then I believe you're trying to change the subject, Mr. Collins. Have you ever read the Qur'an?"

"Yes, I have."

"And?"

"Again, let's just say I'm finding my way," I replied, trying to be as diplomatic as I could.

"If I may be direct, Mr. Collins, you are a young man in great need of Islam. You are, I am sad to say, all alone in this world. You have no wife. You have no children. No faith. No community. That is no way to live, my friend. Why not join us? I would be happy to teach you the path of Islam myself."

"Thank you," I said politely. "I will consider your gracious offer. But I suspect this is not why you have brought me here today."

"Not the only reason, no," he said.

"Then how can I help you?"

"Your most recent article in the *Times*. It bothered me very much."

I took another sip of coffee and braced myself. "I'm sorry to hear that, Your Highness. What bothered you in particular?"

"Among many things, your timing," the prince said. "Didn't President Taylor specifically ask you not to publish a story of this sort at this time?"

I was stunned that he knew such a thing, but then again he and his king were in very close contact with the White House, especially now.

"I believe I made the administration's concerns abundantly clear in the story," I responded.

"Nevertheless, the president and His Majesty are in the very delicate final stages of being midwives to an extraordinary peace treaty," he explained. "His Majesty has been working quietly, behind the scenes, with President Mansour and Prime Minister Lavi and their closest advisors for months, along with your president and his administration."

"For how long exactly?"

"Eight months, maybe nine."

Suddenly the prince began a coughing spell that was so bad I worried he might have a heart attack. I poured him a glass of water. He drank it all, and soon he was quiet again.

"How involved is His Majesty?"

"His Majesty is overseeing the entire process."

"Not the Americans?"

"Everything is done under the auspices of the Taylor administration, of course," he said with a theatrical flair, spreading out his arms expansively. "The president does the talk-talk-talk in public. The Americans take all the credit. But His Majesty is doing the heavy lifting."

"Right here in Amman?"

"Some of it, yes," he confirmed. "But mostly at the palace in Aqaba. It's quieter there. It's off the media's radar. King Hussein used to hold many such secret contacts there. His Majesty learned from his father, peace be upon him."

"And the deal is almost finished?"

"Young man, it *is* finished," the prince said. "His Majesty got an agreement on the final language yesterday. I can't give you any of the details, of course. Not yet. But I can tell you both Lavi and Mansour have signed off. Now they are planning the announcement to the media, which will take place in the region in a matter of days. Indeed, your president is coming soon. It's all very hush-hush, but it could happen by the end of the week."

"This week?" I asked.

"It will be a shock to everyone," he said.

"I'll say."

"Until the last twenty-four to forty-eight hours, the media has been filled with stories that the parties were far from a deal. Now, as you can see, carefully timed leaks are beginning to raise people's expectations. When the announcement is made, your president and secretary of state have made it clear they want lots of pomp and ceremony. A big show for the Arab and Israeli and American media. Then the four principals will fly back to Washington, brief members of the House and Senate, and hold a signing ceremony in the East Room of the White House."

"President Taylor, Prime Minister Lavi, President Mansour, and King Abdullah?"

"Of course, but why do you put His Majesty at the end of the list?" he asked. I could not tell by his tone or expression if he was serious.

Then he began coughing violently again.

"And then comes my article," I said when he had taken another sip of water.

"It was, shall we say, a 'monkey wrench.'"

"Not good news."

"Not good at all."

"But it's all accurate."

"So you say."

"You just didn't want it made public on the eve of the big peace announcement," I said.

"Look, Mr. Collins, this is old news," he said,

his expression becoming more somber now. "The ISIS attack on the base near Aleppo happened weeks ago. No one is certain what they found. Your own reporting says as much. But you and the *Times* have sensationalized the story, made it sound worse than it is, and injected fear into the hearts of millions at a moment when His Majesty is trying to bring quiet and calm."

"With all due respect, Your Highness, fewer than a hundred people on the planet knew about the ISIS attack on that Syrian base until this story. Now the whole world knows. It's very much news, and it should be, especially given recent threats by Jamal Ramzy that ISIS is about to hit a third target."

"But my point is that it's all circumstantial and hearsay," the elderly prince shot back. "If ISIS really had chemical weapons, wouldn't we all know by now? But they've neither used them nor admitted to having them; nor do you have any scrap of credible intelligence that Khalif and Ramzy and their people really have these weapons of mass destruction. You seem to be interested in nothing but selling newspapers and making a name for yourself. I expected more from you. I thought we were friends."

I was stung by the personal nature of his criticism. But for now I ignored his last comments and stuck to the central issue.

"Aren't you worried about the threat ISIS poses to the peace of the region? Don't you think it's possible that ISIS is just holding back these weapons, waiting for the right moment to strike?"

"I am not in the intelligence game, Mr. Collins. I am not a military man. I am a simple follower of Allah, and my time in this world is growing short. My eyes are growing dim. My strength is fading. But I intend to give whatever energy I have left in faithful service to Islam. I may not have much influence, but I intend to do my part for as long as I can. The world is changing very rapidly. Forces have been set into motion beyond the West's control, beyond the media's control. Muslims are looking for hope. Arabs are looking for direction, for a clear sense of mission. My colleagues are doing what they can. In the end, I have no doubt we will prevail. We *will* make this a better world. But frankly, your article is a weapon of mass distraction. And I must say I am disappointed. I had hoped that you would have known better."

Just then my phone started buzzing. A text was coming in. Apologizing, I took a moment to silence my mobile when I noticed who the text was from: Hassan Karbouli, the Iraqi minister of the interior.

I got you your interview, he wrote. **Hope you know what you're doing. Will meet you when you land.**

36

★ ★ ★

All the way back to the hotel, my mind was reeling.

How did the prince not see the seriousness of the ISIS threat? He had been around practically forever. He had seen the region engulfed in war time and time again. Now Syria was collapsing. Iraq was collapsing. How could he not see that the forces of Radical Islam were on the move and threatening to undo all the years King Hussein and King Abdullah had poured into peacemaking and moderation? I couldn't fault him for his loyalty to the king in pursuit of a peace treaty between the Israelis and Palestinians. But calling my article a "weapon of mass distraction"? Saying he was disappointed in me? It wasn't the first time a person of influence had dressed me down for publishing something he didn't want to read. But it seemed awfully reactionary from a man I'd never considered prone to such a response.

Nevertheless, the prince's views were not foremost in my thoughts. Hassan Karbouli's text message was. Was it true? Was it really possible that before this day was over, I could be sitting

face-to-face with Abu Khalif, the most dangerous
terrorist leader on the planet?

What would I say to him? What would I ask
him? He had killed my friends. He had very likely
tried to have me killed twice. Was I going to confront him? Could I maintain a professional composure? Could I actually conduct an on-the-record
interview? Could I really get him to talk about
who he was and what he wanted? How?

At the moment I had no idea. For that matter, I had no idea what Abu Khalif even looked
like. Almost no one in the world did. Indeed, most
people were only just becoming aware of his name
and of the inner workings of ISIS. The profile of
Jamal Ramzy I had written had helped, but mostly
people were learning about ISIS because of the
terrorist regime's blitzkrieg through northern Iraq
and its extraordinary success in capturing major
cities and small towns and thousands of square
miles of Iraqi territory in the face of limited Iraqi
military resistance.

Rare was the occasion before a major interview
that I would ever find myself nervous. I didn't get
stage fright. But this was different. This was a big
get. Huge.

Finally alone, and suddenly quiet, I toyed
with the idea of having a good stiff drink when
I got back to the hotel. I knew it was wrong, and
I immediately thought of Omar doing his best
to keep me sober, one day at a time. A flash of
guilt rippled through my system. But what would
it really hurt? I'd have a bourbon or two, maybe
smoke a fat Cuban cigar, and start jotting down the

questions I wanted to ask Khalif. I needed something to take the edge off my nerves. I wouldn't go crazy, I told myself. I'd be careful.

When the prince's driver pulled up in front of Le Méridien, I thanked him in Arabic, grabbed my leather satchel, and entered the hotel. I put my things through the X-ray machine in the lobby, as required by every hotel in Jordan after a series of horrific hotel bombings in the days of Abu Zarqawi, the first leader of al Qaeda in Iraq. When I had cleared the metal detectors, I headed to the bar toward the rear of the ornate main lobby.

But to my astonishment, the first person I saw as I strode past the main desk was my brother.

"Matt?" I said, having a hard time believing it was really him. "What in the world are you doing here?"

"I got your text," he said. "I wrote back but didn't hear from you."

"But how did you . . . ? I mean, how in the world . . . ?"

I was floored and not a little peeved that he'd found me. I'd taken every precaution to make sure no one knew I was here. It was one thing for His Royal Highness to track me down. He had all the intelligence resources of the kingdom at his disposal. But my brother was an academic on a sabbatical. If he could find me, maybe anybody could.

"It's not rocket science," he whispered, seeing my anxiety. "I called your editor—Allen, right?"

"But Allen doesn't know I'm in Amman," I said, my confusion growing. "I didn't tell him."

"No, you didn't. And he's furious with you. But

he figured you weren't going to hang around in Cairo. He thinks you're probably headed for Iraq, so he guessed you'd route through here. When I told him about your text, he wasn't surprised."

Maybe I hadn't covered my tracks as carefully as I'd thought.

"But how did you find this hotel?"

"I explained to Allen who I was. I told him Mom was terribly worried about you. I said I was trying to track you down and would be grateful for his help."

"And he believed you?"

"Of course he believed me, J. B. It's true. You need to call her. She's worried sick. Anyway, he mentioned a handful of hotels you tended to use when you came through town. I did a little home-work and wound up here. Anyway, it's good to see you. Thanks for your note. I was surprised to hear from you. Grateful, but surprised."

Struggling to contain a surge of conflicting emotions, I asked him how he was and how Annie and the kids were.

"We're fine, J. B.," he said. "But really, how are you? We're worried about you."

"Well, thanks," I mumbled. "I appreciate it. But I'll be fine."

"Fine? Are you kidding? Look at you. You look awful."

"I'm getting that a lot lately," I said.

"Come on, let's have a seat," Matt replied. "Let me buy you a cup of coffee. What time's your flight to Baghdad?"

I hesitated but saw little point in being coy. "Five thirty."

"Good, so we have some time," he said. "And look, I'll even drive you to the airport."

"No, that's okay, Matt. I really—"

"No, come on; I insist," he said. "I'm glad to see you. It's been too long."

I shrugged and said thank you, and we found a couple of comfortable chairs in a quiet corner of the lounge. A waiter came over and took our coffee orders, and then we were alone.

My brother asked me what had happened back in Washington and how I'd managed to survive. I basically shared with him what I'd shared with Yael. Again I skipped the private details of my conversation with Khachigian, though I did share more with Matt than I had with Yael, in part because Matt had known the man as long as I had, and perhaps better. After all, he had actually worked for Khachigian for nearly two years as a legislative aide in D.C. when Khachigian was serving in the Senate, before Matt decided to leave the Hill and go to graduate school at Gordon-Conwell Theological Seminary in Massachusetts. When Matt became an ordained pastor and was called to serve at a church in Bangor, Maine, Khachigian and his wife, Mary, actually began attending the congregation. And when Mary passed away, it was Matt who performed the memorial service and delivered the eulogy. But then Matt and Annie had moved back to the Boston area so Matt could teach at his alma mater, and as far as I knew, he hadn't had anything but occasional e-mail contact with our old family friend.

"I'm going to miss him," Matt said as the waiter delivered our coffees. "He was always so encouraging to me. When I started as a pastor, it felt like I was making every mistake in the book. I had a hard time getting my sea legs, learning how to preach, how to manage a church, how to really care for people. But I could always count on the senator for a kind word."

Matt was the only one in our family who still called Khachigian "senator."

I could see how hard this was on him. In many ways, Khachigian had become the surrogate father Matt had desperately needed when our father left home. Matt and I had gone our separate ways, but he and Khachigian had become quite close.

"Mary was always the more devout of the two," Matt said softly, staring into his coffee. "But after she died, the senator really began to take his own faith much more seriously. He used to come by my office a couple times a week. We'd chat. We'd read the Bible together. We'd pray together. I loved those times. I'd forgotten how much I'd missed them."

He didn't even seem to be talking to me, just thinking aloud. But after taking a sip of coffee, he looked up at me. "The senator grew up in the church—literally," Matt told me. "Did you know his father was an Episcopal priest?"

"Can't say I did," I replied, adding a little cream to my coffee.

"He was, but it didn't seem to take with his

son," Matt said. "After Mary's funeral, the senator told me he'd always been too busy, too proud, too ambitious to focus much on the things of God. But then he admitted he was suddenly afraid of death. How do you like that? All his years in the military, and all those years as a spy for the CIA in really dangerous places, and he'd never been scared of death. But after his wife died, he told me he had no idea if he was going to heaven when he passed on. He was sure Mary would be there, and he wanted to make sure he'd be with her for eternity. So at one point, I just asked if he was ready to pray to receive Christ as his Savior. He said yes. So we both got down on our knees, right in my office, and we prayed. From that point forward, he was truly a new man."

It was a nice story, as far as it went. It certainly spoke to the sincere affection the Khachigians had had as a couple and Matt's sincerity as a pastor. But the trajectory of this story was beginning to make me very uncomfortable. I wasn't Robert Khachigian. And Matt wasn't my pastor. He was my older brother, and he was about to cross a line.

"You know, I really ought to call Mom and let her know I'm okay," I said, setting down my cup and leaning forward in my chair.

"Are you ready, J. B.?" Matt asked.

The question seemed to come out of left field.

"For what?" I asked.

"Death," he said calmly.

The word just hung in the air for a moment as I hesitated to answer. I was about to tell Matt this was too personal. Instead I heard myself saying, "No, I'm not."

Matt said nothing. We just sat there in awkward silence. After a moment, I glanced at my pocket watch. I really was running out of time. I needed to go up to my room and pack and then head to the airport. I had an interview to prepare for—the most important of my career.

I knew Matt believed he had the answer. But I'll give him credit for not being pushy or preachy. He knew me well enough not to overreach. He'd made his point. And he let it sit.

In that way, he wasn't that different from the prince. One was trying to convert me to Christ, the other to Islam. Both were absolutely convinced they had truth on their side, that they'd found the best way to God. Maybe one of them was right. But at that moment I couldn't say which, and I didn't have the time to figure it out.

37

I excused myself and headed up to my room.

I called my mother, but she didn't answer. I left a voice message letting her know I was safe and telling her I'd just had coffee with Matt. Then I packed and headed back down to the lobby.

Matt was waiting for me in a beat-up old Toyota SUV filled with car seats and all manner of kids' toys and not a few fast-food wrappers. He was certainly leading a vastly different life from mine, and though I didn't dare admit it, I envied what he had. A good marriage. Two adorable kids. A measly paycheck but a satisfying profession. Close friends. And a faith that seemed to sustain him and always had.

I threw my bags in the backseat, and we departed for the airport in silence.

What I really wanted to do was ask if I could just go back to their house and crash for the next few days or weeks or months. I had never felt so lost or in so much pain. It seemed almost everyone I knew was dead. I had watched them die. It was killing me inside. I was afraid if I stopped and thought about it too much, I'd lose it—I mean really lose it. So I kept going, kept pushing, trying simultaneously not to think about any of it and yet redeem it as well, make their deaths worthwhile, make them mean something. But sitting here beside Matt, I could feel the tremors of a coming volcano. Raging, volatile, superheated emotions I had long been suppressing were forcing their way to the surface, and it made me want to jump off the grid and hide.

I needed a room to myself. I needed to shut the door and lock it and turn off the lights and crawl into bed and curl up into a fetal position. I needed to weep for my friends and keep weeping and weeping until there were no more tears in me. I couldn't take any more. I felt so alone. I wanted to have it all out with God until he either spoke to me or killed me. The thought of getting on that flight in a few hours and going into Iraq and meeting with the leader of ISIS literally made me want to vomit. I couldn't bear it. It was all too much.

What I needed most of all was time—time to mourn, time to think, time to talk to Matt and Annie. I was sick of eating restaurant food. I was sick of hotels and airports and deadlines and datelines in city after city after city after freaking city. I wanted to eat simple foods cooked by a wife and a mom. I wanted to hear the laughter of little children and sit by the water and lie down in a field and stare at the blue sky and smell freshly cut grass and hear lawn mowers running. I needed time to read Matt's Bible, time to ask a million questions and wrestle through it all and figure out some answers for myself before it was too late.

"Come on, J. B.; it's time," Matt said finally. "Let's pray together. Right now. You and me. Give your heart to Jesus. Let him forgive you and start to heal you and lift all those burdens off your shoulders."

"I'm sorry, Matt. I'm just not there."

"Then don't go to Baghdad."

"I wish it were that easy," I heard myself say in an inexplicable contradiction of everything I'd just told myself. "But I have to go."

"Actually, you don't," he pushed back. "And you shouldn't—maybe not ever, but certainly not until you've gotten yourself right with God."

"It's my job."

"This is not about your job, J. B.," he said. "It's about your soul. Look, you're a great reporter. One of the best in the world. Everyone knows that. I see it, and I'm very proud of you. You meet with presidents and prime ministers and kings and princes. Your articles are read by millions of people, and countless thousands make life-changing decisions because of what they learn from you. But Jesus warned successful people just like you, 'What does it profit a man to gain the whole world and forfeit his soul?' Your soul is at stake here. Please listen to me. I beg you. Don't make another move until you get right with Christ."

I wanted to say yes. I really did. But I just wasn't ready. So I thanked Matt for his concern. I would worry about God later. Right now I had to get ready for Abu Khalif.

38

* * *

BAGHDAD, IRAQ

Royal Jordanian flight 810 touched down in Baghdad at precisely 8 p.m.

Peering out the window of my first-class seat as we taxied to the main terminal, I could see a squadron of Iraqi military vehicles racing across the tarmac and flanking the jet on either side. I could also see snipers posted on the roofs of the terminal, and tanks on the perimeter of the airfield and surrounding the control tower. Security had been tight ever since the liberation of Iraq by U.S. and allied forces in 2003, but it appeared to have been ramped up significantly in light of the rapidly growing threat ISIS forces now posed to Baghdad and the central government.

I powered up my phone and checked the latest headlines. My story on ISIS had been picked up by media outlets all over the world. Agence France-Presse was quoting an e-mail purportedly from Jamal Ramzy "emphatically denying" that his forces had captured or had possession of chemical weapons. Reuters was citing the Russian foreign minister and an unnamed senior U.N. official saying it "seemed unlikely" and "close to preposterous" that ISIS had WMD, given their joint operation to remove all of the Assad regime's stockpiles of sarin precursors and other chemical weapons compounds.

Still, a *Washington Post* editorial, while expressing caution until more facts were known, nevertheless noted, "The assassination of an esteemed former CIA director who was a prime source in the WMD report adds a significant degree of credibility to the *Times* story." The editorial added, "U.S. officials should work to confirm the precise nature of ISIS's capabilities as quickly as possible, given the high stakes. If ISIS really does now have chemical weapons, the next terrorist attack in Washington or elsewhere in the U.S. could result in the deaths of hundreds—perhaps thousands."

Meanwhile, quite aside from the WMD angle, news of Khachigian's murder at Union Station was creating a feeding frenzy in Washington. With two more critically wounded victims succumbing to their injuries in the past twenty-four hours, the death toll had risen to thirty-nine. The White House press secretary was being hounded with questions as to whether there was an ISIS sleeper cell—or several—operating in the U.S. He declined to speculate. The FBI was under fire for not releasing such vital information to the public immediately. The director cut short a press conference after saying, "We're looking into the matter" to twenty-three separate questions. Several members of Congress were calling the administration's refusal to come clean on the foreign terrorist angle a potential cover-up. Meanwhile, an investigative reporter for ABC News had two sources inside the CIA saying the woman shooter was a Jordanian-American who had traveled to Syria twice in the last eighteen months and had suspected ties to al Qaeda.

As I disembarked the plane and headed into the terminal, I heard someone calling my name.

"Mr. Collins, Mr. Collins, over here."

The voice was unmistakably that of Hassan Karbouli. I approached the tall man in an ill-fitting suit. The minister of the interior was surrounded by several very nervous-looking bodyguards who, I guessed, didn't typically do airport pickups. At his side was Ismail Tikriti, the deputy director of Iraqi intelligence.

"Welcome to hell," Karbouli laughed, vigorously shaking my hand.

No one else laughed, and neither did I.

"Thank you for receiving me, gentlemen," I replied, acknowledging Ismail as well. "I appreciate your willingness to help me."

"I hope you'll forgive us for not giving you an answer sooner," Karbouli said. "As you no doubt know, we've been battling ISIS night and day. I haven't slept more than three or four hours a night. Ismail here is probably getting less. I think we're making progress, pushing them back. But I have to tell you, it's been brutal, especially in Ismail's hometown."

The security detail was getting increasingly nervous with us being out among all the other deplaning passengers. At a sign from Karbouli, they quickly whisked us away and led us through a locked door, down several flights of stairs, and along a series of corridors until we reached the airport's operations center. There they directed us to a small conference room. Karbouli, Ismail, and I entered with a single bodyguard. The rest of the security detail waited outside.

"I'm afraid I cannot stay long," the interior minister began. "I have a meeting with the prime minister in less than an hour. But I have asked Ismail to take you to see Abu Khalif. Ismail did most of the initial interrogations of Khalif himself. He'll be a great asset for you. I'm afraid you won't have much time with Khalif, but it's the best I can do."

"How much time?"

"Thirty minutes," he said.

I wanted more, but I was grateful for whatever I could get and I said so.

"How is the new prime minister?" I asked, knowing that there had been a significant political shakeup in Baghdad since I'd last been in the country.

"Off the record?" Karbouli asked.

"Of course," I said. I wasn't planning to write about anything but Abu Khalif on this trip.

"He's in a bit over his head," the interior minister replied. "And I say that with all respect for him. I don't envy the challenges he's facing."

"Fending off ISIS?"

"Yes, of course, but it's more than that. There is a tremendous division inside the cabinet. Some insist the Americans must be invited to come back and help us defend Baghdad and retake the north. Others—including some of the prominent Shias in the government—want to invite Iranian forces to come in to help us."

"And where are you?"

Karbouli shrugged. "I don't want to see the Iranians here. But I don't think your president has the inclination to send forces back here or—to be candid—the stomach to see the battle through even if he did send troops."

"So what's your solution?"

"Well, I tell you one thing for certain: the Shias have really fouled things up. They have no idea how to run the country. They have so marginalized us—politically, economically, socially, you name it—that Sunnis all across the country are absolutely furious with the government. I'm furious. So are my fellow Sunnis in the government. All four of us. We have no say, no voice. The Shias have created the perfect conditions for this ISIS surge. There is tremendous sympathy for ISIS right now. Not in Baghdad, of course. And not among the Kurds or the Christians. But in the north, in Anbar to the west, and in certain areas in the south. People are demanding change, and so far the prime minister and his people aren't listening."

"I've never see you so upset, Hassan," I said.

"You have no idea," he replied.

I looked at Ismail. I was dying to know his take. I was certain it was different from Karbouli's. Ismail, after all, was a Chaldean and a Christian.

But he remained expressionless. Whatever his views were, he was an intelligence officer, not a politician. It wasn't his place to speak his mind—certainly not here and now.

"I'm sorry, but I really need to leave you," Karbouli said, standing. "But tell me one thing. I'm hearing rumors that the Israelis and the Palestinians are about to sign a final peace treaty. Is this true?"

I was taken aback by the question. I'd thought all this was still a closely guarded secret.

"Wow . . . that would be something," I demurred. "What else have you heard?"

"I've heard from several contacts today," he said. "They say it's a done deal, that they're going to be doing a signing ceremony in Jerusalem. And I hear the Jordanians are the architects of the whole thing. You're not hearing this as well?"

"I've heard some rumors," I said carefully, not willing to burn my sources. "But I'd say that's all it is at this moment—just rumors. I guess we'll just have to wait and see."

"Perhaps," he said somewhat cryptically, and then he bid me farewell.

39

★ ★ ★

"Come, we must go too," Ismail said. "We don't have much time."

I followed him out into the hall, where we joined up with the security officers. We exited through a side door into chilly night air. But we were not getting into an armored motorcade. Ismail led me instead to a military helicopter that was already powered up and ready to lift off. Following his lead, I climbed into the back of the Black Hawk, fastened my seat belt, and put on a headset.

"So where are you taking me, Ismail?" I asked over the roar of the rotors as the rest of the detail climbed aboard.

"I'm afraid that's classified," he said. "But you'll see when we get there."

As we lifted off the ground, the head of security pulled shades down over all the windows. I was facing the rear of the chopper, so I couldn't even see through the front windshield. Then again, it was well past sundown and the pilots were flying with night-vision gear, so I wouldn't have seen much anyway.

"May I ask you some questions before we get there?" I asked.

"Ask anything you want," Ismail said, nodding.

I fished a notepad and pen out of my satchel and got to work. "How long have you had Abu Khalif in custody?" I began.

"Sorry, that's classified," he replied.

"Where did you catch him?"

"Classified."

"What was he charged with?"

"I'm afraid I can't tell you that."

"How many ISIS fighters are being held in Iraqi prisons at the moment?"

Tikriti shook his head.

"That's classified too?" I asked.

"I'm afraid so," he said.

"Okay, fine; Karbouli said you did all the initial interrogations of Khalif," I said, scrounging for something usable. "What can you tell me about him?"

"I'm sorry, J. B. I really can't say anything."

"Are you kidding?"

"No, I'm not."

My irritation was beginning to rise. "I thought you said I could ask you anything."

"I never said I was cleared to give you answers," he said.

That was even more irritating. But Ismail wouldn't budge.

He looked nervous. I wanted to know why. I was sure he wanted to tell me something. But he couldn't. Perhaps if we were alone, but not now—not with the pilots and security detail listening in.

I was beginning to wonder whether the only person I was going to get on the record tonight was Abu Khalif himself.

"So how's your family?" I asked, desperately searching for something we could talk about. "I hear ISIS forces seized Tikrit. Were your people able to get out all right?"

There was a long, awkward silence. At first I thought he was going to quip, "That's classified." But the longer he remained silent, the more worried I became.

"Please tell me they're okay," I said.

There was another long pause.

"I'm afraid not," he finally replied. "They were all wiped out."

"All of them?" I asked, aghast.

"Only one of my nephews survived. My mother was raped by ISIS terrorists. Then they shot her in the face. My father and three brothers were crucified. ISIS posted their pictures on the Internet along with photos of hundreds of others they had crucified as well."

I didn't know what to say, so I said nothing.

"These people are animals, J. B., savages—driven by Satan himself."

I was sickened and speechless, barely able to process what he was saying. I had met Ismail's family years earlier. Ismail had taken me to Tikrit to have lunch with them one day, not long after the liberation of Iraq, and what a sumptuous and festive meal it had been. It was Easter. They were all Chaldean Christians, and this was the first time in their entire lives that they had been able to truly celebrate the death and resurrection of Christ openly and without fear of retribution. They were lovely, joyful people.

Ismail's father had grown up with Saddam Hussein and had become a high-ranking general in Saddam's Republican Guard. Because of his connections, the family had been largely immune from the regime's brutality, and Ismail himself had risen to the rank of colonel in an elite unit that provided protection to Saddam's family. But when the American mechanized forces rolled into Iraq in the spring of 2003, Ismail and his father defected and began secretly helping the CIA bring down the Butcher of Baghdad. Now Ismail was one of the highest-ranking Christians in the modern Iraqi security forces. He was also one of the most committed to Iraq's democratization. To think of the price he was having to pay was almost more than I could bear.

"I am so very sorry, Ismail," I said after a few moments.

The words sounded so lame and so hollow, but I didn't know what else to say. He nodded but did not respond.

★ ★ ★

A few minutes later, we began to descend, and my stomach began to churn.

When we finally touched down, the shades went up and the doors on both sides of the Black Hawk whooshed open. Waiting for us were several dozen members of Iraq's most elite special forces unit in full battle gear. Had they been assigned to guard Khalif 24-7, or were they just here to protect us? There was clearly no point in asking, but I couldn't help but be curious.

I exited the chopper amid the glare of enormous stadium lights, but once my eyes adjusted, a chill ran down my spine. I knew exactly where I was, for I'd been here before.

We were in the central courtyard of Iraq's most notorious prison: Abu Ghraib.

It was a sprawling facility covering the better part of an acre on the outskirts of Baghdad. It had once housed more than fifteen thousand inmates, from murderers and rapists to full-fledged jihadists. Until April 2004, most Americans had never heard of Abu Ghraib, nor had most people in the world. Then *60 Minutes* broke the story of the terrible abuses taking place at the prison and revealed the most horrific pictures of American soldiers smiling beside piles of naked Arab prisoners. There were photos of U.S. soldiers beating—or pretending to beat—prisoners, and photos of our troops engaging in all manner of other terrible and offensive behaviors, effectively torturing and humiliating the prisoners in complete dereliction of their military codes of conduct, the Geneva Convention, and common moral sense.

It was a story I should have broken to the world myself, but I admit I was late to understand the gravity of the rumors I'd been hearing for months. The American public was indignant, and rightfully so, when they saw and heard the reports. So was the rest of the world. But the Islamic world—and especially the Iraqi people, many of whom had initially seen the Americans as liberators—were enraged. As news of the atrocities spread, only the jihadists were overjoyed. A handful of American traitors—that's how I saw them, anyway—had given extremists like al Qaeda and later ISIS the ultimate recruiting and fund-raising tool.

"I thought you closed this place," I shouted, since the chopper was only just winding down.

"For a while, we did," Ismail replied. "But we needed the space, so we opened it again not long ago, but only for the most dangerous of prisoners."

"How many is that?"

"I'm sorry, J. B.; that's classified."

"Come on, just give me a hint so I'm not too far off the mark in my story."

"Absolutely not," Ismail responded. "Please don't ask me again. You can say in your article that you interviewed Khalif in a prison in Iraq, but you cannot provide any other details. Are we clear?"

I shrugged, but he grabbed me by the shoulders and looked straight into my eyes. "Are we clear?" he repeated. "If not, we can power the chopper up and get you back to Baghdad right now."

"Yeah," I quickly conceded. "We're clear."

There was no point blowing the interview over details.

40

* * *

Ismail led me into the prison.

He introduced me to the warden, and together the three of us walked down one long filthy corridor after another until they ushered me through a steel door into an interrogation room.

The room wasn't small, but it wasn't large, either—maybe thirty feet by twenty feet. It was made of concrete, with a second steel door directly across from the one I had entered through. There was a two-way mirror in the wall to my right, a steel table in the middle that was bolted to the floor, and two steel chairs, also bolted to the floor, neither with any padding or cushion, facing each other across the table. Two soldiers bearing submachine guns entered behind me and took up positions in the two corners of the room at my back. Then Ismail and the warden brought in metal folding chairs, which they set beside me.

My heart began to pound. I was about to be face-to-face with a psychopathic killer. This was the most important interview of my life, but suddenly I wasn't sure I wanted to be there at all.

"Remember, you have only thirty minutes," Ismail said. "Not a second more."

I turned and glanced at the wall behind me, where I could see two small video cameras mounted high above the door, each with a red light on to indicate that they were live and recording everything we said and did here.

Just then, the steel door across the room opened, and four guards brought in a man in handcuffs and leg irons and wearing an orange prison jumpsuit. He looked like a cross between Khalid Sheikh Mohammed and Charles Manson. He had a long face and an angular nose that looked like it had been broken several times, and he sported a bushy gray mustache and a wild, unkempt black-and-gray beard. He had the beginnings of male pattern baldness that spread from his forehead to the top of his scalp, but behind that he had rather long hair, a dirty brownish gray, tied in a ponytail held together by a pale-red rubber band. His arms were clean of any tattoos, but I immediately noticed that there were large, jagged scars on his hands and forearms. That said, it was his dark-brown eyes that any normal person would notice first, for they were sunken with rings around them as if he got very little sleep, and the moment they locked onto mine, the hair on the back of my neck literally stood erect.

I had with me a digital recorder, a Nikon digital camera, and a reporter's notebook and pen, and I set them all on the table, along with my grandfather's pocket watch so I could keep careful time. When the prisoner sat down in front of me and was chained to the metal chair, Ismail nodded his assent.

I turned on the recorder and began immediately.

"You are Abu Khalif?"

Ismail repeated my question in Arabic.

"I am," Khalif replied in English, catching both of us completely off guard.

"You speak English?" I asked. "I had no idea."

He nodded and glared at me, never once looking at the Iraqi officials.

"My name is J. B. Collins," I continued.

"I know who you are."

"I'm a foreign correspondent for the *New York Times*."

"While you're still alive," he replied in a monotone.

That stopped me cold. In chains, in prison, in the middle of Iraq's most secure facility, this man was threatening to kill me. I fought to keep my composure.

"May I take some pictures?"

He nodded, and I snapped twenty or so photos from several different angles. They bore none of the quality or artistry of Abdel's work, but they would suffice.

"Now, recently I interviewed your deputy in Syria, your cousin Jamal Ramzy."

"Yes, he told me."

"You spoke with him? How?"

"That is none of your concern," he said, leaning forward in his chair. "Or yours, Mr. Tikriti," he added while still looking at me.

I looked at Ismail and the warden, both of

whom were clearly flabbergasted. It was all I could do not to get up from the table, but I was determined not to show fear, though it was rapidly welling within me.

"Very well," I said. "Let's begin this interview so you can make your case to the world. First, a few background questions. You are the spiritual leader and supreme commander of the Islamic State of Iraq and al-Sham?"

"Yes."

"And your name, Khalif, essentially means a political and religious leader of a Muslim state, 'the representative of Allah on earth,' does it not?"

"It does."

"But that is your nom de guerre."

"Yes."

"Your real name is Abdel Diab."

"Yes."

"Diab, the wolf?"

He nodded.

"What year were you born?"

"1969," he said.

"Month?"

"January."

"What day?"

"The fifth."

"Your father was Palestinian, from Ramallah?"

"Yes, peace be upon him."

"And your mother's family escaped from Nablus in 1948 and settled in Zarqā, in Jordan?"

"Yes."

"Who was your great-grandfather?"

"Mohammed Amin al-Husseini, the Grand

Mufti of Jerusalem," he said, straightening his posture.

"The Grand Mufti who allied himself with Hitler."

"Yes."

"Would you align yourself with Adolf Hitler if you could?"

"No," he said without hesitation.

"Why not?" I asked.

Again Khalif did not hesitate. "He would align himself with me."

"Why is that?" I asked.

"Because, Mr. Collins, in the end, I will kill more Jews than Adolf Hitler ever dreamed."

41

There were still more biographical details I wanted to confirm.

Jordanian intelligence officials had told Omar that Khalif's father was killed during the Black September events of 1970—the Palestinian revolt led by Yasser Arafat that attempted to overthrow the Hashemite Kingdom of Jordan. They also said that after Black September, Khalif's mother had escaped with all six children to the United Arab Emirates, where her uncle was living. She never remarried.

Ari Shalit, meanwhile, had told me Khalif himself had been born in Zarqā and raised in Dubai. He returned to Jordan in his teen years and was reportedly arrested numerous times for theft, drug smuggling, and even rape but was repeatedly released from Jordanian jails in a series of prisoner amnesty programs.

Jamal Ramzy, of course, had told me—or confirmed to me—other details of the story: about recruiting his cousin into al Qaeda to fight in Afghanistan and later in Iraq. But how exactly had Khalif risen to power after the death of Zarqawi? What were the specific events that led to his formal break with al Qaeda? What difference if any did the recent death of Zawahiri at the hands of the U.S. government make to the equation?

I wanted answers to these and a hundred other questions. But there simply wasn't time. I wasn't writing a book on Abu Khalif; I was writing a newspaper profile. I had only twenty-two minutes left, and I had to get him on the record on several current and critical issues.

"What has been the biggest ISIS victory so far?" I asked for starters.

"Being disavowed by al Qaeda," he said calmly.

This guy never ceased to catch me by surprise.

"You're saying of all your successes on the battlefield, you consider Zawahiri publicly disavowing you the greatest ISIS victory?"

"Yes."

"Why?"

"It showed the world how weak Zawahiri was. It confirmed that al Qaeda died with Usama bin Laden, peace be upon him. ISIS is the rightful heir to bin Laden's legacy, and we will build the caliphate without the infidels."

I was taking notes as fast as I could. "You consider al Qaeda leaders *infidels*?"

"Of course, and we call on all their jihadis to abandon them and come join us for victory."

"Okay, what was your second-greatest victory?"

"Driving the Americans out of Iraq and cleansing the holy soil of their filthy, arrogant presence."

"You're speaking of the American military withdrawal from Iraq at the end of 2011?"

"Yes."

"What was your strategy to accomplish this?"

"It had four parts," he replied matter-of-factly. "First, we aimed to target and kill as many of America's allies in Iraq as possible."

"Why?"

"To persuade them to leave and thus isolate the United States."

"Which allies?"

"All of them, but especially the British and the U.N."

"What was the second part of the strategy?"

"To target, kill, damage, and destroy as many Iraqi government officials and facilities as possible to exhaust and demoralize the Iraqi government and persuade them to want U.S. forces to leave."

"Third?"

"We aimed to target and kill as many NGO aid workers and government contractors as possible, to exhaust and demoralize them as well and drive them out of Iraq."

"And fourth?"

"To target and kill Shias, destroy Shia mosques, and bait the Americans into the middle of a Sunni–Shia civil war. Zawahiri was opposed to this most of all. He said it would never work. But as you well know, it did. The last American soldier left the seat of our caliphate in December 2011, and then we turned our attention to Syria."

"Why Syria?"

"Bashar al-Assad is an infidel. He had to be taken down."

"Your gains in Syria have captured the attention of the world."

"Our gains in Syria have been a serious strategic failure, though we recovered in time and recalibrated."

"Failure?" I asked. "What do you mean?"

"One of my major objectives was to penetrate the suburbs of Damascus," Khalif explained without emotion. "I believed that if ISIS forces could breach the perimeter of the capital, we could force the criminal Assad to use chemical weapons against us."

"Which he did," I said.

"Yes, and thereby crossed the Americans' famous 'red line.' At that point, I was certain we had won. I was certain that the Americans would unleash their military might against the Assad regime and either bring it down or so weaken it that we could finish the job. Then ISIS would have filled the vacuum and seized Damascus and the rest of the country. But to my astonishment, your president surrendered. He did nothing. He did not launch air strikes. He did not bring down Assad, and consequently it's taken us much longer than we planned to finish the job. That was a serious failure on my part. I vastly overestimated the fortitude of American leadership."

I was surprised but pleased by how responsive Khalif was being. He was talking, on the record. And he wasn't giving me pablum; he was giving me real insights to his worldview and quotes that would make news.

"Zooming out for a moment to look at the big picture, why is ISIS necessary?" I asked. "I mean, you've talked about your disappointments with al Qaeda, but what about Hezbollah, Hamas, and Islamic Jihad? Why is another jihadist group necessary?"

"Was the caliphate established before we emerged?" Khalif asked. "Has Palestine been liberated? Have the infidels been exterminated from the holy lands, from Mecca and Medina to Jerusalem? No. Why not? Because too many leaders who say they are committed to jihad are really businessmen. They are not true warriors for Allah. They are not true revolutionaries. They are running big corporations, large bureaucracies. They are not true believers. They are infidels. They are *kuffār*. If they were faithful warriors, then the hand of Allah would be with them. They would have gotten the job done by now. They would have established the caliphate and restored the glory that once belonged to Islam."

"Do you believe the hand of Allah is with you?"

"Of course. The evidence is clear."

"Ten more minutes," Ismail Tikriti said behind me.

I glanced at my pocket watch. The time was going far too fast.

"So what are your objectives now?" I asked.

"We have many," Khalif said. "We must finish our work here and in Syria. But as my cousin Jamal told you, we are about to open a new front. We are focused on a third target."

"Where?"

"Wasn't Jamal clear?"

"I think the world needs to hear from you directly."

"It is not a secret—we will ignite a Third Intifada in Palestine," he replied. "We will launch a full-scale, all-out jihad against the Zionists, and we will hunt down and destroy anyone who aids or abets them in their criminal occupation of Muslim lands and their enslavement of the Arab people."

"That's rather ambitious, is it not?"

"We submit to the will of Allah."

"Can you be more specific? What are your tactical objectives in the year ahead?"

"We have ten," he said.

"Ten objectives you want to achieve in the next twelve months?"

"They may take a few years to achieve, but I hope to do it in just one—inshallah."

"Will you share them with our readers?"

"Of course," he said. "We aim to capture and behead the president of the United States and to raise the flag of ISIS over the White House. We aim to assassinate the prime minister of Israel. In due course, we will unleash a wave of suicide bombers and other attacks against the Great Satan and the Little Satan and rid the world of these cancerous tumors. But our highest priorities are to rid the region of apostate Arab leaders who have betrayed the Muslim people and the Prophet himself. We will target the leaders of Jordan and the Palestinian Authority and Saudi Arabia, as well as Syria and Iraq—we will find them, kill them, and topple their governments one by one. In the time of our choosing, we will deal with the Egyptians, too. We will unify these liberated lands and people under a single command and reestablish the true caliphate, with me as the emir, beginning in the heart of the Levant but eventually extending throughout the region and soon the globe."

I was writing as fast as I possibly could. I was struck that Khalif was not animated. He spoke without any real emotion. Indeed, it was mostly in a monotone. He looked like a serial killer—creepy, sadistic—but there was an almost-supernatural aura of authority about him, as if he were truly in complete command of not only his own destiny but that of millions of others as well.

"Suicide bombers against the U.S. and Israel—when, how?" I asked.

"You will see soon enough, Mr. Collins."

"Does ISIS have sleeper cells in the U.S.?"

"I will not go into operational details," he said. "You asked for our goals. That's what I've given you. But I will say that we have recruited many Americans, Canadians, and Europeans to the cause of jihad. These warriors have gained real combat experience in Syria and here in Iraq. They are well trained. They look like you. They will blend in easily. And they carry valid American, Canadian, and E.U. passports. They will not be detected by your Homeland Security. I guarantee you that."

I absorbed this for a moment, then changed course. "Why do you hate the United States so much?"

He started to go on a lengthy riff about America's rejection of God and exportation of pornography and Washington's funding of the Israelis (whom he called "criminal Zionists") and lack of support for the Palestinians. Each sentence was a headline unto itself, and I now realized I might need to break up the interview into a series of articles. But when Ismail said we had just three minutes left, I had to cut Khalif off. There was one more topic I had to ask him about and this was it. It was now or never.

"So, Mr. Khalif, I must ask you: did ISIS capture chemical weapons in Syria?"

There was a long silence. Indeed, it was so long and so quiet that I could actually hear my pocket watch ticking over the hum of the fluorescent lights above us. And all the while he just stared at me, without blinking, and I stared back. It was weird—eerie. I'd heard people say they'd been in the presence of evil and it had made their skin crawl. I'd never known what they meant. But now I did. This guy was sheer evil. I'm not saying he wasn't human. But if I had ever been in the presence of someone who was demon-possessed, it had to have been right then.

I could feel the fear rising in me, but I resolved not to give in. This man was a killer. His people weren't just conquering Arab lands; they were slaughtering everyone who got in their way. But I was not going to let him intimidate me. He was the one in chains. I was walking out of here a free man in a few minutes. He'd already given me a huge story. It was going to be the lead story in tomorrow's paper and front-page news around the globe—the world's first interview with the world's most dangerous terrorist. I had what I needed. If he didn't want to talk about the WMD, that was fine. I'd given him his chance, but I wasn't going to beg.

Finally he opened his mouth and stunned me again.

"Yes."

"Yes, what?" I asked, not sure I could have possibly understood him correctly.

"Yes, ISIS forces captured chemical weapons in Syria," he said clearly and directly. "They were precursors, actually, to produce sarin gas. I don't have the exact figures, but my men drove off with hundreds and hundreds of crates."

"Where?"

"At the base near Aleppo, as you reported."

"You're aware of my report?"

"I am aware of and have read all your recent articles."

"You have access to the *New York Times* in Abu Ghraib?"

"I'm in prison, Mr. Collins, not a cave. We are not, let us say, without certain amenities."

I was insatiably curious about how he got his information and how he could continue to run ISIS and stay in touch with Ramzy and his other commanders from behind bars and walls that were eight feet thick. But there was no point asking him in front of the deputy director of Iraqi intelligence. There were certain questions I knew Khalif would not answer.

"We need to wrap up," Ismail said, tapping his wristwatch.

"Just one more question," I said.

"Make it quick," Ismail replied.

He was on a tight timetable, and I could see the security guys getting antsy. They were clearly not happy having a high-level Iraqi cabinet official outside the Green Zone, especially in the presence of the head of ISIS, who apparently had direct communication with his commanders outside.

I was about to ask my final question when suddenly the lights flickered and the table shook.

The warden barked a question or perhaps an order to one of his aides, who immediately radioed someone else, presumably at the prison's security command post we had passed on our way inside.

I turned back to Khalif to pose my question when the steel door behind me flew open and a guard shouted something in Arabic.

"We need to go," the warden said. "Right now."

42

* * *

The moment the door opened, I heard the explosions.

I knew immediately the prison was under attack, and I knew it had to be ISIS forces. But what worried me most was the sudden realization that Abu Khalif had likely been aware the attack was coming and might have even planned its timing.

Ismail Tikriti grabbed me by the arm and shouted, "We must go—now!"

I turned to gather my camera, digital recorder, and pocket watch and threw them into my satchel as the guards were dragging Abu Khalif out the other door, but I will never forget the twisted smile on his face or his cry at the top of his lungs: *"Allahu akbar!"*

Surrounded by soldiers, Ismail, the warden, and I raced through the corridors of the dilapidated prison complex amid the sounds of massive explosions, intense machine-gun fire, and the raucous cheers of hundreds of inmates. We quickly linked up with other heavily armed soldiers who guided us back toward the main courtyard.

328 ★ THE THIRD TARGET

I could hear the Black Hawk powering up and was eager to board and get as far from this nightmare scenario as possible. But just as the doors to the courtyard were electronically unlocked for us, I heard the high-pitched whistle of an inbound mortar shell coming from the southwest. It missed the chopper's rotors by maybe twenty or thirty feet but created an explosion that literally lifted me off my feet and sent me flying through the air. I lammed against a cement wall and landed hard. A terrible pain shot through my back and right leg. I felt blood on my head and was afraid I'd broken something.

A split second later, another shell came from behind us and scored nearly a direct hit. The helicopter erupted into a massive fireball. I covered my head and shielded my eyes, but it hardly did any good. The searing heat was more than anyone could bear. Scraps of molten metal were falling from the sky. The wretched stench of burning jet fuel and human flesh was overwhelming. And the mortars kept coming.

"Let's go, let's go," shouted the warden and the head of the security detail, grabbing Ismail and me by the collars and hauling us to our feet.

I was limping. I was in pain. But I was moving.

Then I saw Ismail. His face was covered in blood. He had shrapnel wounds all over his body. I could see the fear in his eyes, and I knew we were both in a fight for our lives.

We followed the warden back into the building and soon were moving through the corridors as fast as we could, though to where I had no idea.

Were the guards taking us to a safe room to ride out the attack? Or to the motor pool to grab some Humvees and make a break for it? There were no air options at the moment. But Ismail wasn't talking, and the warden was ashen.

We soon reached the security command center. The warden and his men assessed their options while I helped Ismail sit down. I took off my jacket and draped it over him to keep him warm.

Though I'd had several years of Arabic and was conversational in most situations, these guys were talking too fast for me to follow. But amid the fog of war, one thing was clear: our options were limited and rapidly closing.

Though my vantage point wasn't ideal, I had a partial view of a bank of video feeds from dozens of security cameras positioned all over the enormous labyrinth of prison facilities. I could see what appeared to be the remains of a truck—an 18-wheeler or perhaps an oil tanker—sticking out of the main gates of the prison, engulfed in flames. I guessed that an ISIS loyalist might have stolen the truck and used it for a suicide mission to crash the gates and create an opening for jihadists to pour through.

It wasn't just the main gates, however. On the video monitors I could see multiple car and truck bombers had hit all the prison gates, maybe even simultaneously. That, and the never-ending barrage of mortars, had pinned down the security forces inside the prison and created a breach in the outer perimeter for the hundreds of ISIS forces I could now see making their way inside.

That was when I began to get scared. The initial shock of the attack and its magnitude was rapidly giving way to the realization that these soldiers and guards assigned to us might not be able to stave off this onslaught. A prison doctor rushed over to Ismail and began administering first aid. The warden, meanwhile, was on the phone. I couldn't get much of the conversation, but the words *reinforcements* and *air support* cut through the noise. As soon as he hung up, he turned back to me.

"We need to get you men to a safe room," he said calmly.

"Where's that?"

"Directly below us, two flights down. These men will take you there."

I was about to thank him, but the head of the detail spoke first in rapid-fire Arabic. I didn't get much of it but it was obvious he was insisting that the warden go to the safe room as well. There was a brief argument, but when a series of mortars struck no more than a hundred meters from our position, the warden accepted the counsel of his men.

With a dozen soldiers creating a phalanx of security around us, we started moving down the corridor toward a bank of elevators located around the corner to our right. But at that moment we saw a grenade go skittering across the floor of the hallway directly ahead of us.

We dove for cover as it exploded.

Then someone threw two more grenades, which detonated one after the other, shaking the building and filling the corridor with smoke and debris.

The jihadists were in the building.

I told myself not to panic. I was in good hands. The men guarding us were trained professionals.

But then a group of masked men burst through the exit doors in front of us, firing automatic weapons. The soldiers in front of us never had a chance. Four of them fell immediately, dead or dying fast. I hit the deck as the rest of the detail returned fire. I heard an explosion at the other end of the corridor. Turning to look, I saw that an exit door had just been blown to smithereens. Another group of masked rebels was storming toward us.

One by one, the members of our security team dropped to the ground. Most were dead, but some were writhing on the floor in agony. That didn't last long. The commander of the attacking group, wearing a black hood and a flak jacket with an ISIS patch sewn on the front, drew a pistol and shot each of them dead, one by one. And then he turned to Ismail, the warden, and me.

We were all unarmed. There was no way out and no hope of mercy.

Ismail was already badly wounded, but he was a rock. He showed no fear, only a steely determination I found remarkable. But the warden was shaking. His entire body was quivering uncontrollably.

I was just as scared but forced myself to lie completely still. I kept my eyes open, though. I'm not sure why. Instinct. Fear. Shock. I really don't know. But there was no point playing dead. I wasn't going to fool any of these men. They were going to shoot me anyway.

With mortars still landing and one explosion

after another shaking the building to its core, the warden started to beg for his life. But the hooded ISIS commander would have none of it. He ordered his men, who were surrounding us now, to tie up the warden's hands and feet and put duct tape over his mouth to shut him up. They did the same with Ismail. Next someone opened a backpack and pulled out a tripod and video camera. Another fighter opened his backpack and set up two stands of movie lights. Instinctively, I tried to back away until I felt a boot on my neck and the barrel of an AK-47 pressed against my temple.

When I looked over and saw a bloodstained machete in the commander's hands, I shut my eyes and waited for the end. I wish I could tell you that I prayed, that I cried out to God for mercy. But the honest truth is my mind went blank. I was too terrified to think or speak or pray or beg.

Someone kicked me hard in the stomach. I bit my tongue, trying not to cry out, but I doubled up in pain. Then I heard someone shouting at me.

"Collins! Are you Collins?"

I opened my eyes. What else was I supposed to do? The commander was standing over me, a .45 pistol at my forehead. This was it.

Again the commander shouted at me. *"Are you Collins?"* he demanded in a thick Syrian accent but nevertheless speaking in English.

Someone pulled the duct tape off my mouth. I tried to speak. I tried to say yes. But I couldn't. So I just nodded and said nothing.

"Get up!"

Why? What were they going to do? Legs shaking, I struggled to get to my feet.

"Take this!" he said, putting the video camera in my hands. *"Put it on the tripod. The world must know what we've done."*

This couldn't be happening. They weren't just going to make me watch them do it; they were going to make me film it.

I had no choice. I took the video camera and walked a few steps over to the tripod. I set up the camera, turned it on, and waited, but not for long. A moment later, Abu Khalif came around the corner, dressed in his orange jumpsuit.

Khalif walked over to Ismail and the warden and stopped. The terrorists were binding the Iraqi officials' torsos and extremities with ropes and cords of some kind, making it impossible for them to move their arms and legs. The warden's mouth was taped shut, but his eyes told me everything he was thinking and feeling. The only time I'd ever seen someone as terrified was when I watched that Syrian soldier die in front of me in Homs. Ismail, however, remained resolute. He too was bound and gagged. But he wasn't going to beg for his life, not even with his eyes.

Khalif turned and looked at me.

"Start the recording, Mr. Collins," he ordered.

My hands trembling, I did as I was told. What other choice did I have?

Khalif spoke directly to the camera. He wasn't wearing a mask or a hood. He wasn't trying to disguise his voice or conceal his identity. He simply spoke in the same eerie monotone with which he had spoken to me just minutes before.

"I am Abu Khalif, the emir of the Islamic State of Iraq and al-Sham," he began. "In the name of Allah, the Most Gracious and the Most Compassionate, I declare today that the next phase of the liberation of Iraq has begun. We will establish a true Islamic caliphate, governed by Sharia law. We will care for the poor and set the prisoners free. We will drive out the infidels and restore the justice of the sword to those who commit treason against Allah and against the Prophet, peace be upon him."

Someone handed him the machete.

"Today, the faithful and brave forces of ISIS have captured two of Iraq's most vile traitors," he continued. "As Iraq's deputy director of intelligence, Ismail Tikriti is a criminal. He is responsible for the torture and execution of many loyal servants of Allah. He is a betrayer of all that is good and pure and righteous in the world. The warden of Abu Ghraib is equally complicit in these crimes against Allah and against the true Muslim people. These men are the epitome of corruption and arrogance, and today they will face the sword of true justice."

I couldn't bear to watch but was not allowed to look away.

And I knew I was next.

43

I will never be able to erase the memory of seeing a man beheaded.

It was the most revolting sight one can possibly imagine.

In the end, only Ismail Tikriti had been murdered on camera; the warden had been dragged away screaming. At some point, after vomiting so many times that I was dry heaving and gasping for air, apparently I finally blacked out. And when I woke up, I had no idea where I was or how I'd gotten there or how long I'd been unconscious. I was stunned that Abu Khalif had let me live, and I was emotionally traumatized in a way that defies description.

I found myself chained to a wall in a small, dank, chilly room. As my eyes adjusted to the dim light, I realized I was surrounded by filthy concrete walls and men with machine guns—men in hoods, men who began to chatter in Arabic the moment they saw me lifting my head off the wooden planks that served as my bed. Before I understood what

335

was happening, I was hauled to my feet, which were bound in leg irons, and led—handcuffed, with duct tape over my mouth—down a dark hallway. We headed up a stairwell, through a door, and into what appeared to be a modestly appointed living room. There I was told to sit on a tattered, faded-red couch, which I did immediately. It was only then that I realized I had been stripped to my boxer shorts and a T-shirt. But the air in the room was not nearly as cold as it had been below.

As I looked around, I saw that we were on the ground floor of an apartment building. My first impression was that an old retired couple had once lived here. Perhaps we were in the flat of the parents or grandparents of one of the ISIS rebels. But this apartment clearly no longer served as anyone's real home. There were basic accommodations and family pictures on the walls and knickknacks of various kinds here and there and even an old upright piano in the corner. But to my right, the table and chairs had been removed from the dining room. In their place were stacks of wooden crates, stamped with shipping instructions in Russian. I wondered if they were full of weapons. To my left was a cramped kitchen, but whatever appliances and cabinetry had once been there had been removed. The space was filled, instead, with rather sophisticated-looking communications equipment, computers, and hard drives.

This was a safe house.

There were no movie lights here in the living room, no tripods, and no video cameras. There were no plastic tarps on the floors or any sign of a sword or machete so far as I could see. I knew full well that could change at any moment. But since I was still alive, ISIS must want something. What that was, however, I had no idea.

A few minutes later, Abu Khalif strode into the room and sat in an old recliner. No longer wearing an orange jumpsuit, he was now wearing a traditional white robe and black- and white-checked kaffiyeh and looking very much like the Arab emir he presented himself to be, perhaps even a Palestinian one, given the color and design of this particular headdress.

"*As-salamu alaykum,*" he began, the standard Arabic greeting. *Peace be upon you.*

I did not respond, "*Wa 'alaykum-as-salam,*" the standard Arabic reply. Even if I had wanted to— and I did not—my mouth was still taped shut. Several of the guards did it, though, and then Khalif ordered one of them to remove the tape.

I could speak again. I just had nothing to say.

"Welcome to Mosul," Khalif began, taking a seat directly across from me. "Though you too are an infidel, Mr. Collins, I chose to spare your life for one very simple reason—you are still useful to me."

He did not emphasize the word *still*, but it stood out to me all the same.

"I did not want the world to know ISIS had seized those chemical weapons," he continued. "I believe Jamal Ramzy made my wishes very clear, did he not?"

He paused for me to reply.

"He did," I said quietly.

There was no point denying it now.

"There are very few people in this world who defy a direct order from me and live," Khalif went on. "But after your article, I realized there was no point in denying it. I realized I should be proud of our accomplishment, embrace it. We have done what Usama bin Laden and his lackey, Zawahiri, were never able to do—become an army that actually possesses weapons of mass destruction."

I could tell he had more to say, so I remained silent.

"Here is what you are going to do," he said. "You are going to serve the Islamic State and prove your ongoing usefulness by writing the story of my escape from captivity at the hands of the traitors to Islam. The story will be datelined from Abu Ghraib. In addition, I will permit you to write the profile of me that brought you to Iraq. That story will be datelined from Baghdad. Under no circumstances will you mention Mosul. Disobedience of any kind will be punished swiftly and severely."

I knew what that meant. I remembered all too well the way Ismail Tikriti had died.

"You will be given a notebook computer and a quiet place to write," Khalif went on. "When you are finished, you will be given a thumb drive to save the articles. I will personally e-mail the stories to your editor in Washington. You will have no direct contact with the outside world by e-mail, phone, or any other means for twenty-four hours."

Against my will, my stomach suddenly growled, and I realized I was starving.

Khalif noticed. "When you are finished writing, you will be given hot lentil soup, bread, and coffee. Until then you will do nothing but write. Do you understand?"

I was offered no choice; nor did I need one. Khalif knew I would say yes. I had no desire to die in the gruesome manner I had witnessed earlier. Besides, this was precisely the story I'd come to Iraq to get.

The second story, at least. Certainly not the first.

I still said nothing. This was clearly not a dialogue or an interview. He was giving me orders. I was expected to obey, pure and simple. I nodded, and once I did, I was quickly led away by several guards. They took me to a windowless room where I found the computer Khalif had assigned to me. Then they left and locked the door behind them.

I checked but the computer had no Internet connection. Either there was no wireless network in the house, or the computer's ability to connect with it had been disabled. I'm not sure which, and since I'm not particularly tech savvy, all I was left with was the stark realization that I was utterly alone with my thoughts.

Then I noticed my briefcase sitting in the corner. Rummaging through it, I saw that most of my things had been removed. But my notepad was still there, as was the digital recorder. So was the gift from my grandfather, still ticking. I concluded that the sooner I was finished, the sooner I would be able to eat and get out of these claustrophobic surroundings. So I got to work.

For the next several hours, I worked without a

break—without coffee, water, or even the opportunity to use a restroom. I wrote the story of the prison break first, as this was the freshest in my mind. It was a first-person account and included the beheading of Ismail Tikriti, though I did not include the most graphic details. Only then did I set to work transcribing the half-hour interview with the ISIS leader and writing an accompanying profile.

When I was finished proofreading the two pieces and making some minor corrections, I knocked on the door. Two guards led me back to Khalif. He read my work and agreed to transmit it.

"You are a first-rate journalist, Mr. Collins," he said.

I wasn't sure how to receive a compliment from a mass murderer.

He asked me for the e-mail address of my editor in Washington, and I gave it to him. He said he would transmit the article and several of the photographs from my Nikon to Allen along with a note written in my name explaining that I was safe for the moment and writing from a "secure and undisclosed location." Then he said that I should go have some bread and soup and get some rest.

"You will need it," he told me. "You have a big day tomorrow."

I didn't ask him what he meant. I didn't want to know.

44

The guards woke me up before dawn.

They gave me back my clothes and my toiletries and told me to follow them. They locked me in the bathroom and told me to take a shower. The water was freezing cold, so I essentially took a sponge bath instead. When I had dressed and brushed my teeth, I knocked on the door.

They let me out and took me back to the living room. The shades were shut, but I could tell it was still dark outside. As I sat down—once again in handcuffs and leg irons—a deep sense of dread and foreboding came upon me. Whatever Khalif had meant by the "big day" ahead of me had arrived.

I sat there for a while—maybe fifteen or twenty minutes, maybe longer. None of the guards said a word, and I said nothing either. They gave me nothing to do, and with every minute that passed, my anxieties intensified. My mind raced through a thousand what-if scenarios, each more chilling than the last. Finally Abu Khalif entered the room and took his seat across from me while his bodyguards took up positions around the room.

"Now, Mr. Collins, it is time for me to ask you some questions," he began, still without a hint of emotion in his voice. "How is your mother doing? Maggie, yes? What a lovely home she has there in Bar Harbor—Waldron Street, isn't it?"

My stomach clenched. Why was this monster bringing up my mother? And how did he know what street she lived on? I said nothing.

"And your brother—Matt, I believe; and his wife, Annie—how are they? And those precious little children. Is everything well with them? A healthy family is so important. Don't you agree?"

Now it was clear. This was a warning. A direct threat, in fact: play ball or sentence those closest to me to death.

"Feeling a little quiet today, are we?"

I clenched my jaw and said nothing.

"I'm afraid I don't have the time for your resistance, Mr. Collins," Khalif continued. "There are certain things I want to know from you, and I will get answers. To begin with, are the rumors I'm hearing from my sources in Jerusalem and Ramallah true? Is the criminal Zionist Lavi about to sign a treaty with that Palestinian traitor Salim Mansour?"

The question startled me. I'd braced myself for more questions about my family, but it seemed that was just the sadistic preamble to what he really wanted to discuss.

"Why do you ask that?" I inquired.

"No, Mr. Collins, you're not asking the questions today—*I am*," he shot back, his eyes glaring, his voice thick with emotion for the first time.

My pulse began to quicken. It was not wise to make this lunatic angry, but what was the right answer? What did he want to hear?

"Yes, they're true," I replied, concluding if I was going to die anyway, it wasn't going to be for telling foolish lies.

Yet rather than make him angrier, my answer seemed to calm him considerably. He eased back in his seat. The emotions in his face and in his voice seemed to drain away.

"You're saying Lavi and Mansour have hammered out a treaty?"

"I believe they have."

"And it's done, final, complete?"

"That's what I've been told."

"Why haven't you reported it yet?"

"That's not my beat, and I was coming here instead."

"To Iraq?"

"Yes."

"Direct from Israel?"

"No."

"From Jordan?"

I hesitated for a moment but then nodded.

He seemed to chew on that for a moment, then asked, "How soon will the treaty be signed?"

"I don't know."

"What *do* you know?"

"I hear there's going to be a signing at the White House sometime later this month," I said, avoiding any reference to the announcement ceremony that was going to be held within days, presumably in Jerusalem.

"And they will all be there—at the White House—Mansour, Lavi, and President Taylor?"

"Yes."

"And King Abdullah, as well?"

"I believe so."

"That would make sense, would it not, as he has been a key broker of the deal, correct?"

"I'm not sure how the king would characterize his involvement," I said, which was technically true and yet the closest thing to a lie I had uttered so far in this bizarre conversation.

"You don't think the king sees himself as the true author of this treaty?" Khalif pressed. "After all the private meetings he had with the Zionists like Lavi and with a *kafir* like Mansour and with sheer infidels like your president, over and over again for the last few months, you really don't think Abdullah—the betrayer of the Prophet and all that he stood for—not only sees himself but prides himself as the godfather of this so-called peace deal?"

"I really can't say," I replied.

"You can't say, or you won't say?" he asked. "There is a difference, Mr. Collins."

"I can't," I replied. "I have not spoken to the king about this or about anything else. He and I don't know each other. I've never met or interviewed him."

"Your grandfather interviewed his great-grandfather, did he not?"

I found myself both intrigued and unnerved by the intelligence Khalif had on this most top secret of Mideast initiatives, not to mention my own family history. So far as I was aware, not a single reporter in the region, the U.S., or the rest of the world knew the peace deal was done or that the Jordanian monarch was its broker, except me. If some other reporter in any news organization, including my own, had the information, they certainly would have published it. Yet nobody had—not yet, anyway. The *Jordan Times* was furthest out front, giving hints that a deal was in the making. But even they had not been definitive.

How, then, had Khalif gotten such insider information? If it wasn't coming from a reporter, could it be coming from a mole inside one of the four governments involved—American, Israeli, Palestinian, or Jordanian? And how was this lunatic going to use the information?

"Actually, my grandfather never got the—"

But before I could finish my thought, Khalif cut me off. "Oh yes, how could I forget? Fate stepped in. The king was murdered. How sad . . . for your grandfather."

Just then I heard a phone ring several times. An aide entered the living room from a doorway to my right and handed Khalif a satellite phone.

He took it and spoke into it in Arabic, slowly and deliberately. "Not yet. . . . But your preparations are proceeding? . . . Do you foresee any obstacles? . . . And you've briefed the others? . . . Very well, call me again in two hours."

Khalif gave the satphone back to the aide, who now handed over several pieces of paper.

He read them carefully and then passed them

to me. They were printouts off the *Times* website. My articles were both lead stories.

"The news is breaking, Mr. Collins," Khalif said with a slight smile. "But there is so much more to come."

Then he changed directions. "I want to ask you about your profile of me," he said calmly. "Something about it is bothering me a great deal."

I tensed immediately.

"You stated that I 'claimed' to have possession of chemical weapons 'allegedly' captured from a Syrian military base near Aleppo several weeks ago. Why did you use the words *claimed* and *allegedly*?"

"I'm not sure I understand the question," I replied as diplomatically as I could.

"Of course you do," he said. "It's a very straight-forward question. Why did you use these words to describe my statements?"

I was still not following but tried to answer nonetheless. "When I asked you about the chemical weapons back at the prison, you did claim to have them, and you did say your forces captured them from that base."

"Exactly."

"So that's what I wrote."

"No, it's not."

"I'm afraid I don't understand," I countered. "That is what I wrote."

"No, you qualified what I said," Khalif replied. "You made it seem like I merely *said* that I had WMD—as if I were making up a story—when the fact is we do have these weapons, and we will use them when the time is right."

"I was only reporting what you said."

"I get the impression you don't believe me."

"It's not a matter of what I believe," I said. "I was just trying to be a careful reporter of the actual facts."

"ISIS has chemical weapons—*that* is a fact, Mr. Collins."

"So you say."

"Yes, I do say, and that makes it a fact."

"Not in my world."

"My confirming the story doesn't make it true?"

"Not without proof."

"I see."

"I don't know what you want from me," I said. "I reported what you said. I showed it to you ahead of time. You e-mailed it to my editor as is. How can you now be upset?"

"I'm not upset," Khalif said. "I just want a story that makes it clear to the infidels that we are not talk, not spin doctors. We don't simply issue press releases and audiotapes and videos on YouTube. I am not Zawahiri. This is not hype. We are the true mujahideen for Allah, and we want the world to know this clearly."

With this, he stood. "Come, Mr. Collins; I have something to show you."

Two guards pulled me to my feet. They blindfolded me and reapplied duct tape over my mouth, and before I knew it I was being shoved into the back of a car. When we began to drive, someone turned on the radio full blast so I couldn't hear anything but some wretched music the others in the car all seemed to love. I couldn't hear street noises or birds or construction equipment or anything that might give away our route or destination. I couldn't even hear what the others were saying.

I would estimate that we drove for fifteen or twenty minutes, though without any points of reference it was difficult to maintain an accurate sense of time. Finally, however, we came to a stop. The music stopped. I heard doors open. I heard Khalif giving orders in Arabic, and then I was pulled from the car.

When the blindfold was removed from my eyes, I found myself inside a dark garage. By the time my eyes adjusted, I saw a hulk of a man in the shadows and realized Jamal Ramzy was standing in front of me, at Abu Khalif's side.

"Welcome to Mosul, Mr. Collins," Ramzy said. "What an honor. You're the first infidel ever to be permitted inside not just one ISIS base but two."

I nodded slightly but said nothing.

"Now, put this on," Ramzy said, handing me a gas mask.

"Why?" I asked.

"So you don't die—at least not prematurely," he said, and I complied.

Ramzy, too, put on a gas mask, as did Khalif and the dozen armed guards around us. Then Ramzy led the group through a dark corridor and down several flights of stairs to the basement of whatever facility we had come to. We headed through one set of doors that were nothing special, but we quickly came to another set of doors that obviously served as an air lock into some sort of research laboratory. Though my gas mask was fogging up a bit, I could see lots of scientific equipment of various kinds and at least a half-dozen men wearing white lab coats and masks.

Ramzy ushered Khalif and me and one armed guard into a separate room. There was nothing in there—no chairs, no tables, no furniture of any kind—but in front of us on the far wall was a rectangular window with glass that appeared several inches thick. On the other side of the glass was a concrete bunker of sorts. It too was empty, but as I watched, someone with a lab coat entered from a side door to our right. He was carrying a wooden chair. He set it down and went to retrieve another and another and then finally a fourth chair. Working quickly and methodically, he lined up the chairs in a row facing us. Then he was gone.

My heart was racing. Sweat was beginning to drip down the back of my neck. I was feeling claustrophobic in this mask and struggling to breathe. But there was no way out. Abu Khalif was standing immediately to my left. Jamal Ramzy was immediately to my right. And an ISIS thug was standing behind me, in front of the door, holding an AK-47.

Through the window—which I assumed was a two-way mirror—I saw three prison guards from Abu Ghraib appear, along with the prison's warden, whom I recognized immediately. They were all handcuffed and shackled together. When they had been led into the room on the other side of this window, they were unchained and ordered to strip. It was clear that each of them had been tortured severely. They were bloodied and bruised. Their faces were swollen. Two of them had broken noses.

Once they were naked, they were ordered to sit down on the chairs, which they did, each of them trembling. Abu Khalif rapped his knuckles on the glass, apparently giving an order to the man in the gas mask and lab coat, who nodded and quickly left the room.

A moment later, a canister dropped into the room from somewhere above the ceiling. It was emitting something that looked like tear gas, but it quickly became apparent that this was not tear gas. As I watched the men behind the glass, I suddenly realized it was sarin gas. Khalif was going to murder these men just to prove to me that ISIS really did have the Syrian weapons.

Before long the prison guards and the warden were on the ground. They were writhing in pain. They were foaming at the mouth, convulsing violently. The chamber they were in was soundproof, so I couldn't hear their screaming. But when I tried to look away, Ramzy grabbed my gas mask and smashed it against the window, forcing me to watch these men suffer a grisly, painful, horrible death. I wanted to close my eyes, but I couldn't. I was there to witness these murders, to be able to tell the world what had happened and how. This was my job. This was why I was here. As much as I didn't want it to be true, I now had proof that ISIS had chemical weapons, and I had to be a faithful witness. Who else would do it?

These men deserved it. And the world had to know the truth.

I stood there, my bloodless face pressed to the window, for what seemed like hours, horrified as I watched these men die a slow, agonizing, excruciatingly painful death. And I must admit that as much as I didn't want any of them to perish, for me they couldn't die soon enough. That seemed a terribly selfish thought, but I couldn't bear to watch them grasp for life any longer.

Eventually it ended. Only then did Ramzy let me leave the observation room and step back into the larger laboratory. I repeatedly felt like I was going to be sick, but I think the fear of vomiting in my mask and suffocating as a result kept down all that was trying to force its way through my esophagus.

Finally Ramzy took me by the arm and led me back through the air lock. Only then was I permitted to remove my mask. Everyone else removed theirs as well.

No one said a thing, not even Khalif. But perhaps that was because Ramzy was not finished. He led the group to a large warehouse next door. To my astonishment, the rectangular building was filled with artillery shells and missile warheads, most of which were neatly and carefully stacked in crates bearing Syrian military markings, sitting on pallets. Some of the pallets were being loaded onto nondescript trucks.

"This is just a small portion of the chemical weapons and delivery systems we captured near Aleppo," Ramzy told me. "These are awaiting the emir's orders. The rest are being pre-positioned to strategic locations, even as we speak."

When Ramzy was finished speaking, Khalif turned to me and, standing less than a foot from my face, gave me a simple order.

"Write *this* story, Mr. Collins," he said. "Write that we're coming after the infidels. Write that we have the motive. We have the means. All we're waiting for now is the opportunity, and I am supremely confident it will show itself soon. Write that, and then I will decide what happens to you."

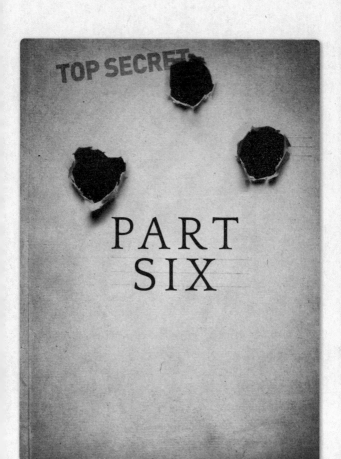

TOP SECRET

PART SIX

45

* * *

My flight from Erbīl landed in Amman.

I still couldn't believe they had let me go.

I had tried to sleep on the flight but couldn't even close my eyes. Every time I did, my thoughts were filled with the most ghastly images. The flight attendants had served me a snack, but I couldn't eat. They'd offered me water and soda, but I couldn't drink. My hands were shaking and I couldn't make them stop.

I powered up my phone and checked texts and e-mails. I saw none that looked urgent. But as we taxied to the terminal, I sent three messages of my own. The first was to my mom, letting her know that whatever else she might read, I was safely out of Iraq and out of the hands of ISIS. The second was to Allen MacDonald, essentially saying the same thing and asking him to coordinate a conference call between him, me, and the chief counsel for the *Times*. I was ready to go to the FBI, to do anything I could to put these monsters behind bars, but I wanted to know if my actions had put me in any legal jeopardy. The third text was to my brother, saying I'd just landed back in Amman and asking if he would come pick me up at the airport as soon as possible.

Then I sent a fourth, to Yael.

Grabbing my things from the overhead bin, I made my way off the plane as I scanned the latest headlines on my phone. My two articles—the first on Abu Khalif and his escape from Abu Ghraib and the butchery of a prominent Iraqi government official, the second on the murder of Abu Ghraib's warden and several staff members during an ISIS demonstration of its sarin gas stockpiles—were the lead stories on the *Times* website.

The other major story on the front page was by Alex Brunnell, the *Times* bureau chief in Jerusalem. Its headline read, **Peace Deal 'Close but Not Yet Done' between Israelis and Palestinians, Says Senior U.S. Official.**

The lead story in the *Washington Post* was by their chief White House correspondent: **President Taylor Announces Surprise Summit on Mideast Peace.**

A *Haaretz* headline out of Jerusalem announced, **Israelis Roll out Red Carpet, Prepare to Welcome Air Force One.**

Meanwhile a *Jerusalem Post* headline was more negative: **Right-Wing Cabinet Members Furious with Lavi over Rumors of Secret Negotiations with Palestinians.**

A tweet from Al Arabiya claimed, **Sources close to PA President Mansour say they are "cautiously optimistic" a deal for a Palestinian state could be closed this week.**

Finally, the *Jordan Times* was reporting, **Aides to**

King Say He Is 'Cautiously Optimistic' about Peace Process, Open to Attending Peace Summit in Jerusalem, if Needed.

Clearly events were moving rapidly. I had missed my window for an exclusive on the peace deal, but I didn't care. I was just glad to be out of Iraq, alive and safe and free. The question was for how long? For the moment, I was useful to Khalif and Ramzy. But that calculus could change any minute. What's more, I was terrified for Matt and his family. They had to get out of Jordan as fast as possible.

As I entered the terminal, I was struck by the much-heavier-than-usual presence of armed Jordanian soldiers and border police. Each passenger coming off the flight was thoroughly checked for weapons and explosives. All luggage was put through X-ray machines, subjected to bomb-sniffing dogs, and then hand-searched. In addition, Jordanian officials were asking questions of all passengers to determine why they had been in Iraq and why they were coming to Jordan. The whole process took more than an hour. But when it was finally over and I headed through the main hall outside to get a taxi, I suddenly ran into Matt, who greeted me with a relieved bear hug.

"Are you all right?" he asked, looking me over.

"I'm fine," I said, truly glad to see him again but wishing he wasn't making a scene. "Thanks for coming to get me."

It wasn't true, of course. I wasn't fine. But I couldn't say anything more, not in public.

"We were worried sick," Matt said. "Annie and

I thought we'd never see you again. And don't even ask about Mom."

"But you let her know I'm out, right?" I asked, guilty for all I was putting her through.

"Of course," he said. "As soon as I got your text that you were here, I called her right away. She said she'd just gotten a note from you as well."

"How is she?"

"She's pretty shaken up. I mean, she's been reading all of your articles, and those were hard enough, but she can read between the lines. She knows it was even worse than you wrote."

"It was," I told him. "Worse than you can imagine."

We headed straight out of the airport to his car. As we got in, he asked me how in the world I had gotten back to Jordan in one piece.

"It was bizarre," I told him. "Late last night, Jamal Ramzy and some soldiers came down to the basement where I was chained up. They blindfolded me and carried me upstairs. I was sure this was it, that they were going to behead me right then. Instead, they threw me, bound, into the trunk of a car and started driving. After fifteen or twenty minutes, they stopped the car, pulled me out of the trunk, and removed the blindfold and shackles. It was night, but there was a full moon. So I could see that we were in the middle of nowhere. That's when I thought they were going to shoot me. But instead, Ramzy handed me the keys to the car and a map. He told me to follow the map out of the province of Nineveh until I got to the border of Kurdistan. Then he told me to explain to the *peshmerga* that I was a journalist who had been covering the war and needed to get to Erbīl to catch a flight to Amman."

"They just gave you the keys?" he asked.

"I know. It was crazy."

"So then what?"

"Ramzy and his men got into an SUV that had apparently been following us, and they drove off into the night."

"Just leaving you standing there."

"Yeah."

"And it worked? The Kurds let you in?"

"I'm sitting here with you, aren't I?"

"Why do you think they let you go?"

"I don't know for sure," I said as we worked our way through the neighborhoods of Amman. "I think they changed their focus. Yes, Khalif and Ramzy would have loved to send my head to the president of the United States via FedEx. But I think they decided they liked the WMD story out there. Maybe they think it makes them look tough. I don't know. But I don't think they're content just having the story published. They want me out there doing radio and television shows, telling people what I saw, that they really do have chemical weapons."

"It's so sickening."

"You don't know the half of it," I told him. "I've never seen anything like Abu Khalif. He rarely shows emotion. He talks in a monotone. But you should have seen the sheer twisted joy on his face when he sawed off Ismail Tikriti's head and when he was watching that sarin gas kill the warden and those three guards. It was sick, Matt, worse than any horror film you could possibly imagine."

"You didn't write any of that in your articles, of course," he noted. "I could tell you were trying to be very careful with your words, and I figured he was watching you write."

"It was the most horrible experience of my life."

"Thank God you're out."

"Thanks again for picking me up. It really means a lot to me."

"Of course. What are brothers for? I'm just glad it's over."

"But it's not."

"What do you mean?"

"It's not over," I said. "I think ISIS is going to strike soon."

"In Israel or back in the States?" Matt asked.

"Actually, I think he's going to strike here."

Matt looked stunned. "Here, where? Jordan? Amman?"

"Yes."

"You think Jordan is the third target?"

"I'm starting to, yes."

"Why? What do you mean? I've seen all the stuff you've written in the last few days. Khalif told you point-blank he was gunning for Israel and the U.S. If I were him, I'd be planning to hit the peace summit in Jerusalem, wouldn't you? It's one-stop shopping."

"I have no doubt Khalif would love to strike the summit in Jerusalem, but I don't think he'd ever get that far," I said. "There's too much security. I think he's coming here first. He's just in Mosul. That's practically right down the road."

"But why here?" Matt asked. "Isn't Khalif Jordanian, from Zarqā?"

"Absolutely, and that's all the more reason," I said. "He hates the king. He believes His Majesty is an infidel. He said as much when I interviewed him."

"Sure, but he gave a laundry list of leaders he wants to kill," Matt replied. "Don't you think he was just talking trash, listing everyone he could?"

"No, I don't."

"Why not?"

"Several reasons," I said as Matt wove through traffic. "First, yes, he gave quite a hit list. But look who's not on it—the prime minister of Lebanon, the emirs in the Gulf, the mullahs in Iran."

"So what?"

"So he wasn't just giving me a laundry list," I explained. "I think he was giving me his list of priorities in order."

"Okay, fine, but that still proves my point," Matt replied. "He said specifically he's going to attack the U.S. and Israel with suicide bombers and chemical weapons. That was the first thing he mentioned."

With that, Matt pulled into his neighborhood and we were at his apartment building, a modest complex in a rather run-down section on the outer eastern edges of Amman. The street was crowded, but we soon found a parking space around the corner.

"Go back and reread the transcript," I said when he had turned off the engine. "I can't believe I didn't see this earlier. Khalif told me exactly what he was going to do."

Matt pulled out his smartphone and brought up the *Times* website. A moment later, he had the transcript.

"Okay, now find the section where Khalif vows to capture and behead the American and Israeli leaders," I said.

Matt quickly scanned through the interview and found the section.

"Got it."

"Good, now read exactly what he says there."

So Matt did.

"KHALIF: We aim to capture and behead the president of the United States. . . . We aim to assassinate the prime minister of Israel. In due course, we will unleash a wave of suicide bombers and other attacks against the Great Satan and the Little Satan and rid the world of these cancerous tumors.

"See?" Matt said. "He couldn't be clearer—he's coming after the U.S. and Israel."

"I know, I know, but keep reading," I insisted.

"KHALIF: But our highest priorities are to rid the region of apostate Arab leaders who have betrayed the Muslim people and the Prophet himself. We will target the leaders of Jordan and the Palestinian Authority and Saudi Arabia, as well as Syria and Iraq—we will find them, kill them, and topple their governments one by one."

"There it is," I said. "Khalif says his highest priority is taking out apostate Arab leaders who have betrayed the Muslim people and the Prophet."

"He's coming after the king of Jordan," Matt said.

"Exactly."

"So you think Iraq and Syria were ISIS's first two targets, and Jordan is the third?" he asked.

"I think so," I said. "And what if it is? Imagine if ISIS attacks Amman with chemical weapons, kills the king, destroys most of the government, and establishes an Islamic state right on the border of Israel?"

"That's terrifying."

"Especially if ISIS ends up in control of all of Iraq and Syria too."

We sat for a moment, trying to make sense of all that. Then Matt said, "I have to admit, I never really thought much about Jordan or its importance until we came here for my sabbatical."

"You're not alone," I said.

"But it's actually quite nice here," Matt continued. "I mean, the king seems pretty moderate. And the country is peaceful, friendly, stable. They've got a peace treaty with Israel. They're probably the best Arab ally America has."

"Absolutely," I agreed. "Plus Jordan is the quiet cornerstone of any peace deal with the Israelis and Palestinians."

"What do you mean?"

"Well, think about it," I said. "The president's entire strategic concept of persuading Israel to give up the West Bank for a final peace deal with the Palestinians is predicated on the Hashemite Kingdom being just what you said—a stable and secure friend and ally on the east side of the Jordan River. But what if the king falls? What if jihadists take over? The entire peace process goes up in smoke, right?"

"I guess so. Hadn't really thought about it that way."

"Sure. A strong Jordan is Israel's buffer against any ground invasion from the east. If the jihadists take Amman, Israel's entire security architecture falls apart. If the kingdom falls and ISIS takes over, the whole West Bank could become radicalized and go up in flames. Suddenly Israel isn't facing a jihadi storm way out in the western provinces of Iraq. Suddenly they've got ISIS forces on the outskirts of Jerusalem. At that point, the U.S. and Israel would be facing a radical Islamic caliphate encompassing all of Syria, all of Jordan, most if not all of Iraq, and very likely allied with Iran, which could soon become a nuclear power."

Matt looked through the windshield, thinking. "Okay, that's a horrifying scenario, I grant you that," he said. "But is that really possible? I mean, Jordan's got a great military. They've got American weapons. The king used to be the commander of the special forces here. Do you really think it's possible ISIS could take over this country?"

"Did you think Mubarak would fall in Egypt?

Ghaddafi in Libya? The guy in Tunisia? Now Assad's on the brink. And I'm telling you, the king is next."

"Maybe you're right." Matt sighed. "Maybe the king's days are numbered. Maybe that's how it's going to happen."

I looked at him. "How what's going to happen?"

"The prophecies."

"What prophecies?"

"You know, what I came here to research."

"I'm not following."

"My sabbatical—the whole reason I came here. Don't you remember?"

"Did you ever tell me?"

"Of course I did," Matt said. "I sent you a long e-mail last year explaining the research I was going to do here and suggesting you might do a story on it at some point."

"I don't remember ever getting that."

"Well, that figures. You never reply to any of my e-mails."

I didn't know what to say to that, so I just asked, "What's your research on?"

"Jordan in biblical eschatology."

"Escha-what?"

"Eschatology—End Times theology."

"What about it?"

"Bad times are coming for Jordan."

"Meaning what?"

"Meaning that aside from Israel, few modern nations are mentioned more in the Bible—and especially in Bible prophecy—than Jordan."

46

★ ★ ★

"Jordan is mentioned in the Bible?" I asked.

"Well, not per se," Matt replied. "*Jordan* is a recent name. But the nation we call the Hashemite Kingdom of Jordan today is actually comprised of territory once held by three biblical nations: Ammon, Moab, and Edom. And the Bible says a terrible judgment is coming against the people who live in these places in the last days before the return of Christ."

"So?"

"So many people—myself included—believe we're living in the last days. Which means the prophecies that describe the epic destruction of Jordan's cities and the apocalyptic devastation of the Jordanian people could come to pass soon. After all, we've already seen so many other End Times prophecies come true."

This was all news to me. "Like what?"

"Like the miraculous rebirth of the State of Israel. Like the dramatic return of the Jewish people to the Promised Land. Like the Jews rebuilding the ancient ruins of Israel. The ancient Hebrew prophets said all these things would happen in the last days. And one by one, they're happening."

"And you're saying the judgment and destruction of Jordan is next?"

"I can't say it's next, but according to the Bible, it's coming. Maybe what you're describing with ISIS will set the prophecies into motion."

"Hold on a minute. What prophecies are you referring to? What kind of 'terrible judgment' does the Bible actually say is coming? How bad are we talking?"

"Catastrophic."

My first instinct was to dismiss this as crazy talk from my crazy brother. A few days before, I would have. But something in me was changing. I had seen too much horror to be able to discount the possibility that more horror could be coming. Besides, I figured, if anyone knew about this stuff, it was Matt. "Keep talking," I said.

"Okay, well, first of all, there are a number of other ancient sites, cities, or regions mentioned in the Bible that are located in the modern-day nation of Jordan."

"Such as?"

"One would be what the Scriptures call 'Mount Seir' or the 'hill country of Seir.'"

"And where's that?" I asked.

"The term *Seir* is actually used to describe a specific mountain, a whole mountain range, and the entire nation or territory of Edom, which is the ancient name for the southern region of Jordan," Matt explained. "Seir was first mentioned in Genesis 14:6 and then again in Genesis 32:3, among other places."

"So Seir is essentially synonymous with Jordan?" I clarified.

"Southern Jordan, at least, yes," Matt said.

"Okay, what else?"

"Well, there's Bozrah," he continued. "Bozrah was an ancient city located in Edom. For a time it was actually the capital of Edom."

"Any others?"

"Yes, there's Sela, which is also thought to have been a capital or stronghold of Edom. In 2 Kings 14:7, we learn that Sela, whose name was changed by King Amaziah to Joktheel, was located in Edom."

"So that's in southern Jordan as well?"

"Right. And here's something interesting: Sela may actually be the biblical name for the city of Petra, the ancient capital city of the Nabataeans. Have you ever been there?"

"No, can't say I have."

"You would love it. Petra was carved out of solid rock inside a narrow canyon, so it was very difficult for foreign armies to penetrate. And it's one of the biggest tourist attractions in Jordan today."

"Okay, fine, the Bible has all these names for Jordan," I said. "But what about these judgments you're talking about?"

"Great question," Matt said. "Should we finish this inside?"

"No, let's talk here," I said.

"But Annie and the kids can't wait to see you."

"And I can't wait to see them," I said. "But that's why I want to finish this now. The moment we go inside, we're going to get caught up in everything else."

"All right, if you insist," he said.

"I do."

Matt paused a moment, then continued. "Okay, one place where the Bible talks quite a bit about Jordan is in the book of Jeremiah, specifically in chapter 49. In verse 2, God says, 'Behold, the days are coming . . . that I will cause a trumpet blast of war to be heard against Rabbah of the sons of Ammon; and it will become a desolate heap, and her towns will be set on fire.'"

"Pretty dark," I said.

"Yeah, but that's not all. In verse 13, the Lord says, 'I have sworn by Myself . . . that Bozrah will become an object of horror, a reproach, a ruin and a curse; and all its cities will become perpetual ruins.' And then, in verse 17, he says, 'Edom will become an object of horror; everyone who passes by it will be horrified and will hiss at all its wounds.' And these are just a few examples of what the Bible says will happen to areas that are within modern Jordan."

"How do you know all this stuff?" I said, not wanting to offend my brother but not sure what to make of any of it either.

"I've been studying this for the past eight months, remember? You have to admit, it does kind of catch your attention—especially when you're living here."

"It's attention-getting, all right," I said. "But

how does all this relate to what could be going on with ISIS?"

"I'm getting to that," he said. "If you do a careful study of this section of Jeremiah, you'll see that the prophecies are eschatological; that is, they concern the End Times. Jeremiah 48 is a prophecy against Moab, which is central Jordan. Most of chapter 49 is made up of prophecies against Ammon, which is north-central Jordan, and Edom, which is southern Jordan. If you look at these two chapters, you see a lot of language like 'days are coming' and 'in that day' and even 'it will come about in the last days.' Still with me?"

I nodded.

"So it's these phrases, which are consistent with other End Times prophecies throughout the Bible, that let us know Jeremiah was not writing—in this section, at least—about prophecies that would take place in his lifetime but rather about things that would be fulfilled in the days leading up to the return of Christ. Does that make sense?"

"Yes, I think so," I said.

"Now, Jeremiah gave many prophecies that did come true in his lifetime or soon thereafter," Matt said. "Most famous, of course, were his prophecies that God was going to punish his people for their disobedience by sending the Babylonians—led by the evil King Nebuchadnezzar—to conquer Jerusalem and destroy the Temple and carry off the Jewish people into exile in Babylon. And these terrible things happened, just as Jeremiah said. Fortunately, Jeremiah also prophesied that the exile of the Jews in Babylon would only last for seventy years, and then God would have mercy on them and restore their fortunes and bring them back to the land and reestablish Jerusalem as their capital. And that's exactly what happened. The Babylonians were conquered by the Persians, and seventy years after the Jews were judged and exiled, the king of Media-Persia set them free and helped them return to the land and rebuild their Temple."

"Jeremiah wrote all that?" I asked, genuinely intrigued.

"Yes," Matt said, "and this is what gives us confidence that Jeremiah was a true prophet from the Lord and that his End Times prophecies will come to pass at the proper time as well. We don't have time to go through an in-depth analysis right now, but just focus for a second on the places I've already mentioned—Ammon, Edom, and Bozrah. We've established that Jeremiah is speaking about the End Times and that he's giving prophecies from the Lord about the future of places we now call the kingdom of Jordan. Right?"

I nodded again.

"Okay," Matt continued. "Jeremiah clearly describes an apocalyptic, catastrophic judgment that falls on the people and cities of Edom in the last days. I already mentioned some of the verses from chapter 49, but there are others. In verse 18, talking about Edom, it says, 'Like the overthrow of Sodom and Gomorrah with its neighbors . . . no one will live there, nor will a son of man reside in it.' And in verses 20 and 21, the text describes enemies dragging off 'even the little ones of the flock.' It says, 'The earth has quaked at the noise of their downfall. There is an outcry! The noise of it has been heard at the Red Sea.'"

Matt was quiet for a moment, presumably to let me absorb what I'd just heard. I was beginning to understand what he had said about bad things being in store for Jordan. But was any of it actually true?

"Look," Matt finally said, "a person can and should study these passages very, very carefully, and use all the tools and resources available to a modern Bible scholar. But it doesn't take a PhD in theology to understand the meaning of the text. The preponderance of the evidence is clear. These biblical prophecies indicate that God has decreed judgment on the people living in Ammon, Moab, and Edom. These are facts. They're not comfortable ones, especially in this modern age. But judgments *are* coming. And if you look at this text, and the many other prophecies about the future of Jordan found in Isaiah, Jeremiah, Ezekiel, Obadiah, Daniel, and elsewhere, you'll find that God gives numerous reasons for such judgments. Because he can see the future, God has declared the people who live in these places in the last days guilty of arrogance, pride, hatred, violence, cruelty, injustice, worshiping false gods, and a profound lack of compassion toward women, royalty, neighbors, and particularly toward Judah, Jerusalem, and Israel."

"And none of these judgments have already come to pass in history?" I asked.

"Some have, sure," Matt said. "But not all."

"How do you know for sure?"

"Well, for one thing, there are still people living and working and prospering in southern Jordan," Matt replied. "But the text clearly indicates that the End Times judgment that is coming on Edom will be utter, final, and irreversible. Verse 13 says, 'All its cities will become perpetual ruins.' Verse 18 says, 'No one will live there.' And of course, the text likens the future destruction to the judgments of Sodom and Gomorrah. Guess where those two cities were located?"

"Jordan?"

"Southern Jordan."

"Ouch."

"Exactly," Matt said. "So while Edom has been conquered in the past, it hasn't experienced the absolute cataclysmic judgment that Jeremiah foretold in this chapter."

"In other words, according to the Bible, this is all coming in the future?" I asked.

"Right—in the future, in the lead-up to the return of Christ," Matt confirmed. "And that's why this is weighing heavily on me. I have come to love this country, and I love its king. I mean, he's not perfect; what leader is? But His Majesty really is one of the good guys. So was his father, King Hussein. These men made peace with Israel. They chose to be close allies with the U.S. and the British. King Abdullah has emerged as arguably the leading Reformer in the Arab world. He actively promotes a moderate, tolerant, peaceful model of Islam. He's reached out to Christian leaders all over the world, Protestant and Catholic. For the most part, Jordanian Christians are treated kindly and with respect. Did you know a few years ago the king created a national park along the east bank of the Jordan River to protect it for Christian baptisms?"

"No, I didn't."

"And that's not all," Matt continued. "The king actually gave land to thirteen different Christian denominations to build churches and baptismal sites along the Jordan River. I've been there, J. B. I've seen hundreds of Christians baptized there since I came to study here."

"Your point?" I asked, not wanting to be rude but not totally following some of his jargon.

"My point is that this king doesn't strike me as a candidate for divine judgment," Matt said. "Now, Isaiah tells us that God's thoughts are higher than our thoughts, and his ways are higher than our ways, and I believe that. So in his sovereignty, God can bring righteous judgment on a nation that isn't following him at any time. And Jordan, by and large, isn't following him. But . . ."

"But what?" I asked, curious why he was suddenly hesitating.

"I don't know," he said, clearly searching for the right words. "After everything you've told me about ISIS, combined with what the Bible says about Jordan, I'm just wondering if this king is going to be toppled. Don't get me wrong; I don't want it to happen. He's a good man, and he's doing a great job in many ways. But I wonder if his days are numbered. What if the Arab Spring erupts here in Jordan? What if the king and his family are brought down and replaced by tyrants who lead the people to war against Israel, to war against the Christians, to the kind of social dynamic that is consistent with these Scriptures? I can't say that's what's going to happen. I don't know that for sure. But what if the return of Christ is sooner than most people think? And what if ISIS is the tool Satan uses to take Jordan down a long, dark path?"

47

We finally got out of the car and headed into Matt's building.

As Matt pressed the button for the elevator, I realized I couldn't procrastinate any longer. "Listen, Matt, there's something else."

"What?"

"You guys need to leave Jordan."

The elevator door opened, and Matt shot me a look. "What are you talking about?"

"You're not safe here. You need to go back to the States—immediately."

"Immediately?"

"Tonight," I said as we stepped into the elevator and the door slid shut behind us.

"J. B., are you crazy? I'm on a yearlong sabbatical. I've still got four months to go."

"No, you and Annie have to take the kids and leave. Don't worry about the cost. I'll cover your tickets."

"Because you think ISIS is going to attack Amman?"

"No, it's not just that."

"Then what?"

"It's Abu Khalif."

"What about him?"

"He mentioned you guys by name. He knows you're here in Amman. He knows where you live. You're not safe here, any of you. Mom's not safe either. Abu Khalif made it clear that when he's good and ready, he's coming after all of us."

The bell rang and the door opened. We stepped out into the hall, but Matt stopped me before we went any farther. "You're serious about this?"

"I'm afraid so. And you've got to move fast."

"But why us? What does Khalif want with any of us?"

"I don't know," I said. "I told you, the guy is a psychopath, a Hannibal Lecter with sarin. I'm just telling you what I saw and heard. What kind of brother would I be if I didn't?"

Matt stood there in the hallway for a moment. I could see him trying to process all that I'd told him and what it meant for him and his precious family.

"Katie turned four last week," he said softly.

"Already?" I said. I desperately wanted to make sure nothing happened to her.

"She's in a Sunday school class at the church we're going to," Matt continued. "She loves it. Can't wait to get there every week. And there's a competition. For every Bible verse she memorizes, she gets a point. Whichever kid gets the most points by the end of the semester gets a prize. Right now, she's in second place."

I nodded but said nothing, not quite sure where this was headed.

"Do you know what her verses were for last week?"

"No," I said. "What?"

"1 John 5:11-12."

"Okay . . . ?"

"Do you remember that from when we were kids?"

"Can't say I do; why?"

"'And the testimony is this, that God has given us eternal life, and this life is in His Son. He who has the Son has the life; he who does not have the Son of God does not have the life.'"

"All right," I said. "I guess I remember something like that, vaguely."

"I'm not worried about us, J. B. The four of us know where we're going. But what about you?"

"What do you mean?"

"I mean Annie and the kids and I have trusted Christ as our Savior," he replied, lowering his voice to almost a whisper. "We have the Son. We've been forgiven our sins and adopted into the family of God—by grace, not because of anything good we did. Have you? We've been praying for you for years. And we were praying for you from the moment you left for Baghdad—for your safety, but more importantly for your soul. So I have to ask you: where are you with Christ right now?"

I tensed. "I appreciate your concern for me, Matt, I really do, but I—"

I suddenly had no idea how to finish that sentence, so I just stopped midflight.

"Look, this isn't some game. Everywhere you go, people around you—people close to you—are dying. Someone's gunning for you. And sooner than later, they may get you. I hope to God they don't. I pray every day and every night they don't, and I won't stop. But the odds are against you, and they're slipping fast. You need to make a choice—heaven or hell, in or out. What are you going to do with Jesus? You're running out of time to decide."

It was a valid question. Especially now. I just didn't want to answer it.

"I don't know," I said, looking away.

"Why didn't you ask Christ to save you while you were in Iraq? Don't you realize how close you came to death?"

"Of course I do, but what do you want me to say? That I had a foxhole conversion? That I saw my life passing before my eyes and decided to accept Christ as fire insurance, just in case?"

"No, of course not. I'm not telling you to make some superficial leap into religion. Certainly not for my sake or Annie's or Mom's. What I'm saying is you need to make a serious decision, on your own, in your heart and in your head, based on the facts. Is Jesus the Messiah or isn't he? Is he the only way to eternal life or not? The stakes couldn't be higher. It's not just life or death; it's your eternity we're talking about. And it's time to choose, J. B. Before it's too late."

"Matt, for crying out loud, why are you pushing me on this?"

"I'm not pushing you."

"Of course you are."

"Okay, fine, I'm pushing you. But what else am I supposed to do? I love you. So do Annie and the kids. We care about you."

"And you're worried for me."

"Of course we are. Aren't you?"

I sighed and looked away. "Yeah, guess I am. But I'm not there, Matt. I'm sorry. I'm just not."

It was quiet in the cluttered, narrow hallway. The only sound was the low hum of the fluorescent lights above us. The whole place was filled with kids' bicycles and balls and dolls and empty soda bottles and various other kinds of family-related litter. It was a long way from the adorable little three-bedroom bungalow Matt and Annie used to live in near Boston before they had kids. A long way from my luxury penthouse apartment in Arlington, Virginia, too. We had very different lives, Matt and I. And now here we were in Amman of all places.

"Okay," he said after a moment. "But I'm not going to stop."

"Fine."

"I'm going to keep praying for you."

"I appreciate it."

"And I'm going to keep asking you. Because at the end of the day, when it's all said and done, the simple truth is I want to be with you and Mom and the whole family in heaven, and I'd never be able to forgive myself if I didn't do everything I could to get you there. What kind of brother would I be if I didn't?"

I sighed. He hadn't changed a bit. I shrugged

and nodded. He put his arm around me and walked me to his front door.

"Come on," he said. "I'm starved, and Annie's making her famous lasagna."

We stepped around all the clutter, and Matt unlocked the door. As we entered the apartment, I expected a warm and enthusiastic greeting from Annie and the kids.

But that's not what happened.

48

* * *

Greeting us were two plainclothes agents from the Jordanian secret police.

With them were two soldiers in full combat gear, sporting automatic weapons. Annie and the kids stood behind them, looking frightened.

"What's the meaning of this?" Matt demanded.

"Are you Matthew Collins?" the lead agent asked.

"Of course. What do you want?"

"I am Ali Sa'id, chief of security for the Royal Court," said the lead agent, who then turned to me. "And are you James Collins?"

"Why are you asking?"

"Are you or are you not James Collins?" the agent repeated.

"Yes, I am."

"Then I need you to come with me."

"Where? What in the world is going on?"

"You'll understand soon enough."

I protested, but it didn't make any difference. These men clearly had their orders and weren't taking no for an answer.

Matt gave me a hug and whispered in my ear, "We'll be on the first flight out tonight."

I said nothing but rather turned and hugged Annie, Katie, and Josh as tightly as I could. I didn't want to let go. I so wanted to spend time with them. I wanted to play with the kids and hear their laughter. I wanted this family to help me get my mind off the terrible things I had seen and heard. After so many years of avoiding my brother, now I wanted to spend real time with him, see his life up close, and ask him a thousand questions. But right now I just hoped they would get out of the country before Khalif's men hunted them down and butchered them like cattle.

The agents led me downstairs and put me in the backseat of a black, bulletproof Mercedes. We peeled away from Matt's neighborhood with an urgency that only heightened my anxiety.

"Where are you taking me?" I asked, but the lead agent didn't answer.

"Am I under arrest?"

Nothing.

"Am I being deported?"

Still nothing.

"Look, I'm an American citizen and an accredited member of the press," I reminded them. "I have a right to know what's happening."

But my pleas fell on deaf ears.

We were heading back into the heart of Amman, I could see, and dense traffic slowed the journey. Given the route, I initially suspected they were taking me to the Interior Ministry. Omar and I had been there numerous times over the years to talk to high-ranking officials, including the minister. Then again, perhaps we might be going to see General Kamal Jeddeh, the head of the General Intelligence Directorate, another occasional source. But soon it became clear that both of these guesses were off the mark.

When we passed through the center of the city and began zigzagging through a series of side streets heading to the city's northwest quadrant, my mind started racing. Was it possible? Were we really heading to Al-Hummar? I'd never been there before, and a visit there now of all times seemed unlikely in the extreme. Yet after a somewhat-lengthy and circuitous drive through the city, we eventually did arrive in the heavily guarded section of the capital where the Royal Court was located. The agents radioed ahead, and before I knew it, enormous steel gates were opening to us and the Mercedes pulled up in front of a huge building I'd seen countless times on television but never in person.

"Welcome to the palace, Mr. Collins," Sa'id remarked before jumping out of the car and opening the door for me. "His Majesty is expecting you."

I stepped out of the car. Baffled yet intrigued by this turn of events, I found myself staring up at a mammoth structure made of beautifully carved limestone with a slightly pinkish hue. I'd always thought of this building material as "Jerusalem stone," but apparently it was common to the entire region. I saw five huge exterior archways, each leading to an equally huge interior archway. Framing the center archway were two flagpoles, one on each side, upon which the distinctive black, red, white, and green flag of the Hashemite Kingdom snapped smartly in the brisk December winds.

At least a dozen soldiers stood guard in front of the palace. I saw several others patrolling the rooftop. Then a half-dozen large trucks—resembling moving vans but unmarked—pulled through the gates, drove past us, and parked to my left. Moments later, a group of workers, presumably employed by the Royal Court, came through a side door and began unloading a series of boxes from the trucks.

Several additional security guards approached and surrounded us as Ali Sa'id asked me to follow him. He led me through one of the archways and two large wooden doors and then we were inside the Al-Hummar Palace.

Under the circumstances, I expected to be thoroughly searched. Certainly I would be directed to pass through a metal detector and have my briefcase and camera bag run through X-ray machines. But no. All the equipment was there, but we passed straight by it. I wasn't even asked to show my driver's license or passport or any other form of ID.

The agent took me down one hallway after another lined with framed portraits of the Hashemite monarchs. The lovely Queen Rania smiled out from one frame, and I saw another featuring Crown Prince Hussein, the king's eldest son. There were also a number of photographs of significant dignitaries meeting with the late King Hussein as well as the current King Abdullah II, including American presidents and secretaries of state and various European and Asian heads of state and foreign ministers, as well as the Saudi king and other Arab presidents, monarchs, and emirs. There was even a recent picture of the king greeting the new pope. It was, in many ways, a monarchy museum, complete with oblong glass cases containing various ancient vases, a gleaming silver saber that looked several centuries old, and other archaeological and historical artifacts from the age of the Ottomans, Roman times, and even biblical times.

On a normal day I might have been interested in some of it or perhaps even all of it. But this was no ordinary day. I was about to meet the king of Jordan for the first time, and I could only imagine why. My stomach was in knots. I hadn't eaten anything substantive in hours. I was suddenly parched, as well, and still battling shock from all that had happened in the last few days. But at that moment, I could only think about one thing: Was this meeting going to be on the record or off?

As I came around a corner, I found Prince Marwan waiting for me in his wheelchair. He was dressed in his traditional white-and-beige robes and wore his traditional red- and white-checkered kaffiyeh like a true Jordanian royal. He was not smiling. Indeed, he not only looked tired and ill but deeply troubled as well. However, he greeted me politely and asked me to follow him. As Sa'id and the rest of the security detail took up their positions around us, two ceremonial guards wearing ornate bedouin military uniforms opened two large doors.

We entered a room I recognized from photos as the king's official receiving room. This was where he typically held meetings with heads of state and dignitaries from all over the world. The walls were covered with rich, dark mahogany paneling. There were two beautiful ivory-and-beige couches straight ahead, one close to the door and the other facing it on the far side of the room.

In the center of the room was a low, modern, rather sleek-looking coffee table upon which were small vases of white flowers and various wooden bowls containing several small archaeological arti-facts. There were two small end tables beside the couch at the back of the room. The one on the right side bore a lamp and a large ceramic ashtray, while the one on the left bore a framed eight-by-ten black-and-white photograph of the late King Hussein wearing a Western business suit and his signature kaffiyeh. Behind the couch near the back wall was an end table with what appeared to be several priceless vases and pieces of ancient pottery, as well as another framed photo of King Hussein.

As I looked around, I saw Kamal Jeddeh, Jordan's intelligence director, a fit, barrel-chested man in his midfifties, rise from one of the couches. We greeted one another, but only for a moment. The prince seemed to be in a bit of a hurry, and he immediately asked me to take a seat on another couch on the left side of the room. I did as he asked, then admired the photographs and other details of the room while we waited several minutes in silence. Jeddeh struck me as uncharacteristically anxious, toying with a pen and glancing repeatedly at his watch.

The prince was not his typically warm self. I wanted to ask why, but at the moment it did not seem appropriate, so I held my tongue. To be honest, I was actually grateful that no one was talking quite yet. The silence gave me a chance to get my bearings, settle my heart rate somewhat, and start thinking about why His Majesty had summoned me and what I wanted to ask him if he gave me the chance.

Suddenly my phone vibrated. I quickly checked. Yael had responded to my text.

James—thank G-d you're safe! Thnx 4 the note. Have been worried sick. We need to talk. Dangerous new developments. Call me ASAP.—Y

Just then a door opened in the back of the room. Several more security men entered. Then the king entered as well, followed by the crown prince. In that moment it occurred to me that I was about to experience something my grandfather never had; I was about to meet a king.

His Majesty wore a finely tailored dark-blue suit, a light-blue shirt, and a red power tie. He was handsome and clean-shaven, and the thought struck me that he could have easily passed for the CEO of a high-tech company or perhaps a university president rather than a sovereign and one of the West's most important allies in the entire Arab world. He was somewhat shorter than me but obviously in excellent physical shape—no doubt the result of discipline gained from his many years in the military—and was clearly in command with a broad smile and warm manner. Although there was no question who was in charge when he entered the room, I didn't detect any arrogance or pomposity as I had when meeting other world leaders.

"Mr. Collins, it is a delight to meet you," he said with an accent that bespoke his years of secondary and university schooling in England, graciously extending his hand. "Thank you for agreeing to meet with me on such short notice."

"It is an honor to meet you, Your Majesty," I replied, not entirely sure of the proper protocol but taking his cue and accepting his firm handshake.

The king introduced me to Crown Prince Hussein as an official photographer snapped several pictures and then stepped out of the room.

"Please have a seat," the king said. "Make yourself comfortable. I have been reading your dispatches. What a harrowing couple of weeks you have had."

"Thank you, Your Majesty," I replied, feeling butterflies in my stomach. "Harrowing, indeed."

The king took a seat on the couch across from me. His son, in his early twenties, wore a black suit with a crisp white shirt and a purple tie and sat on the same couch as his father. Prince Marwan was wheeled into position off to my right, just beyond the coffee table, while Director Jeddeh, in a gray suit and a bland-yellow tie, sat directly to my right, at the other end of the couch. We were served coffee, but as thirsty as I was, I couldn't think about drinking it right now.

The king ignored the coffee as well and motioned for his servants to step out of the room.

"Everything we say here today is off the record. Is that understood?" he began when we were finally alone.

"I would really like to get you on the record," I replied. "No Arab leader has reacted to the Abu Khalif interview. You should be the first."

"Tomorrow," he said. "I will give you exclusive access to me for the day, including a formal sit-down interview. But right now I want to talk with you privately."

I could hardly say no, so I nodded and said thank you.

"I want to start by updating you on the peace process," the king said.

"Not Abu Khalif?" I asked in amazement. "Not ISIS?"

"First things first."

"With all due respect, Your Majesty, I would think ISIS would be your top concern," I responded.

"I am well aware of the risks," he replied.

"Abu Khalif clearly wants to seize control of Iraq and Syria. But he and Jamal Ramzy told me they are now about to strike a third target. And based on everything I have seen and heard, I have come to believe that target may be Jordan."

"We've been dealing with ISIS for a long time, Mr. Collins. We know who they are and what they want. We are ready for them. I am not worried. My focus right now is to help the Palestinians get their state, and I believe that after many tears and much heartache, that time has finally come."

I had tremendous respect for this king, but I wasn't sure this was wisdom. To be sure, His Majesty was highly experienced in surfing the turbulent waves in the region. And of course, he was not only a highly trained soldier, but he had once been commander of Jordan's special forces. Nevertheless, at that moment I was concerned that he and his royal advisors were so focused on the peace process to their west that they might not be sufficiently attentive to the threat rising to their east.

"You are aware that the Israelis and Palestinians are about to announce a final, comprehensive peace agreement that will, after far too many years, finally establish a sovereign Palestinian State in the West Bank and Gaza, correct?" the king continued.

"I've seen mixed reports in the press, Your Majesty," I replied. "But if we are off the record, I will say I have heard the same thing from several trustworthy sources, including President Taylor. I understand you have played a key role."

"Prince Marwan and I have lost a lot of sleep in recent months, but it has all been worth it," he said.

"Every issue has been solved?" I asked.

"Remarkably, yes," he said.

"The borders?"

"The Israelis agreed to relinquish about 94 percent of the West Bank and all of Gaza. There are land swaps. The Israelis will keep all the major settlements but will dismantle and evacuate the smaller ones. In return, the Israelis have carved out sections of the Negev and parts of the Galilee region to give to the Palestinians to compensate for the 6 percent of the land on which the major settlements are located."

"And Jerusalem?"

"The Palestinians will have their capital in East Jerusalem."

"All of it?" I asked.

"Parts of it," the king said. "The Dome of the Rock, the Al-Aqsa Mosque, and the Temple Mount will be managed by a special committee, chaired by Jordan and including the Palestinians, Israel, the U.S., and Saudi Arabia. The Palestinians will have sovereignty over the Muslim Quarter of the Old City."

"What about the Jewish, Christian, and Armenian Quarters?"

"Israel will control those," the king said. "Each side will guarantee access for adherents of all religions to their holy sites. Meanwhile, the Israelis will have sovereignty over Mount Scopus and the Mount of Olives and will control the current tunnel from the West Bank into Jerusalem. The Saudis and Americans will finance the building of a separate tunnel leading from Arab towns into East Jerusalem. And the Palestinians will establish government offices near the Damascus Gate."

"Prime Minister Lavi agreed to all that?"

"Mr. Collins, my good friend Daniel *proposed* all that," the king replied.

I wondered if I looked as surprised as I felt.

"It wasn't such a stretch for him," the king added. "Daniel was on the negotiating teams with

Ehud Barak at Camp David in 2000. He was a key aide in helping Ariel Sharon with the disengagement in 2005. And he was a senior advisor to Olmert in 2008. He's been working on these issues for a long time."

"President Mansour wanted more, no doubt," I said.

"He did."

"But you persuaded him to take the deal?"

"Salim and I had many long talks," the king said. "He is not Yasser Arafat. Nor is he Mahmoud Abbas. They weren't ready for peace. Salim is. The Palestinians are ready. It's time."

"What about refugees?"

"Palestinian refugees will have the right to return to the Palestinian State—as many as want to," the king replied. "But Daniel conceded East Jerusalem as the Palestinian capital on the condition that Salim not insist on the right of Palestinian refugees to return to Israel en masse. In the end, the Israelis agreed to accept fifty thousand refugees—five thousand per year for ten years—so long as each one is vetted by their security services and does not pose a security threat. This was actually the most contentious part of the negotiations and certainly took the longest. The formula is very close to what Olmert proposed in 2008, but Olmert was only offering visas for a total of five thousand Palestinians to enter Israel. This is ten times as many."

"Water rights?"

"It's a complicated formula. It divides the water between the Palestinians, the Israelis, and us, but it's consistent with the treaty my father signed with the Israelis in 1994."

"And what about security arrangements?" I asked.

"The short version is this," King Abdullah replied. "The Palestinian State will be demilitarized. They will have police and border security forces, of course, but no army, no air force—except a specified number of helicopters for surveillance and medical rescue purposes—and no significant navy except patrol boats to protect the Gaza coast. No rockets or missiles are permitted on Palestinian territory. No launchers. No new tunnels. We and the Israelis are responsible for security in the Jordan River Valley. The Israelis will have seven manned outposts in the valley, but they will rent the land from the Palestinians. The Israeli Air Force will maintain security over all airspace west of the Jordan. We'll do the same on the east side. The rest of the security in the corridor will be highly coordinated between all three sovereign governments."

"This sounds a lot like a confederation," I said.

"In some ways it is, yes," the king conceded. "But everyone has specifically agreed not to call it a confederation."

"Why not?"

"Because Salim says that the very word infuriates Palestinians, dishonors them, makes them feel like they don't have true sovereignty."

"And you?" I asked.

"I want to honor our neighbors," the king replied. "If they don't like the term, I'm happy not to use it."

"But you're satisfied the security arrangements will protect your kingdom?"

"I am," he said. "Look, no one has been more supportive of a sovereign Palestinian State than my father and me. My father made a terrible gamble in 1967. He listened to Nasser's lies, and in so doing he lost Jerusalem and nearly half his kingdom. We learned a great deal from that disaster. One lesson was that it was not the will of Allah for Jordan to control the West Bank. That was painful to accept. Very painful. But accept it we have. What we cannot accept, however, is creating a security vacuum on the west side of the river. We want the Palestinians to have a strong security force. We are happy to help fund their training and equip them with whatever they need. But we need to make sure all security issues in the corridor are carefully coordinated. These were not the most contentious elements of the negotiations, but they were among the most time-consuming. In the end, I was and am satisfied."

"So everything is set?" I asked.

"It is," the king said. "In fact, President Taylor called me not ten minutes ago to go over the final details and to review the rollout plan. I told him I was about to meet with you. He asked me to tell you he's glad you are safe and that he looks forward to discussing Abu Khalif with you directly."

"That's very kind," I said. "When does he touch down in Israel? And are you going to Jerusalem for the big announcement?"

"The president is not going to Jerusalem, and neither am I, Mr. Collins."

"Why not?" I asked, wondering what I had just missed.

"The 'big announcement,' as you call it, will be held tomorrow afternoon," the king said. "But it will not be held in Israel. It will be right here, at the palace."

49

★ ★ ★

"Here? Tomorrow? How is that possible?" I asked.

The king smiled. "It's going to take a lot of work, but my team will be ready."

The large trucks and all the workers out in front of the palace now made sense. The staff of the Royal Court was going to be working through the night to prepare for the arrival of the president of the United States, the Israeli prime minister, the Palestinian president—and all the staff, security, and media that were coming with them.

"Does anyone have this story yet?" I asked.

"That everyone's coming here?"

"Right."

"No, not at all," the king said. "Each leader has gone to great lengths to keep any details from the media. In part, that's to create the biggest media impact. It's also for security purposes. But again, tomorrow's events aren't what worry me."

"Why not?" I pressed. "All four leaders here at the same time present a tempting target, do they not, especially to ISIS?"

"Look, Mr. Collins, Jordan's security services

are first-rate. The U.S. Secret Service is helping us. So are the Israeli and Palestinian security services. We'll be fine. What worries me more—and this is absolutely off the record—is that this weekend I am flying to Baghdad for a series of meetings with the prime minister on the ISIS threat and the future of Iraq. Frankly, if ISIS is looking for a window of vulnerability, that is it."

"Can I go with you?" I asked.

"You really want to?"

"Absolutely."

For the first time, the king turned to Prince Marwan and his intelligence director. I couldn't read the signals, but the king didn't say no. Rather he asked for a day to think about it, which I took as a positive sign.

Returning to the issue at hand, I asked why all the media leaks were indicating that the peace treaty ceremony was going to be held in Jerusalem.

"Jerusalem was the original plan—that's why you've seen these leaks in the last twenty-four hours," he explained. "But Salim and Daniel couldn't agree over exactly where to hold it, and in the end, Salim called me and asked if I would host the whole thing here."

"Meanwhile, the Israelis are literally rolling out the red carpet," I said. "But it's all a head fake?"

"It didn't start that way, but now, yes, I guess it is," the king agreed. "We will have a wonderful crowd at the peace ceremony, but none of them know that's what they're coming for."

"Then what do they think they're coming for?"

"There is an awards ceremony beginning at

2 p.m. with about five hundred high school students from all over Jordan and the West Bank. There is even a delegation of Israeli students coming, about fifty, I believe. The brightest students in their schools are supposed to meet with my son and various ministers. Then I am scheduled to deliver the keynote address. All the students arrived in Amman this morning. They're touring the city all day. When they arrive here tomorrow, they will go through security and then learn that they are participating in the most important event of this millennium."

"And the awards ceremony?"

The king smiled again. "Everything has been thought of, Mr. Collins. It will be held at the performing arts center downtown the following day."

"What time do the various government delegations arrive?" I asked.

The king turned to Kamal Jeddeh.

"President Mansour and the Palestinians arrive late tonight," the intelligence director explained. "As a matter of fact, the entire Palestinian delegation is staying at your hotel, Le Méridien. If it is all right with His Majesty, perhaps we can arrange for Mr. Collins and President Mansour to have breakfast in the morning and do an interview."

"Absolutely," the king said. "That's a good idea."

"I'd like that, Your Majesty; thank you," I replied. "And the Israelis?"

The head of the Mukhabarat addressed that question as well; clearly it was his responsibility to keep all these delegations safe.

"As you can imagine, it's difficult for Prime

Minister Lavi to travel without the press noticing. But he'll depart Ben Gurion at 10 a.m., touch down here in Amman around ten thirty, and be brought by helicopter to the palace no later than eleven. His advance team is already here, and most of his security detail arrives less than an hour from now."

I turned to the king. "Could we arrange for me to have lunch with Danny Lavi?" I asked.

"I'm afraid not," the king replied. "He and Salim and I are having an early working lunch. But we'll make sure you get a meeting with him at some point."

"And what about President Taylor?"

"Air Force One touches down at one," Jeddeh said. "President Mansour, Prime Minister Lavi, His Majesty, the crown prince, and Prince Marwan will greet him at the airport, do a photo op, and then all come back here for the official ceremony. I'll make sure we get you a final, detailed schedule in the morning."

"Thank you," I said. "But with all due respect, Your Majesty, what good is the exclusive you're giving me tomorrow if hundreds of reporters will be here from all over the world as well?"

"None of them will have backstage access to the principals except you," the king said. "You'll be in the limousine when we pick up President Taylor. You'll be sitting directly behind me during the ceremony. You'll be privy to conversations and details that no one else will have."

"Why me?"

"Why not?" He smiled. "If you would prefer, I can certainly give this to one of your competitors."

"No, no, don't get me wrong," I replied. "I'm very grateful. Just curious why I've been granted such a favor."

"It is simple, really," the king replied. "You're the only reporter in the world to have actually met and interviewed Abu Khalif. We want to send him a message."

"And what message would that be?"

"That he cannot win," the king said. "That peace and moderation and tolerance will prevail."

Sitting back for a moment, I carefully considered what he was telling me. I was intrigued and impressed with Abdullah bin al-Hussein, both as a monarch and as a Reformer. He was actively trying to lead his small, oil-less, but vitally important nation toward progress and freedom, toward tolerance and modernity. He was keeping close ties with the Arab world. But he was also working hard to maintain a close friendship with the United States and the European Union. On top of all that, he was maintaining his nation's courageous peace treaty with Israel despite all manner of trials. Now he was trying to help the Palestinians and Israelis make peace, even while standing strong against the radical forces in the region. It was not an easy task.

The Radicals—al Qaeda, ISIS, the Muslim Brotherhood, and the mullahs in Iran, to name a few—desperately wanted to topple the king and seize Jordan for themselves. In the last few years, the Radicals had seized Tunisia, Libya, and Egypt, albeit briefly, and they were presently fighting to grab Syria and Iraq too. Would Jordan be next? I hoped the answer was no. But Abu Khalif had told me he planned to strike again soon. And common sense suggested the king was a prime target. Did he not see it this way? I needed to persuade him to go on the record—immediately, for tomorrow's paper. But how?

"Your Majesty, may I ask you a question?" I said finally, leaning forward.

"By all means," he said. The man was nothing if not gracious. The bedouin tradition of hospitality was deeply ingrained in him.

"I realize there is much you don't want to say until all the principals initial the comprehensive peace treaty tomorrow, and I respect that enormously," I began. "But there are two facts I need to address. The first is that my editor expects me to file a story from the region by midnight tonight so it can make it into tomorrow's newspaper. The second is that given the events of the last few days and the threats made specifically against you and your kingdom, I would think that it is important for everyone in Jordan—but especially everyone in Israel—to hear from you directly on how seriously you're taking ISIS and what security measures you're implementing to ensure not only that tomorrow goes well but that Jordan remains the vital cornerstone of security in this corridor over the long haul. So my question, Your Majesty, is simply this: Would you be willing to do a short interview with me right now to explain why you are so confident that Jordan will play a major role in securing this peace, no matter what Abu Khalif is saying?"

50

To my surprise, the king agreed.

I looked at Prince Marwan and Kamal Jeddeh. They, of course, deferred to their monarch. So I fished my digital recorder out of my briefcase, turned it on, and set it on the table. Then I pulled out a pad of paper and pen, and we began.

"Your Majesty, thank you for agreeing to sit down to talk with the readers of the *New York Times*," I began.

"Always a pleasure," he replied, taking a sip of coffee for the first time since entering the room.

"To begin with, how would you characterize this moment in the broad sweep of Middle Eastern history?"

"I would restate the central case I made in my 2011 book, *Our Last Best Chance: The Pursuit of Peace in a Time of Peril*," he replied. "I believe we still have one last chance to achieve peace. But the window is rapidly closing. If we do not seize the opportunity presented by the now almost-unanimous international consensus of the solution, I am certain we will see another war in our region—most likely worse than those that have gone before and with more disastrous consequences."

"You don't consider the carnage inside Syria and Iraq to be regional wars?"

"The situation in Syria is a civil war, and it is very serious indeed," the king said. "Our brothers and sisters in Iraq are fighting a terrorist movement. This too is quite serious. But what I was referring to in my book, and what I am warning of now, is the danger of another full-scale war between Arabs and Israelis. This would be catastrophic, which is why we are working so hard to help the Palestinians and Israelis make peace."

"Is peace at hand?"

"Inshallah," he said. *God willing.*

"You have been deeply involved in behind-the-scenes negotiations between the Israelis and Palestinians, correct?"

"The Palestinians and the Israelis have done all the work," he said modestly. "I have been particularly impressed with President Mansour. He has worked tirelessly to secure a fair and just result for his people. We have played a minor role, tried to encourage him and Prime Minister Lavi as best we could, based on lessons King Hussein learned while making peace with the Israelis back in the 1990s."

"What tangible benefits do you see from the Israelis and Palestinians signing a comprehensive peace agreement?"

"As you know, Jordan has been the region's strongest and most consistent supporter of the creation of a sovereign Palestinian State with its capital in Jerusalem," the king replied. "If this could truly be achieved—and I do say *if*, though we are closer than ever before—then it would be the most important geopolitical development of the millennium. This would be the fulfillment of a dream that eluded my father, Yasser Arafat, Mahmoud Abbas, and one Israeli prime minister after another. It would be a tremendous blessing for the Palestinian people, who have suffered too much for too long."

"And for Jordan?"

"My dream, as I have stated on countless occasions, is to link the economies of Israel, Palestine, and Jordan in a common market—similar to Benelux in Western Europe. Imagine if we could combine the technical know-how and entrepreneurial drive of all three nations to create an economic and business hub in the Levant? The potential for joint tourism is massive, as is the potential for foreign investment."

I was about to shift the conversation to Abu Khalif, but the king was not finished.

"And let me say another word about tourism," he added. "Jordan is a leader in encouraging Islamic tourism not only throughout our own nation but to Mecca and Medina and Jerusalem. But we also know that there are some two billion Christians in the world. Imagine if there was truly peace between Jordan, Palestine, and Israel. Imagine if Christian pilgrims could come and visit the Holy Land— on *both* sides of the Jordan River. What a blessing that would be for Christians, as well as for all the

406 ★ THE THIRD TARGET

people of the region. It is not widely known in the West, but we have in Jordan a small but thriving Christian community that is perhaps the oldest in the world. The place where Jesus was baptized is Jordan's most important Christian site. It is here on the east bank of the Jordan River. This is where Jesus' mission started. This is where Christianity began. Jordan is also where Moses lived and died. This is where Elijah the prophet was taken up to heaven in a chariot of fire. There is so much rich history here, and pilgrims could not only come to see it all, but then cross the Jordan River and visit Jericho and Bethlehem and Jerusalem. They could behold the wonders of ancient and modern Jordan, Palestine, and Israel in ways never before possible.

"On my trips abroad I have met with priests, preachers, rabbis, and imams," he continued. "We have been working hard to build relationships with Christians, the Jewish community, and of course Muslims. We want everyone who shares our heart for peace to come and walk where Jesus and the prophets walked. We are not just *talking* about peace. We are not just *dreaming* about it. We are working very hard each and every day to make peace a reality."

It was time to pivot.

"Have you read the interview Abu Khalif gave to the *Times* the other day?"

"I have."

"How would you respond to the ISIS leader's threats not only to annihilate Israel but to take out any Arab leader who makes peace with the Israelis, yourself and President Salim Mansour included, all to establish a true Islamic caliphate?"

"I am pained by the twisting of my religion by a small band of misguided fanatics," the king replied. "Such people embrace a deviant form of Islam. While claiming to act in its name, they are in reality just murderers and thugs. They constitute an unrepresentative minority of the 1.57 billion Muslims in the world, but they have had a disproportionate impact on how the faith is perceived. These people are *takfiris*, which in Arabic means 'those who accuse others of being heretics.' They rely on ignorance, resentment, and a distorted promise of achieving martyrdom to spread their ideology, turning their backs on over a thousand years of Qur'anic scholarship in the name of what they presume to be the authentic ways of seventh-century Arabia. But the actions of the *takfiris* have nothing to do with Islam and its message. True Islam stands for justice, equality, fairness, and the opportunity to live a meaningful and good life. They seek to destroy these things. In doing so they have turned their backs on the ancient traditions of clemency and compassion.

"My advisors and I have been working for several years to build a broad-based consensus among Islamic scholars and clerics of all stripes regarding the true nature of Islam and the many reasons the *takfiris* are both theologically and historically wrong in their interpretations of the Qur'an. The scholars have produced a document called the Amman Message, which sets out what

Islam is, what it is not, and what types of actions are and are not Islamic."

From memory, he then recited for me a brief passage from the document.

"Today the magnanimous message of Islam faces a vicious attack from some who claim affiliation with Islam and commit irresponsible acts in its name. We denounce and condemn extremism, radicalism, and fanaticism today, just as our forefathers tirelessly denounced and opposed them throughout Islamic history. On religious and moral grounds, we denounce the contemporary concept of terrorism that is associated with wrongful practices. Such acts are represented by aggression against human life in an oppressive form that transgresses the rulings of God."

I was writing as fast as I could. I glanced up to make sure my digital recorder was still working. Fortunately it was.

"One more question, if I may?"

"Please."

"Thank you, Your Majesty. I read your book when it was released in 2011, and I have also read your father's memoir published in 1962, *Uneasy Lies the Head*," I said. "One of the common threads of both books is how often the extremists have tried to assassinate you and overthrow your kingdom. As you know, my grandfather, A. B. Collins, witnessed the tragic assassination of King Abdullah I. Now Abu Khalif, the commander of ISIS, is personally threatening to behead you and destroy the peace process into which you and your family have invested so much. My question is, how can you assure the American people, the Jordanian people, the Palestinians, and the Israelis—along with all those in the region and throughout the world who care about peace—that Jordan will remain a strong and stable cornerstone of regional security, especially in light of the ISIS threat?"

"I would simply say this," the king replied. "The Hashemite Kingdom is the longest-reigning regime in all the Middle East and North Africa. I am not going anywhere. Jordan is not going anywhere. We are here to stay, and we will remain a beacon of peace and moderation in troubled times."

I wrote down his words verbatim. They certainly sounded good. And the king was nothing if not sincere. This wasn't spin. He was saying this from his heart.

I just feared he was dead wrong.

51

* * *

Just before three in the morning, I sat bolt upright in bed.

Shaking and so covered in perspiration that my pillow and sheets felt damp, I got out of bed, turned on the bedside lamp, and made my way across my hotel room to the bathroom to get a glass of water. When I glanced in the mirror, I saw my eyes were bloodshot, but I didn't have a fever. As far as I could tell, I wasn't really sick. I was terrified.

ISIS had threatened to wipe out my entire family. I'd just learned that four of the world leaders Abu Khalif most wanted to kill—the president of the United States, the Israeli prime minister, the Palestinian president, and the king of Jordan— were all gathering under one roof, here in Amman, in a few short hours. The question wasn't "Why had I woken up so early?" but "How had I actually slept at all?"

Death surrounded me.

Matt was right. Everywhere I went, people I cared about wound up dead. I kept telling myself

I was strong and able to keep going in spite of it all. But I was no longer sure that was true. I'd just had the most vivid dream of Matt and his family being killed with sarin gas. I'd seen them writhing and gasping for breath and couldn't do anything to save them. It was all I could do to convince myself it wasn't real. It was a nightmare; that's all. Yet who was to say it wouldn't soon come true?

If there really were five stages of grief—denial, anger, bargaining, depression, and acceptance—I couldn't honestly say I'd even begun. I hadn't even started into denial. I was somewhere between shock and primordial fear. For most of my life, I hadn't been afraid of death because I'd never really taken it seriously. I'd never even thought about it in any depth. I hadn't believed in an afterlife. But now everything had changed.

I was now certain there was an afterlife. I was now certain that heaven and hell were real places that real people went. I couldn't explain how. I just knew. What I didn't know was how to get to heaven. Matt said Jesus was the only way. I wasn't so sure. Which meant he was right about another thing—I was in danger. If I didn't have a route to heaven, didn't that mean I was on the road to hell?

I turned off the lamp, unplugged my mobile phone from its charger, and used the glow of its screen to find my way to the darkened window. I turned on the air-conditioning and then lay down on top of the comforter. I checked the *Times* home page. My interview with the king had just been posted. Allen and I were still communicating only through e-mails and text messages. But he was no longer telling me to come home. I was in the epicenter of the story, and he wanted me to stay put and send him everything I could. That suited me just fine. I had no intention to run from Abu Khalif, even if I had told my brother to.

I checked my e-mails. There were nine, all from various U.S., European, and Israeli reporters. They were all asking for interviews describing my personal take on Abu Khalif. I didn't have time for that. But I did take the next ten minutes or so sending a few quotes to each of them, giving them some tidbits. Most important, I verified that I'd seen ISIS use chemical weapons in Mosul. After all, the only reason Khalif hadn't killed me yet was so I could keep telling the world he had weapons of mass destruction. And that was a story I was determined to tell anyway.

I checked my text messages. There were three from my mom, telling me she was praying for me, asking me to come home, and asking me to read the Twenty-third Psalm. There was a smattering of others from various sources and colleagues, checking on me and asking me to call them. There were no new messages from Yael. I'd called her twice the previous evening—once immediately after my interview with the king, on the drive back to Le Méridien; the other right before I went to bed. I'd texted her too. I was eager to talk to her, to hear her voice, to learn more about the "dangerous developments" she had referred to. But so far, nothing.

There was, however, a text from Matt.

Just touched down in a faraway city, it read simply. **Won't say where for now, but wanted you to know we're safe. Don't worry about us. Kids don't understand what's happening. Think it's an adventure. Annie's fine. Sends her love.**

Two minutes later, another came in.

Annie says read Psalm 3. Thought you might be encouraged by it too. Praying for you. Love you.—Matt

A moment later, another SMS message arrived, this one with a link to Psalm 3 on some online Bible. With nothing else to do at the moment, I clicked on the link and read it aloud in my room.

"O Lord, so many are against me. So
many seek to harm me. I have so many
enemies. So many say that God will never
help me. But Lord, you are my shield, my
glory, and my only hope. You alone can
lift my head, now bowed in shame. I cried
out to the Lord, and he heard me from
his Temple in Jerusalem. Then I lay down
and slept in peace and woke up safely, for
the Lord was watching over me. And now,
although ten thousand enemies surround
me on every side, I am not afraid. I will
cry to him, 'Arise, O Lord! Save me,
O my God!' And he will slap them in the
face, insulting them and breaking off their
teeth. For salvation comes from God.
What joys he gives to all his people."

The heading above the psalm noted that its author was the ancient King David. I wondered how David could lie down and sleep peacefully when ten thousand enemies were hunting him down to kill him the first chance they got. I didn't get it and wasn't sure I ever would.

I got up again and opened my laptop. While I was waiting for the computer to boot up, I thought about the king's upcoming trip to Baghdad and whether I really wanted to go along after all. Professionally, it was probably the right thing to do. But I wasn't sure I could pull it off. How much more of this could I really take? I was emotionally and physically exhausted. My nerves were shot, and truth be told, I had no idea if I could make it through the day. Maybe I should follow my own advice, I thought. Maybe it was time to get out of Jordan—get off the grid and lie low until this whole thing blew over.

It was tempting, but I couldn't just ditch my job now. People were counting on me, and I had to deliver. I had a huge day ahead of me—interviews with the leaders of Palestine, Israel, and Jordan, and perhaps one with the president of the United States as well. I had to ask them about the ISIS threat, but how could I engage them and get them to really make news, not just spit out prepackaged talking points?

My thoughts shifted back to Abu Khalif. How had he known the peace treaty was a done deal? How had he known King Abdullah had been its broker? How had he known Ismail Tikriti was going to be at the Abu Ghraib prison that night, or that I would be there as well? There wasn't a reporter on the planet who had known any of these facts in advance, except me. But clearly someone was feeding Khalif insider information. And if it wasn't coming from the media, it could only be coming from a mole inside one of the four governments involved. Which meant I had to consider the possibility that Abu Khalif not only knew about the king's upcoming trip to Baghdad but might know exactly what was happening later today. If there was ever a time for ISIS to strike and strike hard, it was now. It was here.

I shifted my attention again, this time to scanning more of the latest headlines.

Daily Mail–Another Day,
Another ISIS Crucifixion:
Man Accused of Joining Syrian
Regime Found Hanging from a
Cross in Busy Market Town with
Cryptic Note Pinned to His Chest

CNN–Death and Desecration in Syria:
Jihadist Group Crucifies
Bodies to Send Message

The *Washington Post*–ISIS,
Beheadings, and the Success
of Horrifying Violence

The *Wall Street Journal*–Militants Claim
Photos Show Mass Execution in Iraq

**The *Daily Express*–The New Dark Ages:
The Chilling Medieval Society ISIS
Extremists Seek to Impose in Iraq**

**The *Guardian*–British PM Warns ISIS
Is Planning to Attack UK**

On top of all this were stories about the continuing spike in oil prices that was sending new shock waves through an already-battered and fragile global economy.

I shut down the computer and collapsed on the bed, staring at the ceiling in the darkness.

All the lights in the room were off. Only the red numbers on the digital clock were visible. It was 3:46 in the morning. And that's the last thing I remembered until my alarm went off two hours later.

52

* * *

I had never seen Salim Mansour happy.

Not "so happy." Not "this happy." I'm saying I had never seen him happy.

Ever. Period. End of sentence. New paragraph.

An economist by training, with a doctorate from the University of Chicago, the Palestinian president was not someone I would naturally characterize as an optimist. Once, over a meal of hummus and lamb at a restaurant in Jericho overlooking the Jordan Valley, he had told me—off the record, of course—how despondent he had become by Yasser Arafat's "congenital incapacity to say yes" to any proposal the Israelis offered.

"The U.N. offered Ben-Gurion a fraction of what he wanted in '47, but he took it," Mansour had said, referring to David Ben-Gurion, the founder of the Jewish State. "He didn't demand the whole loaf, even though he wanted it. He took what he could get and he started building. And look where Israel is now. Their per capita GDP is over $32,000. Ours is not even a tenth of that. Their unemployment rate is under 7 percent a year. Ours is almost four times that number. They're becoming a high-tech capital of the world. At times it feels like we're stuck in the Stone Age. We have so much potential. But we've let ourselves get trapped in a cycle of violence and envy and resentment, and where has it gotten us?"

Over dessert, he'd continued his diatribe. "Don't get me wrong. The Israelis have done everything they could to slow us down and keep us back. I'm not absolving them of anything. Every charge Arafat makes against them is true. But when Barak offered him a serious, substantive deal at Camp David in 2000, Arafat rejected it out of hand. Why? How has that helped us? I'm not saying the deal was everything we wanted. Of course not. But think of it—Palestine could have been an independent, sovereign state since 2000. We could have been building. We could have been growing. Instead, we remain in the mire while the Israelis continue to prosper."

Less than a year later, in another off-the-record lunch, Mansour extended his complaints to include Mahmoud Abbas, aka Abu Mazen.

"Arafat was a revolutionary—I get it," he'd said over stuffed grape leaves and grilled chicken. "Arafat aimed for the sky. Abu Mazen's job was to turn the dream into a reality. Ehud Olmert gave him that chance in '08, but he wouldn't say yes. He was too much a disciple of Arafat. Too weak. No creativity. Imagine if he'd said yes—we could have been sitting in a bona fide State of Palestine since 2008. Yet here we are, stuck as ever."

What made him even more despondent, he

said, was the "endemic corruption" and "bureau-cratic incompetence" that he felt had characterized the Palestinian Authority for so long.

"The world is not just going to hand us a state on a silver platter if we can't tie our shoes and pay our bills on time," he had insisted. "Maybe we can't stop the Israelis from occupying us, oppress-ing us, imposing apartheid on us. Not yet. But we can make sure we are building a solid, functioning, serious economy and democracy. And the sooner we do it, the more credibility we will gain in the eyes of world leaders who can then ratchet up the pressure on the Israelis to acknowledge our God-given right of self-determination."

But this meeting was different. Mansour was smiling.

Born in Jenin but raised in Dubai, Mansour had stayed away from the West Bank and Gaza for decades. In 2010, however, he reluctantly accepted then-President Abbas's request that he serve as the Palestinian Authority's finance minister. Facing enormous odds and bureaucratic infighting, Mansour had set about to make the very reforms for which he had been advocating so long. It wasn't easy. Indeed, it was often painful. But it began to work. The Palestinian economy began to grow. The bureaucracy began to function—not great, certainly not perfect, but better than before. The U.S. State Department took notice. So did the European Union. Jordan certainly did. And so did Mansour's fellow Palestinians. As their for-tunes began to improve bit by bit, Mansour's stock began to rise as well. Then came Hamas's repeated rocket wars against Israel and the resultant destruction of Gaza. That had been an enormous setback. Yet in the end, Hamas was humbled and internationally isolated. The rocket wars, as devastating as they'd been, had given the Palestinian Authority—not Hamas—a new lease on life. And when Abbas finally announced he was retiring and calling new elections, there was a groundswell of support for Salim Mansour, the balding, bespectacled economics professor who was offering a serious vision of growth and opportunity for a people long bereft of either.

"It's happening," he now told me over a plate of fruit he wasn't touching and a cup of Turkish coffee that was getting cold. "After all this time, the dream is really becoming a reality."

We were on the record. My digital recorder was on. And despite a deep sense of foreboding I couldn't seem to shake, even I had to smile at Mansour's self-evident joy. "Honestly, Mr. President, I have never seen you happy."

"You weren't at my wedding," he said.

"True."

"Or the births of my four daughters."

"Fair enough."

"Or their weddings or the births of my nine grandchildren."

"My apologies."

"I can be happy, Mr. Collins. I am happy when I have hope, when I see love and fruit and growth and dreams coming true. That's what makes me happy."

"So you're satisfied with this process?"

"Of course not," he said. "It was a circus."

"But you're satisfied with the outcome."

"Hardly," he said defiantly, the smile beginning to fade somewhat. "My people deserve so much more than this. But at the risk of sounding trite, I refused to let the perfect be the enemy of the good. The Palestinian people want a state. They deserve a state. They have fought for one. They have worked for one. They have suffered without one. My job is not to think of a thousand reasons why they cannot have one. My job is to deliver one, and today I have. This is a historic day, one we will not forget for a long time."

"Are you worried about the ISIS threat?"

"No."

"You're not worried that Abu Khalif has threatened to assassinate you and anyone else who makes peace with the 'criminal Zionists'?"

"I am not wasting my time with the mad ravings of a sociopath."

"You know he is calling for a Third Intifada."

"There is no appetite among the Palestinians for another uprising," Mansour said. "Why would there be? We are about to get a state of our own, a true and legitimate state. And once we have it, I believe we will take away the central argument of the *takfiris*, that only through violence will the Palestinian people be liberated. We have been oppressed. And we do need to be liberated. But not through violence. Not through jihad. Today we begin our own liberation. We don't need the help of a rapist and a murderer. We're not seeking a killing ground for jihadists. We're building a real state here, one based on the rule of law and the principles of economic growth, democratic values, and respect for Islam and all religions."

"Do you fear an attack by ISIS using chemical weapons?"

"Of course not."

"Why not?"

"Maybe they don't really have them."

"They do," I said. "I've seen them."

"Then that's what our security forces are for, and Jordan's and Israel's," he replied, a hint of exasperation now rising in his voice. "We have professional security forces, and I have every confidence they will do their job. But this is not our focus today. This is a day of celebration, a day for great joy and optimism, not fear and doubt. Don't spoil this for us with your tales of imminent doom. We have had enough pain to last a thousand lifetimes. We have had enough stormy days. Let us, just this once, have our moment in the sun."

53

* * *

I called Yael again but got voice mail and didn't leave a message.

Then I went to back to my room, wrote up the interview with Mansour, and filed it with Allen.

I pulled out my grandfather's pocket watch and saw it was almost 12:30 p.m. The limo that was supposed to pick me up on the way to the airport to meet President Taylor was late. I was about to call Yael again when my mobile phone rang. But it wasn't her. It was Kamal Jeddeh.

"There's been a change of plans," the Jordanian intelligence director said.

"Is there a problem?" I asked.

"No, just a change," he said. "I have a car waiting for you downstairs. It will take you to the airport. The foreign minister will meet Air Force One and greet the president when he arrives, and the president has requested that you join him for the drive to the palace."

"The king isn't going?" I asked.

"No."

"What about President Mansour and Prime Minister Lavi?"

"They are not going either."

"Why not?"

"Their meeting with His Majesty is running long. That's all I know. But time is short. We must get you to the airport. Please head downstairs immediately."

Something was wrong. The protocol, the timing, every minute of this trip had been mapped out in excruciating detail. I rechecked the official schedule some envoy had slipped under my door earlier that morning. All three Middle Eastern leaders were supposed to greet the American president at Queen Alia International Airport. Why the sudden change—especially one as significant as this? The arrival of the president in Amman under such circumstances would be worldwide news. It would likely be broadcast on live television throughout the region and around the globe. Shouldn't the king be there to greet him? The only thing I could think of that would warrant such a serious deviation from the itinerary was that a last-minute snag had occurred in the peace plan. Was it possible Lavi or Mansour were having second thoughts or reopening some final-status issue that was supposedly already, well, final?

I grabbed my briefcase and camera bag and headed down the hallway. Waiting for the elevator, I quickly sent individual text messages to each of the principals, as well as separate texts to each of their top advisors. On the elevator, I called

Prince Marwan but didn't get him. I called Youssef Kuttab, the Palestinian president's most trusted advisor, as well, but he wasn't picking up either.

Ali Sa'id, on the other hand, was waiting for me in the lobby.

"Ali, my friend, how kind of you to fetch me," I said.

"Of course. Please, come; we must hurry."

We left the front entrance of the hotel and got into the back of Sa'id's government-issue Mercedes. Up front were a driver and a bodyguard. But what really caught my attention was the black Chevy Suburban behind us, filled with a half-dozen additional well-armed men.

"Expecting company?" I asked as Sa'id donned his sunglasses and we started moving through traffic.

"You can never be too careful," he replied.

"Ali, how many Syrians are in Jordan at the moment?" I asked.

"Around 1.3 million," he replied.

That was more than double the number I'd heard. "I thought it was between five hundred thousand and six hundred thousand," I said.

"That's *registered* refugees," he explained. "There are just over six hundred thousand refugees living in the camps we've set up with the U.N. But there are another seven hundred thousand who are not officially registered with the Jordanian government."

"How do you know the number then?"

"They came before the civil war—to work, to visit family, to take a vacation, to study, whatever.

But they were already here when the civil war in Syria got so bad they couldn't go back."

"So they got stuck here?" I asked.

"You could say that."

"So the total number is 1.3 million?"

"Give or take."

"Do you know who those people really are?"

"What do you mean?" he asked.

"You know what I mean," I replied. "Have they been vetted? Are they all safe? Or are there jihadists among them?"

"The honest answer?" he asked.

"Of course."

"You can't print this."

"I understand. I'm just curious."

"Well . . ." He glanced nervously at the other agents in the car.

"You can tell me," I said. "I promise I won't tell anyone."

There was a long pause, and then he finally said, "The truth is we have no idea who they all are."

"You mean there could be extremists among them?"

"Yes."

"A few?"

"At least."

"Many?"

"Perhaps."

"Could there be ISIS rebels among them?"

"Yes."

"Sleeper cells?"

"Probably."

"You just don't know."

"Not precise numbers, no," Sa'id told me. "But even if it's just one percent of the total number of Syrians who have entered the country, that could be more than thirteen thousand *jihadis*."

I winced. "Ready to strike?"

"Perhaps," he said again.

"When?"

"Who knows? Whenever Abu Khalif gives the order."

"Have you captured any ISIS members so far?"

"Just between us?"

"Yes."

"Not for publication?"

"Yes."

"Then yes," he said. "The answer is yes."

"How many?"

"In the last eighteen months, we've captured twenty-four ISIS and al-Nusra cells. We've also captured more than four tons of weapons."

"Four tons?" I asked, incredulous.

"I'm afraid so."

"What kinds?"

"Light arms and ammunition, mostly," he told me. "But also mortars, rocket launchers, and IEDs. Look, Mr. Collins, we know Syrians loyal to ISIS and other radical groups have penetrated the country. But as bad as that is, that's not even our biggest concern."

"What is?"

"Jordanian nationals."

"What do you mean?"

"I mean, think of Abu Khalif himself," he explained as we sped southward along Highway 15 toward the airport. "He's a Jordanian. Obviously he's on a watch list because we know about him. And his predecessor, Zarqawi—also a Jordanian national. Again, we knew about him. We kept a vigilant eye out for him. And in the end, we helped the Iraqis and the Americans find him and bring him to justice. But how many other Khalifs and Zarqawis are out there that we don't know about? How many Jordanian nationals, with Jordanian passports and Jordanian driver's licenses and Jordanian ID cards work directly for ISIS or one of the other extremist groups, and we don't know who they are? That's the X factor, Mr. Collins. And these traitors could be anywhere."

"Sprinkled throughout the government bureaucracy?" I asked.

"Maybe."

"The police force?"

"It's possible."

"What about the army?"

"Less likely, but I wouldn't rule it out."

"Why not?"

"Look—all of us who have served in the military or the security services love the king," he said. "We're very loyal to him. He's an extraordinary man and a great leader. In some ways, he's even more impressive than his father, may God give his soul rest. Some were worried when King Hussein died in 1999. They were expecting Prince Hassan to take his place. But just a few days before his death, the king changed the laws of succession. He made his eldest son the crown prince. And when Hussein died, Abdullah took the throne.

I know the royal family very well. My father and grandfather were personal bodyguards for them. We would give our lives for them. But when the changeover happened, many were nervous. They didn't say it out loud, mind you. But they weren't sure the young new monarch was up for the challenge. He proved them wrong."

"But . . ."

"Unemployment among the youth is hovering around 30 percent," he said as we passed through the last of several military checkpoints and then turned at the airport. "And that's just the official number. The real number may very well be even higher. And then there are army veterans."

"What about them?"

"Their pensions are not that much, and it's hard to find a good job, even when you come out as a high-ranking officer. You're not that old—maybe in your mid- to late forties or early fifties. You still have many years of productive service left in you, but the army doesn't need you. So what are you supposed to do? How are you supposed to provide for your family? I'm not talking about food and clothing. But how do you help your son put together money to get married, to buy an apartment, to buy a decent car? For that matter, how do you help your daughter pay for college? This is not a wealthy kingdom, Mr. Collins. This is not Arabia. This is not the Gulf. The government does the best it can. But guess where most of the benefits go?"

"To the refugees from Syria and Iraq?"

"No, no—that's a new problem," he said. "They

go to the Palestinians—that is, to Jordanian citizens of Palestinian origin."

"Which is about how many people?"

"Some say up to 70 percent of the population," Sa'id said. "Some say it's only 50 percent. Does it really matter? The point is the Palestinians—whom some call the 'West Bankers'—get a lot of the government's time, attention, and resources."

"And the East Bankers?"

"Well, we're the ones who built the country," he said. "We're the ones who run the government and fight in the army and are loyal to Jordan first and foremost, not to Palestine."

"But the West Bankers are getting most of the perks."

"That's how some people feel."

"Enough to join ISIS, enough to actually overthrow the king?"

"I hope not, Mr. Collins," he said as we pulled up to the main terminal and a sea of heavily armed soldiers and secret police. "But these are crazy times. If you'd asked me a few years ago whether the Egyptians would try to overthrow Mubarak, and Mubarak would let them, I'd have said you were crazy. If you'd asked me if the Syrians would rise up against Assad, and Assad would have such a hard time stopping them, I'd have said you were out of your mind. But the world is changing very, very fast. I have no idea what will happen next. And that's what scares me."

54

Air Force One was on approach.

I was standing ten steps away from Jordan's foreign minister, right beside Agent Sa'id, with a front-row, all-access pass to President Harrison Taylor's arrival.

But as impressive as the sight was, I had seen the gleaming blue-and-white Boeing 747 land at foreign airports before. To the enormous crowd of at least ten thousand Jordanians, I'm sure there was electricity in the air as the leader of the free world prepared to land in the country they loved so dearly. For many—indeed, probably for most—all the pomp and circumstance of a state visit was exciting. The bedouin honor guard. The military band. The freshly vacuumed red carpet. The reviewing stand and the camera platform and the klieg lights and the rest of the hoopla.

But all that barely registered for me. My eyes were trained on the United States Secret Service agents and their Jordanian counterparts scanning the crowd for trouble. I was watching the sharpshooters on the roof and the spotters at their sides with their high-powered binoculars. What interested me was the enormous military presence on the perimeter of the airport, the tanks and armored personnel carriers and hundreds upon hundreds of Jordanian soldiers at the ready, as well as the squadron of Jordanian F-16 Fighting Falcons that were streaking through the sky flying CAP—combat air patrol—in airspace that had been closed the entire day except for official travel. Was the king right? Was his upcoming trip to Baghdad more vulnerable than this? Or were the traitors among us, ready to strike when and how it was least expected?

Every face in the cheering crowd looked, to me at least, genuinely excited. News of a final deal had been leaking out all morning. There was a buzz in the air. Peace was at hand. A sovereign if largely demilitarized Palestinian State, fashioned in a confederation with the Hashemite Kingdom of Jordan, was about to be established once and for all. Why wouldn't this nation so filled with West Bankers be overjoyed for their brothers and sisters across the river and even for themselves?

Yet every face on the security personnel, the vast majority of whom were East Bankers, looked worried and grim. They knew everyone here had been screened by metal detectors and X-ray machines. They knew these observers had been patted down and their purses and handbags and briefcases and backpacks thoroughly searched hours ago. But they still had to be vigilant for the unexpected. That was their job. Was there a killer among them?

And if so, were they looking for a lone gunman or a highly trained, carefully coordinated movement?

Sa'id's words on the drive to the airport were bothering me enormously. I had been through Jordan numerous times. I had developed friends and sources among senior government officials. But I was not an expert on Jordan. Like most reporters, indeed like most Americans, I had never carefully studied the nuances of this country. To me, Jordan was a lovely, safe, friendly country, and I rarely gave it another thought. But after Iraq and Syria, was Jordan the third target of the ISIS terrorists? Was this the crown jewel they wanted to help them build their Islamic caliphate?

And what of my brother Matt's words? Was it possible that the future of Jordan was as dark as the Bible seemed to foretell? Could ISIS really be some kind of instrument about to unleash hell on earth? Was today the day?

If so, would a mere assassination or two—even today—satisfy them? How could it? ISIS hadn't simply tried to take Assad out. They were trying to bring his entire government down. They were trying to seize full control of Damascus and the rest of Syria. The same was true in Iraq. For a Sunni extremist like Abu Khalif, merely beheading Ismail Tikriti or any Iraqi official, even the prime minister, who was a devout Shia, couldn't possibly be enough. Khalif was looking for a way to bring down the democratically elected government of Iraq and establish a Sharia-governed state with himself as the emir. So, too, Khalif wouldn't just want to kill the king of Jordan. He would want to obliterate the royal family and the entire government as well. He would want to create the conditions upon which he and his forces could seize full and complete power. Could that be accomplished on the upcoming royal trip to Baghdad? Not nearly as well as it could be if ISIS struck today, I concluded. But when? How? Who?

As Air Force One touched down to the surprising cheers of the crowd—a crowd that obviously now believed the American president was bearing the gift of a Palestinian State—someone tapped me on the shoulder. I turned, expecting to see Sa'id or perhaps a colleague from the *Times*. Instead, it was Yael Katzir.

"Hey, stranger," she said with a gracious smile and a warm hug.

"Yael . . . what are you doing here?" I asked, as baffled as I was pleased.

"Ari sent me with the PM's delegation," she said. "But I also came to see you. I was so worried about you."

"Thanks. That means a lot."

"You don't look so bad, considering."

"I'll take that as a compliment."

"You should."

"I tried to reach you."

"I know. I'm sorry. It's been crazy. Nonstop. I've hardly eaten a thing. And don't ask me the last time I slept."

"Well, you don't look so bad," I said. "Considering."

"Aren't you sweet."

"Where are you staying?" I asked, hoping that didn't sound too forward.

"Grand Hyatt, and you?"

"Le Méridien."

"Nice."

"Beats a safe house in Mosul."

"I bet," she said, then lowered her voice to a whisper. "Speaking of which, we need to talk."

"Dangerous developments?" I whispered back.

"I'm afraid so."

"You're worried there's going to be an ISIS attack today."

Yael raised an eyebrow. "I see we're thinking the same thing. How did you know?"

"Just a hunch, but one I tried to share with the king yesterday," I said.

"What did he say?"

"Told me not to worry—they've got the city sealed up like a drum."

"Same with my PM," she said. "Ari won't rule it out, but we don't have proof. Just the interviews Khalif did with you. Seems to me Khalif made it about as clear as he could he was coming after the king. And if he could take out my PM, Mansour, and your president all in one shot, it seems kind of irresistible, doesn't it?"

"It does to me," I said. "The question is, does Khalif have the means to launch such a massive attack?"

"The PM doesn't think so," Yael said, scanning the crowd from behind designer sunglasses. "And Ari could hardly stop him from coming without solid evidence of an imminent attack.

Lavi insists Amman is the safest city in the world today, between the Jordanian police, the army, the Mukhabarat, the Palestinian security services, the U.S. Secret Service, the Mossad, and Shin Bet. The PM says ISIS would be crazy to launch an attack today."

"Unless they had someone on the inside," I said.

"You mean a mole?"

"Maybe, or maybe more than that."

"What do you mean?"

"Look, there's no question Khalif has someone inside one of the four governments here today. He has to. He knew about the treaty before anyone else. He knew it was a done deal. He knew the Jordanians were involved. He knew the king was the broker. No one could have known all that several days ago unless they had inside access to at least one of the principals."

"But just that knowledge wouldn't be enough."

"No, which means ISIS would have to have a force already on the ground inside Jordan, inside Amman."

"Inside the palace?" Yael asked.

"That's what worries me," I said. "But how?"

A military band was now playing "Hail to the Chief" as the door of the 747 opened and the president of the United States stepped out and waved to the roaring crowd.

"What about al-Hirak?" she asked.

"What's that?"

"You've never heard of it?"

"No."

"What kind of foreign correspondent are you?"

"The kind that has never heard of al-Hirak. What is it?"

"It means 'the movement,'" she said. "It's a secret underground network of Islamists throughout Jordan made up of disaffected East Bankers. They're devout Muslims, over-the-top, and they think the king has gone soft on Islam. They say the royal family and the government are riddled with corruption. They say the king gives too much money and attention to the West Bankers. They think he doesn't care about the East Bankers or about Islam. They want him to govern like a true Muslim. They want Sharia law."

Again I thought about Sa'id's words in the car. It seemed Yael's intel was correct. "So I'm guessing the king is too pro-Western, too pro-American, and too close to Israel for their tastes?" I said.

"Absolutely. They're Salafists. They want to annihilate the Jews, not have a peace treaty with us. And don't get them started on the queen."

"Why? What's wrong with her?"

"Doesn't wear the veil, wears the latest fashions from London and Paris, likes to hobnob with the rich and famous in Davos and Monte Carlo. They say she dishonors Islam and must be humbled."

"So basically they're just like the Muslim Brotherhood?" I asked.

"No, no, much worse. They loathe the Brotherhood, say they're a bunch of sellouts. And the Brotherhood isn't so strong here anymore. They used to be. But they've made some missteps in recent years. Plus, the Brotherhood isn't illegal in

Jordan like they were and now are again in Egypt. They're aboveground here. That's made it easier for the king and the secret service to keep tabs on them."

"So how big is this Salafist movement, this al-Hirak?"

"We don't have any hard numbers, but the analysts that track this stuff back in Tel Aviv, the ones I've talked to at least, say it's metastasizing quickly."

"And these guys are jihadists?" I asked. "They're violent?"

"Hard to say," she said. "They haven't launched any type of operation yet. But our guys are picking up evidence that some of them seem inspired by the message and methods and success ISIS is having."

"You think they're getting ready to launch a coup?"

"That's exactly what I'm afraid of. Alone, I'm not sure ISIS could pull off here what they're doing in Iraq and Syria. But remember, Khalif is Jordanian. He has a lifetime of contacts here. He knows Jordan better than either of the other two countries. He very likely has thousands of warriors stashed around the country using the Syrian refugee crisis as cover. And if he could activate the al-Hirak network . . ."

She didn't finish the sentence, but she didn't need to.

"Could al-Hirak have loyalists inside the police?"

"Probably."

"The military?"

"Possibly."

"The palace?"

"I don't know," Yael told me as the president descended the steps of Air Force One and prepared to address the crowd.

"But that's why you're here."

"Right," she said, "me and the IDF's most elite NBC unit, hoping to God we're not needed."

NBC unit. She wasn't talking about the National Broadcasting Company.

She was talking about a team of specialists trained in handling nuclear, biological, and chemical warfare.

55

* * *

Ali Sa'id turned to me when the arrival ceremony was nearly finished.

"We need to go," he said.

"Where?"

"Just come quickly."

"What about my friend Yael?"

I introduced her as part of Prime Minister Lavi's delegation, though I said nothing about her expertise in chemical warfare. But Sa'id had his orders, and they didn't include an Israeli.

"It's okay," she said, putting a hand on my arm. "I've got my own orders. But I'll see you at the ceremony."

"Great—and what are you doing afterward?"

"Hopefully nothing."

"Maybe we can think of something."

"Maybe."

I turned back to Sa'id. Neither President Taylor nor the foreign minister was saying anything particularly memorable or newsworthy. The military band was about to strike up the music again. It was all pomp and circumstance and precious little substance, and there was no reason to stay. So as discreetly as possible, I followed Sa'id out of the VIP section with our security detail spread out around us.

A moment later, we reached two golf carts. Sa'id and I boarded one along with two other agents while the rest of the detail boarded the other. It struck me how much security had suddenly been assigned to me. I don't think I'd ever had a single bodyguard in my entire life. Now I had nine, including the chief of security for the royal palace. Why? What did they know that I didn't?

I assumed we were going to the motorcade to link up with the president for the ride to the palace. But when we passed the long line of presidential limousines, Chevy Suburbans, military vehicles, and police cars, I was a little concerned.

"Why aren't we stopping?" I asked a bit more forcefully than I had intended. "His Majesty promised I would be traveling with the president."

"And you will be, Mr. Collins," Sa'id replied. "Please be patient."

No sooner had we passed the idling motorcade than we drove through a hangar and came out onto a secure tarmac that could not be seen by the general public. Waiting there were three of the famous green-and-white VH-3D Sea King helicopters. One of them would serve as Marine One and carry the president. The others would serve as decoys to confuse any enemy that might be lying in wait to shoot the president down.

"You're not using the motorcade," I said, more an observation than a question.

"No," Sa'id replied. "The president is going by air. You'll be in the seat right beside him."

★   ★   ★

Ten minutes later, the president greeted me, but he did not look happy.

"You've really made a mess of things, Collins," he shouted over the roar of the chopper as he saluted a Marine guard and boarded the aircraft.

"I'm afraid I don't see it that way, Mr. President," I shouted back, climbing in behind him.

The White House chief of staff and national security advisor boarded after us, along with Ali Sa'id and two Secret Service agents. I took my assigned seat beside the commander in chief and buckled up. I guessed the rest of Sa'id's men would meet us at the palace. Two minutes later we were airborne.

It was the first time I had ever been on Marine One, and it was hard not to be impressed by the sleek design, classy interior, and high-tech wizardry. It was also one of the quietest helicopters I had ever been on, so while we couldn't exactly talk in a whisper, we weren't shouting at one another either.

"Your articles have rattled the Israelis," the president told me, his body language and tone suggesting any delay in the peace process would be my fault. "They've been raising concerns and asking for changes on the documentation all night."

I refused to take the bait. "What are their specific concerns?"

"You'll have to get that from Daniel, not from me," the president said. "The details aren't important. What matters is that the Israelis were locked and loaded, and then your interview with Khalif comes out and then one story after another about chemical weapons and . . ."

"And what?"

"And you've got them spooked."

I had to smile. "Because of *my* stories?"

"You think this is funny?" the president asked, quickly becoming agitated.

"No, of course not," I replied. "I just think it's a bit—I don't know . . . ridiculous to say the Israelis are getting spooked by me. I'm not making this stuff up. ISIS is a real threat. The Israelis have plenty of reasons to be concerned about getting a final status agreement with the Palestinians just right regardless of what I put into my stories."

"Obviously," the president said. "But Daniel Lavi called me yesterday and specifically said all this talk about Abu Khalif was creating enormous pushback from the members of his coalition."

"Does that really surprise you?" I asked.

"No one would be talking about Abu Khalif if it wasn't for you, Collins," the president shot back.

Was he serious? How could he say that?

"Look, Mr. President, I'm sorry you're upset with me. I really am. I'm not trying to rain on your parade. But I truly believe ISIS could be planning an attack today."

"On this event?"

"Yes, sir."

"Based on what?"

"Based on my interview with Khalif. He made it clear he wants to bring down the king, you, and Daniel Lavi and Salim Mansour as well. Suddenly you're all in one place, in a country he knows like the back of his hand. He's got chemical weapons. He's got the systems to launch them. I'm worried, and honestly, I'm surprised you're not."

"Well, I'm not. The Secret Service is well aware of your interview *and* the risks, and so am I. But there's no way I'm going to let Abu Khalif, of all people, stop a peace treaty of historic proportions."

"I understand, sir, but I have to ask you a question," I began, trying to quickly compose my thoughts. "How serious a threat do you think Abu Khalif and ISIS really pose?"

"To whom?"

"To the U.S., to Israel, to our Arab allies in the region."

"They're a threat, sure," he said.

"How serious?"

"I don't know—they're one of many."

"The main threat?"

"No."

"You don't think they'd like to take you all out today?"

"I'm sure they would. But that's not possible."

"Not possible?"

"No."

"So what would you say *is* the main threat in the Middle East, if you don't mind me asking?"

"The lack of peace between the Israelis and Palestinians, of course," he replied. "That's the holy grail, Collins. That's the missing piece. If we can get that right, everything else falls into place."

Marine One began to bank to the left, and then we were heading north. I had always wanted to see Amman from the air, but this conversation was too important to play the tourist.

"And you believe this treaty will bring lasting, comprehensive peace to the Middle East?"

"Of course," the president said. "Why do you think we've worked so hard and for so long to create a two-state solution? And not just my administration but all those who went before me."

"Are you saying you believe the region will become quiet once this treaty is signed?"

"Not immediately, but in time, yes."

"The Iranians will stop pursuing nuclear weapons?"

"Once we conclude our negotiations with them, yes, I believe they will. Why would they need nuclear weapons if the Palestinians have made peace with Israel?"

"What about their vow to 'wipe Israel off the map'?"

"That's rhetoric, not policy," the president said.

"And ISIS—do you believe they will lay down their arms and give up their goal of establishing an Islamic caliphate if the Israelis and Palestinians make peace?"

"Eventually, yes, I do."

"Isn't it possible that the peace deal you've

helped bring about today could actually trigger more war, more violence?"

"How?"

"By enraging Abu Khalif and other militants who have sworn they will stop at nothing to destroy Israel and anyone who tries to make peace with her."

"Are you saying we should stop trying to make peace because some lunatics like Abu Khalif are going to get mad? That's ridiculous."

"I'm not saying you shouldn't try to make peace," I clarified. "I'm just saying a signing ceremony isn't going to stop the jihadists from trying to kill. It is more likely to inflame them. I mean, Anwar Sadat made peace with Israel in '79, and the Radicals killed him for it."

"And King Hussein made peace with Israel in '94 and lived a long and happy life," the president responded. "Look, Collins, I want peace. The Israelis want peace. The Palestinians want peace. The Jordanians want peace. It's what we all want, and a two-state solution is what's going to make it happen. That's what everyone has been demanding for decades, and that's what I'm delivering, beginning today. You guys in the press can snipe and carp and give all kinds of reasons why it won't work and why it's not worth it. But you're wrong. Dead wrong. You're on the wrong side of history."

I couldn't believe how personally he was taking this. "Mr. President, I'm not trying to be cynical or critical. I'm just asking the questions, trying to understand your thinking about this whole process."

"Well, now you know."

"Yes, I do; thank you," I said, taking a deep breath and pulling my digital recorder out of my jacket pocket to turn it off.

"Whoa, whoa, wait a minute—this is all off the record," the president suddenly said.

"What are you talking about?" I replied, genuinely confused. "No, it isn't."

"Of course it is," he shot back.

"You never said that," I responded. "I was told I had an exclusive interview with you. I thought it was going to be in the limousine, but clearly we're doing it here instead."

"No, no, no—absolutely not. I'd be happy to do an interview with you when the ceremony is over, but this is just a friendly off-the-record discussion, nothing more."

"You can't just say that after the discussion is over, Mr. President. That's not how the game is played."

"It's not a game," he replied, incensed. "These are highly sensitive background discussions, not for public consumption."

"Well, I'm sorry, but that's not how it's done," I said, holding my ground. "I'm sorry you think I'm complicating your life. But with all due respect, sir, I'm just doing my job."

"By playing gotcha? By undermining the entire peace process in its final hours?"

"I'm not playing gotcha, and if anyone undermines this peace it will be ISIS, not me. I know these people, Mr. President. I've talked with them face-to-face. I've seen who they are. I've seen what they do. And I'm telling you, ISIS and the rest of these radical Salafist jihadists pose a clear and present danger to the national security of the United States, Israel, Jordan, and everyone who loves peace in this region. And anyone who thinks Abu Khalif is going away after this treaty gets signed ought to have his head examined. He's not going to stop. He's going to redouble his efforts until he wreaks havoc and creates mass carnage throughout this region or until he is hunted down and killed."

"This conversation is over," the president said. "And off the record. If you print it, I swear to you the *New York Times* isn't going to have access to me or my administration in any way, shape, or form ever again. You're playing a game, Collins, but you just went too far."

"I could give a flying leap whether the *Times* has access to you or not, sir. Abu Khalif is a serial killer. He's murdered my friends. He's tried to murder me. He's threatened my family. And he's coming after you and every single leader who signs this treaty. I'm not saying don't sign it. I'm saying you'd better be ready for what comes next. Maybe ISIS won't strike today or this week. Maybe you're right and all the security in place will suffice. But every day ISIS is recruiting more foreign fighters into their movement. And they're not just coming from Arab and Islamic countries. They're coming from Europe. They're coming from Asia. They're coming from America, Mr. President. Americans are signing up for jihad. They're fighting in Syria and Iraq for Abu Khalif and Jamal Ramzy. They carry American passports. If you don't get serious about stopping them, they're coming home to unleash jihad on American soil. And when it happens, it won't be the fault of the *New York Times*. I'm just the messenger. The buck stops with you."

56

★ ★ ★

AL-HUMMAR PALACE—AMMAN, JORDAN

It was deadly quiet in the chopper for the next five minutes.

Then Marine One touched down inside the royal compound. As soon as the engines shut down and the rotors came to a stop, the side door opened and the president was immediately greeted by the king and the crown prince. The three of them chatted for a few minutes, out of my earshot, and then headed inside the palace.

I was now persona non grata, at least as far as the president was concerned.

When it was all clear, Sa'id exited the chopper and I followed him. He gave me a special pin to wear on my lapel and a lanyard attached to a laminated press pass with my photo and media credentials. He explained the combination of these two would give me nearly complete backstage access for the remainder of the day. I put them on and followed him inside.

We entered through a back portico, then turned right and walked down a long hallway to a wing on the northeast side of the building. We stepped into a large, ornate hall. It had enormous crystal chandeliers and original paintings in gold-leafed frames and a massive antique table of polished wood with matching chairs. I couldn't tell at first if it was supposed to serve as a cabinet room or a formal dining room, but it didn't really matter at the moment, for there was no food set out and no drinks were available. Rather, I saw President Mansour chatting with Prime Minister Lavi. I didn't see Prince Marwan, but I did see my old friend Youssef Kuttab talking with some of Lavi's men. I nodded to him, and he nodded back. But I decided now might not be the best time to approach him. He was deep in conversation, and at the moment I wasn't quite sure what was wanted or expected of me, especially after the dustup I'd just had with President Taylor.

To be candid, though, I was excited about the exclusive he had given me. Despite his protestations, his remarks had been on the record, and they provided a fascinating picture into the thinking of a president with whom the American people already had serious and growing concerns. Taylor's approval ratings were dropping steadily. They were lower than those of Presidents Bush and Obama, and it wasn't due solely to the weak economy. Americans were souring on his handling of foreign policy. The latest CBS News/*New York Times* poll found that most people saw the president as "disengaged" and "aloof" on national security matters. They specifically believed he was "on the wrong track" when it came to handling the Middle East, particularly vis-à-vis the dual crises in Syria and Iraq. Those numbers could change quickly, of course, if the new peace treaty was popular. But the rapid ISIS takeover of large sections of Iraq—and now the clear and convincing proof that this al Qaeda breakaway faction actually had acquired, on the president's watch, the very weapons of mass destruction the country had gone into two wars to keep al Qaeda and Saddam Hussein from having—were weighing heavily on the public's mind.

I looked carefully to see if there were any visible signs of discord or disunity between Lavi and Mansour. From my angle, I couldn't see any. They actually seemed quite jovial and relaxed. Whatever concerns had been voiced earlier in the day—assuming the president wasn't spinning me—had apparently been worked out. From all evidence, the ceremony was on.

Ali Sa'id came over and whispered in my ear. "Mr. Collins, we're about to begin. His Majesty would like to get you in place."

"Thanks, Ali," I said. "By the way, where are the king's younger children? I don't see them anywhere."

"The queen sent them to spend a few days with their cousins," Sa'id replied.

That made sense, I guessed, given all that was happening, though I would have liked to meet them. At some point it might make sense to do a story on the entire royal family and how unique they were in the region for being so committed to peace.

For now, I followed Sa'id out a back exit. As chief of security for the Royal Court, he was certainly a senior official in the General Intelligence Directorate in addition to being very close to the king and the royal family. Yet he had been assigned to take care of me in every way, and I was touched by His Majesty's kindness. This was not standard operating procedure. This was special. I couldn't let it skew my coverage, I knew. That had to be straightforward and as objective as humanly possible. But given that the king and I had never met until the previous day, I was certainly grateful on a personal level. I was still anxious something terrible was coming. But honestly I didn't see how. And I did feel safer with Sa'id at my side.

We walked down a series of hallways, and Sa'id was clearly in his element. This was a palace he knew and loved dearly. He gave me a little history lesson along the way, making comments about various paintings and artifacts as well as about some of the interesting leaders he had met over the years.

He also briefed me on various security protocols that were in place, including escape routes if there was a fire or some other incident. He made very clear from the beginning that this information was not for publication, a lesson I thought he might want to share with the president of the United States. Sa'id wasn't giving me any classified or proprietary information. He was just making sure I knew what to do in case of emergency, and he stressed that no matter what, I should stick close to him.

In his own way, he also seemed to be expressing a sense of deep professional pride. I realized that in many ways this palace was as much his home as it was the king's. Sa'id cared deeply about making sure everyone here was secure and cared for. He shared His Majesty's tradition of warm Arab hospitality, and everything he said and did showed it.

It was a much longer walk from that formal dining room to the main entrance of the palace than I had expected. But finally we arrived, and I could hear another military band playing. Then we stepped through a side door into the courtyard where I had been dropped off the day before.

The Mercedes was gone, and so were the large moving trucks and all the workers. I saw the crowd and the cameras and the television lights. I saw the stage and the red carpets and all the Jordanian, Palestinian, Israeli, and American flags, snapping in the crisp breeze. I saw the bleachers filled with five hundred or more smiling, excited, fascinated high school students—Arabs and Israelis, Muslims, Christians, and Jews—and for the first time, I have to say, I was moved by it all.

I can't explain it really, but all my hard-bitten professional cynicism began to melt away for a few moments. This was really happening. This was no longer talk. This was no longer a "backgrounder briefing" about how the parties were going to talk about the ground rules for the discussions about the negotiations. This was the real thing. The Israelis and Palestinians were really going to sign a final, comprehensive peace treaty.

And people were excited. Not just the students but the palace staff and hundreds of other government workers who apparently had been invited to see it all unfold.

I had no idea exactly how it was all going to play out. Nor did anyone else. But this was history in the making, and I was here at the center of it all, and I couldn't really believe it. I can't say I felt pride at that moment. To the contrary, I felt humbled. My grandfather would have loved this, and he would have done an amazing job covering it all. But I was just a kid from Bar Harbor, Maine. Who was I to be a witness to a moment in history as profound as the birth of the Palestinian State? Who was I to become a friend and confidant to presidents and prime ministers, much less a king? I was nobody. But at that moment I felt like God was looking down at me with pleasure. I didn't deserve it. I still wasn't even sure I really believed it. But God did seem to have saved my life countless times and was now opening these doors and seemed to be putting me exactly where he wanted me. And I have to say I felt grateful. I couldn't escape the feeling this was a special moment. I only wished Omar and Abdel could have been here to see it too.

Sa'id walked me to my seat at the end of a riser situated immediately behind the main stage, the signing table, and the speaker's podium, then took a seat directly behind me.

It was an excellent spot. From this vantage

point, while I wouldn't be able to see the faces of the various leaders as they addressed the crowd and the cameras, I still had a commanding view of the environment. I could see what the king would be seeing and how the crowd reacted. It was certainly a much better position than any of my colleagues in the media enjoyed. Plus, seated near me in this VIP section were a number of Jordanian ministers, members of Parliament, judges, and generals, along with their many aides. In part, I'm sure, this was simply because there was no other place to put these dignitaries. The courtyard wasn't small, but there were limitations. I suspected, however, that the royals' media advisors wanted to project TV images around the world of Jordan's government fully behind this treaty, literally as well as figuratively.

The one person I didn't see was Prince Marwan. I wanted to congratulate him on all his hard work. He had a great deal to be proud of, and I wanted to get his thoughts for my next story.

Scanning the crowd, I found the media pool in the back of the large courtyard. They were at least half a football field away, and there were a lot of them, but I was fairly sure I could pick out Alex Brunnell, our Jerusalem bureau chief, standing with the *Times* White House correspondent and chief diplomatic correspondent. At Allen's direction, the Gray Lady was covering this event from all angles, and rightly so.

I realized at that moment that I had absolutely no idea what else was happening on the planet. Surely there were floods and droughts, elections and resignations, weddings and babies being born, and every manner of news being made—"all the news that's fit to print, and quite a bit that isn't," as my colleagues and I liked to joke—but I'd had neither the time nor the capacity to pay attention to any of it. Since entering Homs, I hadn't been able to think about anything but the ISIS threat. But now, finally, I breathed a sigh of relief.

I pulled out my grandfather's pocket watch. It was two minutes before two o'clock. Almost showtime. And then Yael Katzir sidled up beside me.

"Is that seat taken?" she asked, pointing to the empty chair to my left.

"As a matter of fact it isn't," I replied, standing and pretending to doff my cap. "Would you care to join me, young lady?"

"I would be honored, kind sir. Thank you."

We sat down and she scanned the crowd.

"Impressive," she said.

"It is."

"Maybe we're overreacting a little," she added.

"Maybe," I said. "I was half-expecting to see you next in a chem-bio suit."

"It's in the trunk." She smiled, but I couldn't quite tell if she was kidding.

I looked up at the F-16s flying their missions, though they were way out in the distance, not close enough for the roar of their jet engines to disrupt the moment. I looked at the soldiers and Secret Service agents on the roof and tried to pick out the plainclothes agents intermingled in the crowds. Generally, it wasn't hard. Everyone else was smiling. The security guys were not. Plus they had those little squiggly earpieces, of course, a dead giveaway. Still, I was very glad they were there.

Five minutes passed, then ten, but there was still no sign yet of the principals or the prince. Aides continued scurrying around on the plat-form, making last-minute tweaks. They were set-ting out fountain pens, pouring glasses of water, checking the microphones, and resetting audio levels. A newcomer to state events would naturally assume all these things would have been taken care of already, but I knew from years of covering such functions how many details there were to be han-dled, and how rarely such events began on time.

Still, the schoolkids were clearly becoming a bit restless. They had already been sitting there for the better part of an hour, and their chairs couldn't be the most comfortable in the world.

At least it was December, so the sun wasn't blazing down on us all. Rather, there was a blanket of dark-gray clouds overhead and a slight breeze that made it chillier than some might have wanted but also made the flags flutter perfectly for the cameras.

"Everything okay?" I said to Sa'id.

"Of course," he said. "But you know how these things go. I'm sure they'll be out soon."

"Where is Prince Marwan?" I asked. "And where will he be sitting?"

"I don't know where he is—that's a good ques-tion," Sa'id replied. "He should be here by now. He must be conferring with His Majesty. He'll be sitting directly behind the king. Should I radio my men to find him?"

"No, no, they've got enough to do. I'm sure he'll be here soon."

I turned to Yael. "So I guess we have a little time to kill," I said, trying to come up with some small talk that didn't sound completely ridiculous.

"We try not to say 'kill' in this part of the world," she replied. "But yes, I guess we do. Got something on your mind?"

I certainly did. I wanted to ask her out, but I was hesitant to go too quickly. "Well, I'm realizing I hardly know you."

"That's true."

"Where were you born?"

"Up in the Galilee."

"Where?"

"It's a little town called Rosh Pinna. It's up in the hills. It's adorable. You should come sometime."

"Sounds fun. Do you still have family there?"

"My parents are there. They run a restaurant— amazing—best food in Israel. And a stunning view, especially at night."

"Even better. Do you have siblings?"

"I had an older brother."

"Had?"

"He was in a special forces unit. Killed in Lebanon in '06."

"I'm sorry."

"Yeah, well, what can you do?"

We were quiet for a moment, and then she asked, "How about you?"

"What about me?"

"All I know about you is what Ari told me."

"Well, you already know about my parents," I said. "My mom is in Bar Harbor, where I grew up. My dad is gone. But I didn't know him much anyway. He left the family when I was a kid."

"I'm sorry."

"Yeah, well, what can you do?"

"Have you had any contact with your brother since Istanbul? He's here in Amman, isn't he?"

"He was, but he left with his family when Abu Khalif threatened to use them against me."

"So you talked with him?"

"Yeah, we actually had a nice visit. It had been a while."

"And Laura?"

"Oh, well, let's not go there."

"No longer the marrying type?"

"Couldn't we talk about something else?"

"Like what, sarin gas?"

"That would be less painful."

"Ouch."

"Exactly."

She paused for a moment, then asked, "Did she leave you?"

"No, but she cheated on me. A lot. So I left her."

"I'm sorry."

It was quiet again for a bit, and then Yael said, "Let's pick something happier to talk about."

"That would be good. Thanks."

Just then the spokesman for the Royal Court went up to the main podium, tapped on the windscreens for the two microphones. The band stopped playing. Cameras started clicking, and the aide cleared his throat.

"This is the two-minute warning," he said. "I repeat, the ceremony will begin in two minutes."

A newfound surge of electricity rippled through the crowd, myself included.

It was time to get this thing done.

57

★ ★ ★

I checked my pocket watch—it was 2:28 p.m.

I pulled my digital recorder out of my pocket, double-checked the batteries, put it back, and then grabbed my notepad and scribbled down a few observations and a few questions I wanted to ask President Mansour and Prince Marwan after the ceremony.

Again I scanned the crowd. People were actually leaning forward now in anticipation. I noticed a side door open off to my right—the same door Sa'id and I had come through earlier—and a half-dozen agents from the Shin Bet, the Israeli secret service, and another half-dozen agents from President Taylor's protective detail entered the courtyard and took up their positions. I saw one of the agents say something into his wrist-mounted radio and watched to see other agents react. One by one, they seemed to stand up a bit straighter. They were on their toes, ready to prevent anything from going wrong. But what really could?

The king was right. This was essentially a hermetically sealed environment. If there was going to be an attack, it might happen in Baghdad, but it wasn't going to be here. Every person in the courtyard had already been carefully, meticulously screened. The only people who had weapons were Sa'id's team, responsible for the security of the palace and its grounds, and the most trusted agents protecting each of the leaders. What's more, the Jordanian army and police forces were on full alert. Several thousand troops were patrolling the streets of Amman. Security checkpoints were everywhere. The police were stopping cars and trucks and vehicles of all sorts, checking IDs, asking questions, on the lookout for anything suspicious. I told myself to take deep, long breaths and relax.

The words of FDR echoed through my brain: *"The only thing we have to fear is fear itself."*

"Yael," I said after a moment.

"Yes?"

"If you're free this evening, would you like to have dinner with me? You could ask me more painful questions and I could spend the evening dodging them and trying not to look pathetic."

"That's quite an offer."

"I thought so."

She looked at me and smiled. "Sure. That would be nice."

"Eight o'clock?"

"Better make it nine," she said. "The PM has an early state dinner with the other principals and then flies out around eight. I should be clear by nine."

"Then it's a date?"

"It is. Thank you, Mr. Collins."

"My pleasure, Miss Katzir."

I started breathing again. But my heart was racing.

It was ridiculous. I think I was actually blushing. The back of my neck felt hot.

I looked away. It was showtime. I needed to focus. But for the first time in a long time, I actually felt happy. It was a strange sensation, almost surreal, in fact, but nice. I needed a little happiness in my life just now.

I looked up into the cloudy gray sky. A flock of birds flew past and the breeze picked up. It occurred to me that I hadn't been given any prepared remarks for any of the leaders, typically standard operating procedure for an event like this, and I suspected this could be accounting for the delay. They were all probably making last-minute tweaks to their remarks. Then again, I would hear them soon enough. Did I really need a sneak preview?

At that moment, however, two Jordanian F-16s caught my eye. They were flying their combat air patrol, keeping any stray aircraft—Jordanian or otherwise—out of this corridor, which was now restricted airspace. Both were quite a ways off in the distance, but what seemed odd was that while they had been flying from left to right across the horizon, heading from south to north, one of them was now turning right and banking toward the palace. Was that normal? It didn't seem so. Several pairs of fighter jets had been crisscrossing the distant skies for the last half hour or so in the same predictable manner. So why the deviation?

I leaned over to Yael. "What do you make of that, twelve o'clock high?" I whispered, discreetly nodding toward the western sky.

She looked up. "I don't know," she replied. "Ask Ali."

The jet was still several miles away, but there was no question it was headed in our direction. The question was why. I turned and whispered to Sa'id.

"What's going on with that F-16?" I asked. "He's broken off from his wingman."

Sa'id had clearly been scanning the crowd, not the skies, because he didn't immediately respond. But a moment later, he said something in Arabic over his wrist-mounted radio.

"Stay calm, but come with me, both of you," he whispered back a few seconds later.

Startled, I had a hard time taking my eyes off the plane, but when I saw him discreetly get up and walk back toward the doorway from which we had come, I followed his lead.

Yael was right behind me. The band was playing again. Just then, I got a text from Allen back in D.C. **This is exciting.**

He didn't know the half of it.

"Where are we going?" I asked Sa'id.

"The command center."

"What do you think's going on?"

"I'm not sure," he conceded. "But I'm not bringing His Majesty out here until I know."

As he said this, I turned and took one last look at the F-16 before going inside. And at that very moment I saw a flash of light and a contrail.

"He just fired a missile!" Yael said, now motionless.

"Code red! Code red! Everybody down!" Sa'id yelled at the top of his lungs to his fellow agents and the rest of the crowd.

But he didn't dive to the floor or take cover in the courtyard. Instead, he grabbed Yael and me and shoved us through the door. *"To the stairwell—move!"* he said. *"Quickly!"*

He started running and so did I.

As we came around a corner, we nearly ran into the king and the other world leaders who were coming down the hall toward us.

"Through this door, Your Majesty!" Sa'id yelled, pushing open an emergency door and nearly throwing King Abdullah and the others through it. *"Run, Your Majesty! To the safe room! Go, go, go! There's no time to waste!"*

The king's instincts were exceptional. His special forces training kicked in instantly. He grabbed Presidents Taylor and Mansour, the closest men to him, and began pulling them down the cement stairwell toward the basement. The rest of us followed hard on their heels, including Prime Minister Lavi and all the various security agents. A moment later we felt the explosion and then heard its roar.

The force of the blast knocked everyone off their feet. Some went tumbling down the metal stairs. Yael and I were thrown against a concrete wall.

The king was the first back on his feet, and he started shouting commands. *"We can't stay here! Follow me!"*

The security details found their principals and got them moving. In the confusion, Yael and I were shoved to the back. But soon we were racing down two more flights of stairs, trying not to be left behind.

Then a second explosion hit, again knocking us off our feet.

Jordanian soldiers in full combat gear now burst into the stairwell. They grabbed the king and took off. The rest of us scrambled to our feet and hustled to keep up. We raced down one hallway, then another. We were now apparently heading toward a bunker of some kind, something akin to the Presidential Emergency Operations Center located deep underneath the White House.

We passed what appeared to be a command center, not unlike the one I'd seen in Abu Ghraib, though far more modern and sophisticated. Sa'id stopped me there and pulled me inside.

The king and the others didn't stop. They kept moving and passed into what looked from my angle like an enormous bank vault. The moment they were inside, a massive, three-foot-thick steel door was quickly shut and sealed behind them as Jordanian soldiers brandishing automatic weapons rushed to take up positions in front of the door.

Yael, trailing the leaders and agents, tried to join them, but she was too late. The soldiers wouldn't let her in. She protested that she was part of Lavi's team, but they wouldn't budge. The door was locked.

At least the king and the others were safe. That was all that mattered for the moment.

"Where is that?" I shouted. "Where did they just go?"

Sa'id was about to explain, but the explosions just kept coming.

I looked at the bank of security monitors inside the command center, and all the blood drained from my face. I could see the flames and the smoke and the burning, screaming, dying children above us.

But as horrific as those images were, they paled in comparison to the image now on the main large flat-screen on the far wall. It was a live shot of the F-16 screaming inbound. Whoever was flying that plane was on a kamikaze mission into the palace. There was no one to stop him, and all I could think of was Abu Khalif and ISIS.

58

★ ★ ★

With Yael and Sa'id at my side, I stared at the video monitors.

Unable to move and with nowhere to go, we watched as the pilot of the second Jordanian F-16 swooped in behind his rogue wingman and began firing on it. The lead fighter jet bobbed and weaved, dived and rolled, trying to outmaneuver his colleague. But despite the aerial acrobatics, he was still coming in hard and fast.

Though some of the cameras were obscured by fire and billowing smoke, I could see the people who hadn't already been incinerated by the air-to-ground missiles screaming and running in all directions. Then we and the four duty officers in the command post erupted in cheers as one of the second F-16's Sidewinder missiles actually clipped the right wing of the inbound fighter jet.

But it was too little, too late. At the last moment, I instinctively turned away and covered my head as the flaming jet crashed headlong into the Al-Hummar complex, but that didn't stop me from being thrown off my feet by the tremendous force of the blast several stories overhead. The whole complex shuddered and groaned. And I smelled it. The thick, acrid smoke was seeping even into the climate-controlled environment below the palace. Yael and several of the men began choking.

Sa'id took control and threw several switches, presumably activating an air-purification system because some machinery rumbled to life and began to exchange the air quite rapidly.

The video monitors flickered and then went dark. A moment later, all the lights on our level flickered as well, and before we knew it, all power was lost and we were standing in the bunker in complete darkness.

Then came a series of deafening booms, one after another, as the rest of the jet's munitions cooked and exploded in the raging fires above. Framed pictures of the king and crown prince fell to the floor and smashed into pieces.

Down the hall, a pipe burst. I heard water gushing out.

When the explosions ended, we still heard people screaming and dying up above us, their chilling shrieks making their way through the heating and air-conditioning ducts.

Soon we heard emergency generators roaring to life, and low-level emergency lighting kicked in. Some of the video monitors flicked back on as well. Not all of them did, but there were enough to give us a terrifying glimpse of what was happening above us.

I turned to check on Yael. She had a large gash on her forehead and was bleeding profusely.

I called for a first aid kit, and one of the watch commanders rushed to my side with one. As I bandaged her up, though, Yael gasped. At first I thought I had hurt her somehow. But when I saw her eyes grow wide, I turned to see what she was looking at.

In a scene eerily similar to what I had witnessed at Abu Ghraib, I could now see dump trucks and cement trucks loaded with explosives making speed dashes for the outer gates of the royal compound. I watched as soldiers fired automatic weapons at them, but one by one the trucks were hitting their targets and erupting in massive explosions.

Huge gaps appeared in the perimeter fences, and hundreds of fighters in black hoods and ski masks rushed through to engage in brutal gun battles with Jordanian soldiers fighting desperately to save themselves and their beloved king.

"Ali, we can't stay here," I said, turning to Sa'id. "We need to get these men out of here while we still can."

"No, we are safe here," one of the duty officers replied. "We must wait until reinforcements arrive."

"It could be too late by then," I argued. "Look, the rebels are pouring in from the north and the east. But there—screen eight—there are three armor-plated Suburbans parked in the south parking lot. That's just a few hundred yards away. If we can get to them, we can get these men out of this kill zone."

"These men?" the officer asked, incredulous. "You mean His Majesty?"

"And the presidents and the prime minister—all of them."

"No, we have a protocol; we stay here until the army arrives," he insisted.

"You have a protocol for *this*?" I asked, now incredulous myself. "For a catastrophic attack on the palace with the leader of the free world trapped amid an onslaught of ISIS jihadists?"

"I have my orders," the officer shot back. "We wait for the army."

"The army is here, and the ISIS forces are still getting through. We have a chance to get the principals out, but only if we move now. If we wait here, we all die."

Just then we were all startled by the vault door opening behind us. Suddenly King Abdullah was coming out of the safe room and directly toward us.

"Ali, we need to go now," he ordered. "How many men do you have?"

Sa'id stood there for a moment, dumbfounded. Not only was the king standing before him, but Queen Rania, the crown prince, the three other heads of state, and their bodyguards were all waiting in the hallway.

"How many?" the king pressed, white-hot with urgency.

"At the moment, Your Majesty, there are just four duty officers besides me, plus Mr. Collins and Miss Katzir."

"Who is she?"

"She's with me," Prime Minister Lavi said, stepping forward. "Mossad."

"Very well," the king said. "Do you all have weapons training?"

"Yes, Your Majesty," most of them said.

"Good," he said, stripping off his jacket and tie. Then he addressed the duty officer who had been arguing with me. "Get weapons, flak jackets, and helmets for everyone out of the vault. Move, go!"

The man did as he was ordered, and Sa'id and the other officers went with him.

The king turned to me. "Have you ever used a gun, Mr. Collins?"

"Uh, sure. I grew up in Maine, Your Majesty."

"Do a lot of hunting and fishing?"

"Yes, sir."

"Ever use an MP5?" he asked.

"Can't say I have, sir."

"Piece of cake," he said as Sa'id and his colleagues rushed back with weapons and protective gear for everyone.

To my astonishment, the king of Jordan gave me a crash course on how to use a submachine gun. Then he strapped on a bulletproof vest and an ammo belt as everyone else, including the Secret Service and Shin Bet agents and of course the agents of the Royal Court who were directly assigned to protect the king, did the same.

Scanning the video monitors, the king quickly assessed the situation and came to the same conclusion I just had. "We're going to head for those three Suburbans," he said. "Are the keys inside?" he asked.

"No, sir," the head of President Taylor's detail said.

"Where are they?"

"The doors should be unlocked, but the keys will be in the pockets of those dead agents lying on the pavement."

"What's the chance they're using chemical weapons out there?" President Mansour asked. I had been thinking the same thing.

"Don't worry; they're not," the king said.

"How do you know?" President Taylor asked.

"Look at the video monitors," the king replied. "The rebels don't have gas masks on. They're not wearing protective suits. We should be fine."

"With all due respect, Your Majesty," Yael interjected, "the rebels who have penetrated the palace compound may not be planning a chemical attack, but their commanders still might be."

"Miss Katzir is right, Your Majesty," Sa'id confirmed. "We have backpacks in the vault with chem-bio suits, gas masks, gloves—everything you need. I would advise that each person take one."

"Fine, go get them," the king ordered.

Once again Sa'id and his colleagues moved quickly to comply.

"Now, Your Majesty, assuming we get out of the compound alive, where do you suggest we go?" asked the Israeli prime minister, himself a former special forces commando, as he popped a fresh magazine into an MP5.

"The airport," the king said. "My brother is the head of the air force. I'll call him on a secure phone in a moment. I'll tell him to bomb the day-lights out of the palace. I'll also tell him to give us air cover and have the army prepare to meet us at the airport."

"Good," President Taylor said. "I'll order Air Force One to be ready for immediate takeoff when we arrive. I'll take you all out with me. Once we get out of Jordanian airspace and get a U.S. fighter squadron to provide security for us, you can direct a counterstrike from the communications deck."

Everyone nodded.

"Very good," the king said. "There's just one catch."

"What's that?" President Mansour asked.

"There are checkpoints everywhere. Don't stop."

"At which ones?"

"Any of them."

"Why not?" I asked.

"Because right now, Mr. Collins, we have no idea who's on our side and who isn't," the king replied. "If we stop, we die. Clear enough?"

I nodded. So did everyone else. It was ugly, but it was clear.

"Ali, I need a secure satphone," the king said.

Sa'id set down his weapons and immediately unlocked a safe in the command post. He pulled out five satphones and gave one to the king. He gave three to the other leaders and kept one for himself. "These were specially built by the Jordanian military for the Royal Court," he explained. He handed out three-by-five laminated cards with each of the satphone numbers and passcodes on one side and simple instructions in both

Arabic and English for using the phones on the other. Meanwhile, the duty officers handed out the backpacks filled with chem-bio equipment, and we suited up.

"Okay," the king said at last, switching off the safety on his weapon. "Follow me."

59

★ ★ ★

That's when we heard the muffled sounds of automatic gunfire above us.

"They're inside the palace," the king said. "We need to go now."

The king's bodyguards absolutely refused to let him take the lead. They didn't care how long he had served in the army. Nor did they care that he was a direct descendant of Muhammad. Not right now. They had taken an oath to lay down their lives to protect the monarch and keep him alive at all costs, and that's what they intended to do. Thus, four of the king's six protectors moved ahead of him to the front of the pack, while two others covered his back. The rest of the assembled agents and duty officers formed a protective ring around President Taylor and President Mansour and Prime Minister Lavi, as well as the queen and the crown prince. Yael and I brought up the rear, with Sa'id in the very back.

The lead agents decided not to take either of the stairwells back up to the top, assessing them as too risky. Instead, they unlocked an emergency escape hatch on the far side of the bunker and ordered us all to climb up what looked like the inside of a missile silo to the main level. The king went after the lead agents and the rest of us followed quickly behind.

"Where does this lead?" I whispered to Sa'id while I waited anxiously for my turn.

"It opens in a service garage on the south side of the compound," he whispered back. "It won't get us any closer to the Suburbans, but there are only a few people beyond those gathered with us who even know this route exists."

The climb up the metal ladder drilled into the side of the concrete silo, three stories high, was all the more difficult with the bulky and heavy backpacks we were carrying. As we worked our way upward, the sound of the gun battle above us reached a fevered pitch. What worried me, aside from whether Queen Rania had the arm strength to make the climb, was how vulnerable we now were. If an enemy was waiting for us at the top, we'd all be dead before any of us could turn around and get back into the bunker. And what if ISIS rebels got into the bunker behind us?

But that wasn't the only problem. The closer we got to the top, the more intensely hot it became. Within minutes I completed the climb and found out why. The burning remains of the F-16 and the resulting explosions from its suicide mission had created a scorching inferno. The service garage that was supposed to shield us and give us some initial cover was gone. Obliterated. Wiped out in the crash.

The scene at the top of the silo was surreal. I had never witnessed anything like it. It was an image of the apocalypse. Fire was everywhere. Whatever structures had not yet been destroyed were completely ablaze. The flames soared twenty, thirty, forty feet or more into the air. I was immediately drenched in sweat. I could feel the searing heat cooking my skin.

From my right, I suddenly heard screaming. When I turned, I saw one of the king's bodyguards engulfed in fire. And then I heard a burst of automatic-weapons fire and saw three agents fall to the ground.

"Hit the deck!" the king yelled in English.

We all instantly dropped to our stomachs. Yael and a Secret Service agent to my left were the first to return fire. Soon everyone around me with a weapon was firing. Through the leaping flames and the thick, black, nearly blinding smoke, I could make out hazy figures moving here and there. They were wearing black ski masks. They were ISIS, and they couldn't be more than fifty yards away. I aimed my MP5, flicked off the safety, and fired two bursts, then two more.

The masked men ran off, and I heard a Shin Bet agent yell, *"Clear! We're clear on this side! Let's go! Let's go!"*

Turning toward him, I realized four of the agents near me were KIA—two Americans, a Jordanian, and an Israeli. The protective team around the principals was dwindling fast. We were outmanned, outgunned, and running out of time. Our only hope was making it to those

armor-plated SUVs before the enemy did or before
they captured us and cut off our heads.

I was about to jump up to join them when I
saw the flaming wreckage of Marine One at two
o'clock. It looked like it had taken a direct hit from
an antitank missile. There was almost nothing left.

Then I saw someone creeping behind the
burning Sea King. I fired two bursts and was about
to fire again, but then Yael was on her feet. She
dropped her backpack and ran toward the flames,
firing as she went. *What was she doing? Was she
mad?* She had no idea who was back there or how
many more were hidden by the smoke.

As she disappeared from view, I heard an enormous firefight erupt behind the chopper. She was
in trouble. I looked behind me. The principals
and their details were racing for the SUVs. Sa'id
was with them, flanking the royal family and yelling for me to join them. I looked back toward the
chopper as the gunfire intensified. But there was
no question—I had to go find Yael. I couldn't just
leave her to fight alone.

Scrambling to my feet, I shrugged off my own
backpack and ran headlong into the flames and
around the front side of the Sea King. For the
moment, I held my fire. I couldn't see an enemy,
and I'd never forgive myself if I killed or wounded
Yael. Amid the billows of smoke, my eyes were
watering. I could barely breathe. I was starting to
choke. But as I came all the way around to the
other side of the inferno, I stopped dead in my
tracks.

Yael was not more than thirty or forty feet

ahead of me. But she was no longer armed. She had her hands up over her head and was surrounded by three hooded men. Each was pointing a Kalashnikov at her. Why they hadn't killed her yet I had no idea. But they were screaming something at her in Arabic. She began lowering herself to the ground. Soon she was on her knees, her back to me. The men were still screaming something, but she didn't seem to be responding.

I quickly checked behind me and to both of my flanks. I hadn't been spotted yet. And most of the action was well behind me, likely converging against the principals. But I had no idea what to do next. It was clear Yael's only hope was for me to kill these three—and fast—before more terrorists arrived. But I wasn't a trained soldier. I wasn't a sniper or a sharpshooter. The chance of my hitting any of them, much less killing all three of them, without killing her too seemed minuscule at best.

I just stood there frozen. Then one of the terrorists put the barrel of his machine gun on the back of her neck. He barked something at her. She didn't respond at first, so another one drove his boot into her stomach. She cried out and doubled over in pain but he forced her back up to her knees. She tried to raise her hands over her head again but was clearly having a hard time doing it. I could see now that she was bleeding from her left shoulder. And then one of them ripped her shirt halfway off.

Something in me snapped. I yelled at the top of my lungs and charged them as fast as I could run. I started firing—short bursts, one after another.

I might very well kill her, I knew, but it was a chance I had to take. There was no other choice. If I did nothing, she'd be dead for certain. Raped first, probably, and then beheaded. Or crucified. Possibly dismembered. But she wasn't getting out alive unless I did something fast.

Two of the terrorists heard me coming and began to turn, aiming their weapons at me. I pulled the trigger. One of them took a full burst of machine-gun fire to the face and went sprawling. The other took three shots to the chest and collapsed to the ground as well. Yael hit the deck, flattening herself against the ground, facedown. As she did, I was afraid the third terrorist would pull the trigger and finish her off. Instead, when he saw his friends go down, he pivoted toward me. I was coming at him full bore. He was about to open fire. I unleashed all the ammo I had left. His gun did fire but the shots went wild, and he went crashing to the pavement as one of my bullets struck home. The next instant I reached the four of them. Throwing down my MP5, I grabbed the third terrorist's Kalashnikov and unloaded a full burst into his chest.

That's when I heard Yael scream, *"James, look out!"*

I turned but it was too late. Another terrorist was coming around the corner. He had a pistol, not a machine gun, but he got off at least three rounds before I could return fire. One hit me in the left arm, just above the elbow. I spun around and dropped to the ground. The guy kept coming at me and firing, but as he closed the distance, Yael sprang to her feet and tackled him in midstride. They struggled furiously. Yael took two hard punches to the face and then the guy was on top of her. I watched in helpless amazement as she drove her right knee into his groin. I'd never seen a man double over like he did. She added a sharp crack to his neck, then pushed him off her and dove for his pistol. A split second later, she wheeled around and double-tapped him to the chest. He collapsed.

Adrenaline surging, I grabbed my MP5, ejected the spent magazine, reloaded, and scrambled to my feet.

"Come on," I yelled. *"They're leaving without us."*

60

Yael began running flat out, and I followed.

We retraced our route around what was left of
Marine One. On the way, Yael dropped two more
terrorists. But to our horror, when we got past the
flaming wreckage and back to the silo opening, we
saw the rest of our team. They were under withering fire from our right, pinned down in a grove of
trees about halfway to the Suburbans.

Yael didn't hesitate. Without making a sound,
she pointed for me to head right. She would go
left. I nodded and bolted to the cover of a half-
destroyed cement wall on the back side of the palace remains. Drawing no fire, I inched my way
forward. Ahead of me was an inferno, the burning
shell of a three-story wing of the palace. There were
no doors where a double set should have been. I
moved closer, pointing my machine gun inside,
searching desperately for any signs of movement
as my skin baked and my eyes filled with smoke.

Thirty yards to my left, I could see Yael doing
the same thing, moving into the other side of the
building as the firefight between our team and the

ISIS rebels raged another fifty yards to her left. As best I could tell, the rebels were shooting from the cover of this section of the palace. If we could find them, perhaps we could distract them and give our guys a chance to make a break for the armored vehicles.

Yael pointed to me and then to a stairway ahead and to my right. Then she signaled that she would work her way through the ground floor. A flash of fear rippled through me. That gave me two floors to clear and very little time to do it.

Seeing no one yet, I cautiously worked my way up the stairs. I could hear machine-gun fire coming from above, but I couldn't tell from where exactly. The stairs were creaking. I was making too much noise. Anyone waiting for me would cut me down in an instant. So it hardly made sense to go slow.

Abandoning all caution, I bounded up the steps, legs aching, lungs sucking in as much air as they could. I reached the top and swept the MP5 from side to side. But no one was there. Then I heard more machine-gun fire, clearer now, coming from the third floor, almost directly above me.

This time I moved more carefully up the stairs, placing my feet on the extreme edge of each step, hoping they would creak less or not at all. Inch by inch I moved my way upward while all around I could hear nonstop gunfire and men suffering horrible, ghastly deaths. The only good thing was that all the cacophony covered up whatever sounds I was making.

As I reached the top step, the gunfire stopped. I froze in place, my heart pounding through my chest. I heard a clatter. Someone was reloading. But in which room? How many were there?

For a moment I hesitated, trying to map out my next action, when gunfire erupted on the first floor. Yael was all in now. I needed to move as well.

Sliding off my dress shoes, I crept down the smoke- and rubble-filled hallways in my socks. Then the shooting began again. It was coming from one of the last rooms at the end of the hall, the rooms overlooking the courtyard, the grove of trees, and what was left of our team. I wasn't sure if it was the room on the left or the room on the right. Maybe it was both.

Under the cover of the gunfire, I bolted forward as fast as I could and made my bet. Sliding to a halt, I pivoted and burst through the door on the left and started shooting. An instant later, two snipers had collapsed to the ground. I put another two bullets into each to be sure and then turned around.

Was that it? Was it over?

No. I heard more gunfire coming from the other side of the hall. And now I had lost the element of surprise.

Moving carefully, I made my way to the door just as it began to swing open. I aimed at the center of the doorframe and pulled the trigger. A hooded figure dropped to the floor in front of me.

I quickly reloaded and moved into the hallway. Then I burst into the room across the hall only to find that a sniper had just been shot down by someone out in the courtyard. He was rolling around in pain. I switched to single shot, fired two rounds, and it was over.

Switching back to automatic, I returned to the hallway. It looked clear. I started running, desperate to get back to our team. But then I heard Yael yell, *"James, duck!"*

Without thinking, I dove to the floor, just as Yael—crouching in the stairwell—fired a long burst down the hallway over my head. Terrified, I let go of my weapon and covered my head with my hands. Yael fired again. And then all was quiet—in this wing of the building, at least.

"You okay?" she asked, coming up quickly to check on me.

"You nearly killed me!" I said, breathing hard.

"Sorry," she said. "I wasn't aiming at you."

I got up, picked up my gun, and turned to find another ISIS rebel on the floor at the end of the hallway, bleeding out. I had no idea where he'd come from—one of the other side rooms, apparently. I was just glad it was over.

But it wasn't over. The man was lying facedown as the pool of crimson around him grew. Cautiously, my gun aimed at his head, I walked over to him. Yael warned me not to get too close, and she wasn't wrong. I could now see that he was still moving, still breathing. Yael came over and was about to finish him off, but something made me stop her. Perhaps it was his enormous size. Perhaps it was the fact that he wasn't wearing a hood like all the others. But for whatever reason, I drove my foot into his ribs and ordered him in Arabic to turn over. Maybe he couldn't. Maybe he wouldn't. But I told Yael to cover me, and I rolled him over myself.

He was a bloody mess, but there was no mistaking who it was.

This was Jamal Ramzy.

In a blinding rage, I moved in and stuck the barrel of my MP5 in his face.

"Where is Abu Khalif?" I yelled.

He was fading fast, but he could hear me.

I drove my foot down on his right knee and he shrieked in agony. In my peripheral vision, I could see Yael growing edgy, her finger itching toward her trigger.

"Where . . . is . . . Abu . . . Khalif?" I repeated.

"You'll never find him," he replied through gritted teeth.

"Did you bring the sarin?" I demanded. "Are you going to use poison gas?"

Yael was now the frantic one. "Come on. It's over. He's not going to talk. Let's go."

"He'll talk," I said and fired a single round through his left arm, just above the elbow.

Ramzy's eyes rolled back in his head. They closed, then briefly opened again and readjusted. Blood was gurgling up from his stomach and dripping down his chin. I didn't have much time.

"Who's the mole?" I shouted.

But Ramzy refused to speak.

"Who's working for you inside the palace?" I shouted again.

"Burn in hell, kafir!" he screamed as he spat blood in my face. Then he fell back, and his eyes closed for the last time.

"After you," I said as I stood.

61

I just stared at the corpse, not quite believing my eyes.

Jamal Ramzy was dead.

"We need to go," Yael said, turning and heading back up the hall.

But I wasn't through. I reached down and checked his pulse. Sure enough. Ramzy was gone. Then I checked his front pockets. I found nothing. I checked his back pockets. They were empty as well. I patted him down, top to bottom. There had to be something. A wallet. An ID. A plan of some kind. But Ramzy was clean. I pulled out my cell phone and snapped several pictures. This was a huge story, and I needed proof. And as I did, I noticed that Ramzy's enormous left hand was closed tight.

"James, come on," Yael shouted, already at the stairs. *"We've got to move."*

Instead, I set down my weapon and got onto my hands and knees. I pried open Ramzy's thick, bloody fingers, one by one. And there it was. A small cell phone. I quickly flipped it open.

There was nothing in the contacts section. But the call log showed nine calls that had been made and three that had been received. I had numbers, dates, and times.

Pay dirt, I thought.

Yael was frantic. I grabbed my gun and ran. Together, we raced down both sets of stairs and a moment later we burst out the same side door where I had entered this wing. We could see Ali Sa'id beginning to rally what was left of our group and move them from the grove of trees toward the SUVs.

"Let's go, you two! Move!" he yelled when he spotted us.

We retrieved our backpacks and raced to catch up. But suddenly there was another burst of gunfire from our right. I saw two gunmen emerging from the smoke near Marine One. I pivoted and fired three bursts on the run. One of the terrorists fell to the ground, his AK-47 skittering across the pavement.

The other kept running. He wasn't shooting at us, though. He was shooting at the royal family and screaming something in Arabic. The others ahead of me were running hard, but at the rate this guy was coming, I feared none of them would make it in time. So I dove to the ground, rolled to a stop, took a deep breath, tried to steady my aim, and fired two bursts, then three more. Yael was running, but she was firing too, and a moment later the rebel fell to the ground.

"Clear!" she yelled.

I jumped back to my feet. But then Yael yelled

that rebels were coming over the wall about thirty yards to our left. I turned and saw three. One by one, they dropped to the lawn below and started racing for us, raising their weapons and preparing to shoot.

Prime Minister Lavi reacted first. Shooting from the hip, on the run, the former Israeli special forces commando must have emptied an entire magazine. It was a sight to behold, and it worked. Each of the attackers was riddled with bullets and fell to the ground, writhing in pain. They weren't dead. But they weren't coming at us anymore, and for now, that was all that mattered.

"Come on!" the king yelled. *"We have to keep moving!"*

I quickly ejected a spent magazine and reloaded and kept running. I could see the crown prince helping his mother while Sa'id—and now Yael and I—came in behind them. We were all running as fast as we could, but the weight of the backpacks slowed us down. Yael and I were bleeding, too— both quite seriously—but there was no time to do anything about it.

As we approached the SUVs, however, it was a kill box. Rebels were shooting at us from all directions. One agent just ahead of me, providing cover for the queen, dropped to the ground. He'd been shot four times in the face and legs. Two more agents to my right were killed a moment later.

Terrified, yet propelled by a surge of adrenaline, I looked to my right and saw the remains of another garage. I could see one of the king's limos ablaze, but at the moment I didn't see any rebels.

I checked with Yael and Sa'id. They didn't see any either. But it didn't matter, we decided. Rebels or no rebels, we had to get to the SUVs.

Sa'id suggested I fan out to the right. He would go left. Yael would go straight. I nodded and began running. Each of us opened fire and kept shooting until we reached the first SUV. While Sa'id dug through the pockets of the dead driver and retrieved the key, I reloaded, with Yael providing covering fire. Sa'id found the key a moment later, opened the front door to use as some cover, and got the queen and the crown prince safely in the backseat.

The ISIS rebels continued firing back. Agents were dropping all around me. We weren't going to make it. Not like this. I finished reloading and saw several terrorists moving through the flames of the garage. I opened fire. A split second later, Sa'id was at my side, firing back as well. But when he asked me where the king was, I realized I had no idea. The last time I'd seen him, he was on the other side of this SUV. Was he already inside? And for that matter, where was President Taylor? Where were Lavi and Mansour?

"Ali, go find them!" I shouted.

Yael and I kept returning fire. I certainly wasn't the most accurate shot of the group, or what was left of it, but all I was trying to do was buy time until everyone could get safely into the vehicles and we could get out of there.

Suddenly I heard Ali yelling for me to get over to him right away. I fired two more bursts, empty-ing my magazine, reloaded, and quickly worked my way around the back of the truck while Yael covered me. I could hear bullets whizzing over my head. I could hear them smashing into the side of the armor-plated trucks. I could see round after round hitting the bulletproof windows, though fortunately they refused to shatter. But as I came around the far side of the Suburban, I froze in my tracks. Prime Minister Lavi and President Mansour were lying side by side, surrounded by several more dead agents.

The king was crouched over them. I couldn't see what he was doing. Was he trying in vain to revive them or just mourning over them? Either way, it was no use. They were gone. Nothing was going to bring them back. We had to go. We couldn't stay out in the open like this.

At that moment, I went numb. I could feel myself beginning to slip into shock, and I couldn't help it, couldn't stop it.

And then, as if through a tunnel, I thought I heard the sound of someone calling my name.

"Collins, they're alive!" the king yelled. *"They're unconscious, but they're still breathing. They both have a pulse. But we need to get them into the Suburban. Cover us!"*

I couldn't believe it. They weren't dead? They looked dead. They weren't moving. But at the very thought, I snapped to.

Sa'id opened the back of the truck and put down the rear seat to make space while Yael covered his right flank. Then Sa'id helped the king lift Prime Minister Lavi and gently set him inside the SUV.

Reengaged, I pivoted hard to my left and followed my orders. Firing short bursts in multiple directions, I had no illusions I was going to kill many rebels. But I was determined not to let them get to the king or his family or these other leaders. All I had to do was buy time. The question was whether it would possibly be enough.

As the king and Sa'id put President Mansour in the back, I continued firing. Then I heard one of the other SUVs roar to life. For a moment I stopped shooting. I looked to my right and saw two American agents peeling off without us.

"That's President Taylor!" the king yelled as he covered the limp body of the Palestinian leader with a blanket.

He was right. It was Taylor in the other truck. It had to be. The Secret Service wasn't waiting. They'd gotten their man into a bulletproof vehicle and now they were getting him to the airport.

We had to move too, and fast.

"Ali, you drive," the king ordered as he closed up the back. "Yael, you ride shotgun. I'll sit behind you and work the phones. Collins, get in the back with Lavi and Mansour and cover my family."

It was a good plan, and I was prepared to follow it. But as the king disappeared around the other side of the truck to get in behind the front passenger seat, Sa'id was shot multiple times. He cried out in pain. I turned and saw two masked rebels running at us through the smoke. I ducked, aimed, and unloaded everything I had.

Both men dropped to the ground.

"Go, Collins!" Sa'id shouted with the last breath

in him, stumbling backward. *"Don't wait. Take the king and go!"*

I hesitated. I couldn't leave Sa'id behind. He'd already saved my life countless times, starting with getting me out of the courtyard before the missiles hit and the F-16's kamikaze attack. But he wasn't long for this world—he knew it, and he was right. I had to go. I had to save the king's life.

Sa'id fell. I went to my knees to reload. When I was done, I checked his pulse, but Sa'id was gone.

Yael was now climbing into the passenger seat. She was yelling at me to hurry. As quickly as I could, I pushed Sa'id's body out of the way of the truck. I grabbed the keys and satphone from his hands, and his MP5 as well. It felt cruel. It felt callous. But I had no choice and no time.

I opened the truck door, but before I could jump into the driver's seat, I lurched forward. I'd been hit—not once but multiple times. I couldn't believe it. I'd felt the impacts, but I wasn't in pain. Not yet. But that had to be the adrenaline. I'd feel it soon, and then what? Was this it? Was I dying?

"Get in, get in!" the king yelled.

Dazed and confused, it took me a moment to get my bearings. I thought briefly of just slumping back to the ground. I didn't want to hold the king and his family back. He could drive this thing better than I could. But Yael was screaming at me to stay focused and get in. And somehow—I'm really not sure how—I managed to climb into the driver's seat and pull the door shut behind me.

The king then hit a button and locked all the doors.

"Where is Ali?" he asked.

"I'm afraid he didn't make it, Your Majesty," I said.

The king just looked at me for a moment, a thousand emotions in his eyes.

"You've been hit too?" he asked.

"I think so," I said.

But as Yael helped me remove my backpack, handing it to the king to get it out of my way, she noticed something. "Look," she said.

I looked where she was pointing and saw that five rounds had hit the pack, but none of them had penetrated. Yael told me to turn so she could check my back. She looked me over quickly, as did the king, but they found nothing.

"You're okay," she said.

"It's a miracle," the queen said.

I couldn't believe it. "Really? You're sure?"

"I'm sure, Collins," the king said. "But you need to floor it, or none of us is going to make it out of here alive."

62

★ ★ ★

I turned the ignition.

The engine sputtered but wouldn't catch. I tried again, but still nothing.

"Hurry," Yael cried.

"I'm trying—it won't start," I said as I tried again and again.

"Collins, let's move; they're coming," the king shouted.

But nothing was working.

Through the smoke I could see rebels running from all parts of the compound. They were firing everything they had at us. We could hear and feel the rounds hitting the truck. We could see the windows splintering. They had not yet shattered, but it was only a matter of time.

Over and over I turned the key but to no avail. I began to panic. Once more I could feel myself slipping into shock. My hands were shaking and my body felt numb. My throat was dry. My eyes were getting heavy and everything was blurring. I could hear the king shouting at me, but it was as if he were far away. Everything seemed to be happening in slow motion. I tried to say some-thing. I tried to explain what was happening. But my brain couldn't quite send the proper signals to my mouth.

Then finally the engine roared to life. I didn't know why or how but I didn't care either. I hit the gas, and we were moving.

I'd never driven an armor-plated SUV. But two things became instantly apparent. First, because the engine was powerful, I had all the horsepower I needed. But second, because it was so incred-ibly heavy, it didn't handle like a normal truck. I flicked on the lights to find my way through all the smoke. I hit the windshield wipers to clear away at least some of the soot and ash. I was terrified of hitting someone. I knew they were enemies. I knew it was either them or us. But I still didn't want to plow anyone over.

The king was my navigator. He gave me directions, guiding me around obstacles even as he powered up the satellite phone and dialed his brother. A moment later, he was shouting in Arabic. I didn't understand more than a few words. I heard *safe* and *family* and something like *the pal-ace is gone*. I was pretty sure I heard the names Lavi and Mansour mentioned too, but he was talking too fast for me to get much else, and I had to stay focused.

We hit a speed bump—I hoped it was a speed bump—going almost fifty miles an hour and sud-denly we were airborne. I struggled to maintain control as the heavy vehicle crashed back down.

"There, through that hole!" Yael shouted.

"Where? Where?" I shouted back.

"There—on the right!" she yelled.

Finally I saw it. There was a massive breach in one of the concrete walls that surrounded the perimeter of the compound. It didn't have a road leading to it. It was in the middle of a large lawn at the bottom of an incline. But I could see the tracks of another vehicle. I had to assume President Taylor and his team had gone this way as well. The only problem was the hole was guarded by at least a dozen rebels, and they trained all their fire on us now. But there was no other way out.

I gunned the engine and made for the hole, gripping the steering wheel so tightly my fingers and knuckles were white. I forced myself not to duck, not to cover my eyes. We couldn't stop. We couldn't go back. We couldn't look for another way out. There might not be one, and we didn't have time to try. The moment the Secret Service got the president to the airport, Air Force One was going to take off, with or without us. The only chance we had was to catch up.

At the last moment, the rebels dove out of the way. *So much for being martyrs for Allah,* I thought. They'd had a chance to save their own skin, and they'd taken it.

We barreled through the hole and spilled out onto a side street. I slammed on the brakes, but not in time. We smashed into two parked cars on the other side of the street, sending all of us lurching forward. The steering wheel stopped me. But Yael slammed into the front windshield. The gash over her left eye reopened and blood poured down her face.

"I'm fine," she said quickly, seeing the distress in my eyes. "Just get us out of here."

"Which way?"

"Right," the king said. "Go right."

I jammed the truck into reverse, did an awkward K-turn, and hit the gas. We were moving again.

"Left at the light!" he ordered.

I made the turn, barely, though for a split second I thought we were going to spin out or roll over. I glanced in my rearview mirror to see if the king and his family were okay. He ordered me to keep my eyes on the road and not worry about them—they'd be fine—so that's what I did.

For the next few blocks, we barreled down empty streets, cleared by security for the peace summit. Soon, however, we reentered the crush of daily life in Amman. I was weaving through traffic at forty and sometimes fifty miles an hour. The king insisted I not stop for anything, so I blew through traffic lights praying we wouldn't be broadsided.

For a man who probably hadn't driven himself through the streets of Amman in twenty years, if ever, the king seemed to know the roads like a taxi driver. When we hit traffic, he started telling me to take this side street or that, apparently determined to keep us off the main boulevards and thorough-fares. It worked for a while, but all good things come to an end.

"Uh, Your Majesty, we've got a problem," I said, glancing in my rearview mirror.

Yael looked in her side mirror. The king and his family craned their necks to see what was happening.

We had company. A pickup truck filled with masked rebels had picked up our scent and was following us. Not just following—gaining on us. With all the bullet marks, I couldn't see out the back window too clearly, but I was pretty sure at least one of the rebels had a shoulder-mounted RPG launcher.

Yael unbuckled her seat belt, rolled down her window, took her MP5, and began firing at our pursuers, but they immediately moved to their left and out of her view.

"Climb into the backseat," the king told her. "Collins is going to let these guys catch up a bit. Then we'll lower the rear window ever so slightly, and you're going to fire everything you've got at the driver. Got it?"

"Absolutely," Yael said.

Careful not to disturb the Israeli and Palestinian leaders lying bleeding and unconscious in the back, Yael got herself into position, on her knees—her back leaning against the middle row of seats to provide a measure of stability, however small.

"Ready," she said.

I eased up on the gas. The pickup truck surged closer.

"Wait for it," the king said.

I glanced back and could see the rebels closing the gap. This had better work, I realized. And then I saw one of the jihadists raise the RPG and prepare to fire.

"Lower the window, Collins!" the king ordered.
I did.

The king gave the order to fire.

Yael obeyed. She unleashed an entire magazine
into the front windshield of the pickup. I tried
to keep my eyes on the road ahead of us, but I
couldn't help but glance back several times. I could
see the driver behind us being riddled with bullets,
and then the truck swerved wildly out of control
until it finally careened off the road and plowed
into a petrol station.

The explosion was enormous and deafening.
I could feel the heat on the back of my neck. I
quickly raised the rear window as the king directed
me onto Route 40—the Al Kodos Highway—
heading southwest out of Amman.

We were now going nearly a hundred miles an
hour, and we had a new problem. The king was back
on the satphone with his brother, who informed us
that there was a police checkpoint at the upcoming interchange with Route 35, the Queen Alia
Highway. The checkpoint itself wasn't the issue. The
problem, the king said, was that it had apparently
been overrun by ISIS rebels, and they were waiting
for us with RPGs and .50-caliber machine guns.

"How long to the interchange?" I asked.

"At this rate, two minutes, no more," the king
replied.

"What do you recommend, Your Majesty?"
I asked, not sure if I should try to go any faster or
slow down.

"Do you believe in prayer, Collins?" he said.
"Because now would be a good time to start."

63

★ ★ ★

"I'm out of ammunition," Yael said. "Does anyone have more?"

"There's a full mag in my weapon," I replied.

"Where's that?" she asked.

"Here," the crown prince said from the backseat. He picked up my machine gun from the floor, removed the magazine, and handed it to Yael.

"We need to get off this road," the queen insisted, her voice quaking. "It's not safe."

I glanced back and saw the fear in her eyes.

"No, we have to keep going," the king replied.

"But we're out in the open," she countered. "The rebels know we're coming. We're sitting ducks. Let's just pull off. Let's hide somewhere until the army comes to get us."

The queen had a point, but it was not my place to say. I just kept driving. We needed a decision, and fast. In the distance, I could see the interchange approaching. I desperately wanted to know what the king was going to say. Would he accept his wife's counsel, or were we going to try to blow through this checkpoint? That, it seemed, was a suicide mission. And I wasn't ready to die.

A second later the issue was moot. Rising over a ridge off to our right were two Apache helicopter gunships coming low and fast. Yael noticed them first and pointed them out to the rest of us. Now we were all riveted on them, and one question loomed over everything, though no one spoke it aloud: which side were they on?

They very well could be loyal to the king. His brother, after all, was the head of the air force, and we had no doubts about his loyalty. But there were no guarantees. Who were these pilots? How carefully had they been vetted? Did their families have ties to ISIS or al-Hirak? A few hours ago, such a thought would have seemed ridiculous. But that was before a Jordanian air force pilot had attacked the palace.

The checkpoint was fast approaching. So were the Apaches.

"What do you want me to do, Your Majesty?" I asked, easing imperceptibly off the gas to give us a bit more time.

"There's one more exit before the checkpoint," Yael said, her window down, her weapon at the ready. "Let's take it. The queen is right, sir. We need to get off this road before it's too late."

"No," the king said. "Keep moving."

"But, Your Majesty—"

"Salim and Daniel need a hospital," he insisted. "They need massive blood transfusions. We can't stop to save ourselves. We need to think of them first."

"We're not trying to be selfish," the queen interjected. "But if we die at this checkpoint, they die too. If we live, even for another hour, we might have a chance at saving them."

We were quickly running out of time. The checkpoint was dead ahead. So was the exit. If I pulled off, we might all have a shot. What was the king going to do, kill me for disobeying him? I glanced back at the queen. She looked away. She clearly didn't want to disrespect her husband, but it was just as clear she was not happy. I looked at the crown prince, but he was fixed on the Apaches. They had banked to their left and then swooped around and were now coming straight at us from behind.

This was it. At more than a hundred miles an hour, I had only seconds to decide. And then in my mirror I saw the 30mm open up.

"They're shooting at us!" I shouted.

I saw a flash. I knew what it was. I'd seen it a hundred times or more, from Fallujah to Kabul. Someone had just fired an RPG. I could see the contrail streaking down the highway behind us. It was coming straight for us. The queen screamed. I hit the gas and swerved to the right just in time. The RPG knocked off my side mirror and sliced past. It hadn't killed us.

But the next one might.

That was it, I decided. I was taking the exit.

But at that moment I saw another flash, this one from the lead Apache. He too had just fired, and this wasn't a mere RPG. This was a heat-seeking Hellfire missile. There was no swerving or avoiding it. It was coming straight for us, and there was nothing we could do about it. We were about to die in a ball of fire. It was all over.

But to my relief, the missile didn't slam into us. Instead, we watched it strike one of the Humvees at the checkpoint ahead. In the blink of an eye, the entire checkpoint was obliterated in a giant explosion. Stunned—mesmerized by the fireball in front of me—I forgot to exit. I just kept driving. Then we were crashing through the burning remains of the checkpoint, racing through the interchange, and getting on Route 35, bound for the airport.

None of us cheered. We were relieved beyond words, but we all knew this was not of our doing. Forces beyond us were keeping us alive and clearing the way for us. And it wasn't just the chopper pilots.

The Apaches banked hard and came up beside us. One after another, they kept launching Hellfire missiles, clearing checkpoints and allowing us to keep moving undeterred. By now I was topping 120 miles per hour, but there was no way we were going to get to the airport before the president took off. The queen and crown prince had climbed into the back of the SUV. They had found a first aid kit and were doing the best they could to care for Mansour and Lavi. Yael watched for new threats while the king worked the satphone again. He was getting updates from his brother and from other generals. He was organizing a massive counterstrike on the ISIS jihadists.

Soon we saw one squadron after another of

Jordanian F-16s and F-15s streaking across the sky. I had to believe they were headed to Amman to bomb the palace and crush the rebellion. I couldn't imagine how difficult a decision that must have been for the king, but I also knew he had no choice. He was the last of the Hashemite monarchs, and he seemed determined not to go down like those before him.

Somewhere along the way, I had ceased to be a journalist. I was no mere observer of history; I was a participant. I could no longer claim to be objective. Yes, this king had his flaws, and so did his government. No, Jordan wasn't a Jeffersonian democracy. But His Majesty had emerged in recent years as the region's leading Arab Reformer. Where once the presidents of Iraq and Afghanistan had looked like promising Reformers—battling hard against the Radicals—they had not proven themselves up to the task. This king was different, and my respect for him had shot up enormously in recent days.

Maybe my brother was right. Maybe the prophecies indicated Jordan was going to take a seriously dark turn in the last days. Maybe that was coming up fast. But I hoped not. I didn't want the Hashemite Kingdom to fall—not yet, not now. I wanted this king to crush his enemies and help fulfill his destiny as a peacemaker in the region. I wanted him to succeed in making Jordan a model of tolerance and modernity.

As we sped along Highway 35, against all odds, strangely enough I actually began to feel a sense of hope again. We were still alive. We were safe for now. And I had the strongest sense that the king was going to prevail. He had been blindsided, to be sure. But he had enormous personal courage. He had an army ready to fight back, and he had the Americans and the Israelis ready to fight with him.

But when we arrived at the airport, those feelings instantly evaporated.

64

As I surveyed the devastation around us, all hope disappeared.

The gorgeous new multimillion-dollar terminal was a smoking crater. The roads and runways were pockmarked with the remains of mortars and artillery shells that apparently had been fired not long before we arrived. Jumbo jets were on fire. Dead and dying bodies lay everywhere. Fuel depots were ablaze. The stench of burning jet fuel was overwhelming.

Air Force One was gone. The president had left without us.

The Apaches above us went to work. They joined other Royal Air Force helicopter gunships and fighter jets in finishing off the remains of the rebel forces, some of which were still fighting at the southern perimeter of the airfield. But the Jordanian army was nowhere to be seen.

To be precise, there was evidence that the army had been here but apparently had retreated. Why?

All around us were burning tanks and armored personnel carriers. We could see slain Jordanian soldiers everywhere. There were bodies of many ISIS terrorists, too. But why wasn't the Royal Army in full offensive mode? This wasn't the Iraqi army. The Jordanians were highly trained, highly motivated, well-led troops. Why had they fallen back?

None of us said a word, not even the king. We were all aghast. It took us several minutes to absorb the magnitude of the disaster.

It was Yael who first realized what had happened.

"They used the sarin," she said.

There was dead silence in the SUV. No one wanted to believe her. Surely it wasn't possible.

"The mortars and artillery shells that were fired here must have all been filled with it," she continued.

I wanted to believe she was wrong. But as I slowly drove through the fire and smoke, it became clear that the Jordanian troops who had fought here had not died of bullet or shrapnel wounds. As we got a closer look at the bodies—hundreds of them—we could see the vacant eyes and twisted, contorted faces. I had seen such horrors before. I had seen them in Mosul just days earlier. This was the work of Abu Khalif.

There were no words. The queen wept quietly in the back. The crown prince was frozen, his hand over his mouth. The king said nothing either. He just stared at the carnage in disbelief.

Finally he pointed to a half-destroyed hangar off to our left. I drove there immediately at his command. Under what meager cover it provided, I pulled to a stop. We all knew what we had to do.

The crown prince handed us each a backpack. We all put on the chem-bio suits, the gloves, and the gas masks as quickly as we could. Then Yael and I helped the queen and the prince put protective suits on Lavi and Mansour, desperately hoping to shield them from whatever trace of the deadly chemical was still in the air.

As we did, I could hear the roar of choppers. I turned and saw two military helicopters approaching from the east. They were preparing to land not far from us.

Just then, two Jordanian F-15s shot right over our heads. A moment later, four more streaked past.

The king's satellite phone rang. He answered it but mostly listened, saying only an occasional "Yes" or "I understand," and then hung up.

"Who was that?" I asked as I finished zipping up President Mansour's chem-bio suit.

"My brother," the king said as if in a daze.

"And?"

"He sent the choppers," he replied, turning to his wife and son. "The first one is for you both, to get you to safety."

The queen and crown prince appeared too numb to speak.

Then the king turned to Yael and me. "The other is to take Salim and Daniel to Jerusalem," he told us. "You two will go with them. IDF medical crews are on standby. Daniel will go to Hadassah. Salim will be transferred to a hospital in Ramallah."

We watched as the two Black Hawks landed

and teams of heavily armed soldiers in full protective suits poured out of both. The king held his wife briefly. Then he hugged his eldest son and walked them both to the first chopper. I watched as the door was shut and the Black Hawk lifted off while the king waved good-bye to his family.

Then I realized there wasn't a chopper for the monarch. I turned to him and asked, "But, sir, what about you?"

"I'm not leaving," the king said. "My brother is on his way. He's bringing a team of specialists."

"You can't stay here, Your Majesty," I said. "We need to get you someplace secure."

"No," he said. "I need to figure out exactly what happened here and why my men failed to stop it."

"And then?"

"Then we're going to unleash the wrath of Jordan on ISIS," he told me.

"But, sir, James is right—it's not safe here," Yael protested. "Please, we need to get you out of here."

"No," the king said. "This is my home. And these are my people. We're not going to surrender. We're going to fight back. These demons are not going to win. I promise you that."

The king gave us no opportunity for rebuttal. He immediately opened the back of the SUV and with the help of his troops began carrying President Mansour to the second chopper. Yael and I worked with several other soldiers to get Prime Minister Lavi into the remaining Black Hawk as well.

Just then the king's satphone rang again. As he answered it, Yael climbed into the Black Hawk and sat next to her prime minister, checking his vital signs. I was about to get in myself when I saw a strange expression on the king's face. It started off as bewilderment. It turned into horror.

"What is it, Your Majesty?" I asked.

"That was the Pentagon," he said. "Chairman of the Joint Chiefs."

"What did he say?"

"He wants to know where President Taylor is," he replied.

"He's not on Air Force One?"

"No."

"What do you mean?"

"Apparently, when the ISIS attack on the airport began, the president called the pilot of Air Force One and ordered him to get off the ground and into safe airspace until my forces retook the airport and it was safe to come back and get him."

I felt a pain growing in my stomach. "So where was he going to go in the meantime?"

"He didn't say," the king replied. "He just said he and the agents with him would take shelter and hunker down until the coast was clear. Then he'd order Air Force One to come back for them all."

"And?"

"They haven't heard from him since. The chairman says they've been calling every number they have for the president and for every member of his detail. They can't get through to any of them."

"So where is the president?"

"I have no idea."

I just stared at the king. I had no clue what to say.

Then Yael told me to get into the chopper.

They needed to get off the ground and get Lavi and Mansour to safety right away. She was right, of course. But I couldn't go.

"Go without me," I told her.

"Are you crazy?" she shot back.

"No, I'm staying."

"Oh no, you're not. Come on."

"There's no time to argue, Yael. Get this bird off the ground."

Shocked and angry, she turned to the king. "Your Majesty, order him to get on this chopper."

But I shook my head. "I'm staying with you, sir. This is my president. I need to follow this story, wherever it goes and whatever it takes."

The king looked into my eyes but didn't say a word. Then he waved to the pilot, signaling for him to take off. Before Yael could respond, a soldier slammed the side door and the Black Hawk lifted off the ground. It quickly gained altitude and headed west toward Jerusalem with two fighter jets flying escort on either side.

As I stood there and watched them fade into the distance, I became physically ill. I felt hot bile rising in my throat. My body was soaked with sweat. I was suffocating in this suit. The president was missing. Mansour and Lavi were critically injured. Jordan was in flames. ISIS was on the move. And for the life of me, I could see no way out.

Then I remembered Jamal Ramzy's cell phone. I ran back to the Suburban and grabbed it off the dashboard.

"What's this?" the king asked as I put it in his hand.

"A lead, Your Majesty," I replied. "Something you can use. It's Jamal Ramzy's phone."

Then a thought struck me.

I pulled out my own phone and dialed Allen's number in Washington. It rang twice before someone answered.

It was not Allen.

"Hello, Allen MacDonald's office. Can I help you?"

"Where's Allen?" I demanded.

"He's out for the moment. Who's calling, please?"

"It's J. B. Collins calling from Amman with an urgent exclusive. I need Allen right away."

"Hold, please."

The wait that followed felt like an eternity, and the longer it took, the more irritated I became. I was right in the middle of the story of the decade—maybe the century—and Allen was nowhere to be found.

Finally I heard my editor's voice on the line. "J. B., is that you? What on earth is going on over there?"

"What's going on is all hell is breaking loose. Prime Minister Lavi and President Mansour are injured and en route to hospitals via helicopter. The king is furious but resolute and is swearing vengeance against ISIS. But never mind that. Take this down and get it out on the wire, on Twitter, everywhere. The lead is—"

"What?" he asked frantically. "Say again. I can hardly hear you."

"I said, take this down. The president of the United States . . . is missing."

TURN THE PAGE

for an excerpt from the next thrilling novel by

JOEL C. ROSENBERG

New York Times bestselling author

* * * THE * * *

KREMLIN CONSPIRACY

A gripping tale ripped from future headlines!

PREORDER NOW!

Available in stores and online March 6, 2018.

JOIN THE CONVERSATION AT

www.tyndalefiction.com   CP1292

* * *

Louisa Sherbatov had just turned six, but she would never turn seven.

The whirling dervish had finally fallen asleep on the couch just before midnight, crashed from a sugar high, still wearing her new magenta dress and matching ribbon in her blonde tresses. Snuggled up on her father's lap, she looked so peaceful, so content as she hugged her favorite stuffed bear and lay surrounded by the dolls and books and sweaters and other gifts she'd received from all her aunts and uncles and grandparents and cousins as well as her friends from the elementary school just down the block at the end of Guryanova Street.

Strewn about her were string and tape and wads of brightly colored wrapping paper. The kitchen sink was stacked high with dirty plates and cups and silverware. The dining room table was still littered with empty bottles of wine and vodka and scraps of leftover birthday pie—strawberry, Louisa's favorite.

The flat was a mess. But the guests were gone and it was Thursday night and the weekend was upon them and honestly, her parents, Feodor and Irina, couldn't have cared less. Their little girl, the

519

only child they had been able to bear after more than a decade and two heartbreaking miscarriages, was happy. Her friends were happy. Their parents were happy. They were happy. Everything else could wait.

Feodor stared down at the two precious women in his life and longed to stay. He had loved planning the party with them both, had loved helping shop for the food, loved helping Irina and her mother make all the preparations, loved seeing the sheer delight on Louisa's face when he'd given her a shiny blue bicycle, her first. But business was business. If he was going to make his flight to Tashkent, he had to leave quickly. So he gently kissed mother and daughter on their foreheads, picked up his suitcase, and slipped out as quietly as he could.

As he stepped out the front door of the apartment building, he was relieved to see the cab he'd ordered waiting for him as planned. He moved briskly to the car, shook hands with the driver, and gave the man his bag. The night air was crisp and fresh. The moon was full, and leaves were beginning to fall and swirl in the light breeze coming from the west. Summer was finally over, thought Feodor as he climbed into the backseat, and not a moment too soon. The sweltering heat. The stifling humidity. The gnawing guilt of not being able to afford even a simple air conditioner, much less a little dacha out in the country where he and Irina and Louisa and maybe his parents or hers could retreat now and again, somewhere in a forest

JOEL C. ROSENBERG ★ 521

with lots of shade and a sparkling lake for swimming or fishing.

"Thank God, autumn has arrived," he half mumbled to himself as the driver slammed the trunk shut and got back behind the wheel. Growing up, Feodor had always loved the cooler weather. The shorter days. Going back to school. Making new friends. Meeting new teachers. Taking new classes. Fall meant change, and change had always been good to him. Perhaps one day, if he continued to work very hard, he could save enough money to move his family away from 19 Guryanova Street, away from this noisy, dirty, run-down, depressing hovel on the south side of the capital and find some place really lovely and quaint and quiet. Some place worthy of raising a family. Some place with a bit of grass, maybe even a garden where he could till the soil with his own hands and grow his own vegetables.

As the cab began to pull away from the curb, Feodor leaned back in his seat. He closed his eyes and folded his hands on his chest. Yes, autumn had always been a time of new beginnings, and he wondered what this one might bring. He was not rich. He was not successful. But he was content, even hopeful, perhaps for the first time in his life.

He found himself reminiscing about the first time he'd laid eyes on Irina—the first day of middle school, twenty-two years ago. He was so caught up in his memories that he did not notice the car parked just down the street, a white Lada with its headlights off but its engine running. He didn't notice that the front license plate was

covered with some sort of masking tape, revealing only the numbers 6 and 2. Nor did he notice the car's driver, nervously smoking a cigarette and tapping on the dashboard, or the two burly men, dressed in black leather jackets and black leather gloves, emerging from the basement of his own building. When the police would later ask about the men and the car, Feodor would be unable to provide any description at all.

What he did remember—what he could never possibly forget—was the deafening explosion behind him. He remembered the searing fireball. He remembered the taxi driver losing control and crashing into a lamppost not fifty meters up the street, and he remembered smashing his head against the plastic screen dividing the front seat from the back. He remembered the ghastly sensation of kicking open the back door of the cab, jumping out into the pavement, blood streaming down his face, heart pounding furiously, and looking up just in time to see his home, the twelve-story apartment building at 19 Guryanova Street, collapse in a blinding flash of fire and ash.

A NOTE FROM
THE AUTHOR

★ ★ ★

When I started writing *The Third Target*, I had never heard of ISIS.

I knew I wanted to write a series about the threat Radical Islam poses not only to the U.S., Israel, and the West but also to our moderate Arab/Muslim allies in the Middle East and to Arab Christians in the region. I knew I wanted my main character to be a *New York Times* foreign correspondent who sees a grave new threat coming up over the horizon. I also knew I wanted to write about a serious and believable enemy. I just didn't know which one it should be.

To determine that, as I began to sketch my outline in early 2013 I posed two sets of "What if?" questions.

First: What if Radical Islamic extremists were able to seize control of a cache of chemical weapons in Syria that were overlooked or not reported to the U.N. disarmament teams? Which terrorist group would be in a position to do that? What would they do with such weapons of mass destruction once they grabbed hold of them? Who might they use such weapons against? And how might the powers in the region and the international community respond?

Second: What if Radical Islamic extremists chose to target the Hashemite Kingdom of Jordan? What if they tried to seize control of her territory and people to establish a violent caliphate on the East Bank of the Jordan River? What would be the implications for the rest of the Middle East? What would be the implications for America, Israel, Europe, and the rest of the world? And again, which Radical group might be inclined to launch such an attack and be in a position to do so?

I knew going into this project that few Americans spend much time—if any—thinking about the Hashemite Kingdom of Jordan. But over the years I have come to regard Jordan as one of the most important Arab allies the West has in the epicenter.

Since ascending to the throne in 1999, Jordan's King Abdullah II has proven himself to be a moderate, peaceful, wise Reformer who has been a true friend of the United States, Great Britain, and NATO. He has also maintained the peace treaty with Israel and a healthy relationship with the Jewish State, a relationship that began with secret contacts between his father, the late King Hussein, and Israeli leaders as far back as the 1960s. The present king has been actively engaged in combatting the terrorist activity of Radicals via his military, police, and intelligence networks. He has also sought to combat the ideology of Radicals by building a global network of Islamic scholars and clerics who reject the takfiris, violent extremists, and heretics, and who are proactively trying to define Islam as a peaceful, tolerant religion.

At the same time, he has worked hard to make Jordan a safe haven for both Muslims and Arab Christians fleeing from war and persecution in the region. What's more, it has become increasingly clear that a safe, secure, and moderate Jordan is the absolutely essential cornerstone of any serious future comprehensive peace agreement between the Israelis and Palestinians.

As I went down the list of Radical states and terrorist organizations in the region that might be able to gain control of WMD in Syria and might choose to attack Jordan, I conferred with a range of Middle East experts, current and former intelligence officials, and retired U.S. and Israeli diplomats and military leaders. I asked who they thought was the next big threat likely to rise in the region. Without exception, they all told me, "ISIS."

At the time, neither I nor my publisher, Tyndale House, had heard of this group. Yet the more I learned, the more convinced I became that in the following five years or so, ISIS could actually become a global threat and a household name. Indeed, the ISIS threat has metastasized even faster. Now the whole world has heard of ISIS (the Islamic State of Iraq and al Sham), which is also known as ISIL (the Islamic State of Iraq and the Levant), or simply the Islamic State.

Indeed, as I write this author's note, events are moving quickly. The president of the United States has declared ISIS a threat to our national security. Several Sunni Muslim Arab countries have joined a military and political coalition to "degrade and defeat" ISIS. All eyes are now on the epicenter, but it remains unclear just how successful the strategies employed against ISIS by the U.S. and our allies will be. I pray the events I have written about here never take place. I fear, however, that some world leaders may still underestimate the threat. If so, the consequences could be devastating. I hope that those who are able to act will do so before it is too late.

This book is obviously a work of fiction, but I tried to set the fictional events in as realistic a framework as possible. To that end, I included references to a number of real-life people and events. Journalist A. B. Collins is a figment of my imagination, but the assassination of King Abdullah I that he witnessed in Jerusalem in 1951 is a real, historical event. Abu Khalif is a fictional terrorist, but you may see some similarities to Abu Bakr al-Baghdadi, the real-life head of ISIS. Ayman al-Zawahiri, the real-life leader of al-Qaeda, has not been assassinated by the U.S. government—yet—but the tension between his terrorist organization and ISIS is real.

Of course, the most obvious real-life character in the book is King Abdullah II, Jordan's current monarch. I considered fictionalizing him, as I did the leaders of the U.S., Israel, and the Palestinian Authority. After all, it is always sensitive to write about a current leader in dangerous times, and I certainly do not want to offend His Majesty or the Royal Court. But in the end I chose to include King Abdullah II as a character in this novel primarily because I thought it would not be as effective to write about the emerging threat to Jordan without including him directly. People need to understand who this king is, and why he is uniquely important in Jordan's past, present, and future. I hope readers will come to appreciate just how dangerous the region and the world would be if this king is toppled or violently overthrown. To help in this process, several of the things the king says in chapter 50 of this book, for example, are actually direct quotes (or close adaptations) from King Abdullah's excellent 2011 book, *Our Last Best Chance: The Pursuit of Peace in a Time of Peril*. I highly recommend that nonfiction work if you are interested in a true insider's perspective on current events in the epicenter.

Other books I used for research include:

Uneasy Lies the Head: The Autobiography of His Majesty King Hussein I of the Hashemite Kingdom of Jordan

Fighting Terrorism: How Democracies Can Defeat Domestic and International Terrorists by Benjamin Netanyahu

Hussein and Abdullah: Inside the Jordanian Royal Family by Randa Habib

Lion of Jordan: The Life of King Hussein in War and Peace by Avi Shlaim

King's Counsel: A Memoir of War, Espionage, and Diplomacy in the Middle East by Jack O'Connell

Son of Hamas: A Gripping Account of Terror, Betrayal, Political Intrigue, and Unthinkable Choices by Mosab Hassan Yousef

Once an Arafat Man: The True Story of How a PLO Sniper Found a New Life by Tass Saada

The Second Arab Awakening and the Battle for Pluralism by Marwan Muasher

Kill Khalid: The Failed Mossad Assassination of Khalid Mishal and the Rise of Hamas by Paul McGeough

From Beirut to Jerusalem by Thomas L. Friedman

The Case for Democracy: The Power of Freedom to Overcome Tyranny and Terror by Natan Sharansky and Ron Dermer

The Fight for Jerusalem: Radical Islam, the West, and the Future of the Holy City by Dore Gold

As part of the research process I undertook for this novel, I had the incredible opportunity to travel to Jordan in the spring of 2014 to meet with several senior officials. While I have traveled to Jordan numerous times over the years, this was a particularly special trip. I have a deep love and respect for the people of Jordan. This has only grown over time, but never more so than on that trip.

Special thanks to everyone who made time for me and shared with me their perspective as I did research for this book, both on that research trip and others. Not everyone I met and spoke with will agree with what I have written here. Nevertheless, I am enormously grateful for their insights, wisdom, and kindness, and I hope the book is richer for what I learned from them. Among those to whom I would like to express my deep gratitude are:

His Excellency Abdullah Ensour, Jordan's prime minister

His Royal Highness Prince Ghazi Bin Muhammad, senior advisor to His Majesty King Abdullah II

H.E. Nasser Judeh, Jordan's foreign minister

H.E. Hussein Hazza' Al-Majali, Jordan's interior minister

H.E. Nidal Qatamin, Jordan's minister of labor and tourism

H.E. Alia Bouran, Jordan's ambassador to the United States

James Woolsey, former director of the Central Intelligence Agency

Porter Goss, former director of the Central Intelligence Agency

530 * THE THIRD TARGET

Danny Yatom, former director of the Mossad

Hon. Dore Gold, former Israeli ambassador
to the United Nations and president of
the Jerusalem Center for Public Affairs

Yechiel Horev, former Israeli director of
security of the Defense Establishment

Robert Satloff, executive director of the
Washington Institute for Near East Policy

I'm also deeply grateful for the aides, advisors,
and colleagues of those mentioned above who were
so generous with their time and insights. There are
others who were enormously helpful that I am not
able to mention publicly. To them, as well, I say
thank you.

Writing and publishing a novel is a team effort,
and I am so grateful for a number of people who
have helped me on this project as with so many
other books.

Many thanks to:

My wonderful literary agent and good friend,
Scott Miller, and his team at Trident
Media Group

My first-rate publishing team at Tyndale
House Publishers, including Mark Taylor,
Jeff Johnson, Ron Beers, Karen Watson,
Jan Stob, Cheryl Kerwin, Todd Starowitz,

Dean Renninger, Caleb Sjogren, Erin Smith, Danika King, and the entire sales force—and special thanks to my editor, Jeremy Taylor, who has really done an outstanding job on this one

My blessed parents, Leonard and Mary Rosenberg

My excellent November Communications team, June Meyers and Nancy Pierce

My four wonderful sons—Caleb, Jacob, Jonah, and Noah

My dear, sweet, and amazing wife, Lynn, who has blessed me every moment of every day since we first met in college at Syracuse University and has continued to bless me beyond belief through twenty-five fantastic years of marriage! What an adventure we have been on, Lynnie—may it never end!

Most of all, I am grateful to my Lord and Savior Jesus Christ, who loves so deeply the people of Israel, and Jordan, and Iraq, and Syria, and all the people of the epicenter, and for some unfathomable reason loves me and my family, too.

ABOUT THE AUTHOR

★ ★ ★

Joel C. Rosenberg is a *New York Times* bestselling author with more than three million copies sold among his twelve novels (including *The Last Jihad*, *Damascus Countdown*, and *The Auschwitz Escape*), four nonfiction books (including *Epicenter* and *Inside the Revolution*), and a digital short (*Israel at War*). A front-page Sunday *New York Times* profile called him a "force in the capital." He has also been profiled by the *Washington Times* and the *Jerusalem Post* and has been interviewed on ABC's *Nightline*, CNN *Headline News*, FOX News Channel, The History Channel, MSNBC, *The Rush Limbaugh Show*, and *The Sean Hannity Show*.

You can follow him at www.joelrosenberg.com or on Twitter @joelcrosenberg and Facebook: www.facebook.com/JoelCRosenberg.

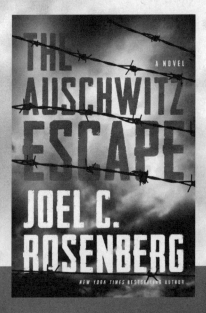

TYNDALE HOUSE PUBLISHERS
IS CRAZY4FICTION!

Fiction that entertains and inspires

Get to know us! Become a member of the Crazy4Fiction
community. Whether you read our blog, like us on
Facebook, follow us on Twitter, or receive our e-newsletter,
you're sure to get the latest news on the best in Christian
fiction. You might even win something along the way!

JOIN IN THE FUN TODAY.

 www.crazy4fiction.com

 Crazy4Fiction

 @Crazy4Fiction

PRAISE FOR
JOEL C. ROSENBERG

"His penetrating knowledge of all things Mideastern—coupled with his intuitive knack for high-stakes intrigue—demand attention."

PORTER GOSS
Former director of the Central Intelligence Agency

"If there were a *Forbes* 400 list of great current novelists, Joel Rosenberg would be among the top ten. . . . One of the most entertaining and intriguing authors of international political thrillers in the country. . . . His novels are un-put-downable."

STEVE FORBES
Editor in chief, *Forbes* magazine

"One of my favorite things: An incredible thriller—it's called *The Third Target* by Joel C. Rosenberg. . . . He's amazing. . . . He writes the greatest thrillers set in the Middle East, with so much knowledge of that part of the world. . . . Fabulous! I've read every book he's ever written!"

KATHIE LEE GIFFORD
NBC's *Today Show*

"Fascinating and compelling . . . way too close to reality for a novel."

MIKE HUCKABEE
Former Arkansas governor

"[Joel Rosenberg] understands the grave dangers posed by Iran and Syria, and he's been a bold and courageous voice for true peace and security in the Middle East."

DANNY AYALON
Israeli deputy foreign minister

"Joel has a particularly clear understanding of what is going on in today's Iran and Syria and the grave threat these two countries pose to the rest of the world."

REZA KAHLILI
Former CIA operative in Iran and bestselling author of *A Time to Betray: The Astonishing Double Life of a CIA Agent Inside the Revolutionary Guards of Iran*

"Joel Rosenberg is unsurpassed as the writer of fiction thrillers! Sometimes I have to remind myself to breathe as I read one of his novels because I find myself holding my breath in suspense as I turn the pages."

ANNE GRAHAM LOTZ
Author and speaker

"Joel paints an eerie, terrifying, page-turning picture of a worst-case scenario coming to pass. You have to read [*Damascus Countdown*], and then pray it never happens."

RICK SANTORUM
Former U.S. senator

THE
FIRST
HOSTAGE

A J.B. COLLINS NOVEL

JOEL C.
ROSENBERG

TYNDALE HOUSE PUBLISHERS, INC., CAROL STREAM, ILLINOIS

Visit Tyndale online at www.tyndale.com.

Visit Joel C. Rosenberg's website at www.joelrosenberg.com.

TYNDALE and Tyndale's quill logo are registered trademarks of Tyndale House Publishers, Inc.

The First Hostage: A J. B. Collins Novel

Designed by Dean H. Renninger.

Scripture quotations are taken from the New American Standard Bible,® copyright © 1960, 1962, 1963, 1968, 1971, 1972, 1973, 1975, 1977, 1995 by The Lockman Foundation. Used by permission.

The First Hostage is a work of fiction. Where real people, events, establishments, organizations, or locales appear, they are used fictitiously. All other elements of the novel are drawn from the author's imagination.

For information about special discounts for bulk purchases, please contact Tyndale House Publishers at csresponse@tyndale.com, or call 1-800-323-9400.

ISBN 978-1-4964-0628-6 (International Trade Paper Edition)
ISBN 978-1-4964-2328-3 (mass paper)

Printed in the United States of America

| 23 | 22 | 21 | 20 | 19 | 18 | 17 |
| 7 | 6 | 5 | 4 | 3 | 2 | 1 |

To our son Jacob, a brave and steady

soul in dark and troubled times.

"Blessed is the man who fears the Lord,

who greatly delights in His commandments. . . .

He will not fear evil tidings; his heart is steadfast."

PSALM 112:1, 7

CAST OF CHARACTERS

JOURNALISTS

J. B. Collins—foreign correspondent for the *New York Times*

Allen MacDonald—foreign editor for the *New York Times*

AMERICANS

Harrison Taylor—president of the United States

Martin Holbrooke—vice president of the United States

Marco Ramirez—lieutenant general, commander of Delta Force

Jack Vaughn—director of the Central Intelligence Agency

Robert Khachigian—former director of the CIA

Arthur Harris—special agent with the Federal Bureau of Investigation

Matthew Collins—J. B.'s older brother

JORDANIANS

King Abdullah II—the monarch of the Hashemite Kingdom of Jordan

Prince Marwan Talal—uncle of the king of Jordan and a senior advisor

Prince Feisal bin al-Hussein—brother of the king of
    Jordan and deputy supreme commander of the
    Jordanian armed forces
Abdul Jum'a—lieutenant general, head of the army
Ibrahim al-Mufti—major general, head of the air
    force
Yusef Sharif—colonel and senior advisor to and chief
    spokesman for the king
Mohammed Hammami—the king's personal
    physician
Ali Sa'id—chief of security for the Royal Court

TERRORISTS

Abu Khalif—leader of the Islamic State in Iraq and
    al-Sham (ISIS)
Jamal Ramzy—commander of ISIS rebel forces in
    Syria and cousin of Abu Khalif

ISRAELIS

Daniel Lavi—Israeli prime minister
Ari Shalit—deputy director of the Mossad
Yael Katzir—Mossad agent

PALESTINIANS

Salim Mansour—president of the Palestinian
    Authority
Youssef Kuttab—senior aide to President Mansour

EGYPTIANS

Amr El-Badawy—general, commander of Egyptian
    special forces

PREFACE

from *The Third Target*

AL-HUMMAR PALACE, AMMAN, JORDAN

Two Jordanian F-16s caught my eye.

They were flying combat air patrol, keeping any stray aircraft—Jordanian or otherwise—out of this corridor, away from the palace and away from the peace summit. Both were quite a ways off in the distance, but what seemed odd was that while they had been flying from left to right across the horizon, heading from south to north, one of them was now turning right and banking toward the palace. Was that normal? It didn't seem so. Several pairs of fighter jets had been crisscrossing the skies over Amman for the last half hour or so in the same predictable manner. So why the deviation?

The jet was still several miles away, but there was no question it was headed in our direction. I turned and whispered to Ali Sa'id, chief of security for the Royal Court.

"What's going on with that F-16?" I asked. "He's broken off from his wingman."

Sa'id had been scanning the crowd, not the

skies, so he didn't immediately respond. But a moment later, he said something in Arabic over his wrist-mounted radio. Then he whispered back, "Stay calm, but come with me, both of you."

Startled, I had a hard time taking my eyes off the plane, but when I saw Sa'id get up and walk toward the doorway from which we had come, I followed his lead. Yael Katzir was right behind me. The band was playing again.

"Where are we going?" I asked Sa'id.

"The command center."

"Why? What do you think's going on?"

"I'm not sure," he conceded. "But I'm not bringing His Majesty out here until I know."

As he said this, I turned and took one last look at the F-16 before going inside. And at that very moment I saw a flash of light and a contrail. The pilot had just fired a missile.

A moment later we felt the explosion.

★　★　★

Inside the palace's security command center, I turned to check on Yael.

The Mossad agent had a large gash on her forehead and was bleeding profusely. I called for a first aid kit, and one of the watch commanders rushed to my side with one. As I bandaged her up, though, Yael gasped. At first I thought I had hurt her further. But when I saw her eyes grow wide, I turned to see what she was looking at.

On the video monitors in the command post, I could now see dump trucks and cement trucks loaded with explosives making speed dashes for the outer gates of the royal compound. I watched as soldiers fired automatic weapons at them, but one by one the trucks were hitting their targets and erupting in massive explosions. Huge gaps appeared in the perimeter fences, and hundreds of fighters in black hoods and ski masks rushed through to engage in brutal gun battles with Jordanian soldiers fighting desperately to save themselves and their beloved king.

Just then the vault door opened behind us. Suddenly King Abdullah was coming out of the safe room and directly toward us.

"Ali," he said, "we need to go now."

★   ★   ★

Outside the palace, I could hear bullets whizzing over my head.

I could hear them smashing into the side of the armor-plated trucks. I could see round after round hitting the bulletproof windows, though fortunately they refused to shatter. But as I came around the far side of one of the U.S. president's Suburbans, I froze in my tracks. Prime Minister Lavi and President Mansour were lying side by side, surrounded by several more dead agents.

The king was crouched over them. I couldn't see what he was doing. Was he trying in vain to revive them or just mourning over them? Either way, it was no use. They were gone. Nothing was going to bring them back. We had to go. We couldn't stay out in the open like this.

At that moment, I went numb. I could feel myself beginning to slip into shock, and I couldn't help it, couldn't stop it. And then, as if through a tunnel, I thought I heard the sound of someone calling my name.

"Collins, they're alive!" the king yelled. *"They're unconscious, but they're still breathing. They both have a pulse. But we need to get them into the Suburban. Cover us!"*

I couldn't believe it. They weren't dead? They looked dead. They weren't moving. But at the very thought, I snapped to.

Sa'id opened the back of the truck and put down the rear seat to make space while Yael covered his right flank. Then Sa'id helped the king lift the Israeli prime minister and gently set him inside the SUV.

Reengaged, I pivoted hard to my left and followed my orders. Firing the MP5 in short bursts in multiple directions, I had no illusions I was going to kill many rebels. But I was determined not to let them get to the king or his family or these other leaders. All I had to do was buy time. The question was whether it would possibly be enough.

As the king and Sa'id put the Palestinian leader in the back, I continued firing. Then I heard one of the other SUVs roar to life. For a moment I stopped shooting. I looked to my right and saw a Suburban peeling off without us with two American agents in the front seat.

The Secret Service wasn't waiting. They'd gotten their man into a bulletproof vehicle and now they were getting him to the airport. We had to move too, and fast.

★ ★ ★

The king directed me onto Route 40—the Al Kodos Highway—and soon we were heading southwest out of Amman. We were now going nearly a hundred miles an hour, and we had a new problem. The king was on the satphone with his brother, who informed us that there was a police checkpoint at the upcoming interchange with Route 35, the Queen Alia Highway. The checkpoint itself wasn't the issue. The problem, the king said, was that it had apparently been overrun by ISIS rebels, and they were waiting for us with RPGs and .50-caliber machine guns.

"How long to the interchange?" I asked.

"At this rate, two minutes, no more," the king replied.

"What do you recommend, Your Majesty?" I asked, not sure if I should try to go any faster or slow down.

"Do you believe in prayer, Collins?" he said. "Because now would be a good time to start."

"I'm out of ammunition," Yael said. "Does anyone have more?"

"There's a full mag in my weapon," I replied.

"Where's that?" she asked.

"Here," the crown prince said from the back-seat. He picked up my machine gun from the floor, removed the magazine, and handed it to Yael.

In the distance, I could see the interchange

approaching. Were we going to try to blow through this checkpoint? That, it seemed, was a suicide mission. And I wasn't ready to die.

A second later the issue was moot. Rising over a ridge off to our right were two Apache helicopter gunships coming low and fast. Yael noticed them first and pointed them out to the rest of us. Now we were all riveted on them, and one question loomed over everything, though no one spoke it aloud: which side were they on?

The checkpoint was fast approaching. So were the Apaches.

And then in my mirror I saw the 30mm open up.

"They're shooting at us!" I shouted.

I saw a flash. I knew what it was. I'd seen it a hundred times or more, from Fallujah to Kabul. Someone had just fired an RPG. I could see the contrail streaking down the highway behind us. The queen screamed. I hit the gas and swerved to the right just in time. The RPG knocked off my side mirror and sliced past. It hadn't killed us.

But the next one might.

I saw another flash, this one from the lead Apache. He too had just fired, and this wasn't a mere RPG. This was a heat-seeking Hellfire missile. There was no swerving or avoiding it. It was coming straight for us, and there was nothing we could do about it. We were about to die in a ball of fire. It was all over.

But to my relief, the missile didn't slam into us. Instead, we watched it strike one of the Humvees at the checkpoint ahead. In the blink of an eye, the entire checkpoint was obliterated in a giant explosion. Stunned—mesmerized by the fireball in front of me—I forgot to exit. I just kept driving. Then we were crashing through the burning remains of the checkpoint, racing through the interchange, and getting on Route 35, bound for the airport.

None of us cheered. We were relieved beyond words, but we all knew this was not of our doing. Forces beyond us were keeping us alive and clearing the way for us.

Soon we saw one squadron after another of Jordanian F-16s and F-15s streaking across the sky. I had to believe they were headed to Amman to bomb the palace and crush the rebellion. I couldn't imagine how difficult a decision that must have been for the king, but I also knew he had no choice. He was the last of the Hashemite monarchs, and he seemed determined not to go down like those before him.

As we sped along Highway 35, against all odds, strangely enough I actually began to feel a sense of hope again. We were still alive. We were safe for now. And I had the strongest sense that the king was going to prevail. He had been blindsided, to be sure. But he had enormous personal courage. He had an army ready to fight back, and he had the Americans and the Israelis ready to fight with him. But when we arrived at the airport, those feelings instantly evaporated.

As I surveyed the devastation around us, all hope disappeared.

The gorgeous new multimillion-dollar terminal

was a smoking crater. The roads and runways were pockmarked with the remains of mortars and artillery shells that apparently had been fired not long before we arrived. Jumbo jets were on fire. Dead and dying bodies lay everywhere. Fuel depots were ablaze. The stench of burning jet fuel was overwhelming.

And Air Force One was gone.

PART
ONE

"Virtuous motives—trammeled by inertia and timidity—are no match for armed and resolute wickedness."

WINSTON CHURCHILL
IN *THE GATHERING STORM*

1

* * *

"The president of the United States . . . is missing."

Even as the words came out of my mouth, I could hardly believe what I was saying. Neither could my editor.

There was a long pause.

"What do you mean, *missing*?" said the crackling, garbled voice on the other end of the line, on the other side of the world.

Allen MacDonald had worked at the *New York Times* for the better part of forty years. He'd been the foreign editor since I was in high school. For as long as I had been with the *Times*—which was now well over a decade—we'd worked together on all kinds of stories, from assassinations to terror attacks to full-blown wars. I was sure he had heard it all in this business . . . until now.

"I mean missing, Allen. Gone. Lost. No one knows where he is, and all hell is breaking loose here," I said as I looked out over the devastation.

Amman's gorgeous new international airport was ablaze. Thick, black smoke darkened the

3

midday sun. Bodies were everywhere. Soldiers. Policemen. Ground crew. And an untold number of jihadists in their signature black hoods, their cold, stiff hands still gripping Russian-made AK-47s. Anyone not already dead, myself included, was wearing a protective chem-bio suit, breathing through a gas mask, and praying the worst of the sarin gas attacks were over.

"But I—I don't understand," Allen stammered. "CNN is reporting Air Force One is safe. That it's already cleared Jordanian airspace. That it has a fighter escort."

"It's all true," I replied. "But the president isn't on it."

"You're sure?"

"Absolutely."

"There's no chance that you misheard."

"No."

"Misunderstood?"

"No."

"Fog of war?" he pressed.

"Forget it."

"Maybe somebody said it as a tactical diversion, to throw off ISIS or other enemies."

"No, Allen, listen to me—the president is not on that plane. I'm telling you he's missing, and people need to know."

"Collins, if I go with this story and you're wrong . . ."

Allen didn't finish the sentence. But he didn't have to. I understood the consequences.

"I'm not wrong, Allen," I said. "This is solid."

There was another pause. Then he said, "Do you realize what this means?"

"No," I shot back. "I don't know what this means. And neither do you. I don't even know for sure if he's been captured or injured or . . ." Now my voice trailed off.

"Or killed?" Allen asked.

"I'm not saying that."

"What, then? Missing and presumed dead?"

"No, no—listen to me. I'm giving you precisely what I know. Nothing more. Nothing less."

"So where do you think he is?"

"I have no idea, Allen. No one does. But my sources were explicit. Air Force One took off without the president."

"Okay, wait," Allen said. "I'm putting you on speaker. I'm going to record you. And Janie is here. She's going to type up everything you tell us."

I could hear some commotion as he set up a digital recorder, cleared space on his desk, and shouted for Mary Jane, his executive assistant, to bring her laptop into his office immediately. A moment later they were ready.

I took a deep breath, did my best to wipe some of the soot from my gas mask, and checked my grandfather's pocket watch. It was now 3:19 p.m. local time on Sunday, December 5.

"Okay, take this down," I began. "The president of the United States is missing. Stop. Air Force One took off from the Amman airport under a U.S. fighter jet escort shortly after 2:30 p.m. Stop. But President Harrison Taylor was not on the plane. Stop. U.S. and Jordanian security forces are presently engaged in a massive search-and-rescue effort in Jordan to find the president. Stop. But at the moment the president's whereabouts and safety are unknown. Stop."

My hands were trembling. My throat was dry. And my left arm was killing me. I'd been shot—grazed, really—above the elbow in a firefight back at the Al-Hummar Palace during the ISIS attack. It had been bleeding something fierce until Yael Katzir, the beautiful and mysterious Mossad agent who had assisted me in getting King Abdullah and his family to safety, had tied a tourniquet on it. That was just after we arrived at the airport, just before she boarded the chopper that was taking Prime Minister Daniel Lavi back to Israel for emergency medical treatment. I was going to need something for the pain, and soon, but I knew Allen required more details, so I kept going.

"The devastating chain of events began unfolding early Sunday afternoon in the northeast suburbs of Amman. Stop. Forces of the Islamic State launched a multiprong terrorist attack on the Israeli–Palestinian peace summit being held at Al-Hummar Palace. Stop. Just before the ceremony to sign a comprehensive peace treaty began, a Jordanian F-16 flying a combat air patrol fired an air-to-ground missile at the crowds gathered for the summit. Stop. The pilot of the F-16 then flew a suicide mission into the palace. Stop. Simultaneously, thousands of heavily armed Islamic State terrorists penetrated the grounds of the palace. Stop. Under heavy fire, security forces evacuated President Taylor, Jordan's King Abdullah II, Israeli prime minister Daniel Lavi, and Palestinian president Salim Mansour from the palace grounds. Stop. Lavi and Mansour were severely wounded and are being airlifted to Jerusalem and Ramallah, respectively. Stop. Witnesses saw a black, bulletproof Chevy Suburban driven by U.S. Secret Service agents whisking President Taylor away from the scene of the attacks. Stop. But that vehicle never reached the airport. Stop. Sources tell the *Times* the president learned the airport was under attack by ISIS terrorists and called the commander of Air Force One and ordered him to take off immediately to protect the plane and crew. Stop. The president reportedly told the pilots he would recall them once Jordanian military forces regained control of the airport grounds. Stop. However, at this moment, senior U.S. government officials say they do not know where the president is, nor can they confirm his safety. Stop. Neither the president nor his Secret Service detail is responding to calls. Stop."

I paused, in part to allow Janie to get it all down, but she was a pro and had had no trouble keeping pace.

"I'm with you," she said. "Keep going."

"I think that's it for now," I said. "We need to get that out there. I can call back and dictate more details of the attack in a few minutes."

"That's fine, but who are your sources, J. B.?" Allen asked.

"I can't say."

"J. B., you have to."

"Allen, I can't—not on an open line."

"J. B., this isn't a request. It's an order."

"I have to protect my sources. You know that."

"Obviously. I'm not saying we're going to include them in the story, but I have to know that the sources are solid and so is the story."

"Allen, come on; you're wasting time. You need to get this out immediately."

"J. B., listen to me."

"No, Allen, I—"

"James!" he suddenly shouted. I'd never heard him do it before. "I can't just go on your word. Not on this. The stakes are too high. A story like this puts lives in danger. And getting it wrong is only half the issue. I'm not saying you're wrong. I can hear in your voice that you believe it's true. And I'm inclined to believe you. But I have to answer to New York. And they're going to have the White House and Pentagon and Secret Service going crazy if we publish this story. So tell me what you know, or the story doesn't run."

2

Allen was right, of course.

The stakes couldn't be higher. But still I hesitated. I couldn't tell him *how* I knew. I could only tell him *what* I knew and that the story—however horrible, whatever the repercussions—was solid.

The monarch of the Hashemite Kingdom of Jordan—King Abdullah II himself—had just hung up from a secure call with the Pentagon. He'd spoken with the chairman of the Joint Chiefs of Staff. And he'd just relayed to me the essential details of the conversation. Did that count as one source or two?

I realized it could be argued that it was only one. After all, I hadn't spoken with the chairman myself. But under the circumstances I was counting the intel as reliable. The king had told me nearly verbatim what the man had said. There was no reason for him to lie to me. I could see in his eyes he was telling me the truth, especially after all we had just been through. And what he told me rang true with everything that was playing out around me. I could see for myself that Air

Force One was gone. I could see that the Chevy
Suburban that had carried the president from the
palace was not here on the airport grounds and was
nowhere to be found. I had heard with my own
ears when the king called his brother, Prince Feisal,
the deputy supreme commander of the Jordanian
armed forces, and ordered a massive search of
Route 35, the Queen Alia Highway, the very road
we'd just taken to the airport and the last known
location of the president.

I knew the facts. But I also knew I couldn't
directly betray the king's confidence. I couldn't run
the risk that if I told Allen these details, some of
them might wind up in the final story. I trusted
Allen, but I wasn't sure I trusted his bosses in New
York. What's more, I couldn't chance any errors.
Allen had mentioned the fog of war, and I'd experienced the phenomenon myself countless times
before. I knew mistakes could happen. I'd made
my share over the years. I didn't intend to make
one now.

I looked out on the burning wreckage of two
jumbo jets as His Majesty strode across the tarmac.
He was about to board a Black Hawk helicopter
that had just landed and was kicking up a huge
cloud of dust. Before stepping aboard, the king
turned and frantically waved me over. He wasn't
going to wait for me. If I was going to stay with
this story, I had to go and go now.

It was suddenly clear to me that I was about
to make a career-altering decision. The king
hadn't specifically authorized me to tell the world
what he'd just told me. But he hadn't expressly

forbidden it either. He knew full well I was a foreign correspondent for the *New York Times*. He had to know I was going to call the information back to Washington. He could hardly expect me to keep this a secret. Still, it was a judgment call. He might have just been telling me as a friend, as someone who had saved his life. Maybe at that moment he didn't see me as a journalist but as an ally. Or maybe he wasn't thinking clearly.

I didn't want to burn a source. I certainly couldn't burn a king. But in my mind there simply was no choice. Americans had to know their commander in chief was missing. After all, weren't there serious national security implications at play here? Weren't there grave constitutional implications as well? Was Harrison Taylor still technically the president? Or in his absence had power shifted to the vice president, even temporarily? For that matter, where *was* the VP at the moment? Was he safe? Had he been briefed? Was he ready for what was coming? Was anyone in Washington ready for this? Then again, what was "this" exactly?

I had no idea. We were in uncharted waters. All I knew for certain at that moment was that the American people needed to know what I knew. They needed to know the facts. They needed to be asking the same questions I was asking. And people at the highest levels of the American government needed to be providing answers.

It was true, of course, that informing the American people that the leader of the free world was missing meant simultaneously informing the enemy. What would ISIS do with such information? Would it give them a tactical advantage in the current crisis? It would almost certainly give them a propaganda victory of enormous proportions unless the president resurfaced quickly, safely, and in full command. But none of that was my concern. My job was to report what I was seeing and hearing, regardless of the consequences to me or anyone else. I just had to make sure I didn't expose my sources.

Running now for the waiting chopper and fearing His Majesty might lift off without me, I shouted into the phone. *"Allen, I'm sorry. I hear what you're saying, but I can't do it. Are you going to run the story or not?"*

There was a long pause. For a moment I thought I'd lost the connection, but as I approached the Black Hawk, I could see that—incredibly—I still had four out of five bars of service and an open line to Washington.

"Are you going to run the story or not?" I shouted again over the roar of the rotors.

Allen's answer knocked the wind out of me.

"No, J. B., I'm not," he shouted back. *"Not until you give me your sources. I'm not a federal grand jury. I'm your editor, and I have a right to know."*

3

★ ★ ★

Hanging up, I jumped into the waiting chopper.

A soldier slammed the door behind me, and seconds later we were off the ground. To my astonishment, King Abdullah was at the controls. He still had his chem-bio suit on, as did we all, but he had taken full command of the situation. We shot hard and fast over the desert floor, then gained some altitude and banked east.

"Where are we going?" I asked the Royal Jordanian Air Force captain who had clearly been asked to relinquish the controls and was now sitting beside me, along with a half-dozen heavily armed special forces operators scanning both the skies and the ground for trouble.

"I can't say," the captain replied.

"Classified?" I asked.

"No," he said into my ear. "I just have no idea."

The king—a highly experienced helicopter pilot, not to mention the supreme commander of Jordan's military—was keeping his cards close to his vest, and given the circumstances, he was probably right to do so. He was in the midst of a coup d'état. Much of his government had just been killed by forces loyal to the Islamic State. His palace, his friends, and the region's hopes for peace had been destroyed by a traitorous member of his own air force. He clearly wasn't taking any chances with who was going to fly his chopper, and he was certainly not going to confide his immediate plans to anyone he didn't implicitly trust, which at the moment had to be almost no one.

Wincing in pain and feeling blood trickling down my left arm, I buckled up and looked out at the billows of smoke rising over Amman. Wherever we were going, I could only hope I could get some medical care when we arrived. I hadn't had time to examine the wound, and Yael hadn't had time to clean it, much less dress it. She'd simply taken the queen's scarf and tied it tightly around the wound before helping the queen and the crown prince into their chopper, bound for some secure, undisclosed location.

I closed my eyes for a moment and tried not to think of the excruciating burning sensation shooting up and down my arm. Instead I tried to turn my thoughts to Yael. Was she okay? She'd been twice punched hard in the face during a struggle with one of the hooded jihadists that had stormed the palace grounds—a struggle that had nearly taken both our lives. She'd also sustained a terrible gash to her forehead while we were escaping from the compound in the king's Suburban. But she'd never complained for a moment. She'd done everything she could to save the lives of her own prime minister and of the Palestinian president, even while protecting the royal family and me. Was she safe now? Were she and her team already on the ground in Jerusalem? Was Prime Minster Lavi going to make it? Was President Mansour?

Opening my eyes, I turned to the window and winced at my reflection. Aside from the cuts and scrapes and bruises on my cheeks and forehead— not to mention across my entire body—the face of an increasingly weathered and tired old man was staring back at me. I was barely into my forties, but a line from a Harrison Ford film echoed in my brain. *"It's not the years, honey; it's the mileage."* That was exactly how I felt. I was a foreign correspondent, a war correspondent, part of "the tribe" of reporters who cheated death and covered the news from the front lines of the most terrifying events on the planet. But death was catching up fast. I was an adrenaline junkie who had always loved jetting around the globe, living out of a suitcase, pushing the envelope in every area of life. But now I was also divorced, a recovering alcoholic, exhausted, and alone. My friends were dead or dying. My family was half a world away, and I barely saw them. I hadn't had a date in years. And no matter how hip and expensive my black, semi-rimless designer glasses were, they couldn't hide my bloodshot eyes. No matter how many years ago I'd shaved my increasingly gray head bald, I was still sporting a salt-and-pepper mustache and goatee. They no longer looked cool, I decided. They just made me look like a guy trying too hard to hold on to his youth.

Unable to take any more of myself, I shifted

focus and tried to make sense of the surreal scene out my window. From our vantage point, south-southeast of the capital, I could see squadrons of F-15s and F-16s streaking across the skies of Amman, dropping their ordnance on the ISIS forces below. I watched the spectacular explosions that ensued and could even feel the impact ripple through my body. I quickly snapped some photos on my iPhone and then took a shot of the king flying the Black Hawk before anyone could tell me not to.

My thoughts shifted back to the president. Where was he? Were he and his security detail under fire? Were they in immediate and over-whelming danger? Or was the Secret Service just lying low, keeping their charge out of sight and off the air until they had more confidence they could truly get him to safety?

Allen's refusal to run my story stunned me. The more I thought about it, the angrier I became. After all these years, after who knew how many stories—many of them exclusives—how could he not trust me now? Did he really think I would run with such a provocative story as the president of the United States being missing in the middle of a coup attempt unless I was absolutely certain? I didn't mind if he added caveats to the story, hedged the language a bit to make it clear this was a fast-developing story and the situation could change at any moment. To the contrary, that was undoubtedly the right thing to do. But he knew I was in the eye of the storm. He knew I was with the highest-ranking leaders in Jordan who were still breathing and fully conscious. Where did he think I was getting this information?

The whole thing enraged me. I felt powerless and cut off. Until I looked down at the iPhone in my hands. I realized we were flying low enough that I still had cell coverage. And just then it occurred to me that I didn't need to wait for Allen MacDonald or the brass at the Gray Lady to get this story out. I could do it myself.

A soldier offered me a bottle of water, but I waved it off. Instead, opening my Twitter app, I began typing and sending dispatches, 140 characters at a time.

EXCLUSIVE: President of the United States missing. After ISIS attacks in Amman, Air Force One took off without POTUS on board. #AmmanCrisis

EXCLUSIVE: Where is POTUS? I saw Secret Service whisk him away from palace, heading for Amman airport. But he never arrived. #AmmanCrisis

EXCLUSIVE: Massive search for POTUS under way using Jordanian military, U.S. Secret Service, U.S. military assets. #AmmanCrisis

Over the next few minutes, I sent nineteen tweets. In many ways, I realized, the story read more dramatically over Twitter than it might on the *Times'* home page. This was the epitome of a breaking news story. Raw. Dramatic. Unfiltered. Fast-moving. And in this case, exclusive. If Allen and the brass in Manhattan wanted to skip the biggest story of our time, they could be my guest. But I had news, and I was going to share it with the world.

After getting out the core of the story, I then sent three more tweets using some cautionary language. I made it clear this was a fluid situation. I stressed my hope that additional reporting from other journalists—and disclosures from U.S. government officials themselves—would shed light on the situation. But in less than five minutes, the story was out there. Now all I could do was wait.

I'd never broken a story via Twitter before. It wasn't my style. In my heart, I guess I was old-school. I believed in filing dispatches and having editors clean them up and make their own decisions about what and when to publish. It wasn't just safer for readers—and for me. It wasn't just the way things had been done forever in the world of responsible journalism. I genuinely believed it was the right approach. It's certainly the way my grandfather operated, and I held him in the highest esteem.

Back in the day, back when Andrew Bradley "A. B." Collins was writing for the Associated Press in the forties, fifties, and sixties, he worked his craft by the book. He wrote up his stories on old-fashioned typewriters (hunting and pecking with just his pointer fingers as, remarkably, he never formally learned how to type). His dispatches were hand-edited by grizzled old men wearing bifocals and smoking pipes or fat Cuban cigars. His stories were rigorously fact-checked and sometimes heavily revised, sometimes even rewritten, before they were finally transmitted over the wires and printed out in the clackity-clack of cacophonous newsrooms the world over. He didn't like being questioned by his editors over his facts or sources. He didn't like being rewritten. No reporter worth his salt did. But he wasn't a rebel. He took his risks in the field, not in the newsroom.

Sure, occasionally when a story was breaking big and fast, he had no time to type it up and cable it to his editors. Sometimes he had to phone in his stories from exotic locales to the news desk in London or New York. But my grandfather would never have even imagined doing an end run around his editors. They were the gatekeepers. Everything went through them. That's just the way it was done. That was the system. And my grandfather respected the system.

I did too. Or I had until now. It had never occurred to me to "publish" my interview with Jamal Ramzy, the ISIS commander in Syria, via Twitter or Facebook or some other social media just moments after I'd finished talking to him. Nor had it occurred to me to tweet out the story of the prison break at Abu Ghraib or the grisly sarin gas tests conducted by Abu Khalif and Jamal Ramzy in Mosul. To the contrary, I knew such stories needed Allen's critical eye and the go-ahead from those above him. If I could convince them of the story's merit, and if they were satisfied with the care I'd taken to write it, then they'd publish it—and not a moment earlier.

But this was different. This story was too big to hold, too important to sit on. I couldn't reach millions of people directly, the way the front page of the *New York Times* or the home page of the official website could. But I had 183,000 followers on Twitter. People all over the country and all over the world were tracking my stories. More importantly, most of my fellow war correspondents and most of the reporters, editors, and producers in Washington and numerous foreign capitals followed me, as did political, military, and intelligence officials throughout the U.S. government, NATO, the Middle East, the Kremlin, and the Far East. I could guarantee they were all tracking their Twitter accounts right now. They were all desperate for any scrap of information from inside the battle zone.

By "publishing" this story directly, at least I could reach people who could reach others—many others—and fast.

4

The story instantly blew up the Internet.

As I scanned my notifications screen, I could watch in real time as reporters and various Middle East experts and analysts started retweeting my news flashes. Their readers then retweeted, others retweeted them again, and the story spread at an exponential rate. The feedback effect was stunning.

Preternaturally, Matt Drudge picked up the scent almost immediately. He and his colleagues quickly cobbled together my tweets into an article of sorts and made this the lead story on his site—complete with his trademark red siren—with a simple yet stunning tabloid headline: **POTUS Missing in Amman.**

Within minutes, Drudge's version of my story became the biggest trending topic on Twitter worldwide. Reporters began instant-messaging me questions, probing for more details. Rather than respond to them each directly, I started tweeting out the photos I'd just taken over Amman and providing tidbits of detail and context as best I could. I couldn't possibly report all that I'd seen and heard over the past few hours. Not 140 characters at a time. But as we shot across the eastern edges of the capital, flying low and fast, barely above the rooftops, I came to the horrifying realization that most if not all of the other reporters who had been covering the peace summit were now dead or dying. Most of the TV crews and satellite trucks providing coverage from the palace had been wiped out in the attacks. Across the world, live streams had been cut off midtransmission. Anchors back in their home studios had been left hanging, unsure at first why their feeds had been cut. What images had gotten out to the world? Any? How much on-the-ground reporting from Amman was actually taking place?

A few minutes later we were on approach to a large air force base located in Marka, a suburb northeast of Amman. I recognized the base immediately. It was named after the first King Abdullah and served as the general headquarters of the Royal Jordanian Air Force and the home base of three squadrons of attack aircraft, including advanced F-16 Fighting Falcons and older Northrop F-5s.

As we touched down outside the main air command center, I put my phone down. I could see that the base was heavily fortified by tanks, armored personnel carriers, and well-armed soldiers. I saw sharpshooters strategically positioned on numerous roofs as well. But I refrained from snapping any photos. There were lines I didn't dare cross.

When the side door opened, the special forces

operators around me jumped out and took up positions around the chopper. They knew the king was a target, and they were taking no chances.

I unfastened my seat belt and then caught a glimpse of Prince Feisal bin al-Hussein. He was flanked by an enormous security detail, and they were moving toward us rapidly. The prince was not a big man, but he was taller than I'd imagined, well built, a classic professional soldier, with closely cropped black hair graying a bit at the temples. He sported a small mustache and a somber expression and wore fatigues and combat boots, not his formal dress uniform. As deputy supreme commander of the Jordanian armed forces, he was the highest ranking officer after only His Majesty himself. He glanced at me somewhat coldly and then at his brother. It was clear he wasn't coming to bring greetings but only to get the king quickly and safely inside the command center.

Abdullah climbed out of the cockpit and removed the chem-bio suit. Following his lead, I removed mine as the king returned his brother's salute.

"Your family is safe?" the king asked.

The prince nodded, then quickly assured his brother that the queen, the crown prince, and the king's other children were safe as well.

"And the president?" His Majesty asked.

"Wait till we're inside," the prince replied, anxious to get the king safely out of any potential line of fire and apparently not prepared to discuss the president's situation in the open.

The king started moving toward the door, then

turned suddenly and said, "Feisal, where are my manners? There's someone you need to meet."

"Yes, Mr. Collins from the *Times*—the pleasure's mine," the prince replied without emotion or any apparent real interest. He clearly knew who I was and had been aware I was coming, but it was also clear in his eyes that he didn't like the notion of my presence at this place at this time one bit.

Even so, he reached out and gave me a firm handshake, but he had no intention of standing on the tarmac making small talk. Again he urged His Majesty to come inside, and the king agreed. With the security detail flanking us, we moved briskly into the lobby of the GHQ—general headquarters—which was filled with more soldiers on full alert, then headed down several flights of stairs until we passed through a vault-like door to a bunker that stank of stale cigarettes. As we entered, the head of the prince's detail prepared to close the vault behind us, but Feisal held up his hand and motioned him to wait a moment. Then he pulled his brother aside and whispered something in Arabic I couldn't hear.

"No," the king said. "Collins stays with me."

"But, Your Majesty," Feisal protested, "given the circumstances, I must insist that—"

But the king would have none of it. "He stays—now lock the doors and initiate your protocols. We are at war, gentlemen. I want a full briefing on current status."

A spark of something flashed in the prince's eyes. Anger? Resentment? I couldn't quite place it, but I was close. Nevertheless, he had just been given a direct order by his commander in chief, and like a dutiful soldier he followed it.

All nonessential personnel were quickly ushered out. I stayed.

As the vault door closed, the king briefly introduced me to the elite few who remained inside the bunker with us. Lieutenant General Abdul Jum'a, head of the army, and Major General Ibrahim al-Mufti, head of the air force, were both likely in their midfifties. Colonel Yusef Sharif, a senior advisor to and chief spokesman for the king, looked like he was about my age, maybe early or midforties. Dr. Mohammed Hammami, an older gentleman, perhaps seventy or thereabouts, served as His Majesty's personal physician. The remaining four men were a young military aide who looked to be no more than twenty-five and three armed members of the security detail. As we shook hands, the king excused himself, stepping into an adjacent washroom.

"Have a seat, Mr. Collins," Dr. Hammami said. "Let me take a look at that arm."

That caught me a bit off guard. Nothing had been said in my presence about my injuries, but the king must have radioed ahead. I did as I was told; as I sat, I noticed for the first time my blood-drenched sleeve. The doctor asked me to take off my shirt, but the pain was too much to raise my left arm over my head. Eventually, with no small amount of difficulty and discomfort, I both unbuttoned and removed the shirt only to reveal the queen's now-crimson scarf-turned-tourniquet. The doctor opened his bag, withdrew a pair of scissors, rubbing alcohol, and some gauze. He cut away the scarf and examined my injuries.

"You're a lucky man, Mr. Collins," he said after a moment. "This isn't nearly as bad as I'd been expecting."

That was comforting . . . I guess.

He asked me a few questions for his chart. "Full name?"

"James Bradley Collins."

"Date of birth?"

"May 3, 1975."

"Height and weight?"

"Six foot one, 175 pounds, give or take."

"In kilos?"

"Sorry—no idea."

"Do you know your blood type?"

"A-positive, I'm pretty sure."

"Any history of heart problems or other chronic medical issues?"

"No."

"Any allergies?"

"None."

"Are you taking any medications?"

"Not currently."

"Are you a smoker?"

"No."

"Good. Any history of alcohol or drug use?"

"How much time do you have?" I asked.

He just looked at me, didn't find me clever at all, and scribbled a few notes. "Past surgeries?"

"Broke my leg in ROTC at the end of my freshman year. They had to do three different surgeries to get it right. And that, my friend, was the end of my career in the American military."

Dr. Hammami wrote it down but didn't seem to care, particularly. Questions finished, he proceeded to clean my wound.

But Sharif, the king's advisor and spokesman, picked right up on what I had said. "You were in ROTC?" he asked.

"It was a long time ago."

"Which branch?"

"Army."

"Did you really want to serve in the U.S. military?"

"Actually, I wasn't sure. A bunch of my friends enlisted. I'd grown up hunting with my grandfather in the forests of Maine. I loved guns. I loved the outdoors. I thought maybe I'd wind up as a reporter for the *Army Times*."

"And then you broke your leg."

"And wound up in a series of hospitals for the next few months, so yeah, that was pretty much a wasted year."

I can't tell you how much at that moment I craved a drink. But I was fairly sure that in a room of reasonably devout Muslims, I wasn't going to find anything suitable, so I did my best to focus on something—anything—else.

I looked around the room. It certainly wasn't the White House Situation Room with its state-of-the-art, high-tech wizardry. Nor was this the handsomely appointed official reception room at the Al-Hummar Palace, where I first met the king. It looked more like a conference room at a Holiday

Inn or Ramada somewhere in the American Midwest: simple, spare, and without any frills. There was a large, old oak table—scuffed up a bit and covered in newspapers and used coffee mugs—in the center of the room, surrounded by twelve executive chairs that looked a little worse for wear. Overhead hung several harsh fluorescent lights. On the wall to my left was a large map of the greater Middle East and North Africa, covered in plastic and marked with notes and diagrams written with erasable pens of various colors. On the far wall was a large map of the Hashemite Kingdom of Jordan and several kilometers of each of its immediate neighbors. Directly across from it on the wall behind me was yet another large map, this one a detailed street map of the city of Amman and its surrounding suburbs, showing all major landmarks and military facilities, including the air base we were at now. These maps were also covered in plastic and even more heavily marked up, showing the current known locations of rebel forces and the movement of Jordanian military response teams. On the fourth wall, to my right, just over the door through which we had entered, were mounted five large television monitors. They were all muted but displayed live feeds from Al Jazeera, Al Arabiya, CNN, and two local Jordanian stations.

The young military aide quickly cleared away the newspapers and coffee mugs and emptied the ashtrays, then replaced them with Dell laptops and thick binders for the king, the prince, and the others. I turned my attention to the TV monitors.

For the first time I could see the images the rest of the world was seeing.

It was immediately apparent I'd been wrong. Many more images of the attacks had gotten out than I'd expected, and they were both mesmerizing and brutally hard to watch. All the networks were replaying footage of the missile strike and kamikaze attack on the palace and the ensuing scenes of horrific chaos and carnage from a variety of angles and vantage points. It was one thing to have seen black-and-white images from the security command post underneath the Al-Hummar Palace, as Yael and I had while the attacks were unfolding. But these chilling images showed far more of the magnitude of the destruction—and in living color.

The generals took seats in front of the bank of phones on the table and went right back to work, presumably getting updates from their men in the field. Out of the corner of my eye, I felt Prince Feisal's glare, though I disciplined myself not to look over at him. Not just yet. He clearly didn't want me there, and I didn't fault him. He had a rebellion to suppress. He knew full well there was a mole somewhere in the system, maybe several of them, who had known enough of the details of the summit to set into motion this devilish attack. He didn't know whom to trust any more than his older brother did. He certainly didn't want to trust a journalist, a foreigner least of all. I had to believe the very notion of having a reporter—a non-Jordanian, non-Arab, non-Muslim, non-Hashemite reporter—in his command bunker while he was orchestrating a massive counterassault against the forces of ISIS and an extensive search and rescue to find the president of the United States must have seemed nonsensical and unbearable.

It made me wonder why, in fact, the king would keep me around. I certainly didn't have the security clearance to be in the war room at such a time as this. Surely the king, who still hadn't come back into the room, was taking a moment to consider his brother's counsel. It was one thing to show me a measure of kindness and hospitality given the role I'd just played in saving his life. But now the king had serious work to do. There was no reason whatsoever to keep me around.

But if—and more likely, when—he kicked me out, what exactly would I do? Where would I go? Would I be stuck in the lobby upstairs with no sources, no access, perhaps not even any ability to communicate with the outside world, in the middle of a base in full lockdown and under imminent threat of attack by the forces of the Islamic State?

It suddenly struck me that not flying out with Yael and the prime minister might have been a serious mistake.

5

* * *

I decided I had to stay in this room, whatever it took.

It was the only way I would be able to cover the hunt for the president, a story of enormous import. But staying in this room meant finding a way to make peace with the prince. He very likely held the key to whether I stayed or was kicked out. But how was I going to win him over? Feisal and I had never met before. He didn't know me, and I knew precious little about him other than his public career.

I did know he was born in 1963 and was thus just a year younger than Abdullah. What's more, I knew the royal brothers had taken similar career paths, straight into the military. Abdullah, of course, had made the special forces his focus and had risen through the ranks to become commander of all Jordanian special forces before his father, the late King Hussein, had appointed him crown prince just days before passing away, thus leaving the kingdom to his eldest son. Feisal, by contrast, had focused on the air services. He, like his older brother, had gone to school in the U.K. and the U.S. Later he'd trained with the British Royal Air Force, completing his studies in 1985 and going on to become an accomplished pilot of fighter jets and helicopters in the Royal Jordanian Air Force. Over time, he had distinguished himself as an impressive airman and strategist. I recalled that in 2001 or 2002, Feisal had been appointed chief of the Air Staff and had been promoted to the rank of lieutenant general several years ago, later becoming deputy commander of all of Jordan's military forces. Beyond that, I knew the prince was married and had several children. But I didn't know what I could possibly say to convince him to let me stay. He was sitting on the other side of the table, working the phones but careful not to let me hear anything he was saying. I couldn't build trust if I couldn't talk to him, and I couldn't talk to him if he was on the phone. My anxiety was rising fast.

Dr. Hammami gave me a shot and then a bottle of pills to manage my pain. Just then, His Majesty reentered the bunker and we all rose. The generals saluted him. I merely stood there, waiting for the ax to fall.

The king told us to take our seats and turned to me. "Mr. Collins."

"Yes, sir."

"I understand you used our flight here to tell the world the president of the United States is missing."

My stomach tightened. "Yes, sir."

"That was a mistake."

I disagreed but held my tongue.

"I told you that in confidence. I never imagined you would tell the world."

"I didn't quote you, Your Majesty."

"You didn't have to," he replied. "The White House and Pentagon know you're with me. They know they didn't release the information. Nor would they. So that leaves me as your source."

I kept my mouth shut.

"Now ISIS knows. Iran knows. So do the Kremlin and Beijing."

No sooner had the words come out of the king's mouth than I saw a breaking news logo appear on the monitor tuned to CNN. The sound was still muted, but the network was clearly now going with the story of the potential death or capture of the American president.

I took a deep breath but maintained eye contact with the king. I wasn't sorry. I was doing my job. But I was pretty sure I was about to be kicked out of the war room, and I knew there was nothing to say that wouldn't make the situation worse.

"Your Majesty, may I make a recommendation?" Prince Feisal asked.

"No," the king said. "Mr. Collins, I need your phone."

"My phone?"

"You heard me."

"Why is that, Your Majesty?"

"Isn't it obvious?"

"Not to me, sir."

"I can't allow you to disseminate any unauthorized information, Mr. Collins. Is that clear?"

Not exactly, I thought.

"Does that mean you're going to allow me to disseminate *authorized* information?" I asked.

The king leaned forward in his seat. "Why else do you think you're here?"

"I honestly have no idea."

"The world needs to know what's happening here," he replied. "They need to hear it from a credible, independent reporter they trust. I've chosen you. You're going to be at my side during everything that happens for the next few days. However . . ."

"Sir?"

"While you're at my side throughout this crisis, Colonel Sharif here will be at your side. Nothing gets published in any way, shape, or form unless he clears it first. Do you understand?"

"That's not exactly the way the *New York Times* operates, Your Majesty."

"Do I look like I care?"

"No, sir."

"Do you want to report from the vortex of the storm or sit in the lobby?"

"I'll take the vortex."

"Very well. Now hand over your phone."

My iPhone was sitting in front of me. I slid it across the table to the king. In return, he slid back a notepad and a pen. We were in business—under military censorship, to be sure, but in business just the same.

The king then turned to his team.

"Okay, now, where are we in finding and rescuing the president?"

The prince took that one. "As you've ordered,

we have a massive aerial reconnaissance effort under way up and down Route 15, Route 35, and the adjacent roads. We're massing ground forces into the area as well. We're coordinating with the Secret Service, the Pentagon, and the American embassy downtown. But so far, nothing."

"How is that possible?"

"I don't know, Your Majesty, but we're doing everything we can."

"And you've beefed up protection around the embassy?"

"Yes, the American compound and most of the rest of the Western embassies too. But we're stretched very thin at the moment and . . ."

"And what?"

"It's a bit delicate, sir."

"You can speak freely."

"Well, sir, we're still not entirely sure whom we can trust."

"I know, but there's nothing else we can do right now. Keep giving orders and watch to see who obeys and who doesn't."

The king now turned to General al-Mufti, the air force commander. "Where are we with the palace?"

"Al-Hummar has been leveled, Your Majesty."

"There's no chance of ISIS getting control of vital papers or communications equipment?"

"No, sir—we've firebombed every square inch."

"And how many ISIS forces are we dealing with?" the king asked, turning to General Jum'a, commander of Jordan's ground forces.

"Our best guess is about fifteen thousand."

"Just ISIS?"

"No, ISIS and al-Hirak."

"The Brotherhood?"

"No—for the moment they seem to be standing down."

"How much of Amman has ISIS taken?"

"Our forces are clashing with them throughout the city. They've taken out the radio stations and captured two banks. But at this point I wouldn't say they control a single quadrant of the city."

"Do we?" asked the king.

6

"It's a very fluid situation just now, Your Majesty," the general said.

It was hardly a satisfactory answer. The capital was under siege. Control of the kingdom itself was in jeopardy.

"What about casualties so far?" the king asked, abruptly changing topics.

"The prime minister is in critical condition," Prince Feisal replied. "Most of the cabinet is dead. The mayor of Amman and most of the tribal leaders we invited to the summit are dead too. So is the White House chief of staff, the national security advisor, and all of the congressional delegation that came with the president."

This was going from bad to worse so quickly I could barely breathe.

"Where is Kamal?" the king asked, referring to Kamal Jeddah, director of the Mukhabarat, the Jordanian intelligence directorate.

"Kamal is dead too, Your Majesty," the prince replied.

I couldn't believe it.

"So is Ali Sa'id."

That much I knew. Sa'id had died at my side. I'd been the one to feel for a pulse and find nothing, and hearing his name in this setting was almost more than I could bear.

"How many casualties overall?" the king asked.

The prince turned to General Jum'a.

"Your Majesty, at this point we're estimating over a thousand people dead within the palace compound—not counting the terrorists, of course," the general reported.

The king was silent. I put my hand over my mouth. I didn't know exactly how many had been in attendance at the summit, but the number of casualties struck me as upward of 90 percent.

"How many survived?" the king asked.

"Fewer than a hundred, Your Majesty," the prince said.

"How many fewer?"

"It's too soon to say."

"How many?"

"Your Majesty, please—we will get you updated figures as soon as we can. But—"

"How . . . many . . . survived?" the king said quietly.

There was another long pause.

"Some, of course, were able to escape," the general said. "And some—thanks be to Allah—were evacuated to area hospitals. The minister of justice, for example, is in critical condition, but I'm afraid he isn't expected to live through the week. I've been told that several members of the Palestinian delegation miraculously escaped, unharmed or nearly so. Youssef Kuttab, for one, and several others. But I really don't think . . ."

He stopped midsentence.

The king waited, but his patience was growing thin. He wanted numbers, and he wanted them now.

Finally the prince stepped in. "Fewer than a hundred, Your Majesty."

"I'm not going to ask again."

The prince took a deep breath. "We estimate no more than fifty survived."

The doctor gasped, as did the young aide standing in the corner.

"This number includes my family?"

"It includes everyone in the vehicle you escaped in, Your Majesty—all seven of you. Prime Minister Lavi and President Mansour too."

"For now," said General al-Mufti.

"What do you mean?"

"It doesn't look good, Your Majesty."

"What exactly do we know about their status?"

"President Mansour is at a hospital in Ramallah," al-Mufti replied. "He was shot in the back. He's just come out of surgery, but it's touch and go."

"And Daniel?"

The prince fielded that one. "The prime minister was rushed to Hadassah Medical Center near Jerusalem. He's still in surgery. I just got off the phone with Ari Shalit. He said . . ."

The prince stopped and looked at me.

"It's okay," the king said. "Mr. Collins isn't going to tell anyone. Right, Mr. Collins?"

"Yes, sir."

"I have your word."

"You do, sir."

"Very well. Proceed."

Feisal hesitated for a moment, but then did as he was asked. "It's pretty grim, Your Majesty. Ari said it's not clear the prime minister is going to make it."

"Why not?"

"Ari said the PM sustained three bullet wounds, two to the back and one to the leg. He lost an enormous amount of blood. They nearly lost him twice on the chopper flight across the river. Apparently it was that Mossad agent, the woman, who saved his life."

"Yael?" I asked. "Yael Katzir?"

"Yes, her," the prince said. "She set up a blood transfusion midflight and performed CPR on him—twice. Still might not have been enough, but . . ."

Feisal didn't finish the sentence. What more was there to say?

The room was silent. I was in shock. I don't know why. I'd known Lavi and Mansour were both in bad shape. When they'd first been shot, we'd all thought they were dead right then. It was the king who'd realized they were still breathing, still had a pulse. But somehow once they were put on the choppers and evacuated back over the Jordan River, I guess I'd just assumed everything would be okay. I couldn't bear the thought that they both might soon be gone—especially after nearly consummating a peace deal they'd worked on so hard for so long.

Suddenly one of the phones in front of Feisal rang. The prince answered it immediately, then handed the receiver to the king.

"Yes," he said without expression. "Yes, I understand. Very well. Good-bye."

I feared the worst and was absolutely stunned by what the king said next. "That was Jack at CIA. We may have found the president."

Everyone instinctively stood. Finally there was some desperately needed good news. *Thank God for Jack Vaughn,* I thought. The director of the Central Intelligence Agency and I had clashed pretty hard in recent days. But I was suddenly thrilled to hear his name mentioned. He and his team were on the case. Maybe things were going to take a turn for the better.

"An American spy satellite has just picked up the signal of the emergency beacon coming from the Secret Service vehicle the president was riding in," the king said. "Jack said it wasn't automatically activated, meaning the vehicle hasn't crashed. It was set off manually. Which is a good sign. Someone is with the vehicle—someone who knows what he's doing, knows that the beacon is in the car and how to trigger it."

"But?" I asked.

"But if it's the agents protecting the president, why aren't they on a secure satphone back to Washington, calling for help and providing a clearer sense of what's happening?"

"Where is the signal coming from?" General Jum'a asked. "I've got extraction teams on standby, ready to go."

"Where would they be deployed from?"

"Here, Your Majesty. They're on the tarmac right now."

"Good," the king said. "Can you redirect ground forces to the site as well?"

"I can, but there are risks."

"We still don't know whom we can trust?"

"I'm afraid not."

"Do you trust these extraction forces?"

"Implicitly, Your Majesty. These are my best men. Bedouins, all. Most are sons of men you trained and served with yourself."

"Can you put them on a secure channel so I can talk with them directly and no other unit can listen in?"

"Absolutely."

"Good, then put them in the air—but don't tell any other unit."

"Yes, sir."

"But, Your Majesty, doesn't Jack want to send in U.S. forces to rescue the president?" I asked, taking a risk by interrupting but trying to understand what was about to play out.

"Of course," the king said. "The Pentagon is deploying a SEAL team off one of the carriers in the Med. But we're closer, and Jack's afraid if ISIS forces have the president pinned down . . ."

He didn't have to finish. The thought was too terrible to contemplate.

"The signal location?" General al-Mufti prompted.

"Near the airport. Get your men in the air. You

and I can give them precise coordinates in a few moments."

"Of course, sir."

"Your Majesty, can I go with them?" I asked, moving toward the door.

"Absolutely not," al-Mufti said.

General Jum'a concurred and the prince was about to, but I spoke first. "Please, sir, I need to see this. You said it yourself—this is why you've got me here."

"It's out of the question, Mr. Collins," al-Mufti shot back. "His Majesty said you'd be at his side during the crisis, not out in the field."

"Please, Your Majesty, Colonel Sharif can go with me," I said. "He'll keep me out of trouble. But I need to go, sir. I need to see the rescue operation. The world needs to hear this story from me, not from a government spokesman."

When the king said nothing, the prince spoke up. "What if it goes badly, Your Majesty?"

"All the more reason," the king said. "Okay, Collins—I want you to go. But Sharif goes with you, and nothing gets published unless he or I approve it."

"Thank you, Your Majesty."

"You're welcome. And may God be with you."

7

Lieutenant General Abdul Jum'a led the way to the tarmac.

Colonel Sharif and I followed close behind and soon found ourselves climbing into the back of an MH-6 helicopter. Known as the "Little Bird," the chopper would serve as the command-and-control aircraft for the unfolding mission as the general directed the movements of six Black Hawk helicopters and the elite SF operators they were carrying. And Sharif and I would be able to see and hear everything that was happening in real time.

We were still buckling up as the two-man crew up front lifted off. Soon we were racing south by southeast to an area not far from Queen Alia International Airport, where the emergency beacon's signal was coming from.

So much was still unknown. Were the president and his security detail out in the open or in an urban area? Were they alone or under assault by ISIS forces? And what exactly was the rescue strategy?

With the president's life potentially in imminent danger, there was no time to develop a detailed and proper plan. Rather than gather all kinds of intelligence and put his men through several hours or days of training, the general was going to have to improvise, and that was going to make a risky situation all the more dangerous.

I had a hundred questions. Was there any way to approach the target by stealth? If not, what would be the best way for the general's men to get to the president and extract him? How was Jum'a going to handle the fact that it was the middle of the day and we weren't going to have the cover of darkness? What if the enemy had RPGs? Would it be possible for the approaching aircraft to be shot down? If that happened, then what? If there was no plan A, what was plan B?

These and other questions were racing through my mind, but for the moment I didn't dare ask any of them. It seemed best merely to keep quiet and observe.

The general was sitting in a row of seats ahead of the colonel and me, just behind the pilot and copilot, before a communications console he was powering up and preparing to use. I had no idea what he was thinking. But nor did I want to bother him. For whatever was unclear at the moment, two things *were* clear: this guy did not want me on his chopper, and time was of the essence.

My job, I knew, was to document everything that happened without getting in the way or complicating a tense situation more than I already was. One thought crossed my mind: I was dying to take some pictures. In times of crisis, readers wanted to see what was happening behind the scenes. They wanted to try to understand how leaders made decisions and what it was like to be "in the room" in moments of great stress and drama. My phone had been taken away, so that wasn't an option. But just then, as if he were reading my thoughts, the colonel nudged me. Without saying anything— only the pilots were talking—he handed me a small backpack he'd brought on board and motioned for me to open it. As I did, I was speechless. Inside the bag I found a nearly brand-new digital SLR camera. And this wasn't any old model. It was a six-thousand-dollar Nikon D4, professional grade, top-of-the-line. As I dug deeper, I found a high-powered Nikkor telephoto lens as well. I couldn't believe it. Sharif hadn't let me head into the field empty-handed after all.

I smiled and slapped the colonel on the back to thank him. This was far more than I needed and probably more than I knew how to handle. I was a war correspondent, after all, not a photojournalist, and this was like handing Tiger Woods's personal clubs to some kid at a miniature golf course. Nevertheless, with the colonel's gesture of permission, I took a few shots of the general at work and then quickly attached the telephoto lens.

Then Colonel Sharif nudged me again. As I turned, he handed me a pair of headphones with an attached microphone. He was already wearing a set and pantomimed that I should put mine on immediately. As I did, I could hear the general's cool, professional, unflappable voice. And he was talking to me.

"Mr. Collins, can you hear me back there?"

"Yes, General, I can."

"Good. Now listen, back at the palace, when you were preparing to evacuate the king and his family, you were one of the last people to see the president, correct?"

"Yes, sir, that's true."

"You saw him get into the Suburban next to the king's vehicle?"

I thought about that for a moment. I wanted to say yes, but it wasn't exactly true. "No, I saw the SUV pull away, but the president and his men were already in the vehicle."

"How many agents were with him?"

"Well, at least two, but maybe not more," I said, closing my eyes and trying desperately to remember every detail. "I saw the driver and another agent in the front passenger seat. But I can't say there were more. Most of them were killed in the firefight, as you know."

"The king just radioed me," the general replied. "He says he's pretty sure he saw an agent in the backseat, covering the president with his own body."

"That could be," I said. "I don't know. I was just trying to get our Suburban started."

As I said this, I noticed the chopper was now banking toward the desert, not toward Amman. And it wasn't just us. All six Black Hawks beside and behind us were changing course too. Why the new course? Why weren't we heading back to the area around the airport? Was the president on the move?

The general relayed the information I had given him to the rest of the troops. The president had at least two agents with him, possibly three. But even if there were four agents with him, which was possible but seemed unlikely, it wasn't going to be nearly enough protection if they really had been found and attacked by ISIS.

Worse, while the Chevy Suburban the president was in was solid—armor-plated with bulletproof windows like all the Suburbans used by the United States Secret Service—it wasn't nearly as secure as the fleet of presidential limousines, each of which was known by agents as "the Beast." These specially designed Cadillacs were essentially luxury battle tanks. Each door was made of reinforced steel eight inches thick, built to withstand the direct impact of an antitank missile. The trunk and gas tank were armor-plated. The windows could withstand armor-piercing bullets fired at point-blank range. Each limo had its own oxygen supply, fire-suppression system, and special steel rims supporting Kevlar-reinforced tires that could continue at high speeds for miles even after being blown out in an attack. Each model also had a supply of the president's blood type on board, the most secure satellite communications known to man, night-vision technology, and even a state-of-the-art system that would allow its driver to navigate through fire and smoke. The Suburban the president was in couldn't possibly compare. How long could he and his men hold out under a direct assault?

Suddenly the king's voice came over the radio. He explained that he and Prince Feisal had just opened up a secure conference call with the American vice president, the director of the CIA, the chairman of the Joint Chiefs, the director of the Secret Service, and the commander of CENTCOM. For the first time, King Abdullah now gave General Jum'a precise coordinates of the beacon's location and explained that momentarily they'd be sending live images of the location from two different sources, a U.S. spy satellite and a Jordanian drone.

"The signal is coming from a warehouse several kilometers north of the interchange between Routes 35 and 15," the king said. "And it's been completely overrun by the enemy."

8

★ ★ ★

One of the monitors in the communications console flickered to life.

Though my angle was partially blocked by General Jum'a, the images I could see were at once compelling and chilling. Clearly visible via a spy satellite feed was an area that was part industrial and part agricultural. I could see a compound composed of seven main buildings. Six appeared to be warehouses. The seventh looked like it housed the main offices for whatever company this was. The entire rectangular site was enclosed by a high concrete wall and surrounded on the north, east, and west sides by open fields, though there appeared to be a factory of some sort just across the field to the west. On the south side was a two-lane road, and across the street there appeared to be a nursery of some sort, as there were dozens and dozens of greenhouses covering multiple acres. Down the road a bit was a major oil depot.

We were patched in on the conference call but could hear only the king and prince, not the principals in Washington or the CENTCOM commander, who I assumed was in Tampa. The king explained that the beacon's signal was coming from the midsize building located in the center of the compound.

The general opened a laptop, connected it to the monitor, and then took a moment to highlight the specific warehouse on his screen and transmitted the image to the men on the Black Hawks around us. "What exactly is this place?" Jum'a asked as he pulled up a GPS map on a separate screen.

"The factory you see on the west side is the SADAFCO plant," Prince Feisal said. "We think the compound we're looking at was recently purchased by SADAFCO as a warehousing and shipping center. But my men are checking on that. Stand by."

I turned to the colonel. I didn't want to talk over my headset microphone as it would be heard by everyone in the chopper and by the king and prince as well. But I had no idea what SADAFCO was. The colonel saw my questioning look and quickly took out a pad and pen and scribbled me a note.

SADAFCO—Saudia Dairy and Foodstuff Company
Largest producer of milk and dairy products in Arab world, or one of them.
Also make foodstuffs—cereals, tomato paste, frozen french fries, etc.
This must be their Jordanian subsidiary.

Why in the world was the signal coming from there, of all places? That was my first thought. My second thought was whether there could be a connection between the ISIS terrorists and the Saudis.

None of that was clear. What was clear—and what made the images so terrifying—was that the place was crawling with heavily armed men. Whether they were ISIS for sure or some other group, I couldn't tell. But I counted more than sixty fighters, all wearing black hoods, and several were holding rocket-propelled grenade launchers. They had taken up positions on all sides of the compound and were using a tractor-trailer truck to block the main entrance. Snipers were clearly visible in the upper stories of the office building, and several more could be seen looking out the doorways of the warehouses. Whoever these guys were, they weren't running a food processing plant.

Another monitor on the communications console now flickered to life. I could see this one a little better, though again my view was partially blocked by the general. But it appeared to be the feed from a drone over the site providing thermal images of the building from which the signal was coming. While it looked to me like a warehouse from the outside, the images suggested it was more of a garage. I could see the outlines of numerous vehicles, including one that potentially could be the president's. I could also see the heat signatures of dozens of people in the facility. Most were grouped in what might have been an office of some kind in the back right-hand corner. Others were clumped in the remaining three corners of the building.

"General, are you seeing the feed from the drone?" the king asked.

"I am, Your Majesty," Jum'a replied. "Is that the president's Suburban on the far right in the back, near the office and all the people?"

"We believe so," the king said. "The Secret Service director says the signal is strong and authentic. It's not being jammed or manipulated. As best he can tell, that's the real thing."

"But am I seeing this right—the doors are open, and no one's in the vehicle?"

"I'm afraid that's right."

"So what do you want to do, Your Majesty?"

"Can your men take that compound?"

"Yes, sir—in less than two minutes."

"Can you get the president out safely?"

"Honestly, Your Majesty, I can't say. There are an awful lot of variables in play here. But an assault is not our only option. We could surround the place and try to negotiate his release."

"No," said the king. "The vice president has ruled that out. The U.S. won't negotiate with ISIS under any circumstances. And Jack Vaughn is worried that if they're given any more time, they will behead him."

The very notion gave me flashbacks of seeing Abu Khalif, the ISIS emir, behead the deputy director of Iraqi intelligence just outside of Baghdad. That was horrifying enough. I couldn't imagine the sight of the president of the United States being beheaded. Surely they would do it on camera. Surely they would post it on YouTube for all the world to see.

I tried to imagine what was going through the vice president's mind at the moment. Martin Holbrooke had been a senator from Ohio for more than thirty years when he'd been tapped by Harrison Taylor to be the VP nominee. He certainly had lots of Washington experience. But was he ready for this? Was anyone?

"This all presupposes the president is even in that building," the general said.

"Right."

"We still don't know that."

"No, we don't—not for certain," the king conceded.

"Can the Secret Service say for sure? Do they have a way to know, like we know where you are at all times?"

"Good question," said the king. "I'm sure they do. But wait one."

He put us on hold, and we waited. But not for long.

"Yes, they have a way to know," said the king. "The president wears a special watch, a Jorg Gray 6500 Chronograph. It was picked out by the president but specially built for the Service. It operates as a panic button and has a tracking device inside it."

"And?"

"And right now none of the American satellites, drones, or other assets are picking up the signal from the watch. They can't say why. Could be any number of reasons."

"You mean the watch could have been removed from him and destroyed."

"Yes, that's possible. But there are other possibilities as well."

"Bottom line—can they say the president is in that building?"

"No, General, at the moment they cannot. But they can't rule it out either."

"Well, it's your call, Your Majesty. What do you want us to do?"

"Give me a moment," said the king. "And make sure your men are ready to go if I give the order."

"Yes, Your Majesty. I certainly will."

Again we were put on hold. We still couldn't hear the conversation between the king and the American leaders. But it was now clear to me why our pilots weren't proceeding straight to the site but were instead circling over the desert. Until the general was sure what his orders were, he didn't want to tip the enemy off that he was coming. So we waited.

And waited. Much longer than the last pause. Two minutes went by. Then five. Then ten.

I said nothing, only glanced at Colonel Sharif. The look on his face said it all. He was just as bewildered by the delay as I was. If the Jordanians were going to strike, they had to move hard and fast. If the president wasn't in that Suburban—and clearly no one was in any of those vehicles in that building—then his life was in grave danger. There wasn't a second to spare. He might be killed in a rescue attempt. But he was going to be killed anyway. The only hope was a forcible extraction. And it had to happen now.

Finally our headsets crackled back to life.

"Okay, General, they want you and your men to go in. God help you. The fate of us all is in your hands."

9

★ ★ ★

I opened my notebook and furiously scribbled down every word.

"The fate of us all is in your hands."

It was a sobering line, one I wanted to ask the king about when I saw him again. It suggested the monarch saw not only the president's personal fate hanging in the balance but his own, his kingdom's, his people's. In many ways, he had prepared his entire life for a moment like this. Yet he was not in the field. He was back in the bunker. He had to trust the men under his command, and if they got it wrong . . .

The general ordered the choppers to bank back toward the target and hit the deck. We were going to come in low and fast. Then he ordered his commanders on the ground to mass tanks and armored personnel carriers at two points, one kilometer east of the compound and one kilometer west, both significantly off the main road and out of sight of all civilians.

"Do you want us to cut off traffic?" one of the battalion commanders asked. "There are a lot of trucks and other vehicles passing through that area."

To my surprise, the general said no.

"We don't want to do anything to tip them off that we're coming," he explained. "Let everything proceed as normal."

But that wasn't all. Jum'a then instructed his special forces teams on the ground to commandeer buses, minivans, and SUVs and be prepared to drive up to the compound at normal speeds, like all other traffic, upon his command.

Next the general asked the prince if there were any calls being made to or from mobile phones or landlines at the target site.

Feisal said both Jordanian and U.S. intel assets were monitoring the site but that they weren't picking up anything. "It's all quiet—oddly quiet," the prince said. "We're trying to monitor Internet traffic at the site too. But so far, nothing. They seem to have shut down the Wi-Fi system."

The general thanked the prince, then gave his men their orders.

"Two minutes out," he said when he was done. "Radio silence from this point forward."

And all was quiet, save the roar of the rotors above us.

Colonel Sharif reached behind him, grabbed an MP5 machine gun, and inserted a fresh magazine. Then he reached for two flak jackets, put one on, and gave the other to me. It suddenly dawned on me that we might not be staying on the chopper. We might be getting off. I pulled out the gold pocket watch I always carried with me, the one my grandfather gave to me before his death. We had less than a minute. I could feel my heart pounding in my chest and a surge of adrenaline coursed through my system.

Suddenly the pilot pulled back sharply on the yoke. Rather than flying barely fifty feet off the ground, we climbed rapidly to two hundred feet, then three hundred, and kept climbing until we leveled out at five hundred feet.

We were less than thirty seconds out. I was pretty sure I could see the compound, but now we banked sharply to our right and began a circling pattern around the target. The Black Hawks didn't follow. Nor had they climbed as high as we had. They were still racing for the compound at an altitude I figured to be no more than a hundred feet.

Just then our helicopter was rocked by a massive explosion. One of the warehouses, in the far left corner of the compound, erupted in an enormous ball of fire. But how? Had someone inside detonated a bomb? Or had someone just fired a missile? I looked to my left and saw nothing. But when I turned and looked out the window to my right, I saw an Apache attack helicopter—and it was firing again.

Two more Hellfire missiles streaked across the afternoon sky. I followed the contrails and watched spellbound as one destroyed the main office building. An instant later, the second missile took out the 18-wheeler that had been blocking the entrance. Then a Cobra gunship swooped in below us and to our left. Its pilot opened fire on the armed rebels patrolling the grounds, then trained his fire on the rebels stationed in the doorways of the remaining five warehouses. One by one I watched men in black hoods shredded into oblivion.

The Apache opened fire again. More Hellfire missiles rocketed down into the compound. They weren't targeted at the buildings, however. Rather, they exploded in the open spaces, vaporizing the remaining visible terrorists but more importantly creating deafening booms and raging fires I had to assume were intended to stun and disorient the enemy combatants inside the main building.

Now the Black Hawks moved into position. Two hovered over the warehouse where the president's Suburban was located. A moment later I could see the king's most elite forces fast-roping to the warehouse roof. Two other Black Hawks broke left. The remaining two broke right. The commandos in all four choppers were soon fast-roping to the ground, then scrambling to secure the perimeter. And that's when the shooting started.

The initial explosions had done their job. They had caught the terrorists completely unaware. They had temporarily thrown the enemy into confusion. But some of the ISIS soldiers were firing back. Within seconds, the fighting had reached a fever pitch. From our vantage point, watching the drone and satellite feeds and looking out the window to our left, we could see the Jordanian commandos in the heart of the compound. They were using Semtex to blow the doors off the warehouse on the north and east sides. Then we watched mesmerized as they tossed flash grenades into the main warehouse.

The thermal images on the second monitor revealed the chaos inside the facility. The king's commandos were now storming in from all directions. They were firing at anything that moved. I could see bodies dropping, including some of the king's men. But they didn't stop. They kept firing, kept pushing forward, kept advancing toward the back office, though they were encountering fierce resistance.

I was feverishly snapping photos through the windows of the Little Bird as well as at the images from the two video monitors. I was also trying to keep track of the radio chatter. But it was in Arabic and it was coming fast and furious. My Arabic wasn't horrible, but I certainly wasn't getting it all. Too much was happening to take it all in. And then, without warning, the Little Bird plummeted. I realized too late it was a planned descent as we hit the ground hard in the driveway just yards from the remains of the tractor-trailer out front, now engulfed in flames.

The moment we slammed to the deck, Colonel Sharif threw open the side door and jumped out. When he shouted at me to follow, for a moment I didn't move. Was he crazy? The situation was hardly secure. There was an intense gun battle under way. In the chopper, we'd had the perfect vantage point. Why in the world would we get out now?

I'm not saying I was scared. Okay, I was scared. He had an MP5. I had a Nikon. He was a trained soldier. I was just a journalist. Besides, I'd had enough excitement for one day. I'd already been shot at—and hit. I didn't want to go back into the fray. I wanted to stay with General Jum'a, high above the action. It wasn't just safer; it was an ideal way to track all the elements of the battle. But now the general was shouting at me to get out. The colonel was unfastening my seat belt and yelling at me to move faster. He wasn't kidding. This was really happening.

I ripped off my headset, grabbed the camera bag, and scrambled out of the chopper after him. And no sooner had my feet touched solid ground than I felt the Little Bird lift off behind me and race out of the hot zone.

"Come on, Collins, let's go," Sharif yelled over the nearly deafening roar of the helicopter blades and the multiple explosions. *"Follow me."*

10

* * *

I did as I was told, though I hadn't much choice.

To my shock, Sharif didn't head for the cover of the perimeter. I guess I'd expected him to put me *close* to the action, at the side of some of the Jordanian forces, to see and hear and smell the battle for myself. Instead, the colonel took me into the heart of darkness.

Suddenly we were racing into the compound, even as the ear-shattering explosions and blistering staccato of machine-gun fire echoed through the courtyard. Sharif didn't take us around the raging flames of the 18-wheeler. He literally jumped right through them, and I had no choice but to follow suit. He was, after all, the only one with a weapon, and I didn't dare get separated.

Inside the courtyard, Sharif was running flat out, and I struggled to keep up. He was in far better shape. I was gasping for air. Just then fresh machine-gun fire opened up from a window above us. Fortunately it wasn't aimed at us but at an armored personnel carrier that was coming in behind us. The ground reinforcements were beginning to arrive, and they were drawing intense resistance.

The colonel broke right, then dove through a gaping hole in the wall of that warehouse. Terrified, I dove too. By a minor miracle, the camera wasn't damaged, though I did drop the bag with all the attachments. I should have worn it like a backpack, but I wasn't thinking clearly. I turned and saw the bag through the smoke, about twenty yards away. I started to go back for it, but out in the courtyard bullets were now whizzing in all directions. A moment before we'd been able to race through unharmed. Now it was a kill box out there, and there was no way I could retrieve it.

Then again, how could we go forward? Gunfire suddenly erupted on the other side of the warehouse floor. I had no idea if it was from the terrorists or friendly fire from the Jordanians. There was no way either side could see us clearly. To them we were only shadows moving through the smoke. That's certainly how they all looked to us.

Scrambling to my feet, I ducked into a row of pallets piled high with canned goods and other foodstuffs. Sharif aimed his MP5 and returned fire. Then he ducked in beside me and took cover behind the pallets.

Why we were in this particular building I had no idea. If we were going to take such risks, then I wanted to be in the main event, in the next warehouse over. That's where the president's Suburban was. That's presumably where the president himself was. That's certainly where the biggest gun battle was taking place. We needed to be there too. Instead, we were hunkered down in a warehouse that, as far as I could tell, had no strategic significance. We couldn't go back. We couldn't press forward. And the raging fires of the main office building were rapidly spreading. The flames had reached this building and were leaping up the walls. The entire warehouse was going to be consumed in the next few minutes. We had to get out.

If that wasn't enough, we knew for sure there were terrorists above us—the ones that had been shooting from the window on the second floor seconds earlier.

Through the flames, I noticed a stairway to my right. When I pointed it out to Sharif, he quickly motioned for me to get down and stay behind him. The reason was fast becoming obvious. The terrorists were either going to be consumed by the fire racing to the second floor or get suffocated by the thick black billows of smoke that were surging into the rafters—or they were coming down those stairs any moment.

The heat was infernal. Sweat was pouring down my face and back. My shirt was already soaked. I mopped my brow, steadied my camera, and started shooting just as Sharif did. Sure enough, three masked terrorists came barreling down the staircase. They weren't expecting us. Sharif unloaded an entire clip. The men were dead before they hit the ground. I'd captured it all, but Sharif wasn't finished. He raced over to the men, checked their pulses to make sure they were really gone, then pulled off their hoods as I kept snapping pictures. Then I rifled through their pockets and came out with cell phones, maps, and other articles. I shot all of it, item by item.

As he began loading the items into his own backpack, I got curious. Looking up the stairwell into the hazy darkness, I hung the camera around my neck, pried an AK-47 from one of the terrorists' death grips, and began moving slowly up the stairs.

When the colonel realized what I was doing, he must have thought I was crazy. He yelled at me to come back. No one in his right mind would be going up those stairs at that moment. The entire building was now on fire. We had maybe a matter of minutes before the whole structure collapsed. But I kept moving, and I'm not sure I can tell you why. If I'd taken some time to think about it, I would never have done it. But I wasn't operating on rational thought at that moment. I was going by instinct, and my instincts were calling me upward.

Every step seemed an act of delayed suicide, yet I couldn't stop. More gunfire erupted behind me, but I kept moving, step by step, into the unknown. I'd thought the heat was unbearable when we'd first entered the building. But it was getting worse and worse by the second. When I reached the top of the stairs, I could barely see. The smoke was nearly impenetrable. It and the flames were sucking out what little oxygen was left in the air. I dropped to my knees, then quickly glanced back. Sharif was no longer with me. From the sound of the gunfire below, he was in full contact with the enemy. I was alone.

Crawling forward, I could barely see the window from which the terrorists had been firing, but I decided this was my destination. I scrambled ahead, stopping every few moments to check my six, terrified someone in a black hood was going to come up and shoot me in the back. Yet the farther I pressed forward, the less I could see behind me. My eyes were watering. I was choking on the smoke and fumes. The gunshot wound to my left arm was throbbing.

I was now crawling on my belly. The only air that was left was down here. The Nikon was on my back. I still held the Kalashnikov, sweeping it forward from side to side as I crawled, just in case.

Why was I doing this? It made no sense. I was moving farther away from the center of the story and putting myself in grave danger in the process. Parts of the roof were collapsing all around me. The holes created new sources of oxygen, giving new fuel to the flames now shooting twenty or thirty feet into the air. I was completely drenched with sweat. I could barely breathe or see. But as I reached the window, I found the bodies of two terrorists. I checked their pulses. They were both dead. I went through their pockets for phones or IDs or anything else useful but found nothing. Was that it? Was this why I'd come? I'd risked my life for what? For nothing?

Cursing myself, I ripped off their hoods and took a few pictures, then turned to leave. But then I began to panic. What if I couldn't make it back? What if I died here, foolishly, without cause and without any idea where I was going next? I thought about my mom. I thought about my brother, Matt, and his wife, Annie. I thought about their kids. I thought, too, about Yael. I desperately wanted to see them. I wasn't ready to die. Not yet. Not here.

As I scrambled back toward the stairs, I stumbled upon something I hadn't seen coming the other direction. It was a leg. A body. But whoever it was wasn't dead. He was groaning. He was bleeding heavily, but he was alive. And this wasn't a terrorist. He was dressed in a suit. I rolled him over and to my astonishment found it was an American. This was an agent of the United States Secret Service. He had a sharpshooter rifle at his side and a gaping wound in his chest. His breathing was shallow. His pulse was erratic.

I threw the strap of the Kalashnikov around my neck so the weapon itself was now slung over my back, side by side with the camera. Then I scrambled around the agent and began dragging him toward the stairs. There was no way I could stand up. The flames along what was left of the roof were coming down closer and closer to the floor. We had only seconds left, so I used every ounce of energy I had to drag the agent across the floor, inch by inch, begging God to allow us to make it to the stairs before it was too late.

But just then the roof above us collapsed, and part of the floor below us gave way.

11

Amid the blazing wreckage, we plummeted toward the first floor.

But we didn't fall the entire way. We dropped, instead, onto a row of pallets, then rolled off and landed with a thud on the concrete floor. My left arm was in excruciating pain. My knees had smashed on the pavement and were killing me. But as I looked up and wiped sweat and soot from my eyes, I could see the agent's suit was on fire. I summoned what little strength I had left, tossed the Kalashnikov to the side, and threw myself on him, extinguishing the flames with my own body. It had all happened so quickly I didn't think the agent had actually suffered any serious burns. But I feared the fall might have finished him off. Again I checked his pulse. It was weak, but it was there. He was still alive, though barely.

I turned to look for the colonel, to call for help, but instead found myself face-to-face with one of the terrorists. Shrouded in a black hood and covered in blood, he was pointing an AK-47 and screaming at me in Arabic.

"Get up—get up and prepare to die!"

Slowly, and with some difficulty, I rose to my feet, my hands in the air, not wanting to make any sudden movements. His eyes were locked on mine, and they were wild with a toxic mixture of rage and self-righteousness. I'd never seen anything quite like it, and I instantly lost all hope that this could turn out well.

And then something changed. I couldn't see his full expression, of course, just his eyes, but behind the rage something was different. Whatever was fueling his emotions at that split second didn't soften, nor did it weaken, but it did alter somewhat.

"You," he said, shaking the barrel of the machine gun at me. "I've seen you."

I said nothing.

"You're . . . you're the infidel . . . the one who interviewed the emir," he said, practically spewing the words out of his mouth as if they were laced with poison. "You filthy *kafir*—you will pay for what you have done!"

I was frozen—couldn't move, couldn't think, couldn't speak. I saw the man's finger preparing to pull the trigger, and I wish I could tell you that I reacted in some way—that I lunged at him or dove for cover or at least closed my eyes and prayed. But I just stood there. Eyes wide open. Waiting for death. And then a machine gun erupted to my right and the terrorist's head exploded.

Before I fully realized what was happening, Colonel Sharif was rushing to my side to see if I was all right. I wasn't, though I told him I was fine.

Smoke was curling out of the barrel of his MP5 as a squad of Jordanian commandos came rushing by.

"Clear," I heard one of them say.

"You sure you're okay?" the colonel asked.

I couldn't answer. Instead I drew Sharif's attention to the agent.

"Who is he?" Sharif asked, dropping to the man's side and checking his vitals.

"I have no idea," I replied.

"Where did you find him?"

"Upstairs, near the window."

"What was he doing up there?"

I just shook my head.

Sharif pulled out a radio and called for a medic. Moments later a team of four men rushed in. They immediately put the agent on a stretcher and raced him out to a chopper that was landing in the courtyard. At the same time, Sharif grabbed my arm and led me out of the inferno—and just in time, for we had no sooner begun to cross the courtyard than the entire building collapsed in a huge ball of sparks and smoke.

I turned and looked at the burning wreckage. I just stood there for a few moments, watching it. Then I heard Sharif telling me to follow him again. I wasn't sure that was a good idea, but it was dawning on me that the entire site was now secure. All of the terrorists must now be dead or in custody.

Soon I found myself stepping inside the next warehouse over. It was cavernous, much larger than the others, and it was swarming with Jordanian commandos. Some were tending to their wounded. Others were collecting clues or taking photos as if it were a crime scene. One soldier was videotaping the scene, presumably for the king and the prince, perhaps even to uplink to the White House Situation Room, the war room in the Pentagon, and CENTCOM. The floor was littered with shell casings, shrapnel, and shards of safety glass from the blown-out windows of one vehicle after another. The metallic, acrid smell of gunpowder hung in the air, mixed with the stench of the fires all around us.

Instinctively, I grabbed the Nikon around my neck and began snapping photos as well.

But Sharif pulled me aside. "Stop," he said.

"Why?"

"It can wait," he said quietly.

"For what?" I pressed. "This is why I'm here."

"Trust me," he replied. "It can wait."

Sharif asked me to come with him. I didn't want to miss anything. I had an unprecedented world exclusive, if only the king—and my editors back home—would let me run with the story. (That, of course, assumed I hadn't been fired yet, though I knew I'd cross that bridge later.) Reluctantly, I did let go of my camera and let it dangle around my neck as the colonel brought me to the very back of the warehouse.

There it was—the president's bullet-ridden Chevy Suburban.

I stiffened. The scene was eerie—haunting, really. The two front doors were open. So were the back doors. The bodies of three Secret Service agents lay before me. I peered into the backseat of the SUV. It was covered with blood. And on the concrete floor was a trail of blood leading away from the Suburban and out a side door.

"Tell me you found the president," I said, suddenly sure they hadn't.

"We haven't," Sharif said, confirming my suspicion.

"Please tell me he's safe."

"I can't."

"Tell me you know where he is," I pressed.

"I'm sorry, Collins; we have no idea."

PART TWO

12

* * *

We landed back at the air base in Marka just after 8 p.m. local time.

It was now one o'clock in the afternoon in New York and Washington, and I knew Allen and his bosses had to be furious at me for not answering my phone.

As we headed into the bunker, I asked Colonel Sharif to brief me on what was happening in the outside world. He might not be authorized to give me back my iPhone, I argued, but I couldn't do my job if I had no idea what everyone else was reporting. He agreed and summarized several of the stories he was reading on his Android.

Agence France-Presse was reporting casualty figures of more than five hundred dead in the attack on the peace summit, though Sharif and I knew the real figure was, tragically, double that number.

Reuters was reporting that Palestinian president Salim Mansour was now in guarded condition at a hospital in Ramallah but was increasingly expected to make a full recovery.

Al Jazeera and the Associated Press were reporting rumors of a major military operation not far from the Amman airport. Interviews with unnamed local residents suggested a heavy concentration of Jordanian ground and air forces and large explosions in an industrial park just off the intersection of Routes 15 and 35. So far, however, Sharif noted, neither story even hinted that this operation might have anything to do with the hunt for President Taylor.

The big story, far and away, was the rumor—driven by the Drudge Report and my tweets—that the president of the United States was missing.

Sharif checked the *New York Times* home page.

"Your story is the lead," he said. "It was posted twenty-two minutes ago."

"So they went with it after all," I said, not sure if I was more surprised or angry.

"How could they not?" Sharif said. "Once Drudge moved it, every news organization in the world picked it up."

"You don't know Allen and the brass."

"What were they going to do?" Sharif asked as we showed our IDs to the MPs guarding the general headquarters building and ran our backpacks, camera gear, and other supplies through the X-ray machine, stepped through metal detectors, and were patted down for good measure. "Their top correspondent in the region broke the story. Sure, you did it on social media, but no one knows the difference anymore. Or cares. And once it was out there, of course the *Times* was going to 'own' it. You're their man, and this is a sensational story.

Terrible—don't get me wrong. But from a journalist's perspective, this is the mother of all news stories. I guarantee your editors are kicking themselves for letting Drudge get the jump on them. And look, no one but you and I and a handful of others even knew they weren't going to run it in the first place."

"I guess," I said. "What about the White House? Are they confirming the president is missing?"

"Not quite," said Sharif, quickly scanning the full story. "But they don't actually deny it either."

"What are they saying exactly?"

"The story says, 'A senior administration official, who asked that his name be withheld as he was not authorized to speak on so sensitive a matter, insisted that Air Force One has landed safely at Israel's Ben Gurion International Airport without damage and without casualties. The official went on to say that the White House is grieving the loss of several senior officials and numerous support staff but is withholding the names of those killed and wounded until their families can be properly notified.'"

"That's it?" I asked. "That's all the White House says about the whereabouts of the president?"

"That's it," Sharif said, gathering his things from the X-ray machine.

"Talk about a nondenial denial," I said. "They can't shoot my story down because they know it's true. But by not providing any other details, they're creating a global firestorm of interest. Why don't they just tell everyone the truth?"

"Who's going to say it?" asked Sharif. "The

White House press secretary is dead. So is the chief of staff. So are the secretary of state and at least a dozen senior White House officials."

"Secretary Murray is dead?"

"Sorry—I thought you'd heard."

"I hadn't."

"He and his team got to the ceremony late," Sharif explained. "Their plane landed about twenty minutes after the president's, just in from Beijing."

"I didn't even see him."

"He was meeting with a half-dozen other foreign ministers in the east wing of the palace. They were going to join up with the principals immediately after the ceremony."

A wave of nausea hit me with the news of the secretary of state's death. Though I'd never interviewed him or developed him as a source, I had met him twice—once when he'd made a surprise visit to Baghdad to hold a press conference with a new Iraqi prime minister, and once with his lovely wife, Bernadette, and their three teenage girls at a Christmas party at the American embassy in Paris. I couldn't imagine what this family was going through, and so many other families like theirs.

There was no time to grieve, however. We headed down several flights of stairs, with soldiers flanking us both ahead and behind. I appreciated the colonel's help. It occurred to me that beyond his name and rank, I really had no idea who he was. We'd had no time to get acquainted. What was his background? Where was he from? And why was he so trusted by the king? I was about to ask him to tell me a bit about himself, but he started talking first.

"You know, your name isn't the only one on the byline. There are three others."

"Really? Who?"

"Conyers from the White House, Baker at State, and Neeling at the Pentagon."

"They're all backups, second-stringers," I said. "What about Fisher, Thompson, and O'Malley?"

"Says here they were all at the summit," Sharif said. "They all died in the attacks."

"What about Alex?" I asked, referring to Alex Brunnell, the *Times*' Jerusalem bureau chief.

"I'm afraid he was killed too."

We were approaching the vault door into the bunker. But I had to stop. I needed a moment. There was too much happening, too much death. I was sure some kind of emotional circuit breakers were going to blow at any second, and I didn't want to see the king until I had gathered myself together. I stood there, just outside the bunker, eyes closed, inhaling and exhaling very deliberately. *Just breathe,* I told myself. *Just breathe, in and out, in and out, in and out.*

What made it all worse was my complete inability to do my job properly. With no phone, I had no way to check my messages, no way to respond to e-mails, no way to track information or stay in touch with my family or my team in the States. And now I had a huge story that would rock the world. The Chevy Suburban carrying the president had been found bullet-ridden and abandoned in a facility swarming with terrorists. The president's entire Secret Service detail was dead or gravely wounded. The backseat of the Suburban was covered with blood. There was a trail of blood leading to a side door. But the president was nowhere to be found. The Jordanians didn't know where he was. Neither did the entirety of the American government.

The door of the bunker opened. Sharif told me it was time to go see the king. I braced myself for the fight that was coming. I understood full well that there were national security implications here. But the American people needed to know. The world needed to know. These were no longer rumors. The president was gone, and the only logical conclusion that could be drawn from the facts at hand was that he was now in the custody of the Islamic State.

13

★ ★ ★

"You're right," said the king.

"I beg your pardon?" I said, unprepared for his response. I'd just completed an extended and somewhat-heated treatise on the importance of being able to write and transmit back to the States a detailed article on the missing president and the failed rescue attempt, but apparently for no reason.

"Why do you think I sent you out there, Collins?" the monarch asked. "Why do you think Colonel Sharif pulled you into the middle of the action rather than staying up in the helicopter? Write the story quickly. As soon as the colonel clears it, you can e-mail it to your editors. I just have two requirements."

"Requirements?" I asked, bracing myself.

"Yes."

"And they are?"

"First, I'm asking you not to speculate," he said.

"Meaning what?"

"Meaning just report the facts. Nothing more. Nothing less. We don't know where the president is. That's a fact. The rescue attempt failed. That's a fact. A massive manhunt for the president remains under way. Also a fact. But you can't say the president is in the hands of ISIS. That's speculation. I know you fear that. We all do. But that's what I mean—don't guess, don't surmise, don't provide commentary or analysis. Not now. Not in the middle of a fast-moving crisis. Let the pundits back in the States or wherever do the speculation. And obviously you can't mention any sensitive military or intelligence information, either, like where I am, what base we're at, and so forth. The colonel will make sure there's nothing classified or sensitive in your piece."

I deeply rejected the very concept of a military censor. I'd fought it all over the world—in Afghanistan, in Iraq, and wherever I went. But there was no time to fight it at the moment. And there was no point. The king understood what I was trying to do. He wasn't asking for me to paint Jordan in a good light. He was just asking me to be a reporter, not a commentator, and under the circumstances that seemed fair enough.

I nodded, then asked, "What's the second requirement?"

"Speed," the king said. "Get some version of the story out fast. To write up the whole battle story will likely take you most of the night. But the American people can't wait for the whole thing. Nor can anyone else. They need to know the most crucial facts right now. So don't write it all up at once. Do a first draft. Get the basic details out there. We'll let you transmit additional paragraphs with more details every thirty to forty-five minutes throughout the evening, if you'd like. It's a world exclusive no matter what. No one else has the story. People will be hanging on every word. The *Times* web traffic will be off the charts. But at least everyone will know the lead right away. Agreed?"

"Photos too?" I asked.

"A few at a time, sure."

"Then agreed," I said.

"Good. Can you give the colonel a first draft in fifteen minutes?"

"I can do it in ten."

"Even better."

With that I was dismissed. Sharif led me out of the bunker, through a vestibule, down the hall, and into a complex of offices where staff members were hard at work coordinating sorties of fighter jets against various ISIS targets and managing the air portion of the enormous manhunt for the president. We came to a small, unoccupied office that apparently had been set aside for the colonel and me. Everything had been cleared from the shelves. The desktop was cleared off as well. But there was a new laptop waiting for me and a laser printer, along with a Keurig machine and a supply of coffees and teas. There was also a small refrigerator, like the kind I'd had in my college dorm room a million years ago, stocked with water and soft drinks.

I soon realized the phone on the desk was disconnected, and while there was Wi-Fi, the colonel said he wasn't authorized to give me the password.

Still, it was clean and quiet and far better than what Abu Khalif had provided me. So I sat down, took some more pain medication for my arm, and got to work.

Ten minutes later, as promised, I was done with the first draft.

Four hours later, I slid the laptop across the desk.

On the screen was the final draft. The colonel, as bleary-eyed as I was, carefully reviewed my copy, struck out only four sentences, and cleared it for publication. Then he plugged in a memory stick, downloaded the file, and took it to another room to e-mail it to Allen MacDonald.

While he was gone, I pulled out my grandfather's pocket watch and wound it up. It was now just after midnight. Over the past several hours, I had spoken to Allen three times, under the colonel's supervision, on a borrowed satphone. After assuring Allen that I was physically okay, I'd explained the unique circumstances under which I was operating. I figured the king's admonition against disclosing my location probably applied to phone calls as well as news stories, so I didn't say exactly where I was. Allen didn't exactly apologize for our dustup earlier in the day, but he was clearly glad I was alive and well and able to keep writing. With the pipeline cleared between us, he began posting my new material every hour or so. Thus far I'd written—and Sharif had cleared—three updates to my original ten-minute story on the ongoing hunt for the president, complete with additional details provided by the king and the prince themselves, including the fact that Egyptian and Israeli intelligence services were now working closely with the Americans and the Jordanians in the search. I'd also written a brief first-person account of being at the palace when the kamikaze attack took place. I'd wanted to write a story about helping to evacuate the king and his family, but the colonel had rejected this concept out of hand. Instead I wrote a detailed, blow-by-blow description of the battle at the SADAFCO warehouses north of the airport.

Every muscle in my body ached. The pills the doctor had given me earlier in the day were dulling the intensity of my gunshot wound, but the pain was still there, still throbbing. My head was killing me as well. I was feeling dehydrated and chugged down two bottles of water before deciding finally to retire for the night and get some desperately needed sleep.

Sharif requested pillows, an air mattress, and a few blankets for me, and they were all graciously delivered within the next ten minutes, along with basic toiletries, including a toothbrush, toothpaste, and some mouthwash. After Sharif said goodnight, an armed MP led me to the restroom, where I washed up, then led me back to the cramped little office. As I lay down, the MP took up his position outside my door. I wasn't going anywhere tonight. Nor was anyone coming in. For now, that was all I needed to know.

I turned out the lights and lay down on the

thin mattress. I pulled the blankets over me, trying to ignore the smell of the dirty carpet and trying equally not to think about the discomfort of not being able to fully stretch out my legs.

Instead, staring up at the ceiling, I thought about my mom back in Bar Harbor, Maine. I knew she was worried sick. But I also knew she was praying for me. I wished I could have called her, but there hadn't been time, and I knew she was tracking the story on the *Times* website. She could see my dispatches. She knew I was alive and kicking. She knew I was doing my job, and I knew she was proud of me. Indeed, I was writing each of my stories with her as my audience—not Vice President Holbrooke or the secretary of defense or King Abdullah or Abu Khalif or anyone else. I was trying to explain what I was seeing and hearing to my mom, in language clear and colorful enough to bring it all alive for her. Still, I wanted to talk to her, wanted to tell her personally that I was okay, wanted to hear her voice. Had she talked to Matt? I hoped he'd called her. I hoped he'd explained why he'd left Amman and reassured her that he and Annie and the kids were safe. Where exactly had they gone? I wondered. I had begged them to leave Jordan immediately. Abu Khalif had personally threatened them and our entire family. I was glad Matt had texted me to let me know they were now someplace safe. I could only hope that was really true.

I was not, by any means, a religious man. That was Matt's thing, not mine. My older brother was the pastor and theologian in the family. I was, you might say, the family's black sheep. But I loved my brother. I truly wanted him and his wife and kids to be safe. I couldn't bear the thought of ISIS getting to any of them. So it occurred to me it might be a good idea to pray for them right then, before I fell asleep.

In the darkness, I closed my eyes and folded my hands like I'd done when I was a little kid, and rarely since.

"So, hey, God . . . how's it going?" I began, then felt foolish for sounding so ridiculous. "Look, I don't really know if you're there. But if you are, I'm asking you to please—you know—keep my mom safe. And Matt. And Annie. And the kids. I'm scared for them. They haven't done anything wrong. But I feel like I've put their lives in danger. And I'm sorry about that. And I just ask that you, well, protect them, and make sure nothing happens to them. Okay? All right, well, thanks, and good night—or amen—or whatever. Anyway, that's it. Okay. I'm done. Good-bye."

I felt like an idiot. That had to be the worst prayer in the history of prayer. If there was a God in heaven, I was sure he was laughing at me. Well, not sure. The truth was I had no idea what God might be thinking. But as intensely uncomfortable and deeply self-conscious as I felt at that moment, there was also, I had to admit—if only to myself—something vaguely comforting in having tried to have a meaningful conversation with God for once in my adult life. I couldn't explain it. I didn't even really want to think about it, much less analyze it. But it was true. And that made me curious.

14

* * *

The next thing I knew, Colonel Sharif was trying to wake me up.

"J. B.? J. B., can you hear me?"

"What time is it?" I groaned, rubbing my eyes and trying to remember where exactly I was.

"It's just after four."

"A.m. or p.m.?"

"A.m.," he said. "Very a.m."

I groaned again, rolled over, and pulled the blanket over my eyes. In this windowless room, there was no evidence it was morning, but regardless, I still needed many more hours of sleep before I could function effectively again.

"Sorry, J. B.," the colonel said, not really sounding that apologetic. "I let you sleep as long as I could. But we have breaking news. You need to come into the bunker."

He handed me a cup of freshly brewed black coffee, a peace offering of sorts. It worked. The aroma alone helped get me to my feet. Given that I was bald, I didn't need to worry about how my hair looked, though a shower and a good shave would have been nice before seeing the king and his brother again. But Sharif insisted there was no time. I needed to move quickly. So I threw on my shoes, gulped down some Sumatran Reserve Extra Bold, and followed the colonel to the war room, a fresh MP at our side.

The bunker was a beehive of activity. The king didn't look like he'd ever gone to bed, but he had changed out of the suit he'd been wearing at the summit into fatigues. He was in battle mode now, the warrior king, and he looked angry.

"Collins, take a seat," he said as he caught my eye and the vault door shut behind me. "Abu Khalif has just sent a new video to Al Jazeera. The network has been told to broadcast it precisely at 6 a.m. local time. But one of their producers contacted the colonel here and suggested we should watch it first."

"Have you seen it?" I asked.

"No, not yet," the monarch said. "None of us. Whatever it is, I thought you'd want to break the story."

"Isn't the whole world going to see it at once?" I asked.

"The video, yes," he replied. "But I want you to report my reaction and the next steps we take against ISIS."

I took a deep breath and tried in vain to steel myself for what was coming. The king ordered Sharif to play the video, and I turned so I could see the monitor. It took a moment before Sharif could get the images from the e-mail on his laptop to the main screen, but a few seconds later, the image appeared. When the video began to play, I felt I could hardly breathe.

The first shot was that of a man who had become all too familiar to me in recent days: Abu Khalif, the emir of ISIS and self-proclaimed caliph, wearing a kaffiyeh and flowing white robes. While I had met him and spoken to him and even interviewed him in person, face-to-face, this image startled me because it was the first video ISIS had ever released with its leader in the starring role. Until a few days earlier, Khalif had been locked away in a maximum-security prison in Abu Ghraib, Iraq, not far from Baghdad. But now, as the world knew because of my reporting, the forces of ISIS had attacked the prison, killed most of its leaders and guards, and freed the spiritual and political leader of the Islamic State. The photos I had taken that had accompanied my front-page story in the *Times* just a few days ago were some of the first the world had ever seen of this barbaric tyrant. Now they were going to see him on television and hear his voice, and I didn't dare imagine what he was about to say.

What struck me in particular was not the dark eyes or carefully trimmed beard of the emir but the setting he'd chosen in which to shoot this video. He was standing in the courtyard of what appeared to be an ancient, crumbling, perhaps even abandoned mosque. There were several decaying arches behind him, though one of the archways had collapsed entirely and was just a heap of stones. It wasn't obvious whether this was from recent bomb damage or from an earthquake centuries before, but it was clear that the video had been shot at night. The partially collapsed structure revealed the night sky, and stars were clearly visible, as was part of the moon. The rest of the courtyard was awash in klieg lights that created harsh and oddly formed shadows in the background.

"I am Abu Khalif, the head of the Islamic State," he began, speaking in flawless, classical Arabic and looking straight into the camera. "I greet you in the name of Allah, the most beneficent, the most merciful. All praise and thanks be to Allah, the Lord of the *'Alamin*, the only owner, the only ruling judge on the Day of Recompense, the Day of Judgment, the day of the glorious resurrection. The Day of Reckoning is coming, the Day of Decision you used to deny."

He was citing various passages from the Qur'an, pretending to be the spiritual and political leader of a billion and a half Muslims worldwide rather than the savage, soulless terrorist he was in reality.

"Truly, all praise belongs to Allah. We praise him and seek his help and his forgiveness. We seek refuge with Allah from the evils of our souls and from the consequences of our deeds. Whoever Allah guides can never be led astray, and whoever Allah leads astray can never be guided. I testify that there is no god except Allah, alone without any partners, and I testify that Muhammad—peace and blessings be upon him—is his slave and messenger. It was this messenger who instructed us in the holy Qur'an that 'he who deceives shall be faced with his deceit on the Day of Resurrection, when every human being shall be repaid in full for whatever he has done, and none shall be wronged.' Tonight judgment has begun for some of the worst deceivers on our planet. As many of you know by now, forces of the Islamic State have launched an operation inside the heart of Jordan, territory that once was held by the dark forces of the Hashemite infidels but has been liberated by our brave forces and is now part of the ever-expanding caliphate."

The image quickly changed to shots of distinctive black ISIS flags flying over various landmarks in Amman as well as over villages that could conceivably be Jordanian but weren't immediately distinguishable from villages throughout Syria or Iraq. I glanced at the king, but he was inscrutable. He was serious and intently focused on both the images and what Khalif was saying, but his expression hadn't changed at all. Colonel Sharif, on the other hand, looked like he was about to become violently ill.

"Presently the warriors of the Islamic State are embarked on a brave and glorious mission to overthrow the wicked regime in Amman, to rid the holy lands of corruption and betrayal of the Qur'an and the Prophet. Our forces are determined to restore this land and its people to the rightful rule of the caliphate and Sharia law. As I speak to you, this operation is already bearing great fruit. For tonight, by the power and greatness of Allah, I announce to you that our forces have captured the leader of the arrogant powers, the dog of Rome, the president of the United States."

An audible gasp went through the command center as the image panned from the emir to a shot of President Harrison Taylor wearing an orange jumpsuit, his hands and feet in shackles, standing in the middle of a grotesque iron cage.

15

The camera zoomed in on the president.

And then, on cue, Taylor spoke directly to the camera.

"My name is Harrison Beresford Taylor," he said slowly, methodically, wincing several times as if in pain. As he spoke, Arabic subtitles scrolled across the bottom of the screen. "I am the forty-fifth president of the United States. I was captured by the Islamic State in Amman on December 5. I am being held by the Islamic State in a location that has not been disclosed to me, but I can say . . . I can say honestly . . . I can say honestly that I am being treated well and have been given the opportunity to give *ba'yah*—that is to say, to pledge allegiance . . . to the Islamic State. I ask my fellow Americans, including all my colleagues in Washington, to listen . . . to listen carefully . . . that is, to listen carefully and respectfully to the emir, and to follow the instructions . . . he is about to set forth for my safe and expeditious return."

I could envision the experts and analysts back at Langley carefully scrutinizing the video in every possible manner. But there was no doubt. The face. The voice. The inflections. He was being forced to read a prepared text, to be sure, but there was no question it was really the president. This wasn't a look-alike. This wasn't a trick. ISIS had really captured him, and it was really, tragically, Harrison Taylor in the cage. For me, the real questions were where exactly this had been recorded and when.

When Taylor was finished, the camera panned back to Khalif.

"Allah has given this infidel into our hands," he continued, once again speaking in Arabic. "O Muslims everywhere, glad tidings to you! Raise your heads high, for today, by Allah's grace, you have a sign of his favor upon you. You also have a state and caliphate, which will return your dignity, might, rights, and leadership. It is a state where the Arab and non-Arab, the white man and black man, the Easterner and Westerner are all brothers. Their blood mixed and became one, under a single flag and goal, in one pavilion, enjoying this blessing, the blessing of faithful brotherhood. So all praise and thanks are due to Allah. Therefore, rush, O Muslims, to your state. Yes, it is your state. Rush, because Syria is not for the Syrians, and Iraq is not for the Iraqis, and Jordan is not for the Jordanians. The earth is Allah's. Indeed, the earth belongs to Allah. He causes to inherit it whomever he wills of his servants.

"We make a special call to the scholars, experts in Islamic jurisprudence, and especially judges, as well as people with military, administrative, and service expertise, and medical doctors and engineers of all different specializations and fields. We call them and remind them to fear Allah and to come to the caliphate so that they can answer the dire needs of their Muslim brothers.

"And I make a special call to you, O soldiers of the Islamic State—do not be awestruck by the great numbers of your enemy, for Allah is with you. I do not fear for you the numbers of your opponents, nor do I fear your neediness and poverty, for Allah has promised your Prophet—peace be upon him—that you will not be wiped out by famine, and your enemy will not conquer you or continue to violate and control your land. I promised you that in the name of Allah we would capture the American president, and I have kept my word. The king of Jordan will soon be in our hands. So will all the infidel leaders in this region. So will all the dogs in Rome. The ancient prophecies tell us the End of Days is upon us, and with it the judgment of all who will not bow the knee and submit to Allah and his commanders on the earth."

Khalif now turned to his right and we had a new camera angle of him, against the backdrop of a shadowy stone wall. When he resumed speaking, it was in English.

"Now I speak directly to Vice President Holbrooke, the new leader of Rome. Fearful and trembling, weak and unsteady, you and the infidels you lead have lost your way. You have three choices—convert to Islam, pay the *jizyah*, or die. You have these three choices, but you do not have time. You must choose your fate and choose it quickly. If you and your country choose to convert, you must give a speech to the world doing so under the precise language and conditions of Sharia law, and you will be blessed by Allah and have peace with the caliphate. If you choose to pay the *jizyah*, you must pay $1,000 U.S. for every man, woman, and child living in the United States of America. I have just sent to the *New York Times* the details of a certain bank account. I am certain they will forward the information to you. Upon its receipt you must immediately deposit the full amount into the account to cover the *jizyah* tax. If you do not, or if you act with aggression in any matter against me or against the caliphate, the next video you see will be your beloved president beheaded or burned alive. From the time of this broadcast, you have forty-eight hours, and not a minute more."

Khalif turned again, back to the first camera, and spoke in a close-up, once more in Arabic.

"The spark was lit in Iraq," he concluded. "It spread to Syria and now to Jordan. Its heat will continue to intensify until it burns the crusader armies in Dabiq. Let there be no doubt. Let all the world understand. Rome is falling. The Caliphate is arising. We are waiting for you in Dabiq."

16

* * *

When the video was finished, the room was deadly silent.

No one spoke for several moments. Everyone seemed to be processing both the chilling words and images. Every minute that went by, I had more questions, but I didn't feel it was my place to ask. Not yet. I wanted to see how the king and the prince and the generals would react to the tape, not to me.

Meanwhile, the young military aide who attended to the king's every need was typing furiously on a laptop. I would soon learn he had been creating a precise transcript of Abu Khalif's words in Arabic and then producing a flawless English interpretation. When he was finished, he printed out copies of both and handed them to each person in the room. I'd gotten most of what Khalif had said the first time. He had spoken slowly and deliberately, so in that sense it was easier for me to process. There was some vocabulary and several theological references that I didn't immediately understand. But reading both the Arabic and the

English versions just moments after watching the video and hearing the words spoken was enormously helpful.

I glanced at the clocks on the wall and then at my pocket watch. The video was going to air across the globe on Al Jazeera in less than twelve minutes. But the king had yet to react.

When he finally spoke, rather than revealing his own thoughts, he asked his war council for theirs. The suspense was killing me, but I held my tongue.

Lieutenant General Abdul Jum'a went first. "I don't believe he is on Jordanian soil, Your Majesty," he began.

"Why?"

"Too risky," the army commander replied. "They know our forces are fully deployed. Yes, we have lost control of some towns and parts of some cities in the north as the ISIS uprising has spread. But they know it's a matter of hours, at most a few days, until we reclaim full control over those places. I don't think Abu Khalif would risk being captured—and the president being rescued—here in Jordan. Not when he has other, better alternatives."

I could hardly process the information. This was the first I'd heard of additional ISIS offensive operations outside of Amman, and certainly no one had mentioned that any Jordanian territory had actually been seized by ISIS in the north—not in my hearing, anyway.

"So where do you think they are?" the king asked.

"I cannot say for certain, of course, but in my opinion the most logical thing to do would be to evacuate the president and take him into Syria or Iraq."

"Dabiq?"

"No, that's too far north—past Aleppo, almost to the Turkish border," Jum'a said. "They wouldn't have had time to get him up there this fast."

"What about Homs?"

"Maybe, but again, that's quite a ways north. And if they were driving, they'd have to make a wide berth around Damascus, given that Assad's forces are still in control of most of the capital."

"Then where?"

"If it were me, I'd take him to southeast Syria, to the heart of ISIS territory, somewhere along the Euphrates, someplace the Americans would never go."

"Deir ez-Zor? Mayadin?"

"Perhaps, though again, if I were Abu Khalif, I'd create my base camp someplace even smaller, a little town or village that was off the radar, discreet, unnoticed. There are a hundred of them up and down the river on both sides."

"And what if they took him to Iraq?" asked Prince Feisal, now on his feet and poring over one of the maps on the wall.

"They wouldn't," the general said.

"Why not?"

"Because you've got too many forces trying to retake northern Iraq," Jum'a explained. "You've got the Kurds, the Americans, the Shia militias, the Iraqi regular forces—they're all trying to retake the north. Why should Khalif take the risk? Why not set up his base camp in Syria? No one's trying to retake Syria except Assad, and he simply doesn't have the strength to get the job done."

"Okay, but what if they did go to Iraq?" Feisal pressed.

"Then they're crazy."

"And they're not?"

"Abu Khalif is crazy like a fox. He's not a lunatic. Take my word for it. He's not in Iraq. He's in Syria."

"But Khalif was just in Mosul," noted the prince. "He was just there with Mr. Collins. They're testing chemical weapons there. They have a warehouse full of munitions, captured from Aleppo."

"*Had,*" the general insisted. "They *had* a base in Mosul. They *had* a warehouse full of chemical weapons. The only reason to reveal it all to Collins and the *New York Times* was if everything was being moved. I guarantee you—none of it is there today."

The prince let it drop.

The king nodded but made no comment before turning to Major General Ibrahim al-Mufti, his air force commander. "Could they have moved the president by air?"

"Not from Amman, Your Majesty," al-Mufti replied. "They would have moved him in the trunk of a car or the back of a van or truck, driven him a few kilometers, switched vehicles, and kept moving like that until they could get well outside our initial perimeter."

"But then, couldn't they have put him on a small plane or helicopter and flown him out of the country?"

"If they had help from locals, yes, I'm afraid they could have."

"Did we detect air activity heading to Syria or northern Iraq overnight?"

"I don't know, Your Majesty. I just sent an e-mail to my intel chief and told him to run the tapes on all air traffic control stations for the last twelve hours. It'll take some time, but I will let you know when I hear something."

For several moments the king said nothing. He showed no emotion. He had a pretty strong five o'clock shadow and was clearly exhausted. He had to be. Yet he struck me as remarkably calm, given that his kingdom was under attack from all sides, much of his government was dead or incapacitated, and ISIS had captured the leader of the free world on Jordanian soil.

"What do you make of the video?" he asked al-Mufti.

The general leaned back in his chair and took some time to answer. "Abdul is right," he said at last. "Khalif is crazy like a fox. He has a plan. He's trying to draw us into a much more dangerous war, a ground war, a war in Dabiq."

"You think he's in Dabiq?" the king asked.

"No, I don't," al-Mufti replied. "But I think he's trying to draw us and the Americans into a ground war there."

The room grew silent again, but I couldn't hold back any longer. "Why?" I asked. "Why Dabiq?"

"Because that's where he believes the last battle will be fought."

"The last battle?"

"The End of Days," said al-Mufti. "The Day of Judgment. It's all going to consummate in Dabiq. That's what they think."

"Who?"

"Abu Khalif, ISIS, all of them," said the general. "They believe the Prophet—peace be upon him—spoke of a final, catastrophic, apocalyptic battle between the Muslims and the forces of Rome that would unfold on the plains of northern Syria in a place called Dabiq."

"The forces of Rome? What does that mean—the Italians, the Vatican?"

"Maybe yes, maybe no," said al-Mufti. "You heard Khalif call the president 'the dog of Rome'?"

"I did, but why? What does that mean?"

"Some Sunnis believe the Americans are the new Crusaders, that Washington is the new Rome, that the president is the new Caesar. The ISIS crowd certainly believes it. No question that Khalif does. Believe me, they're never going to give up the president of the United States, even if your entire country converts or pays the tax. The president is their prize. I wouldn't be surprised if he was dead already."

17

* * *

The king became visibly angry, though he controlled his tongue.

"Don't speak like this, Ibrahim—I will not have it," he insisted. "We have to operate on the assumption that the president is still alive. We cannot give up this hope. There are forty-eight hours left. We need to use them wisely. We need to find the president and rescue him or help the Americans rescue him. The fate of the kingdom hangs in the balance. Now, Abdul, you think Abu Khalif and the president are in southeastern Syria?"

"Yes, Your Majesty, I do," Jum'a confirmed.

"Ibrahim, what about you?"

"Where do I think they are?"

"Yes."

"I'd say Abdul is probably right—Khalif is in Syria."

"And the president?"

"If he's still alive?"

At this, the king's jaws tightened. "Yes," he said carefully.

"I don't think they'd keep the two together."

"Why not?"

"Operational security," Al-Mufti said. "The entire universe is now looking for the president of the United States. It's highly unlikely anyone finds him within forty-eight hours, but if they do—if we do, if anybody does—Abu Khalif is no fool. He's not going to be in the same location."

"Would Khalif send the president into Iraq or just put him in a different safe house in Syria?"

"That I can't say, Your Majesty. But I'm happy to develop contingency plans for both scenarios."

"Yes, do that—work together, both of you," the king said to his generals. "Get your best people working on this. You've got an hour. I want a detailed intelligence analysis of everything we've got so far—the video, the radar tracking of aircraft moving across the Syrian and Iraqi borders, the interrogations your men are doing with ISIS forces captured at the palace and at the SADAFCO plant, signals intelligence, paid informants we've got on the ground in Syria and Iraq—everything. And where are we with Jamal Ramzy's cell phone, the one Collins here pulled off his body at the palace? It turned out to be encrypted, did it not?"

"It was, Your Majesty," Prince Feisal said.

"Have we cracked it yet?"

"They're still working on it."

"Tell them time is running out," the king insisted. "I want to know everything about that phone—what calls were made on it, what calls were received, all of it, when we meet in an hour. Am I clear?"

"Yes, Your Majesty."

"Good. Now get to work."

The king stood, and the rest of us did as well. The generals saluted and then bolted out of the bunker. The prince was about to begin working the phones again, but the king pulled him aside. Colonel Sharif, meanwhile, suggested he and I head back to my temporary office to write up the story of the video.

But as we left, I heard the king ask his brother in a somewhat-hushed tone, "Now, listen—where are we with this mole hunt?"

★   ★   ★

Back in the office, Colonel Sharif opened a safe and pulled out my iPhone.

He let me put in my password, but since I was not allowed to send any messages without his permission, he kept control of the phone. As the phone reconnected to the data service, hundreds of messages began to pour in. But we were looking for just one—an e-mail from Abu Khalif with the details of a bank account to which the U.S. government was supposed to wire more than $320 billion.

"Got it," Sharif said at last.

"Is it from Khalif directly?" I asked, immensely curious.

"It doesn't say," Sharif replied. "It's an anonymous Gmail account."

"No note?"

"No, just the account number and SWIFT code."

The colonel quickly forwarded the e-mail to the king and the prince with a note asking for instructions on whom in the American government to forward it on to. The prince wrote back almost immediately, saying he would take care of it personally.

I spent the next half hour writing up the story of the video. Sharif wouldn't allow me to go back in the bunker to interview the king. But he did step out for a few minutes, and when I was nearly finished, he returned and handed me a typed statement from His Majesty.

This video is further evidence of Abu Khalif's descent into evil. It is proof of his apostasy, his wickedness and barbarism. The forces of ISIS have abandoned all pretense of being Muslims. Such *takfiris* are not practicing true Islam. They have perverted the religion of my fathers and forefathers beyond recognition. The kingdom of Jordan stands against such evildoers. We stand for peace and moderation.

On behalf of all the peace-loving people of my kingdom, I pledge to do everything in my power to assist the United States, our great ally, in safely recovering President Taylor and returning him to his family and his nation.

At the same time, I pledge to bring Abu Khalif and his men to justice. They

are guilty not only of terrorism but
of treason and a host of other crimes
punishable by death. And I will not rest
until they have been captured, tried,
convicted, and eradicated from the earth.

This last part intrigued me. The king was vowing to execute Abu Khalif and the leaders of ISIS.
I asked the colonel to clarify this, given that I was
quite sure Jordan's government hadn't executed
any criminals in years. Sharif confirmed it but
noted that death penalty laws were still on the
books for a variety of heinous crimes from rape,
murder, and drug trafficking to weapons smuggling, espionage, and treason.

I dropped in the king's entire statement, verbatim, toward the end of the article. Normally I'd
include only a line or two, but I figured in this case
it was safer to let the Jordanians see I was transmitting everything they gave me and leave it to Allen
and the brass back in the States to edit it down as
they felt appropriate.

As this was a straight news piece, I led, of course,
with Abu Khalif's demand for the vice president
of the United States to lead his country in conversion to Islam or else pay an ancient tax described
in the Qur'an. The only alternative was to see their
president executed in the most despicable manner possible. I emphasized the forty-eight-hour
deadline and noted that "unnamed intelligence
officials believe the president has most likely been
moved out of Jordan and is probably in Syria or

Iraq, though this could not be confirmed." At first Sharif was bothered by that line, saying it was the very type of speculation the king objected to. But I pushed back, noting that it was the king's own speculation and that of his top military leaders, not my own. In the end, I prevailed and the colonel transmitted the story as written.

By the time Sharif was finished e-mailing the story to Allen and I'd had a few minutes to wash up and get another cup of coffee, we had only about ten or twelve minutes before we had to be back in the bunker to meet with His Majesty and hear the briefings by the generals. I asked the colonel if he'd be willing to scroll through my e-mails and text messages and print out anything from my family, anything from Allen, or anything that seemed either personal or particularly urgent. He graciously agreed and left the room to take care of it. I used the time to lie down on the air mattress for a moment to close my eyes and catch a few z's. But exhausted as I was, I could not sleep.

I found my thoughts turning to the king's question to his brother.

"Where are we with this mole hunt?"

It was an important and frightening question, and with all that had been happening over the past eighteen hours or so, I'd completely lost track of the fact that there was almost certainly a mole within the Jordanian government. The ISIS attack on the Al-Hummar Palace had been exquisitely planned and executed. Surely it had required someone on the inside—more likely several people. The name of the Jordanian F-16 pilot who had fired on the summit assembly and then flown a suicide mission into the palace had not yet been released, but I had no doubt the royal family was doing a full investigation into the man's background, family, associates, and possible connections to ISIS. But the full-blown coup d'état scenario—in which more than fifteen thousand ISIS jihadists had participated—could not have been the work of just a single rogue pilot. Someone else—someone with access, with detailed knowledge of the plans for the summit—had to have tipped off Abu Khalif and his men to the peace summit's location, timing, and other details. But who?

There was a fairly limited list of possible suspects, and most of those people were now dead. The question was who on the list was still alive, still in a position to bring down the king and prevent any possible rescue of the president from being successful?

At that moment it occurred to me that everyone in the bunker—short of the king himself—was a suspect.

18

★ ★ ★

It was just before seven o'clock when there was a knock on my office door.

The colonel entered, but he was not alone. Prince Feisal was with him, along with one of the MPs who had been assigned to me and a half-dozen other elite soldiers guarding the prince.

"Mr. Collins, would you take a walk with me?" the prince asked as we stepped out into the hall-way. "There is a matter of great importance I'd like to discuss with you."

"Hasn't His Majesty asked us to gather in the bunker?" I asked.

"That meeting is already under way," Feisal replied. "I'll join them in a little while. But this matter cannot wait."

"Well, sure, okay; if you insist," I said.

"I do."

We headed up the stairs, trailed by the security detail. When we reached the vestibule, however, we didn't stop. Rather, the prince led me outside and across the tarmac. It was the first time I'd been outside in nearly twelve hours, and it was good to feel the rising sun on my face and a brisk December breeze as well. There were scattered clouds overhead and actual patches of blue between them. Yet to the north, dark thunderheads were rolling in. Another storm was coming.

We paused at the flight line as a squadron of F-15s took off toward the west, headed, no doubt, back to Amman with a fresh payload of missiles and bombs. To our left, two Cobra helicopter gunships were on approach to land, while two more were powering up to lift off and take their place in the fight to reclaim the kingdom. As the last of the Strike Eagles roared past and climbed rapidly into the morning sky, the prince beckoned me to continue walking with him across the tarmac.

"Have you had the opportunity to talk to your mother yet or to your brother?" he asked as we headed toward a series of hangars and administrative buildings on the other side of the base.

"No, not yet, with the time difference and all," I said. "The colonel let me send an e-mail to both of them, though, letting them know I'm okay."

"But not where you are, of course."

"Of course."

"And I understand your brother—Matthew, is it?"

"Yes."

"I understand he and his wife and children left Amman in quite a hurry two nights ago."

"They did."

"Almost like they knew what was coming," the prince said as we passed through a security checkpoint and entered an unmarked three-story office building.

"What are you implying?" I asked, suddenly caught off guard by his tone.

"I'm not implying anything," said the prince, boarding an elevator with me and three of the six members of the security detail right behind him. "I'm simply noting that they just up and left the country—leaving all of their possessions behind— just hours before the worst terrorist attacks in the history of our country."

"And?"

"And how did they know?"

"I warned them to leave."

"Why would you do that?"

"You know why."

"I'm afraid I don't," the prince said. "Enlighten me." He pushed the button for the third floor and the door closed behind us.

This was no longer a friendly conversation. I wasn't about to get an exclusive interview with the second-highest-ranking military officer in the kingdom. This was an interrogation.

I took a deep breath and tried to maintain my composure. There was no point in getting angry—not visibly, anyway. It would only make me look guilty. But angry I was. I could feel my face starting to get red and the back of my neck getting hot.

"Your Royal Highness, you know very well why I encouraged my brother and his family to leave," I said as calmly as I could. "Abu Khalif threatened them by name. He indicated to me that he knew exactly where they lived in Amman. I didn't feel they were safe any longer. And it turns out I was right."

"Khalif threatened your mother as well, did he not?"

"He did."

"Has she suddenly evacuated her home in Bar Harbor?"

"No."

"Did you advise her to leave?"

"No."

"Just your brother. Why?"

The bell rang. The elevator stopped. The door opened on the third floor, and the other three security guards were somehow already waiting for us.

The prince now led us down a long hallway, past one cubicle after another packed with air force officers of various ranks, all hard at work, talking quietly and moving quickly. We were walking briskly, but I could see lots of maps and satellite photos on the walls. I wondered at first if this was a flight-planning and meteorological center, but when we reached the end of the hall, the prince ushered me into a spacious corner office guarded by two MPs. Four of the six security men entered the office with us, while two stayed outside with the guards, and the door was locked behind us.

To my right were a desk and chair and credenza and a Jordanian flag on a stand. Straight ahead was a long set of bookshelves, and to my left were a round wooden conference table and four chairs and a large window looking out over the airfield. The prince led me over to the table and asked me to take a seat. As I did, I glanced at the titles of the books, and it became instantly clear the work being done here was neither aeronautic nor weather-related. This building was part of the Jordanian intelligence directorate, and I was under suspicion.

"Would you like some coffee?" the prince asked, pouring some for himself from a freshly brewed pot on a side table.

"No thank you."

"A soft drink?"

"No."

"Water?" he asked.

"I'm fine."

"Nevertheless . . . ," he said and poured me a plastic cup of water from a pitcher beside the coffeepot and set it down in front of me.

I nodded my thanks and braced myself for what was coming next.

"So," the prince continued when he had taken a seat, "your brother."

"What would you like to know?"

"I'd like an honest answer as to why you told him to leave his home in such a rush, but not your mother."

"Isn't it obvious?" I asked. "Matt was closer to Abu Khalif. He and Annie and the kids were in far greater danger. My mother lives half a world away."

"And you didn't think she was in imminent danger from ISIS?"

"Of course not."

"But you thought it was obvious Amman was going to be attacked."

"Yes."

"And your brother believed you?"

"I'm glad he did," I said. "As it turns out, I was right."

"So you were."

"Matt wasn't the only one I told, Your Highness," I noted. "I told the king I was afraid ISIS would attack the peace summit. He didn't believe me."

"Perhaps he didn't realize you weren't speculating."

"Meaning what?"

"Meaning perhaps you knew for a fact the attack was coming."

"If I'd known for a fact, I would have said so. But I warned the king as clearly and urgently as I could. I warned the president as well."

"When?"

"On Marine One, en route to the palace."

"Did the president believe you?"

"No."

"Did he take you seriously?"

"No."

"Because he thought you were speculating, correct?"

"Apparently."

"He didn't think you knew exactly what was going to happen."

"I didn't know exactly."

"So you say."

"Let's just be clear, Your Highness—are you actually accusing *me* of being the mole?"

19

* * *

The prince glared at me.

"You have to admit, Mr. Collins, the evidence is rather compelling, is it not?"

"How so?" I asked, incredulous but determined to maintain control.

"You really need me to explain it to you?"

"Uh, yeah, I'm afraid I do."

"Very well," the prince said. "As you know, the list of suspects—the people who knew the summit was going to be held in Amman, at the Al-Hummar Palace, who knew the exact time, the precise details—is a very short list indeed. What's more, as you also know, most of the people on that list are dead, strongly suggesting that none of them were the culprits. But you, Mr. Collins—of all the names that remain on that list, you're rather unique."

"How so?" I asked again, not sure what else to say.

"Well, of course, you are the only one who has ever met Abu Khalif face-to-face. You're the only one to have spent time with him. Significant time. And not just with the emir of ISIS but with his senior commander in Syria, Jamal Ramzy. You know them both. You've spoken with them both, at length. You've been to their lairs. You've met their advisors. They've told you their plans. They've instructed you to tell the world certain things, and you've done exactly what they asked of you."

"That's my job, Your Highness."

"Some are beginning to wonder what that job actually is."

"Are you actually accusing me of being an agent of ISIS? Don't you see how ridiculous that sounds?"

"I'm not accusing you of anything, Mr. Collins. I just thought it was only fair to let you know what some are saying about you, so you can, shall we say, disabuse them of their concerns."

"I don't believe this."

"Why not? Being a foreign correspondent for the *New York Times* would be the perfect cover for a mole." The prince stood and began to walk about the room as he explained the emerging theory of my crimes. "Who else has spent time with the leaders of ISIS and repeatedly lived to tell about it?"

"If I was plotting to kill the four leaders at the summit, why in the world would I have warned two of them in advance about such an attack?"

"There could be any number of reasons."

"Pick one."

"Very well," the prince said. "To create plausible deniability. You certainly don't have an alibi. You're consistently in the wrong place at the wrong time, yet you keep surviving while everyone around you keeps dying. By telling His Majesty and the president that ISIS was about to attack—yet providing no proof whatsoever—you could make it look like you were only trying to help."

"That's ridiculous."

"Is it?"

"And the wrong place at the wrong time? I myself was nearly killed each time."

"Of course—but you weren't. You survived."

"Yeah, but—"

"Take Istanbul, for example."

"What about Istanbul?"

"A car bomb goes off in the heart of an Islamic capital," the prince said, still pacing. "A Jordanian national is killed, allegedly a good friend and coworker of yours, but somehow you survive. The prime suspect in the bombing is a mysterious woman you were having drinks with, yet you refuse to give the authorities her name or any details about her."

He paused, but I said nothing. I was in shock.

"Or take Union Station," he continued. "A terrorist group—apparently an ISIS sleeper cell—opens fire in the middle of the train station in Washington, D.C. The shooters target everyone on the top floor of the restaurant—the, uh, the . . . What was it called again?"

"Center Café," I said numbly.

"Right, the Center Café. The shooters kill every patron on the top floor of the restaurant—every FBI agent and a former director of the CIA—and you're the only one who survives. Doesn't that strike you as just a little odd?"

"Are you forgetting that I actually shot and killed one of the terrorists?"

"Oh, you're ready to admit that, are you? I've seen the surveillance tapes. The FBI has seen them too, and from the various angles of the cameras and the lighting and the shadows, it's impossible to tell who actually shot the female terrorist on the ground floor. Very convenient, isn't it? Yet, remarkably, a few moments later, you go running through the crime scene, uninjured, unharmed. The FBI is still wondering, why exactly did you run? If you're innocent, why didn't you go to the police? Why didn't you go to the FBI? Why didn't you go to any of the authorities and explain to them what you'd done if it was really in self-defense and not to cover up a larger crime?"

My anger was rising, but I continued to hold my tongue.

"No, instead you didn't just flee the scene of a crime—the site of a major terrorist attack— oh no, you actually fled the country," the prince continued. "Using a false passport. Using fake credit cards. Using an alias, no less. Where does an innocent man get such things? And then you wind up in Baghdad on the very day—indeed, the very moment—of a coordinated prison break during which Abu Khalif escapes. You come back to Jordan and all hell breaks loose. Yet again, miraculously, you escape unharmed, or nearly so. You see where this is heading, Mr. Collins? You see why people are growing deeply concerned that maybe you're not covering this story—maybe you're causing it?"

I couldn't believe how quickly things were going south. I felt completely blindsided and disoriented, yet I realized there was no point answering the prince's accusations. I was, in essence, being accused of treason, and as Colonel Sharif had recently made clear to me, treason was a crime punishable by death.

"I want to meet with the American ambassador," I said as calmly as I could.

"No," the prince said.

"I insist."

"I'm afraid that's impossible."

"Why?" I asked.

"Because he's dead."

It was as if the wind had been knocked out of me. I suddenly remembered seeing the U.S. ambassador to Jordan in the audience at the summit, sitting with several dozen other ambassadors, most of whom had probably also been killed in the attacks.

"I'm very sorry to hear that," I replied. "Then I would like to speak to the attorney for the *Times*."

"All in due time," said the prince. "I have a few more questions I'd like answers to first."

"These aren't questions," I responded. "This is an interrogation. I'm an American citizen, and I'm entitled to legal counsel before I say anything else."

"You're certain of that, Mr. Collins?" he asked.

"Quite," I said.

"Very well, then; when this whole episode with the president is resolved, we'll see if we can't get the attorney for the *New York Times* to come over to Amman so the two of you can have a chat."

With that, the prince instructed the MPs to handcuff me and take me immediately to the detention center. "Put him on level B, cell number three," he said.

Then he turned and walked away.

20

The door slammed and locked behind me.

I was alone.

Cell number three was a narrow, dark, damp cinder-block room containing only an army cot, a metal toilet without a seat, and a small metal sink that dispensed only cold water—very cold at that, and not much of it. The room was so narrow I could stretch out my arms and almost touch both walls at the same time, though not quite. Oddly, its ceiling was very high, perhaps five or six meters. There were no windows and thus no natural light, only a bare, dim bulb hanging by a thin cord from that high ceiling, far too high for me to reach.

There were no books or magazines or newspapers or reading materials of any kind. There was nothing on the walls—no signs, no markings, and certainly no mirror. Indeed, as I glanced about, the two most noticeable features of the cell were how barren it looked and how cold it felt. One thin green blanket was folded up at the end of the bed, but there were no sheets on the threadbare mattress, and the tiny pillow was made of plastic and had no pillowcase. Nevertheless, I lay down and stared up at the lightbulb and tried to settle my nerves and gather my thoughts.

I'd not been allowed to bring a notepad or pen or any other personal items into the cell. Everything had been removed by the guards when they first brought me into the detention center— everything except my grandfather's gold pocket watch. I'm not sure why they let me keep it. I guess they didn't fear I could use it either to escape or try to harm myself. So I pulled it out, wound it up, and took note of the time. It was just before eight o'clock on the morning of Monday, December 6. The ISIS deadline was just forty-six hours away, and in the midst of the most important story of my lifetime, I was now in prison.

The prince's last words to me rang in my ears. No one was coming to see me, much less get me out of here, until *after* the deadline was over and the president's fate had been decided one way or the other. What was I going to do? No one even knew where I was. Allen knew only that I was in a secure, undisclosed location somewhere near Amman. He didn't know exactly where, and he certainly didn't know I was now behind bars. No one did.

For the life of me, I couldn't even remember the name of the *Times'* law firm. I couldn't remember the name of a single attorney who worked there. And even if I could, how were any of them sup- posed to get to me? Amman's only international airport was closed indefinitely, a smoking wreck- age, its employees murdered by ISIS in a brazen and despicable chemical weapons attack, its runways completely unusable, pockmarked with craters left by enemy mortars and artillery. And even if a sympathetic attorney could physically get not just to Amman but to Marka, to this base, to this makeshift prison, to this cell, why exactly would anyone take such a risk? The forces of the Islamic State were running rampant. People were being slaughtered in the streets of America's most faithful—and until now, most stable—Arab ally. The president of the United States had been captured by ISIS terrorists. What lawyer in his right mind would come here to bail me out?

Theoretically, much could be done by phone, but with whom would a lawyer working on my behalf speak? The king was busy. So were the prince and everyone else on the base. Jordan's minister of justice was on life support in a local hospital and not expected to make it. And even if the Jordanians assigned someone to discuss my case with my lawyers by phone, how likely was it that they were ever going to let me go? The prince was all but accusing me of espionage and treason, both capital crimes. I wasn't going to be released on my own recognizance. There was going to be no bail. With Jordan in flames, I'd be lucky if there was even a trial anytime soon. And what would be my defense?

Upon that thought, I was suddenly on my feet and trying to pace. There wasn't much room, but I certainly couldn't rest. I was utterly exhausted, but sleep was out of the question. I had to figure this out. Someone was guilty of the crimes Prince

Feisal had accused me of, and it definitely wasn't me. But who was it?

I decided to make a list of every possible suspect. From the Jordanians' perspective, clearly, I was at the top. Right beside me, apparently, was Yael Katzir. They didn't have her name yet. Or rather, they hadn't yet connected Yael Katzir, the Mossad agent who had just helped me save the lives of the royal family, with the "mysterious woman" in Istanbul they now considered the prime suspect in the car bombing that had killed my best friend in the world, Omar Fayez. But how much longer would that take?

If they suspected me, wouldn't they soon be suspecting Yael? Once they did, they would undoubtedly "rewind the clock" and play out their theory to its logical conclusion. They would send her photo to the authorities in Washington to see if Yael was in any way connected to the shootings at Union Station. She wasn't, of course, but then they would send her photo to the authorities in Istanbul and ask them to run her face against all surveillance videos of people coming in and out of the airport in the days surrounding the car bombing. Using state-of-the-art facial recognition software, how long would it be before they identified that Yael had in fact been there? A few seconds? A few minutes? Of course, when the Turks cross-checked Yael's face with all the passports processed during her arrival and departure, they wouldn't find one bearing the name Yael Katzir in their database, would they? No. They wouldn't. Why? Because Yael had been using a fake name and a false passport. Why? Because she was on a mission for a foreign intelligence agency. That would lead to even more suspicions by dragging the Israelis into the mix.

My heart was racing. My pulse was pounding. I splashed some water on my face, but it didn't help. I was in danger of hyperventilating. I'd never been claustrophobic in my life, but now I felt like a caged animal, and I was desperate to get out. I needed my freedom. I needed to clear my name, and Yael's, and get back to work.

For it suddenly dawned on me that whoever the mole really was, he—or she—was still on the loose, still at work. This person had already caused the deaths of thousands and could even now be getting ready to kill again.

21

* * *

I woke up in pitch darkness.

Groggy and confused, I had no idea where I was or what time it was. But as I came to, I breathed a great sigh of relief. Clearly, this had all been a terrible dream. I wasn't in Amman. I wasn't in prison. I wasn't facing the death penalty for treason against a king. I couldn't be.

Yet as I felt around, I soon realized that I was not home at my apartment in Arlington, Virginia. Nor in a hotel room in some European or even Middle Eastern capital. I could feel the chilly, damp cinder-block walls. I swung my unshod feet over the edge of the bed and set them down on the cold, dirty floor. I reached out and felt the metal of the sink. And though the bare bulb was not on and thus not visible, I knew it was hanging above me. This was no dream. This was a nightmare.

Lying back down and staring into the great void above me, I did not recall taking off my shoes and socks, much less falling asleep. The last thing I remembered was starting a list of people who might be responsible for this horrific cascade of events. Yael and I topped the list of suspects, but I knew we were innocent. So whom did that leave? It was time to go back to work.

The prince was probably right that some of the most obvious suspects—the most senior aides to President Taylor, Prime Minister Lavi, and President Mansour—could be ruled out since they were dead. It was possible one or more of them was complicit in some way, but it would be difficult if not impossible to prove. For now, I would have to focus on the living. So who had access to the private schedules of all four principals? Who knew the exact details of the summit, including the expected location and movements of the leaders and the precise nature of the security arrangements?

The first name to come to mind was Youssef Kuttab. At fifty-six, he was Palestinian president Salim Mansour's most senior and trusted advisor. Born and raised in Jenin in the West Bank, Youssef had been a longtime member of the PLO before becoming a military aide to Yasser Arafat and later a political aide to Mahmoud Abbas. I knew he was a political mastermind, orchestrating Mansour's stunning electoral victory after Abbas finally decided to step down, then working quietly behind the scenes with the Israelis on the peace deal of the century. He'd been at the summit, of course, at Mansour's side when I'd interviewed the Palestinian leader over breakfast on Sunday morning. Later he'd been in the dining room of the palace, whispering in Mansour's ear just before the comprehensive peace treaty was about to be ratified in front of hundreds of millions of people watching around the world.

Was it all an act? Was Youssef really a closet Islamic Radical, masquerading as a Reformer? I'd known him for years. I'd interviewed him countless times, sometimes on the record but mostly on background. I couldn't imagine he'd be complicit in anything like this, especially when the attack had effectively derailed the treaty he and his boss had worked on so hard for so long.

That said, he had been privy to all the details. He not only knew the summit was going to happen, but I'd been told by multiple sources that Youssef had personally worked in the shadows to persuade the Jordanians to host the summit in Amman, at the palace. Could he actually have been engineering the ISIS attack? Was it possible that rather than supporting the deal President Mansour was striking with the Israelis, Youssef secretly thought the treaty was a catastrophic capitulation, a sellout that betrayed the best interests of his people?

And what of the e-mail he'd sent me just days before the attack? The words now rang in my ears. *I thought you were coming to Ramallah. Things are getting complicated. We need to sit down in person. Where are you?* What, exactly, had been so complicated—a peace deal that might actually get signed, not rejected out of hand by an Israeli prime minister?

I didn't buy it. But I couldn't rule out any theory right now. Everything had to be considered, and anyone running the criminal investigation had to be giving Youssef Kuttab a very hard look.

Also on my list of suspects was Hassan Karbouli, the fifty-one-year-old Iraqi interior minister. Though I considered him a friend and trusted source as well, I was suddenly looking at him very differently. There were several reasons.

First was Hassan's timing. After avoiding me for weeks and ignoring my repeated e-mails and text messages requesting a face-to-face interview with Abu Khalif, Hassan had suddenly and inexplicably summoned me for an interview with the ISIS leader at the Abu Ghraib prison just days before the peace summit. At first Hassan had warned me to stay away from Khalif. But then he'd done a complete reversal, out of the blue. Not only did he offer me an exclusive interview, but he also offered to personally take me to see Khalif. I'd been ecstatic, as had my editors. Now, however, how could the timing not seem suspect? *I got you your interview,* he'd said in his last text to me. *Hope you know what you're doing.* Had he known the prison break was being planned for the exact moment of my interview? Indeed, could he have been involved? How many people besides the Iraqi minister of the interior even knew Abu Khalif was being held in that particular prison, on that floor, in that cell?

Second were Hassan's religion and his politics. He was one of only a handful of Sunni Muslims serving in the predominantly Shia government in Baghdad, and I knew he was increasingly outraged by the moves the Iraqi government was making against Sunnis in recent months. Could he have become not only frustrated but completely enraged? Could he have lost all faith in the concept of democracy in Iraq? Could he have decided to secretly pledge his allegiance to Abu Khalif? Wasn't it possible he could have helped the ISIS leader escape the prison and then get to Mosul? Hassan had been born and raised in Mosul, after all. Who knew the city better than he?

As I lay there in the darkness, I flashed back to my arrival at the airport in Baghdad just a few days before. I could still see Hassan nervously greeting me in his ill-fitting suit. Why exactly had he been so nervous? Why had he changed his plans at the last moment and not gone to the prison with me as I had expected he would? I could still see the anger mixed with fear in his eyes as he railed against his own government. *"The Shias have really fouled things up,"* he'd told me. *"They have no idea how to run the country. . . . Sunnis all across the country are absolutely furious. . . . We have no say, no voice. . . . People are demanding change, and so far the prime minister and his people aren't listening."*

I had never seen Hassan Karbouli so upset. I had never thought him capable of violence. But now I wasn't so sure.

There was a third reason my suspicions were growing, and this one put Hassan in a category of his own: he had known the Israeli–Palestinian peace treaty was coming before anything had been reported in the press. Indeed, he had told me about it himself. He'd pressed me to tell him what I knew, what the precise details were. I'd thought it strange at the time. But even more unnerving was that he had known that the Jordanians were the architects of the whole thing.

"I've heard some rumors," I'd replied, treading carefully. *"I guess we'll just have to wait and see."*

"Perhaps" was all Hassan had said before bidding me farewell.

Had he known more than he was letting on? Was he already deeply involved in plotting against the Jordanians? Did he, like Abu Khalif and ISIS, consider the king and his court infidels, not fit to live or govern any longer?

22

* * *

I suddenly heard a sharp metallic scrape.

Startled, I sat bolt upright in the bed. A sliver of light was leaking in through an open slot at the bottom of the cell door. Someone was sliding in a plate of food and a plastic cup. I jumped to my feet, hoping to talk to whoever was out there, to get my bearings and maybe some news from the outside. But just as quickly as whoever it was had come, he was gone.

It was dark again. I could hear the *tick-tick-tick* of my pocket watch. But there was no point reaching for it. In such darkness, I'd never be able to read it. I was guessing it was around noon, but it was unsettling to say the least to have no idea when the lights were coming back on, when I was going to have contact with another human being, or when I was going to get out of this blasted cell.

My heart started racing again. The claustrophobia was returning. I felt around and found the sink and splashed more cold water on my face and neck. It was no longer chilly in there. Someone had turned the heat on. It was now boiling, and I felt like I was going to suffocate. I pulled off my shirt. Then I rinsed my hands again and trickled some of the brisk water down my chest and back. That helped a bit, but not nearly enough.

My stomach growled. I thought perhaps some calories would clear my head and calm my nerves. Freaking out wasn't going to help me get through this, though I didn't have a clue what would. Feeling around on the floor in the darkness, I found the plastic plate filled with something warm, and the cup, which was empty. Setting the cup in the sink, I repositioned myself in the bed, my bare back against the wall. Steadying the plate with my left hand, I used my right index finger to poke at the food and try to figure out what it was without burning myself. There was about a cupful of steamed rice, what felt like some overcooked vegetables, and a protein bar of some kind.

Famished, I quickly scarfed it all down despite the bland taste. Then I rinsed off the plate in the sink, set it back on the floor by the door, gulped two cups of water, and lay on the bed again in the darkness.

How much time had gone by? What if it was only an hour or two? How was I going to live like this, in alternating heat and cold, in utter darkness, with no one to talk to and no sense of what the future held? I knew I couldn't let myself panic, but I wasn't sure I had a choice. One of the things I valued most in life was my freedom to move, to travel, to roam—around a room or around the world. I'd never been held captive. I didn't know if

I could take it. Mentally. Physically. Emotionally. I wanted to be out. I wanted to be free.

I concentrated on breathing slowly and steadily. I'd never thought of myself as a fearful person. But this was a nightmare, and I didn't know how to wake up. I'd known men who had been held as prisoners of war. I'd interviewed them, written stories about them. Most of them had cracked eventually, I knew, and I feared I might too.

Back to the list, I decided. I had to stay focused, stay sharp.

So who else was a suspect? Who else could be the mole?

I closed my eyes—at least I thought I did, though in utter darkness it was hard to know the difference—and a new face came to mind. Prince Marwan Talal. I tensed. It wasn't possible, was it?

The oldest member of the Hashemite royal family, Marwan was an uncle to King Abdullah II. He was also arguably His Majesty's most trusted advisor, having previously served as a counselor to the late King Hussein, Abdullah's father. I'd first met Marwan through former CIA director Robert Khachigian on a brief trip to London. Khachigian had called the man "a most faithful, stalwart ally in the fight against the extremists in the epicenter." Yet hadn't Khachigian also told me that Marwan was a man who "lives in the shadows"? Hadn't he explained that "few people outside His Majesty's inner circle even know his name"? Then he'd added, *But he knows theirs. He knows where all the bodies are buried. And I mean that literally.*"

Marwan was not just a royal, however. He was

a devout Muslim, a fervent Sunni, a true believer in every possible way. Indeed, on my last visit with him at his lovely, palatial home overlooking the seven hills of Amman, Marwan had actually tried to convert me. He was entering the sunset of his long and storied life, but he still had a fire in his spirit. He was still advancing his goals. Was it even remotely conceivable that his goals included the overthrow of the very monarchy he had helped build over much of the last century?

On the face of it, the very notion seemed preposterous. Yet what if Marwan Talal had come to the conclusion—however painful and however reluctantly—that his nephew was no longer fit for the throne? What if King Abdullah's unwillingness to embrace a purist, fundamentalist brand of Islam was undermining his uncle's devotion to him? What if the queen's refusal to wear a headscarf and her embrace of the most stylish Western fashions had become an odious offense to Marwan? What if the soul and spirit of this elderly prince, this deeply devoted Muslim, this descendant of the Prophet, had heard the call of the caliphate and could not turn away?

As much as I didn't want to believe it, or even consider it, I realized it wasn't out of the question. It had to be considered. *I* had to consider it.

Everything I knew about the man caused me to feel guilty for simply raising such a possibility, even in the privacy of my own heart, even here in the darkness of a Jordanian prison cell. Being a devoted Muslim wasn't a crime. I didn't share Marwan's religious beliefs, no matter how hard he might try to convince me. Yet his fervency didn't make him a member of ISIS, did it? Of course not. The very notion was ludicrous.

Yet it was also true that just because not all devoted Muslims were terrorists, that didn't mean none of them were.

The king viewed Abu Khalif as a man who was perverting Islam. But didn't Khalif see himself as a wholly committed Muslim? Of course he did. Didn't every member of ISIS see himself as committed to the teachings of the Prophet, following his model, rebuilding his kingdom? Without a doubt. And didn't they see the king and all his fellow Reformers as the ones who were perverting Islam, selling it out, undermining its very essence and potency? There was no question of this.

The issue for me wasn't who was right. I wasn't an Islamic theologian. I certainly wasn't the arbiter of what was the true path of Islam. I was merely a reporter. But I was also being accused of a crime I hadn't committed. The question I had to ask was who had the motive to betray the king and usher in the chaos and terror that ISIS had brought.

Viewed from this vantage point, Prince Marwan Talal had to be considered a prime suspect. Who knew more about the king's movements, the details of the summit, the security arrangements, the points of vulnerability than he did? Who likely knew even the names and families of the fighter pilots flying "protection" overhead more than the elder statesman of the royal family? Who could possibly be better positioned not only to pull off a coup but to help provide theological legitimacy for Abu Khalif when the black flags of ISIS were raised over Amman than a direct descendant of the prophet Muhammad himself? King Abdullah would never do such a thing. But was it possible that his dying uncle—approaching eternity, preparing to see Allah face-to-face, with nothing left to lose and paradise to gain—would?

I had to admit it was possible.

And then another thought hit me. Where exactly was Marwan Talal? Hadn't he helped the king craft the very treaty that was supposed to have been signed? Hadn't I been told that many of the secret negotiating sessions had taken place at Marwan's own home? Then why hadn't he been at the summit? Why had he mysteriously disappeared, just before the attacks, as if he knew they'd been coming all along?

23

★ ★ ★

Without warning, the cell door burst open.

"Who's there?" I asked, shielding my eyes as light flooded the cell.

"Dr. Hammami," came the reply.

But he was not alone. There were two MPs at his side.

"What time is it?" I asked, trying to get my bearings.

"Just after nine."

"In the morning?"

"No, at night."

"What day is it?"

"It's still Monday. Now sit up. I need to check your vitals."

I had a hard time processing that. "You're saying fifteen hours have gone by already?"

The doctor nodded and took my temperature.

"How is that possible?"

"I administered a sedative while you were sleeping," he replied, then shone a penlight in my eyes to check my pupils.

"You *drugged* me?"

"I medicated you, Mr. Collins—for your own good. I've been monitoring you. You were in danger of hyperventilating. And you needed the rest. You've been through a great deal in the last few days. You needed to take it easy. You still do."

Take it easy? Was this guy insane? The president of the United States was being held by ISIS and threatened with his life. There were only thirty-three more hours to go before the deadline, and I was helpless either to make a difference or to cover the unfolding drama. How exactly was I to take it easy? "I want to make a phone call," I said, fighting to stay focused.

"Out of the question," Hammami replied as he wrapped a cuff around my arm and began taking my blood pressure.

"I'm an American citizen. I deserve at least a phone call."

"This is not America, Mr. Collins. Now settle down so I can get your readings."

With that I was on my feet. "Forget my blood pressure. I want a phone call. I have rights."

"Sit down, Mr. Collins," the doctor said with a tone I'd neither heard nor expected from him.

"Not without a phone call."

The lightbulb overhead suddenly flicked on. The MPs moved toward me. I immediately thought better of escalating a confrontation. I sat back down and tried a different tack. "Fine, fine; I'm sorry. Look, I'm just not used to . . . I need to speak to Prince Feisal."

"Be quiet and let me take your pulse, please."

"I just need a moment with the prince."

"Your pulse, Mr. Collins."

I stopped talking and tried to settle my frayed nerves as Dr. Hammami checked my wound and changed my bandages. "That's healing nicely."

I was glad about that, but I could also see the doctor was about to leave.

"Please, Dr. Hammami," I said, looking the man in the eye. "You know I saved the king's life, and the queen's and the crown prince's. You know I'm not a conspirator. I'm not a traitor. I'm a reporter. I traffic in information, and there's a critical piece of information I need to tell Prince Feisal. Please. It's a matter of life and death."

"His or yours?" the doctor asked, putting two pills in my hand and not waiting for an answer. "Take this for the pain, and I'll see you in twelve hours."

I protested, but he didn't seem to care. He turned and left as quickly as he'd come. The door shut and locked behind him. A moment later, the slot at the bottom of the door opened and another plate of food was slid to me. Then the slot closed, the footsteps faded, and once again I was alone.

I couldn't believe it. I just stared at the plate of steamed rice and overcooked carrots and potatoes and tried to comprehend what was happening to me. Was there a way out? I couldn't think of one. Wasn't Allen suspicious that I was no longer in touch with him? Was he asking questions? Was he taking action? I very much doubted it. He had too much else happening. And he probably thought I'd check in when I could. Which, I had to admit, had been my modus operandi lately.

Again I stared down at the food. In the dim overhead light it looked singularly unappetizing. But it could have been a fine steak. It wouldn't have mattered. There was no way I could eat.

Instead, I paced about the cell. I felt my blood pressure spiking again. My face and neck were once again hot. I was perspiring all over. Finally I looked at the painkillers in my hand and took them both, washed them down with a cup of water, splashed some water on my face, and then slumped back on the bed. It was clear the prince wasn't coming. I wasn't going to have a chance to warn him about the suspects on my list. I doubted he would even listen if I could. Maybe the doctor was right. Maybe sleeping through this nightmare was my best option. Maybe it was my only option.

I lay back on the cot. As I stared up at the lightbulb and listened to the ticking of my pocket watch, I thought about my mom and Matt and Annie and my niece and nephew. Were they together now? Were they safe? I knew they were praying for me. They couldn't know exactly what I was going through, but I had no doubt they were praying. It was about the only thing I knew for certain. Even little Katie was praying. Though she had only just turned four, I knew she was praying every night for her uncle James—to be safe, to be happy, and to give my life to Jesus. The last time we'd talked, Matt had said they'd all been praying for me, and there was no reason to think Katie was going to give up on me now, even if I was beginning to give up on myself.

It was strange to think a little girl on the other

side of the planet was praying so faithfully for me. Was I praying for them? No—not beyond my awkward prayer last night. I wasn't even praying for myself. But why not? What was really so hard? Why couldn't I turn to God the way they did? I didn't know. And that bothered me.

I tried to remember the Bible verses Annie had asked me to read. I tried to remember the ones Matt had said Katie was memorizing at Sunday school. It was all a blank. And that bothered me too. I had a nearly photographic memory. Yet for the life of me I couldn't remember the Scriptures that had meant so much to them, the ones they'd so wanted me to know and consider.

What was so different between us? I wondered. Why had Matt and I grown so far apart? After Dad had left us when we were kids, we were raised in the same broken family by the same great mom in the same loser little town, in the same lame church. Yet Matt had become a man of true faith. I'd become a man of so many doubts. Why?

This wasn't helping, I decided. All this introspection was just making me feel worse. If God was really up there, if he was really listening to the prayers of my family, then great—I'd be out of here soon enough. But I had nothing to say to him right now—certainly nothing he didn't already know.

And that's when Yael's face came to mind.

24

★ ★ ★

When I woke up—groggy yet somehow content—the light was off.

I couldn't tell what time it was, but I didn't care. It was the pills. It had to be.

Somehow, despite my mental fog, I vaguely recalled I was being held on suspicion of treason against the king. But at that moment, nothing seemed to matter. I couldn't feel my arm. I was in no pain at all. I couldn't even remember being in pain.

But I did have an intense desire for a drink. Vodka. Bourbon. Rum. A beer. It didn't matter. Just something alcoholic.

Before I realized, I'd drifted off.

★ ★ ★

The light was still off when I rolled over and pulled the blanket over my head.

I knew I'd been sleeping again, but I had no idea how long. And still I didn't care. But something had changed. There was someone in the cell with me. Even in the darkness I could see the face of Yael Katzir.

I knew it was a hallucination, yet her presence gave me great comfort. "Hello, Yael," I said to the darkness.

"Mr. Collins, over here," she whispered. "My, my, you're getting soaked. Please, won't you join me?"

It was what she'd said to me the first time we met, back in Istanbul, in front of the Blue Mosque at midnight. She'd been standing there, in the rain, wearing a stylish trench coat and holding a polka-dot umbrella. I could see it as clearly as if I were there.

I remembered thinking she was lovely even before knowing who she was. I also remembered being suspicious. I'd been expecting to meet Ari Shalit, the deputy director of the Mossad. Instead I'd met this striking brunette who somehow knew everything about me. She'd claimed Ari had sent her, and eventually I had believed her. But it had taken a while.

"Nice to meet you, Miss Katzir," I whispered into the darkness.

"Likewise," she whispered back. "Now let's start walking arm in arm, like true lovers."

We had walked together through the streets of Istanbul, the ancient metropolis that once served as the eastern capital of the Roman Empire, holding hands so it seemed natural for us to be out together that late. When a pair of policemen had taken an interest in us, I had impulsively leaned in and kissed Yael. Anything to keep up appearances.

The kiss had been all too brief as the policemen soon turned their attention elsewhere.

Now, in my dark, lonely cell, I relived the kiss. In my semiconscious state, I could actually feel her lips on mine, sense her breathlessness as we pretended to be lovers.

I blinked, and the mirage evaporated in the darkness.

Where was Yael right now? I wondered. Was she thinking of me? Did she remember our first meeting as fondly as I did? Did it matter to her at all?

I doubted it. It might have mattered yesterday, when she'd agreed to have a late dinner with me after the summit, after she put her prime minister on the plane back to Tel Aviv.

Now everything had changed. Everything she'd tried to warn her bosses about—an imminent attack by ISIS, the use of chemical weapons—had been ignored. Yet her worst fears had all come to pass. She'd been right. The world had taken a very dark turn.

And now I feared I would never see her again.

25

★ ★ ★

The electronic locks released.

The door swung open, again flooding the cell with light. Then the lightbulb overhead turned on. Dr. Hammami and the two MPs at his side were back.

"Good morning, Mr. Collins."

"Is it morning?" I asked, certain I couldn't possibly have heard him correctly.

"It is indeed," he replied, pulling out his stethoscope and starting through his routine again. "It's just before 10 a.m.," he said.

"Ten o'clock *Tuesday* morning?" I clarified, still not seeing how this could be true.

"That's right, Mr. Collins—six minutes before ten on Tuesday morning, to be precise. So how are we feeling today? Did we get some rest? How's the arm?"

The patronizing tone alone made me want to strangle him.

"Fine, yes, better," I said, fighting the urge to go ballistic.

Wiping the sleep from my eyes, I did the math.

I'd been locked up for almost twenty-eight hours. That meant there were merely twenty hours left until the deadline. I had to get out, find a phone, let someone know what was happening to me. I feigned grogginess, but with a burst of adrenaline I was wide awake now—wide awake and trying to develop a plan to escape.

"Blood pressure's still a bit high," he said when he'd completed the exam.

It was all I could do not to let the sarcasm fly. The only thing that stopped me was the over-powering urge to break out of this cell. Yet I knew that even if I overpowered the doctor (not a prob-lem) and one of the MPs (not easy but doable), I was still going to have to get the jump on the other MP (which seemed close to impossible). And even if I did succeed, how exactly was I going to get out of the hallway? The doors at both ends were electronically locked, and there were surveil-lance cameras watching 24-7.

"Would you put on your socks and shoes, please, Mr. Collins?" the doctor asked.

"What for?"

"You have an appointment."

"Yeah, right."

"Come now. You don't want to be late. Best get moving."

"An appointment? With whom?"

"I'm not authorized to say."

"Why not?" I shot back, my discipline slipping.

"Let's just put on our shoes and socks, Mr. Collins, and be on our way, shall we?"

"Where are we going?"

"The clock is ticking, Mr. Collins. Let's pick up the pace."

Clearly this banter was going nowhere. He wasn't about to answer my questions, so there was no point continuing to ask. When I did as I was told, my hands and feet were promptly shackled, and I was led down several hallways, through a series of electronically locked doors, to a window-less little room. There I was told to sit on a metal stool on the far side of a rectangular metal table. Both the table and the stool were bolted to the floor, and I was too after the MPs fastened my shackles to steel hooks near my feet. I was reminded of my first meeting with Abu Khalif, which had taken place in a room not too dissimilar from this.

The doctor excused himself. Now it was just me and the two MPs, stone-faced and obviously prepared for any foolhardy escape plan I was idiotic enough to concoct.

The minutes ticked by, and as I waited, I pretended I was in Vegas. I laid down odds for who was going to walk through that door at the appointed hour.

At the top of my list was some Jordanian prose-cutor or perhaps a state-appointed attorney charged with my defense. This was the most logical. But next on my list, with two-to-one odds, was Prince Feisal. I had asked for the meeting, after all, and there was an outside chance he would take a break from the hunt for the president and Abu Khalif to humor me. I was ready for him, prepared to give him my list of suspects and the pros and cons for each. Seeing Colonel Sharif seemed a long shot at best, so I put him at seven-to-one odds. The king was even less likely, certainly not in a room like this, so I put those odds at five hundred to one.

Toughest to calculate were the odds of seeing Allen MacDonald or a lawyer from the *Times*, or someone from the U.S. embassy coming to help me out of this mess. All three were in roughly the same category, though clearly an embassy official had a far better chance of reaching me than the other two. Still, that would require the king or the prince or someone else in that bunker reaching out to the embassy and informing them of the suspicions—if not the charges—against me. Were they ready to do that with everything else on their plate right now? Prince Feisal had assured me the answer was a definitive no. Why would he have changed his mind?

Complicating matters even further was this question: Was the American embassy in Amman even open at the moment? Much of the staff, including the ambassador, had been at the summit, helping coordinate the visit of the president, secretary of state, and other high-ranking officials from the White House, State, and Defense. The ambassador was dead. How many others had survived?

In the end, I decided it was no better than a thousand-to-one shot that I'd see Allen or a lawyer this fast, while someone from the embassy was about fifty to one—possible but unlikely.

But when the door opened and a man I actually recognized stepped into the room, it suddenly became clear that not only was I playing the wrong odds, I wasn't even in the right casino.

26

* * *

"Mr. Collins, we meet again; how nice."

To be clear, I recognized the face. But I couldn't remember his name from Adam. He was an American, in his midfifties, well built, like he'd once been a Marine, a tad over six feet, with a strong jaw and a buzz cut that seemed like a throwback to the days of black-and-white television. He wore a dark suit and a white shirt with a thick dark tie and black wingtip shoes. I knew we'd met in Istanbul, in the hospital, just after the car bombing that took the life of Omar Fayez. He worked for the FBI—that, too, I remembered, but still I couldn't place the name. It was unlike me, and I chalked it up to sedatives and stress.

"Not to worry, Mr. Collins," he said as he watched me racing through my mental Rolodex and coming up blank. "You meet a lot of people."

He handed me a business card and I suddenly had a déjà vu moment. We'd done this before. The card bore the bureau's logo, a local office address in Istanbul, an e-mail address, a phone number, and the words *Arthur M. Harris, Special Agent in Charge.*

"Mr. Harris," I said. "Thanks for stopping by."

Harris didn't smile, not that I'd expected him to. Nor was I really trying to be funny. He wasn't coming to set me free. He was coming to bury me.

Harris sat down on the other side of the table, set his briefcase on the floor next to him, opened it, pulled out a digital voice recorder, and placed it on the table and hit Record.

"Have you been informed of the charges against you, Mr. Collins?" he began.

"Not in so many words, no," I said cautiously.

"Well, I'm here to do that," he replied. "But first, let's review your rights. You don't have to speak to me, of course. You can ask for a lawyer. But I'm hoping you'll first shed some light on what exactly has just happened."

I tried to decide if I should ask for a lawyer— or rather when to ask for one. If I was really facing charges that could lead to the death penalty, I couldn't take any risk in saying something that could be used against me. At the same time, I knew asking for a lawyer would shut down the discussion before it had begun, and I wasn't ready to do that. At the moment, Agent Harris was my only contact with the outside world. To dismiss him because I didn't have a lawyer meant being sent back to solitary confinement while the clock ticked down to the execution of the president. Harris, therefore, was my only hope of gleaning information about what was happening in the hunt for the president and Abu Khalif. He was also my only hope of learning a bit of what was going on with Allen, with my family, perhaps even

Yael, as well as getting messages back to any or all of them.

"By the way, when I refer to charges, I should say 'charges pending' against you," Harris clarified. "No formal charges have been filed. Not yet. Too much is happening at the moment. But the Jordanian authorities have made it clear to the bureau they are building a very strong case against you."

"What case?" I asked. "I risked my life to save the king's and his family's. They're going to charge me for that?"

"They say the royal family survived in spite of your efforts, Mr. Collins. And I have to say, the evidence they've shown me is rather compelling."

"They think I'm conspiring with ISIS against the Hashemite Kingdom?"

"In a word, yes."

"They think the fact that I've interviewed Abu Khalif and Jamal Ramzy means I'm in collusion with them."

"They wonder how you got such 'exclusive interviews.' They wonder how you keep managing to live when everyone else around you dies. They wonder why you were allowed to leave Mosul and get back to Jordan just before the peace summit when no other foreigner has been to Abu Khalif's secret headquarters and come out alive."

I'd heard all this before from Prince Feisal, but the list was no less incredible now. "What do they say about the fact that I was the one who spotted the F-16 breaking off from his wingman, that I was the one who alerted the chief of security for the Royal Court that a kamikaze attack was under way?"

"Too little, too late, they say."

"But it wasn't too late, was it?" I protested. "That 'little' bit of warning saved the king's life, not to mention President Taylor's, Prime Minister Lavi's, and President Mansour's."

"Look, Mr. Collins, I'm not here on behalf of the Jordanian government," Harris replied, deftly changing lanes. "I'm not here investigating the attempted assassination of the king, per se. I'm here investigating the attempted assassination of the president of the United States, along with the murder of the secretary of state and eighty-two other American citizens."

"You can't possibly think I'm complicit in any of that."

"Like I said, Mr. Collins, on a short list of suspects, you're the only one with irrefutable contact with the enemy."

I took a deep breath and fought to keep my composure. "Is the FBI charging me with a crime?"

"Not yet."

"But you intend to?"

"That's not my call."

"Whose is it?"

"The attorney general's—he's in the process of convening a special grand jury."

"And I'm a target?"

"Clearly."

"What are the charges the Jordanians are preparing to make? You never said."

"Murder, attempted murder, aggravated murder, terrorism, and espionage."

I felt sick.

"At the top of the list is treason—'making an attempt on the life of the king, the queen, or the regent.'"

"This is a joke. The only attempt I made was to save the life of the king and queen. A successful attempt, I might add."

"Don't kid yourself, Mr. Collins; this is no joke, and I am told they intend to prosecute all of these crimes to the fullest extent of the law."

"Which is?"

"These are all capital crimes. They are punishable by death."

I knew from Colonel Sharif that Jordan still had a death penalty, but I was pretty sure they hadn't used it in years. Were they really threatening to execute me for crimes I hadn't even committed? "But Jordan doesn't execute criminals," I said hopefully.

"Not true," Harris replied. "There are currently 106 convicted criminals on death row here. And the Jordanian government executed several ISIS and al Qaeda conspirators earlier this year."

If I was going to ask for a lawyer, this was surely the time. Instead, I leaned forward and lowered my voice.

"Agent Harris, I had absolutely nothing to do with these crimes. I'm a reporter, not a terrorist. I've been doing everything I can to understand the enemy and warn my country and the world about their intentions. It was my story with Jamal

Ramzy that warned the president and his senior advisors that a major attack was coming. It was my reporting that made it clear that ISIS had captured chemical weapons. The president wasn't convinced ISIS really possessed them. CIA Director Vaughn told me personally he wasn't convinced ISIS had weapons of mass destruction. It was my reporting—not his or his team's intelligence gathering—that provided conclusive evidence that ISIS had sarin gas. Every step of the way, I have warned American and Jordanian leaders—in print and in person—of grave and imminent dangers to them. Dangers that proved to be true. Dangers that have nearly gotten me killed numerous times. Dangers that got me shot, that led to the deaths of my closest friends. In short, Mr. Harris, I'm not guilty of these horrific crimes. Abu Khalif is guilty. ISIS is guilty. And anyone in a position of authority who didn't listen to my repeated warnings and take appropriate action bears no small measure of responsibility as well."

"Very moving, Mr. Collins, but save it for your summation."

27

* * *

I was getting nowhere fast.

Harris wasn't buying my defense, so I decided to go on offense. It was a risk, especially with a running audio recording, but it was a calculated one, and at that moment I felt I had no choice.

"Look, Agent Harris, like you, like my Jordanian friends, I'm convinced there's a mole at a very high level, a mole that has been feeding information to ISIS," I said, making an enormous concession I was sure no lawyer would advise. "Someone with access to the details of the peace summit must have supplied those details to Abu Khalif and his men in an attempt to kill all four principals and take over the kingdom of Jordan. I categorically deny I am that mole or that I am involved in a criminal conspiracy in any way, shape, or form. But I have been thinking long and hard about this and I want you to consider three possible suspects."

"Shall we begin with Yael Katzir?" he asked, catching me off guard.

"What? Of course not," I said. "She had nothing to do with this."

"How do you know?"

"Because it's ridiculous. Why would you even ask such a thing?"

"That's not a compelling argument, Mr. Collins."

"Yael? You're serious?" I shot back. "She had every opportunity to kill every single principal in the king's palace, but she fought back against the terrorists instead. She could have easily killed the royal family while we were escaping the palace and racing them to the airport, but she risked her life to save them instead. She—"

I suddenly stopped midsentence. I was about to say, "She did everything she could to help me expose the fact that ISIS had captured chemical weapons, including giving me classified Israeli intelligence to help me with my story." But I couldn't burn her as a source. If I wasn't going to tell Allen MacDonald and my editors in New York who my confidential sources were, I certainly couldn't tell the FBI, much less on the record.

Then Harris stunned me by saying it for me.

"Because she was your source for the chemical weapons story, wasn't she?" he pressed. "That's what you were about to say, weren't you?"

"No, it's not," I lied.

"Should I pull out the polygraph and see how you hold up?"

"You know full well I can't talk about confidential sources. And even if she was one—and I'm not saying she was—I couldn't tell you."

"A grand jury could compel you."

"I'm protected by the First Amendment,

Agent Harris—freedom of the press, in case you'd forgotten."

"You think the First Amendment is going to protect you if the attorney general charges you with treason against the president of the United States?"

"The First Amendment, the Fifth, and others—absolutely," I replied. "But I just told you, my reporting was to warn the president and the American government, not to commit treason against them. Why don't you believe me?"

"Perhaps because you're a liar, Mr. Collins," Harris said flatly. "I know you're lying right now. I know Ms. Katzir was your source, or one of them. I know she was the woman in the café in Istanbul, the one who fled after the bombing. I know Robert Khachigian was another source. And I know you fled the scene of a crime when he and a group of federal agents were murdered in Union Station. I know you still haven't bothered to tell your side of the story to the bureau on why you fled, why you left the country, why you immediately went to go see Ms. Katzir. I know Ms. Katzir sent you a text message while you were meeting with King Abdullah, and I know what it said."

Harris reached down, pulled a single sheet of paper out of his briefcase, and slid it across the table. I looked down and read the message, though I already knew every word.

James—thank G-d you're safe! Thnx 4 the note. Have been worried sick. We need to

talk. Dangerous new developments. Call
me ASAP.—Y

"You see where this is heading, Mr. Collins?"
Harris asked, echoing the question Prince Feisal
had asked me. "You see how all this is going to
look before a federal grand jury?"

The man had done his homework. He had the
enormous resources of the American government
behind him, and he seemed determined to crush
me. It was time to launch a counterstrike.

"You're chasing the wrong car, Agent Harris.
Your case is circumstantial at best, not to mention completely illogical. Worse, you're not looking at other, far more compelling suspects—men
who had the motive, the means, and the opportunity to pull off these crimes. And the longer
you try to railroad me, the longer the real conspirators are still out there, still plotting, still
putting our country and our allies in grave danger. Now look, I'm not a Muslim. I'm certainly
no ISIS supporter. I've got no religious motivation to be involved in these crimes. I've got
no political motivation. I'm a lifelong registered
Democrat, same as the president. I've got no
financial or personal motive. Any reasonable jury
of my peers is going to see that every so-called
fact you say damns me is completely countered
by verifiable actions I took to warn these leaders
in order to save their lives. If I was hell-bent on
killing them, I had an MP-5 in my hands and
plenty of ammunition. So did Yael Katzir. We

could have finished them off at any time. But we didn't. So you tell me how it's going to look to a federal grand jury."

To my surprise, he was quiet for a moment. It wasn't clear whether I was convincing him or whether he was simply waiting for me to say more that he could use to further incriminate me. But then he leaned back in his chair and raised his eyebrows, beckoning me to make my case.

So I did. For the next ten minutes, I outlined the case against Youssef Kuttab, Hassan Karbouli, and Prince Marwan Talal, saving the best for last.

But Harris wasn't buying it. "Talk about circumstantial. You're essentially accusing three Muslims for being Muslims."

"You don't think the mole is a Muslim?" I asked.

"Not necessarily, no," Harris replied.

"Someone willing to risk his or her life to help the Islamic State—you don't think religion is a major element of their motivation?"

"Not every Muslim is a terrorist, Mr. Collins."

"I'm not saying they are," I countered. "Don't put words in my mouth. I'm saying that everyone risking life and limb to build the caliphate for Abu Khalif and the Islamic State is motivated above all else by his or her belief in Islam and desire to see Islam spread across the globe."

"So now you're an expert in Islam?"

I felt as if we were playing a high-level chess match, alternately attacking and countering, each of us trying to see five and six moves ahead, trying to set ourselves up for the best possible combinations. "I'm an expert in terrorism. I've been covering it for the better part of my career."

"You've talked to a lot of terrorists."

"Of course."

"Met with them?"

"Yes."

"Traveled the world to find them and spend time with them?"

"It's my job."

"And that makes you an expert?"

"I'd say so, yes."

"I can't wait for the grand jury to hear this. *I'm an expert in terrorism.*'"

"Don't be ridiculous," I shot back. "You know exactly what I mean. You're twisting my words to try to make me look guilty. But you're ignoring perfectly credible suspects. You refuse to look at anyone else but me, refuse to do any digging, any investigating whatsoever. Is burying your head in the sand part of the job description of a special agent for the Federal Bureau of Investigation?"

Harris sat forward. "And you've done your homework, Mr. Collins? You've looked at all the facts? You've been digging, investigating, have you?"

"Well, that's been a little hard to do given that I've been locked away in solitary confinement for the last thirty hours."

"Fine," said Harris. "Of your three suspects, which one do you think is most likely to have done it, assuming for a moment that you're even in the ballpark?"

"You're really asking me?"

"I am."

"And you'll really take it seriously?"

"That's my job. You said so yourself."

The chess match had just gotten more interesting. "Well, then," I said, trying to decide whether he was playing games with me or being serious. "Mind you, this is just conjecture at this stage."

"Of course."

"These are theories—possible theories—not accusations."

"Right."

"All three of these are friends of mine. I hope to God none of them are involved."

"Got it," said Harris. "But if you had to choose one."

"I'm sure the list is longer than just these three."

"I understand—now pick one."

"The prince."

"Talal?"

"Yes."

"Marwan Talal?"

"Perhaps."

"You think the eldest uncle of the king of Jordan is involved in a conspiracy to kill him and everyone in his family and bring ISIS to power in Jordan?"

"It's possible," I said. "More possible than it is that I'm involved."

"No."

"What do you mean, no?"

"I mean it's not possible."

"It's not possible that Prince Marwan Talal is the mole?"

"No."

"Then why was he missing from the summit? Why wasn't he there when he was ostensibly so deeply involved in the crafting of the treaty? That doesn't seem suspicious to you?"

"No."

"Yet my behavior does?"

"Yes."

"Why?"

"Because I know where the prince was," said Harris. "I know why he wasn't at the summit."

"How?"

"Because I've been doing my homework. I've been digging. I've been investigating."

"So where was he?"

"Baghdad."

"Baghdad?"

"Yes."

"The prince was completely out of the country at the moment of Jordan's maximum danger. A little convenient, wouldn't you say?"

"No."

"No?"

"No."

"Because you know why he was there?"

"Yes."

"And why was that?"

"You really want to know?"

"Yes."

"Very well then. He went because the king asked him to go."

I had to think about that for a second. "Why would the king ask his uncle to go to Baghdad?"

"To lay the groundwork for the king's state visit."

"The visit scheduled for this weekend?"

"That's the one."

"You're sure about that? I mean, absolutely certain?"

"The king told me himself," Harris said. "The prince confirmed it. I talked to the Iraqi prime minister, as well. They all tell the same story."

I felt as if the wind had been knocked out of me.

Check . . . and mate.

28

★ ★ ★

It was quiet for several minutes.

I just sat there, not sure what to say. I'd not only made a foolish and serious error, impugning a member of the royal family without any proof whatsoever, but I'd done it in front of an FBI agent who was recording me.

The game wasn't really over. I knew that. But for the first time I really did feel scared. This wasn't a game, after all. This was a criminal investigation. I was accused of espionage, murder, terrorism, and treason. And my life hung in the balance.

"I'd like to speak to a lawyer," I said finally.

Harris turned off the digital recorder. "Not so fast, Mr. Collins," he replied. "You have other options."

"No, really—I don't want to say anything else without legal counsel present."

"Now hold on and listen to what I have to say."

"I'm done listening, Agent Harris. I'd like a lawyer. That's it."

But Harris wasn't done. He leaned close and

spoke so quietly that the guards in the room had no chance of hearing him.

"Listen carefully, Mr. Collins. You're in a heap of trouble. I think we've established that. The only question now is whether you want to be tried in an American court or here in Jordan. And I'd like to recommend you choose option A rather than option B."

"I'm listening," I whispered back.

"You'd rather come home to face the music than stay here?"

"Yes," I replied, oblivious now to the president's fate and completely consumed with my own. I was at that moment no longer a foreign correspondent for the *New York Times*. I was an accused traitor facing death by shooting or hanging in a foreign court system where I had no leverage whatsoever.

"Then I'd suggest you make a call."

"To whom?"

"Jack Vaughn."

"The director of the CIA?"

"Yes."

"Not the attorney general?"

"No."

"Why?"

"You know Jack, right?"

"Of course."

"You've been friends for ages, right?"

"Absolutely."

"You believe he can vouch for your integrity."

"I do."

"Then call him."

"How?"

"I have your iPhone."

I stared at Harris. It felt like the chess match had resumed, but I was no longer seeing five moves ahead. Now I was struggling just to figure out my next move. "And say what?" I finally asked.

"Make your case. Ask him to call the attorney general on your behalf. Tell him to have the AG call the king and make arrangements for me to bring you back to Washington in my custody."

"And why would the king agree?"

"He's the one who lost the president, Mr. Collins," Harris explained. "Right now I think he'd do just about anything the American government asked of him."

"I wouldn't be so sure of that."

"You'll never know unless you try."

He had a point there. "So what's in it for you?"

"Nothing."

"Then why do you care?"

"I don't, since you ask," Harris said. "But you're an American citizen. You're being held for crimes as much against our country as any. And you're being held in a nation that is undergoing a coup. I wouldn't wish that on anyone. If you're guilty, then it should be our government that proves it before an American court of law, period."

I leaned back. I thought about what he was saying and assessed my options. There were only two. Make the call or go back to solitary with no telling what might happen to me next. That was no choice at all. But there was something odd about the whole conversation.

"May I have my phone?" I asked, deciding not to overthink the moment.

"You may."

Harris reached back into his briefcase, pulled out my iPhone, and slid it across the table. For a moment, I just stared at it. I wanted to call my mom. I wanted to call Yael. I needed to call Allen. But apparently I was getting only one phone call today, and I figured I'd better make it count.

"What time is it?" I asked.

"It's twelve minutes after eleven," Harris said.

That meant it was only twelve minutes after four in the morning back in Washington. Twenty-nine hours into the ISIS ultimatum. Only nineteen hours left until the president's execution.

"Shouldn't we wait a few hours until Jack's up?" I asked.

I didn't really want to wait, of course. I wanted to get out of Amman as quickly as possible. But I also needed Jack Vaughn to be awake, alert, and in a good mood. Calling him in the middle of the night didn't exactly strike me as the best strategy.

"This is a onetime offer, Mr. Collins. It's now or never."

I picked up the phone, searched through my contacts, and found the home number for the Vaughn residence in Great Falls, Virginia. I pressed the call button and held my breath.

The phone rang repeatedly, but no one answered. I got voice mail but hung up without leaving a message.

"Try again," Harris said.

"He's not there."

"Just try again," he repeated.

I was in no mood to argue, so I hit Redial and waited. Finally, on the fifth ring, I heard a man's voice on the other end of the line.

"Jack Vaughn," he said, sounding as groggy as he did annoyed.

"Jack, hey, it's J. B. Collins," I began. "I'm so sorry to call you at home, especially at such an hour."

"Collins?"

"Yes, sir."

"Is this a joke?"

"No, sir."

"This is really J. B. Collins?"

"Yes, sir. Again, I'm so sorry to call you so early."

Vaughn sighed irritably. "Where are you?"

"I'm in Amman, sir."

"But you're alive."

"I am, and I need your help."

"Help? You've got to be kidding me. Do you even know how much trouble you're in? I hear the bureau's about to put a warrant out for your arrest."

He was waking up fast.

"That's why I'm calling, sir."

"Look, Collins, I shouldn't even be talking with you."

"Sir, please, you know I'm innocent."

"I do? I don't think so."

"Jack, come on—I did everything I could to warn you and the president about what ISIS was planning. I risked my life to save the president's and the king's. And now I need your help."

Just then I heard a woman's voice.

"Who's that?" she asked.

"Never mind," Vaughn said. "Just go back to bed."

Oh, great, I thought, *now I've woken up his wife.*

"Is that Collins?" she asked. "J. B. Collins?"

"Yes, yes, now just . . . Listen, Collins, I need to go."

"No, wait, sir," I pleaded. "I have one specific favor to ask you."

"Where is he?" I could hear his wife asking him.

"Shhh, I told you, just get back in bed—I'll be there in a minute," Vaughn told her. "So what is it, Collins? Make it fast."

"Jack, I'm innocent of all of this. The evidence will completely exonerate me. But I want to be tried in an American court. Not here. Not in Amman."

"That's out of my hands. Now unless you know where ISIS is holding the president, I can't talk to you any longer."

"Jack, please—I'm asking you to call the AG," I pressed, my tone becoming more urgent.

"The attorney general?" he replied, clearly bewildered. "What for?"

"I want you to ask him to call the king and request that I be extradited back to Washington with the FBI agent who's come to interrogate me. I'll come willingly. I just want my day in court— an American court."

"Where is he?" I overheard Vaughn's wife say again. "Is he still in Amman?"

Just then Harris slipped me a handwritten note.

Just got an e-mail. The king wants to
meet with you in fifteen minutes. Jack
needs to call the AG immediately.

"Jack, listen, the king wants to meet with me
in fifteen minutes. Please, I'm begging you, have
the AG call him. I'm pretty sure His Majesty will
accommodate any request the U.S. government
has for him right about now."

"The king wants to see you?"

"Apparently he does."

"Why?"

"I have no idea, Jack. But that's why I need
you to call the AG right now and have him take
custody of me and this case."

"You know what you're asking?"

"I know, Jack, and I'm sorry. But I'm an
American citizen. I shouldn't be tried in a foreign
court."

"So where are you right now?"

I heard more whispering but forced myself to
stay focused and answer his questions. "I'm on a
military base outside of Amman," I replied.

"Which one?"

"Marka."

"At the general headquarters?"

"Yes. I'm in the detention center, level B, cell
number three."

"That's too much. I don't need all that. I just
want to make sure the AG understands which base

you're at. Who's the agent from the bureau there with you now?"

"Art Harris—do you want to talk to him?"

"No, no, I'm just trying to establish the facts. Are you calling me on a landline?"

"No, it's my mobile."

"What's the number?"

I gave it to him.

"And I can get back to you on this?"

"Hold on a moment," I said. "Let me check."

I turned to Harris and whispered the question to him.

He nodded, so I told Jack, "Yes."

"Fine," Vaughn said. "I need to go. I'll see what I can do."

With that, the call was over.

"And?" Harris asked when I set down the phone.

"And what?"

"Did he say yes? Is he going to get you transferred back to Washington?"

"I'm not sure."

"Did he say yes?"

"Not exactly."

"But he didn't say no?"

"Not exactly."

"So what did he say?" Harris pressed.

"He said he would see what he could do."

"You think he'll at least call the AG?"

"I don't know. I hope so."

"Okay, then," Harris said.

"So now we wait?" I asked.

"No, now we go see the king," Harris replied.

I had already forgotten about his note. "Why do you think he wants to meet with me?" I was certain I was still in great danger and not sure I wanted to look the monarch in the eye just then.

"Don't know," Harris said. "But we'd better not keep him waiting."

29

⭐ ⭐ ⭐

Harris stood and informed the guards we were going out.

Then he asked me for my phone back.

"But I thought you just said Jack and the AG could call me."

"They can, but I'm going to forward your calls to my phone," Harris explained.

"Why can't I keep the phone with me?" I asked.

"Because as far as the king and Prince Feisal are concerned, you're their prisoner. They ordered the phone removed from you, and I don't want to do anything to challenge their authority."

I nodded and Harris proceeded to fiddle with my iPhone to transfer all incoming calls to his phone. I was disappointed. I wanted to scroll through my messages. I wanted to see if Yael had written to me, wanted to send notes to her and to my family letting them know what was happening. But Harris was right. I was in too precarious a position to take unnecessary risks. So I steeled myself for what was ahead as he put my phone in his briefcase, set the briefcase on the table, and pointed me toward the door.

"Aren't you going to take that?" I asked Harris as I got up to follow him.

"Why?" he asked. "There's no point bringing it over to the bunker. The security guys won't let me take it in there. It'll be safe here. I'll get it when we're done."

"Fair enough," I said as the guards came over and released my leg shackles and prepared to escort me upstairs.

Just then, Harris's phone buzzed. I wondered whether it was my phone forwarding a call to his or whether he was receiving a call directly. Either way, when he looked at the screen, the expression on his face completely changed. He excused himself and stepped out into the hallway, and suddenly I was alone again. Unfortunately, that gave me more time to worry about this meeting with the king. How much had Feisal already told him about the case against me? Had they even had time for detailed conversations? On one hand, it seemed unlikely given everything else on His Majesty's plate. On the other hand, the mole hunt was critical to his own survival. I'd personally heard the king ask his younger brother for an update, and how could the two of them not make it a top priority in light of the damage this traitor or traitors had done already?

The minutes ticked by. Harris didn't return. And the longer he didn't walk through that door, the more my anxieties increased. Whom was he talking to, and what was taking so long? Had Jack

Vaughn called him to ream him out for letting me—someone under suspicion of espionage and treason against a foreign government—make contact with the director of the Central Intelligence Agency? Or was it the attorney general on the line, ripping Harris for getting him involved during what was arguably the most sensitive espionage investigation in the history of the bureau?

I glanced at Harris's briefcase. It was sitting there on the table. Was it locked? What else was in it besides my phone? Were there details about my case? I can't tell you how tempted I was to open it and riffle through his papers, even just for a few minutes. My guards had stepped out with Harris. I really was alone. But then I glanced up and noticed a small surveillance camera mounted on the wall, up in the corner, near the door, and I wondered if this was a trap. Were Harris and the Jordanians trying to set me up, trying to lure me into doing something incriminating, only to capture it all on video and hang me for it—perhaps literally?

Louis Brandeis, the renowned Supreme Court justice, used to say, "Sunlight is said to be the best of disinfectants." That surveillance camera was the sunshine, purifying me from all temptation. I had to watch my step, I reminded myself. I had to walk the line. Too much was at stake. Then I started to wonder: was Harris really on a call? Or was he in the control room, watching me on closed-circuit TV, waiting for me to seal my fate?

Almost twenty minutes later, Harris came back into the room. He apologized and told me to follow him, but his demeanor had changed. Why? Was he sorry I hadn't taken the bait? Or had there really been a call? And if so, who had called, and why did the news seem so bad? Every instinct in me wanted to ask him questions. It's what I did for a living, after all—ask people questions, ply them for information. I couldn't help it. It was instinct. But in this case I forced myself to keep my mouth shut. If Harris had something to say, he would say it. But I couldn't let myself be lulled into the notion that he was my friend or ally. He wasn't. He was my adversary. Sure, he wanted the king to hand me over so I could be tried in an American court. But he was still there to bury me, and I couldn't afford to forget it.

We took a right down the corridor and headed through another series of locked doors and maze-like hallways until eventually we were standing outside. Finally I was breathing fresh air. Cold air too. After a gorgeous and warm October with temperatures averaging in the seventies and eighties and a stormy but mild November with temperatures in the sixties, the first few days of December felt unseasonably cold. I hadn't seen a thermometer or heard a weather report in days, but it couldn't have been more than fifty degrees, possibly a good deal less. The patches of blue and rays of sun I'd seen the last time I'd crossed this tarmac were gone. Now the skies were dark and threatening. I tried to remember when I'd last worn my leather jacket. I could have used it just then.

Still, it felt good to be out of doors, even if my hands were still cuffed, even if there were three armed guards watching my every move, even if I was about to see a king and his senior advisors, who believed I had plotted to kill them all. It was strange to think how radically the past thirty hours or so had changed my perspective. No longer was I thinking about my next exclusive story for the *Times*. Now I just wanted to stand here, outside this detention center, and savor every moment out of that cell.

There were no F-15s or F-16s taking off or landing this morning. There were no troop transport planes arriving or departing either. I saw a Black Hawk helicopter powering up over by the main complex of buildings, where the bunker was located, and there was a small Learjet being refueled and serviced. But overall, it seemed awfully quiet for a base operating as central command in a winner-take-all battle to recapture the country from the forces of the Islamic State.

"Come on," Harris said. "We'd better get moving."

"Hang on a second," I said. "I want to ask you something first."

"Ask me while we're walking."

"No, this is important," I said. "Did the king or his people give you access to Jamal Ramzy's phone?"

"What phone?" he replied. "What do you mean?"

"When Yael—Ms. Katzir—and I killed Jamal Ramzy . . ." My voice trailed off. I paused a moment, then looked the agent in the eye. "Did you even know we did that—that we killed ISIS members, including the organization's second-highest-ranking leader?"

"Yes, I knew."

"And it doesn't mean anything to you that I was killing ISIS leaders rather than conspiring with them?"

"It's in the file," he said without tipping his hand.

That didn't give me much comfort, but it was something I'd have to take up with my own lawyers, not with the FBI. "But does it also say in the file that I pried a mobile phone out of Ramzy's bloody hands?"

"No," he said.

"Does it say that when Yael and I got the king and his family safely to the airport and under the protection of his own soldiers, I gave him the phone?"

"No," he said again. "No one's mentioned it."

"Well, you should ask about it," I said. "I gave Ramzy's phone to the king so they could analyze it—calls received and sent, to what numbers, in what countries, what cities and neighborhoods. I suspect there's a treasure trove of information in that phone, information that might even lead you to the president."

"Okay," Harris said quietly. "I'll be sure to ask about Ramzy's phone. Now let's go, or we're going to be late."

We started heading across the tarmac, walking briskly to make up for lost time. Just then I heard a buzzing in the sky off to our right. It was faint, and I barely noticed it at first. But it was getting louder. It sounded like a small plane—a prop plane, maybe a crop duster—not a jet. That was odd because this wasn't a civilian airport. There weren't any crop dusters or Piper Cubs or small prop planes of any kind anywhere near here. But there it was, getting louder and louder. It was coming from the east.

We kept walking, faster now but distracted by the sound. Harris and the guards heard it too, and then one of the guards said it sounded to him like a drone.

That's when we saw a flash in the eastern sky. It was a drone, and it had just fired a missile. I saw the contrail. We hit the deck just as the missile streaked over our heads.

The explosion must have been heard for miles. Burning debris was suddenly raining down on us. I wanted to cover my head, but my hands were still shackled. I turned my head and looked behind me. All I could see was a blazing fire and a smoking crater. The detention center was gone.

And then we heard another missile go slicing past us.

30

The second missile slammed into the central administrative complex.

This was the very building to which Harris and I had been heading, the very building that housed the command center from which the king was prosecuting the fight to regain control of his kingdom. This explosion was even more deafening than the first. A ball of fire soared into the air as the upper stories began collapsing and the main edifice of the structure imploded before our eyes.

"Come on; let's go," one of the guards shouted over the roar of the flames. *"We can't stay here. We need to move."*

He grabbed me and hauled me to my feet. The other two guards and Harris were scrambling to their feet as well, and we sprinted across the tarmac for the nearest hangar. There were no planes or helicopters parked inside, and I guessed this was why the guards were headed there. It was not likely a target and might give us some initial protection from the flames and flying debris. As we ran, I could hear the sound of antiaircraft batteries erupting behind and ahead of me, and moments later I could hear the sounds of sirens. Fire trucks and ambulances were streaming in from all directions, as were armored personnel carriers, military police vehicles, and probably even battle tanks. Moments earlier, the base had seemed so quiet, almost a ghost town. Now it was about to be swarming with soldiers and first responders.

As we reached the hangar, we were rocked by a series of secondary explosions as fuel tankers and other vehicles parked near the sites that had just been attacked erupted in succession. The guards ordered me into a corner. Then they chained me to the side of a tow truck.

Guns drawn, they then set up a perimeter and ordered Harris to hand over his weapon. Harris started to protest but quickly thought better of it. Slowly, carefully, he drew his .45, set it on the pavement, and kicked it gently over to one of the guards.

"Can I make a call?" he asked the lead guard. "I need to reach my superiors in Washington."

"Of course," the MP replied. "You're not under any suspicion, Agent Harris. We just have a protocol we have to follow."

"I understand, gentlemen," Harris said. "I know you're just doing your jobs."

With me chained down and Harris disarmed, the guards turned their attention from us to the possibility that anyone might be trying to help me escape. To me, of course, the very notion seemed ridiculous. This wasn't a breakout. This was simply the forces of ISIS bringing the fight to the vortex of the king's command-and-control operations. Abu Khalif had vowed to behead not only the president of the United States but the monarch of Jordan as well. That meant ISIS jihadists were likely attacking the Jordanian soldiers guarding the base. Would they break through? Would they actually make it here, to where we were now? What then? The only thing I feared more than being tried by the Jordanians was being captured by ISIS. There had been a time when I was useful to Abu Khalif. No longer. I had no doubt the ISIS emir would love watching me die a slow death.

"Op Center Alpha, this is Special Agent Arthur Harris with an emergency override. . . . Yes, sir— my access code is X-ray-Niner-Foxtrot-Three- Seven-Four-Three-Tango-Bravo. . . . Yes, sir. . . . Voice ID: 'Kensington Station.' . . . Yes, sir. . . . I am inputting that number now."

I couldn't imagine how Harris could hear over the triple-A fire, the sirens, and the raging fires. Yet before I could ask him what he was doing, he was dialing another number and talking to someone else. A few moments later, he handed the phone to the lead MP, who nodded a few times, asked a couple of questions, nodded some more, then passed the phone to his two colleagues. When the last one hung up the phone, he handed it back to the leader, who returned it to Harris. After they conferred among themselves, one of them made a phone call of his own. When that call was done, suddenly they were unlocking me from the wall and removing my handcuffs.

"Follow me," the head guard shouted.

I had no idea what was happening, but Harris motioned for me to do what the man said and promised to be right behind me. We started walking briskly, then began running. Soon we were climbing into the back of a Black Hawk helicopter that was already powered up and ready to go.

Harris shouted at me to put on my seat belt and hold on tight. Then we lifted off and shot into the stormy morning sky, rapidly gaining altitude and leaving the chaos behind us. As we banked to our left and took a north-by-northeast heading, I felt numb, staring out the window at the leaping flames and billowing smoke and terrible destruction below. One thing I didn't see, however, was any sign that ISIS forces were striking the Jordanian troops holding the perimeter of the base, which only confused me all the more.

"What in the world is going on?" I shouted at Harris over the roar of the rotors as we reached a reasonably safe altitude and distanced ourselves from Amman. "Shouldn't we be trying to rescue the king and the prince and the others? We can't just leave."

"Don't worry," Harris shouted back. "They're not there."

"What do you mean they're not there?"

"The king and his team left the base yesterday."

"Why?"

"To avoid something just like that."

"Where are they?"

"I don't know."

"What do you mean you don't know?"

"They haven't told me," said Harris. "It's classified."

"But you said we were going to see the king."

"We are."

"I don't understand."

"We weren't heading for the bunker," Harris explained. "We were heading for this chopper. It's taking us to the king, wherever he is."

None of this was making any sense. "I'm not following," I told him. "Why did they remove my handcuffs? It's like they're letting me go."

"That's simple," Harris replied. "You're no longer a suspect."

"What are you talking about?"

"You're no longer a suspect, Mr. Collins—you've been cleared."

"I don't understand," I said again.

"You've been part of a sting operation—an operation that, I'm afraid, just went terribly wrong."

31

* * *

As we shot over the eastern desert, Harris told me a story I could hardly believe.

"You were never really a suspect," he began.

Try as I might, I couldn't process what he was saying.

"Our investigation, and that of the Jordanians, ruled you out almost immediately," Harris explained, "for all the reasons you spent the morning enumerating. We were also able to rule out fairly quickly the people you suggested could be suspects, though we looked at them all."

"Including Prince Marwan Talal," I said, more as a statement than as a question.

"He was actually the easiest to clear," Harris replied. "As I said, he was in Baghdad at the king's request at the time of the attacks."

. I felt terrible. "So you know who's responsible?"

"Yes, and even as we speak, agents are arresting three suspects."

"Who?"

"This all has to be completely off the record, Mr. Collins."

"Of course."

"No, really. I'll tell you because you've been cleared. But there is still a significant amount of work left to do in this investigation. It's under way on three continents, in six different countries. And I believe there are many more arrests still to be made."

"But you've got the mole?" I pressed, dying to know who it was.

Harris glanced at his phone and silently read a text message. "We do, and two of his coconspirators. They were literally just taken into custody."

"So who is it?"

"You're sure we're off the record?"

"Absolutely."

"Because you're involved in this case, you can't write about it at all. I'm sure the *Times* will cover the story. I'm sure the bureau will work with other reporters from the *Times*. But eventually you're going to have to testify in this case, and we can't have you writing about it. Conflict of interest and all."

"I understand. You have my word."

"Can I have that in writing?" he asked, pulling a sheet of paper out of his breast pocket and handing it to me.

"You're kidding."

"I'm not."

I looked at the crumpled piece of paper on FBI letterhead. It was a nondisclosure form, but this was no boilerplate version. It contained detailed legalese written specifically for this case and specifically for me.

I laughed. "You don't actually expect me to sign this without a written guarantee the FBI isn't going to charge me with crimes against the United States or any other government, do you?"

"You're kidding," Harris said.

"I'm not."

He stared at me for a moment, then took the paper and scrawled out such a promise and handed it back to me.

"Now sign it," I said.

And he did.

"And date it."

He dated it.

"And I'm going to need a copy of this before the sun goes down."

"Right."

"I have your word?"

"Yes. Can we get on with it?"

"Fine," I said. "Can I borrow your pen?"

Harris handed me his pen, and I signed. When I was finished, I returned the pen and kept the form.

"When you show me a copier, I'll be happy to give it back to you," I said.

Harris wasn't happy. But to my relief, he didn't protest.

"So, you ready?" he asked.

Honestly, I wasn't sure, but I said yes anyway.

"The mole is Jack Vaughn."

I thought he was kidding. But Harris didn't smile. Harris never smiled.

"Jack Vaughn?" I asked in disbelief.

Harris nodded.

"Jack Vaughn at CIA."

Again Harris nodded.

"I don't . . . I can't . . ."

"Let me be clear," Harris said. "There is no evidence as of yet that Mr. Vaughn intended to betray his country or set into motion such a deadly chain of events. But the evidence is conclusive: he is the mole."

"That doesn't make sense."

"Mr. Vaughn is having an affair," Harris explained. "He and Mrs. Vaughn have been planning to buy a new house, waterfront property on the Potomac River, the Virginia side, a place where they would retire when he steps down from the agency. But along the way, the woman who was their real estate agent began meeting with Mr. Vaughn separately. She would show him various properties while Mrs. Vaughn was out of town. It all seemed harmless enough, but we now know the real estate agent seduced him and they began sleeping together at these various properties while Mr. Vaughn's security detail waited outside."

I still couldn't believe it. "How long has this been going on?"

"Several months," Harris said. "But what the director didn't know was that this wasn't just an 'innocent affair,' if any affair can be called that. It was a honey trap."

"A setup?"

"I'm afraid so," said Harris. "The woman is an American citizen. Her father is American. But her mother is from Qatar. The woman herself was brought up Sunni. For years she raised money in the U.S. for Hamas. But recently she began working for ISIS."

"You're sure?"

"We are. For the last two years, she's been receiving monthly wire transfers from the Gulf through a series of banks in Europe and the Caribbean. But that's not important. What you need to know is she has been buying and selling homes to military officials at the Pentagon, members of the House and Senate, and all kinds of other officials in northern Virginia. She's been using her access to these people's homes to gain classified information and feed it back to her superiors. Six months ago she received an order to approach Claire Vaughn and offer to help her and her husband find a retirement home. She came well recommended by friends in the area, so Mrs. Vaughn agreed. But the woman quickly bypassed Mrs. Vaughn and focused her attention on Mr. Vaughn. And once they started sleeping together, she began learning little tidbits of valuable information."

"Like details of the peace negotiations?"

"Exactly."

"And details of the summit?"

"Unfortunately, yes."

"And she was feeding everything she learned back to ISIS?"

"Yes."

"But you just said something about this being a sting operation that went awry," I noted. "What does that mean?"

"The bureau caught wind of Vaughn's affair a few weeks ago," Harris said. "It wasn't really our place to interfere in a personal matter, but the more we learned about the woman, the more concerned we became. Still, her tradecraft was too good. We were sure she was getting information out of Vaughn, but we couldn't get a judge to give us a warrant to bug his house or the houses where they would have their, you know, liaisons. What's more, we were having trouble finding out how she was getting her information back to ISIS, and without that we felt we couldn't execute an arrest warrant. In short, we hadn't yet built a case that would hold up in court."

"And then came the attack on the summit?"

"Right. At that point, Mr. Vaughn and his mistress were the prime suspects. But we still didn't have conclusive proof. I briefed the king on this, privately—as you can imagine, this is all extremely sensitive. I didn't even tell Prince Feisal. I couldn't. Only the king. I told him our suspicions, and then I told him our plan. What if he arrested you? What if I interrogated you? And what if I persuaded you to call the director and plead with him to help you—at a time where his mistress might be able to overhear the conversation or get the details out of him? My team and I felt certain that if this woman learned where you were and where the king was, she would find a way to feed that information back to ISIS. Once she did, we'd have her red-handed. And that's exactly what happened. Mrs. Vaughn is out of town. The woman was at the Vaughn home tonight. That's the voice you heard talking to him. Just minutes after you got off the phone with the director, my team recorded her making a phone call to a source and telling that source these details. Our theory had worked. What we didn't expect was that this would trigger a drone attack on the base."

"You could have gotten me killed."

"I'm sorry. We didn't anticipate that."

"But why did they hit the detention center?" I asked. "I mean, the main building I get. But the detention center? It doesn't make sense."

"There's only one explanation," Harris said. "They weren't just trying to get the king. They were trying to get you, too. Apparently you've become a bigger target than we realized."

"And they were tracking my phone," I said, suddenly realizing how close I'd come—again—to losing my life.

Harris nodded. "Again, I'm sorry. But thank God you weren't carrying the phone when the missile was fired."

"Or that you weren't."

"Right," he said, staring out the window of the Black Hawk at the vast stretches of desert below us.

"So who was the woman's contact?" I asked, trying to get my mind off my own mortality.

"Her son," Harris said.

"Did you suspect him?"

"No, actually."

"Why not?"

"He served in the U.S. Army, worked for several years at the Defense Intelligence Agency, now works for the NSA at Fort Meade," Harris explained. "I can't say she used him every time. My team is working on that right now. But he's the one she called today, and whomever he called, they obviously moved pretty fast to organize this strike."

My mind was reeling. Then we started experiencing violent turbulence. Hail began pelting the chopper. Lightning flashed all around us. We began descending, but not nearly fast enough for me.

"Do you think Jack knew who the woman was?" I asked. "I mean, do you think he was actively working against the president, working to kill him, to kill the king?"

"No, I don't," Harris replied. "As I said, the investigation is ongoing. But when it's all said and done, I think we're going to find out he was guilty of adultery, not treason."

"So where does that leave me?" I asked Harris, who was suddenly looking for an airsickness bag and not seeing one anywhere.

"You're in the clear," he replied, looking green and holding his stomach.

"And the king knows all this?"

"Most of it, but I'll need to fill him in on the latest."

"So why does he want to see me? Why isn't he sending me home?"

"Honestly, I have no idea," Harris admitted. "But I guess we're about to find out."

PART
THREE

32

★ ★ ★

Jack Vaughn.

I still couldn't believe it. I'd known the man and his family for ages. I'd never have suspected him in a million years. Betraying his wife? Betraying his family? And in the end betraying his country? I felt as sick as Harris now looked.

I pulled out my pocket watch—it was almost twelve thirty on Tuesday afternoon. Just seventeen and a half hours to go before ISIS executed the president.

A brutal winter storm had descended upon the country. Driving rains and hail the size of marbles blown by whipping winds from the northeast buffeted the chopper as we came in on final approach. Sizzling sticks of lightning could be seen on the horizon. Great booms of thunder rocked the craft even more.

I turned to Harris to ask where we were. But he was white as a sheet. "You okay?" I asked.

But it was too late. Harris started heaving his guts out all over the chopper's floor. The stench

201

was overpowering. I turned back to the window. We certainly weren't in Amman anymore.

As the pilot and copilot fought to maintain control, one of the MPs explained that we were arriving at a top-secret facility known as the Muwaffaq Salti Air Base in the Zarqa Governorate, in the desert east of Amman. I'd heard of this place. The base was built in 1976 near a landing strip once used by Lawrence of Arabia during World War I. The modern base was completed in 1980 and named after a Jordanian pilot who was killed in battle with the Israelis.

The first thing that struck me as we got closer—other than the fact that Harris was still puking his guts out—was how crowded the airfield was. Despite the brutal conditions and limited visibility, there were dozens of Jordanian F-16s taking off and landing, no doubt conducting sorties over the capital and some of the outlying towns and villages where ISIS had been making gains. But what really caught my eye was the number of American, Egyptian, and Saudi fighter jets, long-range bombers, attack helicopters, and special operations aircraft—dozens and dozens, perhaps well over a hundred, including a handful of American B-2 stealth bombers—being amassed at a base very few people had ever even heard of. Something was brewing, something big, and I wanted to know what.

The moment we touched down—hard but safe—near one of the hangars and exited the chopper, Colonel Sharif pulled up in an armored personnel carrier. He waved us over.

I turned to Harris. "You all right?"

"I'll be fine," he said, wiping his mouth and his brow.

I handed him a bottle of water. He took several sips.

"Just give me a moment with Sharif," he said. "I need to let him know what's happening with you."

I nodded and waited while Harris briefed the colonel on the latest developments with me and the case against Vaughn. I could see Sharif's eyes grow wide. The man was as stunned as I had been. But time was fleeting. The king was waiting.

"Welcome to Azraq, Mr. Collins," Sharif shouted over the storms and the Black Hawk's rotors. "Thanks be to Allah that you're safe—and innocent."

"Thanks, Colonel," I replied. "You're telling me."

"I'm afraid we can't linger," Sharif said. "Something urgent has come up. We need to go." The colonel asked me to get into the APC. By the time he got in beside me, we were both soaked to the bone and freezing cold.

I looked back and noticed an MP guiding Harris into another vehicle.

"Where's he going?" I asked. "Isn't he coming with us?"

"No," Sharif replied. "He's heading to the infirmary first and then to one of the administrative buildings. He's got a case to manage, and a fast-moving one at that."

Our driver took us around the hangar and across the air base to a nondescript strip of garages housing various tow trucks and other service vehicles. He pulled into an empty stall, parked, and turned off the engine. "We're here," he said, checking his watch, jumping out of the APC, and motioning for us to disembark as well. "There are dry clothes for both of you—fatigues, I'm afraid; that's all they have here. Find whatever fits. There are clean socks and boots of various sizes too. But make it quick."

We did as he suggested, and soon I found myself wearing a private's uniform. I also found a towel and dried off my face and bald head. The colonel changed as well, and then the MP who had driven us here punched a code into a keypad on the only door inside the garage. When the electronic lock released, he led the two of us down a stairwell.

We descended several levels, then reached a security checkpoint manned not by MPs but by elite members of Jordan's special forces. The colonel showed his photo ID and was cleared, but all of my personal possessions were taken from me, including my grandfather's watch. Then we stepped through an X-ray machine and were patted down and carefully examined by a team of heavily armed soldiers before being allowed to proceed.

After being cleared, we headed down a long, poorly lit concrete tunnel and passed through two more checkpoints, each manned by a half-dozen soldiers, all of them toting machine guns, before we finally reached a small waiting area with four more soldiers guarding the vaultlike door to the inner sanctum. A captain checked our IDs again and told us to take a seat.

We did as we were told and for a few minutes said nothing to each other. There was a coffee table but no coffee, and there were no magazines or newspapers, nothing to do but awkwardly avoid eye contact.

Eventually I leaned back and closed my eyes. My hands were shaking. My heart was still pounding. I still couldn't believe how close I'd come to dying in that drone strike. And I still couldn't shake the sick feeling from the reality that Jack Vaughn was responsible for all that had happened. What would have possessed him to have an affair in the first place? And how could he really not have known whom he was shacking up with? The man was the director of the CIA, for crying out loud. Then again, I couldn't for one second believe he had known that his mistress was working for ISIS. A philanderer? Maybe. A traitor? I couldn't get there.

I couldn't bear to think about it anymore. It was all too ugly. So I turned my thoughts to Yael. What was she doing just then? Was the gash on her forehead healing? What about the blows she'd taken to the face? Had the doctors at Hadassah insisted that she stay for several days so they could treat her wounds and so she could get some rest? Then again, hopefully her injuries weren't that bad. Maybe Ari had thanked her for her heroic service in saving the life of the prime minister and the king and given her the week off. I hoped so. She deserved it.

Thinking about Yael made me wonder how her people were responding to this geopolitical earthquake. The Israelis had to be terrified, I imagined. Jordan was a friend, a tacit ally. And now this? A solid, stable, quiet, calm Hashemite Kingdom was the essential cornerstone of the security architecture for this entire corridor, from Jaffa to Jerusalem to Jordan. Now what? Surely the Israeli Defense Forces had mobilized their military after the attacks on the summit. It was now very possible, even probable, that ISIS was going to launch chemical attacks against Israeli population centers at any moment.

Were the Israelis also planning offensive actions against ISIS? They had to be inclined to, and what fair-minded person could blame them? Abu Khalif had just tried to assassinate their prime minister. In the process he had succeeded in killing dozens of Israeli members of parliament and security personnel. But Israeli offensive operations inside Jordan, not to mention in Syria or Iraq, would play right into the hands of ISIS, I worried. Such operations could very well provide the immediate "justification" the ISIS leaders wanted to declare total jihad against the "Zionist enemy."

The vault door opened. The colonel was asked by a young military aide to come inside. I was asked to wait. Ten minutes later, the vault door opened again. This time the colonel beckoned me to join him. I took a deep breath, stood up straight, and followed him inside. I had no idea what to expect. But there was no turning back now.

33

★ ★ ★

I entered the war room.

It was buzzing with activity. At the far end, at the head of the table, was King Abdullah himself. At his right hand was Prince Feisal. Both were talking on separate phones. To the king's left were Lieutenant General Abdul Jum'a and Major General Ibrahim al-Mufti, huddled in conversation as they pored over a map with great concern.

None of them looked up. They neither noticed us nor seemed to care that we had entered. They certainly didn't welcome us, but unlike back in Marka, they weren't the only ones in the room. The colonel whispered that he had just briefed the king and Prince Feisal on the latest developments with me, Vaughn, and the criminal investigation Agent Harris was spearheading. Then he introduced me to General Amr El-Badawy, explaining that he was the commander of Egyptian special forces. After this, he quickly introduced me to Lieutenant General Marco Ramirez, though Ramirez I already knew. He was the commander of Delta Force and a legend in the SOF community back in the States. I'd interviewed him numerous times in Afghanistan and Iraq and once in Tampa, at CENTCOM. Finally, Sharif had me say a quick hello to a Saudi general as well as one from the United Arab Emirates. Then he had me take a seat with him, not at the main conference table but in the back, by the vault door, in a row of seats he said was reserved for aides to the military leaders, though there was only one in the room at the moment, and he was Jordanian.

"Most of these guys just arrived," Sharif whispered, handing me a pad and pen.

"How long ago?" I asked, trying to get my bearings.

"A few minutes ago. I was told the prince is about to give a briefing. That's why we were trying to get you here before it started."

"I don't understand," I whispered back. "I get why General Ramirez is here. But why the guys from Egypt, Saudi, and the Gulf?"

"Your guess is as good as mine," said Sharif. "I suppose we're about to find out."

Prince Feisal asked for quiet. Those on landlines—no cell phones were permitted in this bunker—put them down. The generals who'd just arrived took their seats. The vault door closed and locked behind us. The meeting was under way.

"Good afternoon, gentlemen. Thank you for joining His Majesty and me on such short notice," the prince began. "We will get into the assault planning in a moment. But first I want to bring you up to speed on several important new developments. I wanted you to be among the first to know that CIA director Jack Vaughn has been arrested at his home in Washington by the FBI. I am told by the attorney general that Vaughn will be charged with espionage and possibly with treason."

There were audible gasps around the table.

"While I don't have all the details, I can tell you that Mr. Vaughn was arrested with a mistress who was also at his home—indeed, apparently in his bed," the prince continued. "Allegedly, he told her various classified details about the peace summit as well as about the location of His Majesty and other principals in recent days. What's not clear at this hour is whether Mr. Vaughn knew this woman—of Qatari descent—was working for ISIS."

The men around the table were as stunned as I'd been, and it took a moment for the prince to quiet the room and continue his briefing.

"Furthermore, the FBI has just arrested a suspect at the NSA's headquarters at Fort Meade in connection to this case," Feisal explained. "I'm told this suspect is the son of Mr. Vaughn's mistress. Apparently he was providing the information gleaned from Vaughn back to ISIS, ironically through secure American channels."

"You're absolutely certain of this?" asked the Saudi general, visibly shaken.

"This is what we have been told," the prince said. "Obviously the investigation is ongoing."

At this, the prince glanced at me. But he did not seem angry. Nor did he mention to the others that I had been considered, for a time, a suspect. Apparently I had been fully cleared. Why else would they allow me to be in this of all rooms, with the king of Jordan, no less?

"I've known Jack Vaughn for a quarter of a century," the Saudi general continued. "I cannot imagine him as a mole."

"None of us can," the prince replied. "I'm sure we'll learn more details—including motives—in due course. For now, I'm afraid that's all I have."

"So three arrests thus far?" the UAE general asked.

"Yes—Mr. Vaughn, the mistress, and the son. That's all we've heard about for now."

"But is that it? Is the situation contained, or are the Americans saying more arrests are coming?" the UAE general asked.

"I really couldn't say," the prince said.

Clearly this didn't satisfy the group.

"Wait a minute, wait a minute—you're saying ISIS has penetrated the highest levels of the CIA and the NSA?" asked General El-Badawy from Egypt.

"That would appear to be the case."

"All to trigger an attack on four world leaders, including Your Majesty?" He nodded at the king.

"I'm afraid so."

"I highly doubt it's limited to three people," El-Badawy noted.

"I hesitate to speculate," the prince said.

"Fair enough, but this is an unprecedented penetration of American intelligence. Can we safely assume every member of the conspiracy has been identified and arrested? That seems highly unlikely, does it not?"

No one said a word. I glanced at General Ramirez. He hadn't yet said anything, but I guessed the conversation was about to shift to him.

"Look, this story is going to break to the public in the United States in a few hours," the prince said. "Obviously, as I said, there's still a great deal that we don't know. As we get more information, I will certainly pass it on to you all. For now, however, I suggest we shift to finalizing our war plans. I don't have to remind you that time is not on our side."

"Not so fast, Your Highness," El-Badawy protested. "With all due respect, we can't just shift topics. Clearly there has been a serious breach at the CIA and NSA. Maybe it's been contained, but maybe not. Maybe the FBI has captured everyone involved; maybe not. Either way, as I see it, this raises two immediate and very serious challenges. First, how reliable and secure is any intelligence coming from the U.S. right now? And second, what is Abu Khalif's endgame?"

"What do you mean?" the Saudi general asked. "Haven't the ISIS forces caused enough damage? What more could they possibly want?"

"Are you kidding?" El-Badawy asked. "Abu Khalif wants Mecca. He wants Medina. He wants Cairo. He still wants Amman. And that's just for starters."

A hush fell over the room. The king sat back and, for the moment, remained silent. His expression was inscrutable. I was taking notes as fast as I could. No one had laid down any ground rules, but I assumed we were operating by the same guidelines the king had previously established. Everything had to run through Colonel Sharif. But if he cleared it, I could write it. I knew I couldn't write anything about the FBI sting operation against Vaughn. But what I was watching had little to do with a crime story and everything to do with the rise of ISIS and the collapse of American credibility in the region.

Ramirez cleared his throat. "May I, Your Majesty?" he asked, directly addressing the king.

Abdullah nodded.

"Gentlemen, I understand your concerns, and I share many of them," the American general began. "But we don't have time to get sidetracked. I received this news moments before arriving here. I realize it raises profound and disturbing questions, as many for me as for any of you. But we need to stay focused. The president of the United States is being held by ISIS. By my count, we have only seventeen hours to rescue him before he is executed on YouTube, for all the world to see, if he hasn't been beheaded or burned alive already. I'm not interested in the long-term goals of Abu Khalif right now. I have one mission: get my president back. You all promised to help me. That's why we're here, and for no other reason. Now, are you going to help me or not?"

34

The men all nodded to Ramirez.

Then they quickly returned to the urgent business at hand.

Ramirez began walking the group through the latest U.S. intelligence and analysis. "We believe we've identified the most probable location of the president," he said, "and all signs point to Dabiq."

My ears perked up at the mention of Dabiq. That was the place Abu Khalif had mentioned in his video, the site of the apocalyptic End of Days battle that he and the other ISIS leaders were hoping to trigger, according to General al-Mufti. Clearly the president's captors would have had time to transport him there by now. Was it possible that's where he was being held?

The Jordanian military aide sitting behind Ramirez pulled up a map of the region on the large flat-screen monitor behind the general and marked Dabiq, a tiny city—more of a village, really—in the northwest section of Syria, not far from the border of Turkey.

"Typically, there would be nothing to draw our

attention there," the general continued. "Dabiq is a town ordinarily populated by fewer than four thousand people, but in recent months it's become an ISIS stronghold. We estimate they have amassed about twenty thousand jihadists there, at least half of whom are foreign fighters. They've murdered most of the local men under the age of sixty. They've taken the young girls as sex slaves and murdered most of their mothers. The rest of the able-bodied women are serving the ISIS forces in various capacities—cooking, cleaning, laundry, and the like. But more importantly, many of the heavy artillery, tanks, and other advanced weaponry ISIS has captured from Assad's forces have been brought to Dabiq. They seem to be digging in for a major battle."

The aide now displayed a series of American spy satellite photos showing the buildup of forces over the past several weeks.

"General, do you have actual proof the president is there, or is this a working theory?" El-Badawy asked.

"I think it's fair to say we have very compelling evidence, but I wouldn't call it definitive proof— not yet," Ramirez replied. "Let me explain."

The Delta commander told the generals about the tracking device in the president's Jorg Gray 6500 Chronograph wristwatch. "Our satellites lost the signal coming from the transponder shortly after the president disappeared. But a few hours ago, we started picking it up again. Our tracking indicates it's coming from an elementary school in Dabiq."

"But this isn't necessarily proof of the president's location?" the Saudi general asked.

"No. It's possible the watch could have been removed by ISIS forces and taken to Dabiq, while the president could have been taken someplace else."

"Would ISIS forces know how to disable the tracking device and then reengage it a few hours ago?" asked El-Badawy.

"We don't think so," Ramirez said, "though we can't be certain. Still, there is a growing body of additional evidence that points to Dabiq."

He explained that a mobile phone belonging to Jamal Ramzy, the ISIS commander in Syria, had been taken from Ramzy's dead body during the firefight at the Al-Hummar Palace on Sunday. He didn't mention me. It wasn't clear he even knew I'd been involved in recovering the phone. He did, however, thank the king for making the phone and all its data available to the U.S. government.

"The very fact that the Syrian commander of ISIS was involved in a coup attempt here in Jordan is noteworthy, I think. But it's more than that. Jordanian intelligence experts and our top guys at the NSA have examined the phone thoroughly. It took us a while to get through the phone's encryption. But we now know that the call log indicates a total of nine outbound calls were made from the phone, and three calls were received. Of those, Ramzy—or someone else using the phone—made three outgoing calls to Dabiq and received one call from Dabiq. Not surprisingly, no one is currently answering at any of these numbers. But we have learned that the one call to Ramzy from Dabiq was placed from an apartment building less than six blocks from the school where the tracking signal is now being picked up."

Next, Ramirez shared some good news.

"Mr. Collins, you'll be glad to know that the Secret Service agent you found and rescued at the SADAFCO warehouse is going to live. He's making a solid recovery, and he's talking. As a sharpshooter, he'd been taking out ISIS forces as they converged on the president's position. Unfortunately, he was shot when the enemy swarmed the building he was in. They thought he was already dead, so they left him alone. But in that time, he overheard several of the terrorists talking about Dabiq and the battle that was coming. In fact, he told me that talk of Dabiq was the last thing he remembers hearing before he blacked out."

Then there was the video released by Abu Khalif, Ramirez added, noting that the ISIS leader had said specifically, "We are waiting for you in Dabiq."

"What's more," Ramirez continued, "Khalif denounced the president as 'the dog of Rome.' These, I'm told, are references to some sort of apocalyptic theology held by the ISIS leaders that the last battle in history—sort of their version of Armageddon—will happen in Dabiq. That's when, supposedly, the infidel forces of Rome will be defeated on the plains near this town. Does this ring true to any of you?"

"Of course it does," the Saudi general said. "It all comes from one of the hadiths. The Prophet— peace be upon him—said the Last Hour would not come until the Romans landed at Dabiq. An army of the best soldiers of the people of the earth will come from Medina to confront them, to fight them. This is a very well-known passage among Sunni true believers."

"Now, look, I confess, much of this is new to me," Ramirez conceded—much to my relief because it was completely new to me except for what had been discussed in the bunker the day before, however briefly. "When you say 'the forces of Rome,' does that mean the Italians, or is the language symbolic?"

General El-Badawy stepped in and took that one. "That question is oft debated among Sunni scholars," the Egyptian said. "Some say it's literal. Others say it refers more to the Vatican and the Christian forces of the West rather than to the Roman Empire or to modern-day Italians themselves. Still others say it might metaphorically refer to America, since your country has become known as the world's most powerful Christian nation."

"Clearly Khalif sees the U.S. as Rome," noted the general from the UAE, nodding to Ramirez. "As you pointed out, that's why he described your president as the 'dog of Rome' in the video."

"Indeed," El-Badawy said. "Not all Sunnis share this eschatology, mind you. Or if they do, most don't take action based on their beliefs. But Khalif is convinced that the End of Days has come, that the Mahdi is about to arrive on earth and establish his kingdom of justice and peace and unity under Sharia law. That's what's driving him and his forces. They believe the Romans will be led by the Dajjal, a figure of extreme evil. Some scholars believe this is a specific person. Others believe this represents the forces of the Western powers. It's possible Khalif believes your president is the Dajjal."

"So what exactly is supposed to happen in this apocalyptic battle?" Ramirez asked.

The Saudi answered this. "The hadiths tell us that one-third of the Muslim forces will flee and will never be forgiven by Allah for abandoning the battle. The text says another third of the Muslim forces will die in the battle as 'excellent martyrs.' The final third of the Muslim forces will fight the Romans, win, and conquer Constantinople—which might literally mean modern Istanbul but is more likely code for the West. Before the Muslims win, however, they will turn to Allah in devoted prayer. As they pray, Isa will come to pray with them and then fight with them. The text says Isa will 'break the cross' and 'kill the swine.' Then he will lead the Muslims to victory at Dabiq, then to complete victory over Rome, and then the Mahdi will establish his global caliphate."

I was writing furiously, trying to get it all down, but at this point I leaned over and whispered to Colonel Sharif, "Who is this 'Isa'?"

His answer floored me.

"Jesus."

35

* * *

"What do you mean, Jesus?" I whispered back.

"Isa is Jesus," Sharif repeated. "The ancient prophecies say he's coming back."

"To where?"

"To earth."

"Why?"

"To establish a global kingdom, the full caliphate."

"Muslims believe Jesus is coming back to earth?"

"Of course."

"To rule the world?"

"No, no," Sharif said. "He won't rule the world. He comes before the Mahdi and helps establish the conditions for the Mahdi to rule the world."

"The Mahdi being . . . ?"

"Our savior, our king."

"Jesus isn't the Mahdi?"

"No. He comes—well, you heard the general— he comes to conquer Dajjal, defeat the armies of Rome at Dabiq, and help the Mahdi establish the final caliphate."

I had no idea what the colonel was talking about. I'd never heard any of this before. I was jotting it all down, but I suddenly felt like I was talking to my brother, Matt. We'd had this exact conversation just a few days earlier, but in reverse. Matt had tried to convince me that a bunch of old Bible prophecies indicated that a terrible, cataclysmic judgment was coming upon Jordan and the neighboring nations. Matt said these judgments would fall at the end of history, and then Jesus would come and set up his Kingdom. It had all been new to me. Now these men were saying something so similar, yet so radically different.

". . . and one last thing," Ramirez was saying, wrapping up his presentation. "My team found a sermon by Abu Musab al-Zarqawi, who as we all know was the leader of the Islamic State's predecessor, al Qaeda in Iraq. Zarqawi said of his terror campaign inside Iraq just after the liberation in 2003, 'The spark has been lit here in Iraq, and its heat will continue to intensify until it burns the crusader armies in Dabiq.' Now, as we've just noted, Abu Khalif, Zarqawi's successor, is essentially saying the same thing. So the U.S. is training all our intelligence-gathering assets on Dabiq. We're doing everything we can to confirm that the president is there and that he is alive, and of course we're developing a battle plan to get him out. And that's why I've come here to meet with you all. We could do this alone, but we believe it's better if we work together. We believe it's better if the world sees this as a joint American–Arab operation, and not only to rescue the president but also

JOEL C. ROSENBERG ★ 221

to capture or kill Abu Khalif. Can we count on your support?"

El-Badawy had a question. "Where did the other calls on Jamal Ramzy's phone lead?" the Egyptian general asked.

"Excuse me?" Ramirez said.

"You said three of the calls on Mr. Ramzy's phone were made to Dabiq," El-Badawy said. "Where did the other calls lead?"

"Uh, well, I believe five outgoing calls were to the city of Homs, which is also in Syria, of course."

"To the same number?"

"Yes."

"And what was the number?"

"It turned out to be a switching station," Ramirez answered.

"The calls were transferred elsewhere?"

"Correct."

"To where?"

"We haven't been able to ascertain that yet."

"Did they go to Dabiq as well?"

"They may have, but I'm not sure."

"Why not?"

"The NSA is working on that, but they don't have an answer for me yet."

"Was this person who was just arrested at Fort Meade involved in this case?"

"I don't know."

"Is it possible?"

"I doubt it."

"But you're not sure."

"No, I'm not."

"Well, why should it be so difficult to know

where the calls were transferred to?" El-Badawy pressed. "If your government has confirmed the number is a switching station, surely they can determine to where the calls were switched."

"I'm sorry; I don't know," Ramirez said, looking through a briefing book full of notes but apparently not finding the answer. "I will check on that and get back to you."

"Is it possible the president is being held in Homs?" the Saudi asked.

"We don't think so," Ramirez said.

"Why not?"

"For all the reasons I just explained."

"Because all roads seem to lead to Dabiq?"

"Now that our satellites have reacquired the tracking signal from the president's watch, yes, we think so."

"But a moment ago you said you couldn't be sure."

"I said we had strong evidence pointing to Dabiq, not proof," said Ramirez. "I will stick to that assessment."

"But it is possible—just possible—that the watch was removed from the president and taken to Dabiq to throw us off the scent, right?" the general from the Emirates asked.

"Possible? Sure. Probable? I don't think so."

"Actually, there may be a reasonably strong case that the president *is* in Homs," I said, catching everyone off guard and getting quite a few looks from those who thought I should be seen and not heard.

"I'm sorry, J. B., but the floor is not really

open," Ramirez said. "You're a friend. We've known each other a long time. But we were all told explicitly that you're here as an observer, not a participant."

"I understand, General, and I promise I'll be brief," I said, plunging forward. "I'm just saying I've been to Homs. I've been to Jamal Ramzy's base camp. I've seen it, and it's an ideal safe house. It's underground. It's well protected. It's the perfect place to hide the president and Khalif, and I think it's a serious mistake to rule it out, especially if you have so many phone calls from Ramzy going to Homs."

"Wait a minute; I thought you saw Khalif in Mosul," said the Saudi.

"I did," I replied. "But I first met Ramzy in Homs."

Colonel Sharif leaned over and whispered to me to knock it off, that I was overstepping my bounds.

But El-Badawy wanted to hear more. "Could you find your way back to Ramzy's lair?" he asked.

"Of course not," General Ramirez shot back before I could answer. "J. B. was blindfolded going in and coming out. I read your article."

"Is that true?" the Egyptian asked.

"It is," I said, "but General Ramirez is forgetting one important thing."

"What's that?"

"I might not have known how to get there, but I knew where I was."

"What is that supposed to mean?"

"It means I was told by my contact to meet at

the Khaled bin Walid Mosque," I explained. "It was in a neighborhood of Homs called al-Khalidiyah. My colleagues—God rest their souls—snuck into Homs with me. We linked up with Ramzy's men. They took us to that specific neighborhood and that specific mosque, and from there I was taken through underground tunnels to the meeting with Ramzy. So, no, I couldn't find it wandering around that Dante's inferno of a city. But how hard would it really be for you all to find that mosque with satellites and drones and figure out what kind of activity is under way there right now?"

"And you think ISIS could be holding the president there?" El-Badawy pressed.

"I can't say that definitively, General," I replied. "All I'm saying is that you should take a careful look. I'm not saying it would have been easy for Khalif to get there or for ISIS to have gotten the president there without being noticed. But remember, Jamal Ramzy got himself from Homs to Amman without being noticed. Obviously they've figured out a way to transit back and forth. So we know it can be done. I'm not saying the president is not in Dabiq. Maybe he is. I'm just saying, isn't it a bit foolish to kidnap the leader of the free world and bring him to a town of four thousand people and then tell the world you have him there?"

"Maybe," Ramirez said, "unless you're trying to trigger a battle you believe will bring about the end of the world."

36

Prince Feisal suddenly leaned over and whispered something to the king.

Then he turned to the group and apologized. He explained that the vice president of the United States was on the line and that His Majesty needed to take the call in his private chambers. As the king excused himself and took a guard with him through a door at the other end of the room, the prince asked General Ramirez to walk through his plan to invade Dabiq and explain what role he expected each coalition partner to play in the attack. I was yet to be convinced the president was actually there but was eager to hear Ramirez's plan of attack.

Over the years, I had become deeply impressed with the intellect and courage of this three-star general. Ramirez was the eldest son of Cuban refugees and grew up in south Florida in a family of nine kids. He graduated first in his class from West Point and was recruited by Delta Force early in his Army career. He was one of the first American special operators sent into Afghanistan to fight al Qaeda and the Taliban after 9/11. Later, he was an instrumental player in hunting down and killing Osama bin Laden in Pakistan. He was one of the chief architects of the surprisingly successful "surge" strategy in Iraq, before political leaders far above his pay grade unraveled America's hard-fought gains by precipitously withdrawing all U.S. forces from Iraq in December 2011.

Rumor had it that he and his men were actually responsible for the capture of Abu Khalif several years earlier, though he had adamantly and repeatedly denied that U.S. forces had been involved in that operation at all. It made perfect sense to me that Ramirez and his Delta Force operators were being tasked with the rescue of the president and the recapture (or killing) of Khalif. Few knew the region better—indeed, few knew al Qaeda and ISIS better—than this six-foot-five, 230-pound former defensive tackle whom his colleagues had nicknamed "the Cuban missile." The stakes, of course, could not have been higher. As far as I was aware, this would be the first time in history that U.S. forces would fight on Syrian soil. The very president they were hoping to rescue had repeatedly vowed never to put American "boots on the ground" in Syria. Yet if there was anyone who could pull it off, I had to believe it was Marco Ramirez.

However, just as the general began handing out briefing books and explaining his approach, the colonel nudged me and insisted I follow him out of the war room and back into the waiting area. I assumed this had something to do with my speaking up in the meeting, which to be honest kind of ticked me off. Still, I had no choice. If I was going to get back in that room, it wasn't going to be by making a scene. So I stepped out with Sharif, pulse racing, and prepared to defend myself.

Before I could say a word, however, the colonel led me through a door I'd previously not noticed, down a narrow hallway, and past several more soldiers, where he knocked twice on a closed door, then entered a nine-digit code into a keypad and waved me through.

We were now in the king's spacious private office in what appeared to be the deepest recesses of the bunker complex. His Majesty was sitting behind his desk under a large portrait of his father, a Jordanian flag on a stand by his side. He was already on the phone but nodded to the colonel and me and motioned us to take a seat on the couch. Sharif whispered to me that I should pick up the phone on the end table to my right. Then he reached for a similar handset on the end table to our left and instructed me to select line two and hit the Mute button. I did and watched him do the same.

"Your Majesty, thank you for waiting," an older woman's voice said on the other end of the line. "Vice President Holbrooke will be right with you."

I pulled out my notebook and a pen and tried to calm down and shift gears. I'd been bracing for a fight, sure I was being thrown out of the Ramirez briefing for speaking out of turn. But I'd been dead wrong. I hadn't been thrown out at all. Instead, I'd been invited into the inner sanctum.

My mind raced with questions I wanted to ask Martin Holbrooke. The gray, grizzled, and somewhat-cantankerous seventy-seven-year-old VP was now in an extremely precarious position, and the nation—along with the entire world—was watching his every move.

I'd known Holbrooke for years, but he was a shrewd political operator and Washington insider long before I came on the scene. He'd first been elected to Congress from a district in northeastern Ohio back in the late 1960s. Later he'd won a Senate seat, played his cards carefully, and risen to become chairman of the powerful Armed Services Committee. By the time I met him, he'd become a heavyweight in the Democratic Party, raising enormous sums for his political action committee, investing in up-and-coming progressive candidates, making allies, earning chits, and laying the groundwork for a run for the Democratic nomination for president.

Holbrooke was also an early backer of Harrison Taylor and helped get the software CEO elected first to the Senate, and then, after only one term, elected governor of North Carolina. Along the way, Holbrooke had seen Taylor's popularity rising slowly but surely, both in the local grass roots of the party and nationally. And when the day came for Holbrooke to announce his candidacy for the presidency, he instead stunned everyone by using his announcement speech to become the first U.S. senator to endorse Taylor for president.

The effect was transformative. Taylor, a note-worthy voice on the center-left of the party, sud-

JOEL C. ROSENBERG ★ 229

denly had the full backing of one of the country's most hard-core liberals for one reason and one reason only: Holbrooke was convinced Taylor was the only Democrat who could actually win, and he'd been right. Taylor went on to clinch the nomination and asked Holbrooke to be his running mate. The two won a brutally close race that fall, 50.3 percent to 49.7 percent.

I'd covered Holbrooke when I was a young correspondent for the *New York Daily News* and had interviewed him from time to time throughout my career. He'd always been generous with his time—and his liquor—and could be counted on for newsworthy quotes (as well as spicy off-the-record gossip about his colleagues on the Hill). I'd always found him a compelling, complicated, and often-conniving member of the U.S. Senate; he could write legislation and craft amendments and build unlikely coalitions—and simultaneously yet subtly sabotage his personal and political enemies better than anyone I'd ever seen. But I'd never really been convinced by him as vice president of the United States. The role was, in far too many ways, a complete mismatch of his skill sets. He was a particularly gifted and clever orator, yet his job now was basically to travel the country and B-level world capitals and give banal speeches that purposefully made no news. He was a master in the art of the deal, yet he was no longer tasked with any deals to cut.

And if that weren't bad enough, he absolutely hated to fly. For decades he had insisted on driving himself from his home near Cleveland to

Washington and back, had run his Senate campaigns from an RV traveling back and forth across the Ohio Turnpike, and had complained endlessly when having to travel abroad (which might be why he drank so much with the press when he'd reach his foreign destinations). Yet now he was in sole possession of Air Force Two and had racked up more frequent flyer miles than any other VP in the history of the country.

What concerned me most right now, however, was that he'd undergone triple bypass surgery less than six months earlier. He'd been on bed rest for several months and had only recently gotten back on the road. What's more, his wife, Frieda—his third in as many decades and almost thirty years his junior—had just been diagnosed with breast cancer and was now at the Mayo Clinic going through chemotherapy. Was Holbrooke up for this crisis? Physically? Emotionally? Mentally? He'd never served in the military. He'd never served in an executive capacity. Was he ready to be commander in chief?

37

★ ★ ★

Despite all my questions, I knew the best thing was to simply listen.

I was treading on thin ice as it was, or so I believed, and if this were true, then there was no point risking my position with the king any further. And truth be told, I suspected the VP might be less than candid with His Majesty if he knew I was listening in on their conversation. So I readied my pen and waited quietly until the VP came on the line.

"Abdullah, it's Martin; has General Ramirez briefed you?" Holbrooke asked straightaway, skipping any pleasantries and getting down to business.

"He has," the king replied. "You all believe the president is in Dabiq."

"We do, and the general seems to have developed a pretty solid plan for getting him back."

"He's just about to go through that with us," the king said, glancing at me. "But I have to say, Martin, my team and I are not completely convinced the president is actually in Dabiq."

"And why is that?" the VP asked, sounding

as exhausted as I'd ever heard him. "Our satellites have picked up his signal. We've got the calls from Ramzy's phone to Dabiq. We've got the testimony of the Secret Service agent. We have Khalif's own words in the video. It all points to Dabiq, Abdullah."

"You're not concerned your systems have been, perhaps, affected?" the king asked, raising as delicately as possible the emerging scandal at the highest levels of the U.S. intelligence community.

"Affected?" the VP asked.

"Compromised?"

"You mean this nonsense with Jack?"

"It sounds quite serious."

"It's a distraction. Our intel is solid. Believe me."

"But surely there's a risk that—"

"No," the VP interjected, cutting him off. "I'm telling you, this whole thing with Jack is an isolated incident. It's a nuisance, to be sure, but I have no doubt it will sort itself out in due time. But we can't let that sidetrack us from what we know—that all indicators are pointing to Dabiq."

"Martin, look, you may be right. But your own government has just arrested the director of the CIA. You've arrested a senior analyst at the NSA. Your intelligence systems have been penetrated by ISIS. And who knows who else is involved and where else this leads? These perpetrators have already used American intelligence to launch assassination attempts against President Taylor, Prime Minister Lavi, President Mansour, and myself. They're in the process of trying to overthrow my government and destabilize yours. Don't we have to consider the possibility that whoever is plotting against us is manipulating the very intelligence you're looking at to make critical decisions?"

"What are you saying, Abdullah?" the VP asked, sounding agitated and defensive. "That I can't trust the intel on my desk? Those phone intercepts that are pointing us to Dabiq came from a phone you gave us. The president's tracking signal is coming from Dabiq. Khalif said, 'We are waiting for you in Dabiq.' Those aren't my words—or Jack's—but his. I'm not saying this mess at Langley isn't a problem. Of course it is. But we've got to be able to sift this all through and take an objective read on the data we're seeing. And I'm telling you my guys say all the data is pointing to Dabiq. What more do you want?"

"More," the king said. "I don't have to tell you that if we all move on Dabiq and we're wrong, Khalif is going to behead the president on worldwide television, and all hell will break loose in this region. We will have just handed ISIS the most powerful propaganda tool we could possibly imagine. People will flock to join the caliphate. ISIS will have more money than they'll know what to do with. They could become unstoppable, Martin. The region will become completely destabilized."

"No one understands the stakes better than me, Abdullah. But we're running out of time. If we're going to move, we need to move soon. My guys are worried it may already be too late, that the president may already be dead. I can't operate that way. I'm going to trust that he's still alive until the deadline. But we're running out of daylight."

"I agree," the king said. "But first we've got to be certain we're not being set up."

"The evidence for Dabiq is overwhelming."

"It looks that way. But it all seems a bit too easy to me."

"You think ISIS is baiting us?"

"That's exactly what I'm afraid of. Look, we know Khalif wants to wage the final battle in Dabiq. He and his men have been planning it. They've been prepping for it. They've got an arsenal of chemical weapons that could turn the whole thing into a bloodbath. We have to seriously consider the possibility that this is a trap."

"I grant you Khalif had some chemical weapons. But he's used them already—at your airport. There's no evidence to suggest he has more. We can't let ourselves be paralyzed by Khalif's genocidal rhetoric, not when the president's life is on the line."

The king looked at me. I shook my head, though almost imperceptibly. We absolutely had evidence that ISIS had enormous stockpiles of sarin gas—far more than could have been used at the airport. I'd personally seen a warehouse full of warheads that Abu Khalif and Jamal Ramzy had told me were filled with sarin gas, and I'd seen it tested on Iraqi prisoners. I'd reported as much in my story in the *Times*. The king had read it. Certainly the VP had too. So why was Holbrooke downplaying the threat now?

"Martin, as you know, the *New York Times* reported that Khalif captured a warehouse full of sarin gas," the king said respectfully but without hesitation. "Based on what I saw at the airport in Amman, I think we have to believe not only that Khalif has much more, but that he's ready to use it—and where better than in Dabiq, where ISIS intends to make their final stand?"

There was a pause. "You could be right," the VP said finally. "But my guys say they're ready for anything. We can deal with poison gas. What we can't deal with is sitting on our hands doing nothing while time runs out. I don't have to tell you I'm under tremendous pressure here. This isn't just the president; this is my friend we're talking about."

"He's my friend too," the king said.

"I know, but for me he's not just a friend," Holbrooke added. "He's the constitutional leader of my country. And if you're watching the American press at all, you can see there's already a steady and almost-deafening drumbeat for the attorney general to declare that Harrison is no longer president and to have me sworn in immediately to replace him. That puts me in a very dicey place. I don't want to even consider stepping into the presidency unless I've done absolutely everything I possibly could to get Harrison back safely to his family and to the country."

As the two men kept talking, I could see the strain in the king's face and shoulders. This wasn't some run-of-the-mill Middle Eastern hostage situation. It was, back in the U.S. at least, fast becoming a constitutional crisis.

The VP's comments underscored how cut off I was from all news coming out of the States. I needed access to the Internet. I needed to get up to speed on the political and geopolitical nuances of this fast-moving story. I knew, at least in general terms, that Article II, Section 1 of the Constitution stated that "in case of the removal of the president from office, or of his death, resignation, or inability to discharge the powers and duties of the said office, the same shall devolve on the vice president." I also knew that the Twenty-Fifth Amendment to the Constitution stated plainly that "in case of the removal of the president from office or of his death or resignation, the vice president shall become president." The question was whether the capture of the president by foreign military forces fit the definition of the president's inability to discharge his powers and duties. Did the current crisis warrant removal of the president from office?

It seemed to, on the face of it. But America had never faced such a situation before. Four American chief executives had been assassinated in office since the nation's founding—Lincoln, Garfield, McKinley, and Kennedy. Four more American leaders had died in office of natural causes—William Henry Harrison, Zachary Taylor, Warren Harding, and Franklin Delano Roosevelt. Nixon had resigned the office under the shadow of the Watergate allegations and the prospect of impeachment. But what was unfolding now was completely unprecedented in the annals of American history.

This, of course, was why Section 4 of the Twenty-Fifth Amendment had been written—to cover all potential ambiguities. I couldn't remember the text precisely, but it essentially explained various scenarios under which the vice president could become acting president temporarily and then, with the authorization of the cabinet and Congress, reinstate the president to his full powers once the situation was resolved and he was capable of serving again, or else permanently remove the president from power and give full authority to the acting president until an election could be held.

As far as I was concerned, it didn't take a constitutional scholar to determine that Taylor, even if he was alive, was not currently capable of functioning as president. Thus Holbrooke was for all intents and purposes operating as acting president at the moment. But even from half a world away, I could picture the political weight on Holbrooke's shoulders. He didn't want to trigger Section 4, a provision that had never been invoked before. He didn't want to act—or be seen as acting—precipitously. The nation was operating in treacherous and uncharted waters. Holbrooke, uncharacteristically, seemed to be resisting his standard political instincts of advancing his own interests. He seemed to feel—or at least wanted to be perceived as feeling—a deep sense of responsibility to act carefully, deliberately, and without haste.

Nevertheless, fateful decisions had to be made, and made quickly. The vice president was the only person back in Washington with the constitutional authority to send American military forces into battle, and it was clear he was getting ready to act on that authority.

"Martin, please hear me," the king was saying.

"The president may very well be in Dabiq. I'm not saying he isn't. I'm just saying we need to do everything we possibly can to confirm it beyond the shadow of a doubt and do our best to rule out any other possible scenario. History will never forgive us if we make a mistake."

"I hear that, Abdullah, and as always, I appreciate your concern and your wise counsel," the VP said. "I'll do everything I can to push my team to cross every t and dot every i over the next few hours. I assure you of that. But it's already afternoon over there. It's winter. The sun goes down in a few hours. If we're going to make a move, General Ramirez is strongly recommending we move just after night falls. That means he and his men—and your men and all those who have gathered with you—need to finalize a plan, make sure everything is coordinated, and be prepared to move out in five or six hours, at the latest. That's not a lot of time to make sure everything is done right. It's no time at all."

"No, it's not," said the king. "But we'll be ready. I promise you that. You and I go way back. And I want you to know that above all, I'm with you. My people are with you. The kingdom of Jordan has no better friend in the world than the American people and your government. We will do everything in our power to get the president back safe and sound and to bring these evildoers to justice, come what may. On this, you have my word."

38

* * *

"You're quite the diplomat," I said as the call ended.

"Why do you say that?" the king asked, pressing a button on his desk and summoning a steward.

"I mean, you're not convinced the president is being held in Dabiq."

"Nor are you."

"I'm not the one trying to convince the vice president to tread carefully."

There was a knock on the door, and a steward entered with a fresh pot of tea. He promptly served us all, beginning with His Majesty, and then stepped out.

"You're worried this thing with Jack Vaughn goes deeper than maybe anyone yet realizes," I said when the king, the colonel, and I were alone again.

"I hope not," the king replied. "But it's too soon to rule anything out."

"Because it's possible the intel being shown to the VP could be compromised."

"Perhaps."

"Which could mean someone is trying to lure

us into a fight in Dabiq when the president is elsewhere."

"And Khalif."

"But what if you're wrong?" I countered. "What if they really are in Dabiq?"

"You just heard me. My men are ready to go into Dabiq if that's where the evidence leads."

"And if it's ambiguous and you're out of time and you have to make a decision?"

"We'll follow the vice president's lead."

"Even if he's wrong."

"Yes."

"Why?"

"Because that's what friends do."

"Stand with each other in a fight."

"Absolutely," said the king. "As I said, Martin and I go way back."

"Back to his first Senate campaign, as I recall."

"Longer."

"Really—how long?"

"He and his first wife came on a codel when he was a freshman in Congress," the king said, using insider slang for a congressional delegation. "They came to meet my father. I happened to be home from boarding school for spring break. I was just a kid, but my father insisted that I join the group for dinner."

"When was this?"

"I don't remember exactly, but it was after the '67 war. Things were tense. The Holbrookes were very pro-Israel. But they'd heard good things about my father. They wanted to take his measure, to see if there was a way to deescalate tensions, maybe even to make peace."

"Did you ever think he'd one day be the VP?"

"Off the record?"

"Sure."

"Then no. He was a bright guy—don't get me wrong. One of the smartest men I'd seen enter Congress. But to be honest, he seemed to be more of a businessman than a politician. Very practical. Very pragmatic. A real can-do attitude. I thought he'd never make it in Washington. But what did I know? I was just a kid."

"Of course, you didn't think you'd one day sit on the throne either, did you?" I probed.

He shook his head and stared at the steam rising off the cup of tea in his hands. "Never. Never wanted it. Never sought it. Never even bothered to think it was something I needed to worry about."

"Worry?"

"'Uneasy lies the head . . . ,'" he said.

His voice trailed off, but there was no reason to finish. I got the allusion. He was referencing the title of his father's memoirs, written in 1962. The title was a line from Shakespeare's *Henry IV, Part 2*. I'd discovered the play and fallen in love with it in high school. I'd played the lead in college and still remembered every line.

The king sipped his tea. I sipped mine. Sharif said nothing. I held my tongue. If for only a moment, His Majesty was lost in thought and it was not my place to disturb him.

I thought about the significance of that line from *Henry IV, Part 2*: "Uneasy lies the head that wears a crown." Vice President Holbrooke didn't wear a crown, of course, but he was finding out just how uneasy—and how uncertain—a position of power could be. I hoped for all our sakes he would make the correct decisions in the hours ahead.

"My father watched his own grandfather, my namesake, be assassinated in Jerusalem—watched it happen with his own eyes," the king said eventually, though not so much to me or to the colonel as to himself as he reflected on the almost-unbearable challenges of the dynasty into which he was born. "I grew up seeing one palace intrigue after another, things young boys should never have to see. And now my children are watching it happen all over again. Will such curses never end?"

It was a quiet for a bit. Then I asked him if the queen and his children were safe. He said they were. A moment later, he added that he had sent them out of the country. I asked where. He would not say. I suspected they were now in the States, but it did not seem appropriate to pry any further, so I let it go. Almost.

"And the crown prince?" I asked of his eldest son. "Where is he?"

"In there," he replied, nodding to the door to his left.

"Getting some rest?"

"Well deserved," he said.

"Much needed," I added.

"Indeed."

"May I change the subject?" I asked.

"Please."

"The Egyptians," I said, nodding in the other direction, back to the war room beside us.

"A wonderful people," said the king.

"And the Saudis," I added, "and the Emirates . . ."

"Family."

"And yet the world is not used to seeing you all work together on military matters."

"Or any matters."

"Or any matters—that's true," I agreed. "You have all had many difficulties with each other over the years."

The king nodded.

"Pan-Arab unity was more of a dream than a reality?"

"Unfortunately. But things are changing."

"How so?"

"For one, new leaders with new outlooks have emerged," said the monarch. "For another, we find ourselves facing common enemies."

"ISIS?"

"Of course, but not ISIS alone."

"Iran."

"That is a very sensitive subject," he replied. "We are doing our best to maintain open and cordial relations with Tehran."

"But it's no secret that the Sunni Arab world feels the Shias of Persia could soon pose an existential threat."

"Many believe this, yes."

"Don't you?"

"The Arabs face many challenges on many fronts."

"You don't want me to quote you directly about the Iran threat."

"No."

"Then off the record."

He smiled grimly. "We face many challenges on many fronts."

Given how much access he and his team were giving me, I was intrigued by how guarded the king was in his comments to me. I had earned a degree of trust, and that trust was growing, to be sure, but clearly there were limits; there were red lines beyond which I could not go. Not now. Probably not ever. I wasn't a Muslim. I wasn't an Arab. I wasn't family. I was still an outsider, and a journalist at that. Monarchs didn't typically get close to reporters, no matter from what part of the world they hailed.

"Is it fair to say that Israel is no longer considered the prime and central threat to the Sunni Arab community?" I asked.

"Off the record, that's probably a fair statement—as I said, things are changing. As new and very serious and immediate threats grow, people's perspectives on past problems and conflicts tend to shift."

"There appears to be a widespread reevaluation of Israel's role in the region taking place among the Arabs—at least among Arab leaders, though perhaps not entirely among the people," I said.

"I don't think that's the right way to put it," the king said. "I think it's more a matter of priorities. A leader only has so many hours in the day. What is he going to focus on? Defending himself and his people from attack, from genocide, annihilation, subjugation at the hands of mortal enemies? Or planning to proactively, preemptively attack another nation that is here to stay, that isn't going anywhere? We face many challenges in our region. Poverty. Illiteracy. Economic inequalities. Tribal animosities. A lack of robust manufacturing. A lack of enough advanced, high-tech industries. I could go on, but you know the list. And the so-called Arab Spring was, I believe, a wake-up call for many leaders in this region. The people want us to focus on making their lives better. If we don't, they may turn to revolution. They may turn to dark forces. So no one in this region has the time or energy or resources to wage an unwinnable war in an effort to remove an entire nation and people from the map. Only the extremists want this. The rest of us want to find ways to create peace and prosperity and opportunity for all the people of the region."

"I hear you've become quite close to Wahid Mahfouz," I said, referring to the new Egyptian president.

"We speak often," he said. "We've spoken twice today."

"You went to visit him in January."

"And he came to visit me in June."

"And . . . ?"

"And we are finding common ground."

"You're working closely together?"

"On many fronts."

"Like what?"

That grim smile again. "Many fronts."

I noticed the king glancing at the clock. I wasn't going to have his attention much longer, and no matter what I tried, he remained so guarded.

"I hear Mahfouz is quite close to Daniel Lavi as well," I added, wanting to see if I could get the king to give me some insight into rumors that the Egyptians were developing a close strategic relationship with the Israeli prime minister and his unity government.

"You'll have to talk to Daniel about that," he demurred.

"I hope to—as soon as he recovers," I said. "But something has happened in the last few years. You and the Egyptians and the Saudis and the Emirates seem to be working quite closely together against ISIS, against Iran, and—less noticed by most people—with the Israelis."

"This is a very sensitive subject."

"But I'm not wrong."

"The Egyptians have a treaty with Israel. So do we. You would expect us to be working closely together."

"Not this closely."

"Maybe not in the past, but new breezes are blowing."

"The Egyptians have had a treaty with the Israelis since '79, but after Sadat's assassination, it was always a cold peace."

"Certainly under Hosni this was the case," the king said, referring to former Egyptian president Hosni Mubarak.

"Then came the rise of the Brotherhood in Egypt."

"A very dark time."

"But now that the Brotherhood has been removed . . ."

"That's a question for Wahid," the king said diplomatically. "It's an interesting story. But it's not one for me to tell."

"I understand," I said, disappointed but not surprised.

I didn't really need the king to confirm to me the significance of what I saw happening in the next room. A historic, extraordinary Sunni Arab alliance was emerging. The Jordanians, Egyptians, Saudis, and Emiratis were working together toward common goals and objectives. They were working with the Americans to launch a major military operation to attack ISIS, a Sunni Arab group, in the territory of Syria, an Arab neighbor, to rescue an ally, the president of the United States, who had just tried to complete a peace treaty between the Palestinian Sunni Arabs and the Jews of Israel. And behind it all—arguably driving or at least accelerating this historic move toward unity—was the specter of an even larger threat looming over the entire region: the prospect that the Shia Muslim Persians of Iran might be about to build nuclear weapons.

"Of course, you can't write about any of this," the king said out of the blue.

"Any of what?" I asked.

"The call with the vice president. The players you see in the room next door. The operation being planned for later tonight. These are all extremely sensitive."

"Isn't this why you brought me here?" I responded. "To tell these stories?"

"Not yet, not now," the monarch said. "In a book, perhaps, years from now. I realize this is history and eventually it does have to be told, and I believe you will do a fair and honest job, Mr. Collins. But like a fine wine, it takes many years before it is ready to be sold and sipped and savored, does it not? Or so I'm told."

It was an interesting analogy for a Muslim who wasn't supposed to drink wine, but I think I got his point. Still, I needed a story. I needed to file something, and soon, and I said so.

"I'm not saying you can't write anything," the king clarified. "I'm just saying some things are particularly sensitive."

I needed His Majesty to clarify what he meant, but just then the door to the war room opened. Prince Feisal stepped in, apologized for interrupting, and whispered something to the king, who immediately rose.

"Forgive me, Mr. Collins; something has come up," he said with a new sense of urgency, and suddenly he was gone.

39

★ ★ ★

I glanced at the clock on the king's desk.

It was now just after two o'clock on Tuesday afternoon. Sixteen hours until the deadline. Less than three hours until the sun went down.

"What's going on?" I asked.

"I can't say," said Colonel Sharif, reading an e-mail or a text on his phone, though from my angle it wasn't clear which.

"Why not?"

"I really can't say," Sharif repeated. "We'd better go."

"Where?"

"Upstairs," he said. "I'm supposed to give you a tour of the base."

"I don't want a tour," I said. "I need to go back in there."

"Not right now."

"Why not?"

"If I could tell you, I would. But I can't. So let's go upstairs, and we'll come back when I get the all clear."

"No, Yusef, this is completely unacceptable.

This is precisely why the king brought me here, to cover this whole crisis from beginning to end."

"I understand, Mr. Collins. But there's been a development."

"And you can't talk about it."

"I'm afraid not."

"So where does that leave me?"

"Taking a tour of the base."

"No," I said again. "There's no point and no time. If I can't go back into the war room yet, then I need a phone and a computer and access to the Internet."

"What for?"

I just looked at him for a moment, wondering if he could possibly be serious. "To do my job," I said.

"Let's go upstairs," Sharif replied. "I'll see what I can do."

But I wasn't about to take no for an answer.

"Yusef—Colonel—listen to me. Please. You don't seem to understand. I've been as patient as anyone could expect. I've been arrested, imprisoned, and put in solitary confinement. I've been used to do a sting operation against the director of the CIA. I've had my phone taken away. I've had my computer taken away. I've been made to sign nondisclosure papers preventing me from writing about the biggest story of my lifetime. I've been brought to a top secret military base to sit in on high-level meetings with the military leaders of five countries but prevented from talking to my editors or even to my family. I get the sensitivities of the moment. And I get that you have a job to do. But so do I—and I *have* to be in touch with my editors. I *have* to know what other people are reporting. And I *have* to file a story soon. Which means you have to help me—or let me go."

"I understand how you feel, Mr. Collins."

"But you're not going to help me."

"I'm going to help you as best I can. But there will not be any communications off of this base until this operation to rescue the president is planned and executed. Period. Please understand—I'm not trying to be rude. But the fate of our kingdom is on the line here, and I have my orders. Now, if you'll follow me upstairs, I'd be quite grateful."

The next thing I knew, we were riding the king's private elevator back up to the ground floor. We rode in silence. I was livid but determined not to say anything stupid. There had to be something I could offer Sharif to get him to change his mind. But what? I had no ideas and no leverage.

When the elevator doors opened, we were met by the two MPs who'd brought us here in the first place. They asked us to step inside an armored personnel carrier that was idling in the garage, and soon we were heading back out into the storm, which had not let up one bit. If anything, it had intensified. The clouds were thicker, the sky darker, and the booms of thunder far louder than when we'd first headed down to the bunker. The base was no longer being pelted by hail, but the winter rains were coming down in buckets. Even with our high beams on and the windshield wipers going at full speed, visibility was limited at best, and I couldn't help but wonder how this was going to impact the operation the king and the generals were planning down below.

"How long is it supposed to go on like this?" I asked our driver.

"They're saying most of the night, sir."

"Like this, or is it supposed to let up a bit?"

"Actually, they're saying it's going to get a lot worse."

"How's that possible?"

"I have no idea, sir. But that's what they're saying."

"Is anyone still flying?"

"Not many. Last sorties went out about thirty minutes ago. Should be back soon. But we hear everything else is being grounded."

This didn't bode well for the president, I thought, but decided against stating the obvious. Instead, I changed the subject. "Any word on Agent Harris?" I asked.

Just then the colonel's phone rang.

"Still in the infirmary, sir," the MP in the front passenger seat said as Sharif took the call.

"Is he okay?" I asked.

"Sorry, sir. We haven't heard."

"Could we take a few minutes and go see him?"

The driver shrugged. "I guess, if you'd like."

"I would, very much," I said.

Admittedly, my motives were less than humanitarian. Aside from General Ramirez and myself, Agent Harris was the only other American on the base. If it came time to bail out of the Jordanian orbit—which I increasingly felt was the case—

Harris would be the key. I was fairly certain that if I asked him, he'd be willing to let me accompany him back to Washington. The Jordanians certainly couldn't force me to stay on the base, operating under their rules of military censorship. And as intrigued as I was with watching all this unfold from the inside, if I couldn't report any of it in real time—and had to wait several years until I could even write a book about it all—then there was no point staying.

But I wasn't sure I wanted to head all the way back to D.C. The more I thought about it, the more it seemed to make sense to head to Tel Aviv instead. I very much wanted to see Yael for personal reasons, but I also thought I might have a better shot at being able to cover the unfolding saga in the region using my sources in Israeli intelligence and the IDF than I would by returning to the States. Of course, it now seemed unlikely that Harris and I could even get off the base before daybreak at the earliest. But hopefully we could be on the first flight out of Jordan once conditions permitted.

What's more, I thought, Harris had a phone and thus access to the outside world. Perhaps he'd let me use it to call Allen and touch base with my family and catch up on the headlines.

Brilliant flashes of lightning repeatedly illuminated the desert skies. With each bolt, I saw more of the base and the tanks and APCs blocking every entrance and providing perimeter security. I felt bad for the soldiers standing guard in such terrible conditions but at the same time was grateful they were out there. This base was one of the largest in Jordan, but we weren't that far now from the Syrian border and the genocidal conditions that had emerged within. Nor were we so far from the border with Iraq and the murderous rampage ISIS was perpetrating there as well.

When the colonel finished his call, our driver glanced in his rearview mirror and asked if it was okay to head to the infirmary. But to everyone's surprise, Sharif said no.

40

"Take us to ISR," the colonel ordered our driver.

I had no idea what that meant, but suddenly we were doing a U-turn, then turning onto a service road not far from a row of barracks and pulling up to a long, squat, unmarked, and otherwise-nondescript administrative building. The front door opened and two MPs carrying large umbrellas dashed out to our vehicle, opened the rear passenger door, and rushed us inside. Once we cleared security, Sharif introduced me to the two-star general who ran the facility. The general put us on an elevator, punched a security code, and took us down several floors to meet the rest of his team.

He explained that I was now in the nerve center of the Jordanian air force's ISR command. ISR stood for intelligence, surveillance, and reconnaissance, and it was here, the general told me, that all of Jordan's air operations were planned. At the moment, several dozen staff on the floor just below the main level were planning and analyzing all the air strikes against ISIS targets in the capital, particularly at or near the Al-Hummar Palace.

One floor below them, other staff were designing sorties against ISIS targets in other cities and towns throughout Jordan, particularly in Irbid in the north, which I now learned for the first time had come under heavy assault by forces of the Islamic State.

However, we didn't stop on either floor. When the elevator finally did stop, I could no longer hear the thunder or the rain or wind or any other element of the storm outside. Indeed, one of the first things that struck me as we exited the elevator was the unusual quiet. The overhead lighting was dim, and the staff—all of them young and sharp and serious—worked in small offices and tiny cubicles in front of banks of flat-screen computer monitors and wore big headphones and spoke in hushed voices.

"This is where the general and his team are doing the legwork for tonight's raid on Dabiq," Colonel Sharif explained. "And that's why the king called me and wanted us to come over here. He's got a new crisis he's dealing with at the moment, but he wanted you to see this."

"Why?" I asked, fearing this was part of a tour I had no interest in being on. I didn't care about all this high-tech wizardry. I didn't have time to hang out with a bunch of young air force officers in their twenties and thirties, no matter how important their work might be. It was clear I wasn't going to be allowed to write about any of this anyway, which was why all I wanted at that moment was to reconnect with Agent Harris and nail down a plan to get off this base as quickly as humanly possible.

"The king wants you to start looking at Homs," the colonel replied.

"Homs?" I asked, not sure I'd heard him correctly.

"Yes."

"What for?"

"To see if he's missing something," said Sharif. "Everything seems to be pointing toward Dabiq. But if the president is being held in Homs, the king needs to know, and he needs to know fast."

The colonel then explained the situation to the two-star. We needed an intel suite, his most proficient analyst, real-time feeds of all the satellite and drone coverage he had of Homs, a fresh pot of coffee, and anything else we asked for. The general readily agreed and led us to his cramped office, where he picked up a phone and asked one of his aides to join us immediately. A moment later the aide ushered Colonel Sharif and me into an adjoining room that was about the size of the bedroom I'd had growing up in Maine but looked like a broadcast news control room. The far wall was covered with seven flat-screen monitors, a large center screen with three others above it and three below it. In front of that was a long console that at first looked like an audio mixing board but upon closer examination turned out to be an integrated series of laptop computers, radar displays, and a bank of phones.

There was a quick knock at the door, and the aide introduced us to Zoona, a young lieutenant—couldn't have been older than thirty—wearing glasses and a light-blue headscarf.

The colonel quickly explained the situation. Zoona, in turn, explained that she had been working for the past several hours on analyzing the intel on Dabiq.

"Are you convinced the president is there?" Sharif asked.

"I wouldn't say convinced," she replied. "But it's compelling."

"Maybe you could take a moment and show us why," I said. "Then we can compare it with whatever we see in Homs."

She agreed, and her fingers went to work. She pulled up a range of images and maps and status reports on the six smaller screens, then put a live satellite feed of Dabiq on the main monitor, zooming down from space as if we were using a commercial application of Google Earth.

"Okay, this is the elementary school where we're picking up the tracking signal," Zoona said. "As you can see, it's a fairly simple three-level structure built in a horseshoe configuration. There's the playground on the north side of the compound, and you can see the parking area there on the south side."

"What are those?" I asked, pointing to several large, blocklike images in the parking lot.

"Those are our problem—they're SAMs," she explained, zooming in farther and changing the angle somewhat so I could see the surface-to-air missile batteries more clearly. "Those five are SA-6 units, a mobile model, each with support vehicles and cranes to load more missiles as needed. And that's not all. There are four more batteries in other parts of the compound—three sixes and an eleven—there, there, there, and . . . there."

"That's a lot of firepower for a school."

"Tell me about it," she said. "Each missile fired by an SA-6 can reach a top speed of Mach 2.8 and can hit almost any aircraft up to forty-five thousand feet at a range of up to fifteen miles."

"What about the SA-11?"

"Bigger, farther, faster—let's just say a single missile has a 90 to 95 percent probability of destroying its intended target."

As if this weren't bad enough, she then explained that there were numerous triple-A or antiaircraft artillery batteries in and around the school and the entire village.

"But at least you know where they are, right?" I said. "I mean, you could take all these out with air strikes before they even knew what was coming, couldn't you?"

"Not exactly." Zoona zoomed out a bit and pointed to nine more SAM batteries in a several-block radius around the school, all positioned close to houses, shops, and even a nearby hospital. Her meaning was clear. Any effort to take out the SAMs by air strike would likely cause enormous collateral damage.

"Are people living and working in each of those buildings?" I asked.

"Quite a few."

"Tell me they're all terrorists working on those batteries and guarding that school."

"Some, sure, but we've got video images of women and children living there too."

"How many?"

"Several hundred at least."

"The kids are using the playground?"

"Every day," she said. "From noon to one and then again from three in the afternoon until sundown."

"How come there aren't any there now?"

"For the same reason you're not outside right now," she said. "This storm is hitting the whole region pretty hard right now, Dabiq included. Everyone's inside."

"Can you go back in on the school?"

"Of course."

Using what looked like a video-game controller, Zoona zoomed in again on the three-level structure and then on a particular window in the northwestern corner. I could see the faint outline of a person inside, apparently looking out the window.

"Can you enhance that?" I asked.

Zoona nodded and soon the image came into focus. To my astonishment, looking at a real-time feed from a billion-dollar American KH-12 Key Hole spy satellite operating two hundred miles above the planet, I was staring at the face of a little Syrian boy, no more than five or six years old. He was holding his mother's hand and staring out at the storm that was making it impossible for him to play on the swing sets and jungle gym just a few meters away.

"The tracking signal is coming from the basement of the school," Zoona explained. "And for the last several nights, the kids have been sleeping in the school."

"That's not normal?"

"No."

"What about their parents?"

"Several women are staying at the school each night with them. We assume they are mothers and grandmothers. There are a lot of men in the building as well. Some are probably fathers. But we've also counted at least sixty armed terrorists there."

"Phone calls?"

"We're monitoring everything, but no—no calls in or out over the past few days."

"But the cell towers are working?"

"They are."

"What about e-mail traffic?"

"Minimal and nothing of particular value."

"But you think they're hiding something there," I said.

"Or someone," Zoona concurred. "And they expect we're coming."

41

"What about chemical weapons?" I asked.

"They've got artillery batteries and mortar cannons strategically positioned all over the village," Zoona answered. "So far we can't say whether the shells are filled with sarin gas. But the command has come down from the top that we should assume that's what they've got."

"And prisoners?"

"What do you mean?"

"Are they holding prisoners in the basement of the school or anywhere else?"

"Besides the president?" she asked.

"If he's even there," I said. "But all this is circumstantial evidence at the moment. The tracking signal is the most compelling piece, I grant you, but the watch could have been removed from the president when he was captured or anytime afterward."

"Then, no—there's no sign of other prisoners being held at the school, unless you count the children and their parents."

"And it's not an ISIS command-and-control center?"

"If it is, they're not talking to anyone. No cell calls. Minimal radio chatter. Minimal Internet traffic. Everything's hot; everything's working; there's just no evidence they're talking to each other via electronic means—not much, anyway."

"And the calls to and from Jamal Ramzy's phone?"

"Actually, we just heard from the NSA on that last night. Two of the calls did go to a cell phone at the school. Several others were relayed there from other switching stations. But beyond that, as I said, there's been very little phone traffic not just to the school but to any of the homes within a five-block radius."

"Doesn't that seem odd?"

"It does."

"What do you make of it?"

"I don't know. There's not enough data to support a conclusion."

"Are there any other buildings with this kind of profile in Dabiq?" I asked.

"You mean surrounded by SAMs and triple-A batteries?"

"Right."

"None," Zoona said. "The school has become the security vortex of the entire town. Everything ISIS has done appears designed to protect the school and those inside it from a foreign attack."

"Ground or air?" I pressed.

"Both," she said. "The main roads into the town are blocked by cars, buses, nails, booby traps, IEDs, you name it. And it's not just the main roads. Every street that could possibly be used by ground forces to get to the school is blocked and booby-trapped." She redirected the satellite to show me several examples.

I looked at Colonel Sharif and asked what he thought.

"I'd say she's right," he replied. "It's pretty compelling."

"Okay, can we look at Homs now?" I asked.

"Of course," Zoona said, wiping all the screens clear and reloading them with satellite and drone images of the city that was once Syria's third largest but was now nearly a ghost town. "What specifically are we looking for?"

"The Khaled bin Walid Mosque," I said.

"What part of the city?"

"From the center, it's due east, in a neighborhood called al-Khalidiyah, not far from the M5 highway."

Zoona began typing coordinates into her laptop. Soon she put up on the main screen the live feed from a surveillance drone. I'd never seen the city from the air, so at first nothing seemed familiar. But after a few moments something caught my eye.

"Wait—there, in the upper left," I said, pointing to the monitor.

"What, the playground?" she asked.

"Exactly. Can you zoom in on that?"

"I can, but there aren't any mosques in that neighborhood."

"I know, but I—"

And then there it was. It looked different from the sky, but I was suddenly looking down on the large field Omar, Abdel, and I had crossed to get into Homs. There were the towering yet abandoned apartment buildings ringing the field. There was the old VW van. There was the broken-down school bus and the deserted playground and the burnt-out Russian battle tank.

And then I spotted something else and every muscle in my body tensed. Even from miles overhead, I could actually see the small crater in the ground and the charred grass and soil, the very place where Abdel had stepped on a land mine, the very place where he had—

The horrific images flooded back. I could see the look of stark terror on his face, the panic in his eyes, just before he stepped off the mine. Just before—

The colonel asked me what was wrong, but I couldn't speak. Zoona asked if she should keep searching, but I couldn't reply. I could barely breathe. I felt like I was suffocating, drowning in my own guilt.

Finally I asked for a glass of water. Zoona went to fetch one. While she was gone, I forced myself to look away from the monitor. But all I could think about was that Abdel was only the first of so many colleagues and friends who had died since I'd started to pursue this story about ISIS and chemical weapons. And the deaths just kept piling up by the hundreds and perhaps soon by the thousands.

When Zoona returned, I drank the entire glass of water in mere seconds. Then I asked her to keep searching for the mosque. I knew it was close, but I had no desire to explain to her—to either of them—what I'd seen or what I'd remembered. I felt cold and tired and completely disinterested in what we were doing.

As Zoona kept looking, images of schools and churches and restaurants and shops blown to smithereens or burned to the ground flew by on the monitor. I could see shuttered supermarkets and bodegas. I could see the twisted wreckage of cars and trucks and motorcycles and roads riddled with the craters of bombs and mortars of all kinds. What I didn't see were people. No soldiers. No civilians. No one. Some six hundred thousand people had once lived in Homs. Where were they all now?

"Okay, there's Clock Square," Zoona said. From there, she directed the drone eastward down a boulevard named Fares Al-Khouri, and a moment later there it was. We could see the large green spaces all around the mosque. We could see the two minarets out in front, though only one was still intact. The other had been hit by some sort of bomb and was only half there.

"You're sure that's where you were?" Sharif asked me.

"That's it," I said.

"And that's where Jamal Ramzy was?"

"Not exactly, but he was close," I said.

I explained to the two of them that my colleagues and I hadn't actually walked directly to the mosque. Rather, we'd each been captured by ISIS rebels, drugged, stripped almost naked, and blindfolded before being brought to the mosque. We'd each been grabbed by different teams and likely each taken to the mosque by different routes.

"How did they get you there?" the colonel asked.

"I don't know."

"So how do you know that's really where you were?"

"I had no idea how long I'd been unconscious," I explained. "But I woke up with a bag over my head and tied around my neck. I was freezing. My clothes were gone. My hands and feet were tied, and I was sitting on a cold concrete floor. There was a huge thunderstorm bearing down on the city—not so different from tonight. When someone finally ripped the bag off my head, three armed men covered in black hoods dragged me down a bunch of flights of stairs to the ground level. That's when I realized we were in what was left of the Khaled bin Walid Mosque. It had been shelled and shot up pretty good, but everything about the architecture made it clear it was a mosque. When we reached the ground floor, we stepped into another stairwell and descended to the basement, where we walked down a series of dripping hallways until we reached a mechanical room of some kind."

"What happened then?" the colonel asked.

"One of them shoved the barrel of a machine gun into my back. They forced me to go through an opening in the wall into a makeshift tunnel that had been dug under the city. I remember thinking it was strange because even though most of Homs was blacked out, the tunnel had power and was reasonably well lit. It was no more than five and a half feet high and at best four feet wide, but it was long. It seemed to go on forever. But eventually we wound up under another building. We climbed up a ladder and they sat me down in front of Jamal Ramzy."

Zoona positioned the drone over the mosque and moved it around, and we examined the structure from every angle. It was immediately clear that there were no ISIS forces guarding its entrances. There certainly were no SAM or triple-A batteries anywhere to be seen. In fact, there was no one there. Not a soul. The building had clearly been further damaged since I'd been there last. Upon closer examination, it looked like the south side of the structure had collapsed entirely. It seemed unlikely in the extreme that the president or any other high-value prisoner was being held there.

So we broadened our search. We went building by building, street by street, block by block, looking for any signs of heightened ISIS activity or any activity at all. But we found nothing. Zoona then brought up ten days' worth of archived Key Hole spy satellite images of the mosque and its neighborhood and the adjacent neighborhoods spanning twenty blocks. But there were absolutely no signs of an ISIS safe house to be found. Just utter, catastrophic destruction.

We had come to a dead end. And had wasted almost two hours in the process.

I felt sick to my stomach.

42

It was now 4:17 p.m.

Less than fourteen hours until the deadline was up.

Not even a half hour until the sun went down.

The colonel and I were silent on the elevator ride back up to the main floor, where the ISR command's meteorologists worked, along with most of the administrative staff and technical support team. When the doors opened, the MPs were waiting to take us back to the armored personnel carrier. But as we headed toward them, I noticed a group of young officers clustered together around a TV set. Curious at what they were watching, I peeked over someone's shoulder and found them absorbed by a report on Al Arabiya.

Israeli prime minister Daniel Lavi had just passed away.

I couldn't believe what I was seeing. The anchor repeated several times that the information was still unconfirmed, but he referenced two separate reports—one from the BBC and one from Agence France-Presse—citing unnamed doctors at

Hadassah Medical Center and a senior officer in the IDF, all of whom wished to remain anonymous since they were not authorized to discuss the prime minister's condition.

I couldn't breathe. It wasn't possible. I stopped and leaned in, hoping to learn more, but the rest was just a discussion between the anchor and two political analysts via satellite—one from Cairo and one from Dubai—discussing the possible implications of Lavi's death, "if it is proven true."

I turned to Sharif and told him what had happened. He, too, could hardly believe it and came over to hear more. It was amazing to see how hard the news was hitting each of these young Jordanian military officers and support staff. I'm not saying they had suddenly become Zionists or that they had a deep love for Lavi or his unity government. But they were deeply traumatized by the events that had transpired in their own capital in recent days. They were heavily engaged in fighting to protect their country from the forces of the Islamic State. They knew all too well the pain that they and their people were suffering, and they seemed to identify with the trauma the Israelis were now suffering as well.

"Please, Yusef, I need to be in touch with my office and my family," I whispered to the colonel after he'd had a few moments to absorb the shock of the discussions.

I prepared myself for resistance, for an argument, but to my relief he said, "Of course; I understand. Come with me. Let's find someplace quiet."

Sharif motioned to the MPs that we were going

to be a few minutes; then he led me down the hall and around the corner to a small kitchenette. There he pulled out his smartphone and entered his passcode.

"I'm still under strict orders not to let you call off this base," he said. "But if you want to dictate notes to a few people, I'm happy to send them myself and let your people know they can reach you through me."

It wasn't quite what I was hoping for. I wanted real contact. I needed real conversations, not a few impersonal e-mails. But with zero hour fast approaching, I realized this was the best I was going to get, and I intended to take full advantage of it.

I asked that the first text messages be sent to my mom and brother and gave Sharif their phone numbers. I explained that I was still in Jordan, but safe. I told them that my phone and computer had been destroyed in the attacks but that I had only minor injuries, certainly nothing life-threatening, and that they shouldn't worry. There was no point in telling them I'd been shot. Or imprisoned. Or that I'd killed anyone. Or experienced a sarin gas attack. It was only going to freak them out. There was nothing they could do about any of it, so I figured they didn't need to know. Instead, I told them I was covering the latest developments but had very limited access to the outside world, and I apologized for not being in touch sooner. Finally I told them that I loved them and that I couldn't wait to see them again, and to please keep praying for me and not to let up for a moment.

Sharif typed the message, then showed it to me to make sure he'd gotten it right. I reread that last line asking them for prayer. I wondered if that might give them the idea I was still in harm's way or going back into it. But then again, wasn't that the truth? I was in a forward operating base in the midst of the worst military crisis in Jordan in decades. The fact that I'd narrowly escaped death numerous times in recent days was, I was beginning to think, potentially related to how much my family was praying for me. Regardless of how unclear I was about God and Jesus and my own eternity, I figured I'd be an idiot not to ask for prayer. It was working. They were willing. Why not?

I thanked Sharif and he hit Send.

Then I asked him to send a quick message to Allen MacDonald back at the *Times* D.C. bureau. The colonel agreed but said I couldn't say anything newsworthy or substantive, only that my phone and computer had been destroyed but that I was alive and safe and still on the story—essentially the same as I'd told my family, without the reference to prayer.

"Can I ask if this story about Lavi is true?" I inquired.

"No."

"Can I ask what he's heard about Jack Vaughn being arrested?"

"Absolutely not."

"So that's all I get?"

"Was there someone else you wanted to write to?" he asked.

"Many."

"One more."

"Why just one?"

"Because I just got a text message from the war room," he said. "They want us to come back immediately. We need to move fast. So is there someone else—your wife, perhaps? Laura, right?"

I looked at him sharply. That was not a name I ever expected to hear again—not this far from Washington—and I was completely caught off guard not only by the suggestion but by the fact that a Jordanian colonel whom I had only just met somehow knew so much about me. Did they have a dossier on me? What else did they know? And what gave him the right to bring Laura up at such a time as this?

"Ex-wife," I said coldly.

"Right," said Sharif. "I'm sorry."

"Don't be."

"Should I send her a note, tell her you're okay?"

"No," I replied.

"Then is there someone else? We only have a moment."

There was, of course—Yael Katzir. But I didn't dare say it. Not the name of an Israeli Mossad agent. Not her personal mobile number. Not in such a sensitive moment in relations between Jordan and Israel. Not with Agent Harris on the same base, just a few buildings away, still wanting to talk to her about why she'd fled the scene of the car bombing in Istanbul.

Yet Yael was the one I wanted to reach out to, the one I found myself thinking about in every spare moment I had. I was worried about her, especially after the death of her prime minister.

But that wasn't the only reason I wanted to reconnect. The truth was I missed her. It embarrassed me to think it. But I missed her. I wanted nothing more than to sit with her and have coffee and listen to her talk and pry her for more stories and get to know her better. It wasn't simply a physical attraction, though it was certainly that. There was just something about her that fascinated me, intrigued me, drew me to her, and I wanted to find out what it was. But now wasn't the time or the place.

"No," I said at last. "We'd better go."

The king was waiting for us, though I had no idea why.

43

* * *

"I'm divorced too," Sharif said as we drove back to the war room.

"Sorry to hear that," I said, not exactly in the mood for small talk, if that's what this was supposed to be, and certainly in no mood for baring my soul or having the colonel bare his.

"It's the girls I miss the most," he continued somewhat wistfully as the storm raged around us. "Amira is my oldest. Just turned five."

"That's a lovely name."

"It means 'princess.'"

"You must be very proud."

"You have no idea. And then there's the three-year-old, Maysam, which means 'my beautiful one.'"

For the first time since we'd met, he actually handed me his phone. But it was not to make a call or read the latest headlines. He wanted me to see some digital pictures of his girls, taken at the younger one's most recent birthday party.

"Adorable, both of them," I said, doing my best to be polite. "Congratulations."

I forced myself to hand the phone back to

him. I could see Sharif wasn't smiling. He was just
staring at the pictures and his eyes were growing
moist.

"How often do you see them?" I asked.

"Never," he said. "Well, it seems like never.
Once a month. Maybe twice. They live with their
mother in Aqaba. It's hard for me to get down
there."

"I'm sure. That's quite a drive from Amman.
How long does it take?"

"Four hours."

"But you have the whole weekend with your
girls?"

"No, just an hour," he said, choking back his
emotions. "I leave before sunrise on a Friday. We
have an hour for lunch. I'm back by dinnertime.
But after all this? I have no idea when I will see
them again."

Just then lightning struck a nearby electrical
transformer, creating a small explosion, sparks
spraying everywhere. At almost the exact same
moment, multiple booms of thunder rocked our
vehicle. The storm was directly upon us now, and
even though the sun had not technically set, it was
eerie how dark the skies had become.

I felt bad for Sharif. He was a reserved and quiet
soul, fiercely loyal to the king, proficient at his
job, and overall had been quite decent to me. But
for the first time I realized his mind was far away.
Here we were at a secret base in the northeastern
part of the country, and his heart was nearly four
hundred kilometers away in Jordan's southernmost
port city. I had no idea what the circumstances

were that led to his divorce and ripped him away from the two little girls he clearly loved most in the world. Certainly it was not my place to ask, and it wouldn't have been right to anyway. All the deep and hurtful wounds that he typically kept in check in order to perform his official duties were presently forcing their way to the surface, and I genuinely wished there were something I could do to comfort him.

Yet what advice could I possibly give him? I'd completely failed as a husband. Laura and I had been married for only five years. It had started as a torrid love story. We'd met as interns in Robert Khachigian's Senate office, and I'd fallen for her immediately. We dated all summer, got married that Christmas, and everything had seemed like an intoxicating dream . . . until it didn't any-more. Suddenly she was as cold as ice. Then she announced she wanted some "time away" to figure things out. And the next thing I knew, she was moving in with some hotshot lawyer she'd met at the New York firm where she'd just been hired and was filing for divorce. The whole thing completely blindsided me. I never saw it coming. I still didn't know what I'd done wrong. And ever since, I'd avoided thinking about it, and certainly talking about it, like the plague.

The only sliver of grace in the entire emotional train wreck was that we hadn't had kids. I'd wanted to. Lots. Right from the start. She didn't. Not till she was done with law school. Not till she was with the right firm. Not till she was a partner. If I was being honest, I'd have to admit I resented her for that—and for a million other things—but I had to be grateful we hadn't brought some adorable little souls into this world only to drag them through our selfish, twisted, mixed-up lives.

All that had been a long time ago, of course. Almost twenty years. But my wounds had never fully healed. I couldn't imagine how much worse it would have been with little children caught in the middle.

We pulled into the garage over the main bunker, the door lowered behind us, and the colonel and I were soon on our way back down to the war room. Neither of us said anything, both lost in other thoughts, other troubles, far from this war. But just as the elevator doors reopened, Sharif handed me his phone.

I really didn't want to see more pictures of his children, but nor did I want to compound his pain. So I took the phone and looked at the screen.

There were no pictures of children. Instead there was a text message from my brother.

J.B.—Thank God you're okay—we've been worried sick.

When are you coming home?

We're back in Bar Harbor and staying at Mom's. She sends her love. So do Annie and the kids. We're all praying for you.

Please call ASAP. Something urgent I need to discuss with you. Can't wait. Time sensitive.

Love, Matt

P.S.—Here are the verses the kids are
memorizing this week. Thought you might
find them encouraging too. "Come to Me, all
who are weary and heavy-laden, and I will
give you rest. Take My yoke upon you and
learn from Me, for I am gentle and humble
in heart, and you will find rest for your
souls" (Matthew 11:28-29).

I read the message twice, then handed the phone
back to Sharif and stepped off the elevator. Rather
than taking me into the king's private office, however, Sharif led me down the narrow, dimly lit corridor to the waiting area outside the war room. As
we walked, I wasn't thinking about the discussion
that was coming with the generals. My thoughts
were back in Bar Harbor. All I wanted to do at
that moment was see my mom and make sure she
was okay, catch up with Matt and Annie, hug their
kids, and have a home-cooked meal in that big old
drafty house, even if my whole family did want to
convert me. They'd been trying for years, and it
had annoyed me something fierce for as long as
I could remember. But I knew they didn't mean
any harm. They loved me. They believed Jesus was
the answer to my problems. They wanted me to
believe it too. I still wasn't sure. Religion wasn't my
thing. But I guess I'd finally become convinced my
family meant well. They weren't trying to bother
me. They were trying to help me. And the older I
got, the more help I realized I needed.

Seeing them all in person was not in the cards,
however. Not anytime soon. The best I could

hope for was a phone call with Matt. But even that would have to wait. An unprecedented coalition of Americans and Sunni Arab countries was going to war inside Syria, and I was about to get a front-row seat on the plan and—I hoped—a seat on one of the choppers going into battle as well.

44

"Yael?" I said in shock as I came around the corner.

To my astonishment, she was sitting in the waiting room. Beside her was her boss, the elusive Ari Shalit. They seemed to be making notes in a briefing book, but for the life of me I couldn't imagine why they were here.

"J. B.?" she replied, looking up, removing her reading glasses, seeing me in fatigues, and clearly as surprised to see me as I was to see her.

Before I could respond, she stood and gave me a hug, careful not to press the wound on my left arm, the wound she'd been the first to dress. Her dark-brown hair was wet from the rain, and several drops ran down the back of my neck, but I didn't care. She was warm to the touch and smelled great and looked incredible in a dark-gray suit with a two-button blazer, pleated slacks, an ivory silk camisole, and black flats.

"Wow—what are you doing here, both of you?" I asked, feeling self-conscious for holding Yael a bit too long and turning quickly to shake Ari's hand.

"You'll find out in a moment," Ari replied.

"Well, I'm–I'm glad to see you both," I stammered. "Ari, Yael, I'd like you to meet Colonel Yusef Sharif. He's the king's spokesman and handles all of his media affairs. He's been taking care of me. Colonel, this is Dr. Ari Shalit, deputy director of the Mossad, and his colleague, Dr. Yael Katzir, also with the Mossad, a WMD specialist."

"Pleasure to meet you both," the colonel said, shaking their hands.

"The pleasure is ours," said Ari.

"Dr. Katzir, though we have not had the pleasure of meeting before, I do, of course, know who you are," Sharif continued. "Her Majesty the queen has spoken very highly of you, as has His Majesty. The Jordanian people owe you a great debt for what you and Mr. Collins did to save His Majesty and his family."

"You don't owe us anything. We're friends— allies, even—but you're very kind to say so," Yael replied.

"Actually, we're very sorry to request to see you all with such little notice," said Ari. "As you know, my boss—the director—could not come."

"How is he?" Sharif asked.

"Not well."

"Cancer?"

"Yes, pancreatic," said Ari. "Stage IV, I'm afraid."

"I'm sorry."

"Thank you. And I suspect you've heard the news about the prime minister."

"We just heard some rumors on TV," I said. "Please tell us it's not true."

"I fear it is," Ari confirmed.

"I'm very sorry for that as well," Sharif said.

"All Israel is in shock," Ari said. "But of course Jordan has been suffering far worse in recent days. We are deeply sorry for all that has happened and for all that you and your people are going through right now."

"We are suffering, but we still have our king," Sharif replied. "Please accept my condolences for your terrible loss. Prime Minister Lavi was truly a man of peace and a good friend of His Majesty and the kingdom. He will be deeply missed."

"Thank you," Ari said. "That's very kind."

Ari and the colonel chatted quietly for another few minutes. Yael and I said nothing. But as we listened, I couldn't help but keep glancing at her. Her large, brown, beautiful eyes were tired and full of grief. And I realized that she was wearing makeup. She hadn't worn any in Turkey, and she wasn't wearing much now. It might not even have been apparent to anyone who didn't know her. But I noticed and then realized why. She was covering injuries she'd received during our escape from the palace—the two blows she'd taken to the face when fighting hand to hand with one of the jihadists and the gash she'd gotten on her forehead when our SUV smashed into a car outside the palace gates. I wanted to ask her about it, see how she was feeling, find out whether she'd sustained any other injuries.

But before I could, Ari took me aside. He asked me how I'd wound up here and what I was doing. I gave him a brief summary of what had happened until I realized that what he was really getting at was whether I was going to tell the world he and Yael were here. I assured him that Colonel Sharif was not allowing me to publish anything at the moment and that I would not do anything to burn him. He still didn't look comfortable at the prospect of having a reporter around, but just then the door to the war room opened behind us.

Prince Feisal came out and greeted us somberly, then asked us to step inside.

As we did, the king stood, came around the conference table, and embraced Ari as a brother. They said nothing. Nor did they need to. They were roughly the same age. Both in their mid-fifties. Both sons of the Holy Land. Both had bravely served their countries in the special forces. Once they'd been enemies. Now they were friends. One was a monarch. One was a spy. They knew the fates of their countries were both on the line, and they knew the price of victory.

When the king released Ari, he turned to Yael, took her hands in his, looked into her eyes, and both expressed his condolences and thanked her for all that she had done for him and the royal family. I found it hard to define the chemistry between them, but it was clear that Yael was deeply touched by the king's kind and gracious spirit. She and Ari had come as professionals. They had been welcomed as friends.

His Majesty asked the two to sit next to him at the head of the table and quickly introduced them to the rest of the assembled group. When he got to me, he repeated his assurances that everything said and done on the entire base was off the record and that no reports of any kind from these meetings would be published in the *Times* or anywhere else without his permission. I still wasn't sure that comforted everyone, but he was the king, and it was his room and his rules, so no one said a thing. At that point, he turned the floor over to Ari.

The colonel and I were sitting in the back of the room. Notebook in hand and ready to transcribe everything that was about to unfold, I was positioned directly behind the Egyptian general. Still, even from this less-than-ideal vantage point, I had a decent view of Ari—and more importantly, Yael.

"Thank you, Your Majesty," Ari began. "I apologize for the timing, but it could not be helped. And, gentlemen, I realize that this is a bit unorthodox, having Ms. Katzir and me here with you at such a critical moment. But the purpose of our visit is very simple. We know you believe President Taylor is in Dabiq. We understand the case. We've been studying the evidence. And we agree it's compelling. But in the end my colleagues and I don't believe he's there. We believe it's a trap. The president is not in Syria. He's in Iraq."

45

★ ★ ★

The room fell silent.

"We believe the president is being held in a small village known as Alqosh," Ari continued as Yael set up a PowerPoint presentation.

The first slide they posted was a map of northern Iraq and a red dot marked *Alqosh*, along with two variant spellings: *Al-Qosh* and *Elkosh*.

"Alqosh is an ancient Assyrian town," Ari went on. "Its history dates back before the time of the Babylonian Empire. As you can see on this map, it's located on the plains in the Iraqi province of Nineveh. It's about fifty kilometers north of Mosul, not far from Dohuk, right off Highway 2."

"But Alqosh is a Christian town, not Muslim, isn't it?" asked General El-Badawy.

"That's true, General," Ari replied. "Alqosh has been a Chaldean Christian community, a mixture of Orthodox and Catholic. It has been captured several times in recent years by ISIS, then liberated several times by the Iraqis, but finally retaken by ISIS forces about a year ago and has been held securely by ISIS since then. During these battles, most of the Christians fled. Those who didn't get out in time were crucified or beheaded. The population has plunged from more than three thousand to just a few hundred today, most of whom are ISIS leaders and their families."

"So why do you think the president is in Alqosh, of all places?" the Egyptian general pressed.

"Several reasons," Ari said. "First, let's look at the phone calls made to and from Jamal Ramzy's cell phone."

Ari nodded, and Yael posted the next slide, an infographic detailing the call log.

RAMZY PHONE LOG

Outgoing Calls:

1. Thursday, 25 November: Dabiq, Syria
   (9 seconds)

2. Sunday, 28 November: Dabiq, Syria
   (9 seconds)

3. Monday, 29 November: Homs, Syria
   (4:17 minutes)

4. Tuesday, 30 November: Dabiq, Syria
   (9 seconds)

5. Tuesday, 30 November: Homs, Syria
   (3:54 minutes)

6. Wednesday, 1 December: Homs, Syria
   (2 minutes)

7. Thursday, 2 December: Homs, Syria
   (4:36 minutes)

8. Friday, 3 December: Homs, Syria
   (6:13 minutes)

9. Friday, 3 December: Irbid, Jordan → Fairfax,
   Virginia (12:09 minutes)

Incoming Calls:

1. Tuesday, 30 November: Homs, Syria
   (2:29 minutes)
2. Saturday, 4 December: Homs, Syria
   (53 seconds)
3. Sunday, 5 December: Dabiq, Syria
   (9 seconds)

"As you can see, the log shows that nine out-bound calls were made from Ramzy's cell phone, and three inbound calls were received," Ari said. "Now, it's true that three of the outbound calls were made to a number in Dabiq, including two of the first three calls made. But our analysis shows that each of these calls lasted only nine seconds. It's possible, of course, that Ramzy—or whoever was using the phone—had a brief conversation with someone in Dabiq each time, passing along a small bit of information—a name, a phone number, a date and time, something along those lines. But how likely is it that his conversation lasted exactly nine seconds each time? Not very."

"He was entering a passcode," General al-Mufti said.

"Yes, General, that's what we believe," Ari concurred. "We can't prove it. And we don't know what the code was. But obviously the caller had some reason to dial that number in Dabiq and complete the same procedure each time, a pro-cedure that took exactly nine seconds. The only inbound call from Dabiq also lasted nine seconds. In this case, whatever procedure had been agreed upon in advance was being done in reverse."

Ari looked around the room and then back at the king to make sure everyone was following him. We were, and the king encouraged him to proceed.

"Of course, this doesn't prove the president is *not* in Dabiq," Ari readily conceded. "The phone records show Ramzy calling this number—and it's the same number every time—in Dabiq. Clearly there's a strong connection to Dabiq. But for my team and me, at least, it doesn't make sense that Ramzy was talking to Abu Khalif when he made those calls. Yet Ramzy was Khalif's deputy. They should have spoken several times during this period. At the very least Ramzy should have spoken to someone close to Khalif, someone who could have reliably passed information back and forth between the two. But clearly that didn't happen on any of the calls to or from Dabiq. That leads us to Homs, which I will get to in a moment. But before we do, let's take a look at the last outbound call."

Yael put up a new slide.

FINAL RAMZY
OUTGOING CALL

9. Friday, 3 December: Irbid, Jordan → Fairfax, Virginia (12:09 minutes)
   * Irbid → drugstore
   * Western Union office
   * Two money transfers

"This call is surely the oddest of them all," Ari said. "At precisely five o'clock on the afternoon of Friday, December 3, a call was made from Jamal Ramzy's phone to a number just outside of Washington, D.C. We've been able to determine that the cell tower the call originated from was located on the outskirts of the city of Irbid. So either Ramzy or someone on his team using this phone was operating inside the Hashemite Kingdom, whereas all the calls made or received before December 3 were transmitted from cell towers in various parts of Syria. Everyone still with me?"

We all were.

"Which means Ramzy or his team crossed the border from Syria into Jordan sometime between eleven o'clock on the night of Thursday, December 2, and 8:32 on the morning of Friday, December 3, when the second-to-last call is made from the phone," Ari continued. "What makes the call stand out, of course, is that it's the only call outside of the Middle East. It's the only call to the United States. And curiously, it's to a phone number for a drugstore in Fairfax, Virginia. Now, why is that significant?"

Ari had no takers, so he continued.

"The drugstore is located on Route 123, also known as Chain Bridge Road. Was it a mistake? Was it a wrong number?"

"No," General Jum'a said. "It's the longest call Ramzy made."

"Exactly, General," Ari said. "The call lasted more than twelve minutes. So we have to assume Ramzy, or the person using his phone, meant to call a drugstore in Fairfax. But why? He's not calling in a prescription. He's not checking if they have mouthwash or a certain brand of razor. Why is he calling this drugstore?"

"It's about the money," the Saudi general said, engaging the Israeli agent for the first time.

"Correct," Ari said. "It turns out there is a Western Union office at this drugstore, and when we investigated further, we found that two money transfers were made from overseas to that Western Union branch on that day. The first was for six hundred dollars. It was sent to a nineteen-year-old Indian student from Mumbai who is a sophomore at George Mason University. But the family seems to have no possible connection to terrorism, so we examined the second transfer. This one was for five thousand dollars. It was sent from Dubai to a thirty-four-year-old woman who works as a real estate agent in Vienna, Virginia."

"Real estate?" I asked.

Ari nodded.

"Let me guess," I said, stunned to see how this was unfolding. "This is the woman who was working for Jack and Claire Vaughn, the one having an affair with Jack."

"The very same," Ari said. "We passed this information along to the FBI as soon as we got it."

"Okay, this is all fascinating," Prince Feisal interjected, "but I hope I don't need to remind you we are fast approaching the launch of military operations into Dabiq. So far you haven't convinced us you have a better target."

46

* * *

"My apologies, Your Highness," Ari quickly replied. "I'll pick up the pace."

"Please do."

"This brings us to the calls to and from Homs," Ari continued. "They represent seven of the twelve calls sent or received and a total of twenty minutes of conversation. So putting together what we knew from J. B.'s articles—notably that Jamal Ramzy had a safe house in Homs—we began considering the possibility that Abu Khalif was in Homs and that perhaps the president had been taken there as well. But then our technical team made an important discovery. Yael, would you put up the next slide?"

RAMZY PHONE LOG

Outgoing Calls to Homs:

1. Monday, 29 November: Homs → Mosul
   (4:17 minutes)
2. Tuesday, 30 November: Homs → Mosul
   (3:54 minutes)

3. Wednesday, 1 December: Homs → Mosul
   (2 minutes)
4. Thursday, 2 December: Homs → Mosul
   (4:36 minutes)
5. Friday, 3 December: Homs → Mosul →
   Aleppo → Baghdad → AQ (6:13 minutes)

"What they discovered was that Homs wasn't a base of operations for ISIS," Ari noted. "It turned out the number in Homs was nothing more than a switching station, and all of the calls were being switched to a series of numbers in Mosul."

"A series of numbers?" the UAE general asked.

"Yes," Ari said. "To keep things simple, I didn't put all the data on the slide. But once the calls were routed from Homs to Mosul, they were rerouted again five, six, sometimes seven times before finally connecting. I'm afraid we weren't able to determine where the two inbound calls were coming from before they were routed to Ramzy's phone. But we were able to figure out where each of the outgoing calls was routed to, and the last call becomes the most important."

The next slide showed a blizzard of detailed technical data: certain phone numbers that were used to specific cell towers in Jordan, Syria, Iraq, Syria again, and Iraq again, and so forth. Given the constraints of time, Ari told us he would skip a thorough explanation and just cut to the chase.

"This last call was bounced around the most, a total of nineteen times through three different countries," he said. "In the end they weren't able to throw us off the scent. In fact, by taking such precautions, they revealed that of all twelve calls to and from Ramzy's phone, this was by far the most important. It wasn't as long as the call to the Western Union office in Virginia, but at six minutes and thirteen seconds it was the longest call in the region. It was clearly the call the ISIS team worked hardest to camouflage. Any guess where it went?"

"Alqosh," Al-Mufti said.

"Exactly," Ari confirmed. "Now, I wish I could tell you that we were able to intercept and record the actual call. I wish I could tell you we had Jamal Ramzy and Abu Khalif on tape plotting the assassination of our leaders and their plan to bring the president back to Alqosh. But I can't. Maybe NSA has it. But to be honest, given the high-level penetration of NSA this week, we didn't think discussing it with our friends in Fort Meade was the best move right now. But this is where my colleague Dr. Katzir enters the picture. With your permission, I'm going to hand things over to her now."

The king and prince both nodded, and Yael stood. She straightened her jacket and smoothed back her damp hair. She was moving slowly and seemed stiff.

"Thank you, Your Majesty and Your Highness, for allowing us to come over on such short notice," she began. "Dr. Shalit brought me here today because my specialty—first in the IDF and for the last several years with the Mossad—is weapons of mass destruction and particularly chemical weapons. I have a master's from UC Berkeley and a doctorate from MIT in chemical engineering.

My father was a chemist for Pfizer and now teaches chemistry at Tel Aviv University, which is how I developed my love for the subject. Anyway, a number of weeks ago, as you know from Mr. Collins's reporting, ISIS forces led by Jamal Ramzy's top deputy—a guy named Tariq Baqouba—attacked a Syrian military base near Aleppo. We don't think Baqouba knew at the time that it was a storage facility for chemical weapons. The U.N. had, after all, supposedly moved all of Syria's WMD out of the country. But the Assad regime was still secretly hoarding a great deal of chemical weapons. So when the fight was over and Baqouba and his men gained control of the base, they found—most likely to their surprise—stockpiles of sarin nerve gas and the bombs and artillery shells to deliver them."

I was disappointed that she'd called me "Mr. Collins" rather than "J. B." or "James." But other than that I was enjoying just being in the same room with her, having the chance to look at her for long stretches of time without it seeming odd, and getting to hear her speak with just a mesmerizing hint of an accent.

Ari now put up a series of photos of the Syrian base in question, taken from Israeli drones, but I never took my eyes off Yael.

"As you might imagine, we'd been using drones to monitor each of the sites where we believed the Assad regime had been making or keeping chemical weapons," she continued. "We'd also been monitoring all radio, phone, and e-mail traffic in the area around these bases. Bottom line, we watched Baqouba and his men cart away the sarin precursors, load them onto trucks, and drive away."

Ari now played a video clip showing drone footage of the ISIS convoy of five white box trucks driving away from the base.

"For the next five days, we tracked these five trucks as they drove through Syria, across the border into Iraq, and on to Mosul," Yael explained. "Unfortunately, our drone fleet was stretched thin at that time, and when the convoy got to Mosul, the drivers split off in five different directions. As a result, we lost four of them, but we did follow one, and it led us here."

For the first time, I forced myself to look away from Yael and toward the main monitor on the wall. A new video clip showed one of the trucks exiting a highway, driving down a long country road, entering a small village, and pulling into a heavily guarded compound on the edge of the village, just along a mountain ridge.

"Let me guess," General El-Badawy said. "That's Alqosh."

"It is," Yael confirmed. "Now, when we watched this whole thing begin to unfold, I had never heard of Alqosh. Nor had Dr. Shalit. But he tasked me with learning everything I possibly could about the town: who was there, why ISIS would park a truck filled with sarin gas there, and so forth. So I set up the same type of monitoring operation as I had at the Aleppo base. We started tracking phone calls, e-mails, text messages, anything we possibly could, and of course we kept a steady eye on the drone images. But we had gaps.

I wanted a second drone so we'd have nonstop coverage of the compound. Unfortunately, there weren't any others available. So we had to keep bringing the drone we were using back to Israel for refueling and maintenance. My team and I feared the weapons would be moved out of Alqosh and we'd miss it. Instead, we actually captured on video two more of the white box trucks arriving at the compound a few days after the first, amid numerous cars coming in and out at all hours of the day and night, and we began to consider the possibility that ISIS was actually storing the bulk of the chemical weapons they'd captured at this particular compound in Alqosh."

"This is all well and good, Dr. Katzir, but it doesn't put the president there," Prince Feisal protested.

"I realize that, Your Highness," she said calmly and without seeming to take offense. "I'm getting to that."

"With all due respect, you need to get there faster. The clock is ticking."

47

"Of course, Your Highness," Yael replied.

She leaned forward to pour herself a glass of water. I noticed she winced as she did so and held the glass with two hands. She was in more pain than she was letting on.

"Gentlemen, it's at this point that we intercepted a series of e-mails sent from inside the compound. Both were going to an e-mail address in Washington, D.C., an address belonging to one Allen MacDonald."

Stunned, I looked around the room and then back at Yael. No one else knew whom she was talking about, but I did, and I could hardly believe she was serious.

"Who's Allen MacDonald?" al-Mufti asked.

"He's Mr. Collins's editor at the *New York Times*," Yael explained. "We suddenly realized that Mr. Collins was at that location, writing two articles and sending them back to the foreign desk. When we read the articles, we realized what was happening. ISIS forces had just attacked the Abu Ghraib prison near Baghdad. In the process, they had liberated their spiritual leader, Abu Khalif. They had also captured Mr. Collins, who was writing about these events in great detail. What's more, he was writing about his exclusive interview with Khalif and the demonstration he witnessed of ISIS operatives testing sarin gas on several Iraqi prisoners."

Ari now stood. "I give tremendous credit to Dr. Katzir and her team," he said. "They not only tracked the movement of some of the most deadly weapons in the Syrian arsenal, but they also identified the location of one of the highest value targets on the Mossad's most-wanted list, not to mention each of your own. Because my own boss is so ill and I'm serving as acting director at the moment, I took this to the prime minister at once with a request that we take immediate action."

"What kind of action?" I asked, my heart racing.

"We wanted to neutralize the target," Ari replied.

"Neutralize?"

"Yes."

"You mean destroy?"

"Of course."

"With me inside the same compound?"

"Well, that did complicate the situation enormously."

"I guess so."

"So what did Danny do?" the king asked.

"He put two F-16s on strip alert, ready to hit the compound on his orders, but he also went straight to the security cabinet," Ari said. "They debated it for hours."

"*Hours?* What for?" El-Badawy pressed. "You

had the head of ISIS, likely his top deputies, and a cache of chemical weapons all within a couple hundred meters of each other. Why in the world didn't you take the shot?"

"General, this was exactly my position," Ari said. "The national security of the State of Israel was in grave peril. We didn't know, of course, what was about to happen in Amman. But we knew enough that in my judgment we had to act. And to be completely candid—and completely off the record—the majority of the security cabinet recommended the strike as well."

"But in the end, Danny called it off," said the king.

"Yes."

"And not taking out Abu Khalif when he had the chance cost him his life."

"I'm afraid so, Your Majesty."

I looked at Ari, then at Yael, then down at my notes. But there was one person I couldn't look at just then—the king. He and the Israeli prime minister—"Danny"—had been friends for years. They had also worked together for months on the peace treaty with the Palestinians they had all come so close to signing. And now Daniel Lavi was gone—because of me.

There could be no other reason Lavi had hesitated to attack Alqosh than to protect my life. Ari hadn't said it in so many words, but everyone in the room knew what he was saying. And now hundreds were dead. Many more were wounded. The Hashemite Kingdom was on the brink, and the president of the United States had been captured.

And yet again I had nearly died. When I'd been taken captive by Khalif and his jihadists, I was convinced I was going to be beheaded on YouTube for all the world to see. I never imagined two Israeli fighter jets were on standby, waiting for a single order to drop two five-thousand-pound bombs and kill me and everyone around me before any of us even realized what was happening.

I shuddered at the thought. How many times in recent weeks had I been so close to death, so close to slipping out of this world and into the next? More than I dared count, especially since I knew I wasn't ready to die. My brother was pleading with me to give my life to Christ. He kept telling me that receiving Christ was the only way to heaven. He kept telling me I was going to spend eternity in hell with no way of escape if I didn't. I used to be furious with him for saying things like that. But I no longer believed he was trying to be cruel. I was convinced now that Matt absolutely believed this in the core of his being. I knew he genuinely feared that I would be separated from God and from him and from the rest of our family forever. He loved me. He wanted the best for me. But I couldn't bring myself to do it.

I wasn't even sure that he was wrong. I was actually beginning to wonder if he might be right. But something in me couldn't say yes to Christ. I couldn't have explained why. I'm not even sure I knew. I just couldn't, and yet a fear was engulfing me like I'd never experienced before. My hands started trembling again. I set down my pad and pen on the conference table and put my hands in my lap. I was perspiring and my mouth was dry, but I didn't dare reach for the glass of water on the table before me. I was too afraid of spilling it.

A new video started playing on the main monitor. It was a night-vision shot showing a car and an SUV driving away from the compound.

"That night, we observed two vehicles leaving Alqosh in the middle of the night," Yael said, breaking the awkward silence. "Because we had only one drone operating over the site, we couldn't follow the car. We believed at the time that Abu Khalif was leaving. The problem was that the mandate of my unit was to track chemical weapons, not ISIS leaders per se. It was a brutal call to make. I was cursing my superiors for not giving me a second drone. But I had my orders. I couldn't disobey them. I had to stay with the compound."

"So you didn't know it was Mr. Collins who was being taken away from the town instead of Khalif?" Prince Feisal asked.

"No, Your Highness, I did not."

"Why not?"

"There were tarps over the driveway and carport in the compound, preventing us from seeing faces of people entering or exiting the vehicles inside. And the windows of the vehicle were tinted. Plus it was night. So it wasn't possible to make proper IDs, I'm afraid."

"But if you had known?" the Saudi asked.

"If I'd known what, General?"

"If you'd known Collins had left instead of Khalif, would you have hit the compound?"

"Well, of course, it wasn't my decision to make,"

Yael replied. "But yes, I would certainly have recommended an immediate strike. I know for a fact my superiors would have agreed and taken my recommendation directly to the PM. And I have no doubt that the PM and the security cabinet would have ordered a strike. As it was, we didn't know who had left the compound, so the PM ordered the F-16s to stand down."

"But even without Khalif there, you could have hit the compound anyway," the Saudi pressed. "I still don't understand why you didn't take the opportunity to destroy all those chemical weapons when you had the chance."

Yael said nothing but looked to Ari.

"I wanted to do just that," he replied. "But Dr. Katzir pleaded with me not to."

"Why not? It was a perfect opportunity."

"In some ways, yes," Ari agreed. "But Dr. Katzir argued it would have exposed our knowledge of the site. It would have destroyed all the highly valuable intelligence that was surely at the site. She strongly recommended, instead, that we find a way to send several operatives—"

"Spies?" the Saudi asked.

"Okay, yes, spies, to infiltrate the compound and find out who exactly was there and what their intentions were," Ari added.

"You couldn't have believed that would have really worked."

"It was a compelling case," Ari said.

"This wasn't about intelligence," El-Badawy interjected. "She was trying to protect Collins."

"We did have an innocent American citizen—

a highly respected and accomplished journalist—in the compound, yes," Ari concurred. "It's not our practice to kill innocent civilians, whatever the media in the region say about us."

"But there was a higher mission," El-Badawy insisted. "Wasn't it worth killing one man to save the lives of so many others?"

48

★ ★ ★

"In the end, I took Dr. Katzir's recommendation," Ari said.

"Just to save a reporter?" the Saudi asked, indignant.

"She was the lead analyst on this," Ari responded. "She had an impeccable service record. I've always trusted her judgment. I didn't necessarily agree with her. But I respect her, and at the time I couldn't say definitively that she was wrong."

"But she was."

I couldn't believe what I was hearing. My blood was boiling. The colonel could see it. He reached over and put his hand on my arm, a subtle reminder—perhaps a plea—not to say anything, to let this thing play out without jumping in. I looked at Yael. She was surprisingly calm. I didn't know how she did it. But I could see this was getting to Ari. His jaw was clenched as he carefully chose his next words.

"Dr. Katzir could not have possibly known what was coming, General," he finally replied. "Nor could I. Nor could our prime minister. Nor could any of you. Not that night. Not based on what we knew at that precise moment. We had a judgment call to make. Hindsight is twenty-twenty. But I believe we made the best decision we could, given the imperfect information we had at the time."

I was grateful for the answer. The Saudi general, however, wouldn't let it go.

"But in the end you cannot escape the brutal fact that you chose to risk the lives of thousands—thousands of Arabs, I might add; thousands of Muslims—to save the life of a single man, a single reporter."

"An American citizen," Ari added, "and a friend."

"Ah, and now we get to it," the general said, his face red as he leaned forward in his chair. "This was not just an American and not just a reporter; this was someone Miss Katzir knew personally."

"*Dr.* Katzir."

"Someone that *Dr.* Katzir knew personally."

"Yes."

"Someone she is friends with?"

"You could say that."

"Close friends?"

"Perhaps—they've certainly been through a great deal together."

"And perhaps more than friends?"

"What are you implying?"

"I'm not implying," the general said. "I'm merely asking."

"You're asking if there is some kind of inappropriate relationship going on here?" Ari asked, incredulous.

I glanced at Yael. She was mortified. Her face said it all. And she was growing angry. Her back stiffened. She leaned forward in her seat. For a second, I thought she might unleash on the general. But she was too much of a professional for that. She let Ari defend her, and Ari was doing a fine job. But I was livid, about to explode. Sharif tightened his grip on my arm, silently imploring me to stay calm and let others defend our honor.

"General, these are two people who risked their own lives to save the life of this fine and honorable king from these ISIS monsters," Ari responded. "Perhaps you're not aware that Dr. Katzir killed dozens of the jihadists, or that she was engaged in hand-to-hand combat with them. Perhaps you're not aware that she personally shot and killed Jamal Ramzy or that Mr. Collins was the one who had the wherewithal to recover Ramzy's phone, which has given us such critical intelligence. Or that he was shot and wounded protecting the lives of the royal family. Or that he drove the vehicle that whisked not only the king and his family to safety but also the Palestinian president and my prime minister. Rather than cowardly insinuations, I believe everyone in this room owes these two people a great debt."

The room was silent, but Ari wasn't finished.

"Furthermore, General, with all due respect, you are distracting this group from the real objective, which is to analyze the evidence we have brought you," he continued.

The general tried to speak, but Ari would not let him.

"No, I'm sorry; you can respond in a moment, but I haven't yet completed my presentation," he said as calmly as he could. "Look, all of us deeply regret not seeing these attacks against the summit coming. And we all regret not doing more to prevent them. Personally, if I could do it all over, would I have made different decisions? Of course. We've got three drones over Alqosh right now and, I might add, four over Dabiq. That's what we can do—make adjustments, course corrections, based on what we've all learned. But we cannot look back. We can't get bogged down in finger-pointing and recriminations. Not now. We do not have the luxury. As His Highness has reminded us several times, the clock is ticking. So this brings me to my last and final point. Aside from the vehicles that left the compound in Alqosh to take Mr. Collins to the Kurdish border, we had observed no other vehicles coming in or out of not just the compound but the entire village until around four o'clock this morning."

Yael took a deep breath and put a final video clip up on the main screen. It was more night-vision footage, this time of a convoy made up of three SUVs pulling off Highway 2, heading into Alqosh and right into the compound.

"We believe you are watching the president of the United States arriving at Abu Khalif's lair in the town of Alqosh on the Nineveh plains," Ari said.

The video now switched to thermal imaging of the three SUVs coming to a halt inside the walled compound under the tarps Yael had previously mentioned. So while we couldn't see faces, I counted nine men carrying weapons exiting the first and third vehicle. Then I watched as four more armed men got out of the middle vehicle. I could see them opening the trunk and pulling out a body. At first I thought they were handling a corpse, and my heart almost stopped. But then I saw movement. The person's hands and feet appeared to be bound. But whoever it was writhed and twitched and seemed determined not to go quietly. Was that really him? I wondered. Was that really President Taylor?

"Now, what was particularly curious to us was that within minutes of this particular convoy arriving, communications of every kind in the village shut down completely," Ari noted, and as he did, the video ended and the screen went black. "The lights in the village stayed on. They hadn't lost power. But the nearby cell tower was abruptly switched off. We're not sure how. All Wi-Fi services in the village went dead as well. Since 4:15 this morning, no calls, no e-mails, no text messages, nor any other form of communication has come in or out of the entire village. But we did intercept the last text message sent by a mobile phone inside the main residence in the compound just before everything went dark."

"What did it say?" asked the Saudi.

"'The package has arrived.'"

49

It was now 5:57 p.m.

Just twelve hours until the deadline.

The sun had been down all across the Middle East for more than an hour.

And now the king asked Ari, Yael, the colonel, and me to step out of the room. They had heard the evidence. They had a decision to make and not much time to make it.

I didn't envy the position these men were in. I'd jotted down a list of questions on my notepad, each of which was as vexing as the next.

Were the Israelis right—were the president and Khalif in Alqosh?

Or was General Ramirez right about the evidence pointing to Dabiq?

I found myself leaning heavily toward the case Ari and Yael were making. Perhaps I was biased, but I was trying to analyze the evidence as objectively as possible. And when it came to Alqosh, the pieces fit.

Still, even if Ramirez and the others were persuaded by the Israelis' case, could the U.S. afford not to send forces to Dabiq, given that the tracking signal from the president's watch was unmistakably being picked up from there? What if Ramirez put all his chips on Alqosh and he was wrong—or vice versa?

Then again, did the coalition have enough forces to embark simultaneously on two rescue missions?

And if they did, with the raging storm bearing down on the region, could the coalition's forces get safely to either site and back?

As we stepped out of the war room and into the waiting area, I was eager to get the others' take on all these questions, and there were so many more.

If the storm was too intense to fly special forces teams to either or both sites, was there a realistic ground option that could be pulled off in the next twelve hours?

And if they decided to fly, what would they do if one or more of the choppers went down due to weather or mechanical failure or enemy fire?

What's more, if they could even get to either or both of the sites, how would coalition forces protect themselves against the possible use of chemical weapons?

Above all, what if they were all wrong? What if neither the president nor Abu Khalif was at either site? What if the president was already dead? What if another major attack was coming against Jordan, against Israel, or against the United States?

When we got out into the hallway, the colonel pulled me away from the others and showed me his phone. He now had five text messages and two missed calls from my brother, begging me to call him immediately.

In an instant, my entire perspective changed. "You need to let me call him," I told Sharif.

"I can't," he replied. "You know that."

"Then why show me all these messages?"

"I'm just trying to keep you informed."

"And I'm grateful," I said. "But you have to let me call him. Something's wrong. He's not like this. He never texts or calls this often."

"I wish I could, Mr. Collins. But I'm under strict orders not to let you—or anyone—communicate outside of this base. I've already bent those rules as far as I can. I can't do more."

"Colonel—Yusef—you have to."

"I'm sorry."

"But you don't understand," I pleaded. "Abu Khalif personally threatened my family. What if something's happened to them? Please, ask the king to make an exception."

"Absolutely not. You heard His Majesty. He and his war council are making their final plans. They cannot be distracted by civilian affairs."

"There's got to be something you can do."

"There isn't."

"Think, Colonel—I'm not a prisoner anymore. I'm not a hostage. You can't deny me access to my own family in an emergency."

"The needs of the kingdom rank higher than our own personal needs, Mr. Collins."

"For you, yes, but you're a subject of the kingdom—I'm not," I argued. "I'm an American citizen who has done everything I can to protect the king and his family, not out of obligation but because of the respect I have for them. Surely you can help me protect my family in a time like this."

"The king's command is sacrosanct, Mr. Collins. You may not speak to anyone off this base."

"That doesn't apply to you, though, does it?"

"Of course not."

"You've been in touch with foreign media and foreign officials in the last few days, right?"

"Yes, of course, but what's your point?"

"Call him for me."

"Your brother?"

"Yes, you can call him. Find out what's wrong. Maybe I can listen in but not say anything, or just hand you a note if there's something I need to tell him, and you can decide whether you can pass the message along or not."

Sharif didn't immediately say no. I had five more arguments to make, but I held my fire. I didn't want to push him. And in the end, I didn't have to.

"Okay."

"Really?"

"Yes."

"You'll call him?"

"Yes. Come with me."

Sharif excused himself from the Israelis, encouraged them to have a seat, and said we'd be right back. They were a bit surprised, to say the least, but the colonel didn't wait or discuss it with them. Instead, he led me down the hall to the security command post and into a break room typically filled with off-duty guards. Except that it was empty now. No one was off duty. Sharif pulled the door closed behind us, and we sat down on opposite sides of a small table covered in used coffee cups and napkins.

"Get out your notepad," he said as he found Matt's number and started the call.

"Why?" I asked.

"If there's something you want me to say, write it down and slide it over to me. Otherwise, you keep your mouth shut or I hang up immediately. Got it?"

"Yes."

"No exceptions."

"I understand."

With that, he hit the Speaker button and suddenly Annie's voice filled the room. "Hello?"

"Yes, hello, I'm looking for Dr. Matthew Collins. Do I have the right number?"

"Yes, this is his wife. May I ask who's calling?"

"Of course—I'm Colonel Yusef Sharif. I work for His Majesty King Abdullah. I'm returning a call from your husband. Is he there?"

"Yes, yes, he is," Annie replied. "Just a moment and I'll fetch him."

It was a joy to hear her voice. Her kids were fighting in the background over some toy, and one of them started to cry. Typically things like that annoyed me, but not anymore, or at least not today. Those were the sounds of home, and for perhaps the first time in my life I wanted to be with them instead of on the front lines of a major story.

Then, before I knew it, Matt came on the line. "Hello? This is Matt Collins. Who's this again?"

The colonel greeted him and explained who

he was. "Your brother is okay, Dr. Collins," he told Matt. "He's safe and covering this unfolding drama over here and doing an excellent job, I might add. But I'm afraid with all that's going on, there are restrictions on foreign nationals making calls outside the country, at least those foreign nationals who know where His Majesty is. I hope you'll understand."

"Well, I guess so," Matt said. "But it is really urgent that I talk with him."

"I realize that, and that's why I'm calling you back. Again, it's not that J. B. doesn't want to speak to you. To the contrary, he's dying to talk to you and to his mother, your mother. But for security reasons, no one but government officials are allowed to call out of the location we're currently in. But I can certainly pass along a message."

There was a pause. I could tell Matt was weighing his options. Whatever he had to tell me, it was clearly sensitive. I scribbled down a note and passed it to the colonel. He read it, then looked at me, then closed his eyes.

"Listen, I understand this isn't an ideal way for you two to communicate," Sharif told Matt. "But I'm afraid right now it's this or nothing. I'm not sure I'm allowed to tell you this, but I'm going to because your brother has been a true friend to the kingdom. You should know that your brother is sitting right here with me. He's listening to our conversation. He seems glad to hear your voice and your kids in the background. He's not allowed to speak to you, but I want to assure you that he's not going to miss anything you're saying."

"Really? J. B., can you hear me?"

Instinctively, I was about to respond, but Sharif held up his finger and cut me off. "Dr. Collins, like I said, he's right here, but he's not allowed to say anything. But you can speak to him if you'd like."

"How do I know he's really there?" asked Matt.

"What do you mean?"

"I mean, how do I know you are who you say you are and that he's really at your side?"

"I guess you'll just have to trust me."

"I'm afraid I can't do that, Mister—Colonel—whoever you are. For all I know, you work for ISIS."

50

★ ★ ★

"I don't work for ISIS," Sharif insisted. "I work for the king of Jordan."

"So you say."

"Dr. Collins, I realize you're under a lot of stress right now. But I'm in the middle of a war. I really don't have the time or interest to argue with you. Would you like to pass a message on to your brother or not? I'll remind you that you called me. I'm simply returning your call."

"Not exactly," my brother shot back. "You texted me first. You said my brother was passing along his greetings. But you offered no proof, and you still haven't."

That's my brother, I thought. For all his faults, the man was no fool.

Sharif checked his watch and took a deep breath. "Fair enough, Dr. Collins. Ask your brother a question to which only he would know the answer."

"Really?"

"Yes."

"Okay," Matt said. "What was it that we talked

317

about in the hallway just before we went in to see Annie and the kids?"

Sharif pushed my notebook back across the table. I wrote as quickly as I could and then slid the notebook back to him. He read the note and looked quizzically at me for a moment, but to his credit he read it to Matt anyway.

"You were explaining a bunch of prophecies from the Old Testament, from the book of Jeremiah."

"Go on," Matt said.

I grabbed the notebook and wrote more.

"They were prophecies about the End Times," Sharif told Matt. "You said that in the last days terrible judgments were coming on Jordan. You said you hoped what ISIS was doing wasn't the beginning of the fulfillment of those prophecies. You said you liked the king, that he seemed to be wise and wanted to keep the peace, that he's one of the good guys."

"Okay, fine, but that wasn't actually the last thing we spoke of," Matt replied. "There was something else."

Sharif slid the notebook back to me. This time, I wrote a note on a single sheet of paper and slid that across to him, rather than the whole notebook.

"He says he warned you to leave Amman immediately, that your life was in danger."

"Everybody knows I'm not in Amman any longer, Colonel. You'll have to do better. There was one more topic. The last thing we discussed before we entered the front door of my apartment."

I couldn't think. My mind went blank. Sharif again glanced at his watch. We were running out of time, and we hadn't even gotten to what Matt wanted to tell me yet. I closed my eyes and leaned back in my chair. What was he getting at?

Our conversation had been almost entirely theological, which was probably why I remembered as much as I did. It was so unlike any other conversation I'd ever had. I'd interviewed all kinds of people in my career—presidents and prime ministers, generals and jihadists, soldiers and spies—but I'd never known, much less interviewed, anyone like my brother. I never talked with people about the Bible. No one I knew talked about it. We certainly didn't talk about Bible prophecy or the End of Days. But Matt loved this stuff. He was, after all, a seminary professor, an Old Testament scholar, and the author of a textbook for Bible colleges and seminaries on how to study and teach biblical eschatology. I'd never read it. It had never seemed interesting in the slightest to me. In fact, if I was honest with him—which generally I had not been over the course of our strained and at times contentious relationship—I'd always found the whole subject a bit loony. I mean, really, how in the world could a dusty old book thousands of years old tell us what was going to happen in our times? The very notion seemed insane—except he explained it.

After all these years, Matt was starting to get my attention. I remembered being intrigued when he explained that thousands of years ago the biblical prophets foretold the rebirth of the State of

Israel, predicted that Jews would return in droves to the Holy Land after centuries of exile, and posited that with God's help the Jews would rebuild the ancient ruins and create an "exceedingly great army." Most people considered the idea lunacy for almost two thousand years, including many of the church fathers who thought such prophecies couldn't possibly be true—not literally, anyway. But Matt argued that May 14, 1948, changed everything. Suddenly the State of Israel *was* back in existence. Jews *were* returning. They *were* making the deserts bloom and constructing great cities and building a mighty army.

What could explain such dramatic, unexpected developments? I didn't have an answer. True, there were certain historical and sociological and geopolitical realities that made the rebirth of Israel as a modern nation more likely in the mid-twentieth century than ever before. The collapse of the Ottoman Empire, the Holocaust, the implosion of the British Empire, the rise of political Zionism, and the support of Christians for a Jewish state were all contributing factors. But it was still one of the most unlikely events to ever happen in the history of mankind. What other people group exiled from their homeland for two millennia had ever come back home and reclaimed not just their sovereignty but their nearly dead language? Maybe God did have something to do with it. Maybe there was something to all those old prophecies.

It was intriguing, I'd conceded. But it didn't prove Jesus was the Messiah. It certainly didn't prove that he was coming back to reign over the earth for a thousand years, let alone coming back soon, even in our lifetime. These were bridges I couldn't cross. But Matt really believed such things, and despite the fact that I'd mocked him for years, he wasn't an idiot. Though I was loath to admit it—to him or to others—he was a lot smarter than me. I'd been a decent student back in the day, earning my BA in political science from American University and an MA in journalism from Columbia, my grandfather's alma mater, though I'd partied far too much and almost certainly spent more on beer than books. Matt, by contrast, had five degrees. He'd earned a BA from Harvard, three master's degrees—one in theology, another in Hebrew, and a third in ancient Greek, each from Princeton's school of divinity—and had a PhD in theology from Gordon-Conwell, with an emphasis in Old Testament studies. What's more, he'd graduated at or near the top of his class each time. It made it hard to dismiss my older brother as completely as I'd wanted to for the last few decades.

So when we'd talked back in Amman last week, we'd talked theology. What else? He explained the prophecies about the future of Jordan. He'd said it was possible the prophecies might come to fulfillment sooner than anyone could imagine. It made me wonder what he thought of Khalif's eschatology. Did the Bible say anything about Dabiq? Did it give any clues about the rise of an Islamic caliphate? And what really was the difference between what the Qur'an had to say about the End of Days and what the Bible had to say? I had a feeling Matt knew a lot about this subject. It actually might make an interesting story for the *Times*, especially given Khalif's video message. But that would have to wait for another day.

"Are you still there, Colonel?" Matt asked.

"Yes, I'm still here," Sharif said. "I'm just waiting for your brother to reply. He doesn't seem to remember. And you've got to admit what he's said already could only have been known by him."

"No, he could have told you those things under duress," Matt said. "But I'll give you—or him—a hint."

"Okay."

"It was something Katie said."

I looked up and scribbled a note.

"She just turned four," Sharif said.

"Keep going."

I wrote another note.

"She's in a Sunday school class," Sharif told him. "She loves it. Can't wait to get there every week. And she loves memorizing the Bible. There's some sort of game if you memorize verses."

"What were the last verses she memorized?"

I scribbled down a single sentence—less than that, actually; just a phrase.

"Something from 1 John."

"What was it?"

I winced and shook my head.

"Come on, Dr. Collins, that's enough," Sharif said. "We're running out of time."

"The verse, Colonel," Matt pressed. "I want to hear him say it."

This time I closed my eyes and put my head

down on the table. But try as I might, I couldn't remember. Instead, the most horrific images from the last few weeks flashed through my brain.

Abdel and the mine in Homs.

Omar and the car bomb in Istanbul.

Khachigian in the café at Union Station.

The beheadings in Baghdad.

The sarin gas test in Mosul, which I now realized had actually happened in Alqosh.

The kamikaze in Amman.

And the children. All those precious children.

Suddenly I sat bolt upright. I reached for my notebook and wrote two sentences as fast as I could. My handwriting was so illegible I couldn't imagine how Sharif could decipher it. But he did, and he read it, and I was right.

"'And the testimony is this, that God has given us eternal life, and this life is in His Son. He who has the Son has the life; he who does not have the Son of God does not have the life.'"

51

★ ★ ★

"That's it," Matt exclaimed. *"That's my brother!"*

Just then there was a knock on the door. It was Ari Shalit.

"Colonel, His Majesty is asking for you," the Israeli said.

Sharif thanked him and said he'd be right there.

"It seems he needs you right away," Ari added. "It's fairly urgent."

Sharif nodded but turned back to the call.

"Dr. Collins, you've got one minute," he told Matt. "If you've got something to say to your brother, now's the time."

"One minute?"

"Fifty-four seconds."

I handed Ari a note explaining who was on the phone. He looked impatient but waited by the door.

"Okay, right, well, it's about the video," Matt stammered. "The video that Abu Khalif made, with the president in the cage—you know the one?"

"Of course," said Sharif. "What about it?"

"I know where it was shot."

"How?"

"I've been there."

"Where?"

"Nahum's tomb."

"Where?"

"They shot the video next to Nahum's tomb."

"Nahum who?" the colonel asked.

"You know, the Hebrew prophet, one of the minor prophets, wrote the book of Nahum in the Bible?"

"I guess," Sharif replied, not exactly tracking with Matt's train of thought and not exactly having the time to pursue it.

But Matt kept going. "Okay, well, Nahum was a minor prophet only in the sense that his contribution to the Scriptures was small. His book isn't very long. But it was enormously consequential because he prophesied the coming judgment of the city of Nineveh."

"Nineveh in Iraq?"

"Yes, precisely," Matt said. "You see, God told Nahum to warn the people that their wicked city would be utterly destroyed, but tragically they refused to listen. They didn't repent. And Nahum's prophecies of cataclysmic destruction all came to pass in 612 BC."

"So where is Nahum buried?"

"In a little town, a village really, in northern Iraq, on the plains of Nineveh," Matt explained. "It's a place called Elkosh. Have you ever heard of it?"

I looked at the colonel and then at Ari. They were as stunned as I was.

"Alqosh, you say?" Sharif clarified.

"Yes—have you heard of it?

"We've heard of it," Sharif said. "Tell me more—but make it fast."

"Well, Nahum was Jewish, but he was born and raised in exile, far from the land of Israel, in what was then the Assyrian Empire," Matt explained. "The Bible says Nahum was an 'Elkoshite.' He was born there, and he was buried there as well. There's a mausoleum at the site with Hebrew writing on the walls dating back twenty-five hundred years. I was there a number of years ago with some colleagues from my seminary."

"How long ago?"

"I don't remember exactly—five or six years, I guess—but I actually have pictures of me standing at the exact spot where Abu Khalif was standing, just a few feet to the right of the tomb."

"Can you send me those pictures?"

"Absolutely."

"Then text them right now, Dr. Collins. Please—time is of the essence. We have to go."

"Wait, Colonel; my mom wanted to say hello to—"

But suddenly he was gone. For a moment I thought the call had been dropped. But when the colonel jumped up, headed out the door, and told Ari to follow him, I realized that he'd actually hung up on him, and I was now sitting by myself. But at least I'd gotten to hear Matt's voice. He'd just come through for me in a huge way, and I was grateful.

What were the chances that my brother had

ever been in Alqosh? On the face of it, it seemed preposterous. But of course it wasn't. This was a guy who was in the middle of a yearlong sabbatical in the Hashemite Kingdom of Jordan studying the ancient prophecies of Ammon, Moab, Edom, Bozrah, Mount Seir, and who knew how many others. This was a guy who had taken his wife to Iraq—to the city of Babylon, to be precise—for their honeymoon back in the late 1980s, during the reign of Saddam Hussein, to visit the ancient ruins and see the beginnings of the rebuilding of Babylon—including the famed Ishtar Gate— that Saddam had ordered. It was nutty stuff like that that had caused the rift between us. Now it seemed my brother's nutty ideas were paying off big-time.

I just sat there, closed my eyes, and tried to catch my breath. I was exhausted and the pain in my left arm was growing. I pulled a bottle of pills from my pocket, the ones given to me by Dr. Hammami, and swallowed one without water.

As I worked the pill down my throat, my thoughts turned back to Alqosh. The evidence that Abu Khalif and the president had been there was now almost ironclad. The case that they were still there was intriguing yet merely circumstantial. What if Khalif and his men had taken the president from the compound after filming the video? Could they have slipped out of the village during a gap in the Israelis' drone coverage?

It was possible, I had to admit, but was it likely? And even if they'd managed to leave Alqosh, had they really gone all the way to Dabiq? Wasn't it more likely they were in Mosul, a city of more than a million and a half people, a city completely controlled by ISIS forces? The Iraqis and Americans had been talking about retaking it for months, but they still hadn't. If I were the head of the caliphate, wouldn't I be in Mosul? It was the wrong way to think, of course. I was thinking like a Westerner. Abu Khalif wasn't living in the twenty-first century. He was living in the seventh. He wasn't trying to protect himself. He was trying to follow the path of the Qur'an.

But did that make it more likely that his base camp was next to the tomb of Nahum in Alqosh than in Mosul? So far as I knew, Nahum wasn't a prophet mentioned in the Qur'an or typically recognized by Muslims. So where did that leave me? I had no idea.

"Hey, need some company?"

That was a voice I knew. I opened my eyes and found Yael peeking through the door with a somewhat-shy smile on her face.

"Absolutely," I said, standing. "You didn't go in with them?"

"I think my work in there is done."

Reaching behind her, I closed the door to the break room, and for the first time since Istanbul, we were alone.

"How're you doing?" I asked, standing only inches away from her.

She shrugged.

"Yeah, me too," I said.

We just stood there for a few moments, looking into each other's eyes, neither saying a word. It wasn't that we didn't have anything to say. It was because there was too much to say, and we had no idea where to start. That was my excuse, anyway. I couldn't really read her. I didn't know her well enough. Not yet.

"I'm sorry," I said finally.

"About what?" she asked.

"Danny . . . this . . . all of it."

She nodded and leaned toward me. I could feel her breath on my face, minty and sweet. My pulse quickened, as did my breathing. I can't tell you how much I wanted to kiss her right then. But I knew I shouldn't. It wasn't my place. She was wounded and vulnerable. She was as exhausted and in as much pain as I was. Maybe more. Probably more. I could see it in her eyes. And we hadn't talked, not really. She didn't know how I felt about her. I certainly didn't know how she felt about me. I thought I did. I hoped I did. But that wasn't the same as knowing for certain. The only way to know was to ask, and I didn't know how to ask right then. What if it was all wishful thinking on my part? What if none of it was real? What if it had all been an act? That was her job, wasn't it? To deceive people. To get things out of them. To get you to give her what she wanted and make it feel like you were doing it because you wanted to, not because she was manipulating you.

Yael Katzir was a spy. I was her mission, or part of it anyway. In Istanbul, she'd needed to get my attention and hold it and win my trust and get me to talk, and she'd done it beautifully. What a fool I'd be if I really fell for an act, no matter how convincing. What an idiot I'd feel like when I was rebuffed, as I surely expected to be.

And even if it was true—even if she really did have some feelings for me and I wasn't completely misreading the situation—then what? Ari and the colonel would be back any second. Did I really want them to burst in on us making out? Did I really intend to go back into the war room having discredited Yael in the eyes of everyone in there? It was one thing to contemplate chucking my career out the window to run away with this girl and start a new life. It was another thing to jeopardize everything she'd spent a lifetime working for.

So I stood there and stared into her eyes and forced myself not to kiss her. But then she surprised me by putting her arms around me and leaning her head against my chest. I didn't know what to say. So slowly, hesitantly, I put my arms around her, too, and closed my eyes again.

I forgot where I was, forgot who might be coming through the door at any moment. All the arguments swirling around in my head evaporated, and all I could think about was how warm her body felt against mine and how her hair smelled like strawberries.

I had a thousand questions and finally the privacy to ask them. But I kept quiet. I didn't want to ruin the moment. I just stood there in the break room under the harsh fluorescent lights and held this young woman I'd become so fond of. There was nothing romantic about the setting, nothing nostalgic, nothing personal. It wasn't how I'd imagined it.

But as I held her in the silence, she began to cry.

52

*   *   *

After a few minutes, she pulled away.

She said she was embarrassed. I told her not to be.

"This isn't like me," she said, fishing a tissue out of her purse and wiping away the tears. "I should know better."

"Your secret's safe with me."

She wasn't amused. Well, a little. But only a little. She took a small mirror from her purse and checked her makeup.

"You took a couple of nice shots," I said.

"You too."

"At least no one can see mine."

"That's true," she said. "I saw you noticing the makeup."

"Was I that obvious?"

"Uh, yeah."

"Sorry."

"It's okay."

"I'd never seen you wear makeup before."

"I usually don't."

"How bad is it?" I asked.

"The bruising?"

"Uh-huh."

"Could be worse." She shrugged. "You should see the other guy."

I smiled for the first time in days. "I did." A pause, then I asked, "You on meds?"

She nodded. "Are you?"

I nodded back.

"How bad is yours?" she asked.

"I'll live."

"Me too."

"Good," I said. "I hope so."

"Not all of us have been so lucky," she replied, a sadness coming over her again.

"Danny?"

She nodded and looked away.

"Unreal."

She walked to the other side of the room and stared out the little window in the door to the hallway.

"How's Miriam doing?" I asked of the prime minister's wife.

"She's a mess."

"I can't imagine."

"I was there," she said, "with her, at the hospital, when she got the news."

I said nothing.

"The shriek that came out of her mouth . . . the grief . . . the anguish . . . I'd never heard anything like it. Just total . . . total despair."

Then she said something that surprised me.

"And I knew just how she felt. . . ."

Her voice trailed off. I wanted to ask her what

she meant. But I held back. She wasn't really talking to me. She was talking to herself. I just happened to be in the room.

"The kids are worse," she said, staring at the crumpled tissue in her hands. "They're in shock, all of them . . . except little Avi."

"The two-year-old?" I asked.

She nodded. "He's oblivious," she said, her voice quiet and distant. "Doesn't understand what's happened, just playing with the nanny like he hasn't a care in the world. I mean, he knows Mommy is sad. He can see that. And he was so precious holding her hand and drawing little pictures for her. He just doesn't know what's happened. I'd like to be like that. . . ."

We were quiet for a while.

"Do you have kids, J. B.?" she asked, looking up, completely out of the blue.

The question startled me, but I shook my head. "No."

"Did you want them?"

"I did."

"And?"

The questions were suddenly so personal. But I didn't mind. "Laura didn't."

"Why not?"

I shrugged. What else could I do? I didn't know then. I certainly didn't know now. Not really. Not for certain.

"Do you regret it?" she asked.

"All of it."

"No, not the marriage. I mean . . ."

"I know," I said and looked down at the floor and thought about it more. "Yeah, I regret it."

"You'd have liked kids?"

I nodded but didn't say anything for almost a minute. I didn't know what to say. It seemed like an odd conversation to be having under the circumstances. Strange. Unexpectedly intimate. But surreal. We'd never really had time to talk personally. I realized I knew hardly anything about her.

"What about you?" I finally asked.

"What?"

"You want to be a mom someday?"

"More than anything," she said, still looking out the little window.

Again she'd surprised me. I'd thought of Yael Katzir as the consummate professional. She was completely immersed in her work. She'd labored incredibly hard to get to where she was. She was working among the most highly respected experts in the world in her field and was one of the few women to reach such heights in the Israeli intel community—or in any intelligence, especially since she was only thirty-four.

"Really?"

"Does that surprise you?"

"A little, yeah."

"Why? You don't think I'd be a good mom?"

"No, I'm sure you'd be great. I just . . ."

"Just what?"

"I don't know. You seemed like . . ."

"Too old?"

"No."

"Too self-centered?"

"No."

"Too married to my job?"

At that I hesitated. The last thing I wanted to do was offend her. "So, speaking of married, how come a pretty girl like you never got married?" I asked, almost wincing at how uncomfortable I felt asking such a stupid question and feeling like I'd crossed a line.

"Who said I've never been married?" she asked, raising her eyebrows and giving me a sly look.

"You were married?" I asked, trying not to sound as stunned as I felt.

"Right out of the army."

"How old were you?"

"Twenty, almost twenty-one."

"Oh . . . I had no idea."

"It's not the kind of thing that always comes up on a first date, is it?"

"Have we had a first date?"

"Excuse me, Mr. Collins," she said. "I seem to recall us making out in front of the Blue Mosque."

"I thought that was you being a spy," I said.

"It wasn't."

"No?"

"No."

"But I thought . . ."

"What?"

"I thought you said we had to seem like lovers or the police would think you were . . . you know . . . ?"

"A lady of the night?"

"Something like that."

"Did I say that?"

"Yeah, you did."

"Oh, well."

"What's that supposed to mean?"

She shrugged.

"Was it true?"

She shook her head and smiled again.

"It wasn't true?"

Again she shook her head. Now I was really confused.

"You made it all up? We didn't have to walk the streets like a couple?"

"Nope."

"Why not?"

"It was Istanbul, J. B., not Mecca," she replied. "It's a modern, Western, sophisticated city. They don't care whom you meet on the streets late at night—not if you're not Muslim, anyway."

"So why . . . ?"

"Why what?"

"Why'd you tell me to do it?"

She shrugged again. "Seemed like fun."

"Fun?"

"Wasn't it?"

"Well, yeah, but . . ."

"Come on, it was a rainy, foggy night in Istanbul, under the streetlights."

"Right out of the movies."

"Exactly. And I thought you were . . ."

"What?"

"You know."

"No."

"Adorable."

"Adorable?"

"Yeah, adorable."

"Me?"

"Yeah, you—and it worked, didn't it? The police didn't suspect a thing. Neither did you. So yes, I'd say that was our first date. And it was going rather nicely until . . ."

She caught herself, and it was quiet again. Neither one of us wanted to talk about the car bomb that had killed my friend Omar. I changed the subject.

"So you were married?"

"I was."

"And it didn't go well?"

"No, it went fabulously."

I guess I looked as startled as I felt.

"I was head over heels for him," Yael explained. "We met in the army on the first base I was assigned to, up north in a town called Yoqneam."

"And?"

"And we got married the day after I got out of the army."

"And?"

"And what? He got promoted, became an officer. We were just crazy for each other."

"What happened?"

"Hezbollah happened. Lebanon happened. He was on a patrol along the border, and one day someone fired an antitank missile at his jeep. His buddies survived. Uri did not."

"I'm so sorry."

"Yeah, well, what can you do?"

Her eyes began filling with tears again. I wanted to cross the room and hold her once more—not to kiss her, just to comfort her. But just then we heard footsteps coming down the hall. Then the door opened. It was Sharif.

"His Majesty would like to see you both."

Yael dabbed her eyes with a tissue, composed herself, and stepped out first. I followed close behind. But I had no idea what was awaiting us back in the war room.

53

* * *

Or rather *who* was awaiting us.

Prince Marwan Talal.

He was hunched over in his wheelchair, sitting beside His Majesty at the far end of the conference table, upon which sat a large reel-to-reel tape deck. Wearing his white robes but with a wool blanket wrapped around him to keep him warm, the man looked as bad as I'd ever seen him. His face was gaunt. His skin was sickly pale. Clearly his health had taken a turn for the worse in recent days, and I couldn't imagine the brutal conditions through which he had just returned from Baghdad. Had he actually flown through this treacherous weather, or had someone driven five-hundred-plus miles to get him here?

King Abdullah welcomed Yael and me back into the room, and we took a seat beside each other. Then the king recapped what his uncle and most senior advisor had been discussing with the group, namely that Iraqi intelligence had become convinced that President Taylor and Abu Khalif were now in Dabiq. His Majesty noted that Hassan Karbouli, the Iraqi interior minister, had played for Prince Marwan tape recordings of two intercepted phone calls between two senior ISIS commanders—one in Mosul and the other in Aleppo—discussing preparations to take "the jewels in the crown" to Dabiq. The two commanders had apparently discussed routes, accommodations, fueling stops, and security precautions, and one had insisted that "time is of the essence."

"We've been discussing the meaning of the tapes since you left," the king said, "and how best to move forward."

"And have you come to a conclusion?" I asked.

"We have. First, the group is agreed that our highest priority is to rescue the president. Capturing or killing Abu Khalif is an urgent task, but it must come second to the president's welfare. Second, the group is divided on what the evidence shows. We all now agree the data indicate both the president and Khalif were in Alqosh in recent days."

Then His Majesty addressed me directly. "Mr. Collins, Colonel Sharif shared with us the information provided by your brother, including pictures of him visiting Nahum's tomb."

The photos—which I had not yet seen—flashed on the screen, alongside still images from the latest ISIS video. There was no question both sets of images had been taken at the same place, and that place was the town of Alqosh on the plains of Nineveh.

"We all found your brother's photos conclusive proof the president *was* in Alqosh," the king continued. "Unfortunately, that doesn't prove the president is *still* in Alqosh. Some around this table are convinced the president has been moved to Dabiq. Others are equally convinced that he remains in Alqosh."

"So what are you going to do?" I asked.

"We've decided to launch simultaneous operations against both targets," the king replied. "General Ramirez will lead a force into Alqosh. General El-Badawy will lead the mission into Dabiq. If we can maintain the element of surprise—and synchronize the two assaults—we may just have a shot at success."

The analysis seemed solid. But it was a stunning change of plans. Ramirez had come to Jordan determined to take Dabiq. The vice president had been equally adamant. Now everything had changed.

The king then turned the presentation over to Ramirez.

"For the record," the American general began, "I still lean toward the president being in Dabiq, though I concede the data is not as conclusive as I'd come here believing. And I will be honest with you all that when I spoke to Vice President Holbrooke a few moments ago, I recommended sticking with our original game plan to have me lead the force into Dabiq. But the vice president has decided to accept the counsel of His Majesty, as well as President Mahfouz in Cairo, the king in Riyadh, and the emirs in Abu Dhabi. I know you all believe that if we Americans try to take Dabiq, we will be giving Khalif and his men exactly what they want—a reason to call even more Muslims into the jihad against the infidels of 'Rome.' So given this unanimous opinion that it would be more prudent to have a joint Sunni Arab Muslim force handle the attack on Dabiq, I can support this approach. Therefore, I'll lead a Delta strike on Alqosh. Let's just pray the president is still breathing and that one group or the other can find him and bring him back alive."

I glanced at Yael and at Ari, who was sitting to her left. Both seemed pleased with the decision, as was I, but Ramirez wasn't finished. He explained that the vice president was about to address the nation in a live televised broadcast from the White House Situation Room. The goal was to comfort a country rattled by the events of recent days and to explain the American government's intended course of action.

First, Holbrooke was going to explain his official role as acting president under the current circumstances.

Second, he was going to say that while he had no constitutional authority to require the American people to convert to Islam, he certainly personally had a great deal of respect for "this religion of peace."

Third, Holbrooke was going to say that his military advisors had examined options for trying to rescue the president but had ruled all of them out. He would say the Pentagon was not clear on where the president was being held at the moment and that weather conditions in the region prevented any serious effort to move forward with such a plan, even if one existed.

Fourth, he was going to explain that he was in the process of recalling Congress to pass emergency legislation that would authorize him to transfer several hundred billion dollars to the numbered account in Switzerland designated by the Islamic State. However, he would add that even if the legislation passed, he would not sign it in his role as acting president unless ISIS offered incontrovertible proof that President Taylor was still alive.

"It's all a ruse, of course," Ramirez said. "Under no circumstances is the vice president going to transfer more than $300 billion to a terrorist organization. Nor would Congress authorize such a transfer in the first place. But we've got to create the impression that he is open to capitulating to at least some of Khalif's demands. So members of the House and Senate will start flying back to Washington. The White House will whip up a media feeding frenzy over the possible imminent transfer of the funds. The VP will summon the Speaker of the House, the Senate majority leader, and the minority leaders of both houses of Congress to the White House within the hour. Drafts of the proposed legislation will be leaked. The treasury secretary will confer with the Fed chairman, and so forth—all to buy as much time as possible."

"I'm not convinced Khalif will fall for it," said Prince Marwan, his voice strained and hoarse. He was barely able to lift his head off his chest.

"I'm not sure there's another way," Prince Feisal weighed in, perhaps sparing the king from having to.

The Egyptian general then spoke. "We are pres-

JOEL C. ROSENBERG ★ 345

ently about five hundred kilometers—more than three hundred miles—from Dabiq." El-Badawy clicked a button and brought up a map on the main screen over His Majesty's left shoulder as he spoke. "We're nearly eight hundred kilometers— some five hundred miles—from Alqosh. It would typically take about an hour's flying time to Dabiq, and about an hour and twenty minutes to Alqosh. The X factor right now is the weather. At the moment, the situation outside is so bad that neither General Ramirez nor I believe it is wise to put any planes or choppers in the air. But the meteorologists are telling us we should have a window where things are slightly improved in about four or five hours, and we expect to launch then. In the meantime, we'll work with our men, update them on the changes, brief them on the latest intel, and answer their questions. But first, are there questions from any of you?"

Four or five hours? I glanced at the clocks on the wall behind the king. It was already several minutes past seven in the evening. There were fewer than eleven hours until the deadline. With an hour to an hour-and-a-half flight—perhaps significantly longer because of the weather, even if things did improve slightly—El-Badawy was saying the strikes wouldn't even begin until two or two thirty in the morning. Wasn't that cutting things awfully close? Then again, what more could they do? If Mother Nature didn't cooperate, all these plans could be for naught.

"Seeing none, then I respectfully give the floor back to His Majesty and just want to say what an honor it will be for me to lead this joint Arab operation. May Allah grant us favor and a great and resounding victory."

At this, the king rose from his seat. We all followed suit, save Prince Marwan, of course, who appeared to me to be in great pain and in deep emotional anguish over everything that was happening to his country and to the region. I suddenly felt a renewed pang of guilt for ever having doubted his fealty to the king or the kingdom and hoped he never found out what I'd said to Agent Harris when my own loyalties were being attacked.

"Dr. Shalit and Dr. Katzir, I want to thank you and your government for your immense help," the king said. "The world may not know for many years—or perhaps ever—what a significant role you have played in helping your Sunni Arab neighbors and the Americans prepare for this moment. Especially because I have no intention of letting Mr. Collins go on either of these missions or write about any of these matters going forward. But *I* know. And each of the men in this room knows. And I think your involvement is a testament to the tremendous good that can be done when neighbors work together despite their real and deep and many differences. And I want to personally thank you, in the presence of all these gathered."

Ari and Yael bowed slightly to acknowledge the king's gracious words. But I was livid.

"Your Majesty, may I say something?" I asked, restraining myself as best I could.

"Not right now, Mr. Collins. We don't have time."

"But, Your Majesty, I really must insist you let me cover American forces going into battle to rescue an American president."

"Sorry, Mr. Collins," the king replied. "The answer is no."

"Why the sudden change?" I pressed. "You brought me here to make sure the world had an unbiased view of what was happening."

"The situation has changed."

"I don't see how it has."

"The unanimous view of every single person in this room says it has," the king replied slowly and firmly.

I was about to protest further, to insist they embed me with the Delta team, but as I scanned the faces around the table, I could see there was no point. There wasn't a sympathetic gaze in the bunch. I sensed that Ari was about to say something, but I was certain it was an intelligence matter, nothing to support my case.

But the king was not finished. "There is one piece of unfinished business to which I must attend," he said, turning his attention to Yael. "Dr. Katzir?"

"Yes, Your Majesty?"

"I have a favor to ask of you."

"I am at your service, Your Majesty," she replied.

"Is that a yes?"

"Of course."

"Very well," said the king. "I would like you to accompany General Ramirez and his forces to Alqosh."

I did a double take.

"I beg your pardon?" Yael asked, her countenance betraying that she was as surprised by the king's request as I was.

"You know more about that town, that compound, and the chemical weapons that are stored there than any person in this room," the king explained. "I realize, of course, that it would be politically unwise to have an Israeli Mossad officer formally participating in the invasion of an Iraqi village, especially launching from Jordanian soil. But at my request, General Ramirez is prepared to make you an honorary American for the night. He will give you a uniform to wear and a weapon to fight with, and you'll be at his side for the entire operation."

My stomach clenched. I turned to Yael. The whole room was staring at her. The blood was draining from her face. I knew what she was thinking. She'd thought she was through with all this. She'd done her part; she was finished. She had no intention of going into battle. She just wanted to go back to Tel Aviv and take a nice hot bath and a long, well-deserved break. I could see it in her eyes, in the way her whole body tensed.

That's what I wanted for her too. At the very least, I wanted her at my side here in the war room as we tracked the latest developments in Alqosh and Dabiq. I was still hoping to write dispatches on the operations that were about to unfold, and who better than her to help me make sense of what exactly was happening and its significance? The thought of her going back into harm's way physically sickened me, as I'm sure it did her, especially after the conversation we'd just had, and I was proud of her for her ability to respectfully decline the king's invitation. She'd certainly earned her right to say, "No thank you."

But that's not what she said.

"I'd be honored to, Your Majesty," she said instead.

"Thank you," the king said. "Then it's settled."

"Not quite," Yael added.

"What do you mean?"

"I mean I would be honored to go, but only on one condition."

The room was dead silent. Ari turned and looked at her, as did we all. The king's poker face remained unruffled, but surely rare were the times the king's request for someone to go into battle was met with a condition.

"A condition, you say?"

"Yes, Your Majesty."

"And what would that be?"

"I will only go if Mr. Collins here is permitted to go as well."

PART
FOUR

54

★ ★ ★

EN ROUTE TO ALQOSH, IRAQ

"What if we're wrong?"

My question hung in the air. No one wanted to touch it. Not Yael. Not Colonel Sharif. Certainly not any of the Delta operators around us. And I have no idea why I asked it. Nerves, I guess. It was a pointless question, foolish to ask. If the president wasn't in Alqosh when we arrived, we could only hope he was in Dabiq. And if he wasn't in Dabiq either, then he was not long for this world.

The more important question, the one I should have been asking, was whether either team could get to its target in time. I pulled out my grandfather's pocket watch and wiped away the condensation on its face. It was now 5:02 a.m. The deadline was less than an hour away. The fate of the president hung in the balance, and even if by some miracle he was still alive, I didn't see how either team was ever going to reach him by six.

Nothing had been going according to the plan Generals Ramirez and El-Badawy had mapped out. Starting just after midnight, we'd sat at the end of runway 17R at the Muwaffaq Salti Air Base in Azraq, cooped up in a freezing-cold C-130 Hercules with four more troop transport planes lined up behind us, all battered by gale-force winds and hail the size of golf balls, all waiting for hours for clearance from the tower that I soon feared would never come. Finally, around three thirty, our captain came over the intercom and told us we had a narrow window. The hail had stopped. The winds had dipped somewhat. The meteorologists and the guys in the tower couldn't promise we'd make it to Alqosh. But they were unanimous: as bad as conditions were at that moment, they were as good as they were likely to get. If we didn't take off right then, we never would. So the pilots revved the plane's four turboprops to max power and we hurtled down the runway into the dark and cold of night.

Now we'd been in the air for just over ninety minutes, on a route typically flown by Royal Jordanian flight 822—usually an Airbus 320—from Amman to Erbil. By my calculations we were only a few minutes out, which meant the most terrifying moment of this operation—to me, at least—was coming up fast. We were about to do a HAHO jump into the storm.

HAHO was special ops talk for a high altitude, high opening parachute drop. In covering the American military over the years, I'd heard of them, of course. But I'd never expected to do one. I'd never jumped out of a plane at any altitude. Nor, frankly, had I ever even seriously considered it. When Yael got me into this operation and I'd signed six pages of legal waivers (three for the Americans and three for the Jordanians), no one had said anything about this. But Sharif had made my role clear.

"Mr. Collins, fate and Allah have brought us together for this moment, a moment much larger than any of us or our countries. We've said yes to you being an embedded reporter. You've done it lots of times before. You've got plenty of experience. But this isn't going to be like any of those other times. The good news is that when it's over, the king wants you to tell the world the truth. Exactly what happened. And exactly how. In the meantime, keep your head down and don't do anything stupid, like get yourself killed."

On the one hand, I was thrilled that the king had evidently changed his mind and was now going to let me do my job and not just observe but actually report on the things I was observing. On the other hand, I was starting to realize just how dangerous this mission really was.

Suddenly I felt the plane descending. I glanced at the altimeter strapped around my left wrist like a watch. It was dropping fast. A moment ago we'd been flying at 42,000 feet. Now we were at 34,000 and still descending.

Yael shouted something at me. But I could barely hear over the roar of the propellers and the intensity of the storm, which might have been another reason no one had answered my question a few minutes earlier. Maybe no one had even heard me.

We were all suited up for the jump, wearing

insulated jumpsuits, gloves, and boots to protect us from the subzero temperatures at this altitude. We were also, of course, wearing special helmets, goggles, and oxygen tanks in addition to the rest of our gear—from bulletproof vests to ammo belts and grenades—since there wasn't exactly a lot of air to breathe at such heights. The noise and the helmets and the cold and the constant shaking and rattling of the plane lumbering through the storm had made for a long and lonely journey. We'd said hardly a word to each other. We'd all been alone with our own thoughts and fears and questions, and now the moment of truth had finally arrived.

We were now at 31,000 feet.

30,000.

29.

28.

27.

Yael again shouted something at me, but I still couldn't hear her. We were all wearing comms gear but maintaining strict radio silence. Finally she stood and motioned for me to do so as well. I saw Colonel Sharif and the others getting up as well, so I followed suit. Then Yael motioned for me to turn around; when I did, she turned on my oxygen supply.

Ramirez moved to the back of the plane and held up two fingers. Two minutes to go. I was terrified. I hadn't admitted as much to anyone, of course, not even Yael when she'd finally told me how we'd be getting to our target. To begin with, I didn't think she'd believe me. I was sure she'd tell me the gun battle at the palace and the harrowing race to the airport had been much more dangerous. She'd also tell me I was far more likely to die in the imminent battle for Alqosh than by parachute failure. And I was sure she'd be right. But aside from claustrophobia, there was one primal terror I'd long and carefully avoided at all costs: heights.

The rear ramp of the plane began to open, and every muscle in my body tensed. One by one, the Delta operators gave a final check to their weapons and stepped into formation. Yael helped me put on my pack filled with almost fifty pounds of camera equipment, a chem-bio suit and related gear, bottles of water and PowerBars, and plenty more ammo to go with the MP5 strapped to my chest. I'd insisted I wasn't going to fight, of course. But Ramirez, who'd made it clear he didn't want me coming at all, had insisted that if I was going in with Delta, I had to be armed. In addition to the MP5, Ramirez had given me a .45-caliber Colt M1911A1 with a few extra seven-round magazines. When I protested that I was a journalist, not a combatant, the general had taken his case directly to the king, who in the end had sided with Ramirez, reminding me that I'd been armed at the palace, and that was likely the only reason—aside from the mercy of Allah—that I was still alive.

Sharif turned and attached his harness to mine. This was going to be a tandem jump. There'd been no time to train me. So we'd be strapped together on the way down. I'd be depending on his chute the whole way, though I had a reserve chute of my own—"just in case," as he put it. Not exactly the words I'd wanted to hear.

Ramirez held up one finger.

We were one minute out and stabilizing at 25,000 feet as the entire fuselage shuddered in the storm. The ramp in the back of the plane finished opening. I held the strap above me in a death grip and stared out into the utter darkness. I wondered what my mom was doing right then. Was she praying for me? Were Matt and Annie praying as well? I hoped so. I didn't know how to pray for myself. Part of me wanted to. After all, there was a very real chance I wasn't going to make it out of this thing alive. I knew that, and I was racked with fear over what would happen to me after I died. But I felt like a hypocrite. I hadn't "gotten right" with God. Matt had begged me to, but I couldn't. I just wasn't there. I didn't believe. Not like he did. Not yet. Maybe not ever. I still had too many questions, too many doubts. Yet as I stared into the void, five miles over northern Iraq, the last words Matt had said to me before I went into Iraq the last time rang in my ears.

"Are you ready, J. B.? Are you ready to die?"

The answer was still the same—no, I was not.

55

★ ★ ★

Ramirez jumped first.

Then one by one, his ODA—Operational Detachment Alpha—followed him off the ramp. That meant two teams of twelve men each, for a total of twenty-four Delta operators, plus three command-and-control men, a commander, a radio operator, and an Air Force CCT or combat controller. Yael followed them. And then it was just the colonel and me and the jumpmaster manning the controls by the ramp.

My heart was racing. My legs felt numb. My feet wouldn't move, so Sharif nudged me forward, closer and closer to the edge. There was no longer anything to hold on to. The wind was whipping around me. The rain had already soaked my jumpsuit, and though the plane was flying through thick, dark clouds, I could actually see flashes of light below me. At first, I wondered if the Air Force was dropping bombs. Then I realized it was lightning. The lightning was below us—and we were about to jump into it.

I held up my hand. I needed a moment to

gather my wits and reconcile myself with what was coming. This was now officially the craziest thing I'd ever considered doing, I decided, far worse than sneaking into Syria to find Jamal Ramzy. Sure, Yael had already jumped. But she'd been trained for it. For all I knew she loved jumping out of planes. Maybe she and her first love had done this on dates. But it was different for me. No matter what the stakes were. No matter what the story was. I was just a civilian. It wasn't the same for me. I just had to—

I never finished the thought. Before I realized what was happening, Sharif had kicked me in the back of the knees and launched us out of the plane. And then we were free-falling. Sharif was behind me, so I couldn't see the plane above us. I looked down but couldn't spot the Delta operators below us either. I couldn't see anything except the flashes of lightning. But I could feel the bone-chilling cold. I could hear the wind howling past my mask and helmet. I could feel my stomach in my throat and my heart pounding so hard in my chest I feared it was going to explode. It never occurred to me to check my altimeter and track my descent. It never occurred to me to check my watch and figure out when Sharif was going to pull the rip cord. My mind went totally blank. What few instructions Sharif and Yael had given me were completely gone.

Then my harness suddenly tightened around my armpits and crotch. My head snapped back. It felt like we were being jerked back into the sky above us. I craned my neck and caught a glimpse of the canopy above us. Sure enough, the chute had deployed. I'd never seen a more beautiful sight. We weren't free-falling anymore. We were still descending, of course, but not nearly so fast. Sharif was manipulating the cords to navigate our route and regulate our descent. As he did, my breathing began to slow a bit. So did my heart rate. I could think again.

I remembered what Sharif had told me—that we'd only be free-falling for ten to fifteen seconds. I remembered, too, what Ramirez had said about the whole point of the HAHO being to enter the airspace over Alqosh quickly, quietly, and covertly. With the odds stacked against us, our only chance of success—thirty-three men and one woman versus more than five hundred ISIS fighters—was to seize and maintain the element of surprise. We certainly couldn't afford to let the grumble of the C-130 tip off the jihadists who controlled the village. So we'd jumped almost forty miles out. By now, our plane had already turned back. There were choppers en route, about an hour behind us. They were coming for our exfiltration. There were fighter jets coming too, sooner than the choppers. But for the moment it wasn't safe for them to be anywhere near us. In that sense, the storm was actually helping us—at least we hoped it was—providing low cloud cover to obscure our arrival and plenty of thunder and rain to muffle what little sound we would inevitably make.

Our route hadn't taken us all the way to the Kurdish capital of Erbil, of course. Instead, we'd flown about twenty kilometers north of Dohuk, then essentially done a hook so we'd be headed southwest along a range of mountains that led straight to Alqosh when we jumped. The big problem at the moment was the crosswind, which was whipping us around like rag dolls and had the very real potential, I feared, of blowing us far off course.

Sharif, like the others, had a GPS device strapped to his right arm. He was constantly making course corrections, and I knew I could trust his years of experience in Jordanian special forces. But our drop zone was narrow—precisely 36.735 degrees latitude and 43.096 degrees longitude— and there was no margin for error. To veer even slightly off course could put us dozens of kilometers from our ideal landing site, all of which would have to be made up by walking—more likely running— or could drop us right in the middle of Alqosh and the ISIS forces that controlled it. I knew all too well the stories my grandfather had written when he'd covered D-day for the Associated Press, stories of drops gone badly and untold numbers of American and Allied paratroopers spread out far from each other, behind enemy lines, with little chance of survival much less the chance to link back up with their own. I desperately didn't want to become one of those stories.

For more than twenty-five minutes, Sharif battled the winds, the rain, the lightning, and the cold, zigzagging north, then south, then back north again, trying to keep us on track for our landing site. At precisely 5:36 local time, we slipped under the clouds for the first time. My altimeter showed us at 1,700 feet and coming in red-hot. There were only twenty-four minutes to the deadline.

Just then Sharif tapped me on the back and pointed to the left. In the distance, at about ten o'clock, I could see the lights of a village. There weren't many, and they were faint, but was that it? Was that Alqosh? I didn't have a GPS, so I couldn't be sure. But a minute later—we were now at only 900 feet—Sharif gave me a thumbs-up. Before I knew it, he was kicking my boots. I was confused. That was the sign he'd prepped me for that it was time to land. But at still so high, I thought maybe I'd misunderstood. Then he kicked me again, more urgently this time, and suddenly we were smashing into the side of a mountain.

I was caught unprepared; my feet weren't up when we hit, and I stumbled forward and hit the rocks face-first, pulling the colonel down on top of me. Fortunately, my helmet, goggles, and shin guards took the worst of the impact, but the real problem was that we weren't stopping. The winds were so fierce that we were being dragged along the ridge with no way to self-arrest. The rains were so intense that the granite was too slippery to gain a foothold, and what little topsoil there was so close to the summit had turned to mud. For several hundred yards, we bounced and crashed and scraped across the ridgeline, ripping gashes in my hands and face, tearing my jumpsuit, and slicing up my knees. Rain and blood were streaming down my face, and in the fog I could see almost nothing. I was in unbearable pain now and experiencing near vertigo as we blew and toppled forward like tumbleweeds. I had no idea what to do or how to stop. And then I saw the edge of a cliff surging toward us.

I remember this question flashing across my mind at that moment: *Can I grab something and hold on before we go plunging over the edge, or are we better off going over the edge anyway, since at least we have a parachute?* But no sooner had I thought it than we came skidding to an excruciating and abrupt stop, not thirty yards from the edge.

I lay there facedown in the mud and gravel, in searing pain but suddenly motionless and on solid ground after hours in the air. It took me a moment to catch my breath and look up. But when I finally did, I saw Sharif maybe five yards from the cliff edge, beginning to crawl back toward me. In his right hand he held a bowie knife that glinted in the intermittent flashes of lightning, and it dawned on me what had happened. He'd cut me loose from him, then cut himself loose from the parachute, and in so doing he had almost certainly saved both our lives.

"You okay?" he asked, putting the knife away and scrambling over to me.

"I think so," I lied.

"Nothing's broken?"

I moved my arms and legs, then my fingers and toes. Then I rolled over, sat up, and wiped the blood and mud from my goggles. To my surprise, despite the pain, I hadn't broken anything.

When I shook my head, Sharif grabbed my hand and pulled me to my feet. "That was a close one," he said with a smile, wiping blood and mud from his face and goggles as well.

"Certainly was."

"But you're sure you're okay."

"My arm's killing me."

"Which one?"

"Left."

"The gunshot?"

"Yeah."

"Here, I'll give you something for it." He pulled off his backpack and fished around a bit until he found a first aid kit. Then he gave me some pain-killers and a bottle of water to wash them down. "What else?" he asked.

"My knees," I said.

We looked down and found my knee pads were gone. There were enormous tears in my fatigues on both my left and right knees, revealing bloody gashes smeared with pebbles and dirt. Sharif found some rubbing alcohol and tweezers in the first aid kit and did his best in the fog and rain to clean my wounds, apply some antibiotic cream to them, and then bind them up with gauze pads and duct tape. A moment later, he found another pair of knee pads in his pack and helped me put them on.

It was clear I needed stitches and just as clear it wasn't going to happen anytime soon.

56

* * *

"Gentlemen, we need to move."

I turned as General Ramirez and the rest of his men came up behind us, weapons at the ready. They didn't stop to chat. They were double-timing it to the peak of this ridge, about fifty or sixty yards away. Yael brought up the rear.

"You guys okay?" she asked.

"I'll be fine," Sharif said. "This guy got pretty banged up, but I think he'll pull through."

"You're a mess," she said to me.

I agreed but waved it off and asked if she was okay. She said she was fine, just a bit winded, and I was relieved to see she didn't look any worse for wear. As we scrambled together to the top, she explained that most of the group had landed quite a ways down the slope and had to hustle to regroup.

It was now 5:47. We had only thirteen minutes.

I was moving the slowest, but Yael and the colonel helped me to the top of the ridge, where we found the Delta team on their stomachs, peering down into the village below. Sharif turned on his night-vision goggles and pulled a pair of high-powered binoculars from his pack. A moment later, he handed them to Yael, who looked briefly and handed them to me.

Looking through the binoculars, I could see the compound on the north side of the village. It was no more than five hundred yards down the other side of this ridge. I could see the warehouse where the terrorists were storing the chemical weapons. And about 150 yards to the west, I could see the crumbling mausoleum built around Nahum's tomb. It all seemed so quiet and surreal, hardly noticeable and certainly not an obvious threat to the uninitiated like myself.

But then I spotted the cage. Beside it were a video camera on a tripod and several TV lights on stands. I saw twelve or fifteen armed men wearing black hoods milling about. The president was not in sight, but I feared he might be soon.

"Okay, men, turn on your comms," Ramirez whispered, and his men relayed the message up and down the line.

I fumbled a bit in the darkness to find the switch, but Yael helped me and made sure the volume was set correctly.

"We good? Everyone on?" Ramirez asked over his whisper mic.

"Five by five," came the unanimous reply.

"Cracker Jack, Lucky, you guys have a shot?" Ramirez asked his snipers.

Both men said yes, and Ramirez took another moment to size up the situation. Ramirez's second in command would lead the Red Team to the warehouse. Ramirez would lead the Blue Team to the compound. The colonel, Yael, and I had already been ordered to stick with the Blue Team and help guard their flanks.

"Okay, you know what you've got to do," the general said at last. "Let's move."

Before I'd even gotten to my feet, the two teams were on the move and racing down the southern slope with impressive agility. But soon I was up and moving too. Yael took point. I was in the middle. The colonel had our backs. My injured knees were on fire, but once we started down the mountain, there was no stopping.

The problem was, it was pitch-black. It's hard to describe just how dark it was. With thick cloud cover, there was no moonlight whatsoever. We still had maybe thirty or forty minutes until dawn began to break. There were no streetlights in the village below and no lights on yet in the main compound where we hoped the president was. Nor were there any lights on in the warehouse. This meant we all had our night-vision goggles on. But whereas everyone else was used to running with them on, I was not. As such, I was losing ground to Yael and stumbling often. Several times I tripped over rocks or slipped in the mud and came close to sliding down the mountain. But what worried me most was falling and accidentally making a sound that could draw attention to the team's approach. Fortunately, each time I stumbled, Sharif grabbed my arm and kept me from slipping. Pretty quickly he decided to stay by my side rather than behind to make sure I remained on my feet.

Ninety seconds later, Yael, the colonel, and I had made it down the slope. I was sucking air into my burning lungs as fast as I could, but I still had another two hundred yards across relatively flat ground before I reached the large stone wall on the north side of the compound and the iron gates that led into the driveway. The Blue Team was already there, and they weren't waiting for us. They were scaling the walls. Remarkably, they still hadn't been detected. By now I'd expected the shooting to begin. So far it had not. When I finally reached the wall and peered through the gates, I saw why. Ramirez's snipers had taken out four guards and hadn't made a sound.

There was no way I was going to make it over that wall. But Ramirez had already planned for that. He'd given Colonel Sharif plenty of Semtex and an order to blow the gates off their hinges at the first opportunity. Yael took one side of the gate. I took the other. Together we made sure no one could come around the corner and shoot us from behind. Then came the explosion that told the whole village we were here.

The force of the blast was deafening, and I could feel the heat scorching the back of my neck. I'd stood too close and was grateful I hadn't been hit by any of the shrapnel. For a moment my ears were ringing and I couldn't hear a thing. But then it was as if the volume had been turned back up and I heard automatic gunfire inside the main building. Soon it intensified and spread through two separate wings. And then, on cue, I could hear the high-pitched scream of an incoming missile.

"Hit the deck!" Yael shouted, but it was too late.

The second explosion—far more powerful than the first—lifted me off my feet and sent me hurtling through the air. I landed on my side, rolled for a bit, and couldn't have been more grateful when I not only was alive but still hadn't even broken anything.

I was in the thick of the action. And according to the wristwatch I'd been issued for the mission it was 5:58. The drone strike on the town's only cell tower, located just across the street, had come right on time, just like we'd been briefed back on the air base. The raid was unfolding like clockwork.

I dusted myself off, scooped up my MP5 again, and peered into the darkness. So far no one was coming my way. But I could hear people shouting. The voices were angry, confused, and all in Arabic. Down the driveway and toward the west side of town, lights were coming on in house after house, building after building. Then I heard Yael and the colonel calling for me to follow them. I made one last check of my sector, reported we were clear, and headed into the compound. The sounds of automatic gunfire filled the night.

As I raced through the smoking gates and across the muddy courtyard, I could see through several of the windows the brilliant flash of stun grenades going off, followed by more gunfire and the shrieks of dying men. And then I heard one of the Delta operators say something over the radio that chilled me to my core.

"POTUS isn't here."

57

★ ★ ★

"What do you mean he isn't here?" Ramirez shouted over the radio.

"We've cleared the north wing, sir," one of his commandos reported. "We've got nothing."

Ramirez then demanded a status check from the men clearing the south wing. He got the same reply. They'd checked every bedroom, every closet, every stairwell, every bathroom, every storage area and crawl space, and they hadn't found Taylor.

"What about Khalif?" Ramirez demanded.

One by one his men radioed back that there was no sign of him.

I heard the general order his men to keep looking as Yael and I burst through the front doors of the main house. Sharif was right behind us. Dead ISIS jihadists lay everywhere. Shards of glass littered the blood-soaked floor. The terrorists' weapons—Kalashnikovs, pistols of various types, and several RPGs, along with thousands of rounds of ammunition and rather sophisticated communications gear—had been stripped from them and were in a pile on the dining room table. Two

Delta operators had taken up defensive positions at the living room and dining room windows, all of which had been blown out in the attack. They occasionally fired into the night and fog, trying to keep the ISIS reinforcements at bay while their commander figured out our next move.

Ramirez was pacing in the kitchen and talking on a satellite phone. I could tell he was briefing the king and the commanders back in the war room on the latest developments, and I picked up bits and pieces of his side of the conversation. But the staccato bursts of gunfire made it difficult to catch much.

It wasn't just these operators near me who were shooting and being shot at, after all. Across the street I could still hear a ferocious gun battle going on at the warehouse. I'd heard no radio traffic from the Red Team yet. That could mean only one thing: they were still locked in a brutal fight for control of the chemical weapons. Was it possible the president was being held there? Could Khalif be there too?

When the general saw us enter, he signaled Sharif to take up a position at the front door and make sure no one we didn't know made it inside. Then he waved Yael and me to come to the kitchen. Stepping over the bodies and shards of glass, we made our way from the large entryway toward the kitchen. For such a small village, this was a rather sprawling villa; I wondered who had first built it and who owned it now. Each room was spacious—not palatial, but more than comfortable for even a large family. The chairs and sofas were old and worn. The carpets were not only threadbare but now freshly covered with muddy bootprints. The light fixtures were as dusty as they were outdated. A grand piano stood in one corner of the living room, but it looked like it hadn't been touched in ages.

We entered the large kitchen and found appliances and dishes that looked like they dated back to the seventies. It was clear that whoever owned the place had once had a great deal of money. Yet somewhere along the way that money had apparently dried up and the place was now a shadow of its former glorious existence. How recently had Khalif and his men seized it? I wondered. And had the owners surrendered it willingly, or had they been murdered?

Just then the radio crackled to life. I heard the voice of the Red Team leader. He said they were encountering much stiffer resistance than expected. They'd secured the perimeter of the warehouse along with the main floor. But they'd discovered that the facility had two lower levels, something the intel briefing hadn't revealed. The lower levels, he said, were accessible by one of two freight elevators. There were also two stairwells, one at each end of the building. But with four points of entry to cover with only a dozen men, plus the need to protect the main floor from ISIS reinforcements, they needed backup, and fast.

"They're on their way," the general radioed back. "Stand by one."

I fully expected Ramirez to send Yael, Sharif, and me, especially since Sharif was a full colonel with plenty of combat experience and Yael was the chemical weapons expert of the bunch. We all knew she was anxious to see exactly what Khalif had on location, how much, and whether the sarin gas precursors had already been mixed and loaded into mortars and artillery shells and were ready to be fired. But that would have violated the general's strict rule that we were to remain with him at all times. So he ordered the two commandos in the living and dining rooms to hightail it over to the warehouse and "get this thing locked down." Then he turned to Yael and me. "Get to those windows and shoot at anything that moves. Collins, you always wanted to be in the Army. Don't let us down."

My heart was pounding and my palms were sweaty as I moved to the dining room window. I couldn't dry them off on my pants because I was soaked to the bone. The winds were driving the rains inside the villa through the blown-out windows, and everything was soaked. Yael reminded me to put more resin on my hands to keep my weapon from slipping.

I grabbed some from my pocket and followed her advice—and just in time. The night lit up with a spray of gunfire. I ducked away from the window and pressed myself against the wall. When the shooting paused for a split second, I pivoted around the wall, aimed my MP5 into the darkness, and squeezed the trigger in three short bursts. Then I pulled back and waited for the return fire, which came an instant later. In fact, it sounded louder if that was possible. The jihadists were advancing.

Again I pivoted around the corner and fired three short bursts. Then I ducked back and tried to steady my breathing. I glanced at Yael. I saw her open fire again and then pause to reload. As she did, she motioned for me to put my night-vision goggles back on. They were affixed to my helmet, so I could flip them down into place or flip them up so I could see normally. I'd flipped them up upon entering the kitchen, since a small lamp was on and several candles were burning next to the stove, illuminating the general's laminated map of Alqosh and floor plans of the compound. I quickly flipped the goggles back in place and turned to fire again.

What I saw terrified me. At least four and possibly five armed men were climbing over the eastern security wall not fifty yards from me. When they dropped to the ground, they'd be coming right at me. To my right, at least as many terrorists were scaling the fence closer to Yael. Two were already firing at her. I could see the flashes pouring out of their barrels. There was nothing I could do to help her, so I aimed at the men in my sector, pulled the trigger, and shouted for Ramirez to come help. I felled one jihadist instantly. I downed a second but he wasn't dead. He screamed in pain and started crawling back to his weapon. So I pulled the trigger again, but this time nothing happened. My magazine was empty, and three more jihadists had just cleared the wall.

I ducked back out of the window and against the wall, ejected the spent magazine, and fumbled in the darkness to reload. As I did, Ramirez rushed

to my side, his MK 17 SCAR assault rifle in hand.
He opened up with four quick bursts. I finished
reloading and pivoted back around the corner to
help, but it was immediately apparent the general
had finished off everyone in the yard, including several of the terrorists trying to charge Yael.
Then he let go of his weapon, letting it dangle at
his side, grabbed a grenade, pulled the pin, and
threw it over the wall. The flash was blinding. The
boom was deafening. But the effect was decisive.
We heard screaming for a few moments, and then
all was silent save the gun battle behind us in the
warehouse.

Just then, six Delta operators converged in the
living room and called for Ramirez's attention.
One of them explained that they had left the rest
of their men firing at ISIS forces from bedrooms
in the north and south wings of the building. The
general ordered three of them to replace Yael,
Sharif, and me, and the other three to head up
to the second floor and take defensive positions
there. Then he motioned us to follow him down a
dark hallway in the north wing. We did as we were
told and quickly found ourselves in what looked
like it had once been a master bedroom that had
been converted into a communications center.
There were no beds or dressers but rather tables
lined with shortwave radio equipment, laptops,
printers, satellite phones, and open cases of video
cameras, lights, and sound gear. There were also
three dead bodies on the floor and blood splattered
everywhere.

"When you and your team were surveilling

this compound, did you see ISIS forces moving back and forth between here and the warehouse?" Ramirez asked Yael.

"No, not really," she said. "Why?"

"Doesn't that seem odd?"

"What do you mean?"

"This was clearly the headquarters," Ramirez said. "I suspect Khalif spent most of his time in here and in the adjoining room over there."

He led us through a bathroom to another room, which no doubt had also once been a bedroom. It, too, had been cleared of beds and anything else domestic. Instead, there were several card tables set up, a half-dozen wooden chairs and stools, three additional laptops, a printer, a television set, a large map of Amman on one wall, and a blown-up satellite photograph of Dabiq on another wall. The second map had several buildings marked, including the elementary school. There were also two dead bodies on the floor, clearly recent casualties of the Delta raid.

"Doesn't it seem odd to you that Khalif and his closest advisors never went over to the warehouse, never checked on the progress of the weapons?" he asked. "Never? Not at all?"

"I guess so, yeah," Yael replied.

"Unless we're missing something," Ramirez said.

"Like what?" Colonel Sharif asked.

And then I got it.

"A tunnel."

58

* * *

Ramirez raced for the main stairwell with Yael, Sharif, and me right on his heels.

We headed to the basement, weapons drawn. My heart was racing. But my hopes were fading fast. The longer the president wasn't found, the more likely it was that he was dead or in the process of being killed, or at least being dragged away to another building by forces tipped off by the initial shooting and explosions—if he was here at all. And we still didn't know.

At this point, the only possible clue was the armed men in black hoods who had been gathered around the cage and video camera and lights at Nahum's tomb, just down the road, a few hundred meters from where we were now. Had they been preparing for the president? Or had they simply been planning to kill other hostages they captured and post the footage on YouTube?

Ramirez took point, gun at the ready, and motioned for us to check the rooms behind him on each side of the hallway. Yael took the rooms on the left. I was to search those on the right. Sharif kept our backs.

As I entered the first room, a small bedroom, the MP5 in my hands was shaking. It seemed unlikely to the point of being impossible that the Delta team—with all their training and experience—could have missed any terrorists who were hiding down here, much less the president. But could it be possible that in the darkness and the rush of battle the general's men had missed the entrance to some kind of makeshift tunnel leading to the warehouse across the street or anywhere else? Probably not. In any other circumstances I would have bet everything I had against it. But the truth was, we were down here because their boss thought it very well might be possible after all. So, night-vision goggles on, I was now looking under the beds, behind dressers, under carpets, and in the backs of closets.

I found nothing in the first room, so I moved into the hall and into the room next door and repeated the process. As I did, I couldn't decide whether I wanted Ramirez to be right or not. If he was right, we might find the president after all. But we might also stumble across one or more jihadists ready to shoot or butcher us.

"Clear," I heard Yael shout from across the hallway.

"Clear," I shouted back, referring to the first room, and a few moments later I repeated it to account for the second room.

The next room on my side of the hallway was a rather large but absolutely filthy bathroom. To the right there was a bulky wooden vanity containing two dust-covered porcelain sink bowls along with two sets of rusty faucets. To the left was a shower stall overflowing with bags of trash and a separate bathtub filled with tools and building supplies. I saw bags of cement, boxes of nails, hammers, and numerous other things I didn't have time to identify. Straight ahead but in a small nook off to the right, I spotted a smashed porcelain toilet and a rusty bidet, neither of which had clearly been used in quite some time. The floor tiles were chipped and broken, and the room was cluttered with all kinds of odds and ends, from an old bicycle to mildewed wooden crates containing empty glass bottles to soiled clothes and other random items—everything, that is, except an opening to a tunnel.

"Clear," I yelled again, coming back into the hallway and hearing Yael shout the same.

Sharif was still in the hallway, watching our backs. But Ramirez wasn't. Instead, he had just finished clearing the last bedroom on Yael's side—a rather generous room with three rows of dilapidated bunk beds on one side and two more on the other. Now he was meticulously scouring a storage area on my side of the hallway. His night-vision goggles were off, and he was using a flashlight. Yael came alongside me as I watched the general getting more and more frustrated. He was yelling. He was still quite controlled, but his body language made it clear he was growing angry and perhaps not a little bit frantic.

"No luck?" I asked, turning to Yael.

She shook her head. "Same with you?"

"Yeah—what are we missing?"

"I don't know."

The gun battle at street level was intensifying. The sounds were muffled, but I could tell things were heating up. And it wasn't hard to figure out why. Dawn was about to break over the plains of Nineveh. The storm was dissipating. The winds were beginning to push the system off to our east. The sky was starting to brighten ever so slightly. And every minute that passed made our situation more precarious. The entire village now knew the Americans had arrived, and they knew precisely where we were. Any fighter who had been asleep ten minutes earlier was now awake, dressed, armed, and heading our way. What wasn't clear yet—but would be soon—was whether any calls or other communications had gotten to ISIS forces in Mosul before the drone took out the cell tower. If so, thousands of fighters could be here in the next fifteen to twenty minutes.

A series of explosions shook the foundations of the house. It almost felt like an earthquake, but as I steadied myself against one wall and pieces of Sheetrock fell from the ceiling, Yael said that was the sound of the U.S. Air Force dropping their ordnance on ISIS reinforcements who apparently were getting too close for comfort.

Then Ramirez started cursing up a storm and stomped back into the hallway. He didn't say a word to us. Instead, he began personally rechecking each of the rooms we had just checked ourselves, starting with Yael's. His desperation was palpable and growing, and what little hope I had was draining away fast. Yael offered to stand guard, but I don't think Ramirez heard her. I saw Colonel Sharif step into the first bedroom I'd checked back at the other end of the hallway, and I decided I couldn't just stand there doing nothing. So I started rechecking the rooms I'd just been through. It seemed ridiculous. There was nothing new to find. These rooms had no windows. They had no other doors besides the ones to the hallway. Their closets were small. I'd checked under beds and behind dressers and in every other conceivable place. I was sure I hadn't overlooked anything, but then I stepped back into the bathroom.

And something wasn't right. It's hard to explain. It's not that I saw anything new, but I felt something different. Call it a sixth sense, call it what you will, but I took off my night-vision goggles and started using the flashlight from my belt. Inch by inch, section by section, I reexamined everything—the shower stall, the tub, the toilet, even the bidet. All of it was dirty and disgusting, and I soon began to realize it stank as well, though I couldn't quite place the source of the stench. This time through I noticed there were dead flies everywhere and various insects crawling about. But when I got back to the rusty, filthy double sink, I just stood there and stared. A layer of plaster dust covered everything, and there was more dust lingering in the air now that the fighter jets were dropping five-thousand-pound bombs on our next-door neighbors. But there was something else.

Slowly, carefully, thoroughly, I shone the flashlight over every centimeter of that vanity. I was racking my brain for what was bothering me, but I still couldn't place it. I could hear Ramirez tearing up the other rooms, convinced we were missing the obvious. And then the light caught something on the floor, at the base of the vanity. At first I thought it was just a few pieces of chipped tiles, but as I stooped down to examine it more closely—and poked a bit with my gloved left hand—it began to dawn on me that I was looking at drops of blood. They weren't fresh drops, as if they'd been left here a few minutes earlier. But the spots weren't completely dry either. They were tacky, sticky, like the blood I'd found in the hallway of that bombed-out apartment building back in Homs. These drops weren't more than a few hours old.

I examined the section of the floor in front of the vanity more closely. Everything looked different without the night-vision goggles on. What had previously appeared as streaks of mud I could now see were deep black scrapes in the tiles in two parallel lines, about a meter apart.

"Yael, come here," I whispered, not wanting to attract the general's attention yet.

"What is it?" she asked, coming to the door of the bathroom.

"I'm not sure, but would you hold this for a moment?" I asked as I handed her the flashlight.

"Sure. Why?"

I didn't reply. Not immediately. Instead, I moved my machine gun so it was hanging down my back and wasn't in my way. Then I had Yael shine the flashlight at the base of the large vanity, pulled my gloves on a little tighter, and reached out and grabbed both sides of the wooden base of the sink. Then slowly, cautiously, and as quietly as I could, I started to pull. To my astonishment, it wasn't heavy or difficult. To the contrary, the entire sink pulled away from the wall rather easily. I expected the pipes connected to the back wall of the bathroom to stop my progress any moment. But the pipes weren't connected at all. And when I'd pulled the whole thing completely away from its base and pushed it over beside the shower stall, Yael and I found ourselves staring at a hole in the floor roughly four feet by two or three feet, with a wooden ladder going down at least twenty feet.

59

★ ★ ★

I was about to call to the general when a voice crackled over the radio.

"We have a man down. I repeat, we have a man down."

It wasn't immediately apparent to me who was speaking. I didn't know each of these men well enough to recognize their voices. But I could hear the stress in this voice, whoever it was, and the cacophony of gunfire and grenades going off non-stop was clearly audible over the radio. From this I deduced the transmission was coming from the warehouse.

Whoever it was gave no other details—no name, no rank, no description of how serious the injuries were or whether they were life-threatening. But before Ramirez or anyone else could ask, the same voice came over the radio with an update.

"Cancel that. We have a KIA on level two of the warehouse. I repeat, we have our first KIA. Request more backup if at all possible."

I couldn't believe it. I heard the words but couldn't process them. The heaviness in the voice sucked the wind out of me. A moment earlier I'd been so excited to find this tunnel. Now the angel of death had struck this little team for the first time, and I couldn't imagine how this death would be the last.

I heard the general racing down the hall and bounding up the stairs. At the same time he was asking for a status report on the battle inside the warehouse. I turned to Yael, but she shook her head, pointed back at the hole, immediately clicked off the flashlight, and put on her night-vision goggles. I did the same, then squatted and aimed my MP5 down the shaft. She didn't say it, but I knew she was telling me not to take my eyes off the hole under any circumstances. We had clearly found something we weren't supposed to find, and there was no telling who or what was down there. She slowly lowered herself into a crouch and positioned herself directly behind my right ear.

"I'm going to radio this in and get the colonel to cover us," she whispered. "And then I'm going in."

"Shouldn't we wait for backup?" I whispered.

I highly doubted she had experience in tunnel warfare. I certainly didn't. And Sharif—a trained commando who had served faithfully at King Abdullah's side for years—was in his forties, which was why he was now a spokesman. Surely there were two dozen men more qualified to do this than any of us.

But Yael was adamant. "There is no backup," she said without any trace of emotion.

"What are you talking about? There's got to be—"

But she quickly cut me off.

"Trust me, J. B.," she whispered with a level of intensity in her voice I'd never heard before. "The fight up top is getting worse. They can't spare anyone. We're it. Now make a space. I'm going in."

"Wait a moment," Sharif said from behind us. "I'll go."

I hadn't even heard him enter the bathroom.

"No, you stay here and stand guard," Yael said.

"You have no training for this," the colonel insisted. "I do."

"What, twenty years ago? Twenty-five? I appreciate it, Colonel—really, I do—but we don't have time to argue."

"You're right; we don't," he said. "So step aside. It's a dangerous job. A soldier's job. A man's job. You're brave, Dr. Katzir. But this is something I must do myself."

"Forget it," she shot back, though careful to keep her voice low. "I'm the smallest, and I'm the closest, and I'm going in. Now watch my six."

Before either of us could say another word, Yael slung her machine gun over her shoulder, took out an automatic pistol from the holster on her hip, and disappeared down the ladder even as she radioed the general and gave him a brief description of what we'd found and what she was doing.

I was impressed with her courage, and I could see from the look on Sharif's face he was too. But I was scared for her. Brave was one thing. Crazy was another. And I still thought it was crazy for her to do a job the Delta guys were eminently more qualified for.

Still, I couldn't argue with her logic. With the first of our team killed in action and the general calling in close air strikes, it was becoming clear to me we were in real danger of being overrun. If anyone could hold ISIS back, it was Delta, not Yael, Sharif, and myself. But that meant it fell to us to head into this tunnel and find out what was there.

I looked down the shaft and saw Yael position herself flat on her stomach, pistol out in front of her. She said nothing for a full minute. Then she looked up at me. "We're clear."

"There's no one there?"

"Not that I can see."

"Good, then get back up here."

"No," she said. "The tunnel curves to the left about twenty meters ahead. I need to go see what's up there. I'm going to scootch forward. You come down behind me."

"What?"

"You heard me. I need you."

"For what?"

"Backup. Now get down here, and bring your pistol."

So I pulled out the .45 Ramirez had given me, stepped around the vanity, and made my way down the ladder, heart pounding, sweat pouring down my forehead. I had no idea who or what I was about to find, and my claustrophobia was going crazy, especially when I reached the bottom. Sure enough, the tunnel ran in the direction of the warehouse. However, unlike smuggling tunnels I'd seen on the U.S.–Mexican border, or the ones in Homs, or the one I'd once been to under the DMZ on the thirty-eighth parallel between North and South Korea, all of which had been significantly wider, able to handle several people astride for hundreds of meters, this one was low and narrow in the extreme. At over six feet tall, there was no way I was going to be able to walk erect. Indeed, I gauged the height of the tunnel at no more than three or four feet, which meant I was actually going to have to crawl on my injured knees, and only a few feet wide, which meant I was already feeling cramped. That said, it had clearly been built by people who knew what they were doing. This wasn't a mine shaft from the California gold-rush era with dirt walls and wooden supports. This was made of concrete and actually had a lamp hanging on steel supports in the wall every fifteen or twenty feet, providing plenty of lighting.

I got down on my hands and knees and tried to steady my breathing, tried not to hyperventilate, tried to ignore the pain. I couldn't wait for long. Yael was already crawling forward, and I needed to follow. Every ten yards or so, we would stop, lie flat on our stomachs, weapons ready, catch our breath, and look again for signs of movement. But continuing to see none, we kept moving.

We made the first left and found that the tunnel did not exactly continue in a straight line. It zigzagged a bit, and at each turn I feared what we would find. But turn after turn, we found nothing. No terrorists. No president. No clues.

After six or seven minutes, we were surprised to come upon a T intersection. In front of us was a much larger tunnel, at least eight feet high, and

significantly wider. It, too, was carefully con-
structed of steel and concrete, but unlike the nar-
rower tunnel we'd just come through, this one had
metal tracks, like railroad tracks, running down
its center. They appeared to be tracks for mine
carts, though I didn't see any at the moment. Then
again, looking to my right, it was pitch-black. To
my left, the new tunnel was much better lit than
the tunnel we'd just come out of.

My grip on my pistol tightened. Claustrophobia
was no longer the issue. I realized now that there
was a very good chance we were going to encounter the enemy, and soon.

60

Yael put away her pistol.

Then she took off her night-vision goggles and used the scope of her MP5 to look down the well-lit portion of the tunnel. There wasn't anyone immediately apparent, but here again the tracks curved to the right and we had no idea what was around the bend. As she radioed a status report back to Ramirez, Sharif, and the others, I put away my .45, put my night-vision goggles on, and aimed my MP5 into the darkness behind us.

"Carts," I whispered when Yael had finished transmitting.

"What do you mean?" she said, her back still to me.

"Follow me," I said.

I began walking forward, my weapon at the ready, and the deeper I went into the darkness, the more mining carts I saw. Five, six, seven, ten, fifteen, twenty, thirty—in the end I counted fifty-one carts, leading all the way back to a cement wall, the end of the line. Moving cautiously toward the wall, fully expecting an ambush, I ducked behind the last cart and gave a quick glance inside. To my relief no one was there. Instead, I found at least a hundred artillery shells. I motioned for Yael to move up one side of the tracks. I took the other, each of us checking every other cart. When we came to the front of the line again, we examined the cargo in the first cart. Like each of the others, it contained a pile of shells, but as I looked more closely, I found that they were all marked with skulls and crossbones and the word *warning* in Arabic.

"These are M687s," Yael said.

"What's that?" I asked.

"It's a chemical weapon, a nerve agent," she said. "The M687 is an American design—a 155mm artillery shell with two canisters inside. The first contains one of the liquid precursors for sarin gas. The other canister holds the second. Between them is what's called a rupture disk. When the shell is fired at the enemy, the disk is breached and the two chemicals are mixed in flight. Then when the shell lands: *boom*, death—a very, very painful death for a whole lot of people."

"Did the U.S. ever use them?" I asked.

"Tested them but never used them in combat," she said. "They were eventually banned by the CWC—the Chemical Weapons Convention— and your government destroyed your stores. But the design has been knocked off by lots of different countries—and now by ISIS."

"They've got over five thousand of them here," I said, trying to imagine how many people ISIS could kill if they had the chance to actually use these weapons.

"They're stockpiling," Yael said.

"Why?"

"I don't know," she said. "Maybe to use. Maybe to sell. But either way . . ."

Yael didn't finish the sentence. She didn't have to. I realized both of us had left our backpacks containing our chem-bio suits back in the villa, in the living room. Yael radioed Ramirez to let him know what we'd found. Then she turned and continued toward the light. I followed.

We moved forward, Yael still on one side of the tracks and me on the other, and I suddenly noticed how eerily quiet it was. After the chaos on the surface, we were now at least twenty if not thirty feet belowground, and we could only barely hear the fight above us. Every now and then we'd get an update over our radios, but the bursts of information were few and far between and often in a military jargon that was lost on me. The only thing coming through loud and clear was that the team holding the villa was starting to worry about their supply of ammo, while the team assaulting the warehouse already had one KIA, three men injured, and no reinforcements on the way.

Just before we reached the bend in the track, Yael signaled for me to step behind her. As I did, we got the report that there'd been another KIA in the warehouse and two more injuries.

Yael pressed her back against the wall of the tunnel's right side. I was less than a yard behind her. As she inched forward, so did I. She shot a quick peek around the corner and then pulled back. She said nothing, but all the color was gone from her face.

"What is it?" I asked. "What's there?"

I waited a moment, but she couldn't respond. I asked her again, but she just shook her head. Her hands were quivering. She was taking deep breaths. I'd never seen her react this way, even in circumstances far more dangerous than this.

Slowly, cautiously, I moved around her, took a deep breath, then pivoted around the corner, ready to shoot. But now it was I who could not speak. I felt the blood instantly drain from my face as well, and my hands too began to shake.

There were no ISIS members waiting for us. There was no ambush. We were in no immediate mortal danger. But never in my life had I seen anything like this.

Partially decomposed bodies were hanging from the ceiling on each side of the tracks, their necks wrapped tightly in chains. I counted nineteen men and nineteen women, all of whom I guessed were in their forties and fifties, and twenty-seven children, both boys and girls, ranging in ages from maybe eleven or twelve up to perhaps eighteen or nineteen. But that wasn't the worst of it. Parked on the tracks were a dozen mine carts, and all of them were filled to overflowing with human heads.

For a moment I just stood there and stared, too stunned to think, too paralyzed to move. Then suddenly I turned and vomited all over the tracks near me, again and again until there was nothing left in my system. When my dry heaves finally ended and I had steadied myself against one of the walls, Yael handed me a bottle of water. I took some, swished it around in my mouth, and spit it back out. Then I took some more and swallowed and felt it burn the whole way down my throat. Only then did I notice that Yael had just finished vomiting too.

Wiping my mouth, I gripped my weapon and forced myself to keep moving. Yael started moving as well. Once again, she stayed on the right side of the tracks with me on the left. She picked up the pace, eager to get out of this house of horrors as quickly as possible, but I lagged behind. I tried not to look at the dangling corpses above us or the bulging eyes and gaping mouths of the heads stacked in the carts. As I kept my head down and eyes averted, I couldn't help but notice piles of debris running along each wall. Curious, I finally stopped and took a more careful look, and then I realized these weren't heaps of garbage. These were crosses and icons and Communion cups and Bibles and other holy books. And then I knew who these people were and why they had died such grisly and horrible deaths.

Shaken like I'd never been in my life, I, too, picked up the pace and caught up to Yael just as she was pivoting around another bend in the tracks. There were no bodies this time, nor even any carts. Nor were there any signs of ISIS fighters. But here the tracks and the tunnel began to tilt upward, and we started climbing back toward the surface.

Eventually we came to another bend in the tunnel, and again no one was immediately visible.

But there was something I hadn't expected: a large retractable steel door—almost like a garage door or a blast door—coming down from the ceiling and completely blocking our path. At the base of the door were two rectangular notches about three and a half feet apart that accommodated the rails. As we got closer, I noticed that there was also a smaller door built into the larger one that would permit a person to pass through while the larger door still blocked passage of the mine carts in either direction. Yael motioned for me to move to the right side of the smaller door. She moved to the left. Then she silently counted down from three with her fingers, turned the handle, and cautiously stepped through, her MP5 leading the way. I followed immediately and shut the door behind us.

We were now standing in the pitch dark. I quickly switched back to night-vision goggles, and when I did, I was aghast at what I saw. For here, against each wall—both on the left and right sides of the tracks—were metal cages. Inside each cage was either a young boy or young girl, ranging in age from maybe eight to no more than ten or eleven years old. They were naked, gaunt, and shivering. And now that they knew someone had just entered their hell, they were awake, wide-eyed, backing away, and cowering in fear.

They couldn't see us or each other in the blackness, of course, but they must have been awakened by hearing us open the door, and they had surely seen the light spilling in from the other side as we had entered. Perhaps they had seen our silhouettes as well. None of them dared to say anything. No one called out and asked who we were. But neither did we call out. I didn't dare. I knew they were hostages. They were captives. They were slaves. But they weren't here to work—they were far too young. Which meant they were being held here for only one purpose: to be sex slaves to—and likely to be brutally raped by—their ISIS masters.

An involuntary shudder rippled through my body. I'd rarely experienced the presence—the physical presence—of evil before. But I did now. I'd heard rumors of ISIS members engaging in sexual slavery. I'd seen some unsourced reporting. But I'd never taken it very seriously. I'd certainly never believed any of it. All the allegations and insinuations seemed so outlandish, so far beyond the pale, as to be unworthy of serious attention. This was the twenty-first century, I'd told myself. No one was savage enough to be engaged in such barbaric behavior, I'd convinced myself.

But what else were these children doing here, naked and alone, at such tender young ages?

61

The stench in the place was overwhelming.

The children were living in their own filth. But it was the horror in the eyes of these kids—staring out through the darkness, trembling in terror, unable to see us but knowing we were there—that haunted me most.

The monstrosity of it struck me hard. I grabbed Yael's arm and tried to pantomime what I was thinking, that we should let them out and lead them back through the tunnels. But Yael shook her head, put her finger over her lips, and then pointed forward. We had a mission. We had to stay with it. And of course she was right. These children weren't going to be any safer in the tunnels behind us or up in the villa than they were right now. Their only hope was for us to clear these tunnels of the enemy, link back up with the Delta Force teams, and hold our own until the choppers came to rescue us. Then, just maybe, hopefully, we could get these children not just out of the cages but out of Iraq to somewhere clean, somewhere safe. Until then, they had to remain where they were. And quiet.

So we kept moving. Carefully. Stealthily. My heart was alternating between compassion and rage. But in the end I chose rage. It seemed the only possible choice.

Turning forward, we could see that there was another large steel door, similar to the one we had just passed through, about thirty meters ahead. It too had a smaller door built into it. As we approached, we could hear the sounds of a gun battle growing louder and louder. The good news was that the racket masked what little noise we were making. The bad news was that I suddenly realized we were coming up on the back side of the battle the Delta Force team had been engaged in for the last forty minutes. On the other side of this steel divide was the third and lowest level of the warehouse. This was where several dozen ISIS fighters were holding their own against America's finest. What chance did we have? Going through that door might very well be suicide.

Yael was going anyway, I had no doubt. I saw her back stiffen and her stride quicken as she headed for the small door. I raced to catch up with her and grabbed her by the arm again just before she turned the handle. I shook my head. I couldn't let her go through that door. There had to be another way. We could radio back to Ramirez. We could explain the situation to him. He could send some of his men through the tunnels to link up with us. They could help do the job their colleagues couldn't get done on their own. And we could stay to protect the children.

The only problem was that I couldn't say any

of this. I didn't dare do anything that might alert the jihadists to our presence. We had one ace up our sleeve, and only one, and that was the element of surprise.

But just as I was about to let go of Yael's arm, I looked over her shoulder at the cage not five feet behind her. I had thought it was empty, which seemed odd since it was the only one of sixteen cages that wasn't filled. But at that moment I thought I saw movement. I pivoted her around and aimed my weapon into the cage. Then I saw it again. Something or someone was in there, hiding under a blanket. Yael saw it too, and it momentarily stopped her from going through the doorway. Whatever it was, it seemed too large to be another child. Perhaps it was an animal, maybe a dog of some kind. But then it moved again and I saw a foot slide out from under the blanket—only for a second, and then it disappeared again. But it was definitely a foot. A human foot. A man's foot. A bloody foot.

I moved toward the cage, aiming my MP5 at the center of the mass. Yael didn't stop me. I didn't want to take any unnecessary chances. I handed her my machine gun. Then I handed her my .45. I was going into this cage one way or the other, but I didn't dare run the risk that an ISIS fighter trying to take a nap—or God forbid, having his way with one of these children—might grab one of my weapons and kill me and Yael with it.

Wiping my sweaty hands on my rain-drenched fatigues, more out of instinct than because it dried them off, I reached for the door of the cage. It was cold to the touch. Only then did I notice the padlock. There was no way I was getting this door open without the key. So I started looking around. Maybe it was hanging on a hook somewhere. Yael searched as well. But we found nothing. And when our search was over, we found ourselves standing in front of the cage again. I wasn't going in. That much was clear. Not without killing whoever had the key. So Yael handed my weapons back to me, and I began to back away toward the door, toward the inevitable. We were going through it, come hell or high water. We were going to take ISIS on from behind.

And then, just as I was about to turn toward the doorway, the figure under the blanket rolled over in his sleep. For a moment, the blanket slipped away from his face. Only for an instant, for he shifted again and pulled the blanket back over his face. But that instant was all we needed. It was unmistakable. It was Harrison Taylor.

62

* * *

I stood there in the darkness and couldn't believe it.

Had we really just found the president?

I turned to Yael, and she nodded slowly. She'd recognized him too.

But now what? We were no more able to get him out of that cage than any of these children, and even if we could, we had no place to take him. Seething with rage, I moved to the small door within the larger doorway and motioned for Yael to follow me. There was no point in delaying the inevitable. The only way we were getting out and getting the president and all those children out and going home was by going through that door and killing everything that wore a hood and moved.

Again Yael didn't stop me. So I took a deep breath, put my finger on the trigger, and turned the handle.

The first thing that happened was that I was temporarily blinded. The room on the other side was fully lit, and it felt like my night-vision goggles had just burned holes in my retinas. Yael saw me turn away in pain and quickly removed her goggles and scrambled into position behind me to assess the situation. Fortunately, the gunfire was so intense it masked any sounds we were making.

As I recovered, it was clear we had indeed made it to the bottom level of the warehouse. Through a smoky haze I could see no fewer than nine ISIS fighters. One was close, maybe five yards away. Others were spread out in a row. The farthest was about fifteen yards away. They were all hiding behind mine carts, overturned metal tables, and pallets stacked with steel boxes of some kind and piles of unused artillery shells they'd apparently been filling with sarin precursors before the Delta offensive began. And they were all firing in the direction of exit doors and elevators on the far side of this lower level of the warehouse.

I aimed at the closest fighter, pulled the trigger, and put four bullets in his back. Blood darkened his shirt, and soon he stopped screaming and twitching and fell to the floor, dead. Without waiting, I pivoted slightly to the right, fired another burst at the next closest fighter, and felled him instantly. Yael, meanwhile, fired at the terrorist farthest away and began working back across the room from right to left.

The effect was to create chaos in the warehouse. We had completely caught the ISIS fighters off guard, but we'd blindsided the Delta team, too. They had no idea who we were or where we were coming from or that we were allies. Bullets were flying everywhere. The jihadists were scrambling in all directions. Yael was radioing the general what was happening, but I can't imagine he or anyone else on the comms could hear over the battle.

Several of the black hoods now turned toward us and began firing back. Instinctively, I pulled Yael back through the doorway and slammed the door shut. I could hear a barrage of bullets hitting the door, but none of them could penetrate.

"Red Team Leader, Red Team Leader, this is Katzir and Collins!" Yael shouted over the radio as both of us reloaded. "We've found a way into the warehouse—lower level—from the back. That's us doing the shooting. Over."

"That's you, Katzir?" came the reply.

"That's affirm—press the offensive."

"Roger that. Do you have grenades?"

However hot the firefight had been sixty seconds earlier, it had just gotten exponentially hotter.

"Say again," Yael shouted into the radio. "I repeat, say again."

The terrorists seemed to be unloading everything they had against the smaller of the two doors. And then I realized there was no lock. The bullets were breaking through the steel. But if any of the fighters still alive on the other side decided to open the door, we had no way to stop them except to shoot them point-blank.

"Grenades, Katzir. Do you have grenades?"

"Yes, I have two," Yael replied.

"Get them ready," said the Red Team leader.

"Okay, hold on," she said, then turned to me and told me to back up, aim for the door, and not let anyone past, no matter what. She pulled out a flare, set it off nearby to give us a little light to operate since there was no way we could keep switching to night vision and back again. Then I watched as she pulled two grenades out of her vest.

The children were screaming now. I didn't blame them. But then I heard Taylor's voice, trembling and in shock. "Collins? Collins, is that you?"

"It is, Mr. President. Just hold on."

"How did you find me? And who's this with you?"

"We came with the Delta Force, Mr. President. They're here to rescue you. But I can't explain any further. Not right now. Just move to the back. Stay against the wall."

I saw the president comply as Yael moved to the door.

"J. B., come here," Yael shouted.

Immediately I moved to her side.

"Set your gun down."

"You're sure?"

She nodded. "Set it down."

I did.

"Now hold the handle and when I say go, open it just a crack—just enough so I can toss these through. Got it?"

"Yes," I said and grabbed the handle.

"Okay, I'm ready," Yael shouted over the radio.

At that point I noticed that bullets were no longing pummeling the steel door. I wasn't sure why, but I took it as a positive sign.

"Okay, good; we've drawn their fire back to us," came the response from the Red Team leader. "Now you're going to toss them both through— one to the center, one to the left, on my mark."

"Your left or mine?"

"Mine. Your right."

"So center and my right."

"Yes."

"Ready."

"Good. On my count—one, two, three, go—now-now-now!"

I yanked the door open about half a foot. Yael pulled pin one and tossed the grenade to the right. Then she pulled pin two and tossed it to the center, just as she'd been told. She yanked her hand back and I slammed the door shut. We both reached for our weapons as we heard the explosions go off. And then all was silent.

63

★ ★ ★

We waited for a moment, just to be sure.

Then the Red Team leader said the words we both wanted to hear. *"We're clear."*

For the first time in several minutes, it seemed, I finally started to breathe again. I turned to Yael, but she was already moving back to the door. She readied her weapon just in case and radioed ahead that she was coming in. Then she slowly turned the handle and pulled the door open. Instantly she was hit in the face by a wave of black smoke. She immediately shut the door again but the damage had been done. Thick, acrid smoke poured in, and I smelled the ghastly odor of burnt flesh. I turned away and covered my nose and mouth, but it wasn't enough. My eyes started watering. My throat was burning. I heard the president and the children choking and gagging behind me.

"Mr. President, are you okay?" I asked, moving toward his cage.

"I think so," he sputtered, trying to clear his throat and catch his breath. "Is it over?"

"Yes, Mr. President, for the moment," I said.

"But we still need to get you and all these children out of here. American rescue choppers are inbound. We need to get you aboveground and fast."

"Start with them," he said between coughs. "They've been living a nightmare."

"Of course, Mr. President," I replied. "Let me just tell the others that we've got you."

I radioed to the general and the rest of the Delta team that Yael and I had found the president. He was safe. But we needed medical and logistical help immediately. Then, as Yael lit several more flares to provide some desperately needed light, I explained the situation as we'd found it—the cages, the locks, and the children. Ramirez immediately ordered the Red Team leader to take charge of freeing the president and the children while the rest of Red Team moved back upstairs to the ground floor to aid the men fighting to keep the ISIS forces at bay.

"The choppers are twenty minutes out," Ramirez told us. "Everybody stay focused. Keep fighting. But don't lose heart. The cavalry is almost here."

I didn't find myself rejoicing, however. The strain in Ramirez's voice was clear. The intensity of the gunfire around him was clear as well. A moment later we heard him make a satellite call back to CENTCOM in Tampa and call in the most devastating series of close air strikes so far. *They're everywhere,* we heard him say. *I don't know if we can hold them back much longer.* Then someone next to him told him he was still on comms, and he fumbled to shut off his mic.

A chill ran down my spine. We weren't out

of the woods yet, and twenty minutes suddenly seemed like an eternity.

Just then someone started pounding on the door.

"Katzir, Collins, it's me," shouted the Red Team leader. *"I'm coming in."*

Yael opened the door and let him through, and more billows of smoke poured in with him. She closed the door again immediately and then turned a flashlight on President Taylor. I did the same.

"Mr. President, we're here to take you home," the Delta leader said. "How are you feeling?"

"I'm fine; I'm fine," he insisted. "Just take care of the kids."

"Dr. Katzir and Mr. Collins will do that," he replied. "My job is to take care of you. Now stand back as I get this door open."

"Did you find the keys?" I asked.

"No—I'm afraid they were blown to kingdom come with everything else on the other side of that door."

"Then how are you getting in?"

"Semtex—now stand back."

He pulled out a small piece of the puttylike plastic explosive, attached it to the padlock, and told us all to cover our ears. Then he triggered the detonator. After a small, measured explosion, it was over. The padlock blew apart. The chains fell off. The door swung open. The president was free.

The team leader then handed a small case of the explosives and detonating cords to Yael, who proceeded to blow the locks off all the cage doors.

Meanwhile, I rushed into the president's cage and helped the Delta leader get Taylor to his feet.

"When was the last time you had something to eat, Mr. President?"

"A few days ago, I'm afraid," he said, standing now in the orange jumpsuit we'd seen him in on the video, his legs wobbly and his hands quivering.

"And to drink?"

"Yesterday, a little—or maybe it was the day before," he said. "I'm sorry. The days are running together."

"That's okay," the leader said, handing him a small bottle of orange Gatorade. "Take a little of this, in small amounts. But don't worry. We'll get you back up to speed."

"Thank you, all of you. I can't tell you how grateful I am to see your faces. I never thought I'd see a friendly face again."

"We're glad to see you, too, sir. Can you walk?"

"I think so," Taylor said.

"Good; then I need you to come with me. We're going to get you out of here. Okay?"

"Thank you—thank you so much. I couldn't be more grateful."

The smoke was clearing now, apparently being sucked out by an exhaust system neither Yael nor I had noticed. But the president was still coughing and wheezing. He was also getting emotional. His eyes were welling with tears, and it wasn't simply from the soot or the stench. He had several days of growth on his face. His gray hair was unwashed and askew. And his mouth and lips were trembling. I was sure he was going to break down and start sobbing any moment. I'm sure I would have done the same.

Seeing how fragile the president was physically and emotionally, Yael insisted I accompany him and the team leader back through the tunnels to the villa.

"Forget it, Yael; I'm staying with you and the children," I said.

"J. B., the president needs you," she shot back more forcefully than I'd expected. "You know the way. And I'll be fine with these kids. Don't worry. We'll be right behind you. But move. You don't have much time."

I could see she wasn't going to take no for an answer. So I slung the MP5 over my shoulder and took Taylor's right arm while the team leader took his left, and we started moving.

"Thank you, gentlemen," the president said, still on the verge of succumbing to shock and relief.

"It's an honor, sir," I said as we began walking.

"I guess I owe you an apology," the president said as he limped forward.

"No, sir," I said. "Not at all."

"Of course I do, Collins," he said. "I didn't see it. I didn't see what was coming or how fast. You did. I should have listened, and I'm sorry."

"Thank you, Mr. President," I replied. "I appreciate that. Can I get that on the record?"

"Don't push it, Collins."

"Fair enough, sir. May I ask you a question?"

"Of course."

"Abu Khalif—do you know where he is?"

"I wish," he said. "Last time I saw him was

when they made the video. But we'd better catch him. When we do, I want to personally flip the switch on him."

"Wait till you see what's ahead," I said.

But first, the Red Team leader pulled out a satellite phone and hit speed dial.

"White House Situation Room," said the watch officer who picked up the call.

The Delta team leader identified himself and asked to be patched through immediately to Holbrooke. When the watch officer said the VP was busy, the team leader handed the phone to Taylor.

"This is the president of the United States— put me on with the vice president—*now*."

64

★ ★ ★

News of the president's rescue was relayed back to King Abdullah.

The monarch ordered Jordanian and Egyptian forces to stop their ground operation in Dabiq and to withdraw immediately. Soon we learned that the operation there had been messy, to say the least. Coalition casualties were high, and there was apparently a brutal firefight under way. I had no doubt the king was right to order a retreat. If the president was in Iraq, what was the point in losing the lives of any more coalition soldiers in Syria? The final battle of Dabiq would have to wait.

It quickly became clear the president was badly wounded and suffering from dehydration. For most of the way back to the villa, one of us had to support the president with his arm over our shoulders. He explained that he'd been tortured extensively, beaten on the back, stomach, legs, and feet—anywhere that couldn't be noticed on camera. The hardest part was getting him through the low tunnel. He was simply in too much pain to crawl and probably wouldn't have had the strength anyway. So we ultimately resorted to wrapping him in his blanket, putting my bulletproof vest on him, tying the straps from our machine guns to the vest, and pulling him through the tunnel.

It was 7:13 when we finally got the president back to the villa. Sharif was waiting for us and helped us get him out of the shaft and onto a stretcher. A Delta medic was also waiting for us and immediately began administering first aid, including putting Taylor on an IV to rehydrate him and pump some desperately needed pain-killers into his system. Ramirez rushed down to the basement to greet the president and take a few quick pictures he could transmit back to CENTCOM, the National Military Command Center at the Pentagon, and the White House Situation Room. These were the "proof of life" pictures everyone in the chain of command had been waiting for.

Ramirez wanted to put the president on the phone with the chairman of the Joint Chiefs. But Taylor was exhausted and the general thought better of it. Besides, we were by no means out of danger yet. So Ramirez left us with the medical team and raced back upstairs to keep fighting with his men, ordering Sharif to come with him as they hadn't a soldier to spare.

I could hear the roar of fighter jets streaking over us, and I could feel the building being rocked by the almost-nonstop explosions of American smart bombs taking out approaching ISIS forces.

Part of me wanted to join the general and Sharif and defend our location against the attackers. We had the president. He was in good hands. He was resting. He had a medic. And he certainly didn't need me.

But just then, Yael arrived with the children. I helped her get them up the ladder one by one, then down to a working bathroom. There Yael and I gave them each a quick sponge bath, dried them off, and wrapped them in sheets I ripped off the cleanest beds I could find. It wasn't much, but it was all we had.

I scrounged up as many PowerBars and bottles of water and Gatorade as I could and brought them to the bunk room, where we had decided to keep all the kids for the moment. They were trembling, all of them, terrified by the bombs and the automatic gunfire. We held them and rocked them and told them that it was going to be okay. Neither Yael nor I could be sure it was true, and it was clear none of the kids believed us—if they even understood us. But there was nothing else to be done. The choppers were still several minutes out, we were told, hampered by weather and anti-aircraft fire.

The medic soon came to check on the kids, and when he did, Yael leaned over and whispered in my ear.

"Go," she said.

"Where?" I asked.

"Upstairs to fight."

"No, I'm staying with you," I said. "You need me, and so do the kids."

"They need you more," she said. "And we'll be fine. The choppers will be here soon."

"You're sure?"

"Absolutely; go—and don't do anything stupid."

"Like get killed?"

"Exactly."

"Okay," I said, grabbing my MP5 and giving her a kiss on the forehead. "I'll be back for you soon. I love you."

Then I left.

As I raced up the stairs, I realized what I'd just said. I hadn't planned to say it. It had just come out. And then I'd bolted. I couldn't believe what I'd done or imagine what she was thinking. But I didn't have time to worry about it.

When I reached the main floor, I learned that three more of Ramirez's men were dead. One was critically wounded. All were nearly out of ammunition. They were using the AK-47s stripped off the dead ISIS fighters, but even the ammo in those guns was running low.

"Six minutes," Ramirez shouted. *"The choppers will be here in six. We need to hang on till then."*

I found my backpack and pulled out five full mags. "Here, General. This is all I have, plus the one in my weapon."

"Then keep two and get upstairs," he said, taking the other three off my hands. "Take the bedroom in the southwest corner. Kill anything that moves, but don't waste a shot. We've still got to get up that mountain."

"What mountain?"

"The one we landed on."

"That's where they're picking us up?"

"Yeah. Now move."

"Why not here?" I asked.

"Too dangerous," he said. "Blue Team will take the president and the kids out first. The rest of us will follow. Now get going. We've got men down up there, and more bad guys are coming up that road all the time."

I did as I was told and raced up to the second floor. I found the bedroom to which I'd been assigned at the end of the hall. And inside I found the body of a Delta member on the floor, shot just minutes before. He looked merely wounded, but I checked. He had no pulse. He was definitely dead. But his body was still warm and being pelted by the driving, freezing winter rain that was pouring through both sets of windows, the one facing south and the others facing west.

Perhaps the storm had let up enough to bring the choppers in, but one could hardly tell. The wind seemed as fierce as the last time I'd been aboveground. The rain hadn't abated at all, and the temperature was dropping fast.

The room was a disaster. I couldn't even begin to count all the bullet holes in the walls, door, and ceiling, and the furniture had all been ripped to shreds. But as I moved to the smashed-out windows on the west side, I was even more stunned by the vast destruction of this small village. It seemed every house was ablaze or a smoking crater. What few nearby buildings were undamaged were filled with snipers. I could see the flash of their muzzles and hear bullets whizzing past my head. I took one more glance and then pulled back from the window, images of dead ISIS fighters fresh in my mind's eye. There were bodies and body parts everywhere, hundreds of them, bullet-ridden, bloody, rain-soaked. And yet the fight was so far from over. More fighters were coming from every direction.

65

I opened fire on a group of five coming over the wall.

In three quick bursts, I killed two and wounded two more. But one got past me. I fired again and again but missed every time and now he was inside the building. Panicked, I shouted to my colleagues over the radio only to hear a burst of gunfire directly below me and confirmation from two Delta operatives that the enemy was down.

Two more fighters now sprinted out the front door of a blazing house. I shot them both before they crossed the street. But up the road to my right, about two hundred yards out, I spotted a white pickup truck filled with jihadists racing toward me. I aimed at them, waiting for them to come within range, but they never got to me. Instead, the entire truck, its driver, and all its passengers erupted in a massive ball of fire, and then an Apache helicopter gunship came roaring past.

More frightened than relieved at that moment,

I just stared at the new flaming crater in the road, only to be startled by another burst of gunfire coming from my right. Too close for comfort. I dove for cover as bullets and shrapnel filled the bedroom. When the shooting paused for a few seconds, I scrambled back to my feet, pivoted to the west window, and saw a band of three hooded men huddled behind what was left of a stone wall. I didn't have a clean shot at any of them and didn't dare waste any rounds. Still, they were too close not to engage them.

That's when I remembered the grenades. I drew back against the wall, away from the window, and pulled off my backpack. It was mostly filled with a chem-bio suit and related gear. But there were three grenades at the bottom. I grabbed one and took a quick glance to make sure the three terrorists were still behind the wall. They were, but four more had just joined them. I pulled the pin the way I'd seen Yael do it, then threw a fastball across the courtyard, aiming for the wall so as not to overshoot. It hit just a few feet shy but rolled close enough and detonated an instant later. When I looked again, that section of the wall was gone, and all that remained were charred body parts.

I ducked back to reload the MP5 and heard three shots from a second-floor window across the street. *Crack, crack, crack.*

This time I could feel the rounds passing by my head. If I hadn't ducked when I did, I knew I'd be dead. There was a sniper out there that had a bead on me. He was expecting me to pop back up any moment, but I wasn't going to give him an easy target. I got down on my belly and crawled along the floor, across the glass and the blood and the spent rounds, over to the south-facing window. Then I ejected the spent mag, popped in a new one, steadied my breathing the best I could, jumped out, and aimed for the second-floor window across the street. Two shots. Then I paused. Another shot. Then I paused again and forced myself to wait four seconds. *Beat. Beat. Beat. Beat.* I saw the barrel of his rifle coming back out the window and I let loose. Three bursts at the base of the window and then a fourth, and suddenly the rifle dropped out the window to the ground below.

I started breathing again. But as I pulled back inside for cover, I noticed in my peripheral vision a white blur to my left and the sound of someone gunning an engine. At once curious and worried, I got down low and crawled on my hands and knees away from my post, out the door, into the hallway, and to another bedroom on that side. Here I found another dead body, this time an ISIS fighter, not a Delta operative, and by the looks of him he'd been dead from the moment we'd arrived, almost ninety minutes earlier. But that wasn't what I was looking for. Instead, I raced to the window, popped my head up just for a moment, and was aghast at what I saw.

Three white vans were tearing out of the compound. I watched them clear the front gate and race up a dirt road on the mountain. They had to be going seventy or eighty miles an hour. Then I looked toward the summit where they were heading and saw three Black Hawk helicopters coming into view. The cavalry had arrived. The president and the kids were being whisked to safety, which meant Yael had to be with them. And I had been left behind.

"General, this is Collins; do you copy? Over," I shouted into my headset.

There was no reply.

"General, I repeat: this is Collins; do you copy? Over."

Again there was nothing.

It made sense to me that the general would be in the van transporting the president to safety. But if the rest of us were going to be next, why wasn't anyone communicating over the radio?

I knew I had to get back to my post, so I ducked down and raced back across the hallway just in time to see bullets flying everywhere. Facedown on the floor, I kept calling out over the radio, trying to get the general, one of the team leaders, the medic, or anyone from Delta to respond. But nobody did. Why not? Was everyone dead? Or was everyone in those vans racing up the mountain?

I had to buy more time to figure out what was happening. I jumped up, glanced out the window, and focused on three more ISIS fighters running toward the villa from the south. I didn't hit any of them when I opened fire, but they did scatter and take cover behind the burning wreckage of a van and an SUV. Then they started returning fire. I waited until they paused to reload, then pivoted back to the window and fired two more bursts, one at each vehicle. But before I could duck for cover, I heard two shots from my left side. Then I found myself snapping back and smashing to the ground.

66

★ ★ ★

I landed on my back.

I'd been hit just below my right shoulder. It was impossible to describe the pain. It was a searing, blinding, excruciating sensation like someone had just taken a red-hot poker and driven it into my chest. I instantly dropped my weapon, and the MP5 went skittering across the floor.

I didn't scream. I wanted to, but I didn't dare let the thugs down below know they'd hit me. Instead, I gritted my teeth and fought to stay conscious. If I blacked out now, I knew, no one was going to find me. For all I knew there was no one left in the building. But I had to alert my team that I was in trouble—if any of them were left. I couldn't just lie there alone and bleed to death. I needed to press the wrist-mounted button to activate my microphone, but it was attached to my right wrist, and the burning sensation was rapidly spreading from my chest down my right arm. It would likely be numb in a few seconds, and there was no way I could make my right hand push the button in any case.

Finally, groaning from the pain, I reached over and pressed it with my left hand.

"Man down, man down. I've been hit. Over."

But again, no one responded.

"This is Collins. I need a medic. Over."

Still nothing, and now I began to panic.

"This is J. B. Collins. I'm in the southwest bedroom on the second floor. I've just been shot. I'm bleeding badly—in need of immediate assistance. Is anybody out there? Does anybody hear me?"

My arm was going numb. Inch by inch, it was shutting down, and with it my ability to shoot and my ability to reload—not that it mattered, as I realized I had only half a mag left.

Suddenly the room erupted again in a hail of gunfire. I covered my face with my left arm and rolled over on my stomach. When there was a brief pause, I slid my MP5 across the floor, through the doorway and into the hallway. Then I began pulling myself across the floor after it. If there was anyone left in the villa, I had to find them. Otherwise I was going to bleed out.

I heard a metallic clunk and something bumping across the floor. I turned and saw a live grenade rolling toward me. Instinctively I swatted at it and pushed it away, sending it into the far corner of the room. Then it detonated and everything went black.

★ ★ ★

When I came to, General Ramirez was dumping a bucket of water on me.

"Where have you been?" he screamed at me. "I've been calling and calling you on the radio. You never answered."

"Where am I?" I asked, wiping the water from my eyes and hearing gunfire downstairs and bombs dropping and buildings exploding outside, closer than ever.

"Still in the villa," he replied, pulling me into the hallway. "Now sit tight."

He had a needle in his hand. He was filling it with something and jabbing it in my arm. I winced in anticipation but didn't feel a thing.

"What happened?"

"You got shot and then nearly killed by a grenade, but you did a heck of a job, soldier."

He helped me sit up and drove another needle into my leg. As he did, I looked at myself in horror. My right shoulder was wrapped in a blood-soaked bedsheet. The right side of my uniform was covered in blood, as was much of the room. The other side of my uniform—what was left of it—was scorched, shredded, and smoking.

"I'm not a soldier," I groaned, trying to make sense of it all.

"Yeah, yeah, you're a reporter—whatever. Look, you took out a lot of bad guys from this room and bought us the time we needed."

"Where's the president?" I asked, trying to get up. "Is he safe?"

"He's safe. That's what I'm talking about. You bought us the time to get him out. He's on a chopper with my guys, and he'll be fine."

"And the kids?"

"They're on another chopper, right behind the president."

"What about Yael?"

"Downstairs with three others, holding down the fort."

"She didn't go with the children?"

"I told her to, but she wouldn't go," he said.

"What are you talking about?" I felt like I couldn't completely understand what he was saying. I heard his words but couldn't process them.

"Said she wanted to fight with us. Now look, can you get up?"

"I'm not sure—but why didn't she go with the kids?"

When another bomb exploded nearby, rocking the building, Ramirez ignored my question. He grabbed my MP5 and asked if there was any ammo left in it, and when I told him that there was, he went back to the two windows and fired several bursts. I could hear the screams of the dying, and I knew how they felt.

When he was finished shooting, Ramirez came back, knelt at my side, checked my radio, and cursed. "It's shorted out," he said. Then he grabbed me by the collar, pulled me out into the hallway, and hoisted me to my feet.

"Come on; let's move," he said.

I knew I should be in agony but felt curiously numb. "Why is Yael still here?"

Again he ignored me. I couldn't feel my right arm at all. The left side of my face and body had severe burns, but I couldn't feel them either. The general dragged me downstairs. I could see three of his men firing out three different windows, and then, as Ramirez helped me around a corner, I saw Yael firing out the front door.

"He's alive," Ramirez told her.

She finished a burst, ducked back inside, turned toward me, and gasped. *"Oh, look at you!"* she yelled and rushed to my side.

Ramirez moved to the doorway and kept shooting.

"I'm fine," I lied.

"Oh no, you're not. General, we need to get him out now."

"We don't have another bird."

"What are you talking about?" she shot back. "You said the next one would be here in a few minutes."

"I know. I just got the call," he said.

"What do you mean?" she asked. "What's wrong?"

"The chopper that was coming for us was just shot down."

"Where?"

"About two klicks from here."

"How?"

"RPG—it was coming in low."

"So now what?"

"They're sending another—from Azraq."

"How far out?" she pressed.

"Twelve minutes."

"General, we don't have twelve more minutes."

"I know."

"We're out of ammo, sir. We're being overrun."

Then she turned to look at me. She was bloody

and sweaty and a total mess. She didn't say anything, but I could see in her eyes that she was worried about me. She wasn't sure I was going to make it. She looked back at Ramirez, but he had nothing to say. He killed another few terrorists racing into the courtyard, and then his gun stopped firing. He was out of ammunition and had no more mags. I watched him pull out his pistol and brace for the inevitable.

"There's got to be a way, General," she yelled. "There's got to be a way out of here."

"There isn't."

"There has to be."

I couldn't believe it. This couldn't be the end. We'd come too far. We'd rescued the president. We'd gotten him to safety, and now we were going to be captured and shot—if we were lucky. Or more likely, slaughtered like cattle.

It wasn't possible. It couldn't end like this. Yet the look in Yael's eyes and the tone in the general's voice and the silence from the others and the fact that all but one of them was reduced to firing with pistols made it clear. We were all going to die. And soon. It was not a matter of if, nor even of when, only how.

67

★ ★ ★

"I'm out!" shouted one of the general's men.

I watched as he tossed his pistol aside.

"Here!" I shouted back. "Use mine." I struggled to pull it out of its holster but couldn't manage it, so Yael helped me and tossed it across the room. The commando caught it, and just in time. He fired twice and killed a terrorist rushing across the yard.

"Okay, this is it; I have to make a call," Ramirez said. "We either let ourselves be overrun, or I call in an air strike and end it now."

He fired at two more jihadists trying to penetrate the courtyard, then turned and took a vote. All three Delta operatives voted for the Air Force to go ahead and drop its ordnance on us and finish us off and the attacking ISIS fighters along with us. Reluctantly, Yael did as well.

"Okay—then it's settled," Ramirez said.

"Whoa, whoa, wait a minute," I said. "I didn't vote."

"You want ISIS to cut your head off?" Ramirez asked.

"Of course not," I said.

"Then you just voted."

"No, wait. I have an idea."

"We don't have time, Collins," Ramirez said, firing again and trying to keep three hooded men at bay. "I have to call it in now. I only have two rounds left."

"Wait, wait, listen to me," I said.

"I can't, Collins; I'm sorry. We're out of time and out of options."

Ramirez called Yael over to guard the door. She propped me up against the stairs, then rushed to his side and took his .45 while he pulled out his satphone and speed-dialed CENTCOM.

"General, listen to me. I think there's another way."

"Forget it, Collins. I know you don't want to die. None of us do. But it happens to everyone. The only question is whether we die with honor or are butchered by cowards."

"No, stop—you're not listening," I yelled, unbelievably intense pain shooting through every part of my body.

"CENTCOM, this is General Ramirez, requesting an air strike on my location. Repeat, I'm requesting an immediate air strike on my location."

There was a pause. The soldiers around me were firing their last rounds.

"Yes, sir, I know what I'm asking," Ramirez continued to the CENTCOM commander in Tampa.

There was another pause.

"You can see it on your screen. We're being

overrun. It's over. Take us out, and everyone around us. . . . Yes, I understand. . . . Thank you, sir. It's been an honor. . . . God bless us all, sir, and God bless the United States of America. Over and out."

Ramirez hung up the phone and the room began to spin. I couldn't believe what he'd just done. But I didn't have the energy to stop him. I was getting woozy. I heard myself mumbling, but I knew I was passing out. I saw my mom. I saw Matt and Annie and Katie and Josh. I tried to remember the verses. I tried to remember what Matt had told me, what he'd begged me to accept, but everything was going dark. I couldn't think straight. I was fading. . . .

"What? What are you saying? J. B.—wake up. What did you just say?"

I was looking at Yael's face. I couldn't tell if it was a dream or if it was real. But she was shaking me, hard, and demanding that I tell her what I'd just said.

"I don't remember," I said and closed my eyes again.

"*You do,*" she yelled, shaking me again. "Come on, J. B.—stay with me. What did you say?"

"The war . . . ," I mumbled.

"The war? What war? This war?"

"No, the ware . . ."

"The where? I don't understand."

"The warehouse . . ."

"The warehouse?"

"Yeah."

"What about it?"

"Hit it."

"What do you mean?" she screamed, shaking me even harder.

"The warehouse," I said again, barely able to keep my eyes open. "Hit it."

"Hit the warehouse?"

"Not us."

"Why, J. B.—why?"

"The sheh . . ."

"What?"

"The shells."

"What about them?" Yael asked, pleading with me to stay with her.

I heard Ramirez telling her to let it go. "He's delirious, Katzir. Let him be. It'll all be over in a moment. The F-16s are inbound as we speak."

"No," she shot back. "He's trying to tell us something."

Then she turned back to me, took my face in her hands, and looked me straight in the eye. "What about the shells, J. B.?"

"The M-six . . ."

"M687s?"

"Right."

"What about them?"

"They'll go off."

"If we bomb the warehouse?"

"Right."

"They might, but why? We'll all die if they go off."

"No, just them."

"Who?"

"The bad guys."

"Just the bad guys will die?" she asked.

"Right."

"No, J. B., that's not how it works," she replied, pity in her voice. "The sarin will kill us all—and believe me, that'll be far worse than being bombed or beheaded."

"No, no," I said. "We have the s . . ."

"The what?"

"The su . . ."

"I can't hear you, J. B.—talk to me."

"Suits," I sputtered. "We have the suits."

Then suddenly she got it.

"What is it?" Ramirez asked as understanding dawned on Yael's face.

"We have the chem-bio suits—all of us," she yelled. "Call them back. Redirect the air strike. Have them hit the warehouse. The chemical weapons will detonate. The gas will be released. There's more than five thousand shells down there, and hundreds more on the upper floors. The gas will spread through the entire village. It'll kill everyone. And we just might survive."

"Might?"

"It's worth a shot, General—it's worth a shot. But you've got to call them now."

I saw Ramirez look at me. He hesitated, but only for a moment. Then he hit speed dial and got CENTCOM back on the phone and started barking authentication codes and orders. In the meantime, Yael raced to get her backpack and returned to my side. Then she and Ramirez helped me upstairs and propped me up against another wall while the others grabbed their backpacks and raced upstairs with us.

And soon the bombs started dropping.

Boom. Boom. Ba-boom.

The ground shook like nothing I'd ever experienced before.

"The warehouse," someone yelled, though I couldn't see who. *"They just hit the warehouse."*

He'd done it, I realized. Ramirez had made the call. And the Air Force had responded already. There was just one problem. We weren't ready yet.

An immense burst of adrenaline shot through my system. I was still in enormous pain, but my heart was racing. I was breathing more deeply now. I was starting to refocus, to see and hear more clearly. Ramirez and two of his colleagues took up positions to guard the stairs while I struggled to get my suit on. I can't explain it. Maybe it was the prospect of my imminent death. Maybe it was the prayers of my family. I don't know for sure, but I felt a wave of energy surging over me. I wasn't better. I wasn't healed. But I did suddenly have the will to live and to fight.

Still, with my right hand numb and much of my body badly burned, I couldn't fasten my helmet. Yael tried to help me, but time was running out. If the warehouse had already been hit, then the gas was already spreading. It would be here any moment. She had to move faster or she'd be dead.

"Forget about me," I yelled. *"Get your own suit on—now!"*

68

But Yael wouldn't quit.

As bombs exploded all around us, closer and closer every second, I pushed her away and screamed at her to save herself. But she wouldn't do it. She got my helmet attached, turned on my air tank, and checked to see it was operating properly. Finally she started putting her own suit on.

The deafening, crushing sound of the explosions seemed to bring me to my senses. I forgot about my injuries. I forgot about my pain. I turned and noticed that some of the others were struggling to get their suits on. The general had found a large tear in his. One of his colleagues had a hole in his air hose. Both handed Yael and me their pistols and the last of their ammo and ran off to find other backpacks, other suits, ones left by commandos who'd already been killed.

Time was running out. But there was nothing we could do to help them except make sure not a single ISIS fighter got up those stairs.

I watched down the stairwell as one jihadist after another stormed the first floor. I saw them desperately searching for us. Then one of them spotted the stairs and gave a shout. The moment his foot hit the first step, I started shooting. When his colleagues joined him, Yael opened fire as well. She killed three with six shots. I killed one and severely wounded two, but suddenly I was out of bullets. Yael kept shooting, but there were too many of them. They were coming too fast.

I yelled for help, but no one could hear me. Then I saw that one of our guys was severely wounded. He'd been hit by a round coming up the stairs or through a window. Someone had pulled him down the hallway and gotten him into his suit and leaned him up against a wall. But he was holding his side and doubled over in pain. I also noticed that he had four grenades on his lap, and now he rolled one to me. I grabbed it, pulled the pin, and tossed it down into the living room as fast as I could. The explosion took out six or seven terrorists. But still they kept coming. I looked back down the hallway and my wounded comrade tossed me another grenade. Again I pulled the pin. Again I hurled it into the living room. This explosion took out five or six more. We did this two more times, and then the grenades were gone, and Yael was out of bullets.

That was it, I thought. We'd done as much as we could. And now it was over. I could see no more ISIS fighters from my angle. Not yet. The vestibule and living room were a sea of blood and body parts, and for a moment the hordes stopped advancing. Maybe no one else was down there. Maybe they were down there but thought we had an endless supply of grenades. Either way, we had a respite, though I knew it wouldn't last. They were coming. Soon. And there was nothing we could do.

But now a new barrage of bombs and missiles came raining down on us, and not just on the warehouse and the houses and buildings nearby but on the courtyard and the backyard and even on the north wing of the villa. One after another, the bombs kept falling and exploding and raining down death on everyone coming to kill us. They were dropping closer and closer and becoming louder and more violent, though I could no longer tell the difference. The villa wasn't going to be able to take much more. The structure was shaking and heaving. Walls were cracking. Beams were splintering. And then the section of roof directly above us gave way, bringing with it a fiery downpour. Burning timbers and tiles came crashing down on top of us.

I grabbed Yael and covered her with my body. I might have been yelling. She might have been too. But I couldn't hear a thing. I could barely see, either. The air was filled with smoke and dust. But was it also filled with gas—*sarin* gas? Had it come? Was it here? I had no idea. It was colorless. It was odorless. How would we know?

I could no longer see the two soldiers down the hallway to the north, including the one who'd given me the last of his grenades. I turned to look behind me and saw Ramirez dragging one of his men down the hall in the other direction, toward the south end of the building. I nudged Yael and pointed toward the general, urging her to follow. But she didn't respond. I shook her, but to no avail.

I started to panic. I wasn't sure if she was dead or just unconscious, but I scrambled forward and began dragging her with me. I could use only my left arm. My right arm was completely paralyzed by this point. But as more and more of the roof collapsed, I had no choice. I couldn't wait for Ramirez to come back for us. I had to get Yael to safety.

Screaming at the top of my lungs and straining every fiber of every muscle in my body, I pulled and pulled, desperate to get her through the burning wreckage. And then the floor collapsed as well.

69

★ ★ ★

We landed hard.

Then what was left of the blazing roof came down on top of us—and not just on the two of us, but on all the bodies littered across the living and dining rooms.

My suit caught fire. I furiously rolled and twisted to put it out, then stumbled over all the burning debris to reach Yael. She wasn't moving. Her helmet was cracked, though it didn't appear to have busted open completely. If she hadn't been dead a moment ago, I feared she was now or would be soon. Still, I couldn't leave her there.

I kicked away the burning timbers and used my left arm to pull her through the living room, through the dining room, and down the hallway toward a bathroom I'd seen earlier. It took several wrenching, deafening, terrifying minutes, but I finally got her there, pulled her inside with me, and shut and locked the door. Then I covered her again with my body and prepared to ride out the attack or die trying.

And then suddenly it was quiet. Not completely quiet but eerily so.

I could still hear the raging fires. But the gunfire had stopped. The bombing had stopped. The explosions had stopped. I no longer heard fighter jets overhead. I no longer heard men shouting in Arabic—or in English. I didn't know why. Was I dead? Was it all over? I couldn't see a thing. Everything was black—so black I couldn't tell if my eyes were open or shut. I tried to move my right arm, but nothing happened. I tried to move my feet and toes and my left hand and arm. All of them worked. I wasn't dead, just severely wounded. Trapped, but alive. Hiding from terrorists in a house that was burning down around me. But I wasn't finished yet. There was still time.

I shifted off Yael and tried to turn her over. I still couldn't see. But now I knew it was because the bathroom had filled with smoke. I couldn't smell it through my chem-bio suit filters. But we had to get out of there fast.

I groped around in the darkness and felt Yael's back. I slid my hand up higher and sat quietly for a moment. I could feel her body rising and falling ever so slightly. She was breathing, which meant she was alive. But now what?

I sat there in the darkness, trying to decide what to do. I was still a bit foggy but dramatically better than I'd been a few minutes earlier.

Why had the bombs stopped dropping? The generals at CENTCOM and back in Azraq were surely watching by satellite and with drones. They could see whether the ISIS forces were still swarming all around us. Was it possible the danger had passed?

I moved to the door and decided to peek out. But when I did, I found that several burning timbers had fallen directly in front of the doorway, blocking our escape. There was no way forward, and now more smoke was filling the bathroom. I closed the door and made a decision. I moved around Yael and felt in the darkness for the window above the toilet. I found a latch and tried to open it, but it wouldn't budge. No matter what I did, nothing worked. I heard a beeping in my helmet. It was an alert from my air tank telling me I had less than five minutes of oxygen. We couldn't stay here. We had to get out now. I stood on the toilet, braced myself against both walls and smashed the window with my boot. It occurred to me that I might be making a dangerous blunder, making so much noise and thus giving away our position. But I didn't see I had a choice, and anyway, what was done was done. So I cleared the rest of the glass away with my boot as well.

Very quickly the smoke in the bathroom dissipated. I could see again. I could see and hear the rain pouring down on the courtyard outside. I could also see at least a dozen hooded men twitching and convulsing and writhing in pain and dozens more lying all across the field, lifeless and still.

The air strikes had worked. I could hardly believe it. The gas had been released. The battlefield had been cleared.

Turning to Yael, I knelt down and, using only my left hand, pulled her onto my back. I grabbed the side of the tub to steady myself, then lifted with my legs and got to a standing position. Then I stood on the toilet again, leaned toward the back wall, and rolled Yael out through the window. She landed with a crunch on the broken glass below, but that was the least of my worries. I climbed out the window myself, jumped to the ground, and checked to see if she was still breathing. She was, but her tank, like mine, had less than four minutes of oxygen to spare.

I reached down, picked her up the best I could, and pulled her over my good shoulder in a fireman's carry. Then I started moving through the courtyard, away from the blazing wreckage that had once been a beautiful villa. I decided my only hope was to get to the top of the mountain, away from the sarin gas, away from the flames and any ISIS forces that remained standing. But as I climbed over bodies and twisted, molten pieces of metal—the remains of the missiles and bombs that had, so far, saved our lives—I collapsed. I scanned the horizon for anyone who could help Yael. But all I saw was death in every direction. Those who had been overtaken by the sarin gas released by the air strikes were twitching and convulsing and foaming at the mouth. They were dying a slow and painful and grisly death. But they were dying. They couldn't kill me. And for the moment, to be honest, that's all I cared about.

I struggled to my feet, the excruciating pain

once again spreading across my body. I had no idea how I was going to get Yael up that mountain.

Suddenly someone grabbed me and spun me around hard. I balled up my fist, prepared to strike, but found myself looking into the mask of General Ramirez. We just stared at each other for a few seconds, and finally I started to breathe again. My heart—temporarily frozen in terror—resumed beating.

Ramirez was saying something, but it was muffled at best. But then he took Yael, hoisted her up on his shoulders, and motioned for me to follow him up the mountain.

But he wasn't walking. He was running flat out. I couldn't keep up. My legs and lungs were burning. My head was pounding. Sweat was pouring down every part of my body. Finally, several hundred meters up, I saw Ramirez stop abruptly and set Yael down. When I reached them, he took off her mask and then his own. At first I looked at him like he was crazy. Did he want to die? Was he trying to commit suicide and take Yael with him? But then I heard another beeping sound in my helmet. I had only thirty seconds of oxygen left. It hadn't been five minutes yet, I thought. It couldn't have been. But I checked the meter and realized I'd nearly sucked the tank dry. And if I didn't get this thing off fast, I was going to suffocate. With the general's help, I quickly removed my helmet, tossed it aside, and breathed in the bitter cold air as the rains drenched me anew.

"What about the gas?" I asked, fearing each breath.

"It can't hurt you up here," Ramirez said.

"What do you mean?" I replied.

"Sarin is heavier than air," he explained as he knelt down and checked Yael's pulse and breathing. "Stays low to the ground. We're already almost five hundred feet above the village. We should be fine."

Should be wasn't exactly what I wanted to hear, but we had no choice.

I turned to Yael. "How is she?"

"I don't know," he said bluntly. "We need to keep moving."

Ramirez picked her up again and started for the summit. I followed as best I could, and before long we were at the top amid the whipping winds. The first thing I saw was pieces of two corpses scattered over the top of the ridge. They were the remains of the two Delta snipers who had been laying down covering fire for us. They had apparently been hit with an artillery round or two. I could barely believe my eyes. I wasn't sure how much more carnage I could take.

Ramirez said nothing. His eyes were hard and his jaw was set. He laid Yael down on the north slope, trying to shelter her a bit from the direct force of the wind.

"Where's the rest of your team?" I asked as I sat down beside her.

But the general shook his head and looked away.

"None of them survived?" I asked in disbelief.

"No," he said quietly.

"What about Colonel Sharif?"

Again he shook his head.

"It's just us?" I asked.

"I'm afraid so," the general replied.

I didn't know what to say. The cost of what we'd just done was growing by the minute.

Turning now, I looked down at the unbelievable devastation in the valley. It was like a scene out of the Apocalypse. The town of Alqosh was gone. All of it. Not a single building remained standing, except one, and barely, at that—the mausoleum around Nahum's tomb.

Then I saw a group of five men emerging from the flames of the compound. They were heading our way, running at full speed. They had chem-bio suits on, but a wave of fear washed over me. Could some of the ISIS forces have stripped our guys of their suits and put them on? We had no weapons. We had no way to defend ourselves. But as they approached us, they took off their helmets. They were Delta. Ramirez rushed over and embraced them, amazed and thankful that anyone else had made it out alive.

I greeted them too, grateful beyond words. One of the men was a medic. He and Ramirez and I carefully removed Yael's chem-bio suit, and the medic examined her injuries. She had a major gash on the back of her head, and her left arm was broken. It was bloody and swollen and part of the bone was actually visible. But for the moment there was nothing we could do. We had no first aid kit, no medical equipment, no drugs, just a satellite phone, which Ramirez used to call CENTCOM. He gave them our status and position and requested an extraction.

Meanwhile, I just sat beside this incredible, mysterious woman, held her hand, stroked her hair, and begged God to have mercy on her, whatever it took. I couldn't bear any more loss.

70

* * *

A few minutes later, a Black Hawk roared into view.

Before I knew it, a team of American special operations forces was fast-roping down to us, as there was no place for the chopper to land on the summit. They put Yael on a stretcher and hoisted her back up to the chopper. I was next. Then Ramirez and his team were brought up.

On board, a doctor and a nurse immediately began working on Yael. They strapped me down on a stretcher right beside her. A young African American Army medic, probably in her early thirties, began assessing my injuries. By the time we lifted off, she had put me on an IV and was giving me several units of blood. I tried to ask questions, but the woman attending to me wouldn't allow it. It wasn't my problems I wanted to know about, I told her. It was Yael's. But she insisted that I settle back and rest during the flight, and she promised me it wouldn't be long.

"Where are we going?" I asked.

"You really need to stop talking, Mr. Collins."

"Please," I said. "I just want to know if we're heading back to Amman."

"We're not."

"Then where?"

"You don't take no for an answer."

"No, I don't—are we heading back to Azraq?"

"No," she said as she started cleaning the severe burns I had over much of my body.

"Then where?" I asked. "Because I need to talk to the king."

"That'll have to wait, Mr. Collins."

"Why?"

"We're not going to Jordan."

"Then where?"

"We're heading to EIA."

"Where?"

"Erbīl International Airport."

"Erbīl?"

"Yes."

"The Kurdish capital?"

"Yes, sir."

"But why?"

"I don't give the orders, Mr. Collins. I just follow them. Except to you. I do give you orders, and right now you need to rest."

"But I need to get back to Azraq. It's urgent."

"Then I'm afraid you just got on the wrong flight."

I turned to General Ramirez. A nurse was working on him, too, and only then did I realize that he had been shot as well.

"What happened to you?" I asked.

"Nothing," he said. "I'll be fine."

"But you . . . I didn't . . ."

"Don't worry. I'll be fine," he said again, and he sounded like he meant it.

"You're sure?" I pressed.

"Believe me, Collins, I've been through much worse."

On that, it was hard to doubt him.

"Can you make them tell me about Yael?" I asked.

"They'll tell us when they know something," Ramirez said.

"What's that supposed to mean?"

"It means she's not out of danger yet, Collins. So just stay quiet, let the docs do their job, and we'll all know soon enough."

The satellite phone rang. Ramirez was getting stitches and refusing additional anesthesia, but he still took the call.

"Yes, sir. . . . Right now. We're en route. . . . I don't know—maybe six minutes, maybe eight. . . . Got it. . . . No, sir, we did not. . . . It's possible, but I couldn't say for sure. . . . No. . . . No. . . . I appreciate that, but with all due respect, sir, I need to go back. . . . I understand. . . . Yes, we need to secure it, but my men are back there. We need to get their bodies and get them home to their families for a proper burial. Can you put that together? . . . I'd be grateful. . . . Okay, that's—sir, what's that? . . . Yeah, he's right here with me. . . . No, I think he's going to be fine. . . . Yeah, she's here too. . . . I don't know. Too soon to say. . . . Okay, out."

"Who was that?" I asked.

"CENTCOM," the general replied.

"And?"

"They want to know where Abu Khalif is."

"And?"

"I have no idea."

"Could he have gotten away?"

"He could be a pile of ashes right now for all I know," the general said. "Who knows? We need to put boots on the ground, secure that site, and go over it inch by inch. There may not be much left down there. But we've got to try."

"And get your men back too."

Ramirez nodded. "And get my men back."

There was quiet for a bit, and then I asked him for an update on Dabiq, wincing as the medic cut away more scorched sections of my uniform to treat the burns on my legs.

"Don't go there, Collins."

"Why not?"

"Dabiq is a mess."

"What do you mean?"

"You should rest."

"That bad?"

"Really, Collins, you should rest."

"Just tell me what happened."

"Off the record?"

"Of course," I said.

"I have your word?"

"You do," I assured him, but he didn't seem convinced. "Look, the *Times* will have plenty of coverage of that fight, but I promise none of it will come from me."

Ramirez sighed. "It was ten times worse than this," he said.

"You're kidding," I replied, not sure that was possible.

"I'm not," Ramirez said. "The guys at CENTCOM didn't have time to go into a lot of detail, but they told me ISIS was waiting for our friends. They launched chemical weapons almost the moment the Jordanians, the Egyptians, and the Saudis got there. Our friends fought well, I'm told, but they took heavy casualties."

"How heavy?"

"You have to remember they went in with a much bigger force than we did."

"How heavy, General?"

"It was a bloodbath."

"How many dead?" I asked.

"At least two hundred dead."

I didn't respond. I had no words.

"In the end, it may be more," he said. "The fighting is still under way."

"I thought the king ordered his forces to withdraw once we found and secured the president."

"He did," Ramirez confirmed, "but the bulk of the assault force was already on the ground and moving into the school when the retreat order was given. The men got caught in a wicked cross fire. It seems most of the forces who went in were lost. The rest are fighting their way out, but it doesn't look promising at this point. At least six coalition helicopters were shot down trying to get the men out. And then there's the collateral damage."

"How bad?"

"You don't want to know," Ramirez said.

"Yes, I do."

Ramirez shook his head as the chopper shot across the plains of Nineveh. "First reports indicate all or most of the buildings around the school were filled with civilians, primarily women and children, just like the school itself," he said. "Once ISIS started using the sarin gas, everyone in the neighborhood was doomed. CENTCOM is saying the civilian body count could top fifteen hundred by day's end, maybe more. It's . . . I don't know; it's just . . ." The general's voice trailed off.

"A mess," I said.

"Yeah," he said. "A total mess."

I lay back against the pillow. The scope of the carnage just kept getting worse. The magnitude of the Islamic State's evil was like nothing I had ever seen or heard of. I would have thought by this point in my career I had seen it all. But clearly I had not. Where was it all leading? What was coming next? How would it end? I had no idea.

Suddenly the face of Colonel Sharif came to my mind. I couldn't believe he was dead. I thought of his kids. I wondered who would tell them and when. I wondered how they were going to bear the loss. They'd already been through so much.

The medic leaned over to me and whispered again that I should close my eyes and let myself fall asleep. But how could I? Every bone in my body was in pain. Most of my flesh was burning. I knew I was in good hands. I knew I wasn't going to die. Not in the air over Iraq. Not in the capital of Kurdistan. Not today. But I was still in enormous pain.

And Yael? She was a different story altogether. I still had no idea what was going to happen to her, and that hurt all the more.

71

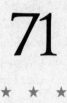

A few minutes later, we touched down next to a hangar.

Then the side doors opened and a team of Air Force doctors met us. They got a quick briefing from the medics who had cared for us and took Yael and me off the chopper on our stretchers. I was about to insist that I could walk well enough on my own, but the African American medic shot me a look that told me I'd better not dare cross her now. So I kept my mouth shut, and as they wheeled us both across the tarmac and put us in a waiting ambulance, I suddenly saw something I would never have expected to see—not today, not in the middle of Iraqi Kurdistan.

Air Force One was waiting for us. The president's gleaming blue-and-white 747 was refueled and ready to go. It was surrounded by dozens of tanks, armored personnel carriers, heavily armed American soldiers and Secret Service agents, and a detachment of the Peshmerga, the Kurdish military force. It was also surrounded by a squadron of American fighter jets.

"I'm afraid this is where I say good-bye, my friend," General Ramirez said just before the EMTs shut the ambulance doors. "It was an honor to fight with you, Collins. You did a heck of a job."

"Thanks, General. Can I quote you on that?"

"You can indeed," he said, though the smile I was hoping to get did not come. There was too much pain and too much loss for both of us. "Don't be a stranger. You're part of the family now. Come see us anytime."

"I'd like that, sir," I said, having to make do by shaking with my left hand. "Take care."

"You, too, Collins. Bye."

He shut the doors, tapped them twice, and the ambulance headed across the airfield. When we got to Air Force One, Yael's stretcher was wheeled onto a lift device, elevated, and brought into the back of the plane. My stretcher followed close behind. I'd only been on Air Force One once in my life, but I couldn't help but notice that the press section in the back where I'd sat had been completely reconfigured. It was now a mobile hospital, and several of the Iraqi children who had been rescued from the tunnels were lying on portable stretchers, receiving, no doubt, the best medical care they had ever gotten.

The first person I recognized was Special Agent Art Harris.

"Mr. Collins, thank God—you made it," he said, rushing over to me immediately.

"You, too," I said. "I was getting worried about you."

"Thanks," he said. "But I'm feeling much better."

"Someone poison you?" I quipped, only half-kidding.

"Nothing so exciting," he replied. "Just airsickness. But what about you? You look terrible. You going to be all right?"

"We'll see," I said, not wanting to talk about myself. "Any news on Jack Vaughn?"

"He was arraigned in federal court a few hours ago."

"How'd he plead?" I asked, trying to picture the scene of a CIA director being arraigned on charges of treason and espionage, for starters.

"Not guilty on all counts," Harris replied.

"And the woman and her son?"

"They'll be arraigned later today."

"Okay. Keep me posted," I said.

"Will do," Harris replied. "You take care of yourself."

"I'll try."

Just then an Air Force officer walked by and insisted Agent Harris take his seat immediately. The crew was kind and couldn't have been more professional, but it was clear they were feeling harried. They were rushing to get Air Force One off Iraqi soil as quickly as possible, and our arrival had obviously slowed them down and complicated matters. Two nurses locked Yael's stretcher into place. Mine was locked in right next to her. We were both strapped in tightly and before I knew it, we began hurtling down the runway.

No one said a word. Even the children were quiet, though it occurred to me that they might have been sedated. I'd overheard a Secret Service agent tell one of his colleagues as we were boarding that ISIS forces were now just a few kilometers from the airport. Tensions were high, as none of us knew what ISIS had planned next.

As we lifted off, I reminded myself that the presidential plane had the world's most advanced countermeasures to defeat ground-to-air missiles. It had also been retrofitted with engines nearly as powerful as those of a spacecraft. Thus, we were now rocketing almost straight up into the sky to get out of missile range as rapidly as possible. The g-forces were making the plane shake something fierce. I wasn't far from several windows, but I couldn't watch. My eyes were shut. My fists were clenched. I knew a dozen U.S. Navy fighter jets were flanking us. They were all from the USS *George H.W. Bush*, the Nimitz-class supercarrier operating as part of Carrier Strike Group Two somewhere out in the Med. They were there to get us out alive and well. But I still couldn't watch.

A few minutes later, we reached our cruising altitude of 41,000 feet. Not long after that, the pilot came over the intercom and informed us that we were now out of Iraqi airspace. I opened my eyes and breathed a sigh of relief as the entire plane erupted in cheers.

Suddenly I heard a familiar voice coming down the aisle. The next thing I knew, President Harrison Taylor was standing beside me, flanked by several bodyguards. "Mr. Collins, how are you?" he asked.

"Mr. President," I said, startled to see him at all, much less on his feet. "I'm fine, sir—how are you?"

"You don't exactly look fine, Collins," he said.

"Neither do you, sir," I replied.

"No, I guess I don't," he conceded. "But they say I'm going to make it."

"Glad to hear it, sir."

"Me too," he said. "And you?"

"We'll see."

Taylor nodded. He wasn't smiling. He'd been through too much, and I could see the pain and exhaustion in his eyes. He looked around the makeshift medical bay and asked if they were taking good care of me. When I assured him that they were, he asked if there was anything I needed. I said no. I saw him glance at the Iraqi children. He thanked the medical crew standing around us for "caring for these kids who really need our love and attention right now." Then he took a few moments to shake hands with each doctor and each nurse and thank them personally for all they'd done for him and his team and these children.

Then the president looked down at Yael. "How is she?" he asked.

"I don't know," I said. "They won't tell me."

The president turned to the lead physician.

"Miss Katzir is stable for now, sir," the doctor replied. "We'll know more in a few hours, but we're going to run a series of tests on her right away."

Taylor nodded and squeezed Yael's hand. I could see him fighting back his emotions, and he was not a man known for having much of an emotional side.

"Take care of these two," he told the medical staff, nodding toward Yael and me. "I owe them my life." Then he turned to me again. "Thank you, James," he said softly.

"Don't mention it, Mr. President," I replied, surprised to hear him call me by my first name.

"No, really," he said, looking me in the eye. "You were right about ISIS, about the summit, about the chemical weapons, about all of it. I should have listened to you. I'm sorry."

"It's okay, Mr. President."

"No," he said, "it's not. A lot of people are dead because I . . ."

He didn't finish the sentence. There was an awkward silence. Then he spoke again.

"Perhaps if I'd listened . . . maybe . . . just maybe all of this could have been avoided."

I didn't know what to say. He was right, but I was stunned to hear him admit it. Thousands of people were dead because he'd failed to take ISIS seriously and deal with them earlier on. I had questions I wanted him to answer on the record, and not just for the American people but for me. But now didn't seem the right time or place—not here on Air Force One, in front of his staff.

Still, I did want to ask him one question: what was he going to do next? ISIS had taken him hostage and broadcast the images of his captivity to the entire world. They had almost beheaded him. They had slaughtered nearly an entire Delta team. They had murdered dozens of American soldiers, not to mention hundreds of Jordanian, Egyptian, Saudi, and Gulf forces in Dabiq. And this was only the beginning. ISIS had scored a propaganda coup of unbelievable proportions. Money and recruits were going to flow in as never before. What's more, Abu Khalif was still at large. So what was the president going to do now? How was he going to learn from his failure to deal with ISIS sooner?

But the moment was interrupted. One of the Secret Service agents got a call on his satellite phone and handed the phone to the president.

"Yeah, it's me," Taylor said. "Okay, put him on. . . . Hey, Marty—what have you got?"

There was a long silence.

"I—that's not possible," he said, and there was another long silence. "What did it say? . . . No, no—not yet. Not till I get back. . . . Okay, let me know. . . . I will. Bye."

He hung up and handed the phone back to the agent. His face was ashen. I couldn't imagine what he'd just learned, and I hoped he didn't tell me. I couldn't take more bad news.

"That was the vice president," he said, looking back at me but saying nothing else.

I nodded but didn't reply. I guess I hoped if I stayed quiet, the president wouldn't tell me whatever he'd just heard. Maybe it was classified. Maybe it was personal. Regardless, he just stood there quietly for a few moments, looking away. Then he patted me on the shoulder and turned to leave.

I started to breathe again. But then he stopped and turned back to me. Every muscle in my body tensed.

"They just heard from the prison where they're holding Jack Vaughn," the president explained, looking down at the floor. "They found Jack's body."

"What?" I exclaimed.

"Apparently he hanged himself with a bedsheet in his cell. He's dead. Just like that. He's dead."

No one said a word. I could see the shock in everyone's eyes. Surely the word had spread through the staff earlier about Vaughn's arrest. I doubted the president even knew about my involvement in the sting operation that had cemented Vaughn's guilt, but clearly the notion of the CIA director being involved in a conspiracy to kill the president had rattled everyone on board. And now this news compounded everything.

"He left a note," the president said, a vacant look in his eyes. "Don't ask me how . . ." His voice trailed off.

"What did it say, Mr. President?" I asked after we had waited nearly a minute.

"The note simply read, 'I'm sorry. Just tell him I'm sorry. I never imagined . . .' And that was it."

What did that mean? I wondered. Tell who? The president? Someone else? Why hadn't Vaughn referred to Claire? Or his children? And "I never imagined"? What was that supposed to mean? That he didn't know his mistress was working for ISIS? That he didn't know he'd be caught?

A hundred more questions came rushing to mind, but the president just turned and walked away.

72

As soon as the president left, the doctors wheeled Yael away as well.

They said they were taking her for tests. I lay there in pain, staring at the ceiling, reeling from all that had just happened, with no way to move and no one to talk to. Rarely had I ever felt so alone.

I closed my eyes but couldn't sleep. All I could see was Jack Vaughn's body hanging, dangling, twisting. I opened my eyes and glanced at the Iraqi children, all of whom were now sedated and sleeping, but all I could see were images of them in those hideous cages. I turned and stared at the ceiling, but all I could see was Yael and Sharif fighting for their lives in that compound in Alqosh—fighting and, in Sharif's case, losing.

An Air Force nurse soon came by to check my IV and vital signs. "How are you holding up, Mr. Collins?" she asked. "Is everything okay?"

Are you kidding? I wanted to scream. *Do you have any idea what we've all been through?* But I just bit my tongue and nodded.

"Blood pressure's a little high," she said, putting

a note in my chart. "Are you comfortable? Can I get you anything?"

I gritted my teeth. Was there anything I wanted? *Of course there is, lady. How about ironclad proof Yael is going to be okay? How about my friends back from the grave? How about the last few days to have never happened? How about a phone to call home, a computer to write the story, and the Wi-Fi to transmit it back to my boss?* But I just shook my head and stared at the space where Yael's stretcher had been. I imagined the doctors working on her, hooking her up to all kinds of hoses and tubes and monitors, and I was scared for her.

"I'm fine," I lied. "But what about my friend—is she going to be okay?"

"We'll know soon enough," she said.

"She took a terrible blow to the head back there," I said.

"Yes, I know," the nurse replied.

"And her arm is broken," I added.

"We're on it," she insisted.

"And she's got severe burns all over her body," I noted.

"Don't worry, Mr. Collins; we're doing everything we can to take care of her," she assured me. "And when we touch down, we'll get her straight to Walter Reed. We've already alerted them. They're going to be standing by with a first-class team when we get there. Believe me, she's in good hands."

I nodded with gratitude, then wondered if I'd heard her right. "Did you say Walter Reed?"

"Yes, sir."

"The medical center?"

"Yes, sir."

"In Washington?"

"Well, Bethesda, but yes."

"We're not going to Tel Aviv?" I asked, somewhat perplexed.

"No, sir," she said. "Why would you think that?"

"Well, I just thought . . . I mean . . . Yael's Israeli, so, you know, I thought we'd be—"

"What, dropping her off?" she asked.

"Yeah, I guess so."

"Sir, this plane is carrying the president of the United States. We've got one priority, and that's to get the commander in chief back to D.C., back to the White House, as quickly and as safely as possible. That's it. That's our mission. Everything else will have to wait."

"Of course," I said. "Thanks."

"My pleasure, sir. Now you get some rest. We've got a long flight ahead of us."

"I can't sleep."

"Do you want me to give you something?"

"No, no, it's not that; it's just . . ."

"I know. You're worried about Miss Katzir. But I'm sure she'll be fine, Mr. Collins. And I suspect she'll be awake in a few hours. Why don't you get some rest? And when she stirs, I'll be sure to wake you."

"You'd do that?"

"Of course, sir. It would be my pleasure."

"Well, thank you," I said, choking up. "I'm sorry. I'm just . . ."

"It's okay, Mr. Collins. You need to rest. That's it. Just lie there and rest. You're safe with us now."

The funny thing, given the circumstances, was that I actually believed her. As I leaned back on the pillow and stared up at the ceiling, I realized I couldn't remember the last time I'd felt safe. But I did now. Sad, but safe. Mourning and hollow and racked with grief . . . but safe. And it was odd. Good, but odd.

Soon my breathing began to slow. My eyes started getting heavy. And for the first time in what seemed like forever, I began to relax. We'd rescued the president. He was safe. We'd rescued all these children, and they were safe too. Yael was getting the best care she possibly could, and so was I. There was nothing else I could do, nothing but rest and resist the temptation to slide headlong into a depression that would just make everything worse.

For a moment, I craved a drink, but I forced myself to think about something else—something, anything—and fast. I began to think about the story I was going to write. I tried to imagine what I was going to tell Allen first, the moment they let me use a phone. I tried to organize my thoughts and imagine how I was going to capture all that I'd been through and communicate it to a world that wasn't going to hear it any other way. This wasn't just a series of articles. This was a book. And I was no longer going to be under a military censor. My thoughts raced.

Soon the cabin lights were dimmed. Conversations turned to a whisper and then quieted completely. The people on this plane were as spent as I was, and everyone began to settle in for the twelve-hour flight. I glanced up the hallway and noticed a young Air Force officer pulling down all the window shades. Before she got to us, I looked out the window nearest to me and noticed that we had started banking west. It took me a moment to realize exactly where we were, but then I saw the Jordan River. I saw the barrenness of the Judean wilderness below us. I knew then that we were clearing the airspace of the Hashemite Kingdom. We were heading into Israel, toward the Mediterranean, and then home.

And then, as we began to level out, I could see the brave young men flying those Navy fighter jets, our escorts. One of the jets was so close I could have waved to the pilot if I'd wanted to.

Then the young officer arrived, and just before she closed the window shade, she turned to that pilot and caught his eye, and she saluted him. And the pilot saluted back.

And when he did, I broke. My eyes welled up with tears. I got a lump in my throat. I tried to hold back the emotions. They embarrassed me. But I couldn't help it. As the officer closed the last of the window shades and darkness settled on the medical bay, I closed my eyes again and began to shake, began to weep. Quietly. Not so anyone could hear me. I was simply overcome with relief and gratitude beyond measure.

And then, though it felt far from familiar, I quietly said a prayer. I thanked God for rescuing me, for giving me another chance. I asked him to take care of Yael, to bring her back to me safely.

And then I wiped my eyes and closed them and thought about those fighter jets at our side, keeping us safe.

I reached over and inched up the shade. Just a crack. Just to be sure.

The fighter escort was still there.

And no sight had ever looked as good.

★ ★ ★

MOSCOW, RUSSIA

Louisa Sherbatov had just turned six, but she would never turn seven.

The whirling dervish had finally fallen asleep on the couch just before midnight, crashed from a sugar high, still wearing her new magenta dress and matching ribbon in her blonde tresses. Snuggled up on her father's lap, she looked so peaceful, so content as she hugged her favorite stuffed bear and lay surrounded by the dolls and books and sweaters and other gifts she'd received from all her aunts and uncles and grandparents and cousins as well as her friends from the elementary school just down the block at the end of Guryanova Street.

Strewn about her were string and tape and wads of brightly colored wrapping paper. The kitchen sink was stacked high with dirty plates and cups and silverware. The dining room table was still littered with empty bottles of wine and vodka and scraps of leftover birthday pie—strawberry, Louisa's favorite.

The flat was a mess. But the guests were gone and it was Thursday night and the weekend was upon them and honestly, her parents, Feodor and Irina, couldn't have cared less. Their little girl, the

only child they had been able to bear after more than a decade and two heartbreaking miscarriages, was happy. Her friends were happy. Their parents were happy. They were happy. Everything else could wait.

Feodor stared down at the two precious women in his life and longed to stay. He had loved planning the party with them both, had loved helping shop for the food, loved helping Irina and her mother make all the preparations, loved seeing the sheer delight on Louisa's face when he'd given her a shiny blue bicycle, her first. But business was business. If he was going to make his flight to Tashkent, he had to leave quickly. So he gently kissed mother and daughter on their foreheads, picked up his suitcase, and slipped out as quietly as he could.

As he stepped out the front door of the apartment building, he was relieved to see the cab he'd ordered waiting for him as planned. He moved briskly to the car, shook hands with the driver, and gave the man his bag. The night air was crisp and fresh. The moon was full, and leaves were beginning to fall and swirl in the light breeze coming from the west. Summer was finally over, thought Feodor as he climbed into the backseat, and not a moment too soon. The sweltering heat. The stifling humidity. The gnawing guilt of not being able to afford even a simple air conditioner, much less a little dacha out in the country where he and Irina and Louisa and maybe his parents or hers could retreat now and again, somewhere in a forest

with lots of shade and a sparkling lake for swimming or fishing.

"Thank God, autumn has arrived," he half mumbled to himself as the driver slammed the trunk shut and got back behind the wheel. Growing up, Feodor had always loved the cooler weather. The shorter days. Going back to school. Making new friends. Meeting new teachers. Taking new classes. Fall meant change, and change had always been good to him. Perhaps one day, if he continued to work very hard, he could save enough money to move his family away from 19 Guryanova Street, away from this noisy, dirty, run-down, depressing hovel on the south side of the capital and find some place really lovely and quaint and quiet. Some place worthy of raising a family. Some place with a bit of grass, maybe even a garden where he could till the soil with his own hands and grow his own vegetables.

As the cab began to pull away from the curb, Feodor leaned back in his seat. He closed his eyes and folded his hands on his chest. Yes, autumn had always been a time of new beginnings, and he wondered what this one might bring. He was not rich. He was not successful. But he was content, even hopeful, perhaps for the first time in his life.

He found himself reminiscing about the first time he'd laid eyes on Irina—the first day of middle school, twenty-two years ago. He was so caught up in his memories that he did not notice the car parked just down the street, a white Lada with its headlights off but its engine running. He didn't notice that the front license plate was

covered with some sort of masking tape, revealing only the numbers 6 and 2. Nor did he notice the car's driver, nervously smoking a cigarette and tapping on the dashboard, or the two burly men, dressed in black leather jackets and black leather gloves, emerging from the basement of his own building. When the police would later ask about the men and the car, Feodor would be unable to provide any description at all.

What he did remember—what he could never possibly forget—was the deafening explosion behind him. He remembered the searing fireball. He remembered the taxi driver losing control and crashing into a lamppost not fifty meters up the street, and he remembered smashing his head against the plastic screen dividing the front seat from the back. He remembered the ghastly sensation of kicking open the back door of the cab, jumping out into the pavement, blood streaming down his face, heart pounding furiously, and looking up just in time to see his home, the twelve-story apartment building at 19 Guryanova Street, collapse in a blinding flash of fire and ash.

ACKNOWLEDGMENTS

★ ★ ★

Over the years, I've been incredibly fortunate to work with an amazing team for whom I could not be more grateful. They are consummate professionals, love what they do, and approach every detail with creativity and excellence.

Scott Miller, my literary agent, and his team at Trident Media Group are the best in the business.

Mark Taylor, Jeff Johnson, Ron Beers, and Karen Watson at Tyndale House Publishers are a great team, and it has been a true pleasure to work with them over the years. They truly get what I'm trying to do and are always helping me do it better. Their colleagues are absolutely outstanding: Jan Stob, Cheryl Kerwin, Todd Starowitz, Dean Renninger, the entire sales forces, and all the others that make the Tyndale engine hum. And I don't know what I'd do without Jeremy Taylor, my editor extraordinaire.

June Meyers and Nancy Pierce on my November Communications, Inc. team always give 100 percent, and I'm so grateful for their hard work, attention to detail, kind and gentle spirits, and faithfulness in prayer.

I'm so deeply blessed by my family. They have all been so encouraging, patient, and helpful on this adventure from the beginning, and I would never want to do it without them.

Thanks so much to:

My wife, Lynn, with whom I just celebrated twenty-five amazing years of marriage and can't wait for a million more!

Our four wonderful sons—Caleb, Jacob, Jonah, and Noah—who are true gifts from our Father in heaven to Lynn and me, and whom we cherish more than they will ever know.

My parents, Len and Mary Rosenberg, who have encouraged me as a writer since I was just eight years old and haven't given up on me yet. They just celebrated their fiftieth wedding anniversary in the summer of 2015 and have set a great example for our whole family of a marriage rooted in Christ.

The Meyers, Rebeiz, Scoma, and Rosenberg families, who fill our lives with so much love and laughter.

Lastly, but most importantly, I want to say thank you to the fans of these books in the U.S., in Israel, and all over the world. I am so grateful for your e-mails, Facebook messages, tweets, and letters. I only wish I could write these books as fast as you all read them. Thank you so much. I just hope *The First Hostage* manages to live up to your incredibly high (and growing) expectations.

ABOUT THE AUTHOR

★ ★ ★

Joel C. Rosenberg is a *New York Times* bestselling author with more than three million copies sold among his twelve novels (including *The Last Jihad, Damascus Countdown,* and *The Auschwitz Escape*), four nonfiction books (including *Epicenter* and *Inside the Revolution*), and a digital short (*Israel at War*). A front-page Sunday *New York Times* profile called him a "force in the capital." He has also been profiled by the *Washington Times* and the *Jerusalem Post* and has been interviewed on ABC's *Nightline,* CNN *Headline News,* FOX News Channel, The History Channel, MSNBC, *The Rush Limbaugh Show,* and *The Sean Hannity Show.*

You can follow him at www.joelrosenberg. com or on Twitter @joelcrosenberg and Facebook: www.facebook.com/JoelCRosenberg.

FROM *NEW YORK TIMES* BESTSELLING AUTHOR

JOEL C. ROSENBERG

"IF THERE WERE A *FORBES* 400 LIST OF GREAT CURRENT NOVELISTS, JOEL ROSENBERG WOULD BE AMONG THE TOP TEN. HIS NOVELS ARE UN-PUT-DOWNABLE."

STEVE FORBES, EDITOR IN CHIEF, *FORBES* MAGAZINE

FICTION

J. B. COLLINS NOVELS
THE THIRD TARGET
THE FIRST HOSTAGE
WITHOUT WARNING

THE TWELFTH IMAM COLLECTION
THE TWELFTH IMAM
THE TEHRAN INITIATIVE
DAMASCUS COUNTDOWN

THE LAST JIHAD COLLECTION
THE LAST JIHAD
THE LAST DAYS
THE EZEKIEL OPTION
THE COPPER SCROLL
DEAD HEAT

THE AUSCHWITZ ESCAPE

NONFICTION

ISRAEL AT WAR
IMPLOSION
THE INVESTED LIFE
INSIDE THE REVOLUTION
INSIDE THE REVIVAL
EPICENTER

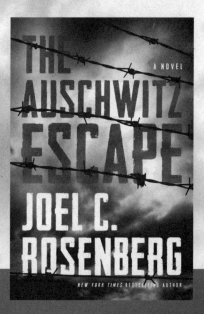

TYNDALE HOUSE PUBLISHERS IS CRAZY4FICTION!

Fiction that entertains and inspires

Get to know us! Become a member of the Crazy4Fiction community. Whether you read our blog, like us on Facebook, follow us on Twitter, or receive our e-newsletter, you're sure to get the latest news on the best in Christian fiction. You might even win something along the way!

JOIN IN THE FUN TODAY.

 www.crazy4fiction.com

 Crazy4Fiction

 @Crazy4Fiction